Vol Four pts 1 & 2.

D. A. SUFFOLK

THE WITCH'S GRANDDAUGHTER
and
THE PLIGHT OF THE PLAQUE MAKER

THE ADVENTURES OF
SAM AND SARAH AND THEIR FRIENDS

THE WITCH'S GRANDDAUGHTER

Being the first part of
the fourth book

and

THE PLIGHT OF THE PLAQUE MAKER

Being the second part of
the fourth book

Adventures of Sam and Sarah
and their friends

Maps Diagrams & Drawings
by the Author.

THE WITCH'S GRANDDAUGHTER
Part One
and
THE PLIGHT OF THE PLAQUE MAKER
Part Two

The Adventures of Sam and Sarah and their Friends

By
D. A. Suffolk

Copyright
© D. A. SUFFOLK 2012
© Maps, Plans, Diagrams and Illustrations D. A. Suffolk 2010
© Anastasi $^{Ltd.}$ 2012

ISBN 978-0-9553077-3-7
EISBN 978-1-909124-22-6

Published by:
Anastasi ^{Ltd}, Leominster, Herefordshire HR6 8TA.
www.anastasiltd-book-matters.com
www.anastasiltd.co.uk

ALL RIGHTS RESERVED. No part of this publication may be reproduced, stored in a retrieval system, or transmitted in any form or by any means, electronic, photocopying, recording or otherwise, without the prior permission of Anastasi ^{Ltd}
A catalogue record for this book is available from the British Library

Cover and page design by: Anastasi ^{Ltd} Design Studio
© Cover design Anastasi ^{Ltd} 2012

Printed and Bound in Great Britain by
Lightning Source UK^{Ltd}

First impression 2012

Author's Acknowledgements.

The author wishes to thank the many friends who have assisted in the preparation of this forth volume in the *Sam and Sarah series*. Especially those who proof read the various drafts and offered comments and suggestions which helped to shape the book's final form. I Also owe a deep debt of gratitude to Tim and Hilly Clement for their unstinting work in preparing it for printing, and to those children and friends who, having read earlier volumes encouraged us to publish the fourth book!

Contents

Author's Acknowledgements............................... 5
About the Author 7
DEDICATION 9
INTRODUCTION 13

Part One
THE WITCH'S GRANDDAUGHTER

Chapter I Tankerville Road.... 15
Chapter II................. 27
Chapter III 35
Chapter IV 43
Chapter V.................. 53
Chapter VI 63
Chapter VII 71
Chapter VIII............... 81
Chapter IX 93
Chapter X................. 101
Chapter XI 109
Chapter XII............... 119
Chapter XIII.............. 129
Chapter XIV.............. 139
Chapter XV............... 149
Chapter XVI 159
Chapter XVII 167
Chapter XVIII 175
Chapter XIX.............. 185
Chapter XX............... 197
Chapter XXI.............. 207
Chapter XXII 217
Chapter XXIII............. 227
Chapter XXIV............. 237
Chapter XXV 247
Chapter XXVI............. 257
Chapter XXVII 267
Chapter XXVIII 277
Chapter XXIX............. 287
Chapter XXX 301

Part Two
THE PLIGHT OF THE PLAQUE MAKER

CHAPTER ONE 311
CHAPTER TWO.......... 321
CHAPTER THREE........ 331
CHAPTER FOUR......... 341
CHAPTER FIVE 351
CHAPTER SIX 361
CHAPTER SEVEN 369
CHAPTER EIGHT 379
CHAPTER NINE 389
CHAPTER TEN 399
CHAPTER ELEVEN....... 409
CHAPTER TWELVE....... 419
CHAPTER THIRTEEN 431
CHAPTER FOURTEEN.... 443
CHAPTER FIFTEEN 451
CHAPTER SIXTEEN 463
CHAPTER SEVENTEEN... 475
CHAPTER EIGHTEEN 487
CHAPTER NINETEEN 497
CHAPTER TWENTY...... 507
CHAPTER TWENTY-ONE . 519
CHAPTER TWENTY-TWO. 529
CHAPTER TWENTY-THREE 541
CHAPTER TWENTY-FOUR 551
CHAPTER TWENTY-FIVE . 563
CHAPTER TWENTY-SIX... 573
CHAPTER TWENTY-SEVEN 587
CHAPTER TWENTY-EIGHT 601
CHAPTER TWENTY-NINE 613
CHAPTER THIRTY 627
CLASS FOUR'S CAMPING TRIP TO SELWORTHY.......... 629
CHAPTER THIRTY-ONE .. 645

About the Author

The author started his working life as a surveyor, but at twenty-one decided to enter the world of education and was, for some thirty-six years a primary school teacher working in an independent Steiner Waldorf Schools movement. He taught in UK, Australia, South Africa and Canada. He retired to England in the early nineteen nineties.

Most of the characters, locations and situations in this volumes and subsequent ones have their origins in the many and varied experiences he has had with children, adults and animals during the years of carrying the spluttering guttering light of learning round parts of the now deceased British Empire.

DEDICATION

This volume is dedicated to my faithful proof reader who gave heart and soul and burnt much midnight oil wrestling with the unwieldy manuscript! Special thanks go to Linda Jo and her daughter Allanque, of Portland Oregon. Who with the American reader in mind made textural adjustments to suit readers on both sides of the Atlantic!

The Author

A Sketch Plan of the Town of Tadbridge

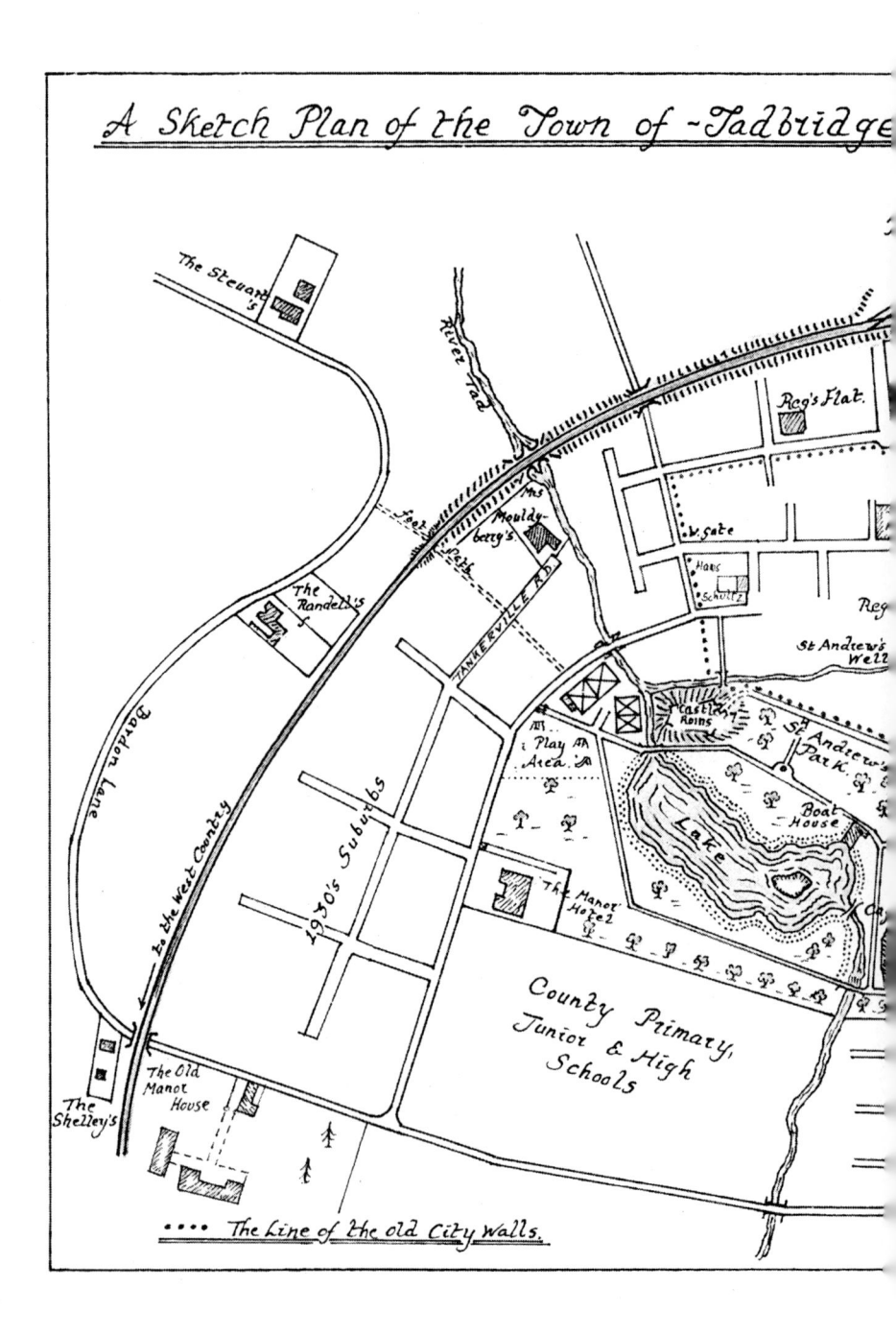

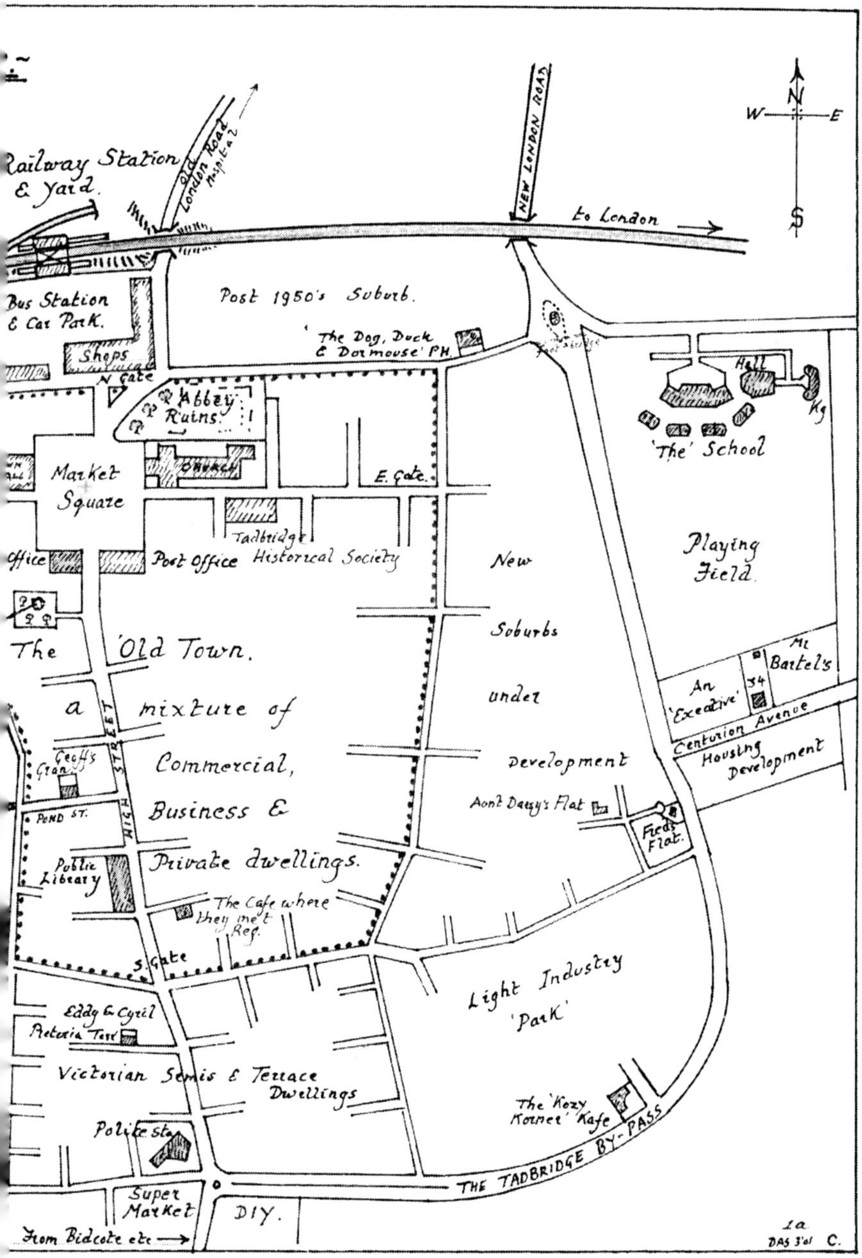
Railway Station
& Yard.
Old London Road
Hospital
NEW LONDON ROAD
to London
N
W
E
S
Bus Station
& Car Park.
Shops
Post 1950's Suburb.
'The Dog, Duck
& Dormouse' PH.
Hall
Kg
'The' School
N Gate
Abbey
Ruins
Market
Square
E. Gate.
Tadbridge
Historical Society
Post Office
New
Suburbs
under
Development
Playing
Field
Mr
Bartel's
An
'Executive'
34
Centurion Avenue
Housing
Development
The 'Old Town.
a mixture of
Commercial,
Business &
Private dwellings.
Geoff's
Gran
POND ST.
HIGH STREET
Public
Library
Aunt Daisy's Flat
Fred's
Flat.
The Cafe where
they met
Reg.
S. Gate
Light Industry
'Park'
Eddy & Cyril
Pretoria Terr
Victorian Semis & Terrace
Dwellings
Police sta
The 'Kozy
Korner' Kafe
THE TADBRIDGE BY-PASS
Super
Market
DIY.
From Bidcote etc
1a
DAS 3'01
C.

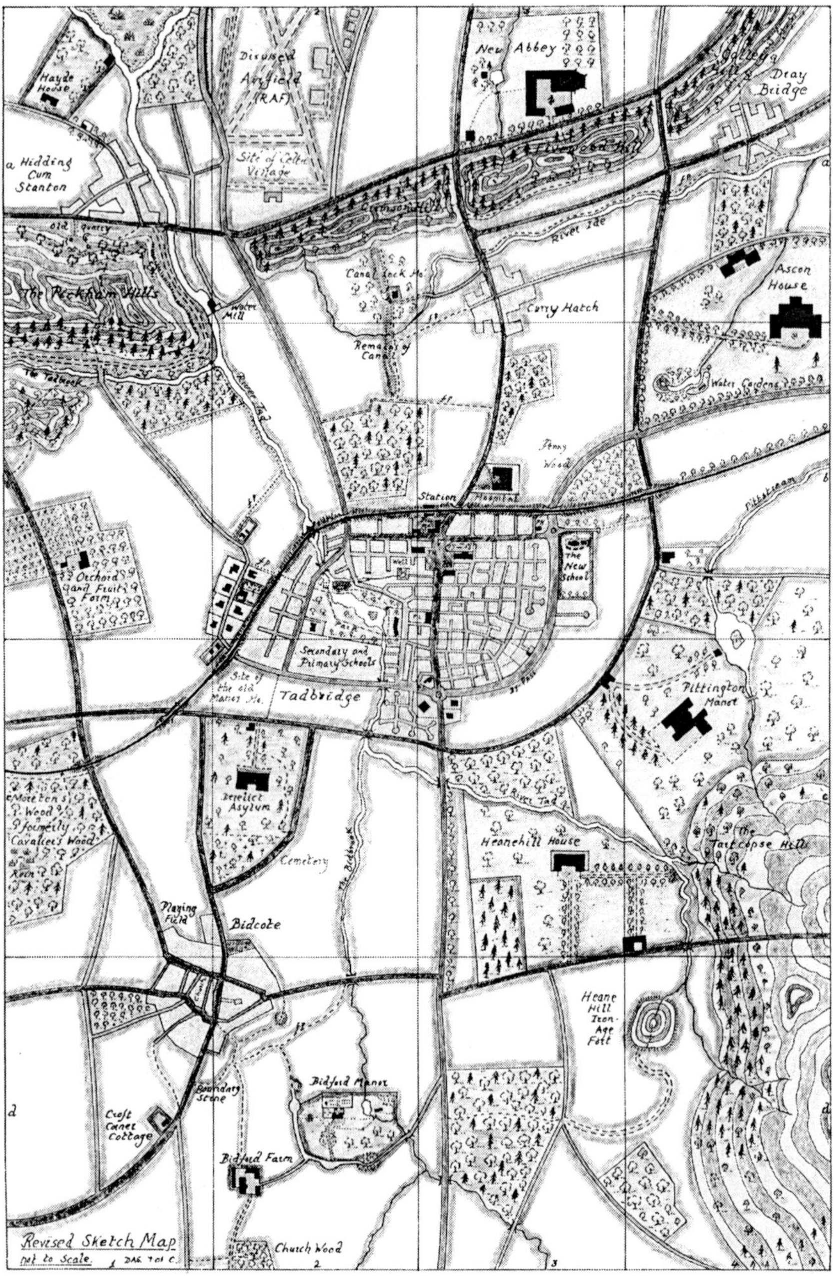

Hayde House
Disused Airfield (RAF)
Site of Celtic Village
New Abbey
Dray Bridge
Hidding Cum Stanton
Old Quarry
The Peckham Hills
Water Mill
River Tad
Canal Lock Ho.
Remains of Canal
Cony Hatch
River Ide
Ascon House
Water Gardens
Penny Wood
Station
Hospital
The New School
Orchard and Fruit Farm
Secondary and Primary Schools
Site of the old Manor Ho.
Tadbridge
Pittington Manor
Derelict Asylum
Moreton's Wood formerly Cavalier's Wood
Cemetery
River Tad
Heanehill House
The Tartcopse Hills
Playing Field
Bidcote
Heane Hill Iron-Age Fort
Boundary Stone
Bidford Manor
Croft Corner Cottage
Bidford Farm
Church Wood
Revised Sketch Map
not to scale.

INTRODUCTION

Once again we enter the lives of Sam, Sarah and their friends. If you have read the three earlier adventures you will know that from the first one, which was mainly involved with Bidford Manor and its surroundings, their circle of both friends and knowledge of the district has gradually widened and this volume will widen it still further.

Thus each story becomes more complex, as new characters and places have to be woven into the original fabric. I trust this has been achieved harmoniously, but if, good reader, or listener, you spot any inconsistencies, please let me know.

Now for a brief word about the characters and places. The inhabitants of Bidford Manor, Bidcote and Tadbridge are based on people I have known, though these are fictional, rather than factual portraits. The names are, for the most part, theirs. As chronicler, this enables me to visualise how they will act or react in certain situations. The animals are real. I have an intimate knowledge of all of them. The places are loosely based on parts of the West Country I am familiar with; however you won't find many of them on any ordnance map. They are an amalgam of several districts and sites.

Much of this is fuelled by a nostalgia for past days and times. I have made very little attempt to be contemporary, except where it proves useful, such as mobile phones and computers! The school is based on a particular educational philosophy, though somewhat modified. That's enough for now; time to start the story!

'Southleigh' Bardon Lane, The Randell's Home

Chapter I
Tankerville Road

At the end of volume three the children were happy in the knowledge that Geoffrey had been accepted into their class. Stephen and Jane had returned to their parents after Geoff's (as he is now called) interview. For, as they had said, 'If you don't come back now you might forget where you live; then we could let out your rooms!' To tell the truth they were happy to go home and hear how things had gone with their Australian aunt, uncle and cousins. The other advantage was that they could always go and stay with Sam and Sarah if their parents became tired of them! Perhaps a few words should be said about their parents–John and Phyllis. John was an estate agent working for a Tadbridge firm called Pinhorn & Pinhorn, a very respectable and long established business. His father — Reg — was their legal advisor, which is why John had joined the firm. He did not want to become a lawyer, preferring to be outside with a tape measure, rather than inside with piles of musty old legal documents. A rather thickset, but well-built man, he walked with a limp, for years ago, when playing in an important rugby match at school, he had sustained a bad injury to his right knee-cap and was unable to bend it properly. He often wore a slightly worried air, as if he'd forgotten something, but could never quite remember what it was. Phyllis blamed this on the twins, who, it must be admitted, had caused more than their fair share of traumas and disasters in the plus nine years they'd been around. Phyllis was tall, with a ready smile and gentle manner. She rarely, if ever, raised her voice, but if she did it was 'look out for squalls'! She had been Mr Pinhorn Senior's secretary; but John had won her heart, and much to the old gentleman's sorrow, she had left to become a wife and mother. Every time he met her it was the same litany.

'Ah, Phyllis, you were the best secretary I ever had. They don't train them properly nowadays. Are you sure you don't want to come back? Part time? No?' He'd then sigh a deep sigh and try the same approach next time he met her.

They live on the western outskirts of Tadbridge in Bardon Lane. Their home is a large detached Edwardian house, 'Southleigh', set in its own grounds, with an adjoining orchard. It is a rambling and many-gabled building with bits tacked on here and there. Inside it has several unusual features. The original builder had an obsession that servants should not be seen, and to avoid visitors meeting them going about their tasks, had the access to the main staircase constructed at the far end of the hallway (see plan), with a door opposite leading out, so that they could go round to the kitchen area without passing through the main rooms. The whole back section of the first floor — the servants' quarters — was cut off from the rest by a heavy green baize door. This area was now the children's bedrooms and for young visitors. Another oddity was up in the attic. In the front room, which they use as a play room, is an old beam running across the middle of the ceiling. Legend relates that it came from Sir Francis Drake's famous ship 'The Golden Hind', in which he circumnavigated the globe. The source of this tale is unknown, but the twins use it as a good story to enthral their friends and schoolmates, more of this later.

There was also a range of outbuildings and stables, useful for games and exploration — a wonderful house for hide and seek and strange corners. The children loved it. Its main disadvantages were a lack of secret rooms and passages, and as far as they knew it did not possess a house guardian. Their father had said he wasn't surprised, as he couldn't imagine any house guardian taking on the job in a house where they lived. 'He'd be a nervous wreck within a few days!' he remarked. In the matter of secret passages they had — at one time — tried to dig one in the back scullery, but had only succeeded in fracturing the water mains with the attendant flooding of the scullery and kitchen.

So it is understandable why they loved being at Bidford Manor almost as much as their own home. Of course Sam and Sarah were another good reason. They were four inseparables, and their teacher, 'Uncle Fred' Atkinson, referred to them as 'The Fatal Four' and sometimes as the 'Quartet' — sent to try his skills, and patience as a teacher and human being. As you already know, the children think he's the most super teacher in the Universe and try their best not to annoy him. Well, at least not more than they can help.

❦

School would recommence on Monday, January the twelfth and as it was now already Thursday, Stephen and Jane were busy preparing their things and complaining to Phyllis that they needed new gym shoes because the old ones were too small and Stephen must have a new set of coloured pencils. (He'd sharpened most of his original set away with the new electric pencil sharpener his father had just bought.) Jane seemed to have lost her lunch box and ruler, so it was obvious there would have to be a shopping expedition today or tomorrow. Panic! Because on Saturday they were going over to Bidford Manor, as they had been invited to a festive New Year Feast at Bidford Farm by the Game family, with who they had become very friendly.

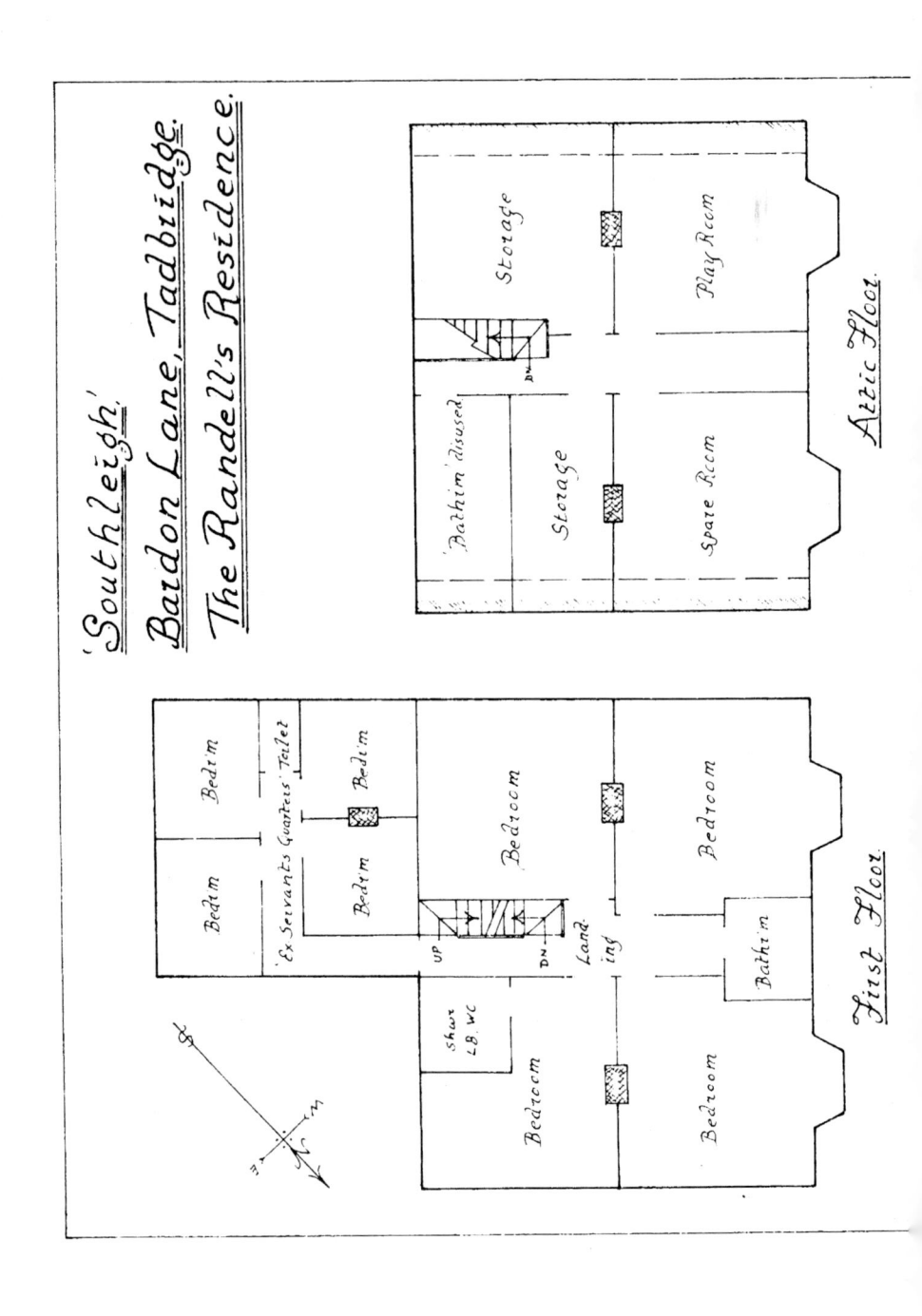

'Southleigh'
Bardon Lane, Tadbridge.
The Randell's Residence.

Attic Floor: Storage, Bathrm disused, Storage, Play Room, Spare Room.

First Floor: Bedrm, Bedrm, Ex Servants Quarters Toilet, Bedrm, Bedrm, Bedroom, Bedroom, Bathrm, Shwr L.B. WC, Landing, Bedroom, Bedroom.

Sketch Plan ~ not to Scale

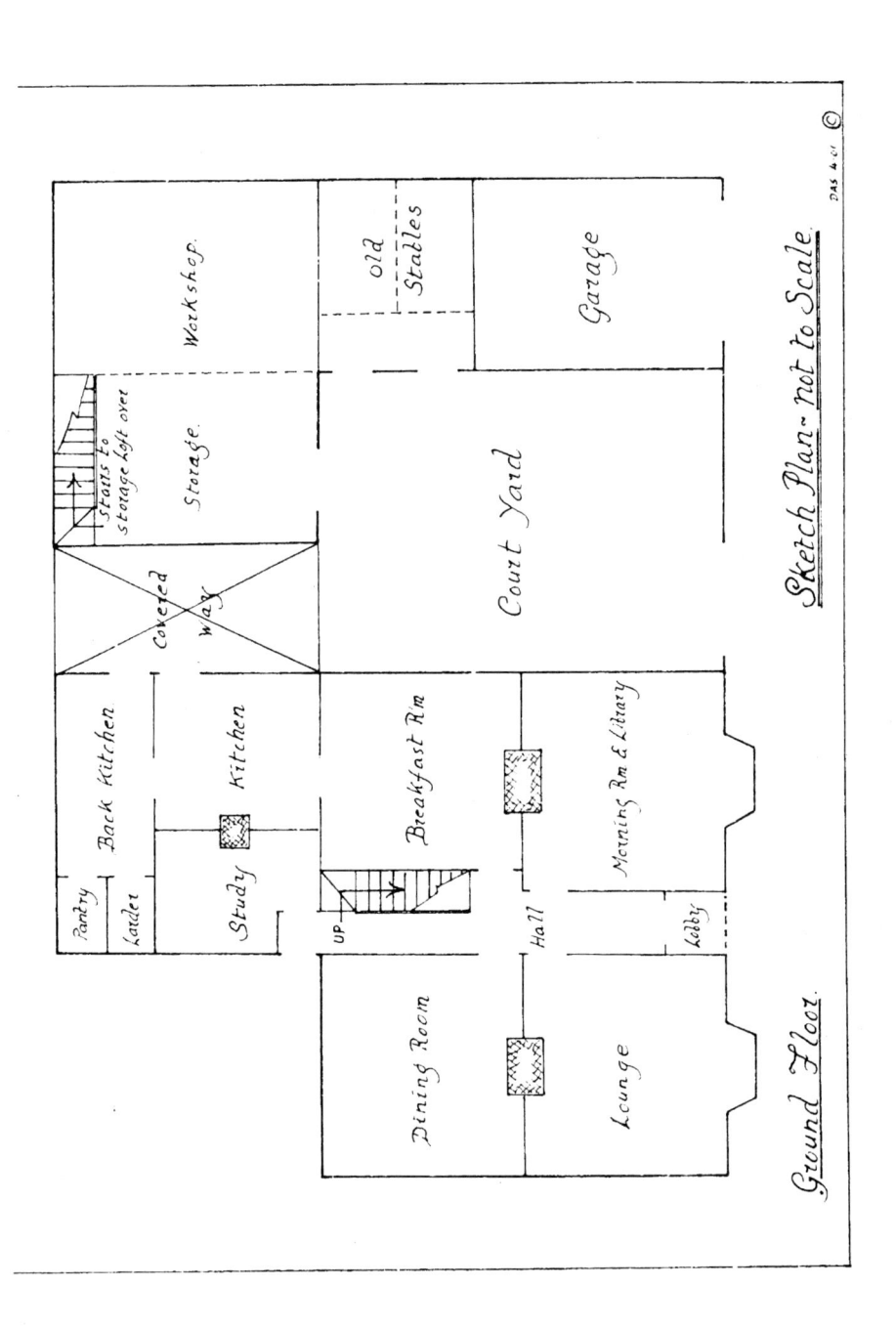

Ground Floor

- Pantry
- Larder
- Back Kitchen
- Kitchen
- Study
- Breakfast Rm
- Hall
- Lobby
- Dining Room
- Lounge
- Morning Rm & Library
- Storage (stairs to storage loft over)
- Workshop
- Covered way
- Court Yard
- Old Stables
- Garage
- UP (stairs)

Meanwhile, at the manor, Sam and Sarah were also preparing for school, with a difference. Geoff had come over for the day and they were explaining to him what he would need and also trying to tell him what to expect at school. He found it all very strange and bewildering and often asked the same question several times to make absolutely sure. On Friday afternoon their mother would take Karen, his mother, and him into Tadbridge to buy the items he would need. The Local Education Authority had already sent a cheque to cover these expenses. The twins had helped him compile a list of the necessities, as they wanted to make sure he was properly prepared.

However, there was another visitor — or rather three visitors — also seeking advice about the school. Mrs Game, with her daughter Jill, who would be starting in Kindergarten this term and 'Tiger' Brian, her young brother, who was not yet old enough for school, but naturally couldn't be left at home. Bess Game was busy chatting with Doreen, their mother, while Jill had found Sam, Sarah and Geoff up in Sarah's bedroom sorting out school things. She attached herself to Sam, for whom she had an unbounded awe, and liked nothing better than to be where he was. She was a very quiet little girl and Sam had grown used to his 'shadow', as the others called her. She would sit and watch or stand beside him, eager to help if she could, though he never took advantage of this. This afternoon she began to ask questions.

'Sam, shall I see you in school?'

He explained that the Kindergarten building was in a different part of the grounds.

She looked crestfallen. But he hastened to add that he could come over and see her during break times. With that she was content for the moment.

The afternoon was wearing on and Geoff announced that he'd better go before it became too dark. Though his new bike was properly equipped with lights, his mother didn't like the idea of him cycling along the narrow country lanes in the dark, even with lights. 'Drivers don't expect boys on bikes cycling round at night,' she told him. He left, saying he'd be back after the shopping expedition tomorrow to show them his new things.

'Mummy's taking me shopping tomorrow as well!' said Jill, 'to buy my "unicorn" and an apron and a lunch box and… …everything!' They tidied up then went downstairs to the kitchen, where Bess was preparing to leave. Brian was protesting because he'd been tickling Binky and when he stopped the little dog would pat his hand with his paw for more. 'Can't go. Must pat Binky!' he announced, but the magic words, 'Daddy will soon be home,' made him quickly change his mind.

'Why don't you come with me when I take Karen and Geoff in tomorrow afternoon?' said Doreen. 'We shall be visiting the school clothiers and there'll be plenty of room for the children in the back.'

'That would be a help,' admitted Bess. 'But what about your two?'

'They don't need to come; I've a list of the things they require. In any case, Derek promised to do some garden planning with them. They want their own plots so they can start planting in the spring.' 'Yes, yes!' echoed the twins. So it was settled that Bess, Jill and Brian would go with Doreen.

'Harry will be glad,' added Bess. 'He's got more than enough to do at the moment without having to gallivant off into town for an afternoon.' She gathered up her two and prepared to leave. 'I'll show you my new unicorn, Sam!' promised Jill as she went out the door.

Derek was busy in his study, as usual. There were several letters to answer, including one from his publishers inquiring if he would be willing to undertake a lecture tour to promote the latest (updated) edition of his book. 'All expenses paid for you and your wife,' he read. 'Why not?' he thought, and hastily dashed off a reply by e-mail to them, then forgot all about it. It was further driven from his mind by the advent of the twins wanting to know about their garden project possibilities. Soon all three of them were bent over plans of the garden seeking out likely spots and arguing over their suitability. 'Not enough sun!' 'Too dry and open!' 'Ugh! Much too wet there!' and so forth.

☙

Meanwhile what of the other occupants of Bidford Manor? These come under a slightly different category: Bill Bluff, JJ and Sir Brian de Tournai. Bill and JJ are 'house guardians', the spirits who protect houses and their occupants. Sir Brian is, on the other hand, what is loosely known as a ghost, though he would hotly dispute such a title. 'Ghost! Ghost! I'm no ghost, not one of your headless, namby-pamby wailing, sobbing miseries, floating around looking like a transparent half-starved slave! Yes, of course I can pass through walls and levitate myself, but owing to a slight miscalculation in the efficacy of a potion, when I died I was inadvertently obliged to remain in the vicinity. That is, until I have prepared the antidote. Which, I may add, I hope to have completed very shortly. A little fine adjustment of the various ingredients and it will be ready!' As he has been working on it for about four hundred years you will realise 'these things take time' — as he is fond of saying. However, with the arrival of JJ and his employment as servant-cum-general assistant, more order has come into his life, and attic study. So now there is hope that — at last — he will achieve his goal and be able to join his distinguished ancestors.

He has been of great help, and a source of much unintentional laughter during the children's previous adventures, and though they hope he will eventually free himself, they know they will miss him. Luckily, this does not seem likely for some time yet.

☙

That afternoon, down the road to the south of Bidcote, in Croft Corner Cottage, a little bird-like elderly lady, called Old Mother Thomas — or Erin to her friends — sits by the fire nursing a large white rabbit on her lap. She's trying to reach her glasses on the side-table without disturbing her pet. She needs them to read a letter she has just received. At last she manages to reach the case and perches the spectacles on her nose, opens the envelope and begins to read the contents. She gives a little exclamation of surprise and then chuckles to herself:

'Well, well! So my old friend and fellow student, Melissa Mouldyberry, is moving to Tadbridge! — — Hm. Oh, I see, her daughter and granddaughter are going to live with her. They need a place, as she and her husband have separated. He was never much good for her anyway. Ah, Rosie, she wants us to go and stay with her for a week or so when she settles in. It will be nice to have a friend nearby. Who knows, perhaps we can practise a few of the old spells again. I wonder what her grandchild is like now? Her mother would never have made a witch. Too fussy, doesn't like getting her hands dirty; always afraid of catching a cold if she went out at night. Well, we'll see when I visit.' She folded up the letter and tucked it in her pocket. 'Upsee, Rosie, I have a lotion to prepare for Mrs Flemming, her rheumatics are playing up again.'

༶

On the same afternoon, Fred Atkinson sat in the staff-room with his fellow teachers at a pre-term meeting chaired by the Headmaster, Neville Harrow, MA. It was mainly a briefing session to inform them of any changes in staff or administration, and to review the new pupils. Geoffrey had been mentioned, also Jill, and the meeting began to break up, as everybody was eager to start preparing their classrooms. Fred rose to go.

'Oh, Fred! Hang on a moment, I'd like a word with you.'

The Head was beckoning him over. Rather reluctantly he followed him to his study.

'Sit down.'

'Thanks.'

He picked up a letter, looked at it, then turned to Fred. 'Could you take another girl into your class?'

Fred sensed this was not as straightforward as it sounded. 'Yes, there's room, I have nineteen students at the moment and we've said the maximum class size is twenty-five. But you know that as well as I. Why did you ask?' The Head looked slightly embarrassed and indicated the letter in his hand.

'This is from an old colleague of mine who is head of a primary school in Plymouth. He informs me that a student from their Class IV is moving to Tadbridge and the mother has expressed the wish for her daughter to attend this school. However, there seem to be a few problems — not that I don't think you won't be able to manage them,' he added hastily.

'What kind of problems?'

'I'll read part of what he says: "Mrs Evard has just separated from her husband and has decided to go to Tadbridge, as her mother is moving there and can provide them with a home. Michelle is a quiet, well-mannered child who works hard and achieves a reasonable standard of performance. However, her interaction with her classmates is not easy. I have to confess I'm baffled by it. She seems friendly enough and yet — well — strange things happen and many pupils appear to be wary of her. I'm sure the methods you employ would benefit her greatly to overcome her anti-social behaviour. Her mother tends to fly off the handle at times. But she does have her daughter's welfare at heart and tries to be as cooperative as possible."

He put the letter down and looked at Fred. 'What do you think?'

'I don't quite know what to think. There's Geoffrey who's

joining us. He may take some time to adjust, though the Court twins have made friends with him and Sarah is especially keen to help him settle in. Anyway, what about Michelle's interview?'

The Head cleared his throat awkwardly. 'Er, well, that's a problem. The actual date they arrive here is not yet fixed. They may be here this weekend—or may be not. Her mother wants us to accept Michelle in any case, with or without interview! Highly unusual, I know. However, as she would be in your class, I leave the final decision with you.'

'That's a fine example of buck-passing!' thought Fred. Then an idea occurred to him. 'Neville, can I have until tomorrow midday to think it over? I'll probably say "yes" but I would like a little time to ponder the decision.'

'That's fine, Fred. If you ring me before two o'clock I can then contact Mrs Evard and let her know if everything's all right.'

Fred left the Head's study and drove back to his flatlet, which was in the newly developed part of Tadbridge. It was late afternoon. He picked up the phone and dialled the Court's number.

'Hello, ah, Derek! How are things going? Good, good. I wonder if I could have a word with Sarah and Sam. Sarah first? They are around? (A loud crash in the background and muffled voices confirmed for him they were.) Yes, I'll hang on!' A few moments later, 'Sarah? It's Fred. Yes, I'm fine. Are you ready for Monday? That's nice! Sarah, I want to ask you something—and Sam, is he there? Can he hear as well? Oh, good idea, he's listening on the hall extension. Hi, Sam! Yes, fine! Now both of you listen carefully!' and he told them briefly about Michelle and her problem. 'I'd like you to tell me what you think. As a class could we help her?' The answer was an unequivocal, 'Yes! Of course we can, especially with you as class teacher! Jane and Stephen would agree too!' they added. That settled it,. When he put the phone down he knew in his heart of hearts that this child, Michelle, belonged in the class.

Melissa's House, The Laurels, Tankaville Road

Chapter II

The Laurels, Tankerville Road, West Tadbridge had been empty for some months since old Mrs Bignell had died. Messrs Pinhorn and Pinhorn had been trying to sell it, but the 'For Sale' board was now leaning at a crazy angle and its writing was weathered and faded. No buyers. And no wonder! The place was dilapidated. These 'desirable properties' had been built in the mid 1930's and the majority had been renovated and modernised; but not Mrs Bignell's. Since her husband had died it had remained in a time warp and still possessed — for example — its original coke-fired hot water boiler, plumbing and wiring, and an 'Ideal' gas cooker. All were now in urgent need of repair or replacement. The whole place needed redecorating both inside and out. The garden was a wilderness. The neighbours knew it was really nobody's fault that it was in such a state and just hoped somebody would quickly buy it and do it up. After all, it lowered the tone of the neighbourhood.

Then, just after Christmas, an agent from Pinhorn's was seen to drive up and help a rather formidable middle-aged lady out of the car and take her round the place. The neighbours' spirits rose. A buyer? Yes! For a few days later the 'For Sale' board came down and a 'Sold' one went up. However, the young man who put it there knew nothing about the new owner, so the locals would have to wait until 'she' moved in.

In the offices of Pinhorn and Pinhorn some heads were also shaking. Whoever heard of a middle-aged lady being delighted with the condition of the house? Who, on entering it, had clapped her hands in ecstasy and cried out, 'Perfect, perfect!' Who drooled over the old boiler, the dripping taps and the fuses, which kept blowing when more than one light was switched on at a time, the dingy old wallpaper and paint work and the jungle-like condition of the garden?

When she came to sign the contract, Mrs M. Mouldyberry had looked appalled when old Mr Pinhorn had suggested several builders who would be only too happy to 'do it up' for her. She seemed horrified. 'Do it up! Whatever for! It's perfect, my dear man, just perfect!' What's more, she had paid the full price without a quiver. Not that it was overpriced, but most people wanted a mortgage. However, not so this lady!

Tankerville Road watched eagerly for signs of redecoration. There were none. Instead, early on that Friday morning, around five a.m. to be precise, there was the sound of horses' hooves and the creaking of iron shod cart wheels making a raucous sound on the tar and gravelled road. Curtains fluttered at upstairs windows as, overcome by curiosity, the neighbours peeped out.

They saw two enormous covered wagons each drawn by two great carthorses trundle slowly up the road and halt in front of The Laurels. They gazed, with some surprise, when the new owner suddenly appeared at the gates and opened them. But where had she come from? The house? The garden? 'It was as if she sort of materialised,' remarked one watcher—of spiritualist leanings—when telling her friends, 'One moment she wasn't there and the next she was!' The carts were backed in for easy unloading and the horses were given nosebags, into which they plunged their muzzles and munched away contentedly. But who put them on? Nobody could remember seeing anybody actually doing it. Further frustration followed, as the high covers of the wagons made it impossible to see what was being unloaded, so no comments, or judgments, could be passed on the new owner's furniture. Then, after what seemed only a short while, the carts moved off and disappeared up the road. Mr Wilkinson, who lived next door, swore they were only there for ten minutes, and he should know, as he was a compulsive clock-watcher. Then who had driven them? Nobody had seen any drivers dismount or remount and they had, according to some, literally disappeared. They'd gone up the road; one minute they were there and the next minute were not! The Laurels looked no different from before, except there were thick net curtains up at all the windows. In ten minutes? Very puzzling. Up and down the road people were making tea in their kitchens and discussing the events they had just witnessed, or thought they'd witnessed.

Later that morning several of the ladies who spearheaded the 'Tankerville Road Residents Development Association' decided they should pay the new occupant a social call. Armed with various plates of home baking, they advanced in a phalanx up the road and paused at the gate. Another shock. The Laurels nameplate had gone, and in its place was one reading: 'Goulhaven'. The ladies sniffed in disgust, how vulgar! However, undeterred, they marched up to the front door and rang the bell. A deep ringing tone, like the tolling of a funeral bell, assailed their ears. The door flew open and Mrs Mouldyberry stood there regarding them with some distaste. Before Mrs Beauville, the leader and Honorary President of the T.R.R.D.A. could open her mouth and say her piece, she spoke, 'I know what you've come for, you nosy lot. I've no time for the likes of you, off you go and leave me alone, I've work to do — which is more than you idle lot have! You can take your plates of stuff away too. Fancy bringing such rubbish! Grown women like you should know better!' With that she slammed the door in their faces. The vigour with which she shut it caused much of the loose plaster in the porch to descend on them, soiling their best morning clothes. But that was not all. When the good ladies looked at the plates of dainties they carried, screams sprang from their mouths and they dropped them in horror. Instead of dainty meringues, cupcakes, fluffy sponges and tartlets, there were wriggling masses of maggots, worms, spiders and other noxious insects. The ladies fled.

No other movement was seen in 'Goulhaven' for the rest of the day — and a strict watch was kept upon it! Then late in the afternoon a taxi drove up and a woman and little girl got out, dragging two large suitcases up to the front door. It opened and they disappeared inside, the cause of further speculation amongst the neighbours!

☙

During that afternoon, as arranged, Doreen drove Karen, Geoff, Bess, Jill and 'Tiger' Brian into Tadbridge to do their school shopping. She dropped them off in the High Street and then went to the supermarket to do her weekly shop. Having put this in the boot, she walked to the High Street to do her own school shopping, then made her way to the cafe where they had met Reg during their first visit to Tadbridge back in early November. The 'Mums' had decided this would be a good place to meet for a 'cuppa' after shopping, as they would all be tired and thirsty. Well, maybe not Doreen, but she could always be counted on to enjoy a sit down and chat over tea. So there they were drinking tea while the children had fruit drinks and nice sticky cakes. Having refreshed themselves, they made their way down to the car park and drove back to Bidford Manor, as Geoff wanted to show off his acquisitions and Jill was still telling all and sundry she was going to show Sam her 'unicorn'. Doreen would then drive Geoff and his Mum home — after another cup of tea, no doubt.

☙

Sam and Sarah had spent the morning making their final preparations for school, apart from adding the items their Mum would bring back from the shopping expedition. After lunch, when she had left to pick up Bess and her children, plus Karen and Geoff, they went round the grounds with their father to pick out the best place for their garden plots. This was a serious business and took quite some time. At last, with Derek's consent, they settled on a section of the old terraced gardens on the eastern side of the main path. At the end there was a shed still in a reasonable state of repair, and the water tap by it still worked. They were on the same level as the old boiler house (see site map).

Once these decisions were made their father went off to struggle with cutting back some over-enthusiastic creepers in the old ornamental garden. The children wandered off in the direction of the summer house; however — on impulse — took the path that led to the Dell first. This was part of the property they had scarcely explored at all. In fact the last time they were there was when Stephen and Sarah had found the old sundial globe. Sam had never really been there, apart from one of the early quick walks round the grounds they had taken on moving in. The path had the Bidbrook on its right and the plantation on its left. Somehow, as they neared their objective, a feeling of unease began to creep over them. They found themselves glancing at the trees as if they expected something to appear and beckon — or worse — leap out and seize them. The brook seemed to rush along in an angry manner, foaming and bubbling, making a strange singing sound as it swirled between its steep banks. Though they knew it wasn't deep, there was the feeling that if they fell in they would be swept away and under into the murky green depths below, seized by scaly arms and carried into dark caverns. Both children shuddered, but continued in spite of these feelings until they reached the Dell. It looked rather forlorn, the saucer-shaped sides were weed-choked, the steps chipped and cracked, and the stone pillar that had carried the sundial looked like the decayed stump of a tooth sticking up out of the mud and debris which surrounded it. The crystal wall was also mud-smeared and in the dull afternoon light seemed to be built of dark grey rocks. Nothing sparkled or glittered vividly in the way Sarah remembered it when she and Stephen had been there. They clambered down the steps and stood hesitantly by the sundial pillar looking at the crystal wall.

'I wonder where the secret passage, whose entrance we saw coming in this direction, leads to?' mused Sarah.

'I don't know, but it must lead somewhere to something, otherwise why make it!' retorted Sam.

'Perhaps there's a secret room under here?' suggested his sister.

'But why, what for?' he asked.

'I don't know, but there must be something, though what, I'm not sure.' she replied.

But even as she spoke there was a sudden tremor under their feet. The ground shook and with a loud crack the old pillar broke off near its base and nearly fell onto their feet. Startled, they jumped back to avoid it. A crack appeared in the paving and a cloud of what appeared to be smoke issued forth. There was a rumbling sound; it closed again with a grinding crunch. Something seemed to brush past them and was gone. For a moment they stood petrified, then swiftly left the Dell and its dismal surroundings, quickly making their way back to the house. The sky had gone strangely dark and a cold wind had sprung up. They met their father coming in as well.

'Funny weather!' he remarked. They were just about to tell him of their experience when the 'toot, toot' of a car announced the return of the shoppers and of course they were soon caught up in the swirl of Geoff wanting to show them his new stuff and Jill begging Sam to see her 'unicorn' and their mother loading them up with the school items they'd requested.

☙

Stephen and Jane had taken the local bus into Tadbridge that afternoon. There were a couple of things that had been overlooked during the morning's shop. Not vital, but it gave them an excuse to go into town again and have a poke round. When their errands were completed they decided to walk back. If they left Market Square by the way to Westgate, where a road to the left crossed the River Tad, it led to a footpath on the right to Tankerville Road and then under the railway embankment into Bardon Lane quite near to their home. This was the way they took. By the time they reached Tankerville Road it was already dusk, so they quickened their pace, wanting to be back before it was dark. A house at the end caught their attention as they crossed the road. There were lights in its windows. Lights quite unlike anything they had ever seen in an ordinary house. One moment they were a livid green, then the upstairs one would become a fiery red whilst the lower windows glowed a strange uncanny blue, flecked with brown spots. They stopped and stared for a moment. It made them feel uneasy, so they quickened their pace down the path. The fences on either side were high and they could not see over them, but as they reached where it went under the railway, there some of the fencing had rotted and fallen, so it was possible to see into the far garden. Stephen caught sight of some movement out of the corner of his eye and halted. Jane also stopped. They turned and stared. Hovering just above fence level in that garden was a broomstick, with a girl astride, bathed in that same weird greenish light. As they watched, she turned her head and saw them. The dim light made it difficult to see her features clearly. Then a voice called out, 'That will be enough for the moment, Michelle, you can come in now!' The light vanished and the twins could no longer see anything or anyone.

They walked on in silence until they were nearly home when Stephen said, 'Did you see her face?'

'Not really,' replied his sister, 'that weird light made it difficult to see anything clearly!'

'I did, just before it went out.'

'And?'

'She looked terrified, and when she saw us she seemed to be trying to say something.'

'You're not making it up are you?' said Jane.

'No, I'm sure of what I saw,' he replied.

They had reached and turned into the gates of their home, Southleigh. It was so solid and comforting and its lights were behaving normally.

Both found it hard to believe what they had seen. Stephen was more convinced about it than Jane, for something told him they hadn't seen the last of the strange frightened little girl on the broomstick!

Chapter III

Saturday dawned a crisp and bright winter's day. Both pairs of twins were up early, as Stephen and Jane had to prepare for their visit to Sam and Sarah, who were also busy preparing for their visit! This was the day of the festive gathering at the farm. Besides the Court and Randell families—for John and Phyllis had also been invited—there would be Reg, Fred, Erin, Karen and Geoff; not to mention Rosie, Binky and Cleo!

❧

The gathering was to begin around two o'clock, but the Randell twins and their parents would arrive at the manor mid-morning so the grown-ups could have a 'good old gossip', as Jane put it. The twins would also have a chance to catch up on things; after all they hadn't seen each other since Wednesday.

Sarah suggested to Sam that upon their arrival they held a meeting in the secret room, then they could tell them of their strange experience in the Dell. Together they prepared a tray-load of 'provisions' to assist in the telling. As soon as the Randells arrived and their parents were all happily drinking tea or coffee in the sitting room, the children made their tray-laden way upstairs, through Sarah's room and up to the little attic room above. Naturally, Binky and Cleo came too; they saw no future in being with the grown-ups who were not nearly so generous as the children with tidbits!

Once they were settled and refreshed, and the animals had contentedly curled up by their feet, Sam and Sarah related their experience in the Dell.

'You say you felt something brush by you as the crack in the paving closed?' queried Stephen.

'Yes, like a breath of warm air, though afterwards it became very dark and cold,' replied Sam.

'Did it feel good or bad?' asked Jane.

'Neither really,' said Sarah, 'more as if some energy, or force was released from where it had been hidden for many, many years, even hundreds.'

They talked about it for some time but came to no conclusion as to what it was, or what it could be. Both Sam and Sarah insisted that the atmosphere in the Dell and its surroundings were 'strange'.

'Talking of strange things,' said Jane, 'we had a funny experience yesterday too.' She told them about the weirdly lit house and the girl on the broomstick. Stephen added his belief that the girl was scared. 'Her name was Michelle,' he added.

'Well,' said Sam, 'I don't suppose we'll ever find out any more about her!' — he was 100% wrong about this! — continuing, 'Once Dad starts work on the passages, we can go down the one leading towards the Dell and maybe find out what caused that mini-quake and, possibly, what it released.' Everyone nodded, but Stephen still looked uncertain. He just could not get the picture of that frightened girl on the broomstick out of his mind. Anyhow, the conversation now passed on to school and how they could help Geoff to become one of their class and also keep an eye on Jill. Then Sarah remembered Mr Atkinson's phone call about the new girl and her 'problems', though he did not actually know what they were. Stephen and Jane agreed with their decision and promised to help.

'What's her name?' asked Stephen.

'It's Michelle,' said Sarah.

There was a silence and they all looked at each other.

Sam spoke first. 'Do you think?' he said slowly.

'Just a coincidence I expect,' remarked Jane. But a glance at her brother told her he thought otherwise.

'It may look like a coincidence,' he said, 'but I don't think it is!'

'Well, we can ask Uncle Fred this afternoon if he knows any more about her,' said Sarah. At that moment the gong went for lunch, so they all trooped downstairs. The animals arrived first.

Afterwards, there was a certain amount of preparation to be done regarding dress, hair, face and hands for both sets of twins, with Doreen and Phyllis both muttering things like: 'I don't know how you manage it! How could you lose a hair-ribbon Jane? You've only been in the car. Stephen, your hands look as if you've dipped them in car-oil!' Or, 'Sam, look at your shoes, they're filthy! What have you been doing? You haven't been outside yet! Sarah! What on earth made you put that jersey on? There are holes in both elbows! I know you like it, but for heaven's sake child, you are going to a party, not a jumble sale!' And in chorus from both mothers to all four of them, 'Go and wash — properly — and brush and comb your hair!' At last everyone was ready, duly inspected and passed. It was now quarter to two and they started off towards the farm, with Binky on his lead and Cleo in the cat basket.

Approaching the farm, they could see two small figures swinging on the gate, from which, as soon as they spotted them, they detached themselves and rushed forwards, making a beeline for Jane and Sam. In a trice 'Tiger' Brian had Jane by the hand and was pulling her excitedly towards the farm and Jill was hanging on to Sam's arm, swinging herself along and chattering away about her 'unicorn', which she was wearing under her coat specially to show him.

In a few moments they were standing in the large kitchen with the great stove and all the various pots and pans upon it giving off the most toothsome smells! However, as this was a festive occasion, the meal would be held in the dining room. They were escorted through the kitchen, along a stone-flagged passage and into a long, low-beamed room with a refectory table, mellow with the polish of ages and laid with gleaming silver, sparkling glasses and shining side-plates. Crisp white serviettes were by each place and crackers, whilst in the centre was a magnificent arrangement of winter greenery and dried flowers. In the large inglenook fireplace a great blaze of logs was scenting and warming the room. They gasped with delight. More voices told them that the other guests had begun to arrive. Sure enough, Fred, Reg, Erin, with Rosie in her arms, and Karen and Geoff now joined them. Soon all were seated on benches along either side of the table. Bess was at the foot and Harry at the head, where he acted as carver of the most enormous roast turkey anyone could remember seeing for many a year. There was much lively talk and laughter during the meal and stretches of silence whilst food was consumed. The dessert was an enormous crystal bowl of trifle and by the time that was empty everybody was sighing with contentment, or as 'Tiger' put it, 'Me full up, right over to above my ears!' Now Harry rose and said, 'To the drawing room everybody, make yourselves comfortable while Bess and I bring in the coffee, the after dinner mints, and so forth.'

The drawing room was another low-beamed room with a view out across the fields towards Church Wood. There were armchairs and sofas one could sink into — just right after such a meal. Soon everybody was happily settled before a roaring fire in the giant hearth. The three animals were stretched out in luxurious comfort before it. They too had been given a special meal and were very content! Tiger was snuggled up next to Jane, looking rather sleepy, but strongly denying it. Jill was next to Sam, looking very smart in her uniform (with his help she'd now got the word right!) which consisted of a tartan skirt with a white blouse, a light blue cardigan and white knee-socks. She talked quietly to him, obviously asking questions about school, which was now only two days away! After the coffee and mints had been distributed, conversations began between different groups. The children had managed to group themselves around Uncle Fred and no sooner had he taken a sip of his coffee when Sarah opened the barrage.

'Uncle Fred, do you know anything more about the new girl, Michelle?'

'Nothing more than what I told you on the phone! Though just before coming here I talked to the Head, saying I would accept her; he told me he'd had a brief call confirming they had arrived in Tadbridge and are in Tankerville Road with her grandmother.' There was a startled exclamation from the other side of the fireplace. Erin had caught the last part of his remark.

'Did you say Tankerville Road?' she inquired.

'Yes, a new pupil, just arrived from Plymouth, but I haven't met her yet.'

'Her name wouldn't be Michelle Evard, by any chance?'

'Why, yes. How did you know?'

'Her grandmother is an old friend of mine; we were students together many years ago, though I haven't seen her for ages. However, I received a letter from her the other day informing me that she was moving to Tadbridge and her daughter and granddaughter were coming to live with her.'

'Apparently there's some problem with Michelle. Do you know anything about it?'

'Well, I saw the child once, years ago, when she was only a baby. But I could imagine a possible problem. You see, her mother doesn't hold with her mother's occupation and the grandmother is determined that if her daughter won't follow in her footsteps, her granddaughter will! She told me that when the child was born.'

'That's odd,' said Fred, 'what is the good lady's occupation?'

Without so much as a blush, or turning a hair, Erin replied, 'She's a witch.'

There was silence while the grown-ups digested this. Then Derek spoke. 'You mean a witch like yourself?' He meant it to be a statement, but it sounded far more like a question.

Erin hesitated before she replied. 'Well, her training was in that direction, but Melissa was always poking round the uncharted fringes of magic. I would call her, regretfully, because I'm really rather fond of her, a grey witch!'

'What's a grey witch?' asked Sam.

'One who has good intentions, but is rather lax on how she achieves them. One who is not above using methods not generally approved of by my fraternity, but who is still too 'good' for the black fraternity. They tend to do things that enhance their power rather than use their gifts to help others. Melissa has a good heart, but is impulsive and impatient. She has invited me for a week's visit once she's settled in, so then I shall be able to judge the situation better. I am concerned about Michelle. If, as you say, she has problems at school, they may be caused by her grandmother's training. I... ...'

Here Stephen broke in, 'Jane and I saw her, yesterday evening. She was on a broomstick in the back garden of their house; she looked terrified.' Jane nodded in agreement.

Fred looked concerned, then grinned at the children. 'We're committed now! How do you feel about taking on a witchlet?' They weren't sure.

Instead, Stephen turned to Erin. 'How can we help her? I mean, suppose she doesn't want to be a witch?' He paused, adding, 'It's all very confusing!'

'It is indeed, Stephen, and until I know more about what Melissa has been up to it's hard to give advice. The main thing is to be kind, gentle and understanding with her. That child has not had an easy life. Her father was a watchmaker—Swiss, I believe—a clever man, but incredibly lazy and unreliable. One day he'd be all over his daughter, the next he'd thrust her away. She never knew how he'd treat her. Her mother's erratic, though has her daughter's welfare at heart, as you've heard. Her grandmother has been the only stable element in her life. So, as I've suggested, do your best to make her welcome and we'll play it by ear at first.'

Geoff had been listening to all this with his mouth open. Now he spoke, 'She'll be new to the school. So am I, but I can't think of a better place for her, especially with friends like you around.' He indicated all the twins. 'I'll help her all I can!' he added.

There seemed to be no more to say on the subject at the moment and the talk shifted to other matters. Final arrangements were made for Jill to travel to and from school with the twins, except on Wednesdays when her mother was in town and could collect her at lunchtime. Then the plans for the rejuvenation of the village were discussed—how the fund was going, and when a committee meeting should be held.

This was rather boring for the children, so they gathered in a corner and chatted quietly until the word 'passages' caught their attention, so they rejoined the grown-ups. Derek was speaking. 'I've had a call from a Mr Hugh Dawes, the builder in Bidcote. He wanted to know if we needed help on our committee; but he also mentioned that as work is slack for him and his men at this time of the year, was there anything he could do for us 'up at the manor'? I asked if he would be interested in clearing out and repairing the secret passages, fixing proper doors or covers and wiring them up for lighting. He said yes, so I've arranged a tentative meeting with him for next Friday afternoon to check out what really needs doing. I thought that evening we could have a meeting with

Bill, Sir Brian, JJ and any of you who would like to be there.'

'Count me in,' said Fred; 'and me,' added Reg. 'Us too!' shouted the children. 'Oh, I'd already counted you lot in,' said Derek with a twinkle in his eye.

'By the way,' said Harry 'we've got a new postmaster. Simm was replaced pretty quickly! A young chap called Roger Fisher, with his wife and three children. He came down today and is staying at the 'Three Feathers'. His family and furniture arrive on Monday. Seems to be a likable chap. Maybe he'll put some life into that miserable building. One of us should visit him soon and tell him about our committee.'

During the latter conversation Bess had quietly slipped out and now reappeared at the door with, 'Tea is ready!' This time the dining room was laid out with a right royal spread of sandwiches, cakes, jellies and an large 'New Year Cake' decorated with icing and symbols for each month of the coming year. Afterwards it was time to leave; gradually coats and hats were gathered and goodbyes said. Fred took Erin home and Reg, Karen and Geoff. The Courts and Randells, plus animals, set off up the farm road back to the manor.

It was a clear, frosty evening with stars twinkling in a deep blue sky. As they reached the lane they could see the manor nestling against the hillside bathed in silvery moonlight; it looked calm and peaceful. But then, away to the right, by the plantation, a strange flickering green light appeared, twisting and writhing up and then plunging earthwards. Suddenly it disappeared, as if swallowed up by the ground. At the same time the children were sure they saw a figure on a broomstick hovering above the spot where the lights had vanished, then it was gone. Stephen turned to the others. 'That light was just like the one Jane and I saw in the windows of the house in Tankerville Road!' he remarked.

Chapter IV

Stephen and Jane had gone home that evening, as everyone was well and truly tired out after such a wonderful afternoon. Their mothers had felt they all needed a day of peace and quiet before school on Monday. Also, Bess and Doreen made the final arrangements regarding Jill. In the morning Harry would bring her over and she would walk up to the bus stop with Sam and Sarah. After Kindergarten finished at lunchtime, she would stay in the care session run for the little ones until the end of school and travel back with the twins, and Harry would pick her up at five o'clock.

Sam and Sarah spent a quiet day. In the morning, as it was clear and mild, they did some clearing of their new garden plots, but made no attempt to go near the Dell. During the afternoon they read and played games and after supper it was bath and bedtime. There was the usual last minute checking of school things and temporary panic for items that had mysteriously disappeared.

'I know I left it on my bed only a minute ago, now it's gone!'

'Is this it?'

'Yes! Where did you find it?'

'Under your bed!' At last everything was ready and they thankfully settled down for a good night's sleep.

For Stephen and Jane it was a similar day of relaxing and

making sure they too had everything ready. However, by lunchtime they had finished, so the afternoon was 'free'. As it was still clear and mild they decided to walk to St Andrew's Park (see map). This meant they could take the short cut, via the footpath, which was their intention. They hoped that by some chance they might get a glimpse of Michelle and possibly her grandmother. They reached Tankerville Road with no sign of anyone, but as it was daylight they could have a better view of 'Goulhaven'. So they walked slowly up to the end of the cul-de-sac as if looking for a particular house. Stephen seemed to be having trouble with his shoelaces. They came undone quite a number of times and he had to kneel down to re-tie them. It was an old trick but highly effective, as Jane could stand by him looking exasperated, but at the same time looking round. The third 'untieup' occurred directly opposite their objective and took some time to remedy. Jane's comments were as follows:

'All the curtains are drawn. The place looks a mess, it needs painting and the garden is a wilderness. Wait a minute; I'm sure I saw a curtain move in one of the upstairs windows. I think we are being watched. Yes! It's in the bedroom over the downstairs front room. I'm sure it's "you know who", Stephen! Oh, a great puff of green smoke just shot out of a side chimney—that must be the kitchen one. Now it's turned a dirty red. It just goes straight up then vanishes! Have you finished yet?' He had, and got up to join his sister. 'Don't look at the place, let's just walk on as if we're in a hurry.'

They did so, turning down the next section of the footpath. Once they were out of sight of the house Jane said, 'I'm sure we were watched, I glanced back as we left the road and there was a woman standing on the front door step staring after us. We'll have to be careful, she didn't look very friendly.'

'Well, we'll have to come back by this path,' said Stephen.

'There are no buses on Sunday and I don't want to have to walk home the long way round.' Seeing Jane's look of concern he added, 'Don't worry, we'll go back while it's still daylight.'

There was a play area by the park entrance, so they spent some time on the swings and slides before walking round the edge of the lake. This would bring them back to their exit. As they passed the boathouse, Jane whispered, 'I think we are being followed, there's a big, funnily dressed lady some way behind us. I'm sure she was the one I saw looking at us from the front porch!'

'Right, follow me!' said her brother, he turned round sharply and began to head back down the path at a brisk trot. Jane almost had to run to keep up with him. Stephen had his head down, but murmured, 'What's she doing?'

'She's stepped off the path and sat down on a bench.'

'Good, we'll go past and see what she does.'

They walked by without looking at their follower. As they crossed the bridge past the castle ruins Stephen glanced back. She'd risen and was coming down the path towards them. 'Wait until she's near the bridge and then we do the same as before,' he whispered. 'There are no seats here so she won't be able to pretend she's resting.'

They idly watched the water flowing under the bridge until the lady turned the corner by some bushes and came into full view. 'Now!' hissed Stephen and they pelted back towards her. This move was obviously totally unexpected and for a moment the mysterious lady stared open-mouthed at the two children running towards her — then, she vanished! The twins stopped abruptly and stared at each other in bewilderment.

'She's gone!'

'No she hasn't, look over there,' Jane pointed across to the large ornamental fountain that dominated this side of the park. There, standing by it, the bizarrely costumed lady could be seen. She looked rather flummoxed. 'Homewards,' announced Stephen and they darted across the bridge, past the play area and out of the gates towards the footpath.

As they entered it, Jane said, 'If she can move herself from one place to another so easily, no matter how quickly we move, she could still catch us!'

'How true,' said a deep husky voice, and there, blocking the pathway before them, was their follower. Stephen's hand plunged into his pocket and drew forth the box Erin had given him at Christmas. Quickly he chanted:

'Little box we've no wish to roam.
Please take Jane and I straight home!'

The next second they felt as if something had wrapped itself round them, plunging them both into a dark comforting place. There was a feeling of movement, a flickering light and they were standing at the entrance gates of Southleigh. Stephen held his box in his hand. He laughed, 'Did you notice the expression on her face when I said the rhyme? She looked really gob-smacked!' Jane was greatly relieved to be safe at home and exclaimed, 'Oh, Stephen, how lucky you had your box!' 'I always carry it with me,' he replied. They went inside and decided not to tell their parents what had happened, but would definitely have a word with Sam and Sarah tomorrow during break.

That evening, in several different homes, children were settling down for the night. Geoff had all his school things neatly packed in a brand new school bag and his uniform folded on his bedside chair awaiting him. Jill's was also beside her bed, together with her lunch box, which she had insisted on taking up with her. Both sets of twins, being old hands at this kind of thing, were ready. But what of the little girl who slept in the room over the porch in 'Goulhaven', was she ready?

༄

Next morning Sam and Sarah were up early and had

finished breakfast well before seven thirty. At seven forty Geoff arrived. He parked his bike in the yard and now stood with the twins on the front porch awaiting the arrival of Jill. A few minutes later Harry appeared with her and they set off up the lane towards the bus stop. Jill was clutching Sam's hand, but she chattered away brightly and did not show any signs of being worried. Geoff was rather silent, but when Sarah spoke to him, he answered readily. The bus arrived on time and they scrambled in, greeting old friends and introducing Geoff to three or four members of the class who also travelled on it. These were Gillian, Vanessa, Billy and Jonathan. Geoff was somewhat bewildered by the way they greeted him so openly and in such a friendly manner. Jonathan told him there was an empty place next to him and he'd ask Mr Atkinson if Geoff could sit there. Soon the two of them were chatting together as if they'd known each other since class one. Sarah breathed a sigh of relief; everything was going to be all right. There were also two Kindergarten children travelling with elder brothers and sisters. The little girl Nola began by talking to Sam, but soon Jill was drawn into the conversation and was happily holding Nola's and Sam's hand when they got off the bus. He took her over to the Kindergarten, and having deposited his little charge, promised to visit her at break time (with permission, of course). Then he raced back to the classroom.

All was happy confusion as usual. Shouts of greeting and, 'What did you get for Christmas? I got a...' were going at full steam. However, when the first bell went, everyone made for their places as Mr Atkinson came through the doorway. Sarah noticed he looked worried. Then she realised—where was the other new pupil, Michelle? As their teacher entered he started to close the door, but it would not budge, as if someone or something was preventing it from being shut. So he looked round to see what stopped him from closing it. From where she was sitting Sarah could see through the partly open door to the passage outside. One moment it had been empty, then two people were standing there, one of them holding the door handle so it could not be shut. She gasped. Where had they come from? How had they arrived? Realising somebody was there, Mr Atkinson quickly let go of the door and apologised to the 'door holder'. This was a lady in her mid-thirties. She was not unpleasant looking, but there was an air of uncertainty on her face, as if she was not sure she should be there. Her clothes were smart, but rather old-fashioned and probably came from a charity shop. She looked quickly round the classroom and addressed Mr Atkinson in a quiet voice, sounding rather out of breath, as if she'd been running.

'Mr Atkinson, the teacher of class four?'

'Yes, that's right, what can I do for you?'

'I'm Mrs Evard.'

She held out her hand. He shook it. 'I must apologise for being late, but I have brought my daughter, who has been enrolled in your class.' She motioned the child forward. 'Her name is Michelle Marguerite.' Michelle was of average height for a nine-year-old with blond hair, but rather skinny. Her eyes were large and melancholy; the corners of her mouth were turned down, making her look sulky. But Sarah sensed she was scared and uncertain. Her gaze was fastened on her new teacher as if she was trying to fathom out how he would treat her. Her school uniform somehow did not look quite right. She had an old-fashioned leather satchel on her back and clutched a brand new lunch box to her chest, as if for protection.

'That's quite all right, Mrs Evard. I understand you have only just moved in. Thanks for bringing Michelle to class. Have you seen the School Secretary?'

'Er no, not yet, should I go to the office now?'

'Yes, it would be good if you would, they'll need some background information about health and other matters for her personal record file.'

'There's an envelope in her satchel, Mr Atkinson, with some of the information you may require. But I won't hold you up any longer.' She turned to her daughter. 'Goodbye dear, be a good girl now (there was a strong emphasis on the 'good'). I shall pick you up at the entrance gates after school.' With that she left, quietly closing the door behind her.

There was an awkward pause. Fred and the class were silent. Geoff was the first to act. He left his place next to Jonathan, where he'd been hopefully sitting and walked over to stand between Michelle and his new teacher. He looked at her and said, 'Hello, I'm new here too!' Then he turned to Mr Atkinson and held out his hand. 'Good morning, Mr Atkinson.' His hand was taken and shaken and a friendly voice replied, 'Good morning, Geoff, welcome to our class and thank you for what you have just done! Stay here, please.' Michelle had followed this exchange closely and now she stepped in front of him and offered her hand. 'Good morning, Mr Atkinson!' Her voice was quite melodious and she spoke clearly. 'Good morning, Michelle,' he responded. 'You are also welcome. We are a mad lot, but you'll soon get used to us. Put your things down on the table for the moment and we'll see about seating you.' Michelle looked round the class. 'I would like to sit over there,' she said, pointing to an empty double desk, but one that had Stephen and Sam's next to it. 'Atty' didn't blink an eyelid. 'Fine, if you think you will be happy there. Later perhaps you might like to have someone beside you.' Michelle picked up her satchel and made her way to her seat. A brief consultation followed with Geoff, in which Jonathan joined, and it was confirmed he could sit next to him. The lesson was now formally opened with the Morning Verse and one of the usual 'Welcome back' speeches. He took pains to include the newcomers and called upon the class to help them when necessary. The first subject block of the term was English for two weeks, then a two week maths block which would carry them up to half-term.

'After that, I hope the weather will have improved enough for us to have 'Local Environmental Studies,' he said. Cheers greeted this, as it would mean excursions and visits to surrounding places of interest.

The class now got down to amending their timetables, as there were a few minor changes. Then, for part of the remaining time a story was told, relating to the work they would be doing. Geoff sat absorbing it all with a look of sheer bliss on his face. Michelle sat bolt upright in her seat, motionless and expressionless. She appeared very tense and looked as if she expected it all to vanish at any moment, as did Cinderella's coach when the hour of midnight struck! The twins glanced at her several times but she ignored them, though Jane caught her staring hard at Stephen with a slightly puzzled look. The lesson ended with a short dictation.

Then it was break time. Sam hurried off to check on Jill, leaving the other three to stroll round by without him. Geoff and Jonathan joined them for a while.

Stephen suddenly said, 'Where's Michelle? I didn't see her come out.'

'I think Mr Atkinson had to get some information her mother had put in her bag,' said Geoff.

'But she must be out by now. Let's go and see if we can find her,' suggested Stephen.

They went back towards the classroom. 'There she is!' said Jane, pointing towards the entrance to their building. Yes, there she was, leaning up against the wall next to the door eating an apple, all alone and looking very solitary.

'Let's go and talk to her,' suggested Sarah, and they began to walk over. At this moment Margaret hove onto the scene. She was in their class and although at times caused much exasperation, definitely belonged to the group. Her main problems were over-enthusiasm and being accident-prone.

In some ways she was rather like a large, playful St Bernard puppy. In painting lessons, when she walked past others' desks, paint pots fell over and water jars flooded their artistic efforts. Books fell off shelves, and in handwork, wool tangled itself into the most impossible knots. And yet she was so good-hearted and eager to help no one could be cross with her for long. But now she was charging like a rogue elephant towards Michelle. The children held their breath. She could send a wisp of a girl like that flying.

'Hi Michelle, how yer doing?' bellowed Margaret, as she thundered towards her. 'I'll play with you if you like!'

What happened next was difficult to see. Michelle looked up — saw what was bearing down on her, and… … ! The next moment Margaret was bowled over backwards and went rolling across the grass for some distance, squawking loudly, while Michelle continued to placidly eat her apple.

'Go and see if she's all right!' said Stephen as they ran down, 'I'm going to have a word with her,' indicating the apple eater. For he had seen something the others had missed. As Margaret had neared her target, Michelle had made a quick gesture with her left hand. It was similar to one he had seen Bill and Sir Brian make. He approached her with some caution. But when she saw him she waited, expectantly, until he came up.

'Michelle, I wouldn't do that again if I were you,' he said very firmly. 'It won't go down well with the class!'

She looked at him quizzically for a second then said, 'You saw, didn't you?'

'Yes, I did!'

She burst into tears, taking Stephen aback at first. 'I didn't want to, but I had to, but she made me!' she sobbed, 'Keeps on saying "I've got to learn to react quickly" — I didn't mean to hurt that girl, really I didn't.' She looked at him hopefully.

'I think she's all right,' he replied. Indeed, at that moment the others came back with Margaret, who looked a little shaken but was otherwise unharmed. She went up to Michelle, held out her hand and said, 'I'm sorry if I startled you, please forgive me.'

It was Michelle's turn to look startled. 'No, it's all right, I hope I didn't hurt you?'

'Oh no! I'm fine!' replied the other and ran off calling after some friends she had spotted.

The others noticed Michelle's tear-stained face and were silent. Then Stephen spoke, partly to them, but mainly to Michelle. 'I don't quite know what's wrong, but if there's anything we can do to help, please tell us!' She looked at them, then smiled sadly.

'You are kind,' she said, 'but I don't think there's anything you can do against her, my grandmother, she's very powerful. You see, she's a witch!'

'Yes, we know,' replied Sam, who'd just joined them. 'Jill's fine,' he added.

'How did you know?' gasped Michelle. But before they could answer, the end of break bell sounded.

'We'll tell you at lunchtime,' said Stephen, 'Come on, we don't want to be late in on the first day back!'

Chapter V

When they entered the classroom, several children were gathered round Mr Atkinson taking excitedly, amongst them Margaret. When they saw Michelle come in with the 'quartet' they stopped, and Margaret looked rather sheepish. She liked a bit of drama and had no doubt been capitalising on her encounter with Michelle. Mr Atkinson smiled when he saw who his newest pupil was with and said, 'Right ho, everyone to your places. Stephen, give out these sheets of paper. Michelle, you go round with him so you can do it next time.' Sam and Sarah smiled, remembering their first painting lesson, when he had told them exactly the same thing. 'Crayons out, form drawing!' Soon they were all busy trying to work out how the half pattern he'd drawn on the board had to be mirrored onto the other half of the paper.

This was followed by French. Geoff was in the same position as Sam and Sarah had been. 'I've never done it before, please, madam!' But as soon as the practical work started he thoroughly enjoyed it. However Michelle was a surprise, she answered and spoke up in good French, shyly telling the teacher that her father had been born in the French-speaking part of Switzerland. She even helped Margaret when she got stuck over a word. The class magic was already working!

Then it was lunchtime. Afterwards, when they were allowed outside, Geoff went off with Jonathan, so the twins and Michelle found a quiet spot under some trees and she told them about her grandmother. It was as they had already heard. Melissa Mouldyberry's daughter—her mother—had not proved amenable to becoming her pupil, so she had fastened her hopes on Michelle. Right from a tiny girl, even when she could hardly toddle, her granny had taught her charms and spells, sat her on her broomstick and had her helping in the art of potion making.

As she grew up the training had become more formal and rigorous. However, being a sensitive child, she'd soon become aware that her granny was tending more towards grey magic, not white. But she was powerless to do anything about it, for even when they lived in Plymouth, the old lady used to visit her on her broomstick of nights and teach her more about the art of magic. Sometimes she was so tired in the morning she fell asleep at school. The other problem was the one they had witnessed. If someone came too near her or was unkind, it was all too easy to work a spell such as she had used this morning. But this did not help her in class, as the other children tended to avoid her. Now that they were living with Granny it was even more difficult, but her mother had heard about the school and insisted that she came to it. She looked round gratefully at them.

'You are the first ones who have seen what I can do and yet neither teased nor told on me,' she said, and paused. Then almost in a whisper added, 'Will you be my friends?'

Sam answered in his usual straightforward way. 'What do you mean be, Michelle? We already are!' She looked at him as if she could hardly believe her ears and then a smile slowly spread over her face. She no longer looked sulky and miserable. 'Thank you, thank you!' she said simply. 'I knew when I saw you the other night,' she added, looking at Stephen and Jane, 'that you could help me, but I never thought I would meet you at school!' She leapt up and touched Stephen on the shoulder. 'You're "it",' she shouted and dashed away. In a few minutes with much squealing and laughter a frantic game of tag was taking place!

They came in for afternoon school rosy-cheeked and breathless. Their teacher noted it with approval, also the transformation on the little girl's face. She seemed a different child — happy, laughing and outgoing. No longer did she want a seat in the corner, but asked if she could sit near Sarah and Jane, which was soon arranged. The afternoon flew by and when school was over they asked her how she was going home.

'Remember, my mum will pick me up,' she replied. 'She'll be waiting by the entrance.'

'But how will you actually get home?' persisted Stephen. 'You could come on the same bus as us.'

'I wish I could, that would be lovely!' she replied. 'Please come and tell her, will you?'

Sam had already collected Jill en route for their bus and luckily, by then Michelle's mother was waiting inside the entrance. She was very surprised when her daughter appeared with five other children, but listened carefully to Stephen's explanation about the bus. 'It would be far more convenient,' she said. 'It's persuading her granny, that's the problem, but I'll try.' They had to run for their buses, but did not see Michelle and her mother walking along the road as they thought they would have done. 'Her granny had a hand in that, I bet!' said Sam to Sarah. At the 'manor' stop the three of them found Doreen and Binky waiting. There was so much to tell that she felt quite ear-battered by the time they reached the house!

༄

That morning Erin had decided to make contact with Melissa. What she had heard yesterday worried her, especially with regard to the little girl. She had also remembered that one of her friend's interests had been the conjuring up or releasing of what were known as 'force' or 'energy' entities.

These were the ancient powers upon which the foundation of the earth had been laid, who slept in hidden places, and if aroused could be wild and terrible. They were believed to slumber undisturbed in remote country areas such as this and Erin had a strong feeling that was one of the reasons why Melissa had chosen to live here. Her daughter's wishes regarding the school for Michelle made a convenient cover. Furthermore, she had been aware over the last few days that 'something' was abroad, though what, or from where, she could not tell. Rosie had also intimated to her that this was so. On Sunday night she had glimpsed the strange lights beyond Bidford Manor, so she was duly concerned.

Had Melissa a telephone, she wondered? Or could she get her by 'other means'? It was worth a try. She sat back in her chair and relaxed, then concentrated on her friend. 'Melissa, Melissa, are you there, are you there?' She repeated this several times, making her mind as receptive as possible. Suddenly it was as if someone had tipped a dustbin of tin cans into it, and a 'voice' came through.

'Yes, who is it? Go away, stop bothering me, I'm trying to get hold of an old friend.'

Erin thought back, 'I am your old friend.'

'My goodness, is that you Erin? I wouldn't have recognised your thought pattern, very subtle indeed.'

'Yours is as active as ever.'

'You mean loud, don't you? No need to be tactful with me. When are you coming for a visit? I was your way on Sunday night; I did think of popping in, but was too busy.'

'I wonder what she was too busy with?' thought another level of Erin's mind.

But Melissa was rattling on, 'I'd like to see you as soon as possible. I've made a remarkable discovery—I'm surprised you haven't picked it up ages ago. Too much slow country life Erin, you lose your sharpness.'

'Slow eh?' thought mind-level two, 'you should have been

here a few weeks ago!' 'Why don't you come over for tea?' she suggested, 'How about tomorrow?'

'Fine, I'll be there,' and with another clatter of tin-can thoughts, Melissa signed off. Erin sighed and patted Rosie. 'There's something afoot. I wonder what Melissa's got herself involved with now?' she murmured. Rosie's ears twitched in a tut, tut manner. 'How do I deal with her attitude to her granddaughter as well? Better see how our meeting goes tomorrow,' she decided, and went to bake a few biscuits, the kind she remembered Melissa liked.

ೞ

Before Geoff left on his bike Sam had a quick word with him. 'Geoff, would you call in on Erin and give her a message, please?'

'Sure, Sam, what shall I say?'

'Tell her about Michelle coming to school today and what happened. Also, that her grandmother is trying to train her. I think she should know.'

'OK, I'll do that. See you in the morning, I can't wait to tell my mum about today, it was great. And I can't wait for tomorrow, either. You bet I'll be here in good time — see you then,' and he was gone.

He called on Erin, who was very pleased to hear how things had been at school and was 'seriously pleased' to receive Sam's message. Now at least she knew how things were regarding Michelle.

Jill's father picked her up around five and was delighted to find such a happy child waiting for him, bubbling over with all the things she had done, and about her new friend, Nola. Jill also explained how Sam had come to see her at break and had promised to do so every morning. She rode home on his shoulders singing loudly, and proceeded to teach Brian all she had learnt in Kindergarten that day.

ೞ

In 'Goulhaven' things were slightly less harmonious.

Melissa was annoyed by her granddaughter's lightheartedness upon her return from school. It was an unbecoming attitude indeed for a trainee grey witch. The anti-attitude was so important. It helped attract negative energies and helped to build up suspicion, cunning and deceit.

Yet here was her young hopeful babbling on about making friends and how kind and helpful everybody had been! What's more, the child's fool of a mother supported this whole-heartedly. How could she carry out the scheme she had long nurtured with all this positive love-energy flowing round? A good talking to, that's what was needed. Make the child see sense. Which reminded her, children. Those two who had been snooping around yesterday, whom she'd followed to the park and whom she'd intercepted on their way home. Yet they'd eluded her! Worrying, children like that wielding such power. Were they being used by other forces to spy on her? Care and caution were needed. However, here Erin could be a help. She was always rather a softie and wasting time helping others instead of improving her own lot. But she knew a great deal, and if she could manipulate her to join forces — it might be possible to achieve her grand scheme.

☙

The next afternoon, while the children were at school, Melissa informed her daughter she was 'going out' and left without telling her where she was going, out of spite!

However, this suited that lady very well, as it meant she could leave early and go to the school to arrange for Michelle's bus pass. Though her mother was a formidable person in many ways, she rarely interfered with something already done. Once the bus pass was obtained there would be no objection to Michelle using it.

In the meantime, Melissa donned her cloak, which rendered her invisible to ordinary mortals and mounted her broomstick in the back garden. She cursed, dismounted and went inside again. She'd forgotten the address and even a broomstick can't take you where you want to go unless you can give it some instructions! Moments later she left, and arriving near her destination glided down, landing in a meadow by a stile and an old boundary stone.

It so happened that Sir Brian had decided — that very afternoon — to take a stroll and have another look at his stone. He, too, was invisible and was very surprised when, just as he came in sight of the stile, a lady suddenly materialised, leaping lightly from a broomstick and throwing a cloak over her arm as she did so.

'Hm, I wonder who she is?' he said to himself, and forgetting all about his original purpose, decided to follow her. Melissa, totally unaware of this, made her way over the stile and down the road to Erin's cottage. She barged in, leaving the gate open and banged on the door with her broomstick.

'Vulgar type,' murmured her follower. Being a gentleman he did not sneak up the path and try to see or hear what was going on. Obviously Erin was expecting her, because she opened the door and let her in. He decided he'd go back to the stone. But the next time he saw Erin he would ask her who this person was. She made him feel distinctly uneasy.

Melissa was ill at ease in the cottage. It 'reeked of goodness' as she put it. Rosie, whom she recognised as a familiar, took one look at her and loped off into the kitchen. Erin, too, was different from how she remembered her, no longer so naive, but steeped in a mellow wisdom that comes only with long years of experience. Nevertheless she had come with a purpose and that purpose she intended to carry out. It proved to be very difficult. Erin always seemed to ask her a question just as she was about to ask one of Erin. She wanted to know how Michelle was and appeared delighted to hear that she had gone to 'that' school.

'I know other children who attend it and they are taught in a most wonderful manner. The teachers are of the highest calibre.'

'Yes, yes,' retorted Melissa, seizing the opportunity to say her piece. 'But my dear Erin, I came here to tell you about my remarkable discovery. It offers both of us an unequalled chance to gain powerful advantages for ourselves, naturally to be used for the good of others,' she hastily added, then quickly continued, 'You know how I was investigating the source of the original energies? Well I have made it a life-long study and came across an old book whilst in London recently, one of those 'District Histories' that were so common some hundred and fifty years ago. In it I found a clue, a clue to one of the sources of such power.' She paused, then giving great weight to her words continued, 'And that source is here in this very district and no more than a mile from where you live. I'm surprised that with all your local knowledge you haven't found it for yourself!'

'If I had' retorted Erin quietly, 'I would have left it alone. You, too, know well enough, Melissa, that such primal energies are not for the likes of us to interfere with!'

'Oh pish, Erin. I have studied this matter for years now and can assure you that, though admittedly not easy, it can be done! I have made all the necessary preparations and only need the chance to try them. On Sunday night I located what I believe to be this source and shall soon investigate it further!'

'I suppose it's no good asking you to give up this scheme?' asked her listener, who had grown more and more uneasy as her friend rattled on.

'Of course not. If you think I'm going to miss such a chance, you must either be too scared or too stupid!'

Erin remained silent.

'However, I'm sure others know this too and are on its trail.' Melissa dramatically lowered her voice. 'Last Sunday two children spied on my house and so I followed them; twice they tried to throw me off their track. In the end I had to resort to some transportation magic to confront them. But the boy had a box—or something—and, listen to this, Erin! They disappeared right under my nose! I wonder what powerful witch or wizard they serve—what on earth are you laughing at?'

For Erin's face had broken first into a broad grin and then she had begun to laugh, softly at first, but now she gave way to unrestrained mirth.

Melissa stood up, affronted. 'Well I see nothing to laugh at; I find your warped sense of humour about such serious matters highly offensive. I tell you a box made them disappear!'

'Yes, I know,' replied Erin wiping her eyes, 'I gave it to him for a Christmas present!'

'Pshaw!' Melissa exploded, 'Living in this out-of-the-way hole has addled your brains, Erin. I shall leave, to allow you to recover your senses. However, for old time's sake I am still willing to entertain you in my new home, and perhaps I shall be able to put some sense into your mind. I shall expect you on Friday, February the thirteenth. Don't bother, I can see myself out.' And picking up her broom from by the door, she swept out in more ways than one. Erin watched her go.

As soon as the door closed, Rosie came hopping back from the kitchen. Erin took her on her lap. 'Well, Rosie girl, we've a problem on our hands; let's hope it can be solved quickly before it becomes too dangerous.'

Sir Brian watched a very irate witch mount her broom in the field, almost forgetting to fling her cloak around herself, and then make an appallingly bad take off in the direction of Tadbridge.

Chapter VI

For the children, the rest of the week passed uneventfully. They soon settled down to the school routine and Michelle and Geoff had fitted in with little or no trouble. Michelle told them her grandmother seemed distracted about something and was leaving her alone, not pestering her to learn more magic or practise broomstick riding. Her mother also benefited from less of Melissa's interference and had become more relaxed. However, the child looked sad when she heard that Stephen and Jane were going to spend the weekend with Sam and Sarah. They felt rather mean about it and promised her that as soon as they could arrange it she should come for a visit. Geoff was going to spend that weekend with Jonathan, so he wouldn't be around either.

After school on Friday they said goodbye to Michelle saying, 'See you Monday!' She smiled back, replying, 'You may see me before then,' but did not elaborate.

'Poor kid,' said Stephen 'I think she's saying that just to be brave. Perhaps we could invite her round to our place soon, Jane?'

Jane looked rather doubtful. 'Suppose her grandmother came after her?' she said.

'We'd pop her in my box until Monday,' he replied and they all laughed.

When they arrived at the manor, Binky gave them a

right royal greeting, and after putting their stuff upstairs they made for the kitchen and afternoon snack. Derek was already there with Mr Hugh Dawes, the builder, a big burly man with an earth-shaking laugh. He stared in disbelief at the two sets of twins that suddenly appeared, and raised his eyebrows. 'No, no!' Derek said hastily. 'Only one lot are mine, the others are their friends from school.' Hugh relaxed. From Derek's cheerful attitude they guessed that he'd struck a good deal with the builder who, having finished his tea, left 'to organise things for Monday,' as he put it. Derek grinned at them and waved a sheet of paper. 'All set to go, his team moves in on Monday to start work by the summer house! You'll hear all the details this evening.'

They spent the intervening hour before supper doing their homework round the kitchen table. Then they did some recorder practise in the sitting room. Just after supper Fred and Reg arrived and Harry came shortly afterwards. He'd also collected Erin and Rosie. Soon everyone was seated round the kitchen table so that Derek could spread out his plans. Just after seven thirty, Bill, Sir Brian and JJ appeared and the meeting commenced.

As usual, Derek had everything worked out, plotted, and drawn up for all to see. Briefly, Mr Dawes' team would fit a proper trapdoor to the secret passage entrance by the summer house. Further tasks would be the bricking up of the hole Sam and Jane had fallen through into the passage by the remains of the old hunting lodge. Repairs would also be made to the passage entrance in the old boiler house. Probably later, in the spring or early summer, the repair and restoration of the Obelisk entrance would be undertaken. For the moment, all the passages explored so far would be cleaned up, repaired where necessary and wired for lighting. This was Stage One. Stage Two would entail searching for the access to the cellars and examining the old tunnel to the Dell. Later, structural repairs would be carried out to the summer house. Derek and his team of helpers—age no barrier—would carry out the decorative work!

When he mentioned this, there was a familiar eruption of throat clearing and Sir Brian arose, saying, 'May I speak?' 'Of course!' said Derek. Sir Brian leaned on the table, cleared his throat again, causing the table to shake, and began.

'I don't want to be a scaremonger or wet blanket, but when you mentioned the Dell, I remembered something. When I took over the old manor building, the passages, such as they were, ran from the house to the hunting lodge and to the summer house. Just before I took occupation, some workmen, during work to widen a bend in that passage, exposed a section of a very much older tunnel running in the direction of the Dell. The foreman told two of the men to take candles and enter to see where it led. They did so, but a few minutes later, terrible cries echoed back and there was another indescribable sound, which turned the blood of those who heard it to ice. The two men came stumbling out. Their hair had gone as white as snow and both were completely out of their minds, gibbering like idiots. Not a word of sense could be got from them. The foreman ordered the tunnel to be bricked up, which was done, and thoroughly, too. But next morning all the bricks were smashed and scattered. The tunnel was open again. Once more it was bricked up. That night on his way home, the foreman's horse shied at some unseen object and he was flung from it, hitting his head against a rock and was killed instantly. The bricks were torn down as before and no one dared to brick it up again or venture down it.'

'That's how it was when I became Master of Bidford Manor.' He continued. 'Naturally, when I heard all about this I went to investigate for myself. Whatever was down there was wild and powerful, like something from the first days of Creation. Not evil, but untameable and deadly. It would destroy anything that came near it that it did not recognise. Instead of bricking up the old section, I caused a new wall to be built across from roof to floor that did not touch this. As I'd hoped, because it joined the newer brickwork, it was not thrown down. Also, the feeling of 'something' lurking there became less noticeable. I performed a few rituals there and in the Dell, which may have helped. I understand that a partial entrance has been exposed again, work of the last Enchainers, I would think. They knew what lurked in there and out of malice may have made the opening, hoping that the Power — as it is known — might be roused and would wreak its anger upon you. Therefore I council you to leave well alone and on no account disturb it. Brick it over again, as I had done!'

Sam and Sarah looked at each other and then Sam said, 'Sir Brian, I don't think that is possible!' and between them they told of their experience of last Friday. Then Erin spoke up, 'I fear, that even if not fully awake, the Power is stirring. What has caused this I'm not quite sure, but my friend, Melissa, has found out where it is and is eager to employ its energies for her own ends. I must tell you she has no idea of what she is getting into or what she may unleash. This is very worrying. I know we can block up the passage as Sir Brian suggests, but from the children's description, it appears that a part has found a way out. Bill, have you any further ideas?'

Bill also looked concerned. 'By my master's time,' he told them, 'the creature that lurks under the Dell was considered to be a mere legend. Since Sir Brian's very wise act, not a sight nor sound had been heard of it. But I'll warrant those who dwelt in the manor were aware of its presence, as were the Enchainers. But even they, for all their evil ways, hesitated to unleash something that might destroy them as well. However, I do believe there is a part of the legend which tells how it may be appeased and returned to its deep slumbers, where it dreams continuously of the Fires of Creation.'

Erin looked up. 'Melissa said something about an old topographical book where she read of this area being one where such a creature — if you can call it such — lurked. It would be helpful if we could find a copy of that book.'

'Could you ask her for the title?' said Reg.

'I could, but whether she will give it to me is a different matter. You see, I upset her scheme last Tuesday by refusing to cooperate. If I now ask her for details of the book, she'll think I'm trying to outsmart her and will probably refuse outright to tell me anything!'

'There's one thing I can do,' said Fred, 'check with the local Historical Society for a list of such books. They have most of them in their own library and I'm sure there's one member whose main line of research is folklore and legend. I'll give it a try!'

Sarah suddenly jumped, causing Cleo to clutch wildly at her knees to avoid falling off. She hardly felt the claws, for an idea had literally struck her.

'The book!' she exclaimed. 'Remember the book you gave to the library, Dad! Perhaps that would have what we need to know!'

'It's possible,' Derek replied, 'I'll ring them up in the morning and find out if I can borrow it. I have to go into Tadbridge to buy some stuff for the builders, so could pop in and pick it up!' Hardly were these words out of his mouth when a vicious gust of wind struck the house, which shuddered under its force. It came from the east, the direction of the Dell. As it died down there was a distinct 'thump' on the window, causing it to rattle in its frame. Luckily, the glass did not break. Fred jumped up and drew back the curtains, but could see nothing. They realised that Bill, Sir Brain and JJ had disappeared; obviously they'd gone to investigate the cause. After a few minutes they returned.

'Nothing, no one about,' reported Bill. 'However, there's been 'something', for all three of us could sense it, but were unable to identify what it is. There's no doubt the mention of the book stirred it into activity. Also, when we got outside there was a slight greenish haze hanging over the Dell.'

'Melissa's trade mark,' exclaimed Erin. 'She's been poking and prying again. Stirring up things best left alone. I may have to visit her myself if she continues this irresponsible meddling.'

'I think when the builders come on Monday their first job will be to act on Sir Brian's suggestion and brick across that tunnel!' said Derek. Everybody nodded in agreement.

There was nothing more to discuss, so the meeting closed and tea was served. However, the atmosphere was tense and conversation did not flow easily. The visitors made to leave, and as Erin picked up Rosie she remarked, 'What we have experienced tonight was scary, but not dangerous. It's as if fragments of energy are flying round, not the full power. Once the wall is up I hope it will die down, provided I can convince Melissa to stop interfering!'

After the visitors had left, Doreen ordered the children to bed. An attempt to postpone it by trying to discuss what they would be doing tomorrow was unsuccessful. 'We'll discuss that tomorrow,' was her firm reply. So it was up to bed and 'Good night, sweet dreams.'

Sarah woke. It was dark; she could hear Jane's gentle breathing in the other bed. What had woken her? Certainly not Jane! She lay there listening. Had she heard a noise? Yes! There it was, a funny clicking sound, like somebody clicking one fingernail against another. Click, Click, Click. On impulse she clicked her nails together twice. Click, Click. Pause, then came the answer, Click, Click. She tried again with four clicks this time. Back came four clicks. She sat up and tried to sense which direction they were coming from. But that seemed impossible, each 'click' came from a different part of the room, as if whatever made them was flitting round. Then the curtains rustled, as if something had passed between them, there was a slight rattle from the window and she knew the visitor had gone. But who or what was it? Still pondering this, she fell asleep.

Sam awoke and listened; a noise had woken him. It wasn't Stephen; he was fast asleep and snoring gently. He strained his ears, it seemed to be coming from under his bed; a gentle, but persistent rustling noise, like dry leaves in the wind. It reminded him of some scaly creature—such as a snake—trying to make itself comfortable. Under his bed? With more courage than many could boast, Sam rolled over and peered over the edge. It was dark and he could not make out anything clearly, but something, a vague shape protruded, a tail, a claw? As he strove to see it more clearly, the bed creaked and the object quickly withdrew. There was a slithering sound across the floorboards towards the window, and like Sarah, he heard the curtains rustle and the window rattle — the strange visitor had gone.

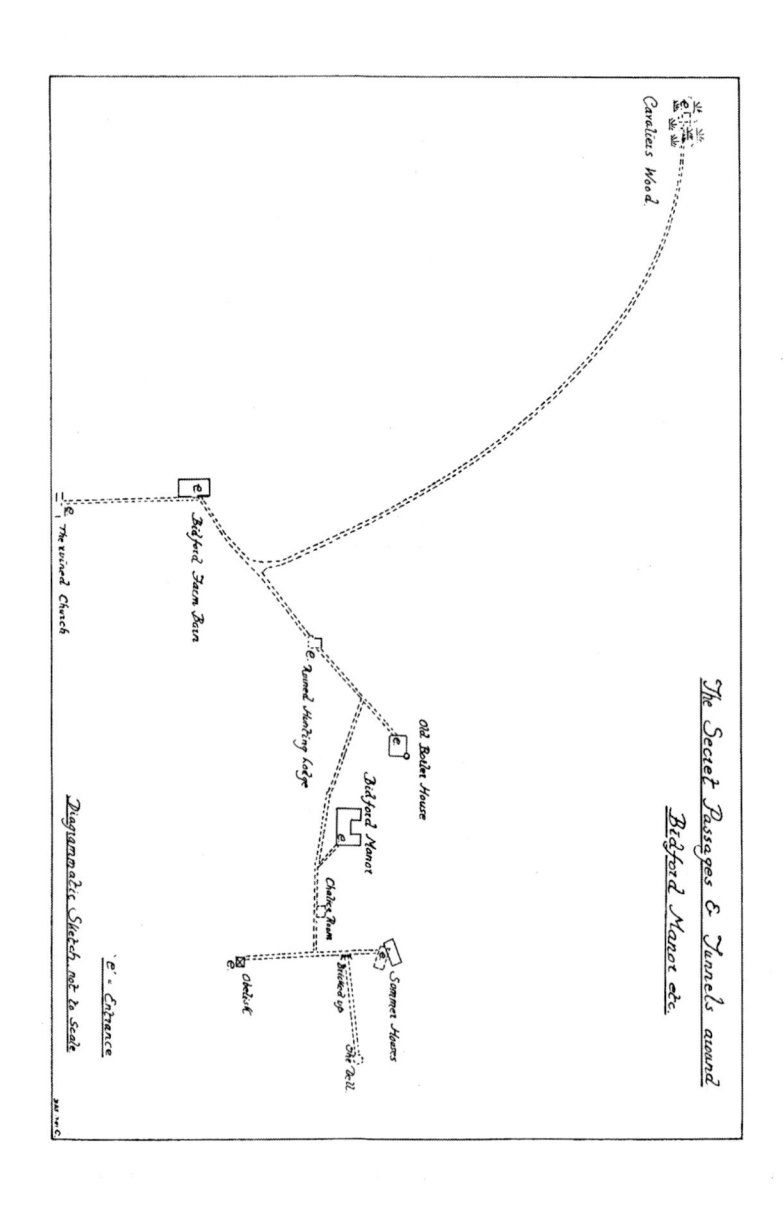

The Secret Passages & Tunnels around Bidford Manor etc.

Diagrammatic Sketch, not to Scale

"e" = Entrance

- Cavaliers Wood
- Bidford Farm Barn
- The ruined Church
- Tunnel Hunting Lodge
- Old Boiler House
- Bidford Manor
- Chalice Room
- Summer House
- Chalice
- Old Well

70

Chapter VII

Next morning Sarah waited until she could have a word with Sam alone about last night's episode, as she did not want to scare Jane. Sam was also relieved, for he could tell Sarah about his experience without upsetting Stephen. They considered what had happened and decided it could be what the grown-ups called a 'manifestation of energies', though why it had chosen them, they weren't sure.

'Maybe because we live in this house?' Sam suggested.

Another surprise awaited them after breakfast when they went into the sittingroom and drew back the curtains; on the glass of an upper sash windowpane was the distinct print of a right hand, as if it had been pressed hard against it. Even the lines and whorls on the fingers and palm were visible. It was not on the inside, or the outside—as they discovered later—but in the glass. They called Derek and Doreen to see it, but they could offer no explanation for the phenomenon, apart from the probability it could have been caused by the thump on the window last night.

While they were discussing this Sir Brian came in, via the ceiling, 'I've just dropped in,' he explained. Then his eyes caught sight of the handprint. 'Good Heavens! How did that get there?' They reminded him of last night's meeting and the violent interruption.

'So that was the thump?' he remarked. 'Well it's a good

thing the glass stopped any further displays of energy.'

'How could glass stop it?' asked Jane. 'It breaks so easily.'

'Ah, my dear, but it does! You see, those entities who come from the beginnings of time are unacquainted with many things we take for granted and glass is one of them. When they come across the stuff they either avoid it or let loose some elemental force to destroy it. This one was cautious, thank goodness!' With that he walked out through the chimneypiece.

Derek rang the library just before he left for Tadbridge. However, there was a setback. The book had been taken out and the copy he had donated was having its binding restored and would not be available until April. As the loan period was now a month they might have to wait nearly four weeks for the other copy to be returned. 'I wonder who took it out?' said Derek.

'Probably Michelle's grandmother,' retorted Doreen.

'Do you really think so?'

'Yes, I do.'

He went off shopping in any case, promising the children that upon his return he would take them into the secret passages, as there were a couple of things he wanted to check. They were delighted at the thought of being able to visit them again. While he was gone they finished off most of their homework, did some recorder tootling and had a mid morning snack.

Derek was back by eleven thirty, and having unloaded the car, putting some of the items on the handcart, he—with the children's help—set off for the summer house. They unloaded the materials for the builders and then gathered round the temporary trapdoor, which had been fitted over the entrance Cleo and Binky had found. Derek now plugged in the electric hand lamps. But Sam suddenly said, 'Wait a moment!' and dashed back to the house, returning in a few minutes with their pocket torches.

'What on earth do you want those for?' asked his father. 'Surely the electric lights are enough!'

'They could go out, or the power might fail,' Sam replied, handing each of them their torch.

Derek tut-tutted, and set about unlocking and lifting the cover. It looked very black at the bottom of the steps and smelt rather damp and musty. But the lights chased away the shadows and they followed Derek's lead down. Stephen brought up the rear with the second lamp. 'Keep in single line and follow me,' Derek ordered. They went towards the Obelisk entrance first, but did not venture too near, as the cracked condition of the walls and ceiling, plus the pile of debris that filled the end of the passage, made it impossible to continue. 'That's going to be quite a tricky job to clear and repair!' remarked Derek. They returned to the left-hand fork, following it to the Casket Room (see volume one), then along the passage to the junction leading up to the boiler house exit on the right, or down to the ruined hunting lodge on the left. Once he was satisfied—though exactly what with they weren't sure—they returned and started up the passage to the summer house exit. Derek stopped when he came level with the narrow entrance to the old tunnel. He wanted to check where the new brick wall could be built across. For a closer examination he lifted his lamp and shone it across the opening. A shaft of light streamed down the narrow tunnel. There was a sudden blinding flash and both lights went out, leaving them in pitch darkness, but not for longer than a few seconds, as the children swiftly brought their torches into action. Derek was staring in disbelief at the burnt out bulb in his lamp. But Stephen's voice jerked them into action, for his torch had flashed briefly down the opening and he'd caught a glimpse of an uncanny creeping mist curling along at floor level—a mist with a purpose.

'Quick, back to the steps and out everybody!' Stephen shouted. Derek made as if to demur, but Sarah grabbed his hand and pulled him sharply towards her. 'Come on Daddy, come on! There's something there!' As they were all running, Derek had to follow or he would have been left in the dark. When they tumbled up the steps into the daylight a noise like a vast grumbling sigh echoed up after them. Derek dropped the trapdoor, bolting and locking it securely. They quickly returned to the house. As soon as Doreen saw their expressions she put the kettle on.

Derek was concerned, what about the builders? Would they be at risk bricking up the tunnel entrance? The last thing he needed would be for an accident to happen to local people. Luckily, just then Bill dropped into the kitchen and Derek put the problem to him. He considered for a few moments then said, 'Something has disturbed this entity. All it wants is to return to its dreams. But having been semi-wakened — I do not think it is fully awake yet — it resents any further disturbances or provocation such as your light flashing down the tunnel. If such things continue, it may come to full wakefulness and then its reactions could be extremely dangerous. At all costs we must try not to disturb it any further. The building of the wall is one method, but of course it has to be built first and that could be the last straw. Lights, noise, talking are all unavoidable. Erin may be able to suggest something, but unless we can make this a silent operation I think there will be a considerable risk.' Not very comforting, alas, but all too true.

'I'll have a word with Hugh Dawes this afternoon and see if he has any ideas,' said Derek. Bill smiled, 'Do, his family have lived in this district for centuries and have always been builders or stonemasons. It's possible he may know of a way to placate such a being. I'll go for a stroll Dellwards and see if things have quietened down.' And off he went.

After some further discussion, the children offered to go and see Erin that afternoon for her opinion and advice, as Bill had suggested. For the rest of the morning they took

Binky for a short run, which he'd been asking for, and then played in the sittingroom until lunchtime.

Derek had contacted Hugh, and he was coming up at two o'clock. Perhaps it would be a good idea for the children to be present for some of the time so they could pass on to Erin how he saw the problem.

Hugh Dawes arrived promptly at two and they gathered round the kitchen table while Derek explained, as best he could, the difficulties. Hugh looked round at their anxious faces when he had finished and smiled. 'I wondered when you'd mention this!' he said. They stared at him.

'You know about it then?' said Derek.

'My ancestors probably helped to build the original Bidford Manor over the centuries and they certainly helped build the present one!' he replied. 'They were well acquainted with the passages from the time of the demolition of the old place and the building of the new. There has long been a tradition in our family that some form of energy, power or force, whatever you want to call it, lurked at the far end of the passage leading to the Dell. The story Sir Brian told you we also know. There is a problem, but not an insurmountable one.'

He turned to the children, 'I understand you are going to see Erin. Tell her my men and I are ready to do whatever she suggests and are fully aware of the risks involved.'

'Can you really do it so as not to wake this creature up?' asked Sam.

'I've every confidence we can,' he replied.

'Off you go now,' said Derek to the children. 'Give Erin my regards; I hope she'll be able to help us.' He turned to the builder: 'Come on Hugh, there are a few other points I'd like to discuss with you about the summer house.' They went off into the grounds.

The children got themselves ready, gathered Binky and set off along the track and across the fields, arriving at Erin's

cottage around three. She wasn't at all surprised to see them and had obviously received foreknowledge of the reason for their visit. Once they were settled comfortably—Binky and Rosie lying side by side in front of the fire, two fluffy white (in Bink's case, nearly white,) animals of the same size, except for the ears and tails–Erin addressed the builder's problem. 'It can be done and done very simply, by using your magic boxes. No, Sam, the box can't produce a wall on its own, but once all the materials are there, then they can be used. The rhyme should be something like:
>'Now my little box do your tricks,
>Build a wall, silently, with these bricks!'

'On Monday, Hugh should have the bricks required on pallets that can be carried down and placed on the floor at the tunnel entrance. Chalk lines must be drawn on the sides of the passage that the wall is to close off, and across the roof. These preparations should be done slowly and with care so that the amount of noise is minimal. This should be commenced as soon as the men arrive in the morning, then left until you return from school. You go with your boxes to where the materials lie ready. Hugh and your father as well, to carry down the two buckets of ready-mixed mortar. When you reach the spot, only illuminate it with one torch. You stand in a line near the building materials where the wall will be. Now the order is important: Stephen on the far right, then Sarah, Sam, and on the far left, Jane. You hold your boxes towards the opening and say the rhyme quietly, clearly and in strict rhythm. As soon as you have finished, take a step backwards and wait. When the work is completed you turn and follow Jane out. The two men bring up the rear. There must be no talking until you are clear of the entrance and the trapdoor has been closed! This is very important!' They nodded. 'Tell Hugh to make sure the amount of bricks and mortar are correct and that his men work with the minimum of talking and noise during the rest of the day. If all goes well these precautions will not be necessary when doing other work in that passage later.'

Having settled this and made sure they understood what needed to be done, the conversation turned to Michelle. Erin was pleased she had made friends with them and hoped it would help her to lead a more normal life, especially if she could come and stay with them from time to time.

Of course her grandmother was still a problem, but Erin hoped she could persuade her to treat her granddaughter normally and would not force her wishes upon the child.

'Give her all the friendship you can,' she told them as they left around four thirty. It was just beginning to get dark, so they hurried along the footpath, eager to tell their father of how matters should be handled on Monday.

As they trotted along, Stephen suddenly said, 'I wonder what Michelle meant about that she might see us at the weekend?'

'Don't know!' replied the others.

'How's she going to get here?' said Sarah. 'There are no buses at the weekend and neither her mum nor grandmother have a car. I think she was just being hopeful.'

'I'm not so sure,' mused Jane. 'There is a way, but whether she could actually use it, I don't know.'

'What, flying?' asked Sam, in jest.

'Why not? retorted his sister, 'Stephen and Jane saw her on a broomstick in her backyard.'

'But she was only practising, and she didn't look very good at it,' added Stephen. By now they had reached the end of the bridle path and were walking down the lane towards the gates of the manor. As they entered there was a good view to the right, looking towards the Obelisk and beyond to the summer house and Dell. They were just about to continue to the house when something caught their attention. A greenish light flickered briefly above the Dell, and then seemed to be drawn down into it. A movement made

Stephen look up. A small birdlike object was hovering high above the spot. Then it swooped down to tree level and shot up again. He realised it wasn't a bird. No! ... ... Surely not! It couldn't be! But there, sharply outlined against the deepening night sky, was the distinct shape of a broomstick and its rider, who was small and obviously not in complete control of its steed.

'Look,' he yelled to the others, 'it's Michelle!' They stared in disbelief, but there was no doubt about it. Stephen was already running across the grass towards the bridge over the stream, waving his hands and calling to her. The others followed, Binky adding his barks to their shouts. Michelle heard them. Her head turned in their direction; she pulled the broom round so it pointed towards them. However, in doing so, she inadvertently caused it to veer over the Dell. Again the greenish flame shot up perilously near her. She pulled the broom sharply upwards and it rocketed away from the danger. But in trying to regain control she now pointed it too steeply downwards. It appeared to be heading straight into the brook! She realised her mistake just in time and attempted to swing up and level out, but misjudged her speed, for although it stopped the headlong descent it was now too low to level out properly and instead ploughed into a bush on their side of the stream. Michelle was flung off and the broom somersaulted a few times then lay still on the grass.

Stephen reached her first. She lay very still with one ankle twisted in a funny way; her face and hands had been scratched by twigs, and blood was trickling down her forehead. As Stephen bent down she opened her eyes and smiled weakly at him.

'I said I'd come, didn't I!' she whispered, then fainted.

By now the others had arrived. The ever-practical Sam had secured the broom on the way and stood by gingerly holding it. However, it remained inert.

'I think she's twisted her ankle,' said Sarah.

'Then we'd better carry her in a bandy chair,' said Jane. 'I'll take the broom, Sam, then maybe you and Stephen can manage to carry her, and Sarah can help to get her seated.'

The boys crossed arms and knelt down while Sarah placed her hands under Michelle's arms and half lifted, half dragged her onto their hands. She draped Michelle's arms over their shoulders and when they stood up she walked behind, steadying the injured girl. Binky had watched all this with great interest and just as they were about to lift her, he had run forward and given her a lick on the cheek, as if to say, 'Everything will be all right now, you are in good hands!' Slowly they made their way towards the house. Jane was in front carrying the broom over her shoulder with Binky in tow; the boys and Sarah, with their precious burden, slowly followed her.

Chapter VIII

Doreen heard the children coming through the yard. Their excited voices told her that something was afoot, so she opened the back door to find out what all the noise was about. Across the yard came the procession: Jane, with a broom over her shoulder and Binky prancing about on his lead. Then Sam and Stephen carrying in a bandy chair a little girl who had obviously fainted. Sarah brought up the rear, holding the child steady. Having taken in this scene she didn't, like some grown-ups would, start asking silly questions like 'Who is it?' or 'Where did you find her?' Or even worse, 'Now don't come in without wiping your feet!' She merely said, 'Carry her through into the sittingroom and put her on the couch. Sam, go and fetch the first aid box. Stephen, please fill a jug with warm water and bring the blue plastic bowl with some ice from the freezer as well. Sarah, run up to the airing cupboard on the landing; you'll find a couple of rolls of crepe bandage on the middle shelf and bring down a blanket as well. Jane, try to ease her shoe and sock off that foot. I'll be there in a moment; she'll need some rescue remedy. No, Binky, down. It's not for you!'

Within five minutes they were all gathered round the couch. Sarah was gently sponging Michelle's face. Stephen took the blanket and spread it carefully over her. Jane, with Doreen's help, had removed the shoe and sock. Now the swollen foot was being packed with ice for ten minutes. 'This should be done three times a day,' added Doreen. Sam had found some more cushions and was trying to make her really comfortable. The first thing Doreen had done was to put four drops of rescue remedy under her tongue. She had spluttered and gradually came out of her faint, but remained passive and quiet while the medical team worked on her injuries. While doing this they told their mother how Michelle had arrived and what had happened. Once she was comfortable Doreen brought her a soothing warm drink, and they sat round (also with soothing warm drinks) until she felt strong enough to tell them how she'd managed her feat of broom flying.

'I said I would try to come, didn't I?' They nodded. 'Well, Granny went out this afternoon to buy some herbs, or something. Mum was busy cleaning and organising her room, so I was free. I'd already decided to use the broomstick. When it began to grow dark I took it from the cupboard and went into the back yard. I've never really flown one any distance. But Granny has often told me how it's done, so I tried. What I wasn't prepared for was the speed it travels and how to keep one's balance! Then when I arrived over here I didn't know what was the best thing to do. I saw a flash of green fire and swerved away from it. Then I heard Stephen and saw all of you. But the broom was difficult to control. You know the rest.'

'Well, dear,' said Doreen, 'you've got yourself a sprained ankle! It will take a few days to heal; in the meantime you'll have to stay here.'

'Hurrah!' shouted the children.

'Hush! Have consideration for the invalid!' said Doreen with a twinkle in her eye.

They duly subsided. At that moment, Derek walked in. He stopped and stared in amazement at the figure on the couch.

'Where on earth…!' he began.

'It's all right dear she's a friend of the children who just dropped in too heavily on a broomstick. She's the granddaughter of Melissa Mouldyberry.' said Doreen. 'Now be an angel and bring us some more juice, it's simmering on the stove.' Derek opened and shut his mouth a couple of times. 'Goldfish daddy!' said Sarah. 'Oh, ah!' he remarked and went to perform the errand.

'But I can't stay here! I must get back!' protested Michelle, panic rising in her voice. 'Granny will kill me if she finds out what I've done, and Mum will be worrying too.' Tears began to trickle down her face.

'Now don't you worry, Michelle,' said Doreen softly. 'We'll ring your mum up and tell her what's happened.'

'But, but we haven't got a phone. Granny won't have one; she doesn't need it in any case!'

Derek had returned at this moment and exchanged glances with his wife. A problem indeed!

'Bill,' she said, 'call Bill!' This was swiftly done and equally swiftly he appeared. Michelle stared at him round-eyed. She'd probably never seen anyone appear so suddenly! He went over to her and patted her head. 'You are a very courageous young lady, though somewhat inexperienced in handling broomsticks!' he told her with a twinkle in his eye. 'Now we have to let your mother know that you are all right!'

'Precisely,' said Doreen, 'but how?' They all waited for Bill's reply.

He paused for a moment, shut his eyes and put his hands together, then opened eyes and hands. 'Done. The phone will ring in a minute; it will be her mother, so you can tell her. Granny will be more of a problem, but I don't think we shall have to deal with her until tomorrow. Good evening!' and he vanished. They were startled by the phone in the hall ringing. Doreen went and answered it. She was back in a few minutes smiling broadly.

'Well, that was your mum, Michelle. She sounded a bit bewildered but told me as she was sitting down to write a letter she suddenly had a number series come into her head, so she wrote them down and realised they must be a phone number. She has had some experience of such things before, so she went out to the nearby phone box and rang it. Of course it was ours. So, I was able to tell her what had happened, and that you were quite safe. She's not angry with you, but I think Granny's going to get the rough side of her tongue when she returns! So relax, my dear. Your gran' can't do anything now, and if she turns up tomorrow we'll be ready for her, thanks to Bill's tip off!'

Michelle looked relived and settled back amongst the cushions.

'I'll go and finish supper preparations. I suppose you lot will want to eat with the invalid!' 'May we?' 'Yes, of course, two of you can kneel at the coffee table and you can use those stools as well. Sam and Sarah come and get the cutlery and perhaps, Stephen and Jane, you can bring in the water and glasses. Binky will stay and keep you company, Michelle. Oh, look out, here comes Cleo!' That young lady had been on mouse patrol but, becoming aware that something interesting was going on inside, had returned early and found her idea of heaven: a nice human child stretched out on the couch just waiting to make room for a hard-working cat to curl up next to. Binky, not to be outdone, jumped up as well and soon Michelle literally had her hands full!

During supper she asked many questions about Bill and the manor. They told her everything and she listened with delight, for she realised these children were involved with the right kind of magic. She was especially interested to hear about Erin and hoped that she would meet her very soon, for she sounded like someone who could deal with her grandmother! Just as they were finishing the jelly and ice cream stage, Bill reappeared. 'I just wanted to check about the broom,' he said. 'Tonight put it in the scullery cupboard and place something iron on it. Then your grandmother cannot recall it. Having it here may be useful tomorrow!'

It was clear after the meal that Michelle was beginning to feel the effects of her escapade and needed to rest. While Doreen bathed her ankle and put more ointment on her cuts and bruises, the others gave Erin's message to Derek. He phoned Hugh and passed it on. Now it was their bedtime in any case. So with much giggling, the invalid was carried upstairs by the boys. Sarah lent her a pair of her pyjamas and gave over her bed to the invalid while she slept on the spare camp bed. Derek also promised to cut a suitable stick for her so that as soon as her ankle had lost its swelling she could practice walking again. In a short while all the lights in Bidford Manor were out!

෴

There is no need to waste time over the words that were said at 'Goulhaven' that evening. Michelle's mother was more than furious and using attack as the best method of defence, told her mother what she thought of her witches training programme in no uncertain terms. It had also revealed to her how much Michelle's grandmother really cared for her granddaughter, as she seemed far more concerned about the loss of her broomstick than the fact that the little girl could have been killed or seriously injured. Melissa was becoming very frustrated; all her plans seemed to be going wrong. She'd found a book in the local library that promised to give her much useful information. But now tomorrow, instead of having a nice quiet read, she'd have to go and get her broom and that wretched child back.

෴

Breakfast at Bidford Manor next morning was a very cheerful and noisy affair. They were up early and Michelle had been carried down on her porta-throne, as they now called it, and deposited at the kitchen table. From there she had watched the whirl of activity that proceeded breakfast and the whirl of activity that went with it and in which she also joined. She already felt and looked much better and somehow even the thought that her grandmother would inevitably appear no longer worried her. She felt safe and cared for in a way she had never known before. When the meal was over she was carried to the couch, where her 'other' escorts—Binky and Cleo—joined her. Once the tidying up had been done, the others returned and they settled for a game of Monopoly to pass away the morning. Michelle proved almost as clever as Jane in accumulating properties and squeezing rents from the other players. 'Can I go into partnership with you?' said Stephen hopefully, as she relieved him of his last two hundred pounds and his remaining property, which consisted of the Old Kent Road. 'Yes, you can be my agent!' she laughed.

They had just finished their pre-lunch snack when the front door bell rang as if it was trying to fuse itself. 'I know who that is!' said Sam. 'What now?' But his mother put her head round the door and said, 'Remain here, all of you, leave this to us!' and shut the door. 'Now we can't hear anything!' said Jane. 'I don't think I want to!' said Sarah and she went and sat on the couch beside Michelle, putting her arm round her. The little lass looked somewhat pale, but unafraid. She hugged Sarah and smiled at the others. 'It won't be easy, but it will be all right,' she said.

Derek and Doreen did not hurry to open the door, which prompted another violent volley on the bell. When they did, Melissa stood—well, actually she was bouncing up and down with suppressed rage—there. She had had to walk into Tadbridge to find a taxi, as she had no phone and there was no phone book in the local phone box. Eventually she had found a lone taxi in the station yard. The driver had not been enthusiastic about driving out to Bidford Manor and when he had hopefully asked if she wanted him to wait—which would boost his fare nicely—she had snapped, 'No!' and retreated into a stony silence for the rest of the journey. In revenge he added another five pounds on the fare. She had been tempted to pay him in false coinage but decided against it and grudgingly handed over the twenty pounds he demanded. He continued to hold out his hand and had the effrontery to add, 'Tip, lady?' All he got was another, even louder 'No!' However, he left happily enough in the knowledge she would probably have to walk back. When the door eventually opened she saw a mild couple about the same age as her daughter standing there. They looked deceptively simple. She fired her first salvo. 'How dare you keep my granddaughter against her will? I'll have you arrested for kidnapping. Give her back. Now—and my broom,' she added, rather spoiling the effect.

Derek smiled at her. 'Er, I don't believe we have met? I'm Derek Court and this is my wife Doreen, Mrs, Mrs?' 'Mouldyberry' it was out of her mouth before she could stop. 'Well, Mrs Mouldyberry,' the quiet voice continued, 'First, we are not keeping your granddaughter against her will. Secondly, she has a badly sprained ankle, which we are treating. The circumstances by which she acquired it are rather interesting. They appear to involve your broomstick.' He stopped and waited. Melissa tried a change of tactic. 'She's an ill-behaved, disobedient child who stole my broomstick and has only herself to blame for what happened. I intend to take her home and punish her severely.'

'Really?' said Doreen, 'and how do you intend to do that?'

Melissa stopped. Yes, indeed. How was she going to get herself and Michelle home? She tried another approach. 'I demand to see my granddaughter to judge for myself whether she is fit to travel or not!'

'By broom?' asked Derek.

'Of course, how else do… …!' She'd given the game away completely.

Derek continued, 'This child was riding an object that can only be described as highly dangerous in the hands of one who has little, or no experience, with it. You were training this child to do so with little or no regard for her safety. She wanted to visit her friends and did — for her — what seemed to be the obvious thing to do. It was lucky she wasn't killed. You may see her, but we have no intention of letting her leave here until her ankle is properly healed. As for your broom, you can have it back afterwards! You may come in!' Angrily she stomped across the threshold and at once realised she was in a place full of powerful white magic.

In the sittingroom the children were waiting for the outcome of the visit. In the meantime, talk had drifted on to other matters and the boxes had been mentioned. Michelle had expressed a desire to see one. Luckily, Stephen, as usual, had his with him. He took it out and showed it to her. At that precise moment the door opened and her grandmother marched in, full of righteous indignation. The first thing she saw was the boy from the other night showing her granddaughter the self-same box she had briefly seen then. At the sound of her entrance he swung round, box in hand, to see who it was. A cold tremor of fear passed through her. The box of unknown powers! Was he about to use it on her? Her mind groped for a counter spell. She began a Latin chant which roughly meant, 'protect me from the magic box.' She was so confused that after the first few words her voice dwindled into silence, for a thunderous throat clearing next to her ear made her jump and drove the remainder clean out of her head. There stood Sir Brian, robed as was befitting to one who studies the ancient magical arts. He recognised her at once.

'Madam,' he roared, 'what do you think you are doing? How dare you attempt to use your puny spells under this roof? You meddlesome, interfering, busybody, be off with you before that lad pops you in his box. And if I ever catch you prowling round here, I'm warning you, I'll… ….!'

Thoroughly unnerved, Melissa turned and fled; as she reached the front door the broomstick was thrust into her hands. She leapt astride it and made an even worse take-off than the one Sir Brian had previously witnessed, banging her head sharply on the portico as she left, causing the broom to swerve, and nearly plunging her into a large sequoia tree on the edge of the drive. From there she steered an erratic course home and said little, apart from telling her daughter 'Michelle's fine!' — something her mother already knew. She retired to her room with some aspirin, as she was now beginning to experience a ding-dong of a headache.

The children were delighted by Sir Brian's appearance and he was now introduced to Michelle. 'That's your grandmother?' he said disbelievingly, 'How come she has such a sensible granddaughter?' making Michelle blush. 'You're in good hands,' he added. 'Couldn't be better, lucky girl!' and left through the wall, much to her amusement.

Derek and Doreen, having witnessed their unwanted visitor's departure, came in and recounted what had happened.

'Michelle,' Derek added, 'you are staying with us until you are better, and what's more, we shall invite your mother to come and stay as well, if she wants to.'

'You can go to school from here,' added Doreen, 'I think our doctor better have a look at your ankle, just to be on the safe side. I'll arrange to take you there first thing tomorrow and then on to school, and I'll pick you up in the afternoon. If there's nothing seriously wrong with it you can probably go in by bus on Tuesday. I can drive you all to the bus stop and pick you up.' Michelle was so overwhelmed by all this she could hardly stammer out her thanks.

'You can borrow one of my uniforms,' said Sarah. 'Oh, and remember Stephen and Jane are coming back with us to perform the wall closing with our boxes,' she added.

The phone rang. Derek took it in his study, where he'd

retreated to in the hopes of finding a little peace and quiet. They heard him call Doreen. A few moments later she called, 'Sam, Stephen, please bandy-chair Michelle to the study. Her mum's on the phone!'

The two stalwarts soon hoisted her up — 'Light as a feather,' Sam said, 'Well almost!' — as they galloped down the passage, lowering her into Derek's swivel chair so she could take the phone from Doreen. The children discreetly made to retire, but she beckoned them to stay. It was not a long conversation, ending with, 'Yes, fine Mum, no, don't worry, we'll pick you up at school tomorrow afternoon!'

She put the phone down and turned a radiant face to them. 'So my mum is coming to stay tomorrow. I can't believe it, everything is happening so fast; it's like all my dreams are beginning to come true. When we moved from Plymouth I prayed every night that I would find real friends and a nice school and…' It was all too much for her; she burst into tears, tears of joy. 'Come on, bearers,' said Doreen, 'carry our princess back to her royal couch where the royal cat and dog impatiently await her.' The tears cleared and there was merry laughter instead.

After lunch she sat with her foot in a bowl of warm comfrey infusion and had her wounds redressed. Then, supported by Stephen, she stood on her good foot and gingerly tried placing the other on the ground. There were a few, 'Ouch, ah!' and 'Oh's!' but she could put it down as long as she kept the weight on the other one. This was very encouraging, though Doreen still thought it a good idea for her to see the doctor.

The remainder of the day was spent checking homework and chatting. She heard all about their adventures since they had come to Bidford Manor last Hallowe'en, and she told them something of her life, which made them all feel rather sad. But then they talked of what they would do once her ankle was better. Late in the afternoon, Geoff looked in. He'd had a great time with Jonathan, but still wanted to see his 'old' friends. He was very surprised to see Michelle and even the more so when he heard how she'd arrived! They warned him not to say too much at school and he nodded understandingly. After a while he went home. Around teatime Harry dropped in with Jill and Brian. He was delighted to meet Michelle and told her in great detail how he'd sprained his ankle when a youngster — trying to fly by wearing paper wings and jumping off the woodshed roof! Jill whispered to Sam that she wasn't going to try flying — no way! Brian offered to demonstrate how he could fly by leaping off the furniture, but was laughingly caught by Jane, with whom he sat chatting until it was time to go.

The house lights went out early; it had been a weekend of the unexpected and they all felt in need of a good rest to be ready for Monday and the week ahead.

Over the Dell all was calm, though high above, a shadow on a broomstick hovered and was rewarded by a flicker of greenish light. Then it sped away towards Tadbridge.

Chapter IX

Monday morning was hectic! Some pretty complicated re-organising was required, as Michelle still had to be helped to get ready. The car had to be woken up earlier than usual (Derek's job). Luckily, Geoff and Jill arrived on time. By some miracle they were all ready and driven up to the bus stop with a few moments to spare, then Doreen drove on to the doctor's. When they arrived at school, Sam and Sarah delivered Jill, with her friend Nola, to the Nursery Class. Stephen and Jane were already in the classroom when they got there. Luckily it was fairly empty, so they were able to tell Mr Atkinson about Michelle's escapade. When they finished he said, 'I'm delighted, not because she had an accident but because she's literally fallen amongst real friends! It's good to hear that her mother is going to stay at Bidford Manor as well.'

They also told him of the advice Erin had given regarding the closing of the old passage and how it would be done this afternoon. He smiled, 'I seem to remember you've been involved with this sort of thing before! Oh, by the way, I've asked about old topographical books and have been put in touch with a Mr James Steuart, who is Fenella's {a member of the class} uncle.'

'She lives up the road beyond us, doesn't she?' said Jane.

'That's right, it's a pity she's away sick at the moment, but

I wondered if you would drop some work in for her tomorrow, if I make up a package?' 'Of course!' was the reply.

Fenella was a cheerful, outgoing child and although she lived near them, as yet they'd not become close friends. She had an elder brother, Andrew, who was a bit off-putting, though as they found out later, he wasn't such a bad sort after all.

When the lesson began, Mr Atkinson told the class that Michelle had been involved in an accident and would be a little late, as she had to go to the doctor's for a check up. About half an hour later there was a gentle knock on the door and when he opened it there stood Doreen supporting a beaming Michelle! She had a crutch, and with a cheery 'Bye, Aunty Doreen!' hopped her way in, making for her desk.

'She's fine!' Doreen assured Fred. 'A simple sprain. By the end of the week it should be as good as new. Oh, could I just have a quick word with my two?'

'Most unusual' said Fred with a grin, 'but of course!' Sam and Sarah quickly went to their mother. 'I just want to tell you that I'm picking up Mrs Evard a little later. Yesterday when she phoned I arranged that she would ring the doctor's this morning to hear how Michelle's foot is progressing. She suggested I pick her up on my way home, which makes sense, as Michelle is able to travel back on the bus now that she has the crutch. There will be more room for their luggage as well. I must fly, I promised her I'd be there as soon after ten as I can.' She flew, a real 'flying mum' as Sam put it.

Having a crutch is quite a status symbol at school, like having your arm in plaster. At break time she was the centre of attention for a while as people came up to ask what had happened. She swung along at a surprising speed with her friends and they chatted away as usual. The remainder of the day flew by, as it always did. When they left, Mr Atkinson wished them 'good luck' and told Michelle to keep them in order with her crutch if they were naughty!

In the meantime, Doreen had driven to Tankerville Road and parked outside 'Goulhaven'. Suddenly she felt uneasy, supposing it was a trick? That Melissa, seeking revenge, had either persuaded or intimidated Mrs Evard and she was walking into a trap? Mere fantasies, she decided and dismissing them from her mind, marched up the front path to ring the bell, which answered with its usual funereal tone. As she suspected, the door was opened by Melissa. Melissa with a big, patently false smile on her face. She could see a couple of suitcases standing in the hall.

'Do come in!' she cooed, 'My daughter's upstairs just collecting a few last items; she won't be a minute, do come in!'

'No thanks, I'll wait here until she's ready.'

A look of anger clouded the smiling face. 'I said DO come in! Now, COME IN!'

Doreen began to feel really uneasy, there was something in the tone of voice she didn't like and the fact that she seemed to have moved up to the door and was nearly over the threshold without realising it frightened her. Was she being hypnotised? She stepped right back to the edge of the porch. Melissa's face went bright red with anger and exertion. She drew herself up to her full height and started again — in Latin — 'I command you to enter!' Doreen felt as if invisible bonds had been thrown round her and she was being drawn nearer and nearer that door where this witch-like person stood, ready to close it behind her. Melissa had a gleam of triumph in her eyes; soon this wretched woman would be within her power.

A voice suddenly cut like a sharp knife across her thoughts. 'Excuse me, Mrs Mouldyberry, Mrs M. Mouldyberry?' The spell was broken, for Melissa's concentration was shattered by this intrusive official voice. Her eyes focussed on its source. A large police officer — none other than one PC Wilby — was standing stolidly on the doorstep. Parked behind

Doreen's car was his police vehicle, and the net curtains were waving up and down the street in a perfect hurricane of curiosity.

Turning his full gaze on this odd woman he continued, 'I must ask you to accompany me to the police station, madam, to answer a few questions concerning an incident that occurred in connection with your last domicile. Please come with me!' Melissa gasped like a stranded fish. Doreen saw an opportunity and took it.

'I'll just go in and help your daughter with her case,' she said brightly, 'is that all right officer?' Having got what he came for, PC Wilby had no further interest in the house or its contents. He nodded, 'Carry on, lady. Now, madam, I hope you are not going to cause any trouble. Will you kindly step into the police car?' In a bewildered dream: 'This can't be happening to me!' Melissa complied with his request and was driven off to muted applause from behind the net curtains.

Doreen left the front door open; who knew what might be lurking in this house. 'Mrs Evard!' she called, 'Where are you?' A thumping noise from upstairs sent her quickly up and into one of the bedrooms. There, trussed up on the bed, was Michelle's mother. In a few minutes she was freed and hurrying downstairs with her rescuer. They grabbed the cases, quickly shut the front door, and bundled them into the boot. Then into the car, Doreen put her foot down and headed for home! On the way, Mrs Evard–Ingrid — related how her mother, suspecting something was afoot between her and the Courts, had slipped a sleeping potion in her breakfast tea, so that when she went up to complete her packing, she passed out. She recovered consciousness to find she was tied to her bed unable to move, with her mother gloating over her, saying she had no intention of letting her go to be with her daughter and how she would trap Doreen, using her as a hostage to get Michelle back into her power.

'You can stay with us as long as you wish,' said Doreen, 'and perhaps we can find somewhere else for you and Michelle to live.' Once they arrived at the manor the famous 'Bidford hospitality' took over, and within half an hour Ingrid felt she'd known the Courts all her life.

☙

The builders arrived just after the children left in the morning. Hugh had already organised things along the lines Erin had suggested and his three workmen, all from the village, knew exactly what they had to do. The lorry arrived a little later with the pallets of bricks and other materials, which were carefully unloaded. Then it was driven and parked at the bottom of the drive. The bricks and other items now had to be carried across to the summer house site, a task they handled quickly and smoothly. The trapdoor was opened and the pallets carried below and placed as Erin had suggested. This part of the operation also went very efficiently and Derek was impressed by the way it was done. By ten thirty all was ready. The trapdoor was closed and work began round the old boiler house, still carried out in the same quiet, almost reverent manner. When they stopped for a tea break Derek learnt that all of them were descendants of builders or masons who had lived in the district for centuries and knew all about the legends and history surrounding Bidford Manor.

Shortly afterwards Doreen and Ingrid arrived, and Derek was told of what had occurred at 'Goulhaven'. They took their new guest up to the spare room and made sure she had all she needed. 'I think Michelle will probably want to stay where she is for the moment,' said Doreen. 'Anyway you may feel happier with your own private space.' Ingrid agreed; for too long mother and daughter had lived in B & B accommodation or pokey bedsits. 'That's why,' she told Doreen, 'in spite of some misgivings, I decided to come and live with Mother. I used to see a lot of her when Michelle was younger but had no idea that she was working on the child. Though at times I did wonder if something was going on. When I split up with Charles and moved to Plymouth we did not see her so often. She always was a little 'odd' and has not changed for the better, I fear. I worry about what will become of her.' Doreen mentioned Erin as a possible source of help and that seemed to cheer her up. They left her alone for a while so she could unpack and make herself at home.

∽

The police were very polite and very firm. There had been a slight unpleasantness when she'd moved from her last domicile over the condition in which the kitchen and bathroom had been left, for she'd used them to concoct her brews and experiments. The landlord demanded compensation for the damage and she told him to redecorate them and send her the bill. He did so, but also had to replace the sink, cooker, bath and hot water heater. She disclaimed any responsibility for their condition and refused to pay, so now the law ground into action. She was required to make a statement, as the matter was going to court. The landlord was suing 'the said Mrs M. Mouldyberry for criminal damages!' It was well after four o'clock before she was allowed to leave, and in spite of hints about her poor feet, had to walk home.

In the end nothing came of it, as the landlord realised a court action would be too costly and the outcome doubtful.

∽

When school finished it was an excited group of children who piled onto the bus. Michelle managed to hop in very nimbly! Jill was fascinated by the crutch and asked Sam why Michelle had a 'clutch'? Doreen met the bus and drove them back to the house. A bit of a squeeze, but they managed. After a snack pause they prepared for the task. Hugh's workmen stood by the entrance. They, with the others, Doreen, Ingrid, Michelle, Jill and Geoff, were to remain outside and some distance away so that the silence could be maintained.

Sarah had fetched the candlesticks. 'Far better than a torch,' she said. 'Dad can hold one and Mr Dawes the other.' As before, candles appeared mysteriously in them when they were left in the kitchen for a moment while the children got ready. Armed with their boxes, they moved off. Binky and Cleo, much to their annoyance, were locked in the back kitchen as a precaution. Stephen led, followed by Sarah, Sam and Jane. Derek and Hugh, with the candles, and buckets of mortar, walked beside them. The trapdoor was unlocked and opened in silence. Jane whispered, 'Enflame!' and the candles flickered into life. The men descended first, the children following. There was a strange oppressive air in the passage that grew stronger as they approached the tunnel opening. It was as if some great monster of the ancient deeps was stirring in its sleep. Dimly it sensed something was going to happen; counter powers and energies were gathering. It strove to awake, but its sleep was indeed deep. Fragments of its energy skittered around but could make no impression.

When they reached the neat piles of bricks, the two buckets of mortar were placed at each end of them and they took up their positions. The candles threw a flickering light on the brick walls, but the tunnel mouth was deep in dark and shadow. Holding their boxes at arm's length they waited for Stephen's signal. He very softly intoned, 'One, two, three':

'Now my little box do your tricks,
Build a wall silently with these bricks!'

They stepped back. A hazy blue mist enveloped the bricks and buckets. There was a soft rustling sound and the mist thickened, swirling ever higher and higher until it reached the roof. All this took less than five minutes. When it cleared, the new wall was before them. It closed the old entrance perfectly, not a brick too little, or too many. Silently they turned and Jane led them out. As they started to move away there was the slightest of sounds from behind the wall. 'It reminded me of a big grizzly bear turning over in his winter sleep,' said Jane afterwards, though her experience of sleeping grizzly bears was restricted to books. They came out into soft evening light. The sun had set some half an hour ago but there was still a rosy glow in the west and the evening star was already glittering brightly in a clear sky. The candles went out of their own accord. Hugh lowered the trapdoor and Derek locked and bolted it. They walked over to where their friends awaited them. All felt it would be wrong to speak. So, maintaining their silence, they turned, with the children holding hands: Jane, Sarah and Geoff, Sam and Jill, Stephen helping Michelle. Then came Doreen and Derek, followed by Hugh and his builders, with arms linked.

Thus they returned to the house and the warmth of the kitchen.

Chapter X

Next morning things were more chaotic than usual. The children were dressed and down in good time, also Ingrid, who came to lend a hand with the breakfast, but somehow things just would not go right! The kettle blew its fuse and it was some time before they realised it wasn't working, meaning the tea and coffee were not ready when they should have been. The timer on the toaster jammed and it refused to turn out other than underdone toast. The milk in the jug had gone sour. Jill arrived early and Geoff arrived late as he had a puncture en route. Doreen had to drive them up to the bus stop in the car, and even so they only just made it! They all went to school feeling somewhat 'ruffled'.

Once they had left quiet descended in the kitchen, and Derek felt he could safely have an extra cup of coffee at leisure and examine the post. Ingrid was clearing up and Doreen decided to nip into Bidcote for some bits and pieces from Mrs Flemming's Store; also to say 'hello' to the new postmaster. The builders would arrive shortly, but they could get on without him for the moment. Being Tuesday there was about a dozen envelopes. Six went straight in the bin, junk mail as usual! The others, two bills, a royalty cheque, a notice about the forthcoming fund raising committee meeting, a reminder that the warranty on his computer would run out shortly and... ... But what was this rather thick and elaborate, best quality, handwoven paper envelope? He opened it and nearly fell off his chair! The letter was from a lecture promotion agency, which was employed by his publisher. They thanked him for confirming, via the publishers, that he and his wife were willing and able to undertake the proposed lecture tour to promote the new edition of his book. The dates were set, venues and hotels booked, travel documents enclosed. The dates were from the sixth to the twenty first of February. His contract would arrive in the next few days, please sign in duplicate and return. He was still staring at it with disbelief when Doreen returned.

'Whatever is the matter?' she said, 'have your publishers gone bankrupt?'

Derek waved the envelope, with its contents at her. She took it and sat down, or rather sank down slowly, into a chair reading it.

'When did this come up, dear?' There was a slight edge on the 'dear'.

'Er, some ten days ago. I e-mailed acceptance; but forgot to tell you.'

'So I observe. Well, what are we going to do about it?'

'Um. Go — there's no way out of it now!'

'Oh, so we drop everything and go, just like that! Never mind the house, children and animals!' Doreen's voice was beginning to rise, a thing it rarely did, except when she was very irate or annoyed.

Derek looked exceedingly uncomfortable. 'Well, dear, there must be some way we can do it, I mean, this place is expensive to run and some extra cash would come in handy. Then we could renovate the master bathroom.'

That was a stroke of pure genius! For this particular bathroom was the bane of her life. The plumbing was ancient and the cheap modern bath, toilet and washbasin that had been installed some years ago were totally out of keeping with its decorative style. The shower had a mind of its own and either dribbled cold water or sent a torrent of boiling water over one. There were no in-between settings as far as they could make out. The floor had tacky vinyl tiles, but why go on? It was awful. Derek saw her hesitate and knew his point had struck home.

'But what about the house the children and pets? We can't just go off and leave them!'

'What about Ingrid? She could look after the house.'

'True, but I'm not sure if it's fair to expect her to cope with Sam and Sarah, plus Binky and Cleo as well. Then there's the business of school, Geoff and Jill. No, it's too complicated, you'll have to go on your own.'

'Impossible, the tour is all arranged for both of us and you are a vital part of the socialising and buttering up of booksellers.'

She thought for a moment. 'Well, perhaps the children could stay with the Randells; I can but ask. But how about Michelle? I don't think it would be much fun for her stuck here on her own for two weeks.'

'Jane told me they were going to ask their mother if she could visit them sometime, so why not now?'

'First we have to see if Ingrid's willing to stay here on her own with the animals, though there will be Bill, Sir Brian and JJ as well. We better make some introductions as soon as possible.'

Ingrid entered the kitchen at that moment and they explained their problem to her. She listened and thought for a minute, then said, 'You know, I rather like the idea. Two weeks on my own would probably be very good for me. There are things I need to sort out, and though the unseen inhabitants come as rather a surprise, I would feel happier to know there are 'others' also keeping an eye on the place. I don't drive, but I know the village isn't far. Yes, I'd be very happy to help. I also agree it would be best if Michelle could go with her friends, if possible.'

'I'll phone Phyllis right now,' said Doreen. 'Maybe Bess or Harry could drive Jill and Geoff to the bus for those two weeks. It looks as if it's going to work out after all.' However, the look she gave Derek warned him he'd better mind his p's and q's for the next few days!

As it turned out, everything went according to plan. Phyllis was more than delighted to have a chance to repay the Courts' kindness for looking after their two over Christmas, and having heard so much about Michelle, she was also welcome.

Ingrid was introduced to the 'other' members of the household and Sir Brian was so gallant he quite won her over. The more sober assurances of Bill that they would keep a close eye on things helped to reassure her. Harry would pop in every day, as in any case he would be picking up Jill from the bus stop in the afternoon. At first she flatly refused to go in by bus without her Sam, but later agreed if he would put her on the bus after school she'd go, as long as Geoff would keep an eye on her and Nola.

Bess said that if there were any domestic problems, Ingrid was not to hesitate to call her. Binky and Cleo had, in their usual manner, assumed that Ingrid had come especially for their sole benefit, so there were no problems there. She liked dogs and cats and had been sad that in many places where they had lived it had not been possible to keep animals. Derek had a word with Hugh and they decided to continue the projected work until the day before his departure, then review how things were going and, if all was plain sailing, carry on. If not, they would start on restoring some of the garden sheds on the terraces.

When the children came home from school they were told what was going to happen. 'Wow! Great!' was the main comment, and Michelle, though at first reluctant to leave her mother, became as enthusiastic as they were when her mother told her she didn't mind being on her own. Just as

Doreen and Derek were finishing explaining all this the phone went; it was Stephen and Jane, of course. They were just as excited as the others.

Ingrid, when alone with Doreen said, 'There's only one thing that worries me. Michelle will be very near her grandmother's place. I hope nothing happens.'

'Don't worry,' replied Doreen, 'I'll brief the twins to make sure she is always with them and never goes out on her own.'

In the meantime, at 'Goulhaven', Melissa was making plans as well. She would invite Erin to visit earlier, not Friday, February the thirteenth, but from Thursday the fifth of February to Monday the ninth. She didn't think she could stand more than a weekend of Erin's goodness, but it should give her enough time to try to obtain her cooperation. Also, she knew the school's half-term started the following weekend and that would give her the rest of the week to make plans and preparations for her grand scheme. It was a good thing her stupid daughter was now out of the way. She would not need the child now, but later. She would deal with that when the time came to use her in this business! She decided to write Erin a nice friendly letter, and set about doing so then and there.

Later on the same afternoon, Erin and Rosie paid a visit to the manor. She wanted to find out how yesterday's tunnel closure had gone and to test for herself its effectiveness. This gave her a chance to meet Michelle and, unexpectedly, her mother as well. The twins told her everything had gone according to plan, and naturally she heard all about the lecture tour and where they would be staying. 'If you wish,' she said to Ingrid, 'I could talk with you about your mother, as I know you have concerns.' Ingrid thanked her and it was arranged she would go and have tea with Erin one afternoon next week.

She now turned to Michelle. 'Michelle, since you are now one of those who has become a friend of the twins' and will no doubt be taking part in their adventures, I have a little gift for you.' She dipped into her bag and produced a small wrapped package. 'I think this may be of help.' It was a box similar to the ones the twins had. 'You'll soon learn how to use it!' she added. Michelle was overwhelmed, and could only stammer out her thanks as the others crowded round to look at it.

'And now, my dears, Rosie and I must take a little walk in the grounds. I want to see what difference yesterday's work has made.'

'Isn't that dangerous?' asked Sarah. 'Do be careful, Erin. We don't want anything happening to you!'

'I'll be careful, don't worry,' was the reply. She said goodbye and headed for the rustic bridge over the stream. It was now fairly dark, though the moon was nearing full and cast its cold light over the scene. Once the bridge was crossed, Rosie poked her head out of her basket and her nose began to twitch. 'What is it, my dear?' said Erin. 'Is it still around?' Twitch, twitch, went the ears. 'Ah ha, not yet. Well, let's go closer and see.' She followed the path towards the Dell. As she drew nearer, strange gusts of warm air began to buffet her. There was an uncanny sense of a being beneath her feet brooding on the past, with an awareness that it had lost something. This was contained, but there were energies emanating from it, like sparks shooting out from a bonfire. Scattered energy. Not dangerous, but it could be if played with, cajoled, flattered, or tempted. A picture of Melissa flashed across her mind and though she knew in one sense the ancient power had been held, there was still the possibility of releasing it by working with what she had just experienced; and that, she felt sure, was what Melissa intended to do!

She stood for a moment longer then turned and made her way back towards the house. She paused; should she go back in? There was a slight rustling sound and Bill stood next to her. 'Well?' he said, expectantly. 'Well enough' she replied. 'It still sleeps, but not totally. There are fragments of its energy active. My concern is if Melissa gets hold of them. Her meddling could cause over-stimulation and they may try to draw more energy from the main source and so awaken the whole from its slumber. She wants me to visit her, then I hope to find out what she intends. Can you and Sir Brian keep a careful watch here and inform me if anything unusual occurs?' 'Of course,' he replied. 'Then I won't go back in. Tell them all is quiet and hopefully will remain so. I shall go home now.' She smiled at him and Rosie popped her head out of the basket. Bill tickled her behind the ears and left to pass on her message; Erin went on her way.

Chapter XI

Next morning Erin received Melissa's bread and butter letter; perhaps bread and treacle would be a better description, as it oozed sweetness. Erin guessed its reason easily enough and decided to accept. At least she would be able to find out what her friend was up to. She had a feeling that the timing was deliberate and in some way connected with half-term and Michelle.

The children at the manor were wildly excited, so were the Southleigh twins. A telephone parental conference had resulted in the idea that instead of Stephen and Jane coming up to Bidford Manor for the weekend, Sam, Sarah and Michelle should go to Southleigh instead. This would give them a chance to get used to the house and its routine and give John and Phyllis the chance to opt out, as Derek put it, if they found the experience too harrowing. Though he was sure — and hoped — they were made of sterner stuff. Jill was disappointed that her Sam was going to be away over the weekend, but cheered up when her father said they might go into Tadbridge on Saturday and spend some time in St Andrew's Park, so perhaps the children could meet them there? It was agreed to confirm this on Saturday morning.

The rest of the week flew by, and Friday morning was almost as chaotic as Monday had been. Bags were packed the previous evening, but as usual there were last minute items to add. Michelle could now manage without the crutch indoors but still felt safer on it when outside. Doreen decided it would be best to drive her and their weekend bags in, while the rest went by bus. Naturally Fred had been informed of what was going on and was prepared for five extra bouncy pupils that day. In fact he taught the class a special bouncy exercise that morning. Geoff also had a bit of news. He and his mother were going to spend the weekend with his granny, so he would be in Tadbridge as well. He said he would keep an eye open for them on Saturday in the park as his gran's house was just across the road from it. Of course, by now the whole class knew what was happening, and Fenella asked them to come and visit her. 'We'll be there all weekend,' she added, 'Dad's got a large advertisement project to finish off, so do come!' Then Christopher, or Chris, chipped in, 'Yes, you know I live down the lane just by the railway bridge, so come and see us as well.' With all these invitations it looked as if they were going to be pretty busy.

At the finish of school Sam collected Jill and saw her onto the bus. She waved goodbye cheerfully, calling out, 'See you in the park tomorrow, Sam,' then the five of them waited for Phyllis, who was coming to pick them up. She arrived a few minutes later, and once their stuff was in the boot they piled in, and she drove to Bardon Lane and home. Sam and Sarah had spent a weekend there just before Christmas. But this was different; they were going to live there in two weeks' time for sixteen whole days. This was a trial run, so they must try and be as helpful as possible. Having Michelle as well made a difference. She had only just met John and Phyllis and was trying hard to be on her best behaviour!

They toured the house from top to bottom and saw where they would sleep. This house had many more, though smaller rooms than theirs, so Stephen and Jane had their own rooms in the old servants' quarters (see plan). Sam would be in one next to Stephen, and Sarah and Michelle shared the room next to Jane's that had bunk beds in it. Michelle had the bottom one, but when they came to stay they would each have one week down and week one up. Then they went for a tour round the grounds, the stables and adjoining orchard. In the stables they were introduced to the two pet rabbits belonging to the twins. They were sleek and dark-coated, in contrast to Rosie, and called Elzevir and Elzevira. During the winter months their hutch was kept inside and put out again in spring. The children ended up hanging over the fence that separated the property from the railway tracks.

'Our dad says when they first moved here there were still express steam trains running on the line. Now all we get are silly little two or three carriage diesel things chugging by,' Stephen told them. They returned to the house and unpacked, then went down to the lounge to chat until suppertime.

Though in many ways Southleigh was a different house in different surroundings from Bidford Manor, its atmosphere of welcome and warmth was much the same. By the time the evening meal was over Sam, Sarah and Michelle felt completely at home and at ease with John and Phyllis. Afterwards they returned to the lounge, and John, who proved to be a good storyteller, entertained them with stories of his youth and how Tadbridge had been some thirty years ago, very much the remote past as far as they were concerned. Before going up to bed it was discussed with the grown-ups what they would do tomorrow. Reg had invited them to visit him at his flat near North Gate for tea; so they decided to go and see Fenella, and maybe Christopher in the morning, then meet the Game family in the park after lunch, phoning them to confirm this before they went out tomorrow. The weather forecast was for a sunny, dry day with seasonal temperatures. Plans made, they were off for a good night's sleep.

Next morning all were up early, but Phyllis beat everybody, and breakfast awaited their arrival. Michelle could now walk on her foot with no trouble, but John suggested she borrow a short walking cane he had for when they went out today. 'You may still feel rather unsteady and uncertain,' he said, 'and you don't want to go falling over and hurting your ankle again!' She agreed, as the cane was rather stylish, with a silver band round it.

After breakfast they phoned the farm; Bess answered and they told her of their plans. 'That suits us fine,' she said, 'Harry is busy this morning and we'd reckoned on coming in after an early lunch. Suppose we meet you by the play area round about quarter past two?' This fitted in well, as they were due at Reg's between four thirty and five. After they had tidied up, a routine the same as at the manor, it was about nine thirty, so they started to walk up towards Fenella's house, past the footpath that led to Tankerville Road and round the curve in the lane to the Steuart's place. This was a new property standing in solitary state until more of the 'desirable plots for sale' around it were taken — a white brick double storey, butterfly roofed, wide windowed house. It would have been more at home on the Cornish Riviera than in its present spot. They knocked on the door and Fenella, who had spied them coming, opened it. She took them into the large lounge-cum-dining room, where her mother was busy working on her laptop at the table. She was a freelance journalist who wrote articles on art and education for a London Newspaper syndicate. She stopped to chat with them, obviously intrigued by the two sets of twins and Michelle with her cane.

'Go and tell Ronald (Fenella's dad) I shall be going out in a moment and I'll switch the phone through,' she said. They followed Fenella into the garden to where her father's studio stood. It was also a white brick building with a large skylight in its sloping roof. Ronald was seated at an enormous drawing easel, upon which was evolving a picture of a sunrise. The visitors gasped, it looked so real. The whole place was littered with paints, paper, pencils, brushes—all the paraphernalia of an artist. Sketches and drawings lay everywhere and paintings were stacked up against the walls. He stopped for a moment to chat and also showed an interest in the duplicated twins. 'You'd be useful for an advertisement, I'm sure,' he remarked. Michelle asked him what the sunrise was for. He quoted a cereal advertisement, 'Popsie Wopsies are the best for you every morning!' 'Yes,' he said, 'this is the background for the front of the cereal box; it will have a cartoon cockerel superimposed on it and the brand name.' He absentmindedly stirred his cold coffee with a paintbrush, took a sip and returned to his work. They returned to the house.

As her mother was going out, they suggested to Fenella that a walk down the road to Christopher's place would be a good idea. She readily agreed, as did her mother, who gave them a bundle of magazines to take down for his mother. So they set off back the way they'd come, past Southleigh and round the lower curve until they reached the Shelley's house next to the railway bridge. It was a complete contrast to the Steuart's, being an old stone built cottage, probably erected for a railway employee. Over the years it had gained several additions: a veranda running across the front and a wooden addition on the left side, which contained the bathroom and a large bedroom. Added on the front of this was another bedroom with a door out on to the veranda. This was Chris's room. The kitchen was a stone outcrop at the rear. In the back garden stood a wooden studio where his father, Ralph, worked. He was a sculptor and commercial artist who specialised in car advertisements.

Chris was busy playing ball with his dog, Rover—a black smooth-coated hound of no fixed breed—in the front garden and welcomed them enthusiastically, as did Rover.

Chris leapt on to the veranda, yanked open the front door and yelled, at the top of his voice, 'Mum, visitors!' From inside came the reply, 'Well don't keep them out there in the cold, bring them in.' They followed him through the living room and into the kitchen, which was as cosy as all kitchens should be and boasted the right kind of table they could all sit around. Chris's mother was a tall, slim lady with reddish hair and a rather wry smile, but very friendly, and she welcomed them heartily. Soon tea and home baked buns had appeared, and she opened the back door calling out, 'Ralph, tea's up. We've got guests, come on, show yourself!' In a minute Ralph entered. He was a big burly fellow with a shock of untidy brown hair and a slightly bemused grin on his face, as if he was thinking of something else most of the time. He examined the assembled company and said, 'I know, you've all escaped from the same zoo that we got Chris from!' After that the verbal fun was fast and furious. When they'd finished snack, he took them out to his studio, which was as messy as Ronald's, though in a different way. Not only was every square inch covered with drawings and the like, but pieces of wood, stone and metal added to the chaos. In the middle stood a large chunk of wood, which he was carving. Near it was a stone block being turned into a bird. They were fascinated, and even more so, when he let them have a go at carving wood and chipping at the stone. But best of all, he showed them how he used a blow torch to fashion metal into different shapes and let them all have a go at bending a strip into strange patterns.

Fenella confided to Jane, 'I like Ralph; he lets you do things! My dad's too fussy; we aren't ever allowed to touch anything. He always says, "You may touch it with your eyes, but keep your grubby paws off!" Chris is lucky to have such a dad!' She sighed.

Afterwards they went and roamed round the overgrown garden playing hide and seek with Rover. They would leave him sitting on the back step, Chris calling, 'Stay, Rover!' Then when they were hidden he'd call, 'Seek us, Rover!' The game was to reach the step without being caught. It was great fun! All too soon they realised it was twelve thirty and time to go home for lunch. They asked Chris if he wanted to come with them to the park, but he declined, inviting them to visit again whenever they wished. His mother endorsed this. As they walked back up the road, Fenella said, 'If I lived in a place like that I don't think I'd want to go out much either!' They agreed with her. She went on to her house while they pounded up Southleigh's drive and got ready for lunch.

Afterwards it was off to the park. They had been quite prepared to walk, though the thought of passing near 'Goulhaven' was rather uncomfortable for Michelle. Whether John was aware of this they didn't know, but as they were about to leave he said, 'I've an errand to do in town, shall I give you a lift? Adding, 'By the way, Reg will bring you back.' This made them all feel better about going. Within ten minutes or so they were being let off at the park entrance near the play area. As they got out, John said, 'Keep your eyes open and keep together; you know what I mean!' They realised that their parents were taking no chances with someone like Melissa!

The first person they met was Geoff, who had come over straight after lunch to see if they had arrived. His gran and mum were, 'doing nothing but gossip' he reported, so he'd left them to it for an hour or so. They sat on the swings waiting for the Game family, who turned up on time, Jill making a rush for Sam and Tiger swooping on Jane. For the next hour they were busy entertaining the little ones, culminating in a walk round the lake, which, by chance, took them to the café, where Harry insisted on buying everybody milk shakes. It was a very pleasant and enjoyable afternoon. At half past four they said goodbye to the Games and walked with Geoff to his grandmother's, as it was on the way to Reg's flat near North Gate.

He lived in an oldish block near the railway station, uninspiringly called 'Railway Apartments.' However, they were spacious, and the owners had kept them up with the times, with a proper heating system, double-glazing and the like. Reg's was a first floor apartment with a large bay window in the living room and another in his bedroom. Both possessed grand views across the town. The place even had what used to be called servant's quarters, a small, self-contained flat within the larger one. Here resided his housekeeper, Mrs Blankenzee, a Dutch lady who had come to England as a refugee during the Second World War. She was short and round, with a cheerful manner, and was ruthlessly efficient. The place was always spotless, and her cooking was renowned amongst Reg's friends. She always made a great fuss of the twins whenever they visited their grandfather, and the arrival of five children really put her on her mettle. She fussed around them, especially Michelle walking with a stick. 'Och, arme dat meiske!' she kept on saying, and Reg had to shoo her back into the kitchen or, as he put it, 'We'll never get any tea!'

They had a great deal to tell him about school, the passages, Erin, Derek's forthcoming lecture tour, Michelle and her grandmother. He listened patiently, asking a question here and there and encouraged Michelle to join in as well. She soon overcame her shyness and asked Jane afterwards if all grandfathers were like him. 'You see, I've never had one,' she explained. Jane offered to share theirs. 'After all, we are his only grandchildren in England,' she told her, 'and many grandparents have lots more, so I'm sure he can manage another one!'

Now Mrs Blankenzee was bustling about and beckoning them to the dining room. 'Kom, binnen Kinderkes, kom.' The spread was magnificent and they had a really great Dutch-English late afternoon meal. Afterwards, they returned to the lounge and talked about their plans for when the Courts and Michelle came to stay in two weeks' time. 'You must come over again,' said Reg, 'and I believe part of your stay will be during half-term. We should arrange a couple of trips or an outing.' There was some talk about where they could go until Reg looked at his watch and said, 'Hm, time flies, it's getting to when I took you home.' They gathered their things, assisted by the housekeeper, who insisted on giving each a hug and a kiss, wishing them, 'Tot zeins.' Soon they were seated in Reg's car being driven back to Southleigh. The general verdict was that it had been a very satisfactory day.

Chapter XII

Next morning no one hurried up, though the children gathered in Michelle and Sarah's room to decide what they would do today. They spread themselves over the bunks three down, Michelle, Stephen and Sarah, and two up, Sam and Jane. They came to no final decision, though it looked as if it was going to be another nice day, and they were still working through various possibilities when Phyllis called up, 'Breakfast in ten minutes, last down does the washing up!' There was a mad rush to get dressed and — John was the last one down! He looked so crestfallen (he was good at faces) that they all offered to help him with his task, then realised there was a dishwasher in the kitchen.

After breakfast there came the business of feeding the rabbits and cleaning out their cage. Also room tidying. Then, as the weather was sunny, Phyllis suggested they go for a walk, adding, 'This afternoon John thought we could take a drive out to Hidding-cum-Stanton. It's an old village and a house on the outskirts has just come onto the market. It's quite an historical place and — as he has the keys — he thought you might like to have a look at it, a kind of private viewing. How does that strike you?' It sounded fun, and as Jane said to them on the quiet, 'When we go on these excursions we usually end up having tea out as well.' It was soon settled!

However, though it was fine to suggest a walk, where? Then Jane thought of the castle ruins situated on the edge of the park. That sounded reasonable. They could also spend some time in the play area, too. In a short while all were ready, but before they left, each made sure he or she had their box, as a safety precaution. However, only when going along the footpath that led under the railway did they remember this would mean crossing Tankerville Road. Now Sam and Sarah had never seen 'Goulhaven', so this would be a good chance to show them Melissa's house.

As they came down the footpath and under the railway line, Stephen pointed out to Michelle and the twins where they had seen her on the broomstick. 'I remember seeing you,' she said, 'Granny had kept me on it for nearly an hour, "to learn how to balance" and I was becoming awfully tired. Then I saw you watching and I was going to try and make the broom come over towards you, but Granny called out, "That's enough" and it dropped to the ground.' They walked on towards the road.

'I tell you what,' said Sam. 'She's only seen us once, and then she was all goggle-eyed on Stephen and his box. You go on quickly down the footpath while Sarah and I walk round the top of the road so we can have a good look at the place!'

'Do you think we should?' queried Sarah, 'Surely that's rather risky, why can't we just take a quick glance as we cross the road?'

'Because we won't see it properly and I want to!' Sam was being stubborn, so Sarah gave in, although she wasn't at all happy about it.

The others went on ahead; after a few minutes the twins appeared, and turning left, walked up the pavement past 'Goulhaven'. The place appeared deserted, and Sam slowed almost to a stop so he could have a good look.

'Oh, do come on!' begged Sarah.

'I'm sure there's no one in,' retorted Sam, 'Don't be such a baby!' He came to a dead halt and stared hard at the curtained house, more out of bravado than curiosity. He did not notice a faint movement of the curtains in the downstairs bay window. They were being watched!

Melissa was no fool. She had kept an eye on the footpath, as she was sure those children might appear again. And she was right, though she missed seeing Stephen, Jane and her granddaughter cross the road, but when she glanced out of the living room window a few moments later she observed a boy and a girl walking slowly along the pavement, obviously looking at 'Goulhaven'. As they came level, the boy stopped and stared hard at the house. The girl seemed to be worried and was obviously trying to hurry him on. Melissa smiled to herself. 'If he wants to see more, he shall!' she muttered and pointing her right hand at Sam chanted in Latin, 'Come here, stupid boy!'

One moment Sam was standing next to Sarah, the next he seemed to have jumped over the low front wall and was moving towards the house. Sarah stared at him speechless with horror. She could see he was trying to resist, but some irresistible force was drawing him inexorably nearer and nearer to the front door, and as she watched it opened a fraction. She knew that as soon as he reached it he would be drawn inside by her! In an agony of indecision she slapped her hands against her sides and felt something square and hard in her right pocket. The box! Sam was now some fifteen feet away from the door, trying to resist, but still being drawn towards it. She dodged behind an overgrown bush so she was well hidden from view, took the box in her hands and the words came to her at once!

'My little box and no other!

Thwart the witch and save my brother!'

Melissa had been concentrating wholly on Sam. She had forgotten about the girl, after all, she was of no consequence.

The helpless expression on his face made her laugh. Before she'd finished with him he'd have a lot more expressions, and she'd have a lot more laughs. She prepared to reach out and drag him in as soon as he was near enough. Then something like an explosion seemed to occur in her head. She reeled back and, unable to stop herself, called out 'release!' The front door slammed shut and she heard running footsteps. By the time she reached the window, the two children were nearly out of sight, running as fast as they could towards the footpath, where the others awaited them. She screamed in frustration; foiled again! These children had also been given boxes by Erin. Wait until she had a word with her. Irresponsible, that's what it was, giving children such things. However, this was only a temporary set back. Now she knew what power they had and she was sure her power and cunning could overcome it.

As soon as Sam leapt back over the wall, Sarah seized his hand and dragged him at a run along the pavement and plunged down the footpath. The others were waiting about halfway down. 'What took you so long?' began Stephen, but when he saw the dazed look on Sam's face and Sarah's agitation, he changed it to, 'What happened?'

'Oh, please, let's get right away from here and into the park where there are people!' begged Sarah; so they hurried on to the park's play area, where they sat down on a seat to hear what had occurred. Quickly Sarah told them.

Sam had recovered by now and explained how he'd felt this irresistible force that pulled him over the wall and towards the front door. Then there'd been a sound and a voice called out one word from within the house. He'd felt a sense of release and ran!

Michelle looked very concerned. 'She nearly got you. We shall have to be very careful indeed!'

Then a voice hailed them, and there was Geoff with his mother and grandmother taking a Sunday morning stroll—much to their great relief! So they decided to put off their visit to the castle ruins, and while the two ladies sat and gossiped they played around on the swings and slides. This gave them the opportunity to tell Geoff of Sam's narrow escape. He promptly suggested that they come back to his granny's because from there they could ring John and ask him to collect them. When he asked his granny she smiled and said, 'Well now, I was going to ask your friends to come back for a snack in any case.' Once there, John was phoned, and agreed without hesitation to come and pick them up, guessing from the tone of Jane's voice that something had happened. So by twelve o'clock they were back at Southleigh and a rather shamefaced Sam was explaining about his escapade. John merely said, 'You were lucky, my lad, that your sister had her wits about her and acted so promptly.' 'I nearly didn't have my wits about me,' said Sarah, 'It was only when I hit my pocket I remembered I had my box!'

One thing was now very clear. The footpath and Tankerville Road had to be avoided at all costs unless they had a grown-up with them. Awkward, but there was no sense in taking unnecessary risks.

There was no reason to postpone the proposed afternoon excursion, as Sam assured them he was all right and it would be better to be doing something than sitting around wondering what might happen next. So, after lunch they piled into the car, Phyllis and John in the front with five somewhat subdued children in the back, and off they went. The weather still held, though a cold wind had sprung up. More snow? It was hard to tell. The journey took forty minutes or so by road, as the village of Hidding-cum-Stanton was north-west of Tadbridge, a few miles off the main Taunton road. On a winter's afternoon it looked very quaint, and very empty. 'Some days in the summer you can hardly move for tourists and cameras!' remarked John.

'And as for a snack, or cup of tea, the cafe has a queue a mile long, but today it will be no problem!' said Phyllis.

'I told you we'd have tea out,' whispered Jane.

The house they were visiting was at the southern end of the high street, a stone built, rather imposing place, set in its own garden and surrounded by a high wall with a massive wrought iron entrance gate. To open this John produced an enormous key and then locked it behind them as they went up the stone-flagged path to the front door. For this he produced another key, not quite so large. The place was cold and dim inside, but everybody was well clad, so it did not worry them. 'I have to check the water system and plumbing to make sure it's still functioning in this cold weather,' explained John. 'You can wander round, but be careful, all the furniture here is mainly original Elizabethan, so no jumping on the beds. Also, leave cupboards and chests of drawers alone, no matter how tempting they look.'

'Yes, yes, we know, Dad!' said his twins. 'Come on, let's explore!'

The place was three storeys high, but only one room deep. The kitchen and 'usual offices' were in an addition at the rear, making the building look like a 'T' with a very short stem. The children decided to start from the top and work their way down. They ran up the broad oaken staircase to the first floor and then up a narrower one to the second. A passage ran along the back of the house with rooms off of it. These were furnished as bedrooms with four poster beds, massive wardrobes, chests of drawers and storage chests. The main bedroom had a small garderobe off it as well. While they were standing in this room, Sarah said, 'I wonder if this house has a house guardian?'

'You mean like your Bill?' asked Michelle.

'I expect it has,' replied Sam. 'See how neat and looked after everything is, and yet John told us it's been empty for nearly six months. It does look as if someone is caring for it.'

'True,' said Stephen, 'and it's not the cleaning lady coming in once a week to spruce it up either.'

No sooner had he said these words than there was the sound of a wardrobe door opening in the bedroom. They rushed in, thinking it had slipped its catch, but no! Standing in front of it was a small figure dressed in Elizabethan clothes looking very pleased with himself. The house guardian! Remembering their manners, the children bowed to him. In return he gave them a stately bow, then spoke: 'I am indeed pleased to meet with young humans who know and appreciate my kind and myself! How did you come by this knowledge?'

'We've a house guardian in our home, Bidford Manor,' replied Sarah.

'May I be so bold as to ask his name?'

'Of course, it's Bill Bluff,' said Sam.

The guardian looked at them with great respect and spoke in a reverent whisper in reply.

'Not one of the Bluffs, surely?'

'I don't quite know what you mean by "the Bluffs", but he told us he comes from a long line of house guardians,' said Sarah.

'The Bluffs are likened to royalty in the world of the house guardians,' he replied. 'You are indeed lucky to have a Bluff in your house.'

'But what of this house?' asked Michelle, 'It's such a lovely old place. It's a shame it's empty.'

'It is indeed, my dear. But I'm confident the right people will eventually come to live here. I'm not putting up with any old riffraff and have already scared off several totally unsuitable buyers!'

'But it all looks so perfect,' said Jane. 'Surely anybody seeing a place like this would fall in love with it and want to buy it straight away.'

'True, true,' he replied, 'but there are ways and means

of discouraging those who think they should own such a place but don't deserve it!'

'But how?' asked the ever practical Sam.

'Oh, quite easy. Would you like me to demonstrate?'

'Yes please!' they chorused.

'Well, take this nice cosy bedroom; it seems very snug. A little cool, perhaps, as the fire is not lit but… …' He flicked his right hand. At once the temperature seemed to drop several degrees, and freezing drafts came through the windows, from the garderobe and under the door. They all began to shiver. He flicked his hand again and things returned to normal. 'Then there's the question of drains. Follow me.' He led them from the bedroom and across into the back portion where the bathroom was. Though old fashioned it was perfectly acceptable and smelt fresh. This time it was his left hand that moved. All at once the whole room looked dingy and drab. What's more, a strange unwholesome smell seemed to rise up from the toilet and bath.

'Yuk!' went the children, and fled back to the landing.

'Of course there's always the matter of structure,' he added, pointing to the stairwell walls and ceiling. 'Built four and a half centuries ago and still as solid as the day it was completed. But… …' both hands this time. The pristine white walls suddenly turned a dingy grey shade with the paint flaking off. A crack, of frightening dimensions, appeared, running down the back wall, and another across the ceiling. Flicker, all was normal again.

'Doesn't that sort of thing upset the agents who show people round?' said Stephen, thinking of his dad.

'Somebody like your father, who is sensitive to old houses, soon realises that there are some people you just don't bring to places like this. The big-town agents are the worst, no respect or idea of who is a suitable person or not. But after they've been a few times they usually give up. Mind you, one was so thick-headed and brought round such awful people, I had to resort to extreme measures!'

'What did you do?'

'I became visible as an Elizabethan gentleman and walked in front of them as they were being shown round. They thought I was some kind of actor hired for the occasion.' He sniffed disdainfully. 'I waited until they were coming up here, then turned round showing them a death's head face. That did the trick! I've never seen six people leave so quickly. That agent never came again.'

'Children,' a voice called up from below, 'time to be going!'

'We are so glad we met you, and thank you for telling us about your duties!' said Stephen. 'We hope the right people soon come along. They are going to be jolly lucky to have someone like you for their house guardian.' The others nodded in agreement and wished him well.

'Please give Bill Bluff the most respectful regards and greetings from Eli Wrink,' he said, 'and good luck to you all.' He looked at Stephen and Jane for a moment, adding, 'and your wish will come true!' Then, like Bill, he vanished.

They pelted down the two flights of stairs and excitedly told John and Phyllis of their encounter with the house guardian. John smiled, 'I guessed there was someone like that here. I've often had the feeling when inspecting old houses that they were cared for by benign beings. Well, in future I shall be jolly careful who I bring to look at this place!'

They left and drove up the village High Street to the cafe, which was definitely not doing a roaring trade, though business was steady. The proprietor recognised John and said, 'No buyers yet?'

'No,' he replied, 'but the right one will appear one day.'

'Yes,' replied the other, 'if they meet with you-know-who's approval! Now what can I get you?'

When their order had been taken and the man had gone, the children asked, 'How does he know about Eli?'

'Because one of his relatives is house guardian in this cafe!' was the reply. They were most impressed. After an excellent scones, jam and cream tea, they returned home, arriving around six thirty. Phyllis prepared a light supper, after which they sat round chatting until reminded that it was school tomorrow and were their things ready? Mild panic ensued, as the visitors had to pack their bags as well. It had been a good weekend and they were looking forward to their lengthier visit in two weeks' time!

Chapter XIII

After school on Monday Stephen and Jane said goodbye to the 'Bidford Manor contingent' and took their bus home. It was very quiet when they thundered in, shouting — quite unnecessarily — 'Mum, we're home!' Phyllis came out of the kitchen and blinked.

'What, only two of you! What happened to the rest?' she said with a twinkle in her eye.

'Oh Mum, have you forgotten? They've gone home!' replied Stephen. 'But they'll be back the weekend after next for two whole weeks.'

'Whoopee!' shouted Jane and proceeded to give a realistic imitation of an Indian war dance, in which her brother enthusiastically joined.

'Oh well, I surrender, tea is in the kitchen,' and their mother led the way. When they'd finished, she asked what they were going to do now, hopeful of some peace, no doubt.

'We've some Atty homework to do,' said Stephen.

'Yes, research for our English period that started today,' added Jane. 'We thought we'd do it up in the play room, as there's those old Arthur Mee's Children's Encyclopaedias on the bookshelves with masses of stuff about poetry, Dickens — and whatever — in them.'

'Good idea, I was up there this morning and switched the central heating on to air the room out a little, so it should be comfortably warm by now,' said Phyllis. 'I'll give you a call when supper's ready.'

'Thanks Mum, come on Sis, bet I get up there first!'

'Bet you don't!'

Thunder, thunder, receding up the first flight and then up the second, followed by the familiar bang of the door being slammed behind them. Phyllis sighed and wondered if she would miss all this in a few years' time. Maybe she would, but then who knew what new horrors teenage twins could inflict on their parents. She decided it was best to be thankful that things were as they were now and worry about the future when it arrived.

Meanwhile, the twins had galumphed into the play room. This was the special attic room (see plan), containing the rumoured beam from Drake's 'Golden Hind' arching its way across the ceiling. It made the room seem different, and the children had always felt it exuded an unusual atmosphere. It certainly stimulated their imagination when playing there. They flung their school bags on the old couch and took out their notebooks, throwing them with great accuracy across the room at and on the table, then descended on the bookshelves.

'I'll take volume one and you start with volume two,' said Stephen.

'All right; shall we just list the literary references?'

'Yes, then we can look up the details when we've decided what we want to do.' They grabbed volumes one and two, raced to the table and began.

For around half an hour they worked in silence, then paused. A frown appeared on Stephen's face; Jane knew that meant he was puzzling over something.

'What's up, Steve?'

'Well, Sis, I was just thinking about what Eli Wrink said, that we would have our wish granted. The only wish I can think of was the one for a house guardian. It makes sense, doesn't it? I'm sure he could find one for us.'

'I think you're right,' replied Jane. 'But how he'll fulfil it I'm not sure, and how will we know when it happens?'

'I don't know either, we'll just have to wait and see. Anyhow, we better get on with our work, or we won't be finished by supper time,' replied her brother.

They worked on, but in a rather distracted manner, as both were still thinking about how, when and where the promised house guardian would appear. Then, above their heads came the most appalling 'crack'. Instinctively they both ducked. It sounded as if the beam was giving way. They looked up. No, it was as firm and solid as ever. Then a strange creaking noise began. 'Just as if it was part of a ship sailing over the open seas,' said Stephen afterwards. This continued for a few minutes then ceased. They looked at each other, what next? However, they did not have long to wait. There was a 'thump' from the far corner where the beam was embedded in the wall and a swirling cloud of blue mist appeared. As they watched, fascinated, it grew denser and began to take on shape and form. A figure with a definite nautical look about it now stood before them! He bowed gravely. They rose and bowed back.

'Welcome to Southleigh' said Stephen, 'are you going to be our house guardian?'

'I do hope you are,' added Jane, 'we do so want one!'

The figure responded with a twinkle in his eye. 'Indeed I am, my hearties, Bob Binnacle by name. Been a ship's guardian for many a year; but the time had come when I said to myself, "Bob my lad, you've sailed the seven seas for long enough. It's time you had some shore leave!" Then, low and behold I gets a call from an old landlubber friend of mine, Eli Wrink. He asked me if I was interested in a shore berth with nautical links. "The house is a mere baby," he told me, "But it has an attachment with the sea that goes back to the days of the Spanish Main, so if ever you feel a longing for your old haunts just spend a few hours immersed in it and you'll soon be your old self again." He's right, you know! This old beam's been round the world and more besides! So here I am and here I stay. I've already a feeling there's something afoot where I can be of help. But first tell me all about yourselves and this place.'

The three of them sat round the table while the twins told him about their home and life there, making special reference to Sam, Sarah, Bidford Manor and Bill Bluff.

Bob was just as impressed as Eli at the mention of his name. 'The Bluffs are as well known at sea as on land,' he told them. 'One of his Saxon ancestors was a ship's guardian on King Alfred's vessel that led his fleet against the Vikings. I shall be indeed honoured to meet him.'

A voice echoed up from below.

'Are you two deaf? I've been calling you to supper for the last five minutes!'

'Oh, we'll have to go, Bob!' They jumped up and made for the door.

'By all means, you need revictualling for your next voyage!' he said with a grin. 'I'll take a look around to get my bearings. I won't disturb you or your parents until you've had a chance to tell them about me. If ever you need me, just call "Bob ahoy! Bob ahoy!" and I'll be with you before you can tie a bowline knot.'

'What's that?' asked Jane.

Bob looked shocked, 'You can't tie a bowline?' he said disbelievingly, 'Oh, I can see I'll have to start teaching you a few things. Now off you go.'

They raced downstairs and into the dining room, where their parents were already at the table and waiting. Flinging themselves into their seats they chorused, 'Sorry we are late, but now we've a house guardian, thanks to Eli Wrink. He's an ex-nautical type and he's going to teach us how to tie bowline knots and lots of things.' All said at top speed and in one breath!

'Does he know what he's let himself in for?' asked John. 'If not, he'll soon find out and no doubt wish he was back at sea in the middle of a raging storm, rather than being Southleigh's house guardian! Give him my deepest sympathy next time you see him.'

'And mine, too,' added Phyllis with a smile.

Their response delighted the twins, as it showed their parents weren't going to make any silly grown-up remarks like: 'When are you two going to stop these fantasies?' Or, 'Yes, yes, we know dears, what lovely fun you must be having!' and then smile knowingly (or unknowingly) at each other in that awfully superior way some grown-ups have.

'You can meet him whenever you like,' explained Jane. 'He's told us how to call him. At the moment he's having a good look round.'

'Excellent,' said their father, 'He sounds like someone who takes his work seriously, just what's needed around here.'

Supper continued very pleasantly and afterwards they raced back to the play room, though they were hesitant about calling Bob, as they felt it would only be fair to let him settle in first. When they went to bed that night they could hardly wait to get to sleep so that the morning would come quicker and they would be able to tell their friends all about him!

Next morning they were up early, and when dressed, went to the play room to grab their school things and to see, if by chance Bob was around, and sure enough he was. He was seated at the table leafing through the Children's Encyclopaedias they had left lying there. Bob smiled cheerfully and held up a page for them to see. It showed great galleons under full sail sweeping across the Spanish Main.

'Ah, those were the days when ships were really ships! It took real skill to sail them, none of your dirty smelly coal or oil.' He sighed, but then brightened up. 'I've had a thorough look round and heartily approve of the way the captain runs this vessel. All very trim and shipshape.'

Captain, captain? Then they realised he meant their father. It was going to take a little while to become used to his terminology. 'However, there is something afoot as well. It lies in a north-easterly direction. Something grey and not very fond of you, or your friends.'

'That's Melissa Mouldyberry,' they told him. 'She's a grey witch!' and told of their encounters with her, also about Michelle and her mother.

'So, there's a white witch as well!' he remarked when the magic boxes were mentioned. 'It seems to me I could be in for a lively time. Still that's much better than having little or nothing to do and just lazing around. I enjoy a challenge!'

A voice echoed up the stairway. 'Are you going to take all day to collect your books? If you don't come right now you'll have no time for breakfast and probably miss your bus!'

'Coming, Mum! Bye, Bob, see you later!'

He chuckled and said, 'Aye, I'll be here when you return to port!'

They caught the bus by the skin of their teeth and tumbled off it as quickly as possible to find their friends. Ah, there they were! Sam was holding Jill by the hand, with Sarah and Michelle beside them. Coming along behind was Geoff with little Nola hanging on to his hand. If Jill had a friend in the 'big' school, why shouldn't she? Geoff looked proud and a little embarrassed at the same time; but in this school it seemed normal for the children of all classes to mix freely, quite unlike his old school, where the segregation of classes and further divisions into gangs or groups had made this quite impossible.

Stephen and Jane caught up with them and began to tell them excitedly about their newly acquired house guardian. This was listened to with great interest. The others congratulated them on their luck and hoped they would meet him when they came to stay.

Suddenly Jill announced, 'We've got one, too!'

'One what?' asked Sam.

'A house-looker-after man!' she replied. 'He's a soldier.'

They were not sure whether she was just copying them, or if the farmhouse really had a guardian, though it was highly probable it did. Next time they visited they would ask Bess or Harry. Having delivered their young charges, they made their way to the classroom, where Mr Atkinson awaited them to continue the exploration of English Literature.

The rest of the week passed uneventfully; however, when Friday came, Stephen and Jane did not go to Bidford Manor as usual. They decided time was needed to really prepare—they informed their parents—for the visitors arriving the following weekend. Also Sam and Sarah wanted to spend this 'last' weekend with their parents before they went away. Now that Michelle's ankle was completely healed they could do some local exploring beyond the manor grounds. However, on Friday night there was a long phone call between them all, to keep in touch, as they explained to parents who wanted to know what on earth they could talk about for so long, since they'd been together all day.

Saturday dawned cold and clear for the last day of January, so the Southleigh twins decided to call on Fenella and see if she wanted to come with them on a visit to Chris. She was delighted at the opportunity, as her father had gone off on a painting trip and her mother was taking Andrew shopping this morning. She would have had to go along too, which, as she put it, 'Would be jolly boring because it's only buying new sports gear that he needs and nothing for me.'

Her mother was also greatly relieved! 'She can come and have lunch with us as well,' said Jane, adding, 'then you won't have to rush back.' Mrs Steuart was duly appreciative, and they promised to return her daughter by five o'clock.

The three of them ran down the lane and were soon at

Chris's place. As usual he was whooping round the front lawn with Rover. When he saw them he let out another whoop, and soon they were all in the kitchen, where his mum was busy baking. Ralph, as usual, was messing about in his studio.

'Better leave him alone for a while, he's finishing off an order for a dozen special copper light fittings. The cat peed on one last night, and he's had to clean and re-polish it,' explained Mrs Shelley. 'So he's not exactly in a good mood at the moment.'

'You're telling me,' said Chris with great feeling.

They chatted and somehow the conversation drifted on to house guardians. Jane claims it wasn't intentional. But knowing her, it's pretty sure she steered it in that direction. Chris listened eagerly and then said, 'We've got one too, haven't we, Mum?'

'Yes,' she replied. 'As you can see this is a very old cottage, originally built before the railway came. Then it was extended and became a railwayman's dwelling. I imagine he had a large family by all the odd additions. Anyway, when we moved here it had been empty for ages and needed a lot of doing up. But it was ideal for us and the price was rock-bottom. When we moved in Chris was only two, so things were pretty hectic. Trying to make the place liveable and in order, plus looking after a small child at the same time, was not easy. Ralph was at work during the day and spent all his spare time trying to fix the place up. I helped too, but soon began to find it all too much. One evening, whilst putting Chris to bed—he was rather fractious, as he was cutting teeth—I really felt I just couldn't go on like this and said, out loud, "I need help, or I don't know what I'll do!" A blue haze appeared in one corner of the room and turned into a young woman. She smiled and came over to the bed, placing her hand on Chris's brow. In a moment he was peacefully asleep. Then she spoke to me: "I am this house's guardian, Sophia Satin by name. You will overcome your present problems and I will help you in many ways, but specially by keeping an eye on the little one." And she did; I could carry on with my tasks and Chris was as good as gold. Not like now.'

'Oh Mu-um!' he said, and blushed, then added, 'Yes, when I was small I remember her being around; it was very comforting, and enabled Mum to help Dad more.'

'Do you still see her?' asked Fenella. 'Not so often now,' he replied, 'but we know she's still about because there's a kind of comfy feeling in the place.'

'Yes, she keeps my studio in order as well!' said a voice, and there was Ralph. 'In fact,' he added, 'she has just helped me to clean the fitting that so-and-so of a cat nearly ruined. Whispered a suggestion in my ear of what to use and it worked! I'm one hundred percent in favour of house guardians.'

They told him all about the arrival of Bob and how delighted they were. Poor Fenella looked rather left out, as her house appeared to be too recent to have one. But Jane promised they would introduce her to Bob and maybe he could do something to help. That cheered her up, and when snack was finished they all went out to the studio and spent a wonderful remainder of the morning messing around with stone, clay, wood and metal until it was time to go back to Southleigh for lunch.

Chapter XIV

After lunch the twins took Fenella up to the play room and chanted 'Bob Ahoy, Bob Ahoy!' It was the first time they had summoned him. He promptly appeared and introductions were quickly made, then Fenella's problem-cum-request was put to him. 'It's rather difficult with new dwellings,' he said. 'You see, they aren't built with the same awareness of the so-called invisible forces and energies that inhabit the site. In olden times the builders knew of these things and took them into account. Often something like an offering or token would be built into a wall or placed under a floor, in the kitchen, for example, to encourage a house spirit to come and dwell there. None of that happens today, except in very rare cases, though there has been some increase of late. But most houses are not even blessed!' Fenella looked somewhat downcast at this, but Bob continued. 'However, my dear, don't worry. House guardians are still available! If those living in a non-guarded house truly feel the need for one and put their thoughts and wishes to that end, the path is opened for one to enter. Also, if those beings that guide us are aware that one is needed for beneficial or protective purposes, they can act to ensure such is provided. The fact that you, my dear child, earnestly wish for a house protector is enough. I shall see what I can do to help. Come back here on Sunday week and I'll let you know what success

I've had. It may take a little time to find the right person, but as there is art and creativity in your home, through your father's work, I don't believe it will be too difficult. Now, if you will excuse me.' He bowed and left. Fenella was enthralled and delighted by his offer to help. The rest of the afternoon was spent chatting and doing a little more literary research in the encyclopaedias. Then they saw their guest home at five o'clock. 'I shan't say anything for the moment to Mum or Dad,' she told them, 'Not until Bob has some definite news!' The twins agreed that was wise. No good getting folk all worked up about things before they happen.

On Sunday, for a treat, John took them to an ice skating rink in a nearby luxury sports centre connected to a large hotel and club complex. Normally they would not have been able to set foot inside the place, as they were not members; but because their father had been involved in the purchase of the site for the owners and had overseen the appointment of contractors to carry out the construction of the centre, he had been made an honorary member with access to all the facilities. Jane and Stephen had skated there before and thoroughly enjoyed it, but chances to do so were few and far between. So this was, indeed, a very special treat. They had a glorious time and returned home that evening glowing and happy!

&

What of the inhabitants of Bidford Manor? How did they spend their weekend? After the triple-way conversation with the others on Friday evening, Sam, Sarah and Michelle decided they would visit the farm in the morning and then take Michelle down to the ruined church. If there was time they would then walk round by the road to visit Erin and Rosie so she could see Croft Corner Cottage as well. This depended upon how her ankle felt. The day was just right for such an outing, as we have already heard. They set off for the farm around half past nine. Binky went with them as a matter of course. Michelle was in charge of his lead (with him on the other end) and he behaved tolerably well. On arrival they found Bess in the kitchen, with Jill and Brian helping her with some baking. Jill was cutting up fruit for a pie and Brian was busy rolling out pastry with much puffing and blowing, but also with a fair degree of success. Bess greeted them cheerfully, 'That school's a real blessing. Jill's never been so contented and cheerful. She comes home full of ideas and keeps Brian occupied too. He wants to do all the things she tells him about. That's why we are baking now. She's showing us what they did yesterday.'

Naturally, work stopped for a while, as the little ones wanted to chat with their friends. Jill took up the matter of house guardian again, telling them that theirs was a soldier. Her mother expanded the story when she finished. 'Yes, it's true. There is one such here. We don't see him often, but the children see him more than us. It's said he was guardian here in the troubled days of the Civil War and took up arms to defend this place. Ever since he has worn his uniform and will not discard it until 'The King Comes to His own Again', whatever that means. Maybe it's all hearsay, but both Harry and I know of and appreciate his presence. Compared with some guardians he's very shy, but faithfully executes his duties.'

There was some further talk about guardians, then they spoke of their coming stay at the Randell's. Bess was delighted to see that Michelle's ankle was so much better and promised her she would 'keep an eye' on her mum while they were away. Harry came in a little later and added his assurances as well. 'I'll be up there every day,' he told her. 'So don't you worry about your mum, she'll be fine!' They had an early snack before leaving for their walk to the church. Jill, for once, did not want to come. They did not press her, as the memory of their last rather unfortunate visit (see volume three) was still fresh in her mind, and anyhow, the baking was not yet finished!

When they arrived and stood before the ruined altar, Michelle felt some of the peace that radiated from it. 'What a wonderful place,' she whispered. 'I could stay here for ever.' They looked around and she was shown where Mr Skurray and his helpers had been 'entrapped' by the monks, and of their capture. As they spoke, both children felt a shiver run down their spines. It could have all turned out so differently if it had not been for Brother Andrew and — of course — Binky! But even as they relived the event the feeling of comfort grew stronger, for coming towards them from his cell was Brother Andrew.

Happy to see him again, they introduced Michelle. He greeted them warmly and they went to the little stone-seated room where they had talked before. He looked keenly at Michelle and then said, gently, 'My child, you carry several sorrows. One concerns your grandmother, who alas, has not followed in the way of the White Ones, but has allowed herself to be distracted by temptations of worldly power. To break the grip it already has upon her will not be easy, but this can be done and you will be the one to do it. Not unaided though, for you have stalwart friends and helpers. Be fearless and courageous, and all will be well.' He turned to the twins. 'You will assist her, and so will others. Help always comes from the least expected quarter in the darkest hour. Always be ready to seize the fleeting chance or the split second opportunity. Now come with me.' He led the way to the altar and said a blessing over them. As he did so, the church no longer seemed to be a ruin, but stood four-square and strong. Courage and joy flowed through them. He smiled, saying, 'Come again whenever you feel like it. You may not always see me, but I shall be here. Now go in peace and strength!' He turned and walked back down the length of the nave. Slowly he became fainter and fainter until he vanished. They stood for a moment before the altar, then quietly departed. Binky, who had been a model of good behaviour all the time they were there now began to frisk and prance around in his usual way, making it quite a job for Michelle to control the little rascal. As it was very near lunchtime, the children jogged back to the manor. They decided to visit Erin in the afternoon.

After lunch — minus Binky this time — they set off along the bridle track and then across the fields towards her cottage. The twins told Michelle of the various adventures that had occurred along their route and they stopped to examine the boundary stone, then turned down the road to where it forked, taking the one that led past her cottage. They went up the path and knocked on the door. Erin answered and was delighted to see them. Rosie came loping out of the kitchen as well and allowed herself to be tickled behind the ears before settling down by the fire. 'I'm glad you called, as there are one or two matters I would like to discuss with you,' said her mistress. They settled themselves comfortably and she began.

'First, as you probably know, Michelle, your mother came and had tea with me a few days ago. We had a good chat and she has told me a great deal about your grandmother and the way she has treated both of you. I don't want to scare you unnecessarily, but you should be aware that for this scheme of hers to harness the Ancient Power slumbering below the Dell, you play an important part. This could be dangerous, very dangerous, and all of you must be on your guard against any attempts she may make to entice Michelle back to "Goulhaven".'

Now, she has invited me to stay with her from next Thursday, the fifth, until Monday the ninth, 'for old times sake'. I believe she wishes to make use of my knowledge to help her with this foolish enterprise. I shall be very careful while I am there. For I'm convinced she will use every means in her power to get what she wants and I am not sure if my strength will be a match for hers. You will all be at Southleigh for two weeks from the sixth and the following weekend your half-term starts. If she is hatching anything I think that weekend of the fourteenth to fifteenth will be when she will try to ensnare Michelle. For any attempt to control the Power must be made before the spring equinox of March the twenty-first. However, I understand Southleigh now has a nautical house guardian! That is good, for he will be aware of any negative force directed against those living there — including visitors. One thing I shall do is confront Melissa about her plans and try to dissuade her from them, though I don't hold out much hope of success. However, I have warned her of the possible consequences if she continues with her plan. Please remember, keep your boxes with you at all times. They have a power that she cannot subdue and will keep you out of her clutches, provided you use them as quickly as Sarah did when she tried to catch Sam. If she attempts to steal a box it will do her no good, as she will be unable to open it, for none of her spells are powerful enough! My advice is simply this: Take great care. Keep together, avoid passing "Goulhaven", and use the footpath as little as possible. It's a nuisance, I know, but better to be safe than sorry.'

'I shall visit your mother while you are away, Michelle, so that she feels supported by as many of us as possible. Though I don't think your grandmother will bother her for the moment.' She smiled. 'Now, enough of that; I've said my piece! How about some refreshment? And a chat about pleasanter matters!' Which is exactly what they did. Then around four o'clock, when it began to get dark, they set off for home.

As they came to the manor gates, Sarah pointed towards the Dell. 'Look! What's that?' Hovering above it in the twilight was something airborne. It was difficult to tell who or what it was, but they could guess! Peering through the gloom they saw the object suddenly shoot upwards. As it did so, something fell away from it and plunged down into the Dell. There was a flash and for a second or two the whole area was lit up with the weird greenish light they had seen before.

'What is she doing?' asked Sam.

Michelle answered him. 'I think she is deliberately trying to disturb the sleeping Power so that when she has her spell ready it will allow her to summon it and arouse it quickly.'

'I wonder if there's a counter spell?' said Sarah, 'Let's ask Sir Brian after supper.'

Later that evening the three of them trooped up to the attics and along the passage to the approximate position of the brass-handled door, which, to their surprise was visible! Sarah knocked politely and it was opened by JJ, who courteously invited them in. The room was wreathed in steam issuing from a cauldron boiling away in the fireplace. The twins had never noticed a fireplace before, because normally the room didn't have one. But with Sir Brian there was no telling what it would have next! The master magician was seated on a stool next to it, stirring away with a large ladle in one hand whilst dropping in what looked like hen's eggs from a large bowl with the other. He was also trying to read from a book perched up against the back of a chair. This was not easy, as the book kept on sliding down, and as he bent his head to follow its contents his glasses would slide down his nose, causing him to jerk his head back violently to keep them from falling off. This meant his aim was erratic and several of the eggs had missed their target and were rolling about on the floor. They did not break, as they were hard-boiled. When he realised he had guests, announced by a discreet 'ahem!' from JJ, he abruptly stopped his activities, put the bowl down, closed the book and muttered something under his breath that caused the fire to obligingly die down to a soft glow. 'Just working on my potion; you know,

I nearly have it!' he announced, 'though I'm not sure about the eggs, they should really be free-range.' He moved over to his desk and motioned them to a bench near it. 'Now, what can I do for you?' he smiled. Sarah explained. He went purple. 'That wretched woman!' he growled. 'Sorry, my dear, I know she's your grandmother,' he added to Michelle. 'But really! Well, there are two things we could do. One is to place a slumber spell over the Dell.' He paused, having noticed its poetic connotations, then continued, 'Though that is not easy, as I would have to research as to the best kind of soothing substance to employ. You see it's a matter of using a liquid that you pour or spray on, or a paste that you spread over the area you wish to calm. The application of either is naturally risky, as the subject, disturbed by your approach and annoyed, may wake up rather than going back to sleep. However, the other method is to deal with the offender. You say she flew over the site then dropped something. Obviously an irritation spell. If we make it so it's impossible to drop anything else, then she can't disturb it! I think that is the best method.'

'But how can it be done?' asked Sam.

Sir Brian grinned, 'It so happens that I have just been working on such a project. When I was Master of the Manor we had trouble with birds attacking the soft fruits in the gardens. I reasoned that an invisible canopy over the bushes would stop this once and for all. The proto-canopy worked very well, though the Spanish Armada put a stop to further experiments. But, I've been looking at it again, as I thought it might help your father in the garden. It also deters slugs.'

'You mean you could make one that would cover the Dell so that if Granny tried to drop things, they would just bounce off?' asked Michelle.

'That's right!' he answered, 'and if I add elasticity, any object hitting it will not only bounce off but bounce back from whence it came!' He began to rummage about on his desk. 'Now let me see! Ah, here we are.' He picked up what looked like a disc cut from paper and held it up for them to see. It glittered and the edge became vague in outline.

'JJ!' 'Yes, Master?' 'Take this and go over to the Dell. When you are near enough, throw it like a discus and say: "Cover and repel!" This is an English spell, none of your fancy Latin ones! Now off you go and you'll know it's in position when you hear a note like a bell.' JJ took the disc and let himself out.

'Don't you worry about your mother, lass, while you're away,' he said to Michelle, 'I'll keep an eye on her, with the others to help, of course.' Michelle thanked him, but couldn't help wondering whether having Sir Brian 'keep an eye' on you was more of a liability? But as he was not going to be the only one, perhaps it would be all right.

JJ was back in about ten minutes and reported all had gone as planned.

'Now we wait and see,' chuckled Sir Brian 'I'll report results to you in due course, good night.'

They knew this was his way of saying 'visiting time over', so bade him good night and JJ showed them out. They felt much easier now and wondered how Melissa would find things on her next visit!

Melissa had decided to continue her annoyance campaign in the hopes that by the time Erin visited the Power would be disturbed to such a degree that it would only require the waking spell to place it at her disposal. She would fly over again tonight and drop another irritation potion over the target. The night was clear and cold. Wrapping up well, she mounted her broomstick at midnight and flew swiftly to Bidford Manor, circling high above the plantation. What she did not know was that on the roof of the manor two pairs of eyes were watching her: Sir Brian's and JJ's. She circled again and dropped her potion-package. It spiralled down and she watched it descend with great satisfaction.

But there was no flash of light. She peered down, trying to see what had happened. Suddenly, she noticed a small object rapidly growing larger as it came shooting back up towards her. She couldn't believe her eyes. Jerking the broom in an evasive manoeuvre she strove to avoid the missile, but it homed in on her, and when directly under the broom exploded with a 'pf-fut' noise drenching her in luminous green liquid. Barely able to control the broom, which yawed erratically upwards and then went into a nose-dive, she fought to gain control, and just before making ground contact managed to steady herself and set course for 'Goulhaven', bedraggled and bewildered!

'I don't think she'll try that again for a while,' remarked a very satisfied magician!

Chapter XV

On the following Thursday Erin was up early to prepare for her trip to Tadbridge to stay with Melissa. Naturally Rosie would accompany her. She decided she would go by bus. There was a service to and from Bidcote twice a day and she would catch the afternoon one. During the morning she walked across the fields towards the manor and met Sir Brian and Bill by the footpath stile on the edge of the grounds. There were a few matters she wanted to discuss with them and some precautions she wished to take. The outcome of their meeting will be revealed later. After lunch she set off for the village to wait for the bus. When it arrived the driver was 'not sure' about Rosie. 'I'm not supposed to carry livestock,' he told her. But she pointed out Rosie was in a closed shopping basket, so who would know? With some reluctance he agreed to say no more about it and let her on. Luckily, the bus route went past the County Schools and up the road near the park so she could get out there, and only had to walk up the footpath to reach Tankerville Road (see map). The outward appearance of 'Goulhaven' did not impress her; there was an air of menace about it that made her decide to be very careful what she said and did. When she rang the bell it tolled dismally as usual. Melissa opened the door and made a great show of welcoming her. But Erin noticed that all the time she was watching her closely and every now and then she would switch her gaze to Rosie's basket. For the signals the rabbit was sending out to its mistress were ones of warning.

Then Melissa, with a show of false embarrassment, said, 'Er, there's one teeny request I must make of you, Erin, dear. Unfortunately, I am allergic to rabbit fur.' She sneezed loudly and blew her nose. 'So I must ask you, and I'm sure you'll understand, to put dear Rosie in the hutch in the garden that I borrowed specially for her.'

Erin paused before answering; she needed time to pick up Rosie's reaction. She heard, 'Agree, but be watchful.'

'Why of course, Melissa,' she replied. 'I'm so sorry to hear of your affliction; when did it start?'

This caught that lady off her guard. 'Oh, er, I've had it for many years. Don't you remember when we studied together I could never work with them?'

'Why yes, of course, how silly of me to forget,' she replied, thinking, 'the cunning hussy!'

While Melissa thought, 'She is silly! It will be easy to get the better of her.'

'I'll put Rosie out there right now,' smiled Erin and picked up the basket.

'While you're doing that I'll prepare some tea,' smiled her hostess.

The back garden was gloomy, for it was overlooked by the railway embankment, and from early afternoon on this threw a deep shadow across it. The hutch stood by the neighbouring fence and was made from a dark wood, giving it a rather dismal appearance. She put the basket down and opened the door.

'Look inside,' was the message she received. On impulse she ran her hand along the top of the doorframe. Her fingers touched something that felt like a piece of metal. She prised it loose with her fingers and examined it closely. It was in the shape of an 'X' and stained a dirty muddy brown, which Erin realised was dried blood! She slipped it into her pocket and popped Rosie in the hutch.

'Fine now,' she picked up. 'Hm, so our dear Melissa tried to put Rosie out of action, did she?' she thought. 'We can't have that!'

Turning round quickly she saw Melissa busy in the kitchen. She looked out, waved and called, 'Nearly ready!'

'I'll just walk round the garden,' Erin called back and did so. She followed an overgrown path that led her to the River Tad, which flowed along the right boundary, and when sure she could not be seen from the kitchen, dropped the offending piece of metal into it. The water hissed as it went under and vanished. A red stain welled up to the surface for a moment then disappeared. Satisfied, Erin returned to the house and a 'cosy' afternoon tea.

○○

That Thursday at Bidford Manor was pretty hectic. Derek was busy turning his study upside down looking for papers he knew he had a moment ago and stuffing them into his briefcase, only to tip them out again later to make doubly sure he'd put in everything he needed. Then a change of mind would occur and he'd start all over again. Doreen was also packing, but she was far more methodical and had already got the suitcases from the attic and was carefully putting in the clothes they would need. Derek's lecturing suit's jacket needed a button sewed on. He tended to fiddle with them while talking, and so they came off at regular intervals. Shoes also had to be checked. Ingrid gave a hand where she could, while at the same time making a list of all the things she had to remember regarding the house. It was in this state when the children left for school in the morning and still like it when they returned home. If anything, it was worse. They took their homework up to the secret room, which was probably the only place not affected by the chaos. For during the afternoon Doreen and Ingrid had turned their attention to preparing the children's cases as well.

At supper the plans for tomorrow were explained to them. They would go off to school as usual, and during the morning their father, or mother, would drive their suitcases over to Southleigh, as there would be no room for them in the boot later with their parent's luggage as well. They would come back from school as usual to gather up their personal bits and pieces, then be driven to the Randell's house around five thirty. Derek and Doreen's train left at seven, so they would have time to offload the children and drive on to Reg's place, as they were leaving their car in his garage, for his flat was only a short distance from the station. The train would take them to Bristol, where the first talk was on Saturday evening. From Bristol they would go on to Birmingham and then to other places in the Midlands and the North.

The next morning, once the children were packed off to school, Derek had a meeting with Hugh about the passage repairs. Since the sealing of the tunnel all had progressed smoothly, so they decided to continue with the clearing and renovation work. The electrician would wire the finished passages as arranged. If they had completed the first phase of the restoration before he returned they would turn their attention to finishing the repairs to the old boiler house and re-glazing the greenhouses.

School felt odd that Friday. Not only was it the 'last' day of the week, but they would be going home only to leave almost straight away! Even though they had already spent a couple of weekends at Southleigh, this would be different. Luckily, Michelle's attitude helped them. She was so used to changes and moving around that she took it all very calmly. This made them try to be the same. After all, they would be with friends and people they knew, not absolute strangers.

When they reached home that afternoon the chaos was subsiding, and in the hall their parents' luggage waited to be loaded up. The car stood at the front door. A quick snack awaited them and then it was up to their rooms to pick up the few personal items they wanted and to say goodbye to Binky and Cleo, both of whom seemed totally unaffected by the departure of most of the household! They had found that Ingrid was a very good animal servant and meant to exploit it to the full while they had her to themselves.

'Ungrateful beasts,' said Sam, for when he told Binky he wouldn't see him for two weeks, all he did was wag his tail furiously.

'Bad as saying "hurrah" or "good riddance", isn't it?' added Sarah. But in a sense it helped their departure. Once they were in the car Ingrid saw them off, promising to ring regularly and tell them how things were, especially with the ungrateful ones!

When they arrived at Southleigh there came the most difficult part for Sam and Sarah — to say goodbye to their parents. Try as they would to keep calm, a lump kept rising in their throats, and tears kept on sneaking into their eyes. However, when they remembered how Stephen and Jane had also had to say goodbye to their parents at very short notice when they left for Australia, they felt better and actually managed the parting very well. Though after the car had gone, they did look rather down in the mouth, until Jane suggested they went up to meet Bob Binnacle.

Derek and Doreen had promised to ring up at least every other day to let them know how the tour was going and where they were.

Once the five of them had gathered round the table in the play room, Stephen and Jane chanted the call, 'Bob ahoy! Bob ahoy!' The beam over their heads creaked alarmingly for a moment, and then Bob materialised, 'beaming' as usual. He welcomed the newcomers to Southleigh and assured them of the best of his service at all times. He asked them to convey his respectful greetings to Bill when they returned home.

'Now listen carefully,' he said. 'As you know, your friend Erin Thomas is staying with the Grey One who lives in Tankerville Road. Already that person has tried to curb her powers by separating her familiar from her. But she found the rune placed in the hutch and destroyed it. Today she was trapped, but managed to escape. There is an uneasy truce between them at the moment. So I am going to have to keep a close eye on things this weekend. Please do not call me unless you really have to. I will report to you here each evening after supper. Don't worry,' he added, seeing the look of concern on their faces, 'Your friend Erin knows a trick or two, and so do I. Now off you go and enjoy yourselves, all will be fine.' He said it so cheerfully and confidently that they felt light-hearted again and ran down happily to unpack and settle in with the assistance of Stephen and Jane.

☙

What of Friday at 'Goulhaven'? Thursday evening had passed in an uneasy truce where Melissa did not broach anything about her objective in having Erin to stay, but nevertheless asked many questions. Erin was very careful with her replies, as she did not want to be drawn into giving away how much she already knew. At last it was bedtime.

'I do hope you'll sleep well and won't be put out by not having your pet with you,' smiled Melissa.

'Oh no, not at all,' she replied. Having removed the spell, Rosie could communicate with her, obviously the very thing Melissa wanted to stop. As soon as she was in bed she had opened her mind, and Rosie came through clearly.

'Be very careful. She is crafty and has stronger powers than you realise.'

'I'm on my guard!'

'The new house guardian at Southleigh, Bob Binnacle, is keeping an eye on Melissa as well.'

'It's good to know I am not alone. Also, I can call upon

Sir Brian, as we arranged.'

'That may be necessary, for tomorrow she will try to enlist your support for her plans and if you don't agree will threaten force; for she will have told you too much for her own good.'

'Will you be able to do your part?'

'Yes, since you removed that charm she has no hold over me. Good night.'

'Good night,' and Erin slept remarkably well for one in an awkward situation.

Next morning after breakfast Melissa took Erin into the front room, which she used as her study. The whole place was in one ghastly mess; the walls and ceiling were covered with stains caused by exploding potions brewed in a filthy fireplace, and the smell was terrible. Her hostess wasted no time in coming to the point.

'Now Erin, dear, I know we had a slight difference of opinion when I visited you some weeks ago, but I want you to understand I bear you no grudge. After all, living as you do — cut off from the mainstream of the latest trends in witchcraft — you can hardly be expected to understand the meaning and significance of what I told you. So now I am going to explain to you once more my main objective and what it could mean for you, as well as for myself.'

She went over her investigations of primal energies, with special reference to what she had discovered in the grounds of Bidford Manor. Erin listened patiently. Then Melissa's voice took on a hard edge as she continued. 'I know it was through your interference the old tunnel was blocked, but it makes little difference. I have already found a method of gradually bringing the Power to waking consciousness. There was a slight hitch last week.' Erin knew all about it, as Sir Brian had told her!-—but she said nothing.

Melissa continued, 'However, we shall overcome that. There's another factor needed for success, which involves my granddaughter. Something will have to be done about her. We'll discuss that later. What I need from you is your co-operation and wisdom. I do not think I can perform the summoning rune single-handed. Two of us would be best! Think of the strength and energy this would give us. We would become invincible. No witch or wizard could stand against such power! They would be our servants. Just imagine, the whole world would be at our feet. What do you say? Surely it must be yes!'

She stopped abruptly and stared hard at Erin, who noticed a glint of fanaticism in her eyes. The Power was already taking hold of her, but in a way far from that she had envisaged. Breathlessly she awaited Erin's answer.

That good lady paused a moment before replying, knowing full well that the reaction she would provoke could be dangerous, but it had to be done now before things got too out of hand.

'Melissa, listen to me carefully, very carefully. What I am about to say I do not say lightly. My heart is heavy and I say it out of concern for you, your daughter and especially your granddaughter. You ask me to aid you with my wisdom to release the primal energies that slumber in the grounds of Bidford Manor. Yes, I could help you to do so. Our combined magical strength would accomplish such a task. But what then? It's easy to wake anybody up, but then can you control their wakening actions? That requires tremendous concentration, which must not falter for one second or disaster will ensue. Have you thought of that? Would this Power allow you, or me, to control it? I doubt it! Once free it will want to remain free and I am fearful of what its uncontrolled energies could do. They could cause untold havoc on physical and mental levels. Then you tell me Michelle has to be involved, but how? Do you think I don't know why an innocent child is needed? Once loosened, only one thing can control it, the innocence of a child.

She would become your mouthpiece, but at a terrible cost. Drained of her own self, in a short while she would be a living husk, nothing more than an imbecile. Then you would need another, is that why you tried to capture the boy? No, Melissa, I can have no part in this mad scheme; it will only lead you to disaster. Give it up now and be content with what gifts you have! Strive to improve them, as I have done with mine. I tell you there are no short cuts to attain the Supreme Power; it's hard work all the way. Stop this business now before it destroys you!

Melissa sat with bowed head for a moment, then leapt up and faced Erin, her face contorted with fury. Her voice became harsh and unreal, spitting out words like projectiles.

'I've said it before and I'll say it again, Erin, you are a fool, a whimpering goody, goody of a fool! You turn down the chance of a lifetime to make yourself famous and powerful, and all you can do is mewl about some brat of a child. There are enough children in the world, one or two, even ten, would not be missed.'

She paused, choked by her own anger, then continued in a low menacing tone, 'Since you will not listen to reason, other methods must be applied! I need your help and intend to have it!' She raised her arms and muttered something under her breath that Erin could not catch.

All at once she found herself held in an invisible grip, which forced her to her feet and propelled her towards the door. 'Take her to her room and keep her there!' she ordered, saying to her captive, 'When you come to your senses, call me and we'll talk again. But if you think you are going to leave this house without agreeing to help me, you are very much mistaken, for my power is already greater than yours!'

The irresistible force dragged Erin up to her room and flung her in. The door closed, the blinds descended, she was trapped. From below, Melissa's triumphant laughter echoed up the stairs.

Chapter XVI

Erin sat up upon the bed. The force with which she had been flung into the room had winded her for a moment, but now she had to act, and act fast. Rosie! She sent her an urgent call. The answer came back at once: 'I know! You must escape before she tries to destroy you.'

'I shall, have no fear, she cannot harm me.'

'Can you get help?'

'Yes, she will be forced to release you before the day darkens. I shall be back.'

Erin sent up a prayer for Rosie's safety and then relaxed. Shortly after, she heard a howl of rage from below and knew Rosie had made her escape. This was followed by much bumping and banging beneath as if Melissa was preparing something in her study, then silence. But Erin could feel that intense concentration was being directed, no doubt, to some unpleasant business.

With Erin safely out of the way, Melissa had decided to get rid of the rabbit. Taking a carving knife she had gone out to the hutch. The rabbit was crouched inside nibbling a piece of carrot. 'Open the door, one quick thrust and it's all over!' she sniggered and drew back the bolt. The door opened all right. It swung open with great force, striking her in the stomach and bowling her over backwards. The knife flew out of her hand and landed in a bramble bush.

Something white flew over her as she lay on the ground and by the time she staggered to her feet there was no sign of the rabbit. Which caused the howl of rage Erin had heard. Annoyed, Melissa came back and shut herself in her study, where she sought to prepare the most powerful spell she knew to strip another's power from them.

Rosie hopped through a convenient hole in the fence, across the next garden, through the broken boards at the end and onto the footpath, under the railway arch and into Bardon Lane, where she hopped down towards Southleigh. Once safe in those grounds, hidden under a bush, her ears began to waggle.

Up in his study, Sir Brian was messing about as usual. He had sent JJ out to find some herbs that grew in the old herb garden and in the meantime was debating how to improve his Dell cover. If that woman tried again he wanted to give her a pretty sharp warning to keep away. Something more drastic than just green dye, he decided. Suddenly a pot of ink rose into the air right under his nose. He made a grab at it, but it avoided his hand and hovered a foot away from his eyes. He stared at it. As he did so, a picture began to form against the background of the ink, reflected on the glass of the bottle. He saw a white rabbit hopping along a road and into the garden of a big house; its ears were waggling. He recognised Rosie at once. Rosie? Erin? Furiously he began to concentrate on the rabbit. After a moment the message came through.

'Erin, trapped in house, "Goulhaven", Tankerville Road! Be quick!'

In a flash he was on his feet, grabbed his robe and wrapped it around himself, jammed his wizard's hat on his head, then slowly began to spin round, faster and faster until he was just a blur of colour. Then he was gone, in a flash of light! When JJ entered the room a few minutes later, he found a note. 'Erin in trouble, tell Bill.' Which, being a good servant, he did.

If Melissa had been looking out of her kitchen window a few seconds later she would have seen what appeared to be a mini-whirlwind at the bottom of her garden; but as she was in her study she didn't. It rotated wildly across the back lawn and shot into the river with a resounding splash. A few seconds later a very wet and irate Sir Brian staggered out and stood for a moment to survey the scene while a large puddle of water formed around his feet. 'Never could get the unwinding part right!' he muttered to himself. His sixth sense told him that Erin was imprisoned in the front upstairs room and that her captor was messing about in the room below. Noticing the water at his feet he said, 'Be dry.' The puddle vanished, but he was still soaking wet. 'No!' he growled, 'Myself, not the water. Got no sense, these modern off-the-shelf spells.' Satisfied that he would not leave any traces, he invisibilised himself and walked through the back wall of the house and through the inner wall, into Melissa's study. The place was in an even worse mess than his den! He had a momentary flash of admiration for somebody who could create more chaos than he thought possible. Then he set about thinking how to turn it to his advantage. Melissa was so intent on what she was doing that she had no inkling he was standing behind her. An open book lay on the table beside her, from which she was reading the instructions for preparing whatever she was preparing. He looked over her shoulder to read the title. 'A Spell for Holding One Indefinitely Against their Will,' he read with horror. The wretch. An idea, or—as he modestly put it later—an inspiration occurred to him. When the hussy had her nose in the cauldron he quietly flipped two pages over to a completely different spell. His supposition that she wouldn't realise this was correct. She looked down the page, and taking the next substance from her stock of ingredients added it, then the next and the next. Sir Brian waited. The mixture began to bubble rather fiercely. Melissa looked surprised, but still flung in the next ingredient. The result was spectacular—far better than he had hoped. There was a thunderous roar and a column of a viscous brown liquid shot vertically out of the cauldron and hit the ceiling, from where it proceeded to spray down on Melissa and the whole room. At the same time, all the doors inside the place flew open and the furniture seemed to come alive. Chairs frisked round the table and fell over each other. Pots, pans and other kitchen items flew round like uncanny insects. Everything in the house went berserk. Sir Brian had moved over to the door as soon as the liquid had started to bubble and so was able to escape the rain of goo. He rushed upstairs and into Erin's room, the door of which had sprung open. She was sitting on the floor looking somewhat bewildered, as the bed had just pitched her off. Visibilising himself he grabbed her by the hand, pulled her to her feet, and they fled down the stairs, through the chaos and out the back door into the comparative peace of the back garden. A column of filthy brown smoke was now pouring forth from the chimney, whilst from inside there came intermittent thuds and crashes as the contents of the house continued their crazy dance. She grinned at Sir Brian, for she'd guessed what he'd done. At that moment, Rosie came hopping through the hole in the fence and up to her.

'Well, you can leave now. Let her stew in her own juice,' said Sir Brian. Rosie's ears twitched and she looked up questioningly at Erin. She listened for a moment and then turning to him said, 'Thank you very much for coming to my rescue. But no, I shall stay here. If I go back, I can soon put an end to the chaos and rescue her. I still want to try—if I can—to dissuade her from this plan.' Sir Brian nodded understandingly. 'Of course, my dear, you are right. However, be careful, she's cunning as a fox, that one.'

'I shall take care,' she replied, 'I hope I won't have to call on you again.'

'My dear lady, if you do, I shall be only too glad to be of assistance,' he replied gallantly and began to rotate slowly, then quicker and quicker until he disappeared. Hopefully his landing at Bidford Manor was successful.

Erin now tucked Rosie under her arm and marched into the house. As soon as she was over the kitchen threshold, she chanted a counter spell and the whole place suddenly became still and silent, except for the gurgling and gasping noises issuing from Melissa, who was covered from head to foot with the gooey brown liquid. The furniture and other items crept back to their proper places rather like naughty children who've been caught rampaging round the place while their parents are out. Without a word, Erin took Melissa by the hand and led her up to the bathroom. She ran the bath, dropped in a pinch of something she took from a little pouch and left Melissa to get on with cleaning herself up. In the meantime, she went down to the study and examined the book that lady had been using. From the expression on her face she did not approve at all of the contents!

Half an hour later Melissa came downstairs; she had changed into clean clothes and generally looked tidier than Erin had seen her for some time. She was contrite and apologetic, a little too much so for Erin's liking.

'My dear Erin, what will you think of me? I really don't know what possessed me to be so rude and unfriendly to you. And in spite of that you rescued silly old me from a stupid error in spell preparation. Oh, and you have your dear rabbit with you too! Well, I can't be an old meanie. I'll put up with a little discomfort. She may stay in the house with you, for I don't know how to begin to thank you.'

There would have probably been much more of this kind of drivel, almost as gooey as the liquid she had been rescued from, but Erin stopped her abruptly with:

'Melissa, you can cut that rubbish out! If you had completed the spell I would not be here now. Luckily, in your pride and hurry you did not notice that two pages had blown over. The resulting miss-mix was a potent one, as you experienced. I ask you again, for the last time, to give up this whole plan of yours and I warn you that if you refuse I shall do all within my power to stop you! Furthermore, as you know, according to our Coven's rules, as I used my powers to save you from your misuse of your powers you are indebted to me, and until that is repaid you have no power over me whatsoever. I shall remain here until Sunday in the hope that you will eventually see reason.'

Melissa was a picture of frustration, which she could not disguise. But there was nothing she could do about it. She had to accept the situation, for she knew the Coven rules — which bound them both — could not be broken without the offender being stripped of their witchcraft degree, and licence to practise. And should they continue to do so, the penalty was 'nether world suspension', the details of which are too long and too terrible to mention here.

However, she was playing for high stakes and knew that if she could harness the Power to do her bidding, she could snap her fingers at the coven! Erin may have the upper hand at the moment, but there was still time. She could wait until the interfering busybody had gone. She put on what she hoped was a genuine smile of resignation and said, 'I'm sorry if I overreacted. By all means, stay a few more days if you wish and we'll say no more about this unfortunate affair.' Naturally this did not take Erin in at all. But it meant a truce and both hoped they could still convert the other.

☙

Saturday in the Randell household was spent shopping in Tadbridge and generally messing around at home. They did not summon Bob Binnacle, knowing he was busy keeping an eye on 'Goulhaven', though they wondered how Erin was managing. However, as promised, that evening he came to the playroom after supper and made his report.

'All is going well. Your friend is in no danger for the moment. In fact, she is in charge and is trying to persuade the other to give up her scheme. There's a kind of truce between them.'

They were relieved to hear this. Good old Erin! 'I'll be back tomorrow morning,' he said. 'As I have some news for Fenella, can you invite her here for ten thirty?' They promised to do their best, and when he had gone, went down to telephone her. Fenella was delighted and promised to be around tomorrow morning on the dot of ten thirty.

And so she was, ringing the doorbell at ten twenty five just to be on the safe side. They trooped up to the attic room. At exactly ten thirty Bob appeared and smiled encouragingly at Fenella.

'Well, my dear, it wasn't easy, but I've found a house guardian who I believe will be eminently suitable for you, your family and your house. Some few centuries ago he was house guardian for a painter called Constable and has always wanted to find another such guardianship. His present post, with a photographer, was the nearest he could get to his ambition. This man has just retired and is moving to a country cottage that already has a guardian, so this fellow is looking for a new placement. He was a little uncertain about the house, as it is so modern, but as your father is an artist, I persuaded him to take it on. His name is Joshua Reynolds and he should arrive later today, around teatime. I suggested that he introduced himself to you first, rather than appear before the whole family. He's a lively fellow. I think you'll get on well with him! Fenella thanked him profusely, also Stephen and Jane for arranging the meeting in the first place. She went home just before lunch, promising to give them a ring in the evening to tell them about Joshua's arrival!

Chapter XVII

Fenella phoned later that evening to tell them Joshua Reynolds was really great! He had already made himself useful by: finding some portrait material her father had mislaid in the studio, locating a manuscript her mother had filed in the wrong drawer of her filing cabinet and a hockey stick Andrew had flung on top of his cupboard that had slipped down the back. The manner in which all these items reappeared were enough to convince the Steuarts—even Andrew—that something other than coincidence was at work. So Joshua was acknowledged as part of the household and not a figment of Fenella's admittedly very fertile imagination.

On Sunday morning, Erin, having had several more talks with Melissa, decided that trying to convince her of the foolishness of her behaviour was useless; so there was no point in staying longer. Time for them to go home. Luckily, there was a bus to Bidcote on Sunday around midday. After breakfast she told Melissa of her plan and noted the look of relief upon that lady's face.

'I'm disappointed we cannot work together Erin,' she said. 'But it's useless. I see things more realistically than you, so we'll go our separate ways. I shall not interfere with your life as long as you leave me to do what I know to be right for me!'

Erin sensed the veiled threat, but made no comment. But she knew what she had to do and would do it. She caught the bus; there were no problems over Rosie on this trip, and by lunchtime they were safely back in Croft Corner Cottage. Incidentally, Bob Binnacle had relayed this piece of information to the children after he had told Fenella about the house guardian. They were relieved to know that Erin was now safely home.

During the week, school moved inevitably towards Thursday and the start of half-term. The English main lesson period was completed and Local Environment Studies would start upon their return. There was also the Open Day to be prepared for and Easter. Mr Atkinson mentioned these in passing when he did the half-term review. It sounded as if they were going to be pretty busy when school reopened on the Monday following it.

When school finished on Thursday afternoon and they were getting ready to leave, he called the 'Southleighans' and their friends over and said, 'I don't know whether you have any special plans during the coming week? My sister is staying with me for three days mid-week and I wondered if you'd like to come over for tea one afternoon to meet her. She's heard about the effect you're having on my peaceful life and wants to meet you! I can't think why.' He grinned at them. 'Would you like to be on show?' They responded with an, 'Oooh yes!' So it was arranged he would contact them as to which afternoon would be best. They wished him a good half-term and raced off to catch the bus home.

On arrival, a surprise awaited them. As soon as they were seated round the kitchen table Phyllis gave each of them an envelope with their name on it. Upon opening they found an invitation inside from Phyllis and John to a 'Valentine's Day Party-cum-Get-together on Saturday!' The general exclamation was 'Gee!' or 'Wow!' 'We thought it would be a good idea as a start for your half-term,' explained John.

'We've invited Reg and Fred, Geoff, Karen and your mum, Michelle. Reg has offered to pick her, Karen and Geoff up. Bess, Harry, Jill and Brian will come too. Also Chris and Fenella. How's that?' 'Great!' was the enthusiastic reply. The party would start early afternoon and finish around eight so it would not be too late for the little ones. 'You can enliven it by thinking up a few games you children can play,' suggested Phyllis, 'and some the poor old grown-ups can join in as well!'

Later they went up to the playroom and set about devising a program of games and other fun. The food side would be well cared for by Phyllis! By supper time they had it pretty well organised. Tomorrow they would have to collect all the various items needed for some of the games and competitions. Jane summed it up for them all with, 'What a smashing start to half-term, I wonder what else will happen besides tea with Uncle Fred and his sister?'

Next morning they set about this task with great zest, using the morning room as a collecting point. The house was scoured for walking sticks, old hats and clothes, shoes, paper and pencils, empty plastic bottles and cardboard cartons, also other various items too numerous to name. Michelle stood by with a list, ticking off each item as it was added to the growing pile on the floor and table. They became more and more excited, and noisy, as things accumulated and by lunchtime were helpless with laughter when they thought of some of the games specially devised for the poor grown-ups! After lunch another meeting was held to discuss the final order of events. The girls were very pleased with it, but Stephen and Sam seemed a little less enthusiastic. Jane promptly asked what was troubling them.

'Well,' said her brother, 'I was just thinking, and I mentioned it to Sam, it seemed a pity, with a place like this, why we couldn't involve the whole house in it as well.'

'Yes,' added Sam, 'like some super-duper game of hide

and seek or something where everyone hides and there's one who's 'it'. He or she has to try and prevent the others from getting to the home base. Something like that, you know.'

Jane looked at Sarah and Michelle. 'What do you think?'

'It would be good to end up with a game that involves everyone, the grown-ups too, if they want,' said Sarah. Michelle nodded in agreement. There was silence for a moment, broken by the buzzing of a fly. They looked up. Flying round the table was a large bluebottle. 'Where did that come from?' said Stephen. 'It's not the time of year for flies!' and he swatted at it with a piece of paper. They began to chase the obnoxious insect, but in spite of its clumsy appearance it dodged all their efforts to bring it down. 'I'll settle it once and for all!' said Stephen and ran out of the room, returning a few minutes later with a can of fly spray. The fly zoomed towards the window and he pressed the button, sending a fine mist of spray after it. They cheered, but where was the fly? It had vanished. Sarah was sure she saw it flying away across the garden. But how had it got out through the window? The others decided it had crawled away into some crevice or corner where it would die and thought no more about it.

But Sarah took Michelle aside as they went for afternoon tea. 'Michelle, can your grandmother turn herself into things like animals, or insects?'

Michelle thought for a moment. 'I'm not sure, I've never seen her do it, but I believe she can transform herself into small creatures, like insects; why?'

'That fly, it was odd that it should be flying round when we were talking. I just wonder if... ...?'

Michelle looked serious. 'Do you think, if it was her, she was listening because she wants to spoil our party?'

'Maybe,' replied Sarah. But she was thinking a game of hide and seek would be an ideal situation in which to kidnap somebody. She did not say this to Michelle, as she did not want to frighten her. She had to tell someone, but whom? Of course, Bob Binnacle.

'You go on in for tea, I'll be down in a minute,' she told her and raced upstairs to the playroom. 'Bob ahoy!' she called twice. He appeared and she explained about the fly and her concerns. He listened carefully and said, 'Good thinking on your part, Sarah. There's a strong possibility she could try something on Saturday evening. Have your boxes with you and if you see anything suspicious or unusual, leave well alone and keep with the grown-ups!'

She went down to tea, and afterwards, when they were back in the morning room, reminded them about carrying their boxes and generally being careful. Stephen and Sam were inclined to take it lightly. 'She wouldn't dare show her face here!' retorted Stephen, and Sam agreed with him. Jane and Michelle agreed they needed to be careful, but obviously thought that with so many adults around it would very difficult for Melissa to do anything.

Meanwhile, what of Melissa? After Erin had left she'd gone round the house sprinkling dirty spells about to counter the awful clean and good feeling Erin spread around. The house now felt suitably horrible and homely once more. Large ugly spiders returned from the garden and began to spin their webs in all the corners. Ah, that was better, much more like it — really homelike! She could now contemplate her next objective: how to get Michelle back into her power. Hm, she needed to know what those children were up to. She knew they had a half-term break and so all those brats would be at Southleigh. But how to find out was a problem, until she remembered that she could transform herself into something small so she could spy on them unobserved. Her choice of a bluebottle fly was not exactly inspired, as it actually attracted attention. A small spider or moth would have been far less likely to be noticed.

So it was on Friday afternoon that she walked to Bardon

Lane, and having reached Southleigh, turned herself into a bluebottle fly. Fine, but if she had been more observant she would have noticed a small boy with his dog walking up the lane. Chris was taking Rover for a walk. He saw a strange woman standing outside the twins' house and the next minute she'd vanished. He blinked and pinched himself to make sure, then ran to the spot. Rover sniffed round and growled. So somebody had been there! He looked up the entrance drive and noticed a small black object flying by the right-hand front window. A fly? That's odd! Chris and Rover went home in a thoughtful mood.

Melissa passed through the window into the room and overheard their ideas for the game of hide and seek. Excellent, that suited her plans very well. She would be able to sneak in, find Michelle and grab her! It was then, through her excited buzzing she attracted the children's attention. She easily escaped their attempts to swat her but had not reckoned on the flyspray! When Stephen returned with the can she made for the window, but was not quite quick enough to avoid being sprinkled with some of the contents. She got away all right and when she reached the bottom of the drive quickly turned back to her proper shape. However, the spray had already started to affect her, and like a fly that has been sprayed, she began to reel about, unable to walk straight or keep her balance. She staggered up the lane towards the footpath, giving every appearance of being totally drunk. Fenella's mother, driving down the road, saw an elderly lady, apparently under the influence of drink, staggering all over the place and eventually, after two or three attempts, finding the entrance to the foot path and disappearing down it.

'Disgusting!' snorted Dorothy Steuart. 'A woman of her age should know better. Making a public exhibition of herself. It's lucky PC Wilby didn't see her. He'd have arrested her on the spot!' She drove on muttering and contemplated writing an article about 'Public Drunkenness.'

Melissa made it to her front door, but the net curtains all around were twitching as if they had St. Vitus dance. It took three tries to get the key in the lock and three more to turn it. As she was leaning on it and the door opened inwards, her entrance was far from graceful, and the onlookers were treated to a pair of feet waving up and down on the threshold before she could drag herself in and push the door shut. By now she had a headache of massive proportions, and after swallowing several aspirins, tottered upstairs and flung herself on to her bed. For the next few hours she took no further interest in the world.

When he arrived home, Chris told his mother what he had seen. She listened and then suggested he phoned Southleigh and told someone about it. He did so, and by a piece of luck, Sarah answered the phone, as it had rung just as she passed by. 'Oh, hi Chris! I hope you're not ringing to say you can't come tomorrow!' she said. He assured her that he would be there, and then told her what he'd seen that afternoon. Sarah was alarmed, but also delighted, as it meant she had been correct about the fly! Alarmed, because it meant Melissa could be spying on them at any time. She thanked him and suddenly had a flash of intuition.

'Chris, can you bring Rover tomorrow?'

'Rover? Are you sure?'

'Yes, very sure!'

'All right, he'll love it. Thanks!' and he rang off.

Sarah realised she hadn't asked anybody whether they'd mind a bouncy dog around. Oh well, she'd just have to go and tell Phyllis now! She found her in the kitchen and confessed. Phyllis looked at her earnest face and guessed there was more to it than just asking Chris to bring the dog for a treat.

She replied, 'Sarah, I believe you have a very good reason for wanting Rover here. I'm not going to be nosy and ask you "why?" or "what for?" I trust your judgment. I'm glad you told me straight away. Now I can prepare a party dish for Rover as well.'

All their activity and preparation meant there were no protests when the words 'time for bed' were pronounced. They went upstairs feeling rather pleased with all they'd planned for the morrow.

Bob Binnacle was on watch; he didn't expect any intrusions tonight, but he wanted to carefully examine the property to note any weak spots where Melissa could sneak in and hide. A thought crossed his mind. Fishing nets—yes, they could be useful, very useful. Tomorrow morning he'd see about getting some. That woman was not going to get the better of an old salt like him!

Melissa awoke with a pounding headache later that night, cursed the children, Stephen in particular, then went back to sleep!

Chapter XVIII

On Saturday morning everybody was up early. Phyllis was already baking and preparing food in the kitchen when the children came down and John had gone into town to see Reg about a business matter, but was also armed with a last minute list of requirements. The children were given the job of decorating the dining room and lounge. They were making sure there were enough chairs, and generally being as helpful as possible. Sometimes their enthusiasm carried them away, such as the incident when Stephen and Sam were putting chairs in the dining room from the morningroom, while Sarah and Michelle were taking them out and putting them into the lounge. However, it was eventually all sorted out and by lunchtime they were prepared as far as ever they could and would be. After lunch there was a pause during which they got ready, making sure each had their box with them before the guests started to arrive.

First on the scene were Chris and Rover. He came early just in case Rover had not been invited and he had to take him home again. He was very relieved when he found it was fine, that Rover was indeed welcome, and fussed over. Next was Fenella, who couldn't wait any longer to get away from her beastly brother who she claimed had been teasing her all morning about a Valentine's Day party.

'Really, he's jealous,' she told the others, 'because he hasn't been invited to one.'

'We could have invited him,' said Jane uncertainly.

'He wouldn't come to a little kids' party, no way!' she replied, so that was that.

The next to arrive was the Game family, Brian absolutely bouncing up and down with excitement and making straight for Jane, on whom he continued to bounce. Jill made for 'her' Sam and asked to be shown round the house so that she knew 'where everything was'. Harry and Bess were soon relaxed in the lounge chatting with John. A cheerful double tooting of horns announced the arrival of Reg with Ingrid, Karen and Geoff; the other was Fred. All the guests had arrived!

The fun and games organisers took over and soon things were happening fast and furious: from pinning tails on donkeys to being blindfolded and having to find one's way round and over various obstacles until a table was reached on which was a plate with cold, greasy spaghetti that they had to eat before returning over the course back to the start.

Another very popular game was standing round in a circle while an object was passed behind one's back from hand to hand and one had to guess what it was. A cold uncooked sausage just out of the fridge caused many squeaks and squeals!

The children were surprised to find that the grown-ups joined in with great zest and thoroughly enjoyed themselves. Even Reg, whom they considered really old, took part in everything. The best game for them Michelle had devised. Two piles of old clothes and a hat were put at one end of the room. Two people had to hop across to them carrying a ball on a table tennis bat. If it fell off they had to go back and start again. Once the clothes were reached they had to put them on and race back with the bat and ball. This caused shrieks of laughter and Tiger Brian was so keen that his dad, who was competing with Fred, should win, that he rushed out to help and only succeeded in getting in the way. This fun continued until supper, when they all transferred to the dining room for a special Valentine's meal with heart-shaped sandwiches, biscuits, cakes and jellies. The drinks were served in heart-decorated glasses and mugs. As Fred said, 'It was all very hearty!' to be met with howls of anguish from his pupils, Geoff making as much protest as the others. Once the meal was over they trooped back to the lounge and settled down for a break before the final game. During this interval Uncle Fred told one of his special stories, which he made up on the spur of the moment. As it included all those present, including himself, and was totally outrageous, it met with hoots of laughter.

By this time it was dark and Stephen and Sam stood up to announce and explain the final game. Sarah was seated near the door when a movement on its frame caught her eye. She looked up and stared. A large, long-legged spider hung there, swinging gently to and fro; a shiver went down her spine. Was it a genuine spider or… …? She heard Rover give a low growl and saw he was looking at it too. However, before she could tell anybody, Stephen started to explain the rules. He was very proud of this game as he had concocted it — on impulse — from various versions of hide and seek, and games of catch.

'Please listen very carefully,' he announced. 'First a catcher is chosen by people drawing slips from a hat. One is marked; the person who gets it is the catcher. Only nobody knows who it is, because… …' He paused, 'because that's part of the game! Now all of you go and hide somewhere. When the catcher rings the gong it means you must leave your hiding place and try to reach home. This room is home. However, the catcher has a choice; he or she can try to catch them in their hiding place, or as they attempt to reach home. But they are not allowed to grab them in the hall, as that wouldn't be fair.'

'If you are found in your hiding place, you are out of the game. The winner is the person who gets back last, or not at all. And the ones who are caught can help him. The catcher chooses the next catcher and we start all over again.'

How much of this his listeners could follow was difficult to tell, for though Stephen's intentions were good, his explanation was far from clear. However, the grown-ups were in an indulgent mood and not inclined to quibble. It was decided that Jane would take Brian with her and Sam, Jill. Though what happened if one of them drew the marked slip no one seemed to know!

Stephen produced the hat and passed it round. Sarah glanced up at the door; the spider had gone. Once everyone had a slip of paper and had looked to see if it was marked they could begin? No, not yet, Stephen had another announcement for them.

'To make it more scary and fun we are going to turn off as many lights as we can and dim the remainder.'

Sam went off to do this and when he returned Stephen said, 'I shall count to ten then turn these lights out and open the door so you can all go and hide. The catcher remains here and strikes the gong after counting to a hundred, then you can start to... ...!'

There was more, but he didn't have a chance to say it, because—by accident—he turned the lights off! There was a mad rush of people leaving the room. Sarah grabbed Michelle by the hand and they raced up the stairs to the landing and through the door to their bedroom. Sarah grabbed her torch and then they ran up to the attic. 'We'll hide in the cupboard in the play room,' she whispered, 'until all's quiet, then try to sneak back to the lounge.' She wanted Michelle to be out of this strange game as soon as possible. The feeling of approaching danger was very strong and the few dim lights did little to dispel the darkness that was gathering. Michelle slipped her hand from Sarah's.

'You use the cupboard, I'll hide somewhere else up here,' she announced, and before Sarah could say anything, she flitted away. Sarah was worried. This was not at all what she'd intended. The last thing she wanted was for Michelle to be alone. If she was with someone else it would make it difficult for Melissa to capture her granddaughter. The gong sounded from below.

'Bother this silly game,' she thought, 'I must keep an eye on her,' and crept out into the passage. At once she knew something had changed. The house was silent, not a sound could be heard. Surely with such a game you would hear something? There was an oppressive atmosphere that made her feel cut off from the others and the rest of the building. She made for the stair head; as she did so, the few remaining dim lights went out, plunging the attics into almost complete darkness. Her sense of unease intensified. Thank goodness she had her torch! Now she must find Michelle and quickly before… …before what?

She felt very cold; the temperature seemed to have fallen sharply. Then from the stairs came a soft movement. She drew back into the angle made by them and the passage, wondering who could it be. In the dimness she saw the figure of a child slip into the old bathroom, then come out and glide past her, up the passage and into the playroom. Was it Michelle? She wasn't sure. Should she wait until whoever it was came back to find out, or should she take a chance and slip down to the first floor? Could Michelle have possibly gone down to their bedroom?

She started for the stairs. As she neared them the oppressive feeling became almost unbearable, for some strange energy was welling up from below, making the atmosphere even more suffocating. Then she heard something coming up them. The sound was uncanny, slow and slithering; they creaked under its weight. It reminded her of a giant slug. She felt a chill of fear, then became aware of a salty smell beside her.

'Bob,' she whispered, 'is that you?'

A reassuring voice quietly replied, 'Aye, lass, it's Bob, all prepared for her, wherever she may be, shh!'

The intruder had reached the stairhead and was slowly moving down the passage. Bob drew his breath sharply. Something indefinable, but emanating a strong sense of evil and malevolence passed them. In the dark it was impossible to make out any shape, and perhaps that was just as well. It disappeared into the right-hand front room. Then the figure that had entered the playroom came out. It was Michelle! Sarah called softly, but the child hesitated and made no effort to move towards her. Then, from the opposite room that awful vague menace flowed into the passage behind her. Sarah had the impression of it rising up to engulf its intended victim. There was a swift movement and Bob rushed forward. He uttered four words, 'Run, both of you!' and simultaneously threw something at the apparition. Michelle ran forward, Sarah grabbed her by the hand, and together they clattered down to the first floor into the old servants' quarters, slamming the door behind them. But the strange atmosphere permeated here as well. It felt as if they were entrapped and being hunted down by an evil power. They ran into their bedroom and closed the door.

'What did you do when you left me?' asked Sarah.

'I went to the stairs, as I thought of hiding down here, but there was someone on the landing. Then I heard them go down and I was just about to creep down myself when there was an odd sound of—well, I didn't know what—so I came back, going into the play room to see if you were still there. It was empty, so I came to look for you. What do we do now?'

'We must get down to the lounge,' Sarah replied.

Now there was that same uncanny sound from the landing and the feeling of being probed for was intense. What now? They were trapped, there was no way out! The passage door creaked open. The strange noise came nearer and stopped just outside the room.

A voice, barely recognisable as Melissa's, spoke. 'I know you're both in there! All I want is a few words with you, Michelle, so come out. If the other girl stays in there no harm will come to her. But, if, Miss Clever, you try any tricks, you'll regret it. I'm not to be trifled with!'

'Talk to her, keep her talking,' breathed Sarah in Michelle's ear, 'I'm going to use my box.'

'What do you want, Granny?' Michelle sounded a lot braver than she felt.

'Only to talk with you, my darling,' came the honeyed tones.

'But what about?'

'Come out, my dear, and I'll tell you.'

'Can't you tell me through the door?'

'No my child, I cannot shout the great secret I wish to share with you.'

The honey had dripped off the voice and it was sounding increasingly impatient. By now, Sarah had the box in her hands. She held it so Michelle could place hers on it as well. Then, very softly, she recited:

> 'My little box, now listen well!
> For a sad tale indeed I tell!
> Trapped are we by one of grey.
> So please help us to get away!
> To the lounge take us with care,
> For all our friends are waiting there!'

At that moment the door burst open, but as it did so, the two children found themselves encircled by a cloud of soft rainbow-coloured light. They were gently lifted up and surrounded by its comforting embrace. A moment later they realised they were at the lounge door, which was partly open. Stumbling in, they found themselves in the brightly lit room with everyone else gathered and waiting for them.

They were greeted with cries of 'Where did you hide?' and 'Jolly good, you didn't get caught!' The shouts and laughter quickly died away when they saw the girls' faces. Phyllis and Ingrid came swiftly forwards and took the children into their arms. Between them they sobbed out their story.

'If it hadn't been for Bob she would have got Michelle,' said Sarah.

Suddenly Bob was with them. He looked somewhat dishevelled and worried. 'She's a powerful witch, that one,' he remarked. 'I caught her in a fishing net, but tough as it was, it could not hold her, so great is her rage. For a while I had to make myself scarce. She's still out there, so do not leave this room. I shall go to seek help,' and he vanished.

They looked at each other in consternation. The temperature began to drop, in spite of the fire, and the ominous slithering noise was heard again, outside the door.

It felt as if some invisible pressure was slowly squeezing the room, and those inside began to feel oppressed and claustrophobic. There was an overpowering desire to open the door and rush out. In fact if it hadn't been for Reg calling out sharply, 'Stay away from the door!' who knows what might have happened?

The distorted voice spoke again, 'Give me the child and no harm shall come to you. Refuse me and you shall incur my wrath.' Then in a sweeter tone, 'Come, my Michelle, why should your old granny want to harm you? I just need to have a friendly little chat. You can help me; surely you wouldn't refuse to do something for your loving old grandmother, who has cared so much for you since you were a tiny baby? Come, my darling, come!'

Suddenly Ingrid spoke: 'Mother, leave my child alone. You have no business using her for your own selfish ends. Be off with you!'

There was a dramatic change in the voice from without.

'You, my daughter, dare to speak to your mother like that? You, who were too scared to follow in the steps of my profession, what do you think you can do to thwart my will? Nothing, you have no power! Now send the child out — at once.'

Ingrid stood before the door, looking, as Michelle put it later, 'fiercer than a dragon!' for she'd never seen her mother look so angry before.

'No power, you say? Well, see how you like this!' Raising her arms she pointed directly at the source of the voice and shouted in Latin, 'Away with you, awful witch!'

Light streamed out from her fingertips and through the door. At the same time a tremendous blast of wind struck the house, causing the front door to burst open, and a strong smell of the sea came in — a welcome relief from the awful stuffiness they had been experiencing.

From without there was a howl of frustration as a voice with a strong nautical flavour sounded over the uproar. 'Heave-ho, me hearties. Haul away, she won't escape this one so easily!' It sounded as if a whaler was sailing up the hallway. There was flash of lightning, followed by a clap of thunder. The wailing died down, the sounds of the sea receded, all became quiet, and Bob reappeared, looking far more cheerful. 'All sound and shipshape, me maties! Netted and harpooned she be. It will be some time before she wriggles out of that lot! Dumped her in her own garden, we did.'

He turned to Ingrid, 'Madam, I applaud your bravery! You struck at the right moment; otherwise we might not have caught our prey. How did you do it?'

Ingrid looked round at them and grinned. 'I may not have lived up to my mother's expectations as a sorcerer's apprentice but I made a point of learning a few chosen items of her repertoire that I thought might be useful. However up to this day I have never used them. However, this evening I knew what to do!'

Michelle ran to her and gave her a big hug. 'There, there now, your dear granny will think twice before trying any more of her tricks,' she reassured her daughter.

Everybody began to relax again and the convivial atmosphere slowly returned, making what had just happened seem like a bad dream. The two girls heard how the rest of the party folk had played the game — or tried to — and had found the rules so confusing, they'd all drifted back to the lounge, unaware of what was happening in the attics.

Bob added, 'She'd been listening, form-changed, as a spider. As soon as you began to hide she used an isolation spell to cut off the top floor, where she knew Michelle would be hiding. What she didn't realise was Sarah had gone up with her. Your presence alerted me. You know the rest.'

Phyllis, Bess and Ingrid now organised a parting snack and drink, as it was already well past eight o'clock, the official finishing time. Everyone was still more or less shaken by what had happened and very relieved that Melissa had been foiled. After some further talk, Fred offered to take Fenella, Chris and Rover to their homes by car so they wouldn't have to walk back in the dark, for which they were truly grateful. Reg gathered his four passengers and left shortly after. Sam and Jane carried two half asleep little ones out to Harry's van and saw them off. When the guests had left, everyone helped tidy up; then the children were packed off to bed, and in spite of all the excitement were soon fast asleep!

At 'Goulhaven' a light burnt late in the study as Melissa searched through her books to seek new ways of pursuing her aims. But she met with nothing but frustration, as none seemed to contain spells with enough power to overcome those ranged against her. This made her even more determined to unleash the Primal Power for her own ends! She was more than somewhat battered and bruised, as whalers are not usually very gentle fellows when dealing with landlubbers!

Chapter XIX

Sunday was a day of rest—a much needed one, which gave time for all concerned to consider, what next? It was obvious that Melissa might still try to kidnap Michelle. Naturally John and Phyllis were concerned about this. Over a late breakfast it was discussed and they decided to seek Bob Binnacle's opinion. Later that morning the grown-ups and children gathered in the play room and Jane summoned him. When he appeared he had already sensed their concern.

'It was a stormy passage last night, but we weathered it,' he began. 'But calms can be deceptive and a storm may blow up at any time! However, one of my mates slipped back last night to pass on some information he thought might be of interest. He heard that woman in her study. She was searching through her spells to find one powerful enough to put an end to our interference and it would seem, from her outbursts of anger, she couldn't find anything. Which means for the moment she is powerless to cause any trouble; and that means Michelle is safe. However, she doesn't give up easily and he heard her vowing to bring the Primal Power under her control, come what may. Then she would take revenge upon all who have thwarted her! If she attempts this—and I'm sure she will—she leaves herself open to dangers she cannot have the faintest notion of, or be able to control. What is worse, such a power, unloosed, could upset the delicate balance between the so-called visible and invisible realities. She has to be stopped! I asked my friend to drop in on Erin and inform her; also to see if she has any suggestions. No doubt she will consult with Sir Brian and Bill. In the meantime, be prudent when you are away from Southleigh and avoid going anywhere near Tankerville Road.'

They thanked him for his advice and felt a certain degree of relief; at least they were safe for the moment. The remainder of the day was passed quietly indoors. The weather had taken a turn for the wet and miserable, so they had no desire to go out.

Halfway through the afternoon the phone rang. It was Chris; he wanted to speak to Jane. Actually he wasn't sure to whom he really wanted to speak and had said the first name that came into his head.

'Oh, Jane! Thanks for the super party last night. Listen, my mum wants to invite the five of you to a Shrove Tuesday pancake do. Come for the afternoon, as Dad says we can mess around in the studio. He's just bought some fresh clay and we can have the old stuff. Then we'll make and toss pancakes for a late afternoon tea.'

A quick consultation with Jane's mum, and her brief chat with Chris's mum confirmed it. Phyllis was just about to put the phone down when it exploded in sound. She listened then handed it back to Jane. 'Chris forgot to tell you something.' Indeed he had — that Fenella was also invited and would call in on her way down so they could all arrive together.

This gave them something to look forward to. However, just before supper the phone went again. This time it was Uncle Fred, who said to Phyllis, 'Any one of the "quintet" who were handy would do.' He got Sam, who was in phone range at the time. Fred invited them to tea with his sister and himself on Wednesday. She was arriving Tuesday and he reckoned she would have recovered from the trip by then and would be strong enough to face their onslaught. They were to get the bus to the police station and walk up to Southgate, where he'd meet them to show the way to his flat, 'For your next visit, if I survive,' he added.

Sam thanked him on behalf of the others. Now they had two days of engagements. They were just sitting down to supper when the phone went yet again. This time it was Reg. Yes, Mrs Blankenzee, knowing it was half-term week had prevailed upon him to invite them for lunch and tea on Thursday. Whatever next? That turned out to be a phone call from Doreen, reporting on the progress of the lecture tour, and that all was going well, though both of them couldn't wait to get home. They would arrive at Tadbridge Station around four o'clock on Saturday, pick up the car from Reg's and come on to Southleigh for a meal, then take their mob home. So that only left Monday to fill in, for on Friday they'd already planned to visit the castle ruins. Geoff had told them he would be at his gran's for a couple of days and would meet them in St Andrew's Park that afternoon. They would then go back to his gran's, as she had invited them to tea.

After supper they gathered in the lounge, the grown-ups as well, to decide how to spend tomorrow. Everyone felt it should be some kind of family day that they could share together. There was much discussion of what to do and where to go. Then John remarked he had an old country house to survey and tomorrow would be a good time to do it. He suggested they all went.

'You children are quite capable of helping me to measure the place up,' he said. 'I know my two are, as they did it with Fred in the class three practical maths block. Then we could go and have lunch locally and spend the afternoon… …? Well, we'll see what turns up.' This plan was unanimously adopted and they went off to bed eagerly, looking forward to tomorrow.

Unfortunately, the weather decided to continue being awful. They awoke to rain beating against the windows and the wind howling round the chimneys. The sky was dark and ominous. John told them at breakfast that the weather forecast offered little chance of improvement.

'Do you think it's still worth going?' he asked.

'Well, let's do the survey and at least we can have lunch out,' Phyllis suggested. 'Then if it's still too bad maybe we could go into Taunton and take in a film?'

'Yes, if the worst comes to the worst, perhaps we could,' replied John. 'Anyway, let's brave the elements. Be ready to leave in half an hour and make sure you've got your thickest woollies on. The house has been empty for some time and will be pretty damp and cold. Better bring your wellies too!'

While they got ready, Phyllis made two Thermoses of tea and cut some sandwiches for elevenses. It wouldn't do to have a car full of hungry youngsters.

The journey was through scenic countryside, but they saw little of it, as the car windows had sheets of rain running down them for the whole trip. At last they swung through some large elaborate wrought iron gates and came to a halt under a covered porch — much to their relief. It was an eighteenth century country house, built of brick and stone, square and solid. John unlocked the door and they trooped inside.

'Hang on here a moment,' he said, 'I'll go and turn the power on, then at least we can warm up the kitchen for our snack.' He disappeared down a passage, returning a few minutes later with cobwebs in his hair. 'Phew, the place is thick with dust,' he remarked and sneezed to prove it.

The actual surveying was not difficult for the mansion was built on a regular plan and once the ground floor had been plotted, apart from minor variations, the two upper floors followed the same pattern. Sam, Sarah and Michelle were novices when it came to using a tape measure compared with Stephen and Jane, but they soon got the hang of it, and with Michelle taking notes, worked as the second team, rechecking some measurements and taking running ones down the corridors, also door widths and heights. By eleven thirty the rough survey was finished and they made their way to the kitchen, where Phyllis had put the oven on, with its door open, to warm the room up and had set the snack on the large kitchen table. The room was as big as Southleigh's dining room and lounge combined. The rain still poured down outside, but they were comfortable enough. There was no need to hurry, as there was little attraction in driving round in the rain for an hour or so before lunch. So while John checked his survey to make sure he had everything he required, Phyllis settled herself with a newspaper beside him. The children, down the other end of the table, chatted amongst themselves.

'An old place like this must have a house guardian,' said Sam.

'Maybe two or more,' added Stephen, 'it's so vast.'

Jane wrinkled her nose, as she often did when thinking. 'Does this place have more than one guardian because it's so big? Then what about Windsor Castle? That's enormous, it must have loads of them.'

'I wonder if the number of guardians depends on the size of the property, or whether a small house has a small guardian, but larger ones have more powerful protectors?' Sarah mused.

'Both suppositions are correct,' a voice said. They looked up, surprised. The other end of the table had vanished into a thick mist. They could no longer see John or Phyllis. Seated beside them was a matronly looking lady in mediaeval garb.

'It all depends,' she continued, 'A house such as this may have one guardian for the main dwelling and another who cares for the outbuildings and servants' quarters. If the owner kept many horses and grooms there would be one who would look after them and their quarters. Likewise, the gardener's cottages, or farmhouse. If the place was compact, one like myself could probably manage the estate single-handed. It all depends upon the circumstances. Naturally, royalty and barons need and expect top service, so the guardianship would be shared round as I mentioned. But for smaller premises one is adequate. Does your dwelling have a house guardian?'

They told her about Bob Binnacle and Bill Bluff. Even here the name 'Bluff' brought a response. The lady nodded knowingly. 'Ah, the Bluffs, yes indeed, they are probably the longest serving house guardians in the country. It's said a Bluff was in residence in the villa of the first Roman Governor of Britain.' She smiled and added, 'Now I must go; give Mr Bluff my regards!' 'Goodbye and thank you!' they replied.

She vanished; the mist cleared. John and Phyllis were visible once more. John looked up. 'What are you saying "goodbye" and "thank you" for? We are still here!'

They realised that the visitor had come out of time and the grown-ups had no inkling of what had happened. They giggled; giggles usually make grown-ups think it was something very silly anyhow and don't bother asking any more awkward questions, which is exactly what happened.

John looked at his watch and said, 'We can go now. By the time we reach the nearest inn they'll be serving lunch. Ready? Let's be on our way. In spite of those excellent sandwiches I feel hungry. They agreed with him and piled back into the car. The rain had eased a little, so had the wind, though it was still not the weather for a pleasant stroll in the country.

John drove to the nearest village and soon they were seated round a table in the old oaken-beamed dining room of the village inn, tucking into a good pub meal! After dessert, while John and Phyllis sipped their coffee, they talked over what to do next.

Of course they could go home, but that would be a very tame ending to the day. Taunton? Hm, it was like all big towns, shop and supermarkets, and Sunday! Phyllis's perusal of the local paper had shown that there was nothing on at the cinema that they really wanted to see, or was suitable for the children.

'We could make a detour and call at the abbey,' said John. 'I think you children would like to see it.'

'What's the abbey?' someone asked.

'A modern community of monks. I was involved in some land purchases for them and became friendly with the abbot. I'm sure they won't mind us dropping in; would you like that?'

'What's the abbot's name?' asked Michelle.

'Father Andrew.'

That settled it; there was enthusiastic agreement for dropping in.

By now the rain had become a drizzle and the wind fitful gusts. The drive took them through fertile valleys and past snug farms and villages. Then, as the car swung round a corner, they gasped with amazement. Rising serenely above the trees and meadows, a stately building of white stone with a dark blue slate roof, glistening from the rain, stood before them.

But what made the children excited was the feeling that this building was in some way connected with the ruined church. Though different, it seemed familiar, and as they drove through the gates the sensation grew ever stronger. Hardly had the car stopped when a robed figure came bounding down the steps to welcome them, shaking John and Phyllis eagerly by the hand and smiling warmly at the children. They stared at him! The abbot could have been the twin brother of their Brother Andrew of the ruined church.

He took them into the refectory and offered everyone tea with freshly baked buns. 'From our own bakery,' he explained. All through this the children could not take their eyes off him. His voice, his manner, everything about him was an exact copy of the spirit of the long-departed monk they knew. At last Stephen could stand it no longer.

'Excuse me, sir,' he said in his politest manner. 'Do you think you could spare us a few moments? There is something we would like to ask you.'

His parents stared at him in amazement. Could this very polite child be their own son? The abbot looked at the five anxious faces and the ghost of a smile flitted across his face.

'Of course, children,' he replied, 'I shall be delighted to answer your questions, if I can.' He turned to the adults. 'Excuse us for a moment. If you require anything further, call Brother William, he is in the kitchen. Follow me,' he said, 'we shall go to my study.'

He led the way down a long stone corridor to an arched door at the end, opened it, and ushered them in. The furnishings were rather like the Headmaster's at school. But on looking round a further surprise awaited them. On the wall behind the abbot's desk hung two engravings. One of a small church set in woods, the other, obviously a copy of a much older drawing, was of a monk. Though invited to sit down, they hardly heard, they were so absorbed in gazing at the picture of their church as it must have looked several hundreds of years ago, and the portrait of Brother Andrew.

'You seem very interested in my pictures,' said the contemporary Father Andrew.

Sarah blurted out, 'Oh yes, we are! You see that's our church or that's as it was, it's a ruin now. But that,' pointing to the portrait, 'is Brother Andrew, the priest who looks after it. You are just like him!' She paused and said hopefully, 'Please explain!'

'First I think we had better sit down and you tell me your

story as clearly and concisely as you can. Then I will tell you what I know,' he replied.

It was lucky that under Mr Atkinson's guidance each morning they had a verbal revision of the previous day's work in which the children were encouraged to retell events as accurately as possible.

Jane said, 'Stephen, you're best at retelling, you start and we'll add in anything else relevant.' 'Right!' said their spokesman, and began. He recounted how they had visited the church with their teacher, how Harry cared for it, and of the episode with Mr Skurray. Also their recent visit with Michelle. The others added further details where necessary. When Stephen had finished, Father Andrew smiled at them.

'I have seldom heard such clear retelling of complicated events, even by an adult. Your teacher is to be congratulated on the way in which he has encouraged you to retell any subject matter. Now I shall try to be just as clear in telling my story. These two pictures were here when I became abbot. They were given to our order many years ago and no one is quite sure who the donor was. Unfortunately, when framed, the framer trimmed the lower edges and the name of both church and monk are missing. The only thing my predecessor knew was that they were linked. Until today, in spite of much research, I have drawn a blank in finding out any more about them. Now you come out of the blue and give me much of the information I have been looking for.'

'Will you please come and see the church?' asked Sam, 'and perhaps meet with our Brother Andrew?'

'Indeed I shall, as soon as it can be arranged. I should like to speak with Harry Game, too, and when I visit I shall want you all to come with me.'

'When will you come?' they asked.

'Before Easter, I hope.' He turned to Stephen and Jane, 'I will let your father know; we can make the final arrangements when the dates are fixed.'

He rose and they knew the interview was over. They stood up and he shook each of them by the hand, then they returned to the refectory where John and Phyllis waited.

'I hope they weren't too much of a nuisance,' said John.

'On the contrary, we have had a most interesting chat and they have helped to solve a mystery for me. I hope to visit the Bidcote area before Easter and shall see you all then. Now, you must excuse me.'

He shook hands once more and they left. During the drive home they told the grown-ups about their talk and decided that as soon as Sam, Sarah and Michelle were back at Bidford Manor they should visit the church to tell Brother Andrew about Father Andrew and his proposed visit.

The day had turned out better than they had dared to hope. After supper they descended on the kitchen and soon Phyllis found herself with the task of explaining how to prepare pancakes. After all, they wanted to help make them so there would be more to eat! One recipe book gave some interesting variations, which Jane noted down so they could add variety to the feast.

The following morning was occupied with further explorations in the world of cooking, their appetites having being whetted on the previous evening. The weather also remained miserable during the morning but began to clear up around lunchtime. One thing they did not know was that Melissa thought she could still spy on Southleigh by using a transformation spell, even if she was powerless to kidnap Michelle. She'd reckoned without Bob, however. Guessing that she might still attempt to snoop around, he had been busy having a word or two with the local wild life.

That very morning she had transformed herself into a bee. Now bees are not usually seen flying around in February, and so once again she could have hardly picked a better way of attracting attention to herself! Upon flying into the grounds of Southleigh it seemed that every bird in the place wanted to make a meal of her and she fled back to 'Goulhaven' very breathless and shaken. She brooded for the rest of the day over what she could do, reluctantly deciding she would have to give up trying to grab her granddaughter for the moment.

After lunch the children got ready and waited for Fenella, who turned up right on time, and the six of them walked down to Chris's place. He was on the look out, and while Felice prepared for the pancake cook-up, they spent a glorious afternoon in the studio messing about with clay, Ralph giving them a hand. He was not exactly a teacher — he didn't tell them what to do, or how to do it — but he had the happy knack of offering suggestions that enabled them to make their models look more like what they intended! When they went inside each carried a small board with their creation on it to show Felice, who generously praised their efforts. Then they got down to the serious business of pancake preparation. It was a great success — the making, tossing and especially the eating. Ralph gave them high praise, saying their efforts were 'out of this world.' When the meal was over, they sat round too content to move while he told them stories of his youth in Australia, where he'd worked as a 'jackeroo' on outback properties. At last it was time for them to go home, so Chris, Ralph and Rover (who'd also enjoyed the pancakes!) walked up the lane as well, and then went on with Fenella to see her home. It had been another well filled day!

Chapter XX

The activities for the rest of the week are soon dealt with! The tea party at Uncle Fred's went off without a hitch. They found his sister, Elsie, regarded him with astonishment and amusement because he had chosen to be a primary school teacher, when, with his abilities and qualifications, he could have secured a highly paid post at any university. But her sense of humour was similar to his and their backchat kept the children in fits of laughter all afternoon. It turned out that she worked for an educational company that supplied computer software to schools and colleges. Fred regarded such technological wonders with caution, and while admitting their use in the modern world, did not consider they had a place in primary school. However, once in high school the children could be shown, and also learn to understand how they worked, then they could be introduced as an educational aid and support, but not as an education in itself.

His sister disagreed, but they'd agreed to differ over this and otherwise got on very well together. After an excellent tea Fred drove them home. This gave them a chance to update him on the latest happenings. 'I'm glad you didn't mention anything at my place,' he remarked. 'Elsie will have nothing to do with such things; she considers them to be mere fantasies of diseased imaginations. However, she's never had any experience of them. If she had, she might change her mind.'

On Thursday it was off to Reg's, though he came and picked them up, as it was raining—again! Mrs Blankenzee was overwhelming in her welcome in her mixture of Dutch, and English, especially over Michelle, even though her ankle was better. 'Dat klein Meiske must met care walk!' she insisted. Each time Michelle got up, the good lady would rush forward to catch her if she fell. Still, it was so well meaning and the meal she had prepared was so delicious, they took it all in good part. Reg was his usual cheerful self and refrained from asking any questions unless one of them mentioned the matter first. The main subject of conversation was the Easter holidays. Reg owned a seaside cottage and wondered if—providing the weather was reasonable—they would like to spend a few days there with him.

oidly looked through the assortment of envelopes: mostly junk and a few bills. Then, a card slipped to the floor. It was from the Tadbridge County Library, informing her that a book she had borrowed was now two weeks overdue and... ...

She read no more. Of course, that library book! She'd forgotten about it. For it had revealed more about the source of the Power she sought and how to harness it. The only problem was, where was the book? She rushed into her study and began pulling all the books and papers off the shelves, opening cupboards and throwing their contents on the floor. Nothing! Like a destructive tornado she whirled through every room in the house, flinging the contents around in her search. It was only when some inspiration told her to look under her bed did she discover, amidst discarded socks, underwear, stale biscuits and dirty cups, the book. She rushed downstairs and into the study. Sweeping stuff off a chair and the table she settled down to search for the information she knew it contained.

An hour or so later she sat back with a malevolently satisfied smile on her face. It was possible to rouse the force without using Michelle! There were instructions — however, the writer obviously did not believe in them — but, for the sake of completeness in retelling what he considered to be a legend, had put them in. If Melissa had turned the page and read the remainder of this passage she would have realised that to control the Power she would need her granddaughter! But she didn't do that! Much to her delight the writer had even explained how to deal with any hindrances or opposition to accessing its physical source. Slamming the book shut, she flung it on the floor and executed a dance of triumph round the room until she slipped on some grease-covered papers and fell over the table, bringing further chaos into the already chaotic room. She now threw everything around again in her search for the materials she needed to prepare the spell that would enable her to — but more of that later.

*

During the time the Courts were away things had been quiet at Bidford Manor. Ingrid had plenty of time to make plans for the future and had enjoyed visits from Bess and Erin, also Harry's daily visits. Time had gone quickly and having Binky and Cleo to look after — though they reckoned they looked after her — provided her with plenty of company. The other members of the household had discreetly kept out of the way, though she was aware of their presence and comforted by it. The builders had proved another diversion and she had spent time chatting with them at tea breaks, learning more about the locality, and Hugh had been helpful with information about possible employment in the area.

The work of passage restoration and the installation of lighting had progressed smoothly, and by the Friday afternoon when the children were having tea with Geoff's gran, stage one was essentially completed. All that remained was for the electrician to link the cable to the mains supply and test that all the points and fittings were functioning. After the usual tea break Hugh invited Ingrid to be present at this event. They gathered at the summer house passage entrance whilst the final connections were made, then the electrician switched on the mains. A soft glow of light came up the stairway. They were just about to descend when there came a loud report from somewhere below and the lights flickered wildly. A smell of burnt cable wafted up to the startled group. The electrician gave vent to some rather spectacular language and as some of the lights were still functioning, went down to trace the fault.

He was back in a few minutes. 'It's the fitting where there's the new brickwork,' he said, 'A short-circuit has blown it clean off the wall and the cable's burnt out for a couple of yards as well.'

'How long will it take to fix?' asked Hugh.

'Should be able to do it in an hour, though I'll have to check every connection to make sure there's no other problems.'

Hugh thought for a moment. 'Tell you what, don't bother about putting a new fitting up. I'd like to have it ready for Mr Court to see this weekend. Can't you just replace the cable and bypass the fitting temporarily? We can give the system a thorough check over next week.'

The electrician accepted this suggestion with relief. After all, it was Friday afternoon and he didn't particularly want to be fiddling around with faulty circuits so late in the day. The burnt out cable was stripped away and a new length inserted as suggested. When switched on it worked perfectly. Relief all round.

While the workmen were packing up, Hugh took Ingrid aside. 'Don't mention anything about this to Derek if he phones, but if you see Erin tell her. That wall blocks off the old passage to the Dell. It's odd it should be that particular light to go. I'm just wondering… …?' He said no more and left with the others.

Ingrid returned to the house and at once felt the presence of—Bill Bluff. He appeared in the kitchen as she entered.

He looked concerned. 'I understand there was some trouble with the passage electric wiring,' he asked.

'Yes,' she replied, 'the light fitting on the new section of wall short-circuited and burnt out a length of cable. Mr Dawes suggested it be bypassed for the moment.'

'A wise suggestion, but I believe your mother is at the bottom of this. Therefore I strongly advise that no attempt is made to replace it.'

'I'll tell Mr Dawes first thing tomorrow,' she promised and Bill departed.

However, the following morning was Saturday and the builders would not be working. So she put the matter out of her head, meaning to tell Hugh first thing Monday. What she did not know was that the electrician felt so bad about the failure of his lighting system and put the blame on himself for being careless. It plagued him all night, so he decided to nip up to the manor in the morning and put matters right. Then Mr Court would have a complete and proper job, not one with a temporary cable on the wall. He had a key for the passage entrance, so did not need to bother the house for one. Furthermore, all the equipment he needed was in the summer house, so instead of coming by van he used his bike, which is why Ingrid was totally unaware that he was on the premises.

He worked slowly and with great care, checking and rechecking every new connection and refixing the cables with solder and junction boxes. Then he re-examined every light fitting he'd installed and double-checked the connection to the mains circuit. At last all was ready. Before sending the current through, he lowered the trapdoor—as a precaution—then put his safety helmet on, and moving over to the mains switch, pressed it down; silence for a fraction of a second. Then the ground shook under his feet, the trapdoor burst open and a blast wave bowled him over and his ears were filled with the roar of an explosion. A jet of acrid black smoke writhed up out of the stairway and there was a strong smell of burning. The electrician picked himself up and stared unbelievingly at the blackened remains of the ruined trapdoor. He was dazed and bruised from where the power of the blast had flung him against the wall of the summer house and his head ached; but if he had not closed the trapdoor he would have taken its full force. There was a slight hum from the mains box and to his amazement the lights in the passage came back on.

With a courage that few would have shown, he picked up a length of cable and ventured down the steps. It was as he expected; the same fitting had blown, but this time not only had it blown itself off the wall, but there was a large hole where it had been and great cracks running in all directions from it. The whole structure looked as if it would collapse at any moment. The air was oppressive and the blackness beyond the hole seemed blacker than any he'd ever seen.

Then he became aware of a noise. Something was moving, slithering, crawling, slowly down the passage on the far side; with it came a strange dank musty smell and with that came fear, uncontrollable panicky fear. He turned and fled up the stairs. Behind he heard the crash of bricks falling. The trap door was useless, but a heavy sheet of iron lay nearby. Fear lent him strength; in a moment he had hauled it over the entrance and piled sacks of cement on top, blocks of stone, bricks, anything he could find. Seizing his bike he pedalled furiously down the footpath and into the courtyard. Flinging the machine down he rushed into the kitchen. Ingrid took one look at him, led him to a chair and grabbed the rescue remedy from the first aid cupboard. While he swallowed this she made a hot cup of strong sweet tea and ordered him to drink it.

When the explosion occurred she had been in the master bedroom checking that it was ready for Derek and Doreen. The smoke was plainly visible from a side window and she guessed what had happened. She promptly rang Hugh and informed him. 'I'll be over right away,' he said, 'Stay in the house, and don't go near the spot.' She had gone down to the kitchen and was wondering what had happened to the unfortunate electrician when he appeared.

As soon as he'd recovered enough to speak she said, 'I guessed what happened, don't worry, it's not your fault. Hugh is coming over, so just sit quietly.' He was only too glad to do so. Hugh arrived within twenty minutes; he brought with him two of his building team. They all looked duly concerned and listened carefully to the electrician's account of what had happened.

'It's nothing to do with your work, Dan,' said Hugh. 'There's other forces at work here. That's why the old tunnel to the Dell was bricked up in the first place. The trouble is that something or someone has tampered with the circuits. Don't ask me how. What we'll do for the moment is fix a new and heavier door on the entrance; luckily we had a spare in the yard. You stay here; we'll take you and your bike home.

'And I'll give you something you can take to soothe your nerves,' said Ingrid.

When the building team returned they were more relaxed.

'No problems,' said Hugh. The doorframe was undamaged, all we had to do was replace the hinges and fix the new door. But we could not do it without moving the stuff you'd put over it, Dan. Heaven knows how you managed to pile on so much; it weighed a ton! It took us some time to shove it off and let the new door drop into place. A funny smell came out, but otherwise... ... Come on lads, we must be going. When do you expect the Courts back?

'This evening,' said Ingrid.

There was a tap at the back door and in walked Erin, complete with Rosie-basket. Hugh looked relieved, 'Well, you've company now, that's good,' and he and his men left.

Erin wasted no time in coming to the point. 'Your mother has managed to find a way through our protective cover! I don't know how, but it seems she does not need Michelle, at least not for the moment. Bill warned me last night that he thought something was afoot and what has occurred is serious. The wall's breached, the Power disturbed and Melissa… …! What her next move will be I don't know. Anyway, I shall stay with you until the family returns. There may be something I can do. Now, how about a bite of lunch?'

All this was completely unknown to those at Southleigh, who were becoming more and more excited, until after lunch Phyllis suggested they go to the play room and let off steam up there. Laughing and chatting, they raced up the stairs and rushed in to be brought up short by the presence of Bob Binnacle, who was seated at the table looking very serious.

'Bob! What's the matter?' exclaimed Jane.

'Sit down, me hearties. We've got to batten down the hatches, it looks as if we're in for heavy squalls,' he replied. Mystified, they joined him round the table. 'Yon grey one has found a way to counter the protective powers,' he told them. 'She's already up to mischief at the manor. The wall you built has been damaged and there's no knowing what stupid trick she'll try next. The problem is, we don't know how she did it. Until we do, things could be very awkward!'

Seeing the looks on Sam, Sarah and Michelle's faces he quickly added, 'You'll be able to go home with your parents, never fear. Bill, Sir Brian, JJ and Erin all working on it. They'll surely find a solution.' But they could tell that in spite of his confident tone, he was worried.

Jane looked at them. 'You three must go to see Brother Andrew tomorrow,' she said, 'I'm sure he can help us; in fact he may be the only one who can!' Bob slowly nodded, 'Yes, lass, I think you're right, though it won't be easy. You three go and talk with Erin. When you reach home, she will be there. Now I must see what my colleagues and I can do to help,' and he was gone. John's voice called, 'Children, time to come down, they've just arrived at Reg's and will be here shortly.'

Chapter XXI

At four thirty the Court's car turned into the driveway of Southleigh and promptly disappeared under a welter of children, who couldn't wait for the occupants to get out. When they did, they were subjected to so many hugs that it was like being embraced by a sleuth of bears, as Doreen remarked to Phyllis later. The bears dragged them into their den — the kitchen — and plied them with so many questions that their heads were soon spinning.

'Dad, you look thinner!' Sarah remarked, having eyed him critically for several minutes.

'He is,' replied her mother. 'Sheer nerves and worry rushing from lecture to lecture; and at most of the buffet do's afterwards so many people buttonholed him he hardly had time to grab or eat anything.'

Derek was muttering to himself, 'Never again, never again, never, never, never!'

The children were just about to start part two of their inquisition when the phone rang. John answered, and turned to Derek. 'For you, it's Hugh Dawes, the builder.'

Derek took the receiver and listened; a frown crossed his face. There was more, then he said, 'All right, Hugh, thanks for letting me know. Erin's there with Ingrid? Good. We'll be back fairly soon. Tell them to ring if anything further occurs.' He replaced the phone and turned to the expectant company. 'Trouble, at least it looks like it. There has been an electrical fault in the passages. It caused an explosion and has badly damaged the wall put up to seal off the tunnel to the Dell. Luckily no one was hurt. But it appears Melissa was partly responsible.' He looked apologetically at Phyllis.

'The meal is all ready,' she replied. 'We can eat in about quarter of an hour if you feel you should get back as soon as you can.'

'Yes, I think we should,' he replied. Though this was sobering news, Sam and Sarah were too excited at having their parents back, and Michelle was glad to be with her mother again, so they were not too concerned about this new problem — for the moment. After the meal the car was loaded with their stuff and having thanked John and Phyllis for putting up with them, and Sam and Sarah said a long farewell to the twins — as if they were going on a slow voyage round the world and wouldn't see them for years! — instead of Monday. They arrived back at Bidford Manor just after half past six. When the car drove up the drive the manor looked peaceful enough. But when they got out all could feel an inexplicable tension in the air. Ingrid and Erin welcomed them warmly with great relief.

As for Binky and Cleo, they went berserk, rushing round the kitchen, dining and sitting rooms barking and squeaking with joy. Each time they came across a family member they launched themselves at them, demanding cuddles and hugs. Of course there was no shortage of these, as all their employees had missed them.

Settled round the familiar kitchen table again they listened to what Ingrid and Erin could tell them about the events of yesterday and this morning. Since the sealing of the summer house entrance all had been quiet. Erin and Rosie had gone up there in the afternoon but could detect nothing. However, as soon as darkness fell they had also noticed a build up of tension.

'Waiting for something to happen, but not knowing what,' as Erin put it. Their main concern was how Melissa had managed to evade the protection Sir Brian and others had placed round the manor and the Dell, in particular. She had consulted Bill and Sir Brian, but they were just as mystified.

'They are watching like hawks,' Erin remarked, 'but when you don't know what you're looking for it's not so easy.'

'Jane thinks we should visit the ruined church and talk with Brother Andrew,' Sarah announced.

'That may prove very helpful, and should be done as soon as possible,' Erin insisted. Derek was doubtful about allowing the children out of the house on their own, but Sam said, 'Dad, if you ring Harry and tell him what we want to do I'm sure he would come with us. You could always drive us to the farm if you don't like the idea of us walking there alone.' Derek had to admit this would solve the problem. As there was nothing else they could do that evening, the car was emptied and everyone set about unpacking. Derek took Erin home and upon return began to open the pile of mail on the kitchen table that awaited him. There were the usual brochures, 'free offers', bills and business mail, there was a package that looked like a book, also an airmail letter with a Southern African stamp.

The children had soon finished their unpacking. (You unzip the bag, turn it upside down and shake it. Remove any personal belongings and put the remainder in the dirty clothesbasket. 'Oh! not shoes? But Mum, they're dirty! Clean them? Why can't they go in the washing machine? Oh, all right, I suppose I'll have to clean them!')

Now they trooped down to the kitchen hoping for the usual snack and to see if there was anything interesting in the post.

Their father, with a puzzled expression, was looking at the package. Had he ordered a book? He read the label: 'From The County Library Service'. Then it dawned on him.

'Children this is the book! Remember? It's been rebound, and since the other is obviously still on loan, they've sent me this copy. Quickly he unwrapped it and there it was, newly bound: *The Histories of the House Known as Bidford Manor and its Surroundings* by the Right Reverend Augustus Montague Sletherby Shape. Doc Lit. M.A. (Oxon.) Published 1857.'

'Handle with care' said Derek grimly, remembering their last encounters with it! 'Tonight I'll have a read through and see what it has to say about this 'Power' that is in the Dell. In the morning I'll scan that part on to disc for the computer. Then the book can go straight back; I don't want it hanging around here a day longer than necessary.'

Putting it carefully to one side he now opened the 'African' letter.

They watched with interest as an anguished expression appeared on his face. When finished he dropped it on the floor and sank back in his chair. A look of hopeless despair came over him and he groaned, 'Oh, no!'

'What is it, Dad?' asked Sam, 'What's wrong?'

'Read it for yourself!' was the reply. Sam picked it up and read the following out loud:

Buana Missionary Station.

My dear Brother Derek,

You will be pleased to hear that I have been chosen to represent our Mission at this year's Easter Conference of the World Missionary Association. I arrive at Birmingham Airport on March the nineteenth and have already booked to travel by train to Tadbridge arriving at eight five p.m. I shall stay with you until the twenty-fifth and then leave for the conference, returning on April the fourth and catching my return flight from Birmingham at eleven p.m. on the eighth. I leave Tadbridge on the four fourteen express.'

'I hope we shall have some decent weather, as living in the tropics for the greater part of my life I tend to feel the cold, and if there is not central heating in my room could I have a heater? Also, I am mainly vegetarian, though on occasion I do eat white meat and fish. But I do not expect any special treatment! One further request, would you kindly raise my bed off the floor on four bricks? I'll explain why when I arrive. I look forward to seeing you and Doreen after what must be some eleven years, and to meet the twins!'

'Your loving sister,

Daisy'

They stared at each other in disbelief and with sympathy at their father. She certainly sounded rather odd and all the stories they had heard or read about maiden aunts who became missionaries made them wary.

'But Michelle's mum is in the spare room!' shouted Sarah triumphantly.

'Mum tells me Mr Dawes has found a job in the village that might suit her and a two-bedroomed apartment goes with it,' announced Michelle, looking torn between that and leaving her friends.

'Well, we shall have to discuss the whole business with your mother,' sighed Derek and tottered off to his study to recover.

When Doreen came back into the kitchen they pressed her for more details about this 'African Aunty.'

'I only met her once,' she told them, 'It was just before your dad and I were married. She was at college, but came back for some amateur theatrical do with the local church, so was at home. Derek and I were going out that evening and I came straight from work to have a meal before we went. She's very much an elder sister, being eight years older than Derek. From what I remember she is a tall, formidable looking lady, who walks around as if she's an ironing board stuck down her back. Her clothes were severely practical and I'm sure she doesn't know what the word "fashion" means.'

The children listened aghast, what would it be like with

such a person round the place, and a relative too?

Then Sam remembered something else. 'Oh, no! She'll be here for our Open Day on the twenty-first; I bet she'll want to come and… …!' his voice trailed away in horror at the very thought of it.

'Hang on, hang on!' said Doreen. 'She may not be quite so bad as you think and anyhow as a guest and relative, we must do our best to make her welcome even if we don't have the same lifestyle as her! Also, she'll be away over Easter. If she really finds us impossible we can always arrange for her to go and stay at the "Three Feathers" in Bidcote.' This cheered them up somewhat!

Ingrid now joined in and told them about the job offer she had received. It was acting as housekeeper for the elderly owner of a large house in the village. Actually this person spent very little time there, having a flat in Bristol. He wanted someone to live in and keep an eye on things and to prepare meals and suchlike, on the occasions he came and stayed. There was a self-contained two-bedroom flat, at the rear, which would be hers. She was meeting him on Monday. If she were accepted, her employment would start on March the sixteenth.

'You'll have to get a bike, Michelle,' said Sarah, 'then you can come over anytime.'

'You'll need one anyway to get the school bus like Geoff does,' added Sam.

They were glad that Ingrid had found work, but it meant the spare room would be available for 'Dismal Daisy' as they had christened her.

Derek returned to the kitchen just before they went up to bed. He'd had a long conversation with Hugh. 'First thing Monday he'll be up here with his men. They'll fix heavy doors to the boiler-house entrance and make sure the Obelisk's entrance is well and truly blocked up and unusable. One of his older workers reckons that because strong metal doors and things like that are unknown to the creature it won't try to leave the tunnel unless provoked, which must be avoided at all costs!' He looked at the three wilting children. 'To bed with you at once! Oh, I forgot to mention, I rang Harry and he'll be happy go to the church with you. I'll drop you at the farm about ten thirty.' That made them feel better; it would be doing something to help. The thought of bed was very welcome and they went without a murmur. Doreen and Ingrid followed a little later, but Derek stayed in the sitting room leafing through the old book, with Binky and Cleo at his feet, enjoying the extra hour or so before the fire.

☙

At 'Goulhaven' Melissa was in an exuberant mood. On Friday afternoon she'd entered the grounds of Bidford Manor undetected. She had been present at the testing of the lights and as surprised as the others at the result. However, it informed her that the power was not fully asleep and would only need a little 'help' to be wakened. She set in motion an ancient charm, which should start things off, and left, meaning to return the following night when all the residents were back. Of course she knew nothing of what happened on the Saturday morning and when she returned at midnight she noticed at once that there was a different atmosphere round the Dell—something very deep and vibrant. Not at all what she had expected. It should have been erratic, nervy and scattered. This was purposeful, though what its purpose was, she could not fathom. The distraction caused her to lower her guard for a second, a second too long! Something, shooting a trail of sparks behind it, came whistling towards her. Quickly she raised her barrier and flew into the plantation. The object followed her. She tried evasive action but it was no good. Once Sir Brian's latest invention homed in on its target, there was no avoiding it. Dodge as she may, it followed her like an unwelcome puppy dog, until in desperation she left the grounds. It stopped following and hovered on the boundary. She moved to the left, it turned in the same direction. The same happened when she moved to the right. She departed. Let them think they'd got rid of her; she'd be back.

The sense of gathering power had also been noticed by Bill and Sir Brian, though the success of his witch remover was busy occupying the latter's mind as to how he could further improve it. Bill was concerned and puzzled by the build-up. It did not have the feel of something that would explode, so what would it do when it reached a critical point? He had to admit he didn't know — neither did Sir Brian.

☙

Next morning at ten thirty Derek drove the three children down to the farm. It was cold and misty, visibility being about fifty yards. Harry met them in the yard. Jill was with him, her eyes a-sparkle at Sam's return. She gave him a hug and then took hold of his hand.

'You've been missed during the past week!' said her father. 'She was very good over half-term, but must have asked us a hundred times a day when would you be coming back. Wild horses couldn't have stopped her coming with us this morning!'

'Shall I pick them up at twelve thirty?' asked Derek. Harry grinned, 'Do you think Bess is going to let them go without one of her meals? Why there's a steak and kidney pie in the oven cooking for lunch — I reckon it has their names on it! Don't worry, I'll walk them back once it's digested.'

Derek drove off. This would give him more time to go through the book. He had been too weary last night and only managed to plough through the boring and lengthy introduction before falling asleep.

The little group was silent as they walked down the bridle path towards Church Wood. Harry did not interrupt their thoughts; no doubt he was thinking some of his own as well. When they turned off into the wood the mist seemed less dense and the damp less penetrating. As the ruin came into view a shaft of sunlight broke through, lighting it up in contrast to the dullness around. This made them feel more confident. Jill tugged at Sam's hand; he looked down. Her face was shining with excitement, 'It's all going to be all right,' she whispered to him, then lapsed into silence.

Once in the ruin, the children stood in front of the altar. Harry placed himself to one side. They sang, and in response Brother Andrew came up the nave. He led the way to the little room and once all were seated waited for one of them to speak.

Sarah nudged Sam, 'Go on, you tell him!'

Her brother looked somewhat uncomfortable, but once started, his fluency returned. He told of their visit to the abbey and Father Andrew's wish to come here. Then he spoke of the recent happenings at the manor. Brother Andrew was interested in the pictures in the abbot's study.

'The portrait is of you,' said Sarah, 'there's no doubt about it.'

'The visit of the abbot will complete the circle; I shall await his coming with interest,' he told them, continuing: 'Now, as to the other matter. This is something I know little about, for such Powers originated long before the time when our monks first arrived here and they had already been here for over a century when I took up my duties. All we knew was by hearsay from the local people. They spoke of something dark and dreadful that lay sleeping within the manor grounds, yet something without which the whole of this area would not exist. As you know it is old, very old indeed. Wakened, its power could be destructive, however, it can also be constructive, if dealt with in the right way. The trouble is your grandmother, Michelle; there's no knowing what she might do. We shall take what steps we can to help, as we did before at the Winter Solstice. This has to be dealt with by the Equinox. Go in peace; do not worry, a solution will be found.' As ever, he blessed them, and before leaving they gave their gift of song. The walk back was cheerful and chatty. The sun broke through and the mist dissolved away. They reached the farm and found Bess and Brian busy laying the table for lunch.

Chapter XXII

The lunch was excellent and they needed at least an hour to recover before starting to walk back to the manor, Harry, Jill and Tiger escorting them. When they parted at the gates, Sam said, 'See you tomorrow, Jill!' That young lady's response was a big grin and she skipped happily around her dad. They went quickly up the drive, on the alert for anything unusual, but all was peaceful. Once inside they went to look for Derek and reported on their visit to the church. They found him in his study; he was excited! 'I think I've found it,' he told them.

'What?' asked Sarah.

'How it was done!'

'How what was done?' echoed Sam.

'The book, the book! It has several chapters on the legends and folk tales linked to the manor and its surroundings, including… …' He riffled through the pages, 'Here we are! "The ancient legend of the Great Primordial Power said to be lying dormant in the grounds of the manor" and further: "Superstitions as to how it may be awakened & tamed or returned to its dormant state." The good Rev. Augustus M. S. Snape does not believe a word of it, but being a conscientious chronicler, puts down all that he's heard. Though his final sentence is worth quoting: "These quaint notions of the ignorant peasantry in this district are indeed a challenge to men such as myself who strive to do the work of the Lord." From what I can make out, he avoided them like the plague.'

'But what does it say?' asked Sarah. 'Please tell us.'

Derek grimaced, 'That's the trouble, it says a great deal in a rather confused way and the good Reverend keeps sticking in his opinionated oar, making it difficult to get to the nitty-gritty. It appears that if one versed in the magical arts wishes to reach the Great Primordial Power, the accepted method to use is "an innocent young person of tender years." Though how, details are not given. The other method, calls for the greatest magical skills and uses "the forces of the higher life-magnetical plane." Unfortunately, here, instead of explaining, our commentator goes off into a tirade about "the false sciences bereft of the light of pure reason," which is no help to anybody. But I reckon with her knowledge Melissa could make sense of it and that's how she got in on Friday and Saturday. Perhaps Sir Brian can enlighten us. Once we are clear what spell she's using I'm sure our friends can counter it.'

'On the following pages there are dire warnings as to what can happen if this Primordial Power is released without the proper precautions in place, and then the method of returning it to a dormant state. Here, the innocent young person is required again.' He closed the book. 'I've copied the whole of this chapter onto disc and the following one for good measure. The book goes back tomorrow; I don't want to have it here longer than necessary. I still have the shivers when I think of that fellow who thrust it into my hands, ugh!' (see volume one) He put the offending item into a padded envelope, sealed and addressed it, then sat back with a sigh of relief.

The children wandered off and went up to the secret room, where they played cards for a while, then started chatting.

'Your Aunt Daisy sounds really gruesome,' remarked Michelle, 'I haven't any aunts so I don't know what they're really like.'

'You can have ours if you want,' offered Sam. 'We can spare her, Mum's got two great sisters who are super!'

'Thanks, but no! I'd rather not have an aunt like Aunt Daisy. I wonder what she looks like?'

Sarah was frowning. 'I'm not sure,' she replied, 'but I think there's an old photograph album somewhere in the dining room bookcase; let's go and look.'

The album was soon located; it was large and leather bound. Plunking it on the table, they leafed through its pages. All the earlier photos, dating from their great grandparents' days, were carefully labelled: who, where and when taken. Later on the pictures had still been stuck in chronologically, but the information underneath grew scrappy, and halfway through petered out altogether. To add to the problem there seemed to be no pictures of their father or his sister when they were young. They continued turning the pages.

'Look, there's mum and dad before they were married!' exclaimed Sam, 'Wow, what old-fashioned clothes.'

They giggled and turned over. A full page studio photograph confronted them; it showed a very formidable upright lady of uncertain age dressed in a heavy tweed suit and wearing horn-rimmed spectacles. She was grim-faced, glaring at the camera. They stared in horror; it could only be one person, Aunt Daisy! However, further searching revealed no more photos of her. There was another young lady, who appeared in group photos, but neither she or the formidable aunt were in their parent's wedding pictures. They put the album away and went soberly to lunch.

Sarah grasped the nettle by the hand. 'Mum, is that big picture in the photo album of Aunt Daisy?'

'Why, yes,' she replied. They were so shocked they failed to notice a twinkle in her eye. For Derek had found a sealed note, which he'd overlooked, in the envelope for her. Upon reading it she had burst out laughing and hid it in her handbag. It wasn't often she had a chance to play a trick on her tricksy family.

The afternoon was spent preparing for school. Michelle was cheerfully packing her bag and putting out her clothes, singing, 'It's school again tomorrow, tomorrow it's school again!' much to her mother's surprise. Never before had her daughter been so cheerful about returning to school.

After supper there was a brief meeting with Bill and Sir Brian. Derek explained about the clues in the book, which threw some light on what Melissa had been up to, but not on how she'd managed it! They both promised to examine the extracts he'd made in the hope of solving the mystery. They were just about to disperse when the lights began to flicker alarmingly. Derek went to check the fuses and reported all was in order.

'Let's find a viewpoint from where we can see the plantation,' suggested Sir Brian. The best place was the side window in the main bedroom. Looking out into the darkness they were aware of numerous flickering, flashing lights darting in and out amongst the trees and over the Dell.

'Will o' the wisps! What do you think?' he questioned, turning to Bill.

'Yes, harmless enough but annoying, especially if they are meddling with the electricity supply!' he replied. 'The stirring of the Primal Power often causes an upsurge in the activity of elemental beings,' he explained. 'They become excited because they can draw energy from such a source. They are not harmful, but can be a nuisance—rather like flies in summer. Do you think it's worth trying to talk with them?' he asked Sir Brian.

'We could try,' was the reply. 'They might have some useful information, who knows?' They bade Derek and the children 'good night,' and left.

The others remained for a while watching the dancing

lights in the distance. 'It was full moon on Saturday,' remarked Derek, 'That could have set them off as well!'

Sam and Sarah exchanged glances. Who would have expected their strictly scientific father of a few months ago to be talking about the influence of the moon on elemental beings!

He smiled at them, 'Right ho, off to bed with you now, it's school tomorrow and I don't want Fred ringing up to complain we've sent him a bunch of sleepy-heads. Shoo!' They fled laughing, as he chased them to their rooms.

In spite of all the preparations made for a smooth start to the morning, things had gone missing during the night and the three of them were rushing round before breakfast searching for mislaid gym shoes, and other such items. Breakfast was fast, as Geoff and Jill arrived during its final stages, and to avoid further chaos Derek piled them all into the car and drove them up to the bus stop. 'I'm not doing this regularly!' he warned, 'Next time you can jolly well walk.'

As usual when they arrived, Stephen and Jane were waiting and when they entered their classroom, it was full of noise and chatter. Chris and Fenella greeted them cheerfully and wanted to know how things were at the manor, and they promised to tell them at break. Mr Atkinson swept in just as the first bell went and they all settled down to listen to what he had to say. After the morning verse he began by speaking about the planned Open Day on March the twenty-first.

'For this, besides an exhibition of work, there will be performances by all the classes,' he informed them. 'We have been requested to do some recorder playing, a song and some poetry connected with our main lesson work. There are four weeks for us to prepare; that should be plenty of time. There will also be an Easter celebration on the day we break up for the Easter recess on March the twenty-fifth.

We'll be doing our usual egg painting and hunt too. I'll tell you what other events there are once they are finalised. For this lesson block, as I told you, we shall be studying local geography. This will involve finding out as much as we can about Tadbridge and its surroundings. During the next four weeks we shall go on local field trips at least once a week. Our first will be this Friday when we shall trace the old city wall and visit St Andrew's Well and the abbey.'

'Four outings!' exclaimed Stephen when they gathered for break, 'Wow, that's more than usual, and there'll be one at end of term as well.' During break the Bidforders told the others of their visit to the ruined church and what was happening in the manor grounds.

'When we left this morning,' said Sarah, 'the builders were just arriving to secure all the passage entrances; you should have seen the stuff they had on their truck!'

They made quite a group now: two pairs of twins, Michelle, Fenella and Chris. Geoff spent more time with his friend Jonathan, but they still counted him as one of them and always told him what was going on. He had an open invitation to join in with their activities any time he wanted to. It was a gesture that he really appreciated and had vowed that one day he would find a way to repay them for all their kindness and help.

Their teacher was on lunch break duty so they were able to tell him about the coming visit of the 'awful aunt'. He listened sympathetically, but like many grown-ups, said, 'She may not be as bad as you think; at least give her a chance!' They promised him they would, though how long the chance would be they could not make up their minds.

The chatter on the school bus was noisy as usual and the driver complained that he needed earplugs to concentrate on his driving. Doreen met them, and when they arrived home, invited Geoff and Jill to stay for a snack. She'd spoken with Bess, and Harry would fetch Jill at half past five.

There was mixed good news too. Ingrid had been for her interview and got the job. She would start on the sixteenth; however, Michelle would remain with them until the Easter holidays so her mother could settle in and also prepare her daughter's room. There were three cheers all round.

When finished, they went up to look at what the builders had done. The old boiler house had a new door with a lock, and the secret passage entrance had also been fitted with one. They trooped down to the Obelisk. Here, the ruined entrance had been further blocked with heavy concrete slabs and a heavy iron mesh frame placed over them. 'Ugly, but effective!' Derek told them. The question he had been debating with Hugh was whether it would be possible to repair the wall closing off the tunnel? Hugh suggested they consult Erin, as she had been involved in its construction. While all this work had been going on nothing out of the ordinary had happened. They assumed that the Power had gone dormant again. If only they could keep Melissa away! Bill and Sir Brian had been examining the pages from the book since this morning, but so far had not come up with any solution to this problem. On return to the house Geoff left on his bike and Harry arrived for Jill. The trio went into the sitting room to do their homework before supper.

They had barely finished the meal when with a loud thud Sir Brian appeared—out of the fireplace— luckily it had recently been swept. Bill appeared more conventionally in the doorway. They both looked very pleased with themselves, and both began to speak at once. They stopped, bowed to each other and said, 'After you!' Then Bill added, 'You first, Sir Brian, you understand these magical terms far better than I.'

'I flatter myself that I have acquired some knowledge of these matters over the last few centuries. However, for the sake of those present, especially the younger members, I shall endeavour to explain things as clearly and concisely as possible.'

Derek rose and bowed to him; the old fellow nodded, then began.

'It took Bill and myself some time to go through the material from the book. The author writes in a most obscure manner. However, at last we managed to figure it out. The Primordial Power, when active, works at a certain basic physical and non-material level, rather like the lowest note on a musical instrument. All other entities work on different levels. For example, Erin's powers are attuned to the Elementals; mine are somewhat higher, therefore the protection I brought about could block out Melissa's 'tone'. The secret the book held was how to change your tone, so that you could 'break through'. If she can do that — and she did — though she couldn't wholly keep up the required concentration the other night,' — he grinned — 'However, if she can eventually reach a basic tone that 'harmonises' with her objective, she'll activate it! As the book indicates, the other, less strenuous method is to use a child because they are able, if tutored by one versed in magic, to attune to almost any creative tone. The point is that a child can also control such a tone. The latter procedure only activates it. If I can find the frequency she's using I can block it, though there's nothing to stop her changing it. But this does mean we can discourage and thwart her crafty schemes for a while.'

Sir Brian's explanation was fairly clear, though how it worked practically was still obscure. But if he thought he could put a spanner in Melissa's works it was all to the good. He promised to work on this, and the children went to bed feeling more hopeful. Sir Brian had indicated that the two of them would have a chat with Erin as well. Before they left, Bill mentioned that they had tried to speak with the Will o' the Wisps but had met with little success. 'They are all of a nervous twitter trying to use up this surplus energy, so we couldn't get a word of sense from them!' he complained.

In the meantime, Melissa was planning her next move. She was very confident that she could still enter the manor grounds without detection. Being by nature impatient she was keen to get on with matters, as it was only four weeks to the equinox. It would be new moon on March the seventh and from then until the twenty-first would be the best time to act. But which date would be most propitious? She knew that certain planetary relationships (aspects) were more favourable than others, so she settled down to some calculating, a subject she had shown little interest in during her training. Now she wished she had. Two pads, several broken pencils and a generous amount of bad language later she had the information she needed: Sunday, March the fifteenth, when the moon, still in the first quarter, had unfavourable aspects to Pluto, Uranus and Venus, as did Mars and Saturn. Added to this, Jupiter was in Scorpio. All, of course, depended on her calculations being correct. Now she had to choose the most favourable time. More calculations and waste paper. It appeared that nine o'clock in the evening was near enough. Excellent, she had twenty days to prepare! Maybe she should just pop over to the Dell to see how things were?

Attuning herself to a tone that differed from that surrounding Bidford Manor, she mounted her broomstick and headed in its direction. This would be a high-level surveillance operation. It would need care and concentration and no distractions or interference. She was confident there would be none of that. The night wind was chilly and scraggy clouds skittered across a disseminating moon. She gained height as she neared her objective and could see the dark shape of the plantation looming up below. She began to pick up subtle vibrations, but as yet she could not attune to them. There were lights flickering about the ground, very low grade, feeding off the local energies. She decided to ignore these, continuing her flight over the Dell.

Then all the flickering lights coalesced into one flaring wall of flame—and she was heading straight for it! She pulled her broomstick up sharply, but as she did so a blast of heat struck her, flinging her broom round so that it headed back towards 'Goulhaven'. Bewildered at first, she now realised that someone or something had sought out her tone and repelled it. What's more, the tail-twigs of her broom were singed!

Chapter XXIII

The following morning Erin attended two consultations. She arrived at the manor after the children had gone to school and made her way up to the summer house, where Derek, Hugh and the building crew awaited her. Their question concerned the damaged wall. Was it best to leave well alone, or should it be repaired to restrain the force emanating from the Dell?

'I have already given this some thought,' she told them. 'Remember it was built by non-human hands and so did not disturb the dormant one. Now owing to the electrical short circuit and subsequent damage on two successive days, the spell is dispersed. It would have to be repaired in the normal way. The elemental activity you mention is no threat. It merely indicates some basic energy is being given off in that area. Rosie has confirmed this. For the present I feel we should leave well alone. However, I think with Melissa involved it may be necessary to repair the damage, for who knows what mischief she may try now? I suggest that all the necessary materials are made ready at the entrance, and your men on standby, should they be needed. I will also place a restraining charm on any new work, though it appears that, for the moment, Sir Brian has found a way of countering Melissa's attempts to invade the grounds. I'm now going to have a word with that gentleman and Bill.' Hugh and

Derek thanked her for her advice and the former went to organise the required materials.

'You'll drop in and have a cup of tea with us afterwards, won't you?' said Derek. 'Of course!' she replied, 'I'll see you in about half an hour,' and set off towards the old ornamental garden where they had chosen to meet.

Bill was already there, but Sir Brian was apparently finishing off one of his latest spells, which was at a crucial boiling stage. How crucial they never knew, for hardly had Erin arrived when there was high pitched whistling noise and a loud splash in the ornamental pond, from which the spell-maker now scrambled out muttering angrily. 'Why can't they put the measurements on products in pounds and ounces or pints and gallons? I'll never get the hang of these metric mitres and letres —or whatever they call them!' He looked at his wet robe and said 'Dry!' and it was, but not ironed.

They sat on a stone bench under a rose arbour and Bill told her what the book had revealed. She nodded and said, 'As you know, my powers do not extend so far. Melissa was always ambitious and she is quick to spot any spell or charm that will give her an advantage. Her weakness lies in the fact that she is impulsive and I could imagine that she never turned the page to see how to control the Power! This will be our problem: how to know when will she try to rouse it? When I find the sleep rune, and we are well and truly prepared, I would use Michelle to put the Power back into its centuries' old slumber. No harm would come to her if the rune is used properly. I need to talk with the children when they are all here, which will probably be next weekend.'

Bill thought for a moment and then said, 'One thing is certain, she must act before the spring equinox, for during spring and summer not even one so foolhardy as her would dare to disturb it!'

Sir Brian nodded, 'Since all these things are connected

with the heavens and the movements of the planets it should be possible to find out when is the best time to try and awaken the Power.'

'Could you make such a forecast?' asked Erin.

'Yes indeed, madam, I have studied such in the past. The only difficulty is there may be several propitious days and times. Also, we do not know what particular planetary combinations she may choose. However, I shall do my best.'

With that the meeting closed and Erin made her way to the kitchen to chat with Doreen and Ingrid. Derek joined them around the third cup. She told them about the conversation with Bill and Sir Brian and the possibility of finding out when Melissa intended to carry out her plan. Derek had always been interested in astronomy and of late had been studying the hypothesis that the planets and stars do have an influence upon the earth.

'I could do some calculations as well,' he remarked.

'That might be a very good idea,' agreed Erin. 'Not that I don't trust Sir Brian's arithmetical powers, but an independent check would help to establish the probable date and time.'

So it was settled that Derek would also make the calculations on his computer. She continued, 'Please tell the children I should like to speak with them at the weekend. Stephen and Jane will be here too, won't they?'

'Yes,' replied Doreen. 'Their main lesson now is local studies. There's an excursion this Friday and they want to work up their notes over the weekend.'

'Good, I'll drop in on Saturday morning at about half past nine.'

Doreen noted this on the message board.

The next few days at school were very busy preparing for the excursion and doing some research in the school library. Mr Atkinson also arranged for a member of the town tourist promotion board to come and give a talk about 'ancient Tadbridge', which included a video on the local ancient and historical sites. By Friday morning they were all ready and eager to go. The day turned out sunny, but cool, though should remain dry, according to the weatherman. The class gathered as usual and the route they would take was gone over briefly — once more. (You can check it on the town map.)

'Right class, listen carefully. I don't want to have to send out search parties for missing students. We leave the school and cross over the bypass, using the footbridge, past the 'Dog, Duck and Dormouse' and down the road on the left following it until we reach South Gate. Remember to note down anything of interest and keep a sharp eye open for any signs of the old wall. Some fragments are incorporated into modern buildings. The next stretch takes us round by the park to the castle ruins, then on to West Gate and round to North Gate. We go through Market Square and visit St Andrew's Well. Our next stop will be the church and the abbey ruins, back past the 'Dog, Duck & Dormouse' arriving at school by lunchtime. Ah, I knew that would brighten some of you up! We'll have our morning break in the park. Everyone quite clear about the route? Any questions? No, then let's get going!'

They paired off and left the school in an orderly fashion. They did not need to be reminded that how they behaved when out would be noted, and those who still were suspicious of the school would pounce on any misbehaviour as an example of ill-disciplined pupils!

The first part of the excursion did not reveal a great deal in the way of the old city walls. Too much change had affected the eastern side of the town with the post-war growth of industry and new suburbs. Every so often there was a plaque fixed on a building indicating the line of the wall, but above ground nothing remained. However, when they reached South Gate there was a section of it on both sides of the

High Street and one of the original towers still stood on the left. This was open to the public and the class spent a pleasant half-hour exploring it under eyes of a very tolerant guide. Then they moved on, still following the line of the walls to the park for break. Afterwards a visit was paid to the castle ruins and back to the High Street via the West Gate, which, alas, no longer existed. From the High Street the children went to St Andrew's Well, a small park down an alleyway just off the main shopping area. In it stood an old well, fed by an underground spring. In troubled times when Tadbridge had been besieged, this was the town's only water supply and often enabled the defenders to hold out until relief came. Originally it had been part of a property connected with the abbey, but with the Dissolution of the Monasteries, passed into private hands. However, the legend that the abbot, a local 'St. Andrew,' had miraculously discovered the spring during a long drought persisted, many claiming the water had curative powers. It was a peaceful place and most of the older inhabitants of the town preferred to sit here rather than in the main park. When the class arrived the place was deserted and they were able to closely examine the well and its surroundings. On their teacher's instructions, notes and sketches were made. The wellhead was covered with a heavy iron grid. Above it a pipe trickled water in from the spring. On the stone coping was a metal plate with facts about the capacity and flow, plus a few dates. These were carefully copied down.

Tadbridge did not possess a museum. Several times the Council had proposed one, but that's as far as it ever went. There were two collections of artefacts and pictures: one housed in the library and the other in the entrance vestibule of the Town Hall. There was also a collection of relics from, and connected with, the abbey ruins in a small hall adjoining the church. These could be viewed on request and Mr Atkinson had made such a request; so it was to the church they now made their way. The verger received them with some trepidation; twenty-two nine-year-olds were not his usual visitors. Generally they were more likely to be in the ninety age range! But the children were so interested in everything and so well behaved that his reserve soon thawed and he was delighted to have such an appreciative audience. There were cases with coins, buttons and other small artefacts, also church plate and vestments. The walls were hung with pictures of the abbey before it was dissolved and of the church. There were also pictures of the various abbots and the vicars who had served there, and two or three representations of St. Andrew as well. But, as their guide explained, nobody really knew what he looked like. Stephen asked if there had been any connection between the ruined church and the abbey.

'Not that I know of,' the verger replied, 'There were many small Christian communities dotted throughout the country in early Saxon times. It was only when Christianity became the accepted religion and Rome sent missionaries and monks to open monasteries and larger groups began to form. Then many of the smaller communities would join a larger one. It was safer, for this was the time of the Viking invasions. The interesting thing is that the first abbot here was English. This is very unusual; mostly they were sent from Rome. It was only later in late Saxon and early Norman times that English leaders were chosen. Our one may have already had local standing and so in a remote area like this would have been an obvious choice.'

Seeing the quintet's deep interest, he took down a large bound book from a shelf.

'This is a very unusual scrapbook. It was made in the sixteenth century by a vicar of this church and is full of pages from old manuscript books that were probably from the abbey library that was dispersed and, alas, mostly destroyed at the Dissolution. At least he had the desire to save something and these scattered pages show what kind of books were here. All the children gathered round and he stood on a small bench to turn each page so that they could all see. The detail and decoration, drawn in colours as bright as the day they were applied, drew gasps of wonder from his audience. But it was as he turned the last page that the quintet gave their special gasp of amazement! There was a delicately coloured drawing similar to the engraving in the abbot's study, though it was not so stiff and stylised. This one was alive with movement; there were figures working in the fields, ploughing, sowing and bird-scaring. In the church porch there stood an imposing figure in his vestments; he held a crosier in one hand and the other was raised in blessing. His face, in spite of the minuteness of the drawing, looked with reverence over the scene — it was Brother Andrew, there was no doubt of it!

'Do you know when this was drawn?' asked Sam. 'Not exactly,' was the reply, 'but the style is late Anglo-Saxon, so possibly around 900 AD.'

'We could ask… …' began Sarah, but stopped herself. To say they could ask Brother Andrew would require some explanation! Michelle quickly supplied a revised version.

'We could ask the abbot of the New Abbey; he may know something,' she told the verger.

He nodded, 'Yes, that's a possibility. If he does have any further information, perhaps you would ask him to contact us. We are always on the look out for more facts or information about our exhibits.'

They promised to do so and then said goodbye, as their party still had to visit the abbey ruins, where more sketches and notes were made. Then it was a brisk walk back to school in time for lunch break. As they passed the 'Dog, Duck and Dormouse' a police car drove into the parking lot. A police officer got out and was about to enter the pub. Noticing the passing procession of children, he stopped to watch. Suddenly he waved to the little group lagging slightly behind the others; they saw him and waved back.

'Do you know that man?' asked Michelle.

'Oh yes!' they replied, 'That's PC Wilby; we know him quite well!'

The afternoon was spent discussing the morning and deciding what each group would write up. The class would also prepare a wall display for the Open Day. The quintet bagged the abbey ruins and the church. Fenella and Chris's group got St. Andrew's Well. Geoff and Jonathan's, the eastern section of the wall and South Gate. The fourth, the castle ruins and the western wall.

'We've three weeks to prepare the display,' Mr Atkinson reminded them. 'It will mean some really concentrated work, as the main lesson books also need to be ready.'

Then added, 'Next Friday we shall be visiting the old water mill on the river. This is about five miles to the northwest of the town. Our purpose is to see how water was used for transport and power in olden times.'

School over, there was the usual frantic rush to collect their stuff, and for Stephen and Jane to bring their overnight bags. Soon they were all on the bus and eagerly looking forward to the weekend.

While seated round the kitchen table—snacking—Doreen told them of Erin's request to speak with them in the morning. This gave them something to look forward to; chatting with Erin and Rosie was always interesting and they guessed that it would have to do with the Dell. Afterwards they took their sketches and notes up to the secret room so that when they got round to it work could be carried on with no disturbances—apart from sorties to the kitchen for brain nourishment. As there was still some time before supper they took Binky out for a walk down the drive, up the lane and back via the footpath that went past the ruined hunting lodge. This also helped them to work up more appetite.

After supper there was a note sorting session and an apportioning out of the various plans and sketches they wanted to make. Then it was bedtime. 'But Mum, it's the weekend, we don't have to go to school tomorrow!' (Will grown-ups never learn?) However, upon being reminded of Erin's visit, though they did not really agree that an early night was a good idea, they accepted it so they would be fresh and ready for her.

Bill was on patrol that night with JJ. Sir Brian was still at his calculations and had used up more paper and patience than Melissa. Also, being older, he had a much wider and varied vocabulary and if the expression, 'making the air blue with language' had been literally true his study would have been a deep indigo by now.

The watchers went up to the high ground overlooking the pond, as it gave a good view of the summer house and Dell area. Apart from a few flickers of light all was quiet. Then JJ nudged Bill, saying, 'Look at the pond!' He did so; the water was being violently agitated, rising up and then falling back. Spray and water vapour now began to rise from it. 'More elemental activity?' JJ suggested. 'Probably,' returned Bill. 'It's more than likely there's an underground water source that's picking up the energies.' They watched for a little longer then returned to the house.

Chapter XXIV

Next morning the children were up early, as they had decided to put in some study before breakfast. However, it seemed they'd hardly started when they were called to the kitchen. The reason for this was that most of the time had been spent discussing who was going to draw what, then who would be best at drawing which, and then what they were going to draw for the illustrations. The only positive outcome was a desire to go back and examine some of the items in the church collection. Sarah undertook to ask Mr Atkinson for the telephone number of the verger so they could arrange this.

After breakfast Erin and Rosie arrived. They met in the sitting room and, as usual, Binky and Cleo joined the company. When they were settled Erin told them of her meeting with Bill and Sir Brian and how matters stood regarding Melissa.

'Once we have an idea of the date and time she's chosen we can act. But we still have to be prepared for the possibility of her managing to waken the Power. Our task will be to return it to its dormant state before its energies are let loose. From the old book we have learnt that the only sure way of achieving this is to use a certain ancient rune, or charm. However, that has to be recited by: 'One who is young and has some training in the magical arts.'

She looked keenly at Michelle, as did the others.

The little girl blushed then replied, 'That's something I have. What do you want me to do, Erin?'

That good lady smiled. 'You have courage, my dear! But you will not be alone. Everyone here will help, as they are well acquainted with supernatural forces. Your task will be to recite the rune. I shall act as your mentor. There is risk involved, as there is in all things magical. But consider our friends and allies: Bill, Sir Brian and JJ, Brother Andrew. Quite enough to deal with Melissa!'

She hesitated, 'Though I must tell you, compared to the Power's it is like that of a sparrow to an eagle.' She looked at them. 'I asked you once before to undertake a difficult task. Are you willing to do so again?' and received a wholehearted, 'Yes!'

'Good, first I shall give Michelle the rune charm to learn. We must practice how you stand in relation to her and there are movements that the rest of you make while she recites. Provided this preparation is done well away from the Dell, and quietly, it should not activate any unwanted energies; but we still have to be careful. It would be best if we rehearse on Monday afternoon when you come home. Perhaps Stephen and Jane could come up on Wednesday and at the weekend. Can you arrange that?'

They reckoned they could. 'One more matter, I shall call in on Bess tomorrow. I would like Jill to come with you. You don't mind, do you, Sam?'

'Of course not!' he replied, 'but why do you want her?'

'That child has remarkable latent powers; in the olden days she would have been tutored to develop them by one like myself. I feel that her presence may be vital to the success of our task. Now I shall have a word with Doreen, and we shall meet again over elevenses.'

They went back to do some more work on their project in the meantime; managing at last to sort out the problem of who was going to do what for the wall display.

While this meeting had been going on, Derek had shut himself in his study, loaded an astronomical programme into the computer and commenced to examine the planetary movements over the next few weeks. He noted down the various possibilities and then printed out the charts for comparison. As his knowledge of such things was limited, he now had to refer to an astrological book.

'Who would have thought,' he muttered to himself, 'that Derek Court, writer of a popular science book would, within six months of its publication, be studying one of the very things he scorns in it? Oh well, now let's see!'

An hour or so later he had a pretty good notion of the suitable day and time. Luckily there was very little choice, which made the task easier. Having finished he sat back, saying thoughtfully, 'I need to check this against somebody else's calculations, but who? Of course, Sir Brian!'

He made his way up to the attics to see if he could locate that worthy's room—something he'd never done before. He stood in the passage and wondered what to do. Should he knock on the wall, or call out? Suddenly, under his nose the brass-handled door appeared, opened, and JJ popped his head out. 'You wish to see my master? He has just asked me to come and fetch you! Pray enter!'

Derek did so and found himself in the most unusual room he'd ever been in. Sir Brian was not a great one for tidiness and even JJ had trouble in maintaining some form of order, owing to his master's habit of starting one task and halfway through switching to another, and then to another.

At present the room was awash with paper and broken quill pens. The wild-eyed and wild-haired master sat at his desk muttering away and scribbling furiously. Upon realising he had a guest, he sat back, realigned his spectacles and greeted Derek with,

'Ah ha! Done the calculations, thought you might like

to check them through for me.'

'Certainly, Sir Brian, I've also been working on the same problem and have brought along my computerised results for comparison.'

'Your com-pluto-sized whats?' exclaimed the sage.

Derek remembered; his host had no knowledge of computers. Should he explain further? Instead he placed the printouts on the desk, saying, 'There, does this tally with yours?'

Sir Brian stared at the neatly printed sheets. He scrabbled around on his desk until he found a sheet of paper covered with his spidery scrawls. He held it vertically, then horizontally and eventually got it the right way up. He squinted fiercely at his, then at Derek's work, and then looked at him with bewilderment.

'Remarkable, your com-whatever-it-is agrees with my calculations; how many hours did it take?'

'Three minutes for the positions over three weeks,' he replied.

'Come, come, you must be joking! That's impossible, even the most advanced mathematician would need a day to work that lot out.'

'No, Sir Brian it's true, a computer can perform the most complicated calculations, provided it has the correct data, far quicker than the human brain.'

The messy mathematician looked thoughtful. 'Hm, maybe I should get one. It might enable me to finish that spell of mine. I'm a bit stuck over some quantity proportions.'

'Come down and have a look at it some time,' suggested Derek.

'Indeed I will. But now let us just double check my workings against those of your complutoer.'

The details can be skipped. Their final choice was Sunday, March the fifteenth, and the most propitious time nine o'clock in the evening, GMT. A study of the aspects showed no other day had so many malefic influences. Sir Brian was duly elated and bringing his fist down with a crash on the desk, causing further chaos amongst the papers and a bottle of ink to tumble floorwards and shouted:

'We've got it! Now we have her!'

'Erin's chatting with Doreen, shall we go and tell her?' suggested Derek.

'Of course, this very instant!' and he grabbed up a handful of papers and made for the doorway. Derek collected his and followed.

Sir Brian had decided on a short cut and was already halfway through the floor, making one of his vertical descents. He stopped and hauled himself back. 'Sorry,' he muttered, 'I forgot you couldn't do that!' and led the way down the stairs to the kitchen.

Here they found the kettle on the boil and Doreen had just called, 'Children! Come and get it!' They did, charging in as if they were the Household Cavalry, not a bad description of the quintet moving at speed. When they saw Sir Brian the brakes were applied and he was duly greeted. He acknowledged them with a gracious nod. Once everybody had been catered for, Derek explained their findings, accompanied by encouraging grunts and snorts from Sir Brian.

Erin smiled, 'I congratulate you both on your good work. Now we know how long we have before the day of crisis. I can start my preparations with more certainty. No doubt, Sir Brian, you have some ideas as well?'

'Yes indeed,' he replied.

'There's one thing we shall have to be careful of,' added Derek.

'What's that?' they asked.

'Well, we are dealing with a very cunning person and the last thing we want is for her to have any inkling that we know her intentions.' He turned to Erin, 'Would it be possible to mislead or lull her suspicions?'

'A good point, a few red herrings along a false trail should do the trick! I think we should show some activity to distract her from our plans. Let's think it over and meet tomorrow evening to see what ideas we have come up with.'

'Right ho!' promised everybody.

Erin picked up Rosie and set off for home. Derek retreated to his study. Sir Brian did likewise and the children went back to their project until lunch.

They discussed other matters too, and when they came, at the gong's summons, for lunch, asked if they might go to the farm to talk with Bess about Erin's remarks concerning Jill. They also wanted to visit Brother Andrew and tell him of the date and to ask if he could help clear up the verger's problem. They set off directly after the meal, taking Binky with them. The weather was dull but dry, pleasant enough for walking — as long as you kept moving — and they were soon at the farm. Bess welcomed them and without further ado they told her the reason for their visit. Jill was already sitting on Sam's lap listening, wide-eyed, while they talked. Bess's answer was as expected.

'Anything Erin suggests I've no problem with, whatever it is,' she replied. 'If Jill's with the five of you I know you'll take great care of her. Perhaps you would ask her to call in some time and tell me if Harry and I can also help.'

They told her Erin would be popping in tomorrow to see her. Bess continued, 'I know Harry's worried about the thing in the Dell, for it could bring disaster to the farm as well as the manor. You say you're going to Church Wood now? Well, if you've no objection, I'll come too and bring the children. They could do with some fresh air.'

They were delighted to have her company, as they still felt some unease at going there on their own.

Harry was visiting a neighbouring farmer who wanted to consult him about the forthcoming lambing season, so Bess would tell him of their visit when he returned. As soon as the younger ones were ready they started down the bridle track, Binky tugging the way. It seemed he knew where they were going and was as eager as they were to get there. They sang, and Brother Andrew appeared; he welcomed Bess in particular.

'Let us walk a little,' he suggested, 'I think you would find the stone seats rather too cold for comfort today.'

He led them along a path that went from the west end of the church and through the wood towards the bridle track. They stopped at the wood's edge and gazed out across the peaceful winter countryside. First the children told him about the date.

'It is as well that I know it,' he replied. 'If there is need I shall be there; in any case we here shall pray for a rightful outcome to this affair. All our strength will be focused to this end and those who are involved.'

He looked with gentle concern at Michelle, then all of them.

Binky let out one of his 'what about me?' noises; Brother Andrew bent down and patted him on the head. 'I hadn't forgotten you, or Cleo. You will have your parts to play too!'

The children wanted to know what parts? But he merely replied, 'You will see!'

They now asked him about the connection between the abbey in Tadbridge and his church. 'It is true, as the verger told you, that the original church was built back at about 400 AD. It was destroyed during Saxon times but rebuilt around 800 AD. These remains are of a church that stood here in the fourteenth century. There are fragments of older buildings in it. The drawing you saw, from which the engraving was made, shows it in the year 952 AD, when I was vicar. We had a young novice who had artistic skills. He drew it as decoration at the end of a commentary upon the Gospel of St John. Alas, the rest of the book was destroyed during the Dissolution, as was the church. It is also true that I became the first abbot of Tadbridge Abbey. Indeed it was unusual for an Englishman to be chosen. Preference usually went to men of Rome. But Tadbridge was a small place and in a farming area. It was not rich, so rather than waste greater talents, I was appointed. One day, when the shadows that beset us now are dispersed and we have more leisure, I will tell you more about this church and the abbey's history. Documents from my time do exist, hidden in some diocesan archive. Maybe you can find them.'

The sun was beginning to set and the air turning chilly, so they retraced their steps to the church and having sung, walked back to the farm. Actually, Brian was carried by horsie Jane and Jill rode her trusty Sam-steed! They did not go in as it would soon be dark and it was preferable to be home beforehand.

There was talk of tomorrow at supper but nothing definite was planned. 'Let's wait and see what it turns out like,' suggested Derek, 'then we can make up our minds.' His idea was to go to somewhere that would tie in with their present studies.

That night the manor and its surroundings were quiet. No lights, no swirling waters and—no Melissa!

To their delight next morning turned out to be bright and sunny. There had been a mild frost overnight and the grass and trees sparkled in the sun.

'That settles it,' said Derek, 'the sooner we leave the better.'

'Where to, where to?' they clamoured.

'Well, since your teacher is taking you to the old mill this coming Friday, I thought we might continue looking at the way water was used for transport. Did you know that back in the 18th century there was a plan to link Tadbridge to the sea by canal?'

They confessed they didn't.

'Neither did I until reading a *History of Canals in the West Country* recently. It appears that some enterprising, but not very practical local businessmen decided that if Tadbridge could be so joined it would be good for their businesses. The plan was to link up with the Taunton-Bridgewater Canal at some point and out through the Parrett Estuary into the Bristol Channel so goods could be sent by barge to Avonmouth and Bristol. The actual distance of new canal would have been some ten to twelve miles. Unfortunately, they had no real knowledge or experience of waterways and their construction. They chose a local engineer to oversee the project and he had even less knowledge and experience than theirs. Stocks in the "Tadbridge, Taunton and Bridgewater Canal Company" were sold and several local merchants invested their capital. The engineer surveyed the route — on a map — as it was later discovered.

About five miles to the north of Tadbridge there's a two hundred foot ridge of limestone running east west. The engineer had overlooked this fact. The canal would either have to go through or over it! This meant a tunnel or a series of locks. The projected costs trebled over night. The engineer discretely disappeared — to America — it was rumoured. The stocks became worthless and the investors lost most, if not all of their money. Work had actually begun and a three mile stretch of it still exists north of the town, complete with a lock and a lock keeper's house which was never used as such.

Your father, Stephen and Jane, knows the owner of this unique place, so I rang him last night to find out if we could pay a visit. He'd be happy to show us round and has invited us to lunch.'

There were appreciative gasps from everybody and Doreen murmured with great relief:

'Thank goodness, no sandwiches to prepare!'

Derek continued, 'He has collected information about the construction and has old maps and diagrams too. What's more, he'll come with us on our walk to point out important features and the like. Now no more chatter (Chatter? Derek had been doing all the talking!) off you go to get ready, and bring your notebooks.'

There was the usual rush, and soon, with the quintet giggling in the back, Derek at the wheel and Doreen as navigator, they set off towards a small hamlet called Curry Hatch.

The drive was a pleasant one and in half an hour they were driving through Curry Hatch, which consisted of a few houses and an inn; of occupants there was no sign. Half a mile beyond it they turned down a narrow lane on the left that wound its way gently downhill. In the distance away to the right, the low limestone ridge upon which the project had foundered was visible. The lane crossed a small stream and they were on flatter ground. There, ahead of them, rising in solitary state out of the meadows, stood the most remarkable house they ever had seen. It was octagonal with a steeply pitched slate roof out of the peak of which rose the most magnificent and elaborate brick chimney. The walls gleamed white in the wintry sun and all the windows were pointed at the top. 'Gothic style,' Derek told them. The building was elevated on a slight mound and surrounded by a red brick wall with a stone coping. The gates were open and as they swung up the short drive the children caught sight of the name proudly displayed on one of the gateposts: 'Canal Lock House.'

Chapter XXV

As their car stopped by the front door it flew open, and a short, rather rotund man with grey hair came quickly down the steps to meet them. He was closely followed by two children, a fair-haired pigtailed little girl of about seven, and her darker haired brother of five. As they got out, their host-to-be greeted them warmly.

'I'm so glad you could make it today. We don't have many visitors in winter. I'm William Bennett, but usually answer to Will or Will B. These two shrimps are Judy and Nigel, but we call him Nicky, though heaven knows why.'

Introductions were made and they went inside to be given a conducted tour of the remarkable building. Its external octagonal shape made for some unusually shaped rooms inside. The side facing the lock had a projecting room with a large bay window so that the lock keeper had a clear view in both directions. There was a large pulpit desk at which he would have stood. Open on it was a large ledger.

'In this he would have recorded all the barges that passed through and the toll they paid to use the lock,' Will explained, 'Upstairs used to be mainly for storage of ropes, tackle and items for maintaining the canal locks. Now it's bedrooms. Strange to think that it never served its true purpose. Those directors must have been optimists, for they put up the lock keeper's house before the canal and the lock.'

'Do you know what happened to it when the venture collapsed?' asked Derek.

'Yes, there was an enquiry held in which the engineer was severely censured, not that it worried him; he was already en route to America! Naturally, all the assets were sold to help recompense the unfortunate shareholders. This dwelling was bought by a local gentleman who used it for a retreat when his wife was entertaining her relations, whom he could not stand! He had a housekeeper and her son living here. He made the upstairs alterations and the place remained in the family until the early nineteen twenties, when it was sold to defray death duties on the estate. An uncle of mine bought it, and when I was a lad my twin sister and I used to come here for holidays. My uncle was a bachelor and when he died, left the property to us. I have always been fascinated by the 'canal that never was' ever since childhood. My sister did not have the same enthusiasm for the place, so I bought out her share and Joyce and I have lived in it for some twelve years now. Judy and Nicky were both born here. Enough chatter, come to the kitchen we'll have a warm cuppa something before I show you the actual canal—what there is of it!'

Joyce welcomed them into the spacious kitchen, and once fortified with warm drinks and biscuits they set out to explore. Directly outside the house was the lock. Which though it had been built, its gates were never fitted, but the brickwork with its stone capping and the massive iron hoops into which the gate pins would have fitted were still there, as were the two massive iron wheels equipped with handles, which would have been used to open and close them. The lock's floor was covered with a shallow pool, as Will had built small retaining walls across either end so one could have some idea of what it would have been like if it had ever been used. Looking towards Tadbridge they could see a shallow depression, the line of the canal. There was a footpath running alongside it, which they followed. The growth of waterweeds and rushes was thick and many willows and other trees overhung it. Now and then there were stretches of water.

'How did that get there?' asked Doreen.

'When the initial trench had been dug they diverted the stream that you crossed over to fill it, and it still supplies water in winter, even though much of it is clogged up.'

They reached a small footbridge that crossed the stream and noted some old brickwork at the junction.

'There was a sluice gate here to control the flow,' he remarked. It was a fascinating walk, for their guide told them many things about it and canals in general.

'I hope I can remember all he's told us,' Sarah whispered to Michelle, 'so I can write it in my notebook when we get back for lunch.'

There was a peaceful atmosphere as they walked along the old towpath. It was hard to imagine that some three hundred and fifty years ago this would have been a scene of great activity — men digging and the shouts of the drivers encouraging their horses hauling carts away laden with soil from the excavation. In some parts there were the remains of low stonewalls that bounded the towpath. Then suddenly the canal ended and unbroken fields stretched before them.

'This is as near as it came to Tadbridge,' remarked Will, 'In the other direction it goes for half a mile and then stops abruptly like this end — roughly three miles and a half in all. There's some more brickwork on the other part where the road to a farm was to be carried over it by a bridge. The abutments were built, but not the bridge.'

They turned back and were at the house in time for an excellent lunch. Afterwards the children sat around the kitchen table with their notebooks and quizzed Will for more information, which he willingly gave. His two children sat by him, listening quietly.

Once they had all the information they wanted, he said, 'Wait a minute,' and went into his office, returning with five A3 sheets, giving one to each of them. They were photocopies of the survey plan for this section. 'There, that should help you with your project,' and went on to ask them about their school. He seemed impressed with what they told him and added that if Mr Atkinson wanted to bring the class here on one of their trips, he was welcomed to do so. They thanked him and promised to pass the message on.

The weather had dulled over after lunch and so they did not walk the northern section, but stayed chatting. Judy and Nicky wanted to show the children their playroom and bedrooms; so while the grown-ups conversed they went up to the first floor and duly admired them. It was clear from Judy's manner she had something she wanted to tell them, so they sat on the playroom floor and she began with all the confidence of a seven-year-old.

'There are four of us who live in this house, but really there are five!' She paused and looked at them anxiously.

'What do you mean?' asked Sarah gently, though she already had an idea of what Judy was leading up to.

'Well,' the little girl continued. 'There's another sort of person, but he doesn't live with us and he doesn't have a bedroom. He's, well—we don't know if he eats—but he looks after the house and us when Mum and Dad are busy.'

'Ah, a house guardian!' said Sam, and the others nodded.

Judy looked delighted and jumped up, saying, 'You know about them?'

'Yes,' they replied and told her about Bill Bluff and Bob Binnacle, also mentioning Chris's and Fenella's house guardians.

'I'm so glad you have them too,' she said and her brother nodded in agreement. 'You see I don't think Mum and Dad really believe in him. They think it's a game we play. I told one of my friends at school, but she teased me and so did some other children.' She looked unhappy. 'They called me "soppy Judy" when the teacher wasn't around.'

Stephen got up and put his arm around her. 'Never you mind,' he said, 'we know it's true and are your friends. You and Nicky must come and stay with us sometime and we'll introduce you to Bob, and to Bill!'

'That would indeed be most kind and comforting for the children,' a voice remarked, and from the corner stepped a ruddy-faced fellow dressed in the working clothes worn in the eighteenth century.

'Jim Barrow, at your service!' he announced with a bow. 'Been here ever since the place was built. Of course I came expecting heavy work, but I can't say I object to my lot, and these two.' He indicated the little ones, 'They keeps me busy enough!'

As usual, information was exchanged on their respective guardians and Bill's name caused the usual appreciative comments. Then, with another bow, Jim disappeared.

Voices called from below. 'Come on children it's time we left.' They clattered downstairs and thanked their hosts for their kindnesses.

Then Stephen said, 'We'd like Judy and Nicky to come and visit us one day.'

'And us,' added Sam.

Will looked at his two, who were jumping up and down with excitement. 'The answer's plain!' he said, 'They'd love to!'

'And we'd like it, too, if you'd all come,' said Doreen. Phone numbers were exchanged so a visit could be arranged in due course. There were hugs and goodbyes all round and soon they were heading back for Bidford Manor.

While supper was being prepared they went into the dining room and settling them-selves round the table began to write up their notes. They wanted to surprise their teacher with an outline of what they had discovered about the canal and its origin. With it would go a copy of the map.

'If the canal had reached Tadbridge, I wonder where it would have finished?' mused Michelle.

That set them all thinking, so they borrowed a local ordnance map from Derek to see if they could spot the most likely site. Stephen added, 'You know, I'm sure there was an argument about that! I mean if you were a merchant investing in it, you'd want it near your manufactory or warehouse.'

'Yes,' said Sam, 'and so would all the others who had shares. I'll bet there were some first class rows over it!'

'Yes, but how can we find out?' asked Jane. She thought for a moment and then added, 'I know, we'll ask Gramps; he'd know where any old documents may be kept about it.' She promised to ask him as soon as there was a chance.

Having settled this, more work went into the wall display: Sarah and Stephen doing the notes, while Jane and Sam started the accompanying map. Michelle sketched the layout and additional decorations. This kept them nicely out of mischief—as Derek put it—until it was time to clear away and lay the table for supper.

They were just finishing the meal when a most peculiar sound was heard; it was as if somebody had trodden on the cat's tail, though it was considerably louder and longer. They stared at each other wondering, 'What on earth?' when it abruptly stopped and Sir Brian popped out of the fireplace looking very pleased with himself.

'Did you hear anything?' he asked. He was emphatically told they had and would he kindly explain what it was and why?

He looked surprised, 'I thought you would have guessed, wasn't it obvious?' Heads were shaken. 'Why, it's my vagrant early warning system. Set up round the grounds, it will alert us at once to anyone entering them!'

'But if it's for anyone it will go off when the milkman comes, or even one of us!' exclaimed Derek. Sir Brian opened his mouth, shut it, and looked perplexed. Then said, 'Er, yes, it does, er, wouldn't it? Quite right, of course. But you see this is a prototype, it needs further refinement and adjustment. But once these are made… …!'

Doreen made a suggestion: 'Sir Brian, there's really only one person we need to know about entering unannounced, Melissa Mouldyberry. If you can adjust it to her wavelength or frequency it would be perfect.' She emphasised the 'perfect.'

'Of course, madam,' he replied with a low bow, 'I shall go and work on it with that in mind.' He looked at Michelle, 'Tell me, young lady, what does your grandmother detest most in the way of food and in the realms of nature?'

'Easy,' she answered, 'she can't bear porridge and hates small dogs, especially poodles,' said with a grin at Binky.

'Ha, excellent!' said the inventor. He turned again to Doreen. 'Madam, can I request from your larder some porridge oats and from that brave houndlet a tuft of his curly coat?' He was soon furnished with these and left chortling away to himself, doing one of his vertical take offs through the ceilings to his part of the attic.

'This should be interesting!' remarked Derek. 'I wonder what he has in mind? Will it, upon her approach, throw ladles of sticky warm porridge at her and tickle her nose with poodle hair, causing her to sneeze, thus activating the alarm?' Little did he realise how near to the truth he was, but more about that later.

After the clear up it was time for Monday morning preparations and bed.

Later that night Sir Brian and JJ made a circuit of the boundaries. Every so often they stopped and JJ dug a little hole into which his master spooned out, from a large pot he was carrying, a large blob of some very nasty looking gooey substance. The hole was then covered up. A short verse was muttered over it and they moved on to the next chosen spot. As the moon began to set they finished and looking very satisfied, returned to the manor.

When they arrived at school the quintet could hardly wait to tell of yesterday's outing. They weren't the only ones! Quite a few of their classmates had visited places of interest in the district, including Chris and Fenella, who had gone with her father on one of his trips, as he had been commissioned to paint an old barn for a local grain company. Mr Atkinson was very pleased with the enthusiasm and energy his class were putting into this period and told them that if they kept it up he thought class four's display would be outstanding. They were fully occupied for the rest of the morning!

At break, the quintet cornered him and passed on Mr Bennett's offer and told him something of what they had seen. They also presented him with their write-up and diagram, 'So you'll have an idea what it's like,' they explained. He was duly appreciative and would reschedule one of the proposed outings so they could go there. They were delighted.

Then Sam mentioned their conversation with Brother Andrew and what he had told them about the drawing of the church and how he became the abbot of Tadbridge Abbey.

'We want to go and sketch some of the artefacts for our display,' he explained. 'Can you give us the verger's phone number? Then we could tell him what we've found out.'

'I'll give you the phone number, but I should wait until you've spoken with Father Andrew before telling him anything that Brother Andrew has told you! You see, some members of the church look upon matters of "communication with the dead and spirits" with great mistrust. So it would be better if you avoided it.'

'You would have thought that churchmen would have been eager to know about the past straight from those who were there,' said Stephen afterwards as they walked round the school grounds during lunch break.

'I wonder what they're frightened of?' mused Sarah.

'I think they used to know these things but over the centuries have forgotten them,' remarked Michelle. 'Now days they only believe what is written in their books, and even then they don't always agree.'

'I think the verger is a nice man,' Jane argued, 'I'm sure we could tell him.'

'You heard what Mr Atkinson said,' retorted her brother, 'we should wait until we've talked with Father Andrew!'

'You don't have to keep telling me,' snapped his sister.

Luckily the bell went and this argument was not continued. This was the first time Sam and Sarah had heard them come close to quarrelling.

After school and their return home they prepared for the rehearsal with Erin, who arrived shortly after they did. It had been decided to use the sitting room. Though Stephen and Jane could not be there, it had been arranged they would come over on Wednesday afternoon and also be present at the weekend, as would Jill.

The main action rested on Michelle, supported by the twins. First Erin gave the rune to her, going through it and emphasising the correct pronunciation and the rhythmic stress. Then — with the twins standing on either side of her — the child repeated it while Erin instructed them in the special arm movements. Afterwards, the three of them were tutored in their foot movements. None of this was difficult, but they knew it had to be exact, and real concentration was needed to achieve precision. Erin was pleased with their efforts and suggested that they try it on their own tomorrow. She also gave them a sheet with instructions for Stephen and Jane so they could have an idea of what they would be doing, and could practise before Wednesday's rehearsal.

Meanwhile, Melissa was not idle. Over the weekend she had worked at the waking rune and found another tone level, which she was confident the protectors of the Dell would not know. She would try it out one evening during the week, just to make sure. This time she would approach at ground level rather than flying. Surely they would never think of her doing that. For in spite of all the setbacks she had met with, she was confident she would succeed in the end. Then she would show Erin what real witchcraft was!

Chapter XXVI

As arranged, on Wednesday afternoon Stephen and Jane came back to the manor for a rehearsal. They were very excited about it and had been practising for ages—as Jane put it—the previous evening. Jill would also stay. Erin had arranged with Bess that she would be picked up by her dad later. As usual, she remained close to Sam, chatting away happily about helping Aunty Erin, who arrived shortly after them, and having been refreshed, they trooped into the sitting room. First Erin put each one in their place on the form. To begin with she said a short verse calling on the Higher Powers to assist them in their task, then the rehearsal began. Carefully they went through the rune sequence with the movements. Erin was delighted with the way they managed, and Michelle's manner of reciting the words.

Jill was an onlooker for the initial run-through. Then Erin gently led her through her movements. She started by standing in front of Michelle. Then, as she began to chant the rune, Jill circled round her. When she came back to her starting place, she now circled round the pair standing on either side of the chanter, and eventually round all five of them. This brought her to halfway through the verse. For the remainder, she moved along the front and then the back of the row, pausing for a moment in front and behind each of them. Upon returning to in front of Michelle, she moved to Sam's right side and remained there holding his hand. This was practised two or three times and Erin pronounced that she was highly satisfied. The next rehearsal would be on Saturday morning.

They returned to the kitchen and Erin left when Jill's dad picked her up, Harry having offered her a lift.

Half an hour later John arrived. 'Any spare sets of twins?' he inquired.

'Will we do?' asked Jane.

He looked hard at her and Stephen. 'I think I've seen you before. Yes, you'll do, I'll risk it.'

However, he had some news as well. 'Father Andrew rang this morning. He sends you all his regards and will be visiting us this Sunday. He plans to arrive at our place mid-morning. We'll have an early lunch then drive over, and you can take him to see the ruined church.'

'Then when you return we'll all have supper!' said Doreen.

'Thanks, that will be great,' John replied. 'He has to catch the eleven p.m. express to London and can rest for a while when we get back. If you two want to return on Sunday you may, since you do live with us,' he added.

'We'll see, that is if Aunty Doreen doesn't mind,' they replied. John grinned and left with his offspring.

After supper the Bidford Trio worked on their projects and then made ready for bed. The weather was turning unpleasant. 'It looks as if we are in for a nasty spot of it!' said Doreen as she wished them good night.

Melissa decided to put her new tone to the test on Wednesday night. It was indeed a night for witches! A strong north-east wind was blowing, bringing with it flurries of sleety rain. Ragged clouds swept across the sky, through which the moon shone fitfully. Most sensible folk were well tucked up at home, as were the inhabitants of Bidford Manor. By ten thirty the place was in darkness; even the usual watchers were relaxed. Sir Brian now had three protective devices at work: the Dell cover, his repeller and the boundary alert; he was confident this witch-woman could not get anywhere near her objective without the alarm being raised. He was particularly proud of his latest device, his boundary alert. However, he had overlooked one deficiency, as is often the case with his inventions!

Melissa travelled by her usual method, broomstick, but touched down in the disused quarry on the north-west side of the grounds. Hiding the broomstick under some bushes, she made her way onto the ridge that led to the manor's gardens. She moved very cautiously and some twenty yards from the boundary hedge drew a small crystal ball from her cloak pocket. She held this in front of her, moving it to and fro horizontally. It became opaque then cleared as she swung it to the right, then opaque again. Carefully she moved it back until clear. Then she ran swiftly forwards at that point, keeping close to the ground. In a flash she was through the protective barrier! She paused for a moment, but there was no reaction. All remained still, wet and silent. With a chuckle of triumph she moved round the perimeter of the old stone circle and up to the summer house, slipping inside to be out of the wind and rain.

The cause of the protective barrier's failure was rain and damp. In this particular spot where he had buried some of his mixture, the rain and water soaking down the slope had washed it out of the soil, dispersing it and diluting its effectiveness — one of those minor matters the inventor had overlooked.

She now used the ball again, holding it at arm's length in the direction of the Dell. At the same time she began a low monotonous chant, part of the waking rune. All the time she kept her eyes fixed on the ball. After the first few words it began to gleam palely and once more grew cloudy. As she continued the cloudiness grew more and more agitated, swirling wildly, as if being lashed by an invisible wind of great strength. She drew near to the end of the first part. Now the ball began to feel uncomfortably hot in her hand, forcing her to jiggle it up and down. As she chanted the last words it cleared suddenly and for a fraction of a second something stared out of the depths at her. She uttered a strangled cry of terror and staggered back; the ball went dark and fell from her hand, rolling across the floor into a dark corner. But she was past caring, for a dreadful fear had seized her and the one overpowering thought was to get away. Outside, the rain was now coming down in torrents and the wind had reached gale force. Its centre seemed to lie in the Dell. She sped through the gap and was soon in the quarry, leaping on her broomstick and away home.

On arrival, she remembered the crystal. Well, it had served its purpose and was no longer of any use. Something else would be needed now. In the messy, but comforting surroundings of her own home, the fear gradually left her and was replaced by triumph. It had worked. She hadn't bargained for what had revealed itself in the crystal, but she had disturbed its slumber and knew that the full rune would definitely wake the Power. There were still a few minor preparations to be made, but she saw no difficulty in being fully ready by the fifteenth. One thought crossed her mind—a child—perhaps it would be a good idea to have a child, just in case. Time enough though to think about that later. A very smug and contented Melissa went to bed. But her sleep was broken by the image of what she had seen. In her dreams it floated before her, becoming larger and larger until she felt it would engulf her and the whole world. She would wake up, trembling. It took quite a time to get to sleep again and then once more the image would occur. As daybreak drew near, it weakened and finally, with the rising sun, vanished, leaving her looking as if she had the great-grandmother of all hangovers.

The sudden increase in the wind and rain had not gone

unnoticed at the manor. Sir Brian, dozing at his desk, was awakened by JJ. 'Master, Master, there's something strange going on in the grounds.' At the same time Bill appeared and reported he too had been disturbed by the sudden change in the weather; and on glancing out of his window had seen some object moving fast and low across the parkland towards the western boundary.

Sir Brian leapt up. 'Come on, what are we waiting for?'

Bill cut in. 'Ah, whoever it was has long since gone and I think we all know that could only be one person. It's more important to find out what she's up to! I suggest you and I, Sir Brian, make our way to the summer house area and JJ makes for the boundary to see if he can pick up any trace of how the intruder entered, then joins us. Let's go!'

Nearing the summer house, both noticed the flickering lights over the Dell once more.

'Meddling no-good!' muttered Sir Brian, 'She's been up to something, heaven knows what mischief has she done now.'

But Bill was listening intently. He touched his companion on the arm. 'Can you hear anything?' he said. The rumbler stopped in mid-rumble and listened.

'Yes, I can. Whatever is it? Sounds like a sobbing mouse.' He turned his head, 'It's coming from the summer house.' They were just about to enter when JJ joined them.

'She slipped through at a point where the rain had washed the protective matter away,' he reported. 'I followed the trail and found she had hidden her broomstick in the old quarry.'

'Come with us now,' said Bill, 'there's something in the summer house she's left behind.'

'A trap?' queried JJ.

'No, I don't think so, come on!' said Bill.

They entered the building; it was dark inside but the strange squeaking noise was stronger and a feeble greenish light glimmered in one corner. Bill made as if to go towards it.

Sir Brian held him back. 'Er, allow me, I am more conversant with these witch's baubles than you, Bill. They can be tricky, but I can deal with them!' He crept across the floor, both hands outstretched and when he was within a few feet of the object, sprang at it with a cry of 'gotcha!' But he hadn't, for as he leapt his foot slipped in some gravel dropped by the builders and he landed flat on his face. The object rolled out of his reach and came to rest at Bill's feet! By the time he'd scrambled up, Bill was holding the now silent crystal ball, examining it with interest.

'A very useful item,' he remarked, 'It acts like a sensor; that's how she found her way through your latest invention, Sir Brian. But I think she used it in here, as well.' He held the ball at arm's length and slowly moved it round. Its glow increased and then at a certain position the interior went cloudy. Bill remarked, 'In line with the Dell, I think,' adding, 'It's warming up and I believe it senses some very powerful force. Why, it's becoming quite hot!' He put it down and turned to the others. 'She was trying to disturb the Power as part of her plan to waken it.'

'I knew she was a meddling, interfering nuisance of a witch!' snorted Sir Brian. 'But she's a cunning one,' he grudgingly added. 'It's not often a mere witch can get the better of me!'

Bill was thinking. After a few minutes he said, 'Aren't we wasting valuable time and energy trying to keep her out? It seems if she wants to get in she can. I believe it would be better if we let her do as she pleases and concentrate on how we deal with her on the fifteenth.'

'What, let her come and go as she likes!' snorted Sir Brian. 'I, I... ...!' He spluttered to a halt, looked at Bill, then said, 'But I see your point. If she can come and go she'll think she's got the better of us and will become careless. It's a risk, but one worth taking.'

'I'll speak to Derek in the morning,' said Bill, 'Now let's

get back inside and we'll take this little plaything with us; we may learn more from it.'

'If it's so useful, why did she leave it behind?' asked JJ.

'I think she saw more than she intended and dropped it in fear. But it's in her nature to discard anything once it's served her purpose.'

The three of them went back to the house. The sky was clearing and the wind had dropped. A faint glow in the east heralded the sunrise. How different it looked from a few hours ago.

The following morning Bill sought out Derek in his study and related the happenings of the previous night. At first he was concerned about the ease with which Melissa had entered and left, and he began to speak about 'stiffer measures'. Bill now told him of his suggestion for a new approach, pointing out their need to concentrate on her plan rather than wasting time and energy trying to keep her out.

'If she can gain entrance at will, I hope she will become overconfident and give us the loophole we need for counter measures!' he added.

Derek thought long and hard before answering. It was risky, but made sense. 'All right, Bill, I leave the planning up to you. Just keep us informed. The children are already working with Erin, as you know. At least we shan't be disturbed by more of Sir Brian's protective measures!'

There was a sequel to this. Later during the morning that gentleman decided to check his boundary protectors to see if any others had been spoiled by rain or damp. Bill had gone to find him, wanting to discuss their new approach. He saw the warrior in the distance and made his way towards him. Suddenly there was a peculiar 'Ker plop' noise and a familiar muffled roar of anger. The inventor rose out of the long grass where he had fallen, his face covered in porridge while a disembodied yapping could be heard at his feet. 'Ouf, pah, augh! Get away, you wretched animal!' he cried, aiming a kick at the invisible dog, while trying to scrape the sticky mess from his face. 'Not even sweetened,' he moaned, tasting some. Bill waited until the yapping ceased and most of the porridge had been removed. 'Why was it activated by you?' The inventor looked sheepish. 'Well, you see, I don't like porridge or small yappy dogs and I forgot to specify that it was only for a particular person.' Bill tried hard not to grin and explained why he wanted a word with him.

In the meantime, Derek went to have a chat with the builders. Since the discussion with Erin on Monday they had been working on the old boiler house and green houses. Now they would suspend all work until after the equinox and then decide what to tackle next—and when. There was the possibility of reopening the passages as well.

&

On Friday the class made its visit to the Old Water Mill as planned. The weather was typical March–a blustery wind blowing, but dry and not unpleasant if one was well wrapped up. The coach took them along the 'old route' to it. This would have been used by pack horses and carts taking grain to be ground and then collecting the flour. It was a narrow, twisting road and it was lucky they didn't meet any other vehicles.

The mill had been restored and was in working order. They watched the great wheel turned by the power of water, the millrace and pond. Then inside to gasp with astonishment at the great millstones turned by waterpower. There was an exhibition of old tools and farming implements and a large wall display on Water and Windmills. Then, to their great delight, they all climbed into a restored hay wagon drawn by two beautiful carthorses and were taken for a ride round the neighbouring lanes. Mr Atkinson enjoyed it as much as they did.

'Do you know,' he told them, 'I have never been for a ride by horse and cart in my life!'

Some of the class stared in surprise. They'd always regarded him as ancient, growing up in a world with no cars, electricity, radio or TV, so maybe he wasn't that old after all! When the wagon returned to the mill they had lunch, then the coach took them back to school. Everyone now had another mass of notes to sort out and write up, but it was worth it after such an interesting day. The quintet were delighted that they would be able to carry on together with their project and invited Geoff to come over on Saturday afternoon if he needed any help. His group was working on the eastern wall section and South Gate. They would check his work and he would check theirs. An independent opinion would be helpful. So when school finished it was on to the bus and heigh-ho for Bidford Manor.

Just before the children returned, Derek and Hugh had removed the obstructions from the trapdoor, unlocked, and opened it with great care. No sounds reached their ears. Taking a powerful flashlight they descended the steps and made their way along to the damaged wall.

'Hm, that was some force!' remarked Derek.

'Yes, it will take some repairing; really it ought to be taken down and rebuilt,' said Hugh.

'That would be risky,' said Derek. 'But it occurs to me that if there was some work obviously in progress, a certain lady might be attracted to perform her dark deeds in this place, in which case we can also be present. I'll have a word with Erin; she's coming over tomorrow morning.'

'Give us a ring if there's anything we can do,' said Hugh. 'The sooner all this business is over the quicker we can complete the job for you.' They went back, closing the trapdoor carefully behind them.

Chapter XXVII

Erin arrived promptly on Saturday morning and found the children waiting for her, including Jill. The words and movements were repeated, and apart from a few minor corrections they managed very well. Though Erin was not effusive with her praise, they sensed she was pleased at the progress made since Wednesday. The star performer was Jill; she seemed instinctively to know what was required of her and in a subtle way held the group together. They planned to meet again tomorrow morning, for the vital day was but a week ahead. As they finished, Derek popped his head round the door and asked Erin to have a word with him for a moment. The children took Jill with them and headed for the kitchen.

Derek outlined Hugh's and his visit to the passage and mentioned his idea to her. Erin smiled. 'Excellent! I think that could be just what's needed to bring Melissa here, where, as you say, we can keep an eye on her. Yes, let it be known that the wall is going to be repaired and she'll be around for sure!' Then she left; for as she put it, 'I have other duties to attend to.'

Derek made his way back to the study to find Sir Brian there bending over the computer. He started guiltily as Derek entered.

'Just looking, you know. Fascinating things. When this

other business is over you must show me how it works,' adding, 'I came to tell you something, though. Bill and I decided it's all very well having that witch-woman poking around the grounds. In the house is a very different matter. We couldn't speak freely to each other and every spider would be a suspect snooper. So, we worked out a house protection cover.'

Seeing the look on Derek's face, he hastily added, 'It's foolproof, at least as far as we can make it. If she tries to enter, she won't be able to. Simple as that; it was mainly Bill's idea, I just helped to set it up.' This made Derek feel easier. He thanked Sir Brian, who then left, as he too had 'other things to do.'

Shortly after lunch Geoff arrived and they went up to the secret room and worked away until teatime. Geoff read the notes his group had made and showed them the sketches of the wall and South Gate. They made comments and suggestions and he did the same for them. It was a very constructive and successful session and they decided to do it again the following weekend. After tea they went to the sitting room and chatted. Sarah wanted to know if Geoff had had any contact with pupils from his old school and if so, how had it been. 'Oh yes, I've seen some of them. They made a few silly remarks, which I ignored and now they leave me alone. Though there are one or two I would still like to be friendly with. I think they would too, but don't dare to because of the others.'

'Couldn't you ask them to your house?' suggested Sarah.

'I could,' he replied, 'but they'll probably be watched and picked upon at school. But I've got lots of new friends now!' he added, brightening up. 'There's all of you, Jonathan, and lots of the children in our class are really friendly! There's Nola too. She's a funny little thing, but I like her; it's like having a kid sister. I met her mum recently and she's invited me to go and have tea with them one afternoon!'

He looked round cheerfully. 'I'm fine, and my mum is delighted with everything I do at school. The people I collect groceries and run errands for keep on telling me I'm much more cheerful and helpful than I used to be, and with the bike… …!' He gave a big grin and expansively spread out his hands. A few minutes later Doreen called up, 'Geoff, time you were on your way, it's getting dark. Your mum will start worrying.' 'Right ho!' he yelled and they went down to see him off.

Usually he took the track that led across the fields to the village. But as that was rather muddy, owing to the recent rain and cattle tramping along it, he decided to use the road. Leaving the manor, he turned left down the lane and cycled in that direction, going through the wooded hollow. As he came up out of it and rode towards the bridge over the Bidbrook he saw a strange flash of light from round the coming bend. He dismounted and switched his dynamo off. Then, pushing his bike, he began to walk cautiously forwards. Upon reaching the bend he paused and peered carefully round it. The bridge was empty, but even as he looked, there was a swishing noise and a woman appeared in its middle. Having heard Michelle's description of her grandmother, he knew at once who it was. She was chuckling and chortling to herself. Geoff noticed a gap in the hedge. Leaving his bike in the ditch he scrambled through and keeping low crept forwards until near the bridge, but still under cover of the hedge. Now he could hear her.

'This time I've done it. No resistance, nothing! I slipped through like a hot knife cutting butter. Now I can enter at will, nothing and no one can stop me. On Monday I'll be there first thing to listen to what those builders are up to. Then I'll enter the house and see what's going on! Let me see, a fly should be an adequate disguise, not a big one, just an ordinary house variety!'

Geoff found a gap and peered through. The woman was

chuckling and hugging herself. She began to spin round, faster and faster until she was a whirling blur, then she vanished!

He quickly grabbed his bike and cycled back to the manor. As he clattered into the yard he met Derek going to the wood store. He blurted out what he had just seen and heard. A smile of grim satisfaction crossed the face of his listener.

'Wait here,' he said, 'I'll get the car keys and drive you home. The bike can go in the back.'

'But I can cycle, really I can!'

'I'm not taking any risks, and neither are you!' replied Derek.

As soon as he returned he made his way to the sitting room and called Bill, telling him what Geoff had heard. 'I'll tell Sir Brian and we'll pass this on to Erin. Luck's with us, it appears.'

At supper the children heard of Geoff's adventure. Afterwards they relaxed with a fierce game of Monopoly, as Jane was dying to get even with Michelle's recent victory. It was an evenly matched contest and nobody was an outright winner. When shooed off to bed, a reminder was given that Father Andrew would be with them after lunch tomorrow and they would be taking him to visit the ruined church.

'There's your rehearsal first, then you can amuse yourselves for the rest of the morning,' Doreen told them.

౭౧

Back home, Melissa was riding high on her success, so much so, she planned to visit again, in broad daylight, early tomorrow morning and would make her way into the house just to prove to herself how clever she was.

Sunday began as: 'One of those days when the weather could do anything!' But that did not deter Melissa, who started out as soon as she had gulped down her breakfast. The house was chaotic and filthy, as was the garden, for items she had no further use for were flung out the back door—odd scraps of unwanted food, bits of paper, anything! This morning several pieces of severely burnt toast joined the mess together with the empty bread wrapping, and then she was away, landing in the lane by the bridge as she had done the previous evening. There was no sign of life in the grounds, though if she had looked more carefully at the manor she might have caught a flicker of movement on the roof. She squeezed through the gap where the bridge parapet and hedge met, then paused. Nothing happened; she was in!

Slipping behind a bush, she muttered a transformation spell and a moment later a small housefly buzzed towards the manor. As it did so, a thrush, watching from a branch of a nearby tree, flew off and made for the watcher on the roof, upon which the watcher—Sir Brian—muttered a few words and leaned back against a chimney to await results.

Inside, breakfast was just finishing. A slight tremor and darkening of the light made them look up or stop what they were doing. Bill appeared. 'Nothing to be alarmed about, the protective screen round the house has just been activated, as herself in the shape of a housefly is approaching!'

'Should we do anything?' asked Sam.

'No, just carry on as usual; we'll let you know what happens.'

Melissa discovered two things on her way to the house: it takes a long time for a fly to cover such a distance against a head wind and, flies are not used to the raw cold of a March day. This made her feel lethargic and flying in a straight line proved daunting. After fifteen minutes of struggle, she neared her objective and launched herself forwards with renewed vigour; soon she'd be in the warm, soon she'd... THUNK! She hit something solid that sent her reeling back with a throbbing head. Dazed, she settled on a twig and examined the house. Nothing, nothing to be seen. She took off and flew more cautiously. Thump! She contacted it again. Not so hard this time, but after several tries she realised there was some barrier round the place that she could not penetrate. For a moment the old anger boiled up inside. Then she thought, 'What does it matter? I'm in the grounds; I don't really need to go into the house. As long as I can reach the summer house and the Dell that's fine! Better not push my luck too far.'

She turned round and flew back towards the bridge. The roof observer smiled and muttered again. The thrush flew from his shoulder and went back to its tree.

Arriving at the bush, the fly became its human counterpart and made her way towards the exit point. As she reached the hedge she felt a slight pressure on her legs, like brushing aside long grass. There was a 'kerplop' and she was hit full in the face by what felt like a blob of cold, wet, sticky porridge. To add to her discomfort, a high pitched yapping started round her ears and something like dog's hair tickled her nose, making her sneeze uncontrollably. Sneezing and gasping, she blundered through the hedge on to the lane and propelled herself back home. An hour or so was spent in scraping and scrubbing off the very adhesive mess. She reasoned that she must have carelessly set off one of the old warning devices, but was still confident she could carry out her plans unhindered.

As she left, the thrush flew back to the roof; Sir Brian chuckled at its report. It was nice to know that his device did work even if it was now no longer necessary. He made a note to disconnect the others, just in case there were other porridge and poodle haters around.

Bill reported the results to the house. Shortly after, Erin arrived with Jill, whom she had collected on the way. The rehearsal went very smoothly, and more were arranged for Tuesday and Thursday afternoon. Then Erin took Jill home and promised to tell Harry about the meeting with Father Andrew at around two o'clock. For the remainder of the morning they got on with their various tasks and prepared for his visit.

The Court household lunched early, and afterwards the children went up to the secret room, where they could use the telescope to watch for the arrival of their guest. The weather was still unsure what it was supposed to be doing, but at least it had remained dry. Just after two o'clock, Sam, who was on watch, spotted the car coming down the lane. They rushed downstairs and out the front door. Then began to feel rather uncertain as to how to greet such a distinguished guest.

'Do we bow and curtsy?' Sarah asked her mum.

'Be your usual self, well almost your usual self. Just tone it down a bit!' she replied.

They need not have worried, for as soon as Father Andrew jumped out of the car, greeting them cheerfully, their shyness vanished and they rushed forward to greet him.

John and Phyllis now joined them and Derek and Doreen were introduced. They went inside for a few moments before Father Andrew remarked, 'I know my young friends are anxiously waiting; and as the main purpose of my visit is to see this church, we should go now before the sun sets.'

'We'll call in at the farm so Harry and his two children can come with us,' Sarah explained.

No more words were wasted. Their guest put on his cloak and they set off. As usual, Jill and Brian were swinging on the gate waiting for them. Brian was a little cautious of the 'man in the flappy thing,' but when his father appeared he regained his courage and asked, in all seriousness, 'Can he fly?'

Harry and Father Andrew walked at the back of the group chatting quietly while the children went on ahead. By now Brian was mounted on Jane's back, but Jill preferred to hold Sam's hand. 'I'll have a ride on the way back if I feel tired,' she told him.

It did not take long to reach the wood and Father Andrew took a lively interest in what Harry could tell him of its history.

'We sing when we reach the old altar,' Jane explained. 'It's a sort of "thank you" song. Our teacher taught it to us.'

'I shall be most interested to hear it,' their guest replied.

When the ruin came into view Father Andrew gasped. He looked questioningly at Harry, who nodded and said, 'Every time I come here it's the same; I can't put the feeling into words, but in me a deep longing arises for something long past, yet not lost.'

'I know,' replied the other, 'Only very special places have such an atmosphere, and this is surely one of them.'

The children had now reached the altar and had started their song; Father Andrew and Harry bowed their heads. When the last verse had died away, the priest said, 'It's a pity there are not more of such songs that breathe a sense of gratitude for all the wonders of this world and its Maker.'

Jane and Sarah were looking round with some concern.

'I wonder if Brother Andrew will come?' began Sarah, 'He may be scared of… …' She stopped in confusion, 'I didn't mean…!'

But a quiet voice reassured her. 'I am here, Sarah,' and there stood Brother Andrew; he smiled at the children. 'Your singing becomes better each time!' he remarked. Then he turned to his namesake, bowing deeply, 'Welcome, my Lord.' Father Andrew bowed in return, 'I thank you, but you are the master, I am a mere follower.'

The children watched with interest. The first abbot of Tadbridge Abbey and the present abbot of the 'New Abbey' were now deep in conversation. They left them to talk in peace and wandered around the ruin, looking at the first signs of new spring growth that was beginning to appear among the stones. A little while later the two reappeared.

'Thank you for your patience,' said Father Andrew, 'I have

learnt much and I believe I now know where that archival information might be found, in which case you could safely pass the information on to your friend the verger. Now we should return.'

He bowed to his counterpart, 'I shall definitely visit again; it is seldom one finds a place with so much spiritual nourishment.'

'You know you can come whenever you wish and will be welcome,' was the reply.

They parted, the Brother turning to walk back down the nave and the Father to join Harry.

'Grown-ups are forgetful,' thought the children as they took up their places and sang 'The Spacious Firmament on High' to the tune of Tallis' Canon for their farewell, while the two men stopped and waited.

Brian was still puzzling out the two Andrews. At last he asked the present day one, 'Is he your daddy-man?'

'Well, kind of!' was the reply, which seemed to satisfy him. When they arrived back at the manor—having said goodbye to Harry, Jill and Brian—supper awaited them.

Father Andrew now relaxed, keeping them amused with stories of the funny side of monastic life. All too soon it was time for the Randells to take him to catch his train, but not before he had promised to visit them again. Stephen and Jane decided to stay over and return on Monday as usual.

'You see, we've all got so used to it, so we don't want to upset Aunty Doreen's routine.'

John grinned at the Courts, 'I'll bequeath them to you in my will, I think!'

'Strange you should say that,' replied Derek, 'I'd thought of leaving our two to you, with Michelle thrown in for good measure!' Laughter all round and cheery farewells.

'Wow it's Sunday, and already eight thirty!' There was the usual scramble to prepare for Monday, and by nine, well maybe nine fifteen, they were all safely in bed!

Chapter XXVIII

On Monday morning around nine o'clock a housefly settled on a window ledge near the door of the summer house. It watched with interest the workmen pushing up wheelbarrows laden with bricks and bags of mortar, dumping them by the entrance to the passage. It also listened carefully to the conversation between the two men standing in the doorway near its perch.

'Lucky I kept a record of how many bricks and bags of mortar were used when it was bricked up the first time,' said the builder. The other man, the owner, nodded.

'Good,' he replied, 'now it's all there we can start at any time. But what about the removal of the remains of the first wall?'

'We'd better go careful on that,' responded the other, 'because of the you-know-what! I think I'll give that job to old Bert, he's a steady, reliable chap. A bit slow, but that might be a good thing on this job. He won't make a lot of unnecessary noise.'

'How long do you think it will take?'

'Let's give it a week, there's plenty to keep the other fellows busy round the boiler house and Obelisk!'

'Fine, then the bricking up could start next Monday?'

'I'd say about then.'

They shook hands and the owner went back towards the

house while the builder started to give orders to his colleagues. The fly flew off.

Back at 'Goulhaven' an elated Melissa hugged herself with glee. Matters could not have worked out better. The tunnel entrance would be clear on Sunday, so she would have free access and could perform her incantations unhindered. This reminded her that there were still a few details to be settled. Certain items would be needed, special herbs to be burnt. She'd need something to burn them in. Perhaps she should make a list? These things would have to be transported to the place, and hidden somewhere until she needed them. This was going to be a busy week, but well worth it. Once she had the Power, untold possibilities opened up. She wouldn't need this grotty little house. Well, it could be sold, though she wouldn't need the money. She wouldn't need money ever again! She chuckled at the thought of magically emptying all the filth and rubbish in the house and garden onto the surrounding ones. That would teach the snooty, interfering lot! When they found it she'd be long gone and the house vacant — what a joke! In an extremely good mood she commenced the final preparations.

At Bidford Manor there was also some cause for satisfaction. Bill had been experimenting with the crystal ball. He'd wondered if it had some link with Melissa and had been examining it — by chance — on Sunday morning when she had tried to enter the house. He noted that within it a flickering image appeared, rather like an indistinct insect. He watched as it fluttered, and then, after being repelled, slowly vanished. The crystal also emitted a low humming tone when she was near. So that morning they had been warned of her approach and had been able to start the hoodwink Melissa scheme-cum-programme. Erin was informed, by rabbit courier; so the week had started well in their favour. However, there was no feeling of complacency.

Erin also started to finalise her plans. She knew they

needed to do nothing further with the rune incantation, for the children were well prepared. She realised that Melissa had to have certain items and reasoned that she would try to bring the stuff over during the week and hide it somewhere. Not that she had any intention of meddling with such, but to know what she was using could be of help if things went wrong. Erin had two objectives: one to keep the Power dormant and two, to rescue her ill-guided colleague from almost certain destruction, though she had not told the others. Knowing this would have definitely produced a mixed reaction!

Hugh, once he was informed that the fly-spy had gone, told his men the real plans. Yes, old Bert would demolish the remaining fragments of wall, and the materials would be put down there, and the Obelisk entrance would be partially opened to let them in. However, it would appear to any casual observer that its closure was being reinforced. Three of the workmen were also to come up to the manor on Sunday—late afternoon—about five o'clock. They might be needed to block the tunnel. Hugh wasn't sure, but it was best to have them handy. Naturally they would receive an overtime bonus, and more!

The rehearsals were held as planned on the two afternoons and Erin was completely satisfied that everyone knew their part perfectly. However, she warned them that the conditions under which they would have to act would be very different from the sitting room. 'Concentrate on your parts and don't worry about what may be lurking in the dark before you,' she told them.

Support came from other quarters too. On Wednesday morning a letter addressed to them all arrived at Southleigh. It was from Father Andrew; he enclosed the address of an archivist who may be able to help in the search for the old abbey and church records. He suggested they ask Reg to write for the information, which he was only too pleased to do, as his twins had already asked him to search. But there was more:

'Knowing something of the problems which face you and what you will be called upon to do this weekend, I felt I must tell you that all at New Abbey will be thinking of you and praying for your success.' Somehow, knowing that a whole group of people were supporting them boosted their courage and confidence.

On Friday class four had their third outing. This time it was to the railway station, where they heard some of the history of the Great Western Railway and how the remaining line through Tadbridge was but a pale reminder of the network that had once criss-crossed the whole countryside. In the now hardly used sidings sat three old GWR coaches, being restored by the local railway enthusiasts. One of them took the children through a carriage, where they admired the polished woodwork, brass fittings and rich upholstery. A further treat was in store; for when taken into the old engine shed there stood a 4-2-2 tank engine dating from 1883, which was also undergoing restoration. The class was able to gain a real hands-on experience of a steam locomotive. Standing on the footplate it did not take too much imagination to be hurtling down the track at full steam, whistle sounding, as a level crossing came in sight!

As Stephen exclaimed, 'Nowadays it's tootling, little, smelly, diesel-powered coaches puttering along the tracks that these mighty beasts once thundered over.' The railway enthusiast nodded most approvingly at his comments!

The stationmaster then took them into his office and unrolled on a plan table sets of engineers' diagrams of track layouts and even a couple of engine construction plans. What's more, he had made some photocopies for their display. When they left he insisted on shaking hands with them and remarked to Mr Atkinson that it was a real treat to show round such a well-behaved and interested group of children.

'I only wish that some of the classes from other schools in the district were so polite!' he remarked, no doubt speaking from bitter experience.

They were back at school by lunchtime and the afternoon was spent in rehearsals for the Open Day, which now loomed very close.

As the 'septet' got ready to leave, Atty said, 'I shall be phoning Derek tonight. I'm free on Sunday and thought my presence might be useful?'

'Of course it will!' they chorused. 'We'll tell Dad; you don't need to phone, you know you can always come!'

'Well, it's only fair to let your mother know there's another ravenous mouth to feed!' he replied.

Knowing he would be there gave their courage a real lift! When they reached home there was another surprise; Reg had phoned to say he thought it was time he came over to check they were all behaving properly. But of course they knew what he really meant — another ally to defend the cause.

A further encouraging sign was the behaviour of Binky and Cleo. They became much more protective and followed everyone around as if they thought they were going to lose them. This proved difficult at times, because if the children separated, Binky would be thoroughly confused as to whom he should follow. He usually went with the group Sam was in. Cleo tended to go with the last person who had fed her or on whose lap she'd just been. It was much easier when the children were at school, as with only Derek, Doreen and Ingrid in the house they could easily keep an eye on their human servants.

Bess and Harry were another couple that wished to be counted in. After all, their daughter had an important part to play in this affair. As on previous occasions, a feeling of solidarity began to permeate the atmosphere, making them all feel more sure of the outcome. On Friday afternoon, before cycling off, Geoff said to Sarah, 'I know there's something important going on here on Sunday. I just want you all to know that if I can be of any help, give me a call and I'll be round like a shot.'

She smiled and said, 'Thanks, Geoff, come in the afternoon anyway and we can do some more project work,' adding, 'It happens after supper. Tell your mum we'll bring you home!'

Usually before such events there were meetings at which every member of the manor took part. This time there were none. Life was to appear as normal as possible so as not to arouse any suspicions. The only new news was a message from Brother Andrew saying that he and his fellow monks would be ready to assist if required. The evening was spent quietly; the children worked away at the wall display and became so absorbed with it they forgot Sunday for a while. The fascination of all that had gone into the making of the Tadbridge they knew completely enthralled them until it was time for bed.

When they came down for breakfast next morning there was a feeling of anticlimax. How could they pass the day? Stephen came up with one of his cheerful images, which reflected how they felt.

'It's like the day before going into hospital for a serious operation from which you may not recover!'

They nodded in agreement.

'Yes,' added Jane, not to be outdone, 'You wonder if you'll ever see your home and friends again.'

How this would have ended there's no knowing, but Doreen broke in, 'Now, now what's all this doom and gloom for? Off you go and make your beds and tidy up. And you'll do it tomorrow as well, even if you do reckon you won't come back!'

She shooed then out, saying, 'And don't dare return before eleven.'

Oh! She expected them for snack?

'Of course!'

'Goody.'

They departed feeling much more cheerful. Surprisingly enough the time passed quickly and they returned to the kitchen in a far less gloomy mood. The phone rang at the second or third biscuit stage; Sarah got there first.

'Hello, oh, Fenella, hi! What? Why, yes! Great! Hang on, I'll ask Mum, MUM! Oh sorry, I thought you were still in the kitchen. It's Fenella; her dad's driving out this way after lunch. He wants to do some sketching in Bidcote and wondered if he could discard his daughter and Chris—who's coming with them—for a couple of hours with us. Do say yes, Mum, please!'

'Yes, of course, I can't think of anything better than for you to have company this afternoon.'

'Fenella, are you still there? That's fine; tell your dad. When will you be here? Two o'clock? See you then!'

The anticipation of having two of their classmates over meant a conducted tour for them and probably a discussion on the class project. The remainder of the morning whizzed by, as they spent it making up an entertaining program for their visitors—A Magical Mystery Tour!

Fenella and Chris arrived on the dot of two. Mr Steuart popped in briefly to thank Doreen for accepting the guests thrust upon her—as he put it—and in return was invited to join them for tea when his sketching was done. The first tour was round the house, ending in the secret room, and here Fenella revealed the reason for their unexpected visit.

'It was our house guardian's and Chris's one's idea that we should come. Apparently yours from Southleigh had spoken with them. He said things were taking place here this Sunday which could have a great effect on the whole of the district and that you would need all the support you could get. So here we are!'

Chris added, 'Yes, and here we are!'

Briefly Sam explained what it was all about and of their delight at further allies.

'But what can we do!' asked Chris.

'Just send us all your "good thoughts" tomorrow, especially around nine in the evening,' said Sarah. 'Also, lots and lots for Michelle, as she's got the most difficult task!'

Both promised to do so and were then taken on a tour of the western side of the grounds, as it was best to keep away from the 'sensitive area' as Derek called it. Still having some time before tea, they wandered down to the farm and spent an hour or so with Bess and her children looking round. Jill and Brian were delighted at this surprise visit and the two horsies were given plenty of exercise! As they walked back to the manor they met Fenella's dad by the gates and piled into his car for the last hundred yards. Tea was very pleasant and Ron Steuart proved to be just as entertaining as Chris's dad. As they were leaving he turned to the children and said, 'I hear you've an important day tomorrow! I wish you good luck.'

They stared — how did he know? 'It was whispered in my ear by a friendly fellow called Joshua,' he told them. So even the grown-ups knew! Chris reckoned his father did too, as he had sent special greetings to them. All this helped to increase their confidence a hundred percent plus and for the rest of the day there was almost a light-hearted atmosphere round the house. They went to bed that night feeling much better than they had in the morning.

Saturday at 'Goulhaven' was also extremely busy. Melissa was up early and spent the first part of the morning checking and rechecking the procedure for the wakening spell. The seven part rune gave her some trouble. It was not long, but she had to remember where the pauses came and the things to be done at each one. Basically this consisted of throwing various combinations of herbs and odd items like spider's legs, ant's wings, wasp's spit and feathers from a dead crow into a shallow bowl over a brazier of glowing coals. She had one, but it would need transporting. The seven combinations were packed and ready, plus a bag of charcoal. She decided to take the brazier plus the charcoal over now and hide them near the summer house. Readjusting her tone, she mounted her broomstick and set off. Now, travelling faster than sound on such a vehicle is not without some discomfort, but to do so carrying an iron tripod and bowl is not the easiest of tasks and she had several hair raising narrow misses because she really needed three hands. She had tried to tie the stand on to the back of the broom, but it objected, pointing out it was licensed as a grade one (humans only) carrier, not a grade three (humans and miscellaneous items) carrier. However, if the human carried the items they would still be within the law. Melissa grumbled, but the broomstick was firm. It knew its rights and wasn't going to be put upon.

Her invisible approach may have concealed her from ordinary folk, but it did not fool Sir Brian. He was on patrol and had her crystal ball with him. As soon as it began to hum he noted the direction and took up a concealed position by the summer house. A moment later there was a thud followed by a jangling noise and a curse as the rider became visible, seated on the ground with her broom sticking in the grass at an angle and her legs tangled up in those of the tripod. The bowl was on her head and the bag of charcoal on her lap. After some struggle she gained her feet, and noticing a large laurel bush nearby, hastily shoved the three items under it and took off. Sir Brian waited a few minutes then strolled over and examined them. He guessed they were to do with the incantation. He thought for a moment then took a strangely decorated gold ring from his finger and — muttering a few strange-sounding words — held it over the bowl. Satisfied, he returned to the house, where he told Bill what he had seen and done. 'A ring retard spell may slow things up a little, which could be to our advantage.' Bill agreed.

When she reached home Melissa had one more run-through, packed everything carefully into a shoulder bag, then toasted her success with a six-pack of Messrs Wiccans' 'Witches' Brew Old Foul Ale'. A lethal concoction, which was not exactly the best thing to drink the day before a very complicated task that would need every ounce of concentration and alertness if it was to come off successfully. Some people will never learn.

Chapter XXIX

The children were awakened early by the animals. Binky whined and scratched outside the boys' room and Cleo — for her part — performed a miraculous acrobatic feat of climbing, demanding to be let in through the girls' window. Carrying a very self-satisfied cat they made their way to the adjoining bedroom, where Binky greeted them with great enthusiasm.

'I bet they planned this!' yawned Stephen, who was not quite fully awake, until Cleo jumped on him and started kneading his knees with her claws.

'I think they want to tell us of their undying loyalty!' said Sarah.

'Maybe, but Cleo doesn't have to rip my knees apart,' grumbled the victim.

'I think they want to know what they have to do this evening,' said Sam. He paused. 'What do they have to do?'

A good point. In all their previous adventures these two had always played a part. What would it be this time?

Jane thought for a bit. 'They know the passages well. Remember how they found us before? I think when we go down to await Melissa's arrival they should come with us.'

'Yes, but we'll be busy with Erin, so who's going to look after them? You know how Binky gets over excited and Cleo goes berserk. They could spoil everything!' protested Sam.

'What about Geoff?' suggested Michelle, 'He wants to help. What if he came with Binks on his lead?' She paused. 'Then there's Cleo. We can't put her on a lead or in a basket; she'd yowl the place down.'

'She's always good with Mum,' said Sarah. 'Some of the grown-ups are going to be by the summer house; Geoff could be with them. If Mum had Cleo in her arms I'm sure she'd be good until she's needed. When that happens no one could hold her anyway.'

They dressed quickly and trooped down to the kitchen to ask Doreen's opinion. She was quite willing to do as they suggested.

'Reg and Ingrid will stay in the house to make it appear occupied,' she told them.

'After breakfast your dad will explain where everyone should be. I think he's worked it all out by now.'

As they sat down to eat, Sam exclaimed, 'Gee, look at the sunshine; it's like spring!' and indeed it was. The day had dawned clear and mild; March was in a lamb mood today. Of course there was no guarantee it would remain so all the time, but it waa good sign.

'I vote we do some gardening this morning,' he suggested. 'We've been so busy and the weather has been so rotten we haven't looked at our plots for ages!' He looked at the others, adding, 'Y'know we could do with some helping hands!'

When Derek heard of the idea he agreed wholeheartedly. 'Just the job!' he said, 'I'll come out too. There's some pruning to be done on the terraces, and now's the time to do it. We can discuss the other matters later, when our supporters arrive.'

Soon they were up on the terraces where Sam and Sarah's plots were, and were soon busy with spade, fork, rake and wheelbarrow.

Derek set to work pruning the trees and bushes along the back wall. calling at intervals for the barrow to remove the clippings. Binky snuffled and searched for 'somethings' and dug holes here and there. Cleo pounced on leaves, or hid behind clumps of grass and jumped out at the workers. The birds sang from the safety of the trees, much to her annoyance. The sun warmed them gently while they worked and before they realised it Doreen called them for tea break, so they hurried down to the kitchen.

On arrival they found Reg and Fred sitting there. They had just arrived, having come over in Fred's car. After snack the children returned to the gardens. But the three men went off to the summer house for a chat, rejoining them later. Reg took on the task of advisor, while Uncle Fred joined in the work of preparing the beds with great zest.

'This reminds me of the times when my sister and I helped our parents in the garden. On Sunday Dad used to have a garden project going in the morning, while Mum cooked the lunch, then in the afternoon we'd be off for a drive in the car to somewhere in the country, go for a stroll, ending up in a tea room for a cream tea!' The work and chatter was only brought to an end when they were called for lunch.

୧୨

The bright rays of the rising sun streaming through a gap in the curtains woke Melissa early. Far too early! Her head ached terribly and her tongue felt like sandpaper. She had the most awful hangover from her triumphal drinking session. She staggered down into the kitchen and made herself a strong, sweet black coffee, then collapsed on the sofa in the lounge. Every sound went through her head like a nail being driven in by a large hammer! She was not happy, not happy at all. She had planned to visit Bidford Manor to do some snooping, for at the back of her mind there was a shred of doubt. Were things really going so well? Perhaps that wretched inventor fellow had some other trick up his sleeve. She didn't underestimate Erin, either. But in her present state she couldn't care less and certainly was in no condition for such a trip. A thrush flew down and perched on a branch just outside the lounge window. It peered at the prostrate form lying there, gave a cheerful warble, which made her wince, then flew away.

Sir Brian had redoubled his vigilance that morning, for this was something he had anticipated. However, there was no indication of that lady's presence whatsoever. He dispatched a scout, who returned with the news that she wasn't going anywhere for the moment. He thanked the thrush.

About three o'clock Melissa rolled off the sofa and found she could stand without the room trying to revolve round her. A wash in cold water cleared her mind but didn't improve her temper. Carefully she gathered together her seven packages of the necessary magical combinations and repacked them in the shoulder bag. She added some kindling and matches, also a torch. She could have lit the charcoal with a spell, but she needed all her powers concentrated on the spell, not frittered away on party tricks. She checked her broom, and even gave it a rub down with a duster, at the same time threatening it with all manner of punishments if it let her down tonight. She had decided to land in the old quarry and hide it there again. Once she had the Power she could summon it to her. All this work had made her hungry so she made up a snack and sat in her so-called study, dreaming of how different things would be tomorrow.

☙

At Bidford Manor, after a good lunch they all went into the sitting room to relax. The children embarked upon a game of cards while the adults chatted. A slight tension began to rise, for in seven hours' time it would be nine o'clock. Around two thirty Geoff arrived and they went upstairs to do some more work on their projects. Fred was impressed with their zeal, asking to see the results; but was told, in no uncertain terms, that he would have to wait until it was completed before he would be allowed even a quick peek! While they were upstairs the grown-ups met with Bill, Sir Brian and JJ to plan for the evening.

Just after tea the three builder's men arrived with Hugh. Though they were assured no snoopers were around, it was decided to wait until darkness before they entered the tunnel from the Obelisk end, and then to do so singly, not in a group. The building materials were already in place at the passage junction. Supper was at five thirty and just as they started, Erin arrived with Rosie. She had used her broomstick, which was now safely locked away — as a precaution — in the broom cupboard. Rosie communed with Binky and Cleo while they ate. Jill arrived with her dad just as they finished. Erin took them all into the sitting room for a few minutes' meditation and then they were ready. Geoff had Binky straining on his lead and Doreen was nursing a very contented Cleo. It was now dark, but the night was clear and the moon, in its first quarter, hung gleaming in the sky. Erin led the children quietly down to the Obelisk and they too moved up to the junction, positioning themselves in the passage some ten meters nearer the damaged wall. Doreen, Derek, Fred, Harry, and Geoff, with the animals, made their way to the summer house. The trapdoor to the passage was closed, but not locked. Building materials lying around gave the impression that work was about to begin the next day. The non-corporeal watchers were placed so: JJ by the old ornamental gardens, Bill by the summer house and Sir Brian in the grounds in front of the house. Inside, Ingrid and Reg had switched on various lights and during the evening would go round turning them on and off so that it would appear the family was at home. Now all they could do was wait.

At six o'clock Melissa checked all her materials again and changed into a very fetching rusty black long garment, embroidered with strange signs, and large black cloak fastened with a brooch carved from a human finger bone at her throat. She wore black shoes with buckles in the shape of skulls. Further fashionable additions were a necklace of human teeth and a tall black steeple hat also covered with magical signs. She had blue lipstick and her cheeks were rouged a delicate shade of green decaying flesh. This lady certainly meant business! Then she grabbed her long-suffering broomstick and hurtled out into the night. The fact that it was so clear annoyed her. She'd hoped it would be dark and cloudy. Nothing could be done about it for the moment, but soon she'd control the weather as well. She landed in the old quarry, sticking her broom under the bush she'd used before and made her way towards the manor grounds, taking her usual path. JJ spotted her, and as soon as she was out of sight, went to the quarry and removed the broomstick.

She sped across the lawns, duly observed by Sir Brian, over the stream and towards the laurel bush where she had hidden her equipment, observed by Bill. This brought her very close to the summer house, but so intent was she upon her task that she never gave it a glance. Staggering under the unwieldy tripod and brazier, to say nothing of the bowl and bag of charcoal, she made her way over to the trapdoor. She put down her ironware with exaggerated care and cautiously tried to lift it, letting out a gasp of relief when it opened easily. Gathering up her bits and pieces she went down the steps.

In the summer house there were sighs of relief and praise for the two animals who had remained obediently quiet in spite of the clashing of assorted ironware and the mutterings and mumblings of the carrier. As soon as he was sure she had really descended into the depths, Bill joined them with the news that JJ had appropriated her broomstick. 'She won't be able to make a quick getaway now,' he remarked. They waited a few minutes longer before coming out and standing quietly by the trapdoor. All was quiet below. The real waiting now began.

Stumbling down the steps in the dark wasn't quite what Melissa had bargained for. She had assumed the passage would be lit up — but it wasn't. She congratulated herself on bringing a torch and fished it out of her bag. It gave her enough light to reach the ruined wall and, once her set-up was working, would also provide enough for her purposes. Unpacking the shoulder bag, she arranged the seven packages in order on a pile of bricks, then set up the tripod and brazier facing directly down the tunnel and prepared it for lighting. No point in doing that yet, there was over an hour to go. But it would have to be lit in good time so that there was enough heat to consume the 'herbs and other items'. She felt very relaxed and the only thing that puzzled her was a faint draught of air coming up the passage from the right. She dismissed this as unimportant.

Now came the most nerve-wracking time for everyone: to wait and remain quiet. The builders were probably the most relaxed group. The grown-ups were tense, but for the children it was far worse. To sit cramped up in a dark, smelly passage, not daring to move — for more than an hour — would be nothing short of sheer torture!

However, this had been one reason why Erin had gathered them together before they left the house. She suggested each should think of some joyful occasion and try to relive it as vividly as possible. Even little Jill could do this. She'd already announced that she would think about when Sam and Sarah first visited the farm. And, to their surprise, the time went quicker than expected. At a quarter to nine Erin stood up and signalled them to do the same. They stretched, in an effort to rid themselves of their stiffness and formed a line in the order she had arranged. This was done in complete darkness by touch. They knew that as soon as light and sound began from up the passage they would start to move forward. Though what would happen next, no one could tell.

Melissa also found it unnerving. She tried sitting, standing, and swaying, but having to keep quiet was a severe strain. A feeling of unease began to possess her. It was rather like having somebody looking over her shoulder. She whipped round sharply several times, but nothing was there. She put it down to nerves and the after-effects of the hangover.

At a quarter to nine she started her preparations in earnest, placing the kindling and charcoal in the brazier and lighting it. There was a fair amount of smoke at first, which made her cough and splutter. Those down the passage also caught whiffs of it; luckily it wasn't enough to cause coughing and it alerted them to the fact that Melissa had commenced her task. Once the charcoal was glowing nicely she stood before the bowl and opened the first packet. At precisely nine o'clock she began to recite the opening section of the wakening rune. On reaching the first pause she cast the contents of her hand into the now glowing bowl. There was a hiss and flicker of flame as it was consumed. From the depths of the tunnel there came a slight tremor and a sound like a deep sigh. The tremor turned to a rumbling vibration that filled the passage with a strange rhythmical throbbing.

Those by the summer house heard and felt it. Binky's ears pricked up, and he tensed, and Geoff prepared to release him. Cleo lifted her head and Doreen felt her relaxed body begin to stiffen. Below, the children, following Erin, began to move slowly up the passage towards the glow. The builders also stood prepared and ready.

Melissa continued chanting the second part of the rune; again she flung the contents into the bowl. There was a blinding red flash of fire and a strong acrid smell flowed down the tunnel. The throbbing ceased for a moment, then came the sound of something of unimaginable size stirring, uncurling, stretching. The previous sound recommenced, but louder and more insistent. The tunnel and passages echoed with it.

Melissa could now sense the impact of the energy that streamed out of the tunnel towards her; it was overpowering. She began to feel less confident. She'd only spoken two sections; there were five more and even now she could scarcely stand the force of the energy that was bombarding her. For those down the passage it had a numbing effect; but Erin, moving in front, acted as a shield protecting them from its full force.

Melissa's voice was far more uncertain when she started the next section and flung the contents of the third packet into the bowl. This time there was a green flash and a thunderclap of sound that flung her back against the passage wall, knocking her hat off. From the far end of the tunnel came the noise of splintering wood and a wave of fetid air billowed up it, making her gag. Peering into the darkness she could make out two tiny pin-points of light moving slowly to and fro — the eyes in the head of 'it'? Something dragged itself up and then descended with a thud on the floor of the tunnel. In spite of her gathering fear, Melissa felt a surge of triumph. It was moving, coming in response to her summons. Hastily she began the fourth section, ending it with the same action as before. There was another vivid flash and the floor rocked beneath her feet. The points of light grew brighter and the ponderous forward movements continued, accompanied by a low rumbling tone: the mutterings of something disturbed, something coming unwillingly, being forced to obey a call it could not ignore or refuse. She chanted the fifth section as it crept nearer and nearer. There were other noises too; it was being followed by other 'things'. Waves of energy swept over her and something even greater, darker and more dreadful was looming behind all this psychic activity. As she pronounced the sixth section it dawned on her with horror that what she had thought was the Primordial Power was merely an outer form. These unimaginable energies now stirring were from the real source. They filled her mind and she realised it was taking her over. It was going to use her. Seized by panic she frantically tried to get away, to escape. But she was held, held in a vice-like grip over which she had no control. Fascinated, she listened as her almost unrecognisable voice recited the last lines and her reluctant hand flung the powder into the basin. The next minute she was picked up with terrible force and hurled against the side of the passage. The last thing she heard before she lost consciousness was laughter, terrible inhuman laughter.

Those above ground could only guess at what was going on beneath their feet. But they realised there was some rhythm involved as the clamour below grew in intensity. Sir Brian counted, and with seven the ground shook so violently that they were almost knocked off their feet. Geoff felt Binky struggling to escape, so swiftly bent down and unclipped his lead. At the same moment Cleo leapt from Doreen's arms and the two of them vanished down the steps. Fred made as if to follow, but Bill restrained him with,

'No! Not yet, wait. Give Erin a chance!'

Hugh and his workmen, somewhat shaken by the cacophony, gripped their spades more firmly and prepared to do battle—if necessary. But, like Bill, Hugh ordered them to wait.

Erin had led her group nearer and nearer the strange sounds. They could hear Melissa's voice clearly now. After each pause it became more strained and unreal. The seventh time it sounded wild and hysterical, with no resemblance to a human voice.

'It's taken her over!' murmured Erin. There followed the crash of the knocked over tripod and a thud as she hit the wall, followed by the terrible crescendo of laughter.

'Now!' she commanded and led them forwards to the

tunnel junction. A strange reddish glow emanated from its mouth, growing stronger by the moment. They saw the overturned tripod and bowl and the huddled form of Melissa against the wall, her hat lying crushed beside her. But they had no time to stand and stare.

'Into your positions, quickly!' whispered Erin, 'Remember to look straight ahead and above all keep going, don't stop!'

Suddenly there was an unexpected diversion. Two familiar four-legged forms came running down from the entrance. Without any hesitation they rushed into the tunnel, barking and yowling at full volume.

The Power, having disposed of the creature that had woken it, became vaguely aware that other, similar creatures were now gathering. It sensed they would try to stop it from gaining its freedom and prepared to deal with them as it had the other. Just as it was about to unleash an energy field to strike them down, two small, and very noisy entities rushed into the tunnel. It could not fathom what kind of beings these were, and paused, trying to identify them. The racket they made was very unsettling, making it difficult to think clearly. Doubt and uncertainty began to fill its long dormant mind.

'Now!' At Erin's command they began. Michelle, standing as straight as she could, looked very thin and frail, but when she began to recite the rune her voice was strong and clear, echoing down the tunnel. At the same time the others commenced their movements and the whole complex pattern came to life. They felt safe within its form. It protected them and sent waves of calming energy down the tunnel. The final line rang out and they stood silent. Within the tunnel the animals had ceased their clamour and become quiet. Deep from the depths came a long sigh — a ponderous slithering noise, which gradually grew fainter, then silence.

Even as it struggled with the baffling problem of these noisy beings, the Power became aware of a new sound: a voice, chanting like the last one. But this was different, it was young and fresh, soothing, telling of wondrous dreams and visions of the world as it was before it descended into matter. A comforting drowsiness engulfed it. The desire to sleep and live with these dreams became strong. A great sigh broke forth and it slowly dragged itself back to the place where it had slept until so rudely disturbed. Sleep returned quickly, as did the silence.

The little group remained standing quietly until Binky and Cleo came trotting back out of the darkness, both looking very pleased with themselves. Soon they were being hugged and praised by the children.

A groan behind them drew their attention to Melissa. Swiftly Erin knelt beside her, and taking a small phial of liquid from her pocket, poured the contents down her throat, at the same time she muttered a restorative rune over her. The bedraggled witch opened her eyes and stared in astonishment at Erin.

'You, you?' her head turned towards the tunnel, 'Is it?' A dreadful look of fear crossed her face.

'No, it's at rest again,' she was told. A look of relief came over her features and she passed out. At that moment the lights were switched on from above. Then they heard voices and the grown-ups came tumbling down the steps. Erin put her finger to her lips, as quietness was still essential. Hugh and his men appeared and began the task of quickly bricking up the tunnel entrance once more, while they made their way back to the house, Doreen and Erin supporting Melissa. The work was soon completed and the builders also returned to the manor.

As soon as the inert form of her mother was carried through the kitchen and placed on the sitting room sofa, Ingrid took control.

'I think she'll be all right,' said Erin. 'She's had a colossal shock and been hurled against the passage wall, which knocked her out, to say nothing of her mental state. Give her rescue remedy at regular intervals and some soothing restorative. She should be fine in a couple of days. Then I'll come and have a chat with her.'

Ingrid nodded. 'Tomorrow I move into my new flat. It has two bedrooms; Michelle is staying here until after Easter, so Mother can come with me. She'll have plenty of peace and quiet and time to recover.'

In the kitchen everybody was gathered round the table drinking tea, cocoa or coffee. Not all at once, but according to preference. Conversation was muted and when Erin returned all looked expectantly at her.

'I thank all of you for your assistance in this business,' she began. 'It was a very close thing and if it had not been for these two scamps!'—indicating Binky and Cleo—'the outcome might have been very different. Melissa was incredibly lucky that the Power was still waking. If it had been fully conscious it could have wiped her mind out and would have probably killed her. Now it slumbers its ancient sleep again. The danger is passed.'

Hugh and his workmen now departed. Once they had gone, Bill, Sir Brian and JJ joined them.

'Now I can dismantle all my protective devices!' said their inventor.

'Well, you'd better do it soon, or you might receive another face full of porridge!' said Bill with a grin. Everybody laughed, including the victim. Erin gathered up Rosie, who had remained with Reg and Ingrid, rescued her broom from the cupboard, congratulated the children again and left. Fred looked at his watch.

'Ahem, it's past ten o'clock!' he said, 'I must be going; Geoff, I'll drop you off.' He looked at the children. 'I shall not be surprised if you are a little late for school in the morning. Come when you feel ready!'

He grinned and was gone, taking Reg with him. Harry

took a very sleepy little girl back to the farm, and the remaining children were soon in bed and swiftly fell asleep. The grown-ups soon followed their example.

Chapter XXX

In spite of their teacher's suggestion, the children woke at the usual time and were soon up, dressed, and hurtling downstairs for breakfast. After all, this was the week before the Open Day and there was so much to do. Not to go, unless one was really sick, would be letting the class and teacher down. It could mean the postponement of their last excursion. The canal one, arranged with Will Bennett. No! They just had to be there!

Melissa slept erratically that night, troubled by menacing dreams, something coming towards her, vague, indistinct, but dreadful in its malevolent energy and just as it was about to overwhelm her she would wake. Someone would then gently mop her sweating brow and give her a soothing drink. She would fall asleep, but the dream would return, though gradually it grew less intense. When morning came and she awoke in daylight she became aware of a massive headache and her back felt sore and ached from where she had been flung against the brickwork.

'How do you feel now?' said a familiar voice, and there was her daughter bending over her.

The answer was a groan and the one word, 'Awful!'

'I'm not surprised,' Ingrid commented, adding. 'Later today we'll be moving to the house in Bidcote where I'm going to be housekeeper. There's a two-bedroom flat attached and I'll be able to look after you until you feel fit enough to return to your own home. It will be quiet and you'll have plenty of time to think matters over.'

Melissa had a twinge of guilt. Yes, there was a great deal she would have to think over.

'Do you feel like a bite to eat? I can cook up some broth if you like,' said her daughter. Suddenly she felt very weak and tired and could only nod. Left alone she listened to the noises of the house waking to a Monday morning. Children's voices, the thunder of five pairs of feet on the stairs. A dog's bark. Grown-ups in conversation.

She must have dozed off, for a gentle pressure on the arm woke her. 'Here you are, Granny, your broth, shall I feed you?' Opening her eyes she met the worried gaze of her granddaughter. 'How do you feel?' she asked.

Melissa couldn't speak. After all she had done, or would have done to this child. Yet here she was, eyes full of gentle concern, no anger, no 'serves you right' attitude, only forgiveness and compassion. Melissa burst into tears; all she could say was, 'I'm sorry, so sorry!' and groped for her granddaughter's hand. Michelle took it and squeezed it softly, saying, 'Don't cry, Gran, everything's going to be all right,' adding, 'I must go now, it's time for school. But I'll come and see you tomorrow at the flat. I expect you'll feel much better by then.' She kissed her on the brow and ran lightly from the room, pausing at the door to blow her a kiss.

There followed the clatter and noise of departure; now silence descended. There were still sounds, but they could hardly be classed as noise. Ingrid returned to collect the bowl. She sat down on the couch and said, 'Derek will drive us round to the village after lunch. I'm finishing off my packing now; you just lie here and relax, no one will disturb you. I'll leave the door ajar, and if you want me, just ring this bell.'

In that she was wrong, for hardly had she left the room

when there was a patter of feet and a cold nose was thrust into her hand. There was Binky, forepaws on the couch, poking at her and wagging his tail with vigour. She began to stroke him. Then came a 'purr!' and Cleo leapt on to the couch and settled down contentedly beside her. When Ingrid looked in later her mother was asleep, one hand resting on Binky, who was curled up by the couch, the other on Cleo, who was stretched out luxuriously next to her.

Mr Atkinson was not surprised to see the quintet arrive. They had been given an option and had made their choice. He gave each an extra warm handshake and could see they had appreciated his support yesterday. The morning was a busy one, as the week's programme had to be worked out to allow space for rehearsals and the setting up of the exhibition, to say nothing of completing the main lesson work.

'I've spoken with Mr Bennett,' he told the class, 'and asked if we could visit on Thursday rather than Friday. We should really be here then. He's quite happy about it. So the coach is booked.' Cheers, then it was down to work.

At eleven Ingrid took her mother a cup of tea and sat with her for a while. They did not talk much, but just before she left, Ingrid said, 'Erin will be coming to see you tomorrow, Mother.' Melissa looked very uncomfortable, remembering all the things she had done to that good lady. 'Don't you fret about it,' said her daughter, guessing what was on her mind. 'Erin wants to help you, not tick you off. Though you deserve it!' she added with a grin. 'Now just rest and relax; Doreen and Derek would like us to have lunch with them and after he'll drive us over.' Seeing a look of reluctance she added, 'You've got to start meeting people again sometime and I can't think of any folk better for you to begin with.' Melissa nodded; Ingrid was right, she usually was.

It turned out to be a very pleasant meal. She was treated like a convalescent and not one word of recrimination was said. Afterwards Derek loaded Ingrid's belongings into the car and took them to the flat. Then he said to Melissa, 'Look, I'm sure you'll want some of your own stuff, so as soon as you feel up to it, let me know and I'll drive you over to collect whatever you need.' She thanked him and found the world was becoming a better place than she had ever realised it could be!

The children who arrived home that afternoon were remarkably spry, but as soon as they sat down to snack began to yawn and when spoken to would reply, 'What? Sorry! What did you say? (yawn).' 'I think,' said Doreen, 'you all better go up to your rooms and have a little snooze; we don't want your heads pitching into your dinner tonight.' There were some half-hearted protests, but secretly they were glad, and within five minutes of 'just lying down for a second or two', they were asleep.

Outside, the builders were finishing off the tunnel wall and generally tidying up. They would wait a few days — on Erin's advice — before continuing more restoration work underground, though it would now be concentrated on the western side of the house.

Bill, Sir Brian and JJ deactivated the various devices round the property, and as predicted, Sir Brian was only hit once by a porridge missile, though he was yapped at twice. On the whole it was a successful operation. The one problem was what to do with Melissa's broomstick? They decided it was best to retain it for the moment and consult with Erin after she had talked with Melissa. It could tempt her into her old ways if placed in her hands too soon.

The children were awakened by the supper gong and came bounding down the stairs much refreshed. Though naturally they had to say, 'Why didn't you wake us earlier?' The answer was simple. 'Because you needed a good rest after all you've been up to!' Derek was very cheerful at the table. Now that business was over he could get down to some serious work round the estate, catch up on those articles, and maybe start to prepare the amendments for the third edition of his book. After supper he wandered back to his study before joining the others in the sitting room. 'I'll just see if there's any fresh e-mail,' he told them as they left the table.

It was pleasant to relax by the fire and they were all beginning to feel drowsy again when the door burst open and Derek stood there, hair ruffled and an expression usually described as 'looking like a dying duck in a thunderstorm' on his face. In his hands he clutched a printout.

'Whatever's the matter?' asked Doreen, 'You look as if there's an impending disaster about to descend upon us.'

'There is, there is!' he replied, dramatically, thrusting the paper at her. 'Read that!'

Doreen took it and read: 'Confirming arrival Thursday, meet me at station eight four p.m. Daisy.'

'I'd clean forgotten about her visit!' groaned Derek. The children stared at each other in horror; so had they! Only Doreen seemed unperturbed. 'I'll prepare the guest's room tomorrow,' she said. Then, looking at their appalled faces, added, 'Goodness me, I don't know why you all think she's the herald of doom and destroyer of joy all rolled into one. Wait and see.'

'But Mum, the picture,' said Sam, 'I mean, look at it, just look at it. How could... ...!' He became lost for words. 'I have looked at it!' said his mother placidly. There was a twinkle in her eye, but she would say no more.

Derek regarded her suspiciously. 'It's all very well for you,' he moaned, 'she's not your sister. But I'm supposed to have an obligation to entertain her on these — thank goodness — rare occasions when she visits the 'Old Country'. I was only nine when she went to Bible College and don't remember much about her, because as a teenager she had her own friends and I was just a nuisance of a kid brother. But I do remember being scared stiff of her at times and I still feel uncomfortable at the thought of her being around!' He looked gloomier than ever and the children felt really sorry for him. However, they were also worrying about what her impact would be on them. If she were arriving late on Thursday and may be even later, knowing the train services, they would probably be in bed before she descended, 'Like a wolf on the fold!' as Sarah, who had a poetic turn of mind on such occasions, put it.

'If you feel like that, would you like me to go and pick her up at the station?' offered Doreen. Derek brightened up. 'Would you? Would you really?' he said. 'You don't mind?' 'No,' she replied. 'Perhaps I could explain a few things to her which might help ease her stay.' 'Great!' he replied, 'Now let's forget about her for the next few days.'

However, that was easier said than done. They found themselves wondering, when they did something boisterous, like sliding down the banisters, or yelling to each other from their rooms, 'What would Aunt Daisy say about that?' The next two days were spent in a great deal of speculation; the only person who did not seem duly perturbed was Doreen, who was, according to Sam, far too cheerful in the face of this disaster that was about to strike them!

On Tuesday Erin visited Melissa at the flat. They had a long conversation in her room. Afterwards the three of them had tea together and Ingrid noticed that her mother was in better spirits. 'We talked a few matters over and I'll pop in again tomorrow afternoon,' said Erin; Melissa nodded in agreement. After she had left, the only comment to her daughter was, 'I'm glad that's over. I feel much easier now.'

Michelle also visited her that day, after school.

On Wednesday Derek took her over to 'Goulhaven' to pick up some clothes and small items. 'Do you mind waiting in the car?' she asked him. 'The place is in such a mess I'm ashamed to invite you in!' 'Not at all,' he replied and settled back with the paper. Hardly had he read the headlines when she came dashing out, a look of wonder on her face. 'Come and see,' she cried, 'I don't believe it, some good fairy must have been about!' Curious, Derek followed her. The place was spotlessly tidy, so was the garden. 'Erin!' she announced. 'I know it was Erin. I mentioned something about the place yesterday and she told me not to worry. Now I see what she meant. She's coming over this afternoon, so I'll be able to thank her!' It didn't take long for her to pack what she needed, and they were back in Bidcote well before lunch.

That evening the children were all excited over the class excursion and had little thought for the visitor's arrival late tomorrow. But Derek had! He became gloomier and gloomier, and when Doreen said, 'Darling, you haven't seen her for eleven years and she may have changed! Stop worrying and remember you are no longer a little boy of nine. You are a much respected scientific author, so for heaven's sake behave like one!' He was about to reply, 'It's all very well for you!' when he caught the look in her eye and decided to remain quiet.

THE END OF PART ONE

THE PLIGHT OF THE PLAQUE MAKER

Being the second part of book four

In The
Adventures of Sam And Sarah
And
Their Friends

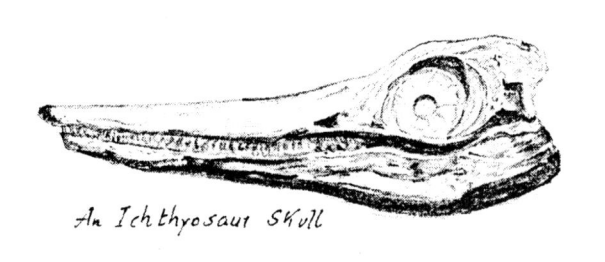

EXPLANATION

For reasons of length —and the endurance of the readers— I decided it would be best to divide this book into two parts. We hear the consequences of the arrival of the dreaded Aunt Daisy and follow the adventures of the children during their holiday on the Dorset Coast and the consequences of a strange find in a rock pool. The class camp and two *very* important sets of birthdays are also celebrated. Now read on!

The Author

CHAPTER ONE

There was no doubt about it! Thursday was going to be a very interesting day for the Court family in several different ways. Breakfast was hectic as usual with last minute preparations for the class outing to the old canal site. Sam couldn't find his backpack and Sarah had mislaid her hardback notebook. Panic was about to set in when Michelle appeared in the kitchen carrying the missing items, casually remarking:

'Are these what you are looking for?' Sighs of relief and hurried thanks, 'Where did you find them?' and 'Thanks Michelle!' Jill and Geoff's arrival added to the excitement and they were only just in time for the bus. When they reached school, the coach hired to transport them to Canal Lock House was already waiting, and after the usual briefing by their teacher the class took their places in the vehicle and soon were on the road to Curry Hatch.

It was a typical spring day — unsettled: sunshine one minute, dull the next, enlivened by a sharp shower — over in a few minutes — accompanied by a biting cold wind which would spring up and die away the next moment. Luckily the class was well prepared for all contingencies, including boots and rain gear. The driver was rather dubious about taking the coach over the small bridge, also eyeing the muddy narrow track beyond. So Mr Atkinson suggested they walk the remaining half a mile or so and the coach could return to and wait at Curry Hatch. When they were ready to leave he would phone the driver, for there was a phone in the coach. He drove off with obvious relief and now the children had a chance to try out their boots in the very interesting puddles that spread invitingly over much of the track.

They made it to the gates of Canal Lock House with no major mishaps, apart from Margaret, who misjudged the edge of the track and plunged one boot into a well-filled ditch, getting it full of water. Michelle came to her aid and acted as a holding-post while she emptied out her boot and wrung out the saturated sock. Her foot was damp but not soaking — as she put it. Will Bennett was waiting for them and in a few minutes the class was crowded into the kitchen, boots lined up neatly outside the back door and Margaret's sock being dried on the stove while Joyce produced a pair of hers to take it and its companion's place. In the absence of Judy and Nicky, who were at school, Will took them over to the lodge, ending up in the lock keeper's office where he explained what his duties would have been and showed them the engineer's proposed plans for that stretch of canal. During this explanation the weather had put on a spectacular heavy shower, so it was just as well they were inside. However, now the sun came out so he suggested that they walk the shorter northern stretch and — if the rain held off — the southern section after snack time. The quintet was happy with this arrangement, as the former was the section they had not explored on their previous visit.

Boots were hauled on, rainwear grabbed and the class set off. The old towpath was *very* wet and muddy as they squelched along it. Ahead of them loomed the limestone ridge, which had been the undoing of this ambitious venture. After about a mile and a half, the path and shallow ditch, which represented the initial canal excavations, stopped some hundred yards or so from the rising ground. As they stood gazing at the ridge the sun went behind a cloud and the scene took on a melancholy aspect. The children could imagine the despair and frustration of those honest, but simple-minded merchants of Tadbridge who had been hoodwinked by their glib engineer.

Will agreed, but added that in the early days of the Industrial Revolution there were many such schemes that came to naught. Noticing another ominous cloud coming up, he hurried them back to the lodge kitchen for snack. Only just in time! They managed to fit round the kitchen table, and while biscuits were munched and warm juice drunk, he told them more about the canal and how he had come to live here with his family.

Luckily, the shower eased off again so they were able to explore the lower section. Though the quintet had already been there, it was good to visit it again, as they picked up some new information for their notes. Then it was back to the lodge for lunch, during which Will had a word with Mr Atkinson, the outcome being an invitation for him and his family to attend the school's Open Day. The quintet was delighted; this meant they would be able to show Judy and Nicky round. Sarah then remembered the envelope her mother had given her for Joyce and fished it — somewhat crumpled — out of her backpack.

'It's an invitation for you to come over one Saturday after Easter,' she explained. 'Mum says, if you like, Nicky and Judy can stay for the weekend and we'll bring them back on Sunday.'

Will and Joyce grinned at them. 'Ever since you five have been here they've talked of nothing else but your visit and when are they going to see you again? It was only with great difficulty we persuaded them to go to school this morning. We explained it wasn't a visit, but a school trip you were on. We've had such here before, so they knew they must not interfere. But we are going to have to give a minute by minute account of what you said and did while you were with us!'

There was some more diving into packs and bags as the five produced the drawings they had made for the children. These, they were assured, would 'make the children's day' when they returned. After lunch, there was a discussion and note-taking session. Then Mr Atkinson looked at his watch and asked if he could phone for the coach. This was done, and the class gathered up their belongings and with many 'thank you's' prepared to leave. Margaret returned the borrowed socks in exchange for her own and the party set off at a brisk walk to the now waiting coach on the other side of the bridge and they were back at school within three quarters of an hour of going home time. This was spent writing up notes and preparing neat copies of the sketches they had made.

'Tomorrow it's all hands to setting up the displays and a final rehearsal,' they were told. 'Don't forget to bring any material you still have at home. If you don't, it won't be on display.'

When the bell went and the children started to leave, Mr Atkinson grinned at Sam, Sarah and Michelle as he shook their hands. 'I shall be very interested to hear all about Aunt Daisy tomorrow!' Three faces fell; they'd forgotten all about her!

'We may not see her,' said Sarah hopefully. 'We'll most likely be in bed before she arrives and Mum thinks she'll probably want to lie in on Friday to make up for the jet lag, or whatever it's called. So we won't see her until late afternoon!' She sounded distinctly relieved. Then added, 'But you'll meet her, because she'll be coming to the Open Day *and* she's a teacher too!' This was said with a certain amount of satisfaction.

If Aunt Daisy was *that awful* why shouldn't they share her

with their teacher? He caught the glint in her eye and said, 'You little horrors, trying to involve me, are you! If you're not careful I'll paint a picture so awful that she'll probably give you extra lessons *all day* while she stays at the manor.' This said with a twinkle in his eye. Sam interrupted: 'It doesn't really matter does it? We've *got to* put up with her and you'll *have to* meet her. So we are all in the same boat.' (I bet it's called the 'Titanic', he added under his breath.) They left, for Jill still needed to be collected from afternoon care. As the bus rattled its way towards their stop the feeling of gloom descended ever deeper.

Stephen and Jane had been very sympathetic, but obviously greatly relieved they did not have the dreaded aunt staying in their house. Even Geoff was aware of their gloom, for as he picked up his bike he said, 'Look, if you want to get away from you-know-who you can always come to my house. I know Mum won't mind!' They thanked him, but how to escape was a problem they would first have to solve. Jill was also concerned; the concept of an 'un-nice' aunt was a hard one for her to grasp. All her aunts were 'nice'. She suggested putting this one in the dustbin for 'the men to take away' and she'd lend them one of hers so they would still have 'an aunt' for Easter. When her father came to collect her she was still explaining her idea and no doubt he heard all about it on the way home.

Derek had shut himself away in his study and Doreen was in what could be described as a preoccupied state. When the children asked her a question she did not seem to hear it at first and then would jerk herself back to the present and ask them what they had just said. After three attempts to attract her attention they gave up. Then suddenly she addressed them as if being aware of their presence for the first time: 'Tonight we'll have supper in the kitchen; your father is busy on some project and does not want to be disturbed, so I'll take his in on a tray. As you know, Aunt

Daisy's train is due in at eight four and I'm going to pick her up. We'll eat at six thirty and I'll leave around seven twenty. I'd like you three to clear up and then get yourselves ready for bed *and* be in bed by eight sharp. Whether your aunt will want to see you I don't know. It all depends on the train being on time and how she feels after such a long flight and train ride. I shall also try to persuade her to remain in bed until you lot have hurtled off to school in the morning. Remember, when you get up, to be *quiet,* so don't try holding conversations through closed doors, or incite Binky and Cleo to run riot! Close doors softly and come down the stairs as if they are stairs and not a cliff to be leapt down.'

She paused, having run out of 'don'ts' and breath.

Sarah spoke up for them: 'Of course we won't, Mum, we'll be as quiet as mice. She won't even know we exist!'

The truth of the matter was, the last thing they wanted was to confront this terrible person early in the morning. That would completely spoil their day! Doreen looked doubtful, knowing the memory span of her two was alarmingly short on such points as 'How to behave when we have guests', but she said no more. They galloped upstairs to do their final bits and pieces of preparation to take with them tomorrow, and having finished, talked about the inevitable.

'I wonder what Bill and Sir Brian will make of her?' mused Sam. He brightened up. 'Maybe we could ask Sir Brian to invent an 'awful aunt' disposal machine?'

'I think she might dispose of him instead,' said Sarah, 'Remember how Erin dealt with him at Christmas? He was like some little child caught doing something naughty. I'm sure Aunt Daisy would only have to look at him like she looked at the poor camera in that photo and he'd run for his life, well, the life he had, I suppose.'

'But what about Bill?' said Michelle, 'I'm sure he won't be so intimidated.'

'No, indeed I won't,' said a voice at her elbow, and there stood Bill, smiling at them in an amused manner.

'It's all very well for you,' began Sam in an aggrieved tone.

'Tut, tut, Sam, the good lady hasn't even arrived and you judge her upon the evidence of a photo taken over twelve years ago!' he admonished. 'Far better to wait and see *what* she is like before putting one of Cleo's offerings, such as a dead mouse, in her bed.' Sam blushed, that's exactly what he had been thinking of!

'No,' continued Bill, 'my advice to you is wait and see, then act accordingly.'

'But if she is really dreadful and interferes with *everything*, could you, would you, do something?' asked Sarah.

'If necessary yes–I could. As you know, house guardians have ways and means for getting rid of unwanted owners and anyone who makes trouble for the true occupants.'

His reassurance on this point satisfied them, and as they were then called to supper, Bill left them, no doubt to report to Sir Brian on their chat.

Eating in the kitchen without their father was an unusual experience anyway and the animals also found it disturbing. Binky made several attempts to go to the study every time the door was opened and only ceased when he was threatened with banishment to the back kitchen. They ate in an absent-minded fashion and it's doubtful whether any of them could have told you what they ate for supper! Doreen was constantly looking at her watch and at last said brightly (much too brightly, Sam thought), 'Well dears, I must be off. Be good children and clear up nicely and leave the kitchen tidy. When you've done that it's off to bed. *On no account disturb your father!* Just call out 'good night' *once*, as you go upstairs. Oh, and shut the animals in the back kitchen. I'll let them out when we return.' With that she took the car keys from the hook on the dresser, picked up her handbag and was gone.

The children tidied up *very* carefully, for they did not want their mother getting into trouble for having an untidy kitchen. There was a slight hitch before going upstairs, as Binky and Cleo resented being put to bed early and led them a merry dance round the kitchen before they managed to herd them through the door into the back one. They called 'good night!' to Derek, receiving a muffled 'G'night,' from the other side of the door in reply and then pounded (for the last time for goodness knows how long?) up the stairs to their rooms and prepared for bed. A last minute meeting was held in Sam's room regarding procedure next morning. They *must not* let Mum and Dad down, whatever happens. As for the dread aunt, they would meet her soon enough!

Meanwhile, Doreen had arrived in good time at Tadbridge Station, only to find, when she walked on to the platform, a notice leaning against the ticket collector's booth. "Owing to unavoidable circumstances the eight four express from London is running three quarters of an hour behind schedule. Emergency track repairs south of Frome will cause a further delay of twenty minutes. Estimated time of arrival, nine nine." Doreen was more concerned for the unfortunate traveller rather than her enforced wait. Also it would mean the children would definitely be asleep when they returned. That was a relief. She took her mobile phone from her bag and called Derek to tell him of the delay. He sounded greatly relieved. 'I'll probably be in bed by the time you come back,' he remarked, 'I feel *very* tired.' Doreen made no comment, but wished him good night and rang off. She made her way to the snack bar, a cup of coffee, perhaps? It was closed. The only alternatives were to sit in the dismal waiting room on a hard wooden bench or walk up and down the draughty platform. An hour to wait, was it worth going into the town to see if a cafe was open? Then she remembered the car's parking ticket would need renewing, as she'd bought one for half an hour. At least she could do that. So she did and was relieved to find that there was a trailer in the bus terminus area selling tea, coffee and snacks. At least that helped pass some time, and feeling warmer inside and more cheerful, she made her way back to the station. The notice had been changed; it now read: "The London Express is now due at eight fifty". The station clock informed her that this was in six hours, as it had stopped some years previously. Her watch was more cooperative and indicated a wait of fifteen minutes. She settled down on the cold bench. Then three mournful looking passengers materialised out of the waiting room and stood there hemmed in by their luggage. A porter also appeared. The signal turned to green and sixteen minutes later the diesel express lumbered alongside the platform. Several people got out. Doreen stood up and scanned the arrivals. Ah, there was Aunt Daisy just emerging from a coach a little way down the platform. She had a large suitcase on wheels and a shoulder bag. Doreen made her way towards her. Daisy, seeing her coming, waved and soon they were embracing. But who *is* this tall, cheerful, well-dressed lady in her early forties? Where is the formidable tweed and spectacled, 'hair pulled back in a bun' grim enlightener of the heathen? Why are the two of them giggling and laughing—is it at some private joke? Why does her patting of the shoulder bag cause yet more mirth? They leave the station and are soon driving back towards Bidford Manor, still laughing. What *is* the joke? Wait and see!

CHAPTER TWO

Doreen drove home the 'long way' so they would have time to chat and straighten out a few matters. Aunt Daisy was highly amused to hear that the children, having seen the photograph of her dressed for the part of an elderly spinster in a local amateur theatre production, had jumped to the conclusion *this* was how she looked. Equally amusing was the fact that her brother seemed to have a similar idea about her personality.

'I must admit I was pretty horrible to him at times, but then, when I was sixteen, he was eight and a real little brat! His main memories of me would be from that time. When he was a teenager I was already living away from home, first at college and then working in an orphanage. We didn't have many holidays and so I was rarely at home.

The time you and I met — just before you were married — was my longest for years; that was because I was off to Africa. But surely the children saw the other photos of me. I remember them being in the album.' 'Yes,' replied Doreen, 'there are, but your dear brother was too lazy to label them and the children were so shocked by *that* picture they hardly gave the others a glance. But I'm glad you agree to my little bit of fun. Things are working out well for it. Derek will be in bed when we return and the children will be up early and away to school. I've warned them to be quiet. You can probably do with a lie-in after your trip. Then you can dress up, give Derek a scare and be ready for the children when they return in the afternoon from school! We'll see how it goes, then decide how long to keep up the deception. It would be rather fun to go to the school's Open Day like it, if you feel you could carry it off. Maybe the revelation could follow?'

'It's a great idea!' chuckled Daisy. 'I always enjoyed dressing up and acting. I can practise getting in character tomorrow morning, on my dear brother.' The conspirators laughed heartily, for by now they were turning into the familiar lane leading to Bidford Manor.

The car's return did not pass unnoticed. Bill and Sir Brian had decided to observe the dread aunt's arrival. They were standing in the shadow of the porch, not that this was necessary, as both were invisible. Doreen and another lady got out, taking the luggage from the boot. Bill stared at the stranger. She did not at all fit the description the children had given. He sensed this person was gentle, kind and fun loving. Then he heard Doreen say, 'I can't wait to see you disguised as the 'awful aunt' I'm sure you'll be superb in the part!' and they both laughed as they went indoors.

'So that was it,' thought Bill, 'a trick!' He chuckled to himself. No, he wouldn't spoil the fun. He turned to tell Sir Brian so, only to discover that the noble warrior was staring at the car, eyes popping from his head. He clutched Bill by the arm. 'Look, look! Whatever is it?' Bill looked—from the boot a strange shape seemed to be materializing: a human-like figure with very long arms and legs and a long narrow-shaped head. Its features were African and it wore a shirt and trousers that, to put it mildly, were *vividly colourful*. 'Wha, what is it?' stuttered Sir Brian. 'I don't know,' replied Bill, 'but I imagine it came with her and is some kind of protective spirit from the African land where she lives. Let's go and ask.' His companion hesitated. 'Er, do you think that is wise? It may be fierce and not understand our peaceful intentions. I don't like the look of that spear!' Indeed, the creature held a broad-bladed assegai and was looking round nervously.

Bill 'visibilised' himself and stepped forward both hands held up, palms outwards, to show he carried no weapons. 'We welcome you to Bidford Manor!' he said. There was a tense silence for a moment while it scrutinised them. That is, as much of Sir Brian as was visible from behind Bill. Then the spear was lowered and a broad smile spread across its face. 'Thank you, my brothers,' it replied in a deep, melodious voice.

'I am the house guardian for this property and all those in it. Your lady shall also be protected whilst under our roof,' announced Bill. 'And this is a nobleman of great learning and wisdom who also resides in this place.'

'Ah, a Witch-Doctor-Chieftain,' exclaimed the other.

There was a spluttering noise from Sir Brian. 'Witch what?' he muttered. 'Never been called a witch before, odd place this fellow's country of origin must be! I...'

Bill cut him short. 'Excuse my ignorance, my honoured friend, but may I enquire what your lineage is and where you come from?' He bowed and Sir Brian also appeared to do the same behind him. Actually, he ducked, not wishing to be exposed to that nasty looking assegai.

'I come from Southern Africa, from the tribe "Tokoloshi". We, too, are house guardians and look after those who dwell in them. Usually we sleep under their beds, which the owners place up on bricks so there is room for us. We also undertake to protect those whom our people regard as great and good, such as the madam I have the honour of serving — I should go to her now.'

Bill realised this was the Tokolosh's way of asking for permission to enter his domain. 'Most certainly!' he replied. 'All that lies under my protection is yours as well. Perhaps tomorrow, when you are rested, we can meet and learn more about your far distant country?'

'Why yes, indeed,' replied the other, 'and I too wish to hear more about this land, which is the birthplace of my madam.' With that it drifted through the door.

'Do you think?' began Sir Brian, but Bill smiled. 'I know a loyal spirit when I see one. Come and join us for that chat, you may learn something!' and Bill also went through the door. Sir Brian stood spluttering on the porch for a moment, shrugged his shoulders and followed.

Meanwhile, Doreen and Daisy were seated in the kitchen over a good pot of strong tea! She sighed contentedly, 'Ah, a good old English cuppa. I think that's the one thing I miss. No matter how I try to teach our helpers to make it properly, they never seem to get the hang of it.' Here she was interrupted by a series of bumps and thumps on the back kitchen door. Binky and Cleo, hearing voices and scenting biscuits, were demanding to be let in. 'You'd better meet them now, or there'll be no peace,' Doreen told her and opened the door. The two animals made straight for the visitor and soon were being duly appreciated and treated to pieces of biscuit. Then they settled down in front of the stove.

Daisy continued in a more serious vein. 'Did you put my bed up on bricks?' 'Yes,' replied Doreen, 'That also helped your "eccentric spinster" image, convincing the children you are very odd indeed.'

'Well, it has a practical purpose,' Daisy continued. 'You see in Southern Africa the natives believe in a kind of guardian for one's dwelling, called a Tokolosh — a spirit that keeps an eye on the house and its occupants. These beings protect and serve witch doctors and tribal chieftains, too. Also those who the inhabitants consider to have helped them in times of trouble. As a result, I have such a guardian. It has come with me and will sleep under my bed, thus the bricks.'

She looked at her sister-in-law. 'You think I'm barmy, touched by the sun, don't you?'

'Not at all!' Doreen replied. 'Here we are well acquainted with such beings. This house has a "house guardian", as do those of several friends. They used to be very common several centuries ago, but with modern ways have almost died out. How do you reconcile them with your religious views?'

Her sister-in-law smiled. 'One learns many things during training. However, when you are in the middle of nowhere and surrounded by people who fervently believe in, and experience such beings, you do not call it a load of superstitious rubbish! One cannot be dogmatic. If you want to be so, then stay in England. Now I think it's time I went and unpacked and got to bed. It will be a busy day tomorrow.'

Doreen took her up to her room and said good night, then made her way to the master bedroom. Derek was sitting up apprehensively in bed.

'How is she?' he asked.

'Fine, you'll meet her in the morning and I advise you not to try and avoid her. She was not exactly pleased that you weren't waiting for her on the doorstep!' Continuing, 'I've suggested she doesn't come down until the children have gone, anyhow. We shall breakfast with her at nine o'clock precisely.'

Derek groaned, 'Very well, dear, I'll be there.'

Having unpacked a few essentials, Daisy was thankful to slip between the sheets of her comfortable bed. Before she dropped off to sleep she heard a faint but unmistakable snore from underneath. Her Tokolosh was in residence.

Michelle woke early the next morning. She sat up in bed and looked across at Sarah. She was still asleep. What was the time? Just gone six; she lay back but felt so wide awake she just couldn't go back to sleep. Then she remembered they must take all their exhibition materials back this morning. Yesterday all the material had been collected from the secret room, but maybe something had been overlooked? It would do no harm to nip up and check. She slipped out of bed and padded, barefooted, softly across the floor. The little door to it had to be opened with care, as it tended to squeak; but all went well and in moment she was up and going through the bits and pieces scattered on the table. Ah ha! What a good thing she'd looked. For here was one of Sam's sketches of the abbey ruins that had been overlooked. There was nothing further, so taking the drawing she went quickly back down and out of the bedroom—Sarah was still asleep—intending to take it downstairs to slip into the folder waiting in the dining room. It was very quiet as she crept along the landing towards the staircase…

Last night, as he was preparing to get into bed, after the final discussion about the dreaded aunt, Sam suddenly remembered he'd promised to take his old roller skates to school to lend to Chris. After some poking round in his 'junk' cupboard he found them.

'I'd better put these some place where I don't forget them in the morning,' he said to himself. 'I know, on the landing, at the head of the stairs. Then I'll be sure to see them when I go down for breakfast.' So saying, he put them there and retired to bed, satisfied with his excellent scheme.

Now, from the girls' room, when you went onto the landing, the staircase was on the right. To go downstairs meant a sharp right-hand turn was necessary. Sam had placed the skates at the top. Alas, Michelle, intent on being as quick as possible, and not expecting any obstacles, swung round the corner and walked straight into them. One skate trundled away across the landing. The other ricocheted off its companion and bounced down the uncarpeted stairs. Being sturdily constructed of metal, its progress shattered the calm of the early morning.

Startled and with a throbbing big toe, which had contacted the skates, Michelle didn't know what to do at first.

Luckily the rogue skate came to rest at the half-landing on its side so would not cause any further noise. Quickly she ran down and grabbed it, then froze as a door opened above. *The door to the guest room!* In horror she slid round the corner and crouched down on the lower flight. 'Hm, children!' an icy voice remarked. 'What's this, a skate? Most careless, I shall take charge of it!' and the door closed.

After a few minutes, Michelle, holding the other skate, cautiously climbed the stairs and made her way back to the bedroom. She realised she still had the drawing, but did not wish to tempt fate any further.

As she entered, Sarah was just sitting up in bed. 'Oh hello, Michelle, where have you been, did I hear a funny noise just now?' She was informed of what had happened.

'Gosh! The mean old thing, fancy taking one of Sam's skates. But what on earth were they doing out on the landing anyway? Stupid boy, I'm going to tell him off.' She leapt out of bed disappearing through the bathroom and into Sam's room. A series of thuds and muffled yells followed with Sarah's voice predominating at first. But then Sam got into his stride and an evenly balanced shouting match started. Michelle charged through, hushing madly. But they were so involved in their argument they didn't hear her.

In the end she shouted, 'Shut up, both of you, or you'll wake Aunt Daisy!'

They both turned and looked at her.

'Then why are *you* shouting?'

'Because you two were making so much noise you couldn't hear me,' she retorted.

'We were just talking, what's noisy about that?' replied Sam. Michelle gave up. Sometimes the twins were…well, *the* twins.

Another diversion was caused by Sam's alarm clock, which he'd forgotten to switch off. It started to inform all and sundry it was six forty-five. The three of them leapt at it frantically trying to jab the silencer. In the scuffle the clock was knocked off the table and rolled under the bed from where it continued its merry jangling. They dived after it, scrabbling and sneezing amidst the fluff, dust and a fine collection of Sam's dirty odd socks. At last somebody managed to silence the beast. Exhausted, they collapsed on the bed.

'Well if *that* didn't disturb her, she must be deaf!' exclaimed Sam.

Doreen poked her head round the door. 'Time to get dressed,' she said. So far you've been pretty quiet; keep it up.'

She left them staring disbelievingly at each other, 'pretty quiet'? If that was pretty quiet—well! You never know where you are with grown-ups.

Sam was philosophical about the skate. After all, he pointed out one skate wasn't much good and if *she* wanted to skate then she'd need the other one and if she didn't want to skate what would be the point of keeping it? He could always give them to Chris tomorrow. They got dressed and crept down to breakfast, carrying their shoes. Once the kitchen door was closed, sound level returned to normal. But the door was good solid oak and the walls were thick, so Aunt Daisy would sleep on in peace, *if* she was asleep.

Their departure for school *was* quieter than usual, mainly conducted in loud stage whispers and elaborate lifting and placing of stockinged feet. When Jill and Geoff arrived they set off down the drive. 'Remember *not* to burst into song until you are well on the way to the bus stop,' warned Doreen. They managed it, almost, for upon leaving the gates they gave three loud (Loud? who said they were loud? *That* was subdued, we cheer *much* louder at school!) cheers, then let out huge sighs of relief. Normal behaviour for the next eight hours—but then?

Derek now put in an appearance and helped Doreen lay the table in the dining room for an 'English breakfast'. Punctually at nine Derek rang the gong and a few minutes later footsteps were heard on the stairs and into the room sailed the Aunt Daisy of the photograph. Even Doreen was taken aback; the character make up was perfect. Before them stood the epitome of the Victorian spinster bent on doing good, no matter what the cost. The apparition glared at Derek and spoke: 'Ah, brother Derek! Not changed, I see. Where is your tie, man? Surely you do not expect to come to breakfast in a state of undress? Go and put one on at once!'

Derek's mouth opened and shut a few times. 'Hurry, I have no wish to sit down to a lukewarm meal.' He scuttled off. Doreen was still marvelling at the transformation, even the tone of voice had changed. This was going to be fun! Derek returned and passed inspection, though there were some tart comments about his choice in ties after her long and rambling grace. The meal began and was dominated by Aunt Daisy. Each time Derek tried to say something he was shut up or totally ignored while she expressed her views on the wickedness of the world to Doreen. At last, when the meal was finished the good lady rose and announced she was going to retire to her room to write a few letters. Derek breathed a sigh of relief; too soon as it turned out, for hardly had he helped clear up, when an imperious voice summoned him to the stairs. On the half landing stood his dreaded sister, holding a roller skate between her fingers at arm's length.

'Derek Court, what is the meaning of this object being left on the landing at the head of the stairs? Do you not inculcate tidiness and a sense of order into your children? I shall speak severely to the boy upon his return this afternoon. Take it!' and she threw it at him. Luckily, Derek was used to fielding such sudden throws from both Sam and Sarah, and so caught the offending object. The thrower returned to her room, where she took off her wig and collapsed into a chair, helpless with laughter.

Derek returned to the kitchen. 'She's far worse than I

ever thought she could be!' he moaned. 'I hardly recognised her. If that's what twelve years in darkest Africa does to one, I'm glad I never felt the call. The trouble is, I still recognise most of her mannerisms, but now she has changed—for the worst. I feel sorry for the children, and you!' he added hastily.

'The next few days are going to be pure hell,' and he took refuge in his study.

Binky and Cleo were puzzled. The lady who came down to breakfast and had demanded they be instantly removed from the dining room looked different but smelt the same as the nice lady they had met last night. All very confusing!

As soon as she'd washed up, Doreen slipped up to Daisy's room and they both had a really good laugh over Derek's reaction. 'Now for the children,' grinned Daisy.

CHAPTER THREE

At the time of the dreaded breakfast the children were just beginning main lesson. They had arrived early enough to give Stephen, Jane, Chris, and Fenella an account of the morning's happenings, admittedly somewhat dramatised, and met with much sympathy.

'And you have to go home to *that!*' exclaimed Fenella.

'I wish we were spending the weekend with *you!*' said Sarah to Jane.

'Well at least tomorrow she won't be able to bully you all day because we'll be at school!' she replied.

Indeed this would be so, as Mr Atkinson explained. It had been arranged that the school bus would run an hour later than usual to collect those who lived out of town.

The Bidforders would be picked up from their stop at nine fifteen. What a relief! The official opening would be at twelve thirty, but there were still some final preparations to be made. As for today, the main lesson was spent in the final assembling of the class wall display. Books for inspection had to be collected and set out on desks in the classroom, and a selection of their paintings hung on the walls. Various notices were made and positioned, and many other details attended to. In fact, the first part of the morning was soon over. After break there was the final rehearsal of class presentations in the hall, then lunch and a final general tidy-up of the grounds and classrooms in which the whole school took part. Now it was time to go home.

Never did three children board the school bus with so much reluctance.

'Far, far worse than going to the dentist, or hospital or anything!' announced Sarah as they drove off. Jill was most concerned for 'her' Sam and kept on telling him he should come home with her. When they got off, the driver reminded them to be ready for him tomorrow, adding that he had heard so much about what was going on he would be coming to the Open Day as well.

They set off down the lane, Jill hanging on to Sam and Geoff reminding Sarah and Michelle that they could always hide at his place. As they neared the gates they met Bess with Brian, who had come to collect Jill (all part of the plan). That young lady was most indignant until her mother whispered something in her ear. Her eyes grew round and she let out a loud 'Oh!' then took her mother's hand and off they went.

'I wonder what that was about?' said Sarah.

'Whatever it was it made her forget about m..., us,' said Sam dolefully.

They plodded up the drive, going slower and slower, seeking to put off the dreaded moment.

'I won't come in,' said Geoff, 'I'll just get my bike from the yard and be off.' He looked relieved that he could avoid the dread aunt. They watched him collect his machine and ride off.

Then they squared their shoulders and entered via the back kitchen. Here Binky and Cleo greeted them enthusiastically. But what were they doing shut out here? Usually they had the run of the house. As they went to open the intervening door their mother called, 'Keep the animals out there, please.' Easier said than done, as both of them were experts at scooting through small openings.

Somehow they managed and stumbled through into the kitchen. But where was their afternoon snack?

'We're having tea in the lounge,' Doreen informed them. ('Lounge? Lounge? Oh, sitting room. So we call it that for now?' 'Yes.') 'Go and put your school things in your rooms, tidy yourselves up then come down *quietly*. Please knock on the door before you enter. Also, remember you are *Samuel and Samantha,* and don't forget it when she speaks to you. Now hurry, I said we would have tea at four fifteen and it's four twelve already.' They rushed towards the door.

'Wait!' hissed their mother, 'Take your shoes off first and put on your indoor ones before you come down.' They crept upstairs, appalled. This was far, far worse than anything they had imagined.

'Far, far more awful than *even* my grandmother!' exclaimed Michelle as the three of them washed their hands and tidied their hair. Actually, Sarah and Michelle tidied theirs and then Sam's. He always had difficulty in making comb-contact with his. There was another slight delay, as he couldn't find his indoor shoes. Somehow they had hidden themselves under a pile of miscellaneous items in his cupboard.

Ready at last, they all took a deep breath and went down to knock at the lounge door. Sarah gave a soft tap-tap.

'They won't hear that!' said Sam and rapped smartly. From inside came a startled exclamation and the sound of falling china. 'Come in,' called Doreen; they entered. Derek was down on his hands and knees frantically mopping up tea and picking up the cup and saucer he'd dropped on the hearthrug. They stared at him until a throat cleared. 'Ahem!' It sounded like a gunshot. They spun round and there, seated on an upright chair was Aunt Daisy. They goggled; not only was she the image of the photograph, she was worse, a hundred million thousand times worse. Stiffer, starchier and far grimmer. She looked at them as if they were unsavoury objects and spoke. The voice was the one Michelle had heard that morning, but if icy then, it was now vying with the coldest temperatures known to man or beast.

'So, these are my nephew and niece with their little friend.' Pause. Another ironing board seemed to slip down her back. 'Well, where *are* your manners, have you not been taught how to address visitors?' This, and the look on their mother's face, jolted them into action.

'Er, good afternoon, Aunt Daisy, we hope you had a pleasant journey,' chanted the twins. Pause. Aunt Daisy turned and stared at Michelle.

'Er, oh, good afternoon Aunt… I mean Miss Court. Did you have a pleasant journey?'

'I shall have a word with your teacher about the need for children to learn the proper mode of addressing their superiors and betters,' was the tart reply. They stood there, not knowing what to do next.

'Well are you going to stand there all afternoon like statues? Make yourselves useful and hand round the cakes and kindly add some *really hot* water to this tea for me.'

Eager to oblige, Michelle and Sarah made a grab for her cup. Sam swooped on thecake stand. Sarah, realizing that Michelle would reach the waiting cup first, rapidly altered course and also made for the cake stand. Unfortunately, at this moment, Derek finished his clearing up and started to get up. Sarah tripped over his outstretched leg and in an effort to save herself from falling, grabbed at Sam, who had just extracted the plate of cream cakes from the stand. Caught unawares by Sarah's grab, he teetered wildly for a moment and staggered back, jerking the plate sharply upwards. It rained cream cakes. Michelle was making for the tea tray when Sam's stagger brought him into contact with her. They both cannoned into the small table with the tea things on it; luckily the contents were the second best silver-plated tea set. However, it made a fine old sound, like a stack of empty cans falling over. Derek was flat on his face, for Sarah had literally knocked his leg from under him. She, Michelle and Sam were in a heap on the floor, the cake stand had fallen on top of them, shedding a jam sponge that split in two and rolled majestically across the carpet to end up both parts jam side down.

Suddenly a loud burst of laughter rent the air. They sat up amazed to stare at Aunt Daisy. It could not have been her, for perched squashily on top of her immaculately groomed head was a cream cake, the cream slowly oozing down past her left ear. She sat, stern and immovable, then stood up, carefully so as not to dislodge the addition to her hairstyle, saying, 'Excuse me for a moment, I seem to have something in my hair.' And she swept out of the room. On reaching the door she turned and surveyed the scene. 'When I return we shall continue to refresh ourselves,' she added. They heard her mount the stairs and her door close. Doreen was already picking up the tea things and Derek, with the children tried to restore order to the cake stand.

'My God,' said Derek. 'I can just imagine her in the jungle when some ghastly, deadly poisonous snake drops out of a tree on to her head, saying to her listeners, "Excuse me a moment, I seem to have something in my hair", shaking it off and belting it with her umbrella!'

This made things worse, as they got the giggles. But peace and order were soon restored, just in time, for Aunt Daisy could be heard returning. The children had been deposited on chairs and told only to move if asked to and threatened with dire and dreadful punishments if they disobeyed. To their horror they realised they were seated in a row facing *her* chair. Her entrance was calculated to strike fear into the stoutest heart. She sat down in slow motion and examined the children with her sub-sub-zero degrees stare. Doreen proffered her tea and Derek handed round the side plates and serviettes. What about the cakes? Not yet, first the inquisition.

'So, Samuel and Samantha, I understand you have recently started at a rather unusual school. I shall be interested to visit it tomorrow to see the results and to converse with your teacher concerning educational matters. 'I've just started there too,' said Michelle, 'It's great, I'm ever so happy there.'

The dread gaze swung to focus on her. 'I am not aware that I was asking you, young lady, and let me inform you that happiness has nothing to do with school whatsoever!'

She turned her attention back to the twins. 'Though I am pleased that you can live in the country, that is no excuse for sloppy behaviour or a lowering of standards. I shall observe carefully your general behaviour and amenableness to being of assistance to your parents. If necessary I shall take the required steps to improve your manners and such matters as I deem need further attention.' She clapped her hands, making everyone start.

'Derek! You are not setting your offspring a good example! Hand round the cakes at once. Never ever let a guest be left with an empty plate unless they have specifically expressed the fact that they have partaken of an elegant sufficiency.'

Derek hastened to obey.

'Doreen, the tea! Once a guest has a cup, it is your duty as hostess to see that it is at the correct temperature and milk and sugar are supplied, if required.' Doreen poured out and handed round the tea. The children were paralysed; they ate and drank like automatons.

'Derek, please take the milk jug and refill it,' said Doreen.

'OK,' he replied.

This provoked another salvo about the misuse of our language and setting the younger generation a good example. When finished, Derek fled. They heard him enter the kitchen and open the door to the back kitchen, rapidly followed by a yell and a crash. The next minute, two streaks, one white, the other black and white, hurtled through the lounge door. Delighted at their unexpected release, Binky and Cleo were determined to show the nice guest how pleased they were to see her. Binky took a flying leap. Only when halfway through the air did he realise it was not quite whom he thought it was. It's not easy to change direction in mid-flight. He tried but it was no good. He caught Aunt Daisy's hand holding her cup and saucer, sending them flying. By some fluke, Doreen managed to catch them, though how she did it she never quite knew. He then landed heavily on her knees, scrabbled madly to keep hold and fell off on top of Cleo, who was just about to join him up there. Doreen reacted quickly.

'Time to do your homework, children—off you go NOW!' They knew that tone, there was no hesitation; they hastily stood up, and remembering their manners said, 'Good afternoon Aunt Daisy/Miss Court, thank you for having us,' and rapidly left the room.

The door was closed very firmly behind them. As they went upstairs they heard it open again and caught the words '...and you also need to learn to act your age!' The door closed and peeping over the banisters they saw Derek disappear into his study.

The children knew Doreen had said homework to get them out of the way, or off the hook, as Sam remarked. They didn't have any because of the Open Day. Anyhow, they took their school bags up to the secret room and then sat round the table chatting. The initial shock of Aunt Daisy was wearing off and they began to wonder about her.

'There's something fishy about the whole thing,' said Sam. 'Mum's hiding something, I'm sure, because she's going around like she does before our birthday and Christmas when there's going to be a big surprise.'

Michelle joined in, 'You know, she's almost *too* much like her picture, kind of over-real. Almost a caricature, like an actor.'

'That laugh when the cakes went everywhere,' mused Sarah. 'Who was it? Not any of us, or Mum, or Dad. It could only have been her—but?' She paused and then looked at Michelle, 'I think you are right, she's acting!'

'But why?' argued Sam, 'What's the point? She is what she is, though maybe she's overdoing it a bit. She could be nervous as she hasn't seen Dad for donkey's years.'

They continued to discuss the matter, but came to no real conclusion about the true state of Aunt Daisy. Then the light began to glow in the corner and Bill appeared.

'I've come to let you know that we have another guest as well as your aunt,' he informed them. 'Her house-cum-general guardian has come too. I thought it would be a good idea if you met him. We had a long conversation this morning, which proved to be most interesting.'

They nodded. 'All right,' he called, 'You can appear, N'humba, it's quite safe.' Another flash of light and there, in his dazzling outfit, bowing low to them was the Tokolosh.

Sam could not restrain his amazement. 'Wow, *where did you get those clothes!*'

N'humba looked pleased. 'A friend of mine works in a clothes shop in the nearby settlement. When she heard I was going overseas, she says: "N'humba, you've got to show those folk we knows how to look as smart as they do." You like it, yes?'

They all agreed they did. At that moment the gong sounded for supper and they trotted demurely down to wash and prepare themselves for another ordeal with the aunt.

Their mother met them at the foot of the stairs. 'For heaven's sake, *try* and behave!' she said. 'Whatever you do, stay on your seats, speak only when you are spoken to and remember to say "yes, Aunt Daisy" and "no, Aunt Daisy" when she speaks to you. I've told her you have to be at school early tomorrow and so as soon as dessert is finished you will be excused. Would you give Cleo and Binky their supper and a bit of fussing; then go up to your rooms and *play quietly until* eight thirty, then get ready for bed. I've put out your clean uniforms; it's probably best for you to have breakfast in your dressing gowns and dress afterwards. Breakfast latest, eight fifteen. Can you remember all that?' They nodded and went in for dinner.

Aunt Daisy sat at one end of the table, Derek at the other, Doreen and Michelle on the left side, Sam and Sarah on the right. Sam, much to his disgust, was next to the guest. She was already seated, and as soon as everyone else was, she said grace—an extremely long one. The meal was a very good, a kind of Friday evening-cum-Sunday dinner, as Sarah described it later. Luckily the eating of it was a full time occupation and there was little if any talk apart from an occasional: 'Elbows off the table, child!' or 'Hold your knife and fork properly!' and 'Take the glass in one hand. Now up to your mouth, not your mouth down to it! Goodness me, you are not a horse.'

The food received grudging approval, though Derek's carving of the joint, he was told, would hardly do credit to the lowest kitchen-boy back at the mission. After the main course came trifle for dessert. Everybody had been served and were all ready to start when Aunt Daisy's nose twitched and... ...

'Doreen, do I detect *alcohol* in this trifle?'

'Er, yes, there's a drop of sherry in it.'

Deathly silence, then... ... 'and you intend to allow these innocent children to partake of it? Setting them on the path to perdition and ruin! I am deeply surprised that you, Doreen, could be so unthinking. As for Derek, he always was a weak vessel and succumbed to its lure long ago. I suggest you remove their plates to the kitchen and give each of them an apple from the fruit bowl instead. I shall, out of respect for all your hard work, attempt to eat some of my portion; but should the alcoholic content prove too strong,

I shall leave the remainder.'

Horrified, the children watched as their plates were removed and each received an apple instead. They noticed that Aunt Daisy did full justice to her trifle. She did leave some, the glazed cherry and a few crumbs.

'Now children you may say good night and off you go; remember what I told you,' Doreen added.

They stood up and pushed their chairs in.

'Pick them up, pick them up, you'll ruin the carpet!' snapped their aunt. Somehow they managed to say 'good night, Aunt Daisy' as if they meant it and left, heading for the kitchen, fuming! However, this quickly abated when they entered, for there on the table were their bowls of trifle and a note saying, 'enjoy,' which they did. The animals were attended to, then they went upstairs, getting ready for bed by the time their mother had requested. As they talked before climbing between the covers, Sam said,

'You know, I'm sure there's something fishy going on. Sitting near her tonight, well, she looks "funny-peculiar", I can't explain it exactly, but Binky's reaction got me thinking. When he rushed in, he jumped straight for her, as if she was a real friend; it was only when he saw *her* that his attitude changed. Odd, very odd!'

The girls agreed, but pointed out tomorrow was more important now and they could investigate this mysterious *aunt* at their leisure after the Open Day.

CHAPTER FOUR

It seemed strange preparing to go to school on a Saturday morning, even if they were leaving later! This was further complicated by the need to be very quiet, as Aunt Daisy was 'resting' and must, on no account, be disturbed. However, with parental help, they were up at the bus stop in good time. The bus was full of very excited children and when they arrived at school the driver breathed a sigh of relief.

Stephen and Jane were waiting for them and were treated to an even more highly dramatic account of yesterday afternoon's happenings.

'You'll see for yourselves when she arrives with Mum and Dad,' said Sam. 'She has requested to meet you too,' he added with some satisfaction.

'See what you can make of her,' said Michelle. 'There's something odd, but we haven't been able to discover yet what it is.'

'She's just *too* much an awful aunt,' explained Sarah.

There was no time for any further conversation, as they had reached the classroom and soon became involved in the last minute preparations. By eleven thirty Mr Atkinson was satisfied and allowed them a break. A large plate of cream buns also appeared — as if by magic — for the class.

'You need to keep your strength up,' he remarked.

At twelve o'clock everybody was allowed to go and wait

for their parents and the guests, with strict instructions to be in the hall at twelve thirty for the official opening and a short presentation by the four lower classes.

The quintet took up a position by the car park. Stephen and Jane's parents arrived first and were directed to the hall. Next, much to their surprise was Michelle's mother and her grandmother. That lady looked quite different now and greeted them warmly; Erin was with them, and seeing a slightly apprehensive look on their faces whispered,

'We came by taxi, not broomsticks.'

Next came the Bennetts, young Judy making a beeline for Stephen, while Nicky stood shyly by his mother. They too went to secure seats in the hall, for by now the car park was filling up and there were also many folk arriving on foot.

'Where can Mum and Dad be?' complained Sarah, 'It's nearly twelve thirty and we'll have to... ...'

But at that moment the family car drove in at a steady ten miles an hour. They ran over to it. Derek scrambled out and held open one of the rear doors. Slowly and majestically Aunt Daisy rose from the interior. Doreen was already waiting to escort her to the hall.

'Good morning, Aunt Daisy, please come quickly, it's about to begin and we have to go!' said the children; and before she could reply or reprimand them, they dashed off. They learnt afterwards that she had insisted Derek drove no faster than twenty mph into town and ten mph when in town!

Once the four classes were in position behind the stage the Principal stepped forward:

'Welcome parents and friends to our Open Day I... ...'

'Speak up man, if you *are* the Principal of this school. Don't mumble!'

There was a shocked silence and the Head stared glassily at the imposing figure of Aunt Daisy, who had risen from her seat while making this remark. Hastily he finished his welcome and introduced class one's teacher, who explained what they would be performing. Aunt Daisy had sat down, but continued to mutter audibly, much to the annoyance of her neighbours, and to the acute discomfort of Doreen and Derek.

However, she lapsed into silence while class four performed and nodded as if satisfied. The presentation being over, Mr Atkinson informed the parents that a buffet lunch would be served in the kindergarten building at one fifteen. At two the classrooms would be open for inspection and the upper classes would perform at three. Tea at four and the proceedings would close at five. The children could join their parents for lunch, but would be required in their classrooms at one fifty-five.

Once free, the children made their way to the kindergarten to find their parents. Much to their delight, they had all managed to gather at a long table in one corner of the large play area. While the men went off to get the food, the ladies had settled down for a good chat about the school, their children and heaven knows what else. It was an impressive group: Doreen, Phyllis, Bess, Ingrid, Melissa, Erin, Karen, Joyce and a lady they did not know, but were told later she was Cherry, wife of the new postmaster at Bidcote. Then the Shelleys and Steuarts joined them.

There were small children in plenty: Jill, Brian, Judy, Nicky and the three little girls belonging to the postmaster: Shirley, just nine, Wendy, seven, and Ann, five. While the children ran round or talked among themselves, Aunt Daisy sat bolt upright at one end of the table registering disapproval at the unseemly levity of whole affair. But no one took much notice of her, apart from the occasional: 'Oh yes?' or 'Really!' when she managed to put in a remark.

Even Sam, Sarah and Michelle felt less intimidated. However, she still had to be reckoned with, and her imperious command: 'Samuel and Samantha, please come here!'

made them groan. However, before she could say anything further, the men returned with trays full of food and everyone set to. The children noticed she had an excellent appetite. When finished, as they made ready to return to the classroom, she spoke again:

'Samuel, Samantha! I shall accompany you, as I wish to have words with your teacher before he is too occupied with other parents.'

There was no getting out of it. They set off like a flotilla of tugs shepherding a stately 'Queen Mary' into Southampton Docks. On arrival they found Mr Atkinson busily organising some children to act as guides to the visitors. Aunt Daisy wasted no time.

'Are you the teacher of class four?'

'Er, yes.'

'I want a word with you; I have considerable experience in the inculcation of learning into the young and from what I have seen and heard so far there are certain basics, yes, basics, young man, that are sadly lacking!'

With that she took him firmly by the arm and led him over to a far corner of the room, barely giving him time to tell the children to 'carry on.' They stood aghast.

'How could she, how could she be *so awful!*' gasped Fenella who had witnessed the way their beloved teacher had been treated.

'I don't know how she can, but she does,' Sam replied gloomily, 'and we have to put up with this until Wednesday *and* she's coming back for five days *after* Easter.'

Fenella was deeply sympathetic. 'You *poor* things,' she said.

At that moment Aunt Daisy released her victim and with a curt nod left the building. They rushed over to comfort him. 'We told you so, she's really *awful* isn't she? What do you think of her now!' 'I think... ...' he began but got no further, as a gaggle of parents entered and swooped on him.

The children were soon involved with parents and visitors too, telling them about their lessons and other activities. One very interested family was the Fisher's and their three daughters. Then Will and Joyce Bennett with their children came in, and were deeply attracted by all they were shown and told, Judy announcing very firmly that she wanted to come to 'Stephen's school!'

Will grinned, 'I reckon she's got the right idea!' he said, 'I must say what we've seen and heard today makes me think this is just the place for both of them. Let's drop into the office to have a chat with the secretary and pick up a couple of registration forms, Joyce.'

She nodded in agreement and off they went. There was a slight lull and Mr Atkinson came over to them. He looked tired but pleased.

'It's going very well,' he told them. 'But your aunt!' he shook his head and laughed — *Laughed!*

'How can you laugh?' said Michelle, 'seen for yourself what she's like.'

He grinned at five very puzzled faces and said, 'Wait and see,' adding, 'You can skip off now for a bit to be with your parents.' They skipped. Then he turned to speak with Geoff's mother, and several other parents hovering in the background.

The senior classes' display was now under way. Owing to a shortage of space, only parents of the children concerned and visitors were admitted. But there was still plenty for the others to see and fellow parents or inquirers to talk with.

They found theirs going into the kindergarten for tea. But Aunt Daisy was not with them. Wild hopes were raised. Perhaps she'd been kidnapped, or eaten by a dragon conjured up by Melissa? Though they felt sorry for anyone who kidnapped her and for any dragon that had eaten her — it would surely get the most awful indigestion.

Doreen, upon seeing them, said, 'Your aunt's gone off to

the cloakrooms. Would you *all* go and wait there to guide her back here, please.

'But she knows where we are,' retorted Sam.

'Never mind, she particularly requested that you do this.'

Now what, they wondered, what new tortures and humiliations had she in store for them? Glumly they went over to the cloakroom block and stood outside the 'ladies' section.

A few minutes passed and there was no sign of any aunt.

'That's odd,' said Jane. 'If your mum said she'd already gone in there, she must have been there for some time before we came. Whatever can she be doing, or has she come out and we've missed her?'

'She's probably deliberately staying in longer so we don't get any tea,' remarked Sam. 'That's the sort of thing she would do.'

'Well, Mum said "wait", so wait we'll have to,' announced Sarah.

'Why don't one of you girls go in and see what she's up to?' suggested Stephen.

'Go in and see what she's doing,' retorted his sister. 'Do you think we're barmy! Would *you* like to do that?'

Stephen admitted he wouldn't. Five minutes went by and ladies of various sizes and ages went in and out but still there was no sign of Aunt Daisy.

'Perhaps she's fainted and the door's locked so no one would know,' said Michelle.

'Well let's ask the next person who comes out if they've seen her in there. They couldn't mistake *her*, could they?' said Sam.

As he spoke a cheerful, tall, rather comfortable looking lady in her early forties came out.

'Excuse me,' said Sarah, 'have you seen a rather, well, formidable lady in there?'

'Formidable?' she replied, 'What exactly do you mean?'

'She's tweedy, stiff and awful,' said Sam without thinking.

The others murmured 'Oh, Sam!' But the lady appeared not to have heard. 'I'll go and have a look,' she replied.

As she vanished inside, Michelle turned excitedly to them. 'Did you see, did you see?' she said.

'See what?' they asked.

'The shoulder bag she was carrying?'

'So what? Lots of ladies carry shoulder bags.'

'But do they all have a Southern African flight baggage check-in label on them?'

'Why?'

'Because the one Aunt Daisy has is the same colour and has the same label!'

Before they could react to this, the lady reappeared.

'Well, children, I've had a good look round and there's no lady answering to your description in there,' and she turned to walk away.

For a moment they were nonplused, then the apparently disembodied voice of Aunt Daisy spoke: 'Well, what are you all standing there gawking at; where are your manners?'

They jumped, and looked round anxiously for that dreaded person. However, the only person in sight was the lady they had just been speaking with. She had turned round and was walking slowly back towards them, smiling broadly.

'It is, it is, it is!' cried Michelle triumphantly, 'It's Aunt Daisy!'

'Quite right, my dear, I am indeed Aunt Daisy!'

'B, bu, but how and why?' exclaimed the perplexed children.

'Come along, let's go over to the kindergarten and have some refreshment; then your mother and I will explain,' she smiled.

Upon their arrival there were some surprised faces, the most surprised being Derek's! Explanations were soon given. The children learnt that when they had told Doreen about the dreadful photo of Aunt Daisy in the album it reminded her that it had been taken for publicity when she was acting an 'old battleaxe' part in an amateur theatre group production. She had mentioned it in a letter to her sister-in-law, who in reply, had suggested it would be a shame to disappoint them — and Derek — if she did not live up to the photo.

'I really had great fun playing that part all those years ago *and* for the last couple of days,' she told them.

Just then Mr Atkinson appeared, 'Ah ha! The secret is out,' he chuckled.

'How did you know?' they asked.

'Your aunt told me when she lectured me after lunch.'

'We thought there was something strange about you, and Mum's behaviour was odd too,' explained Sarah, 'but we never ever thought that you weren't you, if you know what I mean.'

'It was a super trick,' agreed Sam, 'Could you teach us how to make up like that and fool our friends?'

'I don't think you'd fool *us*,' said Jane.

'Nor me,' added Jill, 'I'd *know* Sam anywhere!'

Perhaps the most relieved person was Derek. It was as if a great weight had been lifted from him. He became the life of the party, joking and teasing his sister with memories of the boyfriends she'd had as a teenager.

After tea there was a chance for the public to have one last look around or visit the office for further information. Aunt Daisy made a point of seeking out the Principal and apologising for the dreadful behaviour of the 'other' Aunt Daisy. At first he couldn't believe it, but when she put on the voice he began to laugh and agreed with the children it had been a wonderful leg-pull for all concerned.

At five people began to leave, and some reorganisation of transport would be required to get everyone back to the manor and Bidcote. Harry reckoned he could squeeze in a couple of children, taking Sam and Geoff. Sarah and Michelle went in the family car, while Reg gallantly offered

Ingrid, Melissa and Karen a lift.

The children should have been exhausted—according to Derek—after such an exciting day, but their discovery of a real aunt buoyed them up so much they were still as fresh as daisies, as Doreen remarked, no pun intended!

However, in spite of the hundreds and hundreds of things they wanted to ask their aunt, shortly after supper they began to yawn and wilt, so were packed off to bed.

Their protests were met with, 'Your aunt is here until Wednesday *and* she's coming back! So you'll have plenty of time with her, if she has time for you.' Which, she hastened to inform them, she had!

CHAPTER FIVE

After the excitement of the previous day everyone had fully intended to take it easy on Sunday morning. However, there were two members of the household who had had a very boring Saturday and, in their opinion, had not been given nearly enough attention by their human servants upon their return. Binky and Cleo woke early and let it be known, very clearly, that they were awake and ready to get going. Luckily Sam had just wakened and hearing their initial woofs and squeaks nipped downstairs to get them. It was just about eight when he let them out and ordered, 'Upstairs, and quietly!'

They were used to this and scampered up and into his room. Just as he was about to cross the hall, the phone rang. He grabbed it.

'Jane? Oh, hi! What? Reg is coming out this way and you can come too! Super, when? About ten? I'll tell Mum and Dad and the girls. 'Bye!'

He put the phone down and charged upstairs, any thought of being quiet now gone. He found Sarah had already let the animals into her bedroom and he quickly followed.

'Guess what, Jane just rang and Reg is driving out this way to see a client. So they asked if they could come with him and be dropped off here for the day, and he agreed. He'll pick them up on his return. I'll go and tell Mum and

Dad they are coming!'

He went and knocked on their parents' door, and without waiting for a reply, walked in. Binky and Cleo rushed in too. Derek and Doreen were sitting up in bed looking slightly startled.

'What is it?' asked Doreen, 'an earthquake?'

'No,' Sam replied, 'the twins are coming over for the day.'

'That's as good as an earthquake,' retorted Derek.

'When?' queried Doreen.

'Uncle Reg is bringing them at about ten. He's visiting a client nearby.'

By now Sarah and Michelle had joined them. 'I suggest then it would be a good idea if you went and got dressed, taking these exuberant animals with you, while your father and I do the same. First ready starts preparing breakfast.'

'Yes, Mum.' The bedroom quickly emptied.

With the children it was a dead heat. Binky and Cleo had already gone back to the kitchen.

'What about Aunt Daisy?' said Sarah, 'Shall we wake her?'

Michelle was doubtful. 'Maybe we should leave her until everything is ready, then call her,' she suggested.

Sam suddenly sniffed, and sniffed again. 'Can you smell what I think I smell?' he said.

They sniffed. Toast, distinctly toast. But who, and how? They rushed down to the kitchen and there was Aunt Daisy happily preparing breakfast. The table was laid and the kettle just on the boil.

'Good morning, all of you. I thought after all the waiting on I've received, I should do some for a change.'

Binky and Cleo were already scoffing down their breakfast, tail wagging and purring contentedly.

'First come, first served!' she remarked. 'Now, Sam, perhaps you'd go and ring the gong to let your parents know. Sarah and Michelle, just check the table and see that there's everything we need.'

The next moment, if anybody was still asleep in the house, they would have been awakened with a vengeance. Sam was an expert on the gong and its tones were probably heard to the farthest corners of the grounds.

Derek and Doreen appeared very promptly. Once everyone was seated and enjoying the meal, Aunt Daisy asked what their plans were for the day. She was told of Stephen and Jane's visit and Doreen added:

'I had a long chat with Roger and Cherry Fisher at the school. He's our new postmaster,' she informed Daisy. 'They are coming over at eleven for morning tea, as Ann, the youngest girl, is ready for kindergarten. Bess and her two will come as well. I hope you will help look after them,' she said to the children.

'Sure,' they replied, 'It looks like being a nice day we can take them round the grounds.'

'You can count me in as well,' remarked Aunt Daisy. 'I'm ready for a conducted tour.'

As soon as the children had done their share of tidying away the breakfast things, they went up to 'do' their rooms, then met to discuss plans. Last night Sarah had had a *brilliant* idea and though there would be unexpected visitors, they felt there was no reason why it shouldn't be put into practice. This involved the pond through which the Bidbrook flowed. The pond was situated just above the rustic bridge to the summer house. They remembered that Stephen and Jane had already played in the stream, so could be relied upon to share their experiences. If Aunt Daisy was there she could keep an eye on the little ones. The plan? Sam had discovered an old remover's wooden pallet in the long grass on the streamside of the terraced gardens. When he told Sarah she had made her brilliant suggestion; now all they had to do was… …!

When Reg arrived they were waiting and almost before the others got out of the car were busy explaining their plan.

Stephen's comment was 'Great!' and Jane added, 'Yes, the pond's fairly deep, especially on the summer house side. Stephen and I fell in last summer. We didn't realise the long grass at the edge was growing out and trod on it. We got soaked! Luckily it was a hot day so we took off our clothes and dried them in the sun while we ran about to dry ourselves.'

'It's not going to be very warm today,' retorted Michelle. But the others were too carried away by the excitement of their project to be worried about that. By now they were in the kitchen, where Doreen and Aunt Daisy were preparing the morning tea.

'Hands off those chocolate biscuits, you'll have your share in due course!' they were told. As there was still some time before the guests arrived, they took Aunt Daisy into the dining room and hauled out the old photo album to show her the picture. She laughed, as they all did now.

'You looked even worse than that,' said Sam. When they examined some of the other pictures they realised that the unknown young lady in them was the real Aunt Daisy.

At eleven Bess arrived with her two and a few minutes later a small Land Rover arrived with the Fisher family. Roger was a tall, dark-haired rather quiet man with a slow manner and a most infectious chuckle. Cherry was small and delicate, like a little bird; she laughed a lot. Shirley, their eldest, was, like her father, rather shy and quiet. Wendy was a curly haired miniature edition of her mother and never seemed to stop moving or talking. Ann, the youngest, was fair-haired and a mixture, sometimes quiet and then chattering away like a magpie. Being just a little younger than Jill, she soon struck up a friendship with her and they wandered round hand in hand. Wendy happily attached herself to Michelle, chattering away nineteen to the dozen. Shirley held back for a while, staying close to her father. However, when Jane asked her if she would like to come outside with them into the grounds, her eyes lit up and she eagerly answered, 'Oh, yes, please!'

'She's a real outdoor girl,' explained Roger. 'Never happier than when she can be in the garden.'

First there was elevenses, then they made ready to go out. 'I'll join you shortly,' said Aunt Daisy, 'I'm just going to clear up while your mother talks with her guests.' Meanwhile, Derek took Roger off to his study, having discovered he had an interest in engineering.

The children made their way towards the pond. It was sunny, but not very warm, as a chilly wind was blowing. Luckily they were well wrapped up. Upon reaching the pallet, Sam and Stephen hauled it from the long grass, dragging it over to the pond's edge. Sarah had borrowed a length of clothes line for a painter — even though their vessel had no bow — this was securely fastened on before its launch.

However, first, like all good ships, it had to be christened. Sarah had come prepared for this event and produced a small bottle containing blackcurrant juice. The others gathered round while she solemnly tipped it over the bow, saying in a loud voice,

'I hereby christen this ship "HMS Pallet", may good luck go with her and all who sail thereon!'

The launch now took place. This proved to be rather difficult, as the banks of the pond were steep and there was no place where it could be slid in gently. Giving Wendy the painter to hold, and ordering the younger children to stand well back, the five older ones, with Shirley's help, managed to part lift, part drag and then balance it precariously on the edge. They went to the stern and it was 'One, two, three, heave!'

HMS Pallet lurched forward, teetered on the brink and then plunged in with a most satisfying splash, its weight causing it to completely submerge. It rose sluggishly to the surface just below the bank.

Now the question was: 'Who goes first and how many passengers?' After some discussion, Sarah, as the originator of the idea, was chosen as skipper, with Stephen as first mate. Michelle, because she was sensible, was appointed as deckhand and Wendy as a passenger, for Shirley firmly shook her head when offered a berth. The painter was passed over to Ann for the moment. She promptly coiled up as much as she could, then stood on it. Sam had found a long pole and used it to hold the craft steady while the crew boarded. This was tricky, for they had to drop on backwards from the bank. For Sarah, being first, this wasn't too hard, but she had to cling to an overhanging clump of grass to keep it steady when Stephen jumped on, for HMS Pallet wallowed about in an alarming manner as the deckhand and passenger dropped down. The younger children edged forward to watch and Ann stepped off the rope to get a better view.

The bold crew knelt on their craft wet knees being preferable to wet bottoms. Then Sam gave a push with the pole to send them out into the middle of the pond. The idea was that once that crew had had enough, HMS Pallet would be hauled back to harbour and the next crew would embark. There was a flurry of water as it left the shore followed by a splash. No, nobody had fallen off, but the coil of rope, as the vessel pulled away, was dragged forward over the edge into the water, where it promptly sank. HMS Pallet continued on course to the middle. There it became caught in an eddy and rotated slowly round and round, the crew unable to do anything except kneel and stare at the distant shore. Even Wendy stopped chattering. Sam called out,

'Stephen, wind in the painter, coil it up and throw it to us; then we can pull you in.'

Easier said than done. Eventually he managed to haul it back, but several times it became caught on some underwater obstruction. At last it was on board and Stephen knelt upright as far as he dared and threw. Unfortunately, as the craft was still rotating, the rope described a circular arc landing well short of the shore. What's more, the vessel lurched dangerously, nearly pitching him off and causing everyone on board to get very wet knees, and more.

On shore Ann started to cry, 'I want my Wendy, I want my Wendy!'

'I'm fine, Ann,' yelled her sister, but this only made her howl louder.

Sam was now lying on the bank, Jane and Shirley kneeling on his legs, while he stretched out as far as he dared, trying to hook the rope with his pole.

Jill also began to sob, as she was afraid Sam was going to fall in. No matter how much he tried to hook the rope, the loop would slither off back into the water. They were so engaged in the attempted rescue that it was a few minutes before a loud, 'Ahem, ahem!' made them aware they had been joined by Sir Brian, who, luckily looked very real and solid. He took in the scene in a flash.

'Ha, adrift on the foaming main. What are you doing, me boy?' he said, turning to Sam.

'Trying to fish out the rope end so we can tow them in,' he replied, somewhat shortly. Couldn't the old numskull *see* what he was doing?

'Good idea, but not working very well?' was the next comment.

'No.' Pause. Sir Brian looked up at the sky then down at his feet.

'Maybe you should try something else?' he suggested.

'What?' Sam's thoughts were now quite unprintable.

'Well, if you had a boat you could row out and rescue them.'

'Sir Brian, we haven't got a boat. Can't you do something to help?'

'I've made several useful suggestions,' came the huffy reply. Then suddenly he shouted, 'Of course! Here, give me that pole of yours.' The girls got off his legs and Sam staggered to his feet, handing over the pole.

'Now, quite simple, I shall use it to vault lightly on to the vessel and then pole it back to safety.'

'Wait a moment, that's not going to work.'

'Rubbish, my boy, of course it will. The mere simplicity of it guarantees success!'

Holding the pole before him he took a few steps back and then ran forwards, perhaps lumbered would be a more accurate description. Taking off with the grace of a cross-eyed bandy-legged duck he plunged the pole into the water. It went down, and down, and down; so did Sir Brian with a resounding splash and a loud yell. His head broke the surface and clutching the upright pole he began shouting, 'Help, help, I can't swim.'

A calm voice said, 'Whatever is going on here?' What a relief! There stood Aunt Daisy. Attracted by the general uproar she had made her way directly to the pond.

'Help, I'm drowning,' yelled Sir Brian.

'I think I'm going to be sick,' sobbed Wendy as HMS Pallet continued its slow rotation.

'Boo-hoo, I want Wendy,' howled Ann.

'I don't want my Sam to fall in,' wailed Jill.

The three older children stood in a bewildered group.

But the mere sound of her soft voice made them feel better. She put her arms around the two sobbing little girls and walked forward to the edge of the pond. She regarded Sir Brian with some amusement, then said:

'Excuse me, but are you not standing on the bottom?'

He stopped in mid-yell and looked down. 'Er, yes. How very observant of you, madam.'

'Well, if you use the pole, from there you should be able to reach the rope if Stephen coils it and is able to throw it over its end. Try, Stephen!' she added. He did; the first attempt failed, but on the second he flung the coil over the raised pole. 'Three cheers!' called Aunt Daisy and they did, even Sir Brian.

Once the rope was passed to shore it was only a matter of moments before the —damp kneed, and other parts— mariners were back on dry land. The rope was then passed to Sir Brian and he was hauled out with much puffing and blowing—from Sir Brian.

'I don't think we've met,' smiled Aunt Daisy.

'No you haven't,' said Sarah quickly. 'Sir Brian's a *very old* tenant, some four hundred and fifty years, in fact!'

'Ah! You're the lady that young fellow from Africa accompanied,' said the dripping figure and he bowed gracefully. A shattering sneeze rather spoilt the effect.

'You go straight in and change at once,' ordered Aunt Daisy, sounding rather like her other self.

'No need,' he replied, 'No problem for one with my magical arts,' and spreading his arms wide he chanted,

'A trifle… a trifle wet I am you see.

Powers of warmth kindly dry me!'

There was a peculiar squelching thud and Sir Brian appeared to have had a large bowl of trifle emptied over his head.

'No, no!' he bellowed, '*Not* Trifle! Don't you recognise a pause when you hear one? Bah! This off the shelf stuff is useless! I've said it before and….'

He got no further, for the next moment a miniature whirlwind picked him up and to the amused lookers he appeared to be tossing about in an invisible clothes drier. After a five minute spin he was dumped on the ground, dizzy but dry. Muttering, 'goodbye!' he vanished.

The quintet was very impressed by the unflappable way Aunt Daisy had handled the pond problem and Sir Brian.

Jane said, 'You realise he's a sort of ghost, don't you?'

'Of course!' she replied. 'I know you also have house guardians.'

'You do?'

'Yes, my own one, N'humba, has accompanied me on this trip. He felt I might do something rash if he didn't keep an eye on things.' The thought of Aunt Daisy doing something rash seemed highly improbable; she was *so* sensible.

'But we can't stand about here chatting or the crew will be getting pneumonia!' she added. Indeed, they were already beginning to shiver. 'I'm afraid you won't fit in the clothes drier,' she remarked, 'but the kitchen stove should do quite well,' and with Ann and Jill on either hand, she set off at a brisk trot towards the house, the others following.

CHAPTER SIX

Their arrival in the kitchen was greeted with a mixture of concern and amusement. However, as no one had drowned, and apart from four rather damp-kneed — and beyond — children, none were any the worse for their adventure. So their parents, apart from issuing a 'Don't do it again' warning, took no further action. Some explaining was required about Sir Brian, as the Fisher girls excitedly told their mother: 'A funny man came and helped, fell in and dried himself in an invisible tumble drier, then vanished like magic.'

Cherry seemed quite happy to accept his betwixt and between status, saying that in their experience of living in different parts of the country there were many strange things town dwellers would find hard to believe. Once they had changed and Wendy was lent a spare pair of Sarah's trousers, pinned on and rolled up, they were ready for… …?

'A walk round the grounds,' announced Aunt Daisy. This was a more normal affair, apart from Binky accompanying them. The wind had now eased and it was pleasant in the sun, provided they kept moving. This time the route lay to the *other side* of the grounds, through the old ornamental gardens, round past the ruins of the hunting lodge, across to the treed mound, out on to the track and back through the gates. As they walked, the children told of the adventures that had occurred there since their arrival at Hallowe'en.

Aunt Daisy listened to their accounts with great interest, as did the three Fisher girls. When they returned to the house it was nearly lunchtime, and as the good ladies had gone on talking somewhat longer than intended, Doreen invited everyone to stay for a snack lunch. Bess rang the farm telling Harry to come over and Roger, seeing that Cherry and the children were enjoying themselves so much reckoned, 'The post office can manage without us a bit longer.'

After lunch the Fishers left amidst cries of 'come again' and 'you come and see us'.

Derek had told Roger about their encounter with the late postmaster, Mr Theophrates Simm, also his son, Ethelbert, and he was interested to hear more. A tentative visit was arranged for the following Thursday afternoon. This was later confirmed. Harry and Bess also departed taking Brian, who was ready for his afternoon rest. Jill was allowed to remain, much to her delight, and Sam promised they would walk her back before dark.

The rest of the afternoon was spent with Aunt Daisy in the sitting room, where she enthralled them with her stories of life in Southern Africa and the people she worked with. Then she showed them some of the games played by the African children she taught. Afternoon tea was looming up when there was the sound of a car arriving; it was Uncle Fred. 'I thought I'd drop in to see how things were going,' he said.

Naturally he heard all about the HMS Pallet episode and counted them to make sure the quintet was intact. Aunt Daisy took the chance to ask him some questions about the school and its teaching methods. The children were allowed to stay because she also wanted to hear how they felt about it. When they'd finished she sighed and said,

'If only something like this could be brought to the children I teach, I'm sure they would really flourish.'

'There are things you can do yourself,' Fred told her and

he made some suggestions.

'I can't stay to supper,' he said in reply to Doreen's question. 'As you know we break up on Wednesday and I have to prepare for our Easter Festival. Perhaps when you return I could come over and we'll have another chat?' he remarked to Aunt Daisy which, she agreed, would be a good idea.

'I tell you what,' he said, addressing the children as well, 'Why don't we arrange a day trip? I'll pick up Stephen and Jane and then we can all go off and show your aunt some of the local sights.' This was greeted with much enthusiasm. 'Magical Mystery Tour for overseas aunts!' he said with a grin as he drove off.

Reg arrived just before supper and was forced to stay under threats of having his tyres let down. He did not need *too much* persuasion, though he insisted they left straight afterwards as the twins would have to get ready for school tomorrow. 'Don't look so mournful,' he told them. 'If I know anything about it you'll be back here next weekend, which, being Easter, should prove interesting,' and he winked at Derek and Doreen. But they could get nothing more from him. 'I almost wish I could stay, too,' said Aunt Daisy. 'You must tell me all about it when I return!'

When the Randell twins had left, it was the usual Sunday evening procedure.

The next two days at school were spent tidying up after the Open Day, reviewing it and preparing for the end of term. However, on Tuesday their class was having an egg blowing and decorating session and Mr Atkinson was going to bring in a small tree in a pot upon which they would hang the eggs. On the Wednesday there would be a short Easter Festival first thing followed by a grand scrambled egg brunch for the whole school — an end of term picnic.

Much to the quintet's delight, school finished around lunchtime so the school bus would bring them home by two, in plenty of time to say goodbye to Aunt Daisy before she left for her conference. Perhaps if they were good they might even be allowed to go to the station as well. However, the ways of grown-ups are indeed strange and they learnt on Tuesday evening that instead of coming home on the bus the three of them would go to Southleigh and they would all go to see her off. Then Doreen would take her brood home.

Wednesday dawned bright and clear, even warmer than expected. In their classroom a magnificent 'egg tree' stood for all to admire. The assembly was short, with a few musical items and some Easter verses and songs.

The Principal thanked everyone for their part in the Open Day and informed his audience that all the enquiries had generated at least five definite enrolments and possibly more. Then the whole school gathered outside where several barbecues had been set up, one for each class, and soon large containers of scrambled egg were being cooked by teachers with more than enough class cooks to help them; luckily it wasn't broth. The feast was great and the children dispersed at one o'clock. Phyllis picked them up, a giggling, 'hurrah for holidays' group of very happy children. They spent the early afternoon playing games. At three thirty they were driven to the station and there, already on the platform, was Doreen with Aunt Daisy.

They rushed over and hugged her, sad she was going, but glad she was coming back.

'Next time you come,' said Sarah you *must* be with us if it's Christmas, or Easter, or whatever.'

'I don't know when I shall come again,' she replied softly. 'It may not be until I retire and by then you will all be grown-up.'

All be grown-up? Impossible! How *could* she stay away so long? (Afterwards Doreen told them that the religious nursing and teaching order she belonged to had very strict rules and work came before any personal considerations.)

Suddenly Michelle looked directly at her and said, very

softly, but convincingly, 'You will be back next year!'

Aunt Daisy looked startled. 'What, how do you know?'

Michelle blushed, 'I don't know what made me say that, but I just had to,' she replied.

A blast on one of those awful diesel sirens announced the arrival of the train and after loading her luggage on and by the time everyone had kissed or been kissed, it was ready to leave. Aunt Daisy leaned out of the window.

'See you Friday week,' she called. 'Oh, by the way, N'humba has decided not to come; he reckons there will be enough protective magic around. So he's taking a break, apparently he gets on very well with your Bill,' and with that, the train was gone.

The children were very quiet during the journey home. They were going to miss Aunt Daisy, but luckily she would be coming back. Still there were Easter cards and gifts to be made—and only tomorrow to do it! They would be busy with no time for moping.

Next morning, just as they were finishing breakfast, Michelle's mum walked in. Her daughter greeted her happily. Soon she was sitting with them having a late cuppa.

'Well, Doreen, Mother is much better and feels ready to return home as arranged after Easter. I shall need a day or so to get the room reorganised for this young lady, but by next Thursday she can come home! Michelle looked delighted and yet a tad sad as well.

Ingrid smiled, 'I know, dear, you'd love to stay here. But you'll still be able to see them and maybe we can invite them over to stay with us some time.'

Sam spoke, 'A bike, like Geoff's; you need a bike, Michelle, then you can come over whenever you want to. Also to get here for the school bus.'

'We'll have to see what we can do,' said Ingrid.

Sarah turned to her brother, 'That's all very well, but what about us, where are our bikes? We have one each,' she added. 'Mum, do you know where they are?'

Doreen looked perplexed. 'Funny, I haven't seen them since we moved here,' she mused.

At that moment Derek came into the kitchen.

'Darling, have you seen the children's bikes?'

He paused and scratched his head. 'Bikes, bikes? Let me think.' He began to tick off possibilities on his fingers. 'The garage, no. The old storage shed, no. The yard storehouses, no. The old boiler house, no. The greenhouses, no.' He paused, 'Can you think of anywhere else, Doreen?'

She shook her head.

Sam's face was a study. 'You don't think? It's not possible, did, did, the removers leave them behind?'

'I'll ring up the new owners right now,' said Derek and went to the study.

In a few moments he was back. The look on his face prepared them for the worst.

'I spoke with Mrs Reuben; she said her husband found a couple of old children's bikes at the bottom of the garden, hidden under some bushes. He assumed they were junk and put them for the garbage collection.'

There was a horrified silence and Sam went bright red. He looked at Sarah; she went very pink.

'You'd better tell us,' said Doreen quietly, 'What did you do?'

'Well, you see,' said Sam. 'The day before we moved we were playing cops and car thieves. The bikes were in the garage with the other stuff waiting to go. We *really* meant to put them back. Anyway, Sarah was the cop and I'd stolen a Rolls Royce and a Jaguar and hidden them in my secret hideout. Sarah had to find them.'

'I was just starting to search with my faithful bloodhound (Binky) when you called us to come with you to go and say goodbye to old Mrs White, who lived opposite. She gave us tea and when we returned it was already dark.'

'Yes,' added Sam, 'and we forgot all about the bikes. Next morning we were so busy that…!' Silence.

'Your father and I will talk this over later,' said Doreen. 'Those bikes were only about a year old.'

Another pause, interrupted by the phone. Derek took it in the study. It was a lengthy call. When he returned he looked amused and exasperated.

'You two are impossible, yet like Cleo, always fall on your feet! That was Mr Reuben. His wife phoned him at work and told him about your bikes. He was very apologetic that he did not think to contact us first before throwing them away. In spite of my protests he insists on replacing them for you. He's putting a cheque in the post this morning. So, you lucky little horrors, we can buy you new bikes after Easter. And you'd better take really good care of them this time, *or else!*' They knew better than to ask him 'or else what?' when he spoke in that tone.

He turned to Ingrid, 'We can buy one for Michelle at the same time, I think your mother owes her granddaughter a present,' he added.

'She can certainly afford it,' Ingrid replied.

'Perhaps we could go Saturday morning if the cheque arrives, because some shops will be open, like the DIY store in Tadbridge, and they sell bikes!' said Sam, hopefully. But Derek was making no promises apart from 'We'll see.'

After lunch the three of them were packed off to get ready for the visit to the Fishers, and having been sartorially checked and approved of by Doreen, and Ingrid, they set off in the car, dropping Ingrid at her flat on the way.

Stopping in the parking area near the shops, especially Mrs Flemming's, brought back memories to Sam and Sarah. For Michelle this was all new, though they had told her of their adventures linked to the boundary stone. To their surprise, the post office looked quite different. It had been given a new coat of paint, the large window had been cleaned and an attractive display of stationery and cards placed in it. Upon entering, it was light and bright, for it had been redecorated in pleasing colours—no longer dark, dusty and dingy. A new counter and post office section had been installed and there was Roger behind it with a friendly welcoming smile.

'I'll call Cherry and the girls,' he said and pressed a button by the till. 'Safety device,' he added, 'so I don't leave the shop unattended.'

In a moment Cherry appeared with the girls in tow and took them through to the back. It was so different from how Sam remembered it. No longer untidy heaps of boxes and the like lying around, all spic and span. A peep into the backyard showed an amazing transformation into an already neat little garden with rose bushes and other plants. A dilapidated old shed had vanished and there was a flowerbed in its place.

'Shirley's work,' remarked her mother. Afternoon tea was a pleasant affair and while the two mums chatted, the children went and explored upstairs. When they went up to the attics Sam explained how he'd been caught, imprisoned and how he'd escaped.

The bedroom on the lower floor from which Jill had rescued him was now Shirley's and much more inviting. Later they drove home well content, for the Fishers had been invited to the Sunday Easter egg hunt.

CHAPTER SEVEN

Good Friday dawned cool and cloudy with a hint of rain in the air. It had been decided yesterday evening, before bedtime, that they would attend the eleven o'clock service at Bidcote Church. They would walk there across the fields and Ingrid, with Melissa would meet them in the village, returning to have lunch at the manor.

Breakfast was a quiet, reflective meal and afterwards the three children helped to prepare the dining room for lunch and then got ready.

Binky was most indignant when he saw everybody preparing to go out and not a hint that he was going too!

'Don't worry, Binks,' said Sarah 'We'll take you for a walk this afternoon.'

He wagged his tail, as if to say, 'That's all very well, but *why* can't I come with you *now*?'

'Because dogs aren't allowed in church!' said Sam. But he put down some of Bink's favourite biscuits and they left him chewing at one end and wagging at the other.

The walk was very pleasant in spite of the weather, and as they approached the stile by the boundary stone they met Erin also going to church. So she too received an invitation.

When the village was reached it was obvious that most of the villagers were going to the service. Ingrid and Melissa were waiting for them by the lychgate.

Melissa looked *so* different the children could hardly believe she was the same person. They entered, and once seated had a chance to look round, spotting Geoff and Karen, Cherry and Roger, with their children, also Mrs Flemming — without Mr Tibbles!

During the service Sam and Sarah had a strong feeling that there were others present, no longer in their earthly garment, but taking part with the same reverence. During the final hymn, 'The Bellman's Song,' they were *sure* other voices, deep and strong, joined with the choir and congregation. When finished there was one of those moments of suspended time when there is the feeling that something deep within has been touched in a way that only happens on special occasions.

Sam, turning his head slightly, was sure that out of the corner of his eye he glimpsed Brother Andrew and his companions gliding out through the open west door. As they vanished, the sun came out and shone through the stained glass window in the south transept, flooding the interior with shimmering coloured light. There was a gentle sigh from the congregation, and as the organ voluntary began, people started to leave. Soon they stood outside, blinking in the sunlight. The clouds had rolled away and the afternoon promised to be fine. Having exchanged greetings with the vicar, and others they knew, the Court's party started on their way home: Erin and Melissa arm in arm chatting away cheerfully, Ingrid talking to the parents of the twins, the children talking of the experience they had just had.

When they arrived, Doreen and Ingrid vanished into the kitchen, while the two elderly ladies were escorted to the sitting room. Derek disappeared into his study and the children went up to change into something more suitable for the proposed walk with Binky. On coming downstairs Derek was waiting for them.

'Guess what!'

'What?'

'There was a message on the answering machine from John Randell; Father Andrew is in Tadbridge tomorrow and will have lunch with them. Then, at his special request, they will come over in the afternoon.'

'Wow, that means we'll have Stephen and Jane with us. Let's go and ask Mum if they can stay overnight. That would save them having to return for the egg hunt.'

There was a concerted rush into the kitchen and a babble of voices, above which rose the patient tones of their mother. 'For goodness sakes, one at a time, *please*! How do you expect me to understand anything with the three of you all talking at once?'

They fell silent, then all started talking at once again.

'Right! Now quiet; Sarah, let's hear from you first. Jane and Stephen? Yes, yes, of course I understand what you want. Give me some time to think about it. No, don't come back in half an hour, I'll need longer than that.' They retreated back upstairs.

'Mum will probably say "yes", it's only when she says "no!" straight off that she means it,' said Sam.

Sure enough, when they went down for lunch she nodded, 'You may phone the Randells and ask if Stephen and Jane can stay overnight tomorrow.'

This was done directly and met with much approval, as John and Phyllis had been invited out Saturday evening and — to date — had not been able to find a 'twin-sitter'.

Binky had his walk, which included a visit to the farm to deliver some homemade Easter cards, also receiving ones in return from Jill and Brian. They stayed for afternoon tea, then returned home.

On the way back a council of war was held and a strategy worked out regarding the bicycles. This consisted of Sam remarking at regular intervals that '*If* Mr Reuben's cheque comes tomorrow maybe we could go to the Tadbridge DIY in the morning, really early, and see what they have to offer.'

At first this was received with little or no enthusiasm, but then an unexpected ally joined their cause, Melissa.

'What a good idea,' she said, 'I've decided to buy Michelle a bike. Could I come along as well?'

This put Derek on the spot and apart from saying, 'We'll go *if* the cheque comes!' The matter was settled.

Next morning that much wanted piece of paper *did* arrive, enclosed was an apologetic note for the children from Mr Reuben regarding his disposal of their bikes and he hoped the enclosed would enable them to buy suitable replacements. When they saw the amount on the cheque — £260, they let out a gasp of amazement and were sure it would! So shortly after breakfast they drove to Bidcote, picked up Melissa and twenty minutes later were examining the bikes in the DIY store. Luckily they had a large selection of children's models and after trying several different types they settled on a model with a Y-frame, twenty inch wheels, front and rear calliper brakes, five-speed gears, a drinks bottle(!) and pneumatic tyres. Sam opted for a red model, Sarah a green one, while Michelle chose blue. Derek bought them new cycle helmets, including one for Michelle, and a cycle carrier for the car. Melissa contributed a shackle lock for each bike, also a puncture outfit and pump. Sam hazarded the need for lights, but Derek pointed out summer was coming and they'd see about that in the autumn.

On arrival at home the forecourt to the garage was turned into a bike adjustment area as saddles were heightened, or lowered, brakes and gears checked. Then came the first tentative rides round the yard, the whoops of joy and yells of:

'Watch me.'

'Bet I can go faster than you.'

'Can you turn sharply, like this?'

'Race you down the drive. Come on!'

By mid-morning they were pronounced super-perfect

and the twins solemnly promised to write and thank Mr Reuben for his generosity. Michelle gave her grandmother a big hug and kiss that startled and gratified that good lady.

Until lunch they had a glorious time up and down the drive and the lane. They cycled to the farm and showed them off to Jill and Brian. Brian announced loudly, 'Me want cycly too!' Jill was not so sure, perhaps a tricycle first? Upon returning for lunch they all had the knee-wobbles when they dismounted. The bikes were carefully put away in the garage, securely padlocked to an old iron ring in the wall.

After lunch, before they could sneak out to have another go, Doreen caught them, sending the cyclists to tidy themselves up before the arrival of Father Andrew. They could hardly protest over this, but they did!

'I'm sure he won't mind if we're a little oily, after all we do have new bikes. That's no excuse? Oh well, if you say so. We don't have to change though? Goody!'

Once checked by Doreen they went to fetch the bikes, lining them up by the front porch.

Just after two the toot-toot of the Randell's car was heard and 'Here they are!' was yelled through the front door. The car had hardly stopped before Stephen and Jane had tumbled out and were examining the bikes.

'Gee, how super; they're like ours.'

A deep voice added, 'I wish such bikes had been about when I was a youngster, I'd have enjoyed riding one of those.'

They turned in some confusion. 'Sorry, Father Andrew, we sort of forgot about you.'

He laughed, 'When you have such fine new bikes it's understandable. Come on now, show me how well you can ride them.'

For the next five minutes or so they circled round him demonstrating their skills and receiving applause and encouragement, also from John, Phyllis, Derek and Doreen. Stephen and Jane ran round with them and were given goes on Sam's and Sarah's.

Then Doreen called, 'Enough!' and the grown-ups went inside while they put them away.

Father Andrew was very relaxed and did not ask any direct questions regarding the events centred round the Equinox. He remarked how well they looked and was given the cards they had made, in somewhat of a hurry, when they heard he was coming. He thanked them gravely and said:

'Ah, that reminds me! Please pass my briefcase. Thanks.'

He took out five small plain cardboard boxes and handed one to each of them with 'A Happy Easter to you!' In each box was a beautifully decorated papier mache egg.

Upon opening it they found a tiny silver image of St Andrew with a chain so that it could be worn round the neck. They thanked him gratefully.

'The eggs were made in our craft shop and the silver figurines come from our silversmiths atelier in Bristol,' he told them. He asked a few questions about school and was interested to hear of the Aunt Daisy episode, which still made Derek blush. Then he had to be off as there was an evening convocational meeting to attend. Stephen and Jane fetched their overnight bags and they bade the guest farewell from the front porch.

Then, having flung the bags upstairs they all rushed out to have another go with the bikes!

Upon arriving in the garage they found Bill, N'humba, JJ and Sir Brian gazing at them with great interest.

N'humba was familiar with bikes. 'Oh yes, many of my people have such machines but none are as so beautiful as these; you are indeed very lucky children!'

Bill and JJ nodded in agreement, but Sir Brian snorted. Now what idea had he got in his armour-plated head?

'They've only two wheels, you can't ride on two wheels, won't balance, unless they are side by side. You'd fall off.'

'No, no!' said Stephen, 'Once you are going fast enough

the bike stays upright. Show him, Sam.'

Sam unlocked his machine, wheeled it into the yard, jumped on and cycled round a few times.

'Must be done with mirrors,' muttered the sceptic, 'I tell you it can't be done!'

Even after Sarah and Michelle had ridden theirs he was still unconvinced.

'I know,' said Sam, 'Amongst the junk in the old store room there's an old grown-up's bike. It's all rusty and the tyres are flat but if you sat on it, Sir Brian, and we all pushed, you'd have an idea of how it can work.' Sam and Stephen went to get it and soon returned wheeling a very old, rusty ladies' 'sit up and beg' style of bike.

Sir Brian eyed it suspiciously. 'You want me to sit on *that?*' he asked.

'Yes, it's quite safe,' said Michelle, 'we'll help you.'

Bill, N'humba and JJ stood by, watching with some amusement. 'Wait a moment, I must prepare myself!' insisted the rider. He muttered a few words under his breath. There was a clanging noise and there he stood clad from head to foot in a suit of jousting armour. 'Can't be too careful,' said a muffled voice from within the helmet. This, from a protective point of view was fine—for him. But for the pushers, the added weight posed a problem. They decided that the yard was not the best place to gain sufficient momentum and chose the drive with its gentle downhill slope instead. Going round to the porch they placed the bike against the steps so that he could mount, and then Sam and Stephen took the handle bars on either side and the three girls moved behind: Jane and Sarah on either side of the saddle and Michelle pushing the back mudguard. They explained about the pedals and Sir Brian placed his armour-encased feet on them and they started off. His weight and the flat tyres did not make it at all easy, and Sam, realising that unless they got up some speed, it would topple over, shouted, 'Pedal, Sir

Brian, pedal!' Sir Brian did; the chain was stiff and rusty but the sheer weight of his feet set it and the wheels turning. Once started there was no stopping them, especially on a down slope. In a few moments they could no longer hold on and the bicycled knight shot off down the drive, most peculiar sounds coming from within the helmet.

'Turn the handlebars, steer it,' yelled Sam. But the cyclist, pedalling rhythmically, continued until the drive began to curve. Then the message penetrated the helmet and he yanked the front wheel sharply to the right. This took him up the path that led into the old ornamental garden; in a flash he had disappeared between its overgrown hedges. The children began to run after him. They were too late. From within the hedges they heard a clunk followed by a noise like a thousand tin cans hitting the ground, then a loud splash. When they arrived at the ornamental pond, the bike, with a dented front wheel, was lying by the pond coping and Sir Brian was just arising from the green slimy waters, puffing and blowing like a grampus. He had pitched off the bike, bounced on the coping and ricocheted into the centre of the pond. Luckily it was shallow.

They helped him out and he stood by the bike with water pouring out from every joint of his armour. He looked like a well-perforated water tank on legs. Bill and JJ helped remove the helmet and a truly bedraggled head appeared. N'humba was so helpless with laughter he could offer no assistance. Stephen and Sam picked up the bike and were trying to straighten the front wheel. The waterlogged knight now pronounced one of his charms again.

'Take this armour off and away, A trifle…!
No! Don't take any notice of that!
A little wet am I,
Pray make me dry!'

This time the trifle landed on the back of his neck and trickled down inside the armour. However at the same moment when it disappeared, two large rotating brushes, like those in car washes, appeared on either side of him and closed in. For a few moments there were loud 'Ows' and 'Ouches'. Then they withdrew, leaving a well scrubbed and dry object standing there. 'Hrrmph!' was its only comment. The children began to explain and apologise for his misfortunes, however, he did not seem to care, but kept on murmuring,

'Remarkable, only two wheels. Never would have believed it.' Then he turned to JJ saying, 'Come on my lad, there's some research needed here. Much more economical than a horse, eh?' and off they went.

'I've never seen a knight in armour ride a bike,' chuckled N'humba.

'Nor I,' added Bill.

The boys took the battered machine back to the storeroom and they went in for supper.

Their adventure was received with qualified mirth, though Doreen pointed out, 'It could have been much more serious!' Though how, they weren't sure. After all, Sir Brian could well look after himself, and if he was dead, how could he do himself any further harm? They suspected Doreen was concerned that they might try a similar experiment on a living person.

After supper Derek read them an Easter story from a book of Easter legends. Then it was the inevitable bed. But tomorrow there would be the egg hunt. So there were no protests!

CHAPTER EIGHT

Easter Sunday dawned clear and mild. Sunrise had been at five forty-five and when the household rose at about six thirty, it had taken cover behind some thin cloud, giving it a hazy appearance. Easter Sunday breakfast had always been a special occasion for the Courts, with a decorated table, including an egg-tree, spring flowers — depending on what was available — and boughs of catkins and branches just about to break into leaf. The meal included a special Easter bread that Doreen baked from an old recipe of her great-grandmother. Naturally there were eggs, too. The meal commenced with the singing of 'Christ the Lord is Risen Today' and the first part of the meal was eaten in comparative silence. No unnecessary talking was the aim. But after the breaking and eating of the bread there would be normal conversation, mainly directed to the forthcoming egg hunt, then the singing of the carol 'Easter Eggs'. All this was new to Michelle, not so much so for Stephen and Jane because of the school's Easter festivities they had taken part in right from kindergarten.

However, Michelle joined in with her usual enthusiasm. Just as breakfast finished, singing was heard approaching the dining room, and *through* the door came N'humba, Bill, JJ and Sir Brian. They were singing an old Latin Easter chant, with N'humba doing an harmonic improvisation, as he did not know the words. But it was Sir Brian who attracted their attention! He was clad, or swathed, in green. Round his ample waist was a broad belt decorated with patterns of spring flowers. He wore a wreath fashioned from stalks of spring corn and carried a large bunch of it in his right hand. This was making him sneeze heavily and rather spoilt the effect. After one particularly tremendous sneeze he managed to say his piece.

'I represent the spirit of the new life, the coming of Spring!' He went over to the fireplace and laid the sheaf in it. 'May this be a reminder of the harvest to come, the glory of summer and the fruits of Autumn.'

This last statement was spoilt by a particularly violent sneeze as he put the sheaf down. It caused his wreath to shoot off and also land in the fireplace. The little group then sang 'Now the Green Blade Riseth', and as the children had learnt it at school, they joined in. At the end every one called out, 'Merry Easter!' before the entertainers departed.

This year the egg hunt would be more elaborate, as more children were taking part and there was a much greater choice of hiding places. Upon returning from morning church they would each be given a decorated basket and be shown where the Easter Hare had visited. Once the search was over there would be lunch and then… But more of that later.

The church was now arrayed in all its Easter finery and the service one of joy and thanksgiving. They returned across the fields feeling elated and all ready for the hunt. Their invited guests had been at church, so they all came back together. The children were told to wait in the hall, where their baskets awaited them.

Brian wanted to know why his basket wasn't bigger because he was going to look for a 'Normous' egg. Jane told him that the Easter Hare brought eggs of all the same size, otherwise it would not be fair. Having thought about this he agreed—as long as the Hare brought 'lots and lots and lots of eggs.' He was assured there would be plenty. The younger children were paired off with the older ones. Jill with Sam, Brian with Jane, Ann with Sarah, Wendy with Stephen and Shirley went with Michelle.

Derek now appeared and announced to the little ones that as he was walking back he saw the Easter Hare *just* hopping along in the old ornamental garden, so maybe they should look there. Swinging their baskets and lustily singing the Easter Egg Carol, off they went.

The sun had now dispersed the light cloud and shone down on them. As yet it had little warmth, but bathed the grounds in a gentle light. Led by Derek, who walked on tiptoe and constantly said 'Shh!' so that they did not disturb the Easter Hare—who *might* still be hiding eggs—the procession made its way into the ornamental gardens.

Suddenly Brian let out a shrill yell and dragged Jane forward, for there, sitting on a large square stone just inside the entrance was a brightly coloured egg. 'Me the first finderer!' he proudly announced, putting the egg in his basket. Now they split up and the search began in earnest. Soon squeals of delight could be heard from every corner of the garden. Derek kept a watchful eye on things and would suggest to those whose baskets were not as full as they might be, 'Why not look over there?' or 'What about under those old rose bushes?' Strangely enough he was always right. After an hour's hunting, they brought their baskets to the entrance, where Doreen solemnly counted them and consulted a 'note left by the Easter Hare'. She then announced that they had found *every one* and so could go indoors to examine their booty, before lunch.

After lunch came another surprise. Derek called them out, grown-ups included, up to the terraced gardens. At the foot of the steps everyone was given a fork or trowel and a bag containing a handful of corn seed. He then led them up to one of the long beds, which had been carefully dug and raked over. It was scored with furrows and marked off in sections. Each had a peg bearing a name. 'Find your section,' he told everyone.

'Sprinkle your seeds in the furrow and carefully cover them over.' Brian and Ann were helped by their mothers, especially Brian, who tended to be rather too vigorous with his scattering and raking. When the task was completed all stood in silence while Harry recited an old farming blessing for newly sown crops. To finish, they sang 'Now the Green Blade Riseth' again.

In the evening, after the guests had gone and supper was finished, they gathered in the sitting room to talk over plans for the coming week. After all, with the children on holiday, some changes were necessary. So far the only known event was Michelle moving into her mother's flat on Thursday. However, the most important matter was the Bank Holiday Monday — tomorrow — what could they do? The weather forecast was favourable, which would mean busy roads, and long trips were best to be avoided. Derek had been consulting the local paper for 'what's on' and now made his suggestions:

'There are three large country houses nearby which will be open to the public tomorrow, all within easy distance of here and of each other. Also, if we buy entrance tickets at any one of them, they grant us admission to the other two, but only for tomorrow. We don't have to visit all three, but it does give us a wider choice. The nearest one is Heanehill House, to the north of the Iron Age Fort. Then almost adjoining it is Pittington Manor, on the next right turn off from the Tadbridge Road, and the third is to the east of Curry Hatch, Ascon House. We could take a packed lunch. They open tomorrow morning at ten, so we could start with Heanehill House and move on to the next when we feel we've seen enough.'

Everybody liked the sound of this and Derek's plan was adopted unanimously with one abstention, Cleo, who for obvious reasons could not come. Binky, on the leash, was welcomed in the grounds of all three properties and he would be quite happy to remain in the car some of the time, or be in Doreen's company while the others had a look round. Doreen was not over fond of trotting along miles of stately passages in stately homes.

'We'll prepare the food straight after breakfast, then we can be at Heanehill House when it opens,' she said. 'If you lot lend a hand there should be no rush.' So it was arranged and they retired for the night with a pleasant sense of anticipation for the morning.

For once, the weather forecast turned out to be correct, on a bank holiday too! As the sun rose in a cloudless sky, they were up early preparing for the day. Doreen, with her three persistent assistants, soon had the lunch ready and packed *before* breakfast, which meant it could be a really leisurely holiday affair. Remembering there would be a further local environment main lesson before the end of term, the children decided to take their notebooks, just in case. Derek found a local guidebook as well. Then they went upstairs to get ready.

Here a surprise awaited them, for standing in the lobby between their bedrooms was N'humba dressed in his gaudy outfit, smiling from ear to ear.

'Mr Bill has been telling me all about the great houses you are going to visit. He says there are many guardians in such places and I would like to meet them. So I'm coming with you.'

They looked at him and… … 'Will you be invisible to people?' asked Jane, hopefully.

'Most of the time,' he replied. 'But surely some of the inhabitants would be interested to meet an African Tokolosh?'

'They might,' said Stephen, 'and they might not. You

would surprise them, folk here aren't used to your kind of outfit.'

'Ah, then I show them we are setting, how do you call it—the fashion? I see you there. Don't worry, you will see me but not others; Sir Brian kindly gave me a potion, "Selective Invisibility, Potency Five." It is infallible.' With that, he vanished.

They groaned; the last time Sir Brian had used such a potion had been at Alwick Wild Life Park, with mixed results! (see volume two Sir Brian, Beasts and Brooches) There was nothing to do but hope for the best.

They set off in good time. That was just as well, for when they reached the Tadbridge Road, it was already full of traffic in both directions. It was quite a few minutes before a gap occurred so they could join the northwards flow. Then it took even longer to get across the southbound one onto the road for Heanehill House. As they swung across, a police car parked in a lay-by facing southbound switched on its flashing lights, pulled out and followed them.

༒

PC Wilby sat in the police patrol car in a southbound layby on the Tadbridge Road. He was in a 'why me' mood. Why, on a bank holiday, had it been his lot to be out on traffic control? Last year it had been the same. All the duty officer could say was, 'Because Easter is early this year, and that's the way the roster works out!' So here he was, on a glorious day, stuck in a stuffy car. If he opened the windows all the petrol fumes wafted in. Nothing ever happened, it was a waste of time it...

Suddenly he tensed in his seat. A car was just crossing the oncoming traffic turning down the lane to Heanehill House. It looked vaguely familiar; the back was full of children and a white toy poodle. Yes, he'd met *that* lot before! Then he shot bolt upright, for seated on the boot was the most extraordinary figure he'd ever seen: a brightly clad

African with incredibly long arms and legs, grinning and waving. He shot out into the line of traffic and swung down the lane in hot pursuit.

'That's funny,' said Derek, 'There's something wrong with the balance, it feels as if there's a heavy weight on or in the boot.'

Jane turned to look out the back window, only to be confronted by the grinning face of N'humba looking in. She let out a startled squawk. At the same moment the sound of a police siren rapidly approaching was heard, and as it drew alongside, the driver made signals for Derek to pull over. 'What on earth now?' he muttered. Jane had whispered her discovery to the others and they looked cautiously out the rear window. However, there was no sign of N'humba. The police car drew in ahead of them and PC Wilby got out and plodded back.

Derek leant out the window. 'What's the matter officer, I made all the correct signals when I crossed.… Oh, it's you!'

Once you've seen PC Wilby you never forgot him. He could have said the same about the contents of the car. Binky also recognised him and let out a positive volley of barks. 'Shut up, Binky,' ordered Sam.

Having recovered from the shock, the good policeman went into operation.

'No, sir, it's not your driving I pulled you over for. It's allowing dangerous riding, it is. How could you let someone ride on your boot, very dangerous, very dangerous indeed.'

'*Ride on the boot* officer. You must be joking.'

'I'm not joking, sir, I saw him with my own eyes.'

Doreen joined in. 'If you saw *him* with your own eyes why didn't other drivers see him and where is he now? I don't see *anybody* on our boot.'

PC Wilby paused. Where indeed was the mysterious rider? Could he have dropped off and hidden, and if others had seen him why hadn't they reacted? He glared at the occupants; why, whenever he met them, did he come off second best?

'Well, I'm warning you, don't let it happen again,' he snarled, and stomped back to his car, turned round and shot back to the main road. He arrived just in time to see a large caravan yaw across the road and sideswipe a passing truck that swerved into the path of an oncoming mini. In a moment he had his hands full sorting out the mess, trying to direct the traffic round the obstruction and phoning for help. The affair of the figure on the boot was forgotten for the moment.

'That man's hallucinating, he does it every time we meet him,' said Derek. As they swung into the tree lined drive leading up to Heanehill House, the children remained quiet. They were directed to the parking lot, and then went to purchase entrance tickets.

'Three, er, no, two adults, five children and a dog,' said the cashier.

'What do you mean by *three adults*?' said Derek. 'Surely you can see there's only two of us!'

'Well as you was walking up I could have sworn there were a funny looking coloured gentleman in very bright clothing,' he replied, scratching his head, 'but when I looked again he wasn't there. Must be the sun, I should have brought a hat.'

They walked across the front terrace. 'What is going on?' said Derek. That's the second person seeing someone who's not there.'

Then he turned suspiciously to the children. 'You're all very quiet about it! Come on, tell, what do you know about this?'

'It's N'humba,' said Sarah, 'Aunt Daisy's Tokolosh. He didn't go with her to the conference as he didn't think he'd be needed, so Bill suggested he remained behind for a holiday.'

'Yes, and Bill thought he'd like to meet other house guardians, so he's come along with us,' explained Jane.

'Sir Brian gave him a potion so that we can see him, but others can't. The only trouble is that it doesn't always work properly,' added Stephen.

'Great!' said Derek, 'Right, where is he now?'

They looked round, but there was no sight of N'humba.

'Perhaps he's gone inside to meet the other guardians,' suggested Sam.

'Well, the moment you spot him, tell me,' said his father, 'and we'll go in the opposite direction.'

'There's no need to be so touchy, dear. I'm sure he won't cause any problems,' soothed Doreen.

They started down another tree-lined avenue that led to a circular area overlooking the River Tad. From here they could see across to the grounds of Pittington Manor, which looked even more imposing than Heanehill. Walking back there was a sign pointing down a gravel road to their left saying: 'To the stables and cart rides'.

Promptly a clamour of 'please, please!' arose from the children.

'All right, off you go,' said Derek, 'Here's two pounds each; that should cover the ride and leave you something over for ice creams. We'll go back to the house and meet you on the back terrace. There are seats and tables so we can lunch in comfort!'

When they reached the stables there were several equipages harnessed and waiting to go. They chose a brightly coloured carriage that seated three on either side plus the driver. He turned out to be a friendly young stableman who did not seem to mind answering their questions.

'We go along the road and then up the main drive, along to the river lookout then back down the gravel road,' he explained to them.

With a crack of the whip they were off. The driver was

busy concentrating on the road as there was a great deal of traffic about. Jane, who was sitting with Sam on one side suddenly felt a slight pressure beside her, and there was N'humba, looking very excited.

'My goodness me!' he said, 'I never thought I would be riding around in England in one of these. My madam uses one when she travels on the veldt.'

'Shh,' said Jane, 'If the driver hears you he'll wonder how an extra passenger sneaked on.'

Unfortunately, just then the driver looked round. His eyes grew round and his mouth dropped open in a similar shape. He nearly fell off his seat. At that moment an impatient driver who wanted to overtake this wretchedly slow, 'Never should be allowed on the road' vehicle gave a blast on his horn causing the horse to shy, and he had to give his full attention to controlling it. He also gave vent to his feelings, roundly cursing the driver as he roared by. The children listened with interest. After all, one should enlarge one's vocabulary at every opportunity.

Then he turned his attention back to them, but N'humba had disappeared.

'It *is* hot in the sun today, isn't it!' said Michelle. 'Really, you should be wearing a hat.'

He looked at her rather queerly and said, 'Er, yes, I suppose you are right.' The rest of the ride passed without further incident. When leaving they thanked him profusely and were relieved to see he looked less bewildered. 'Don't forget a hat!' called Michelle as they turned up the road.

On the back terrace Doreen and Derek had found a table, and lunch was already spread and waiting. So was Binky.

CHAPTER NINE

They were having lunch early so that there would be plenty of time to visit the other houses. It was very pleasant sitting on the sunny terrace of a gracious country house. Many other visitors were also taking advantage of it. They were seated at the far end in front of a big bank of azalea bushes. At a nearby table sat a large, imperious, tweedy lady who reminded the children of Aunt Daisy in disguise. She sat facing her two friends, who had the bushes behind them and was in full flood about the 'disgracefully high entrance fee'. Then she abruptly stopped and stared beyond her friends into the depths of the greenery, letting out a shriek that virtually brought everyone around to a full stop.

At the same time, the children, who were also seated facing the bushes, saw the cheerful face of N'humba peering through at them; he waved, then disappeared. The shrieker had now decided to have hysterics and her friends were frantically trying to calm her down. She had a fine sense of drama and was using it to full advantage.

'I saw it, I saw it! A horrible face peering at me! Really evil it was.' Pause, for more hysterics, then, 'I demand to see the manager. Have they no control over whom they let in? I've always said these places should not be open to the ragtag and bobtail of society; it's disgusting. I demand a refund!' followed by another round of hysterics.

From somewhere a managerial looking lady, almost as formidable as her, appeared and said, in an icy tone, 'Would madam kindly control herself and stop disturbing the pleasure of her neighbours. If you have a complaint, kindly follow me to the office where it can be dealt with in a reasonable manner.'

Quivering with righteous indignation the objector followed her with her two very embarrassed friends in tow.

'What *is* the matter with people today?' complained Derek in a bewildered tone. 'It must be bank holiday madness.'

Peace was now restored and they continued their meal. But not for long. Out of the blue came a loud yell, followed by a crash and the sound of breaking crockery.

From out of the large French windows, which opened onto the terrace, appeared — visible to all — N'humba running as fast as he could, pursued by a varied selection of very irate figures wearing anything from full suits of armour to Elizabethan, Stuart or Georgian finery. There was a sense of unreality about them, but they were seemingly real enough to cause chaos among those seated there. N'humba was weaving in and out through the tables in an attempt to throw off his pursuers as they charged recklessly after him. Luckily they did not cause much harm, as they passed *through* any obstacles in their path.

There was a lot of shouting too: 'Varmint, villain, insulter of the fair sex! Wait until we catch you. You shall be taught how to show respect for M'lady!'

To which was added the barking of all the assembled dogs, Binky's high-pitched yap being well to the fore. Having reached the far end of the terrace, N'humba took a flying leap over the bushes and vanished. The hunters stopped abruptly, apparently satisfied he had gone, shouted a few more insults after him, then disappeared.

There were now several ladies having hysterics and being pacified by the house staff. The remainder were gathering up fallen sandwiches, broken crockery and the like, saying to each other:

'Did you see that?'

'Must be some kind of show!'

'Well they could have warned us!'

When order was restored, the icy managerial lady reappeared and called for everyone's attention. She apologised for the 'unforeseen disturbance' and added that, if those who felt their pleasure had been spoiled would care to go to the cashier, a third of the overall entrance fee would be refunded. A good move, for as a ticket cost £5.00, £2.00 for children and £1.00 for dogs, it would seem rather petty to go and demand £1.65. 66p or 33p. They noticed very few people did so.

Derek suggested they move on to Pittington Manor, where, hopefully, things would be quieter. They made their way to the car park and there, seated on the bonnet, was N'humba, luckily only visible to the children. When Derek began to manoeuvre the car out of a rather tight parking place, he jumped off and explained the cause of the uproar to them. Yes, he'd found the house guardians. They had welcomed him and took him to meet the lady who was in charge, 'a very grand person, oh yes, very grand indeed'.

He had been asked by a 'fat whiskery gentleman dressed in tin' what he thought of her.

'I answered honestly,' he exclaimed in a puzzled tone. 'I said she was much too thin and could do with a lot more fat, especially on her behind and under her chin. I was going to say more, but all the men started to chase me. I cannot understand why.'

The children soon told him why! Michelle explained, 'Ideas of beauty differ in other countries. You said the most insulting thing you could have said about her!'

Poor N'humba looked very crestfallen.

'Don't worry,' said Sam, 'just be careful what you say if

you meet any more guardians.'

The car was ready and they piled in. Luckily PC Wilby had managed, with the help of his colleagues, to untangle the traffic, and by the time they reached the main road it was flowing normally. However, the police car was still in the lay-by. As soon as he saw *that* car appear he shut his eyes, muttering, 'No, not again, there's nothing there, everything is normal.' He didn't reopen them until he was absolutely sure the car was well down the road.

The drive to the next turnoff was easy, as the traffic had thinned out and they were before the time when the afternoon trippers would be on their way. Pittington Manor was soon reached, and they drove through the portalled gatehouse and up another long and imposing drive. The glory of these gardens was a large artificial lake with a gazebo looking out to a man-made island covered with flowering shrubs and trees. The southern edge of the property was marked by the Tartcopse Hills. The manor house could be described as: 'Late Georgian with Victorian-Gothic accretions', making it look like an over-decorated wedding cake. The house only had a few of its main rooms open to the public, so they strolled round the grounds. Though when the children took charge of Binky it was hardly a stroll, as there were *so many* scents he wanted to follow, and their progress was somewhat erratic. Of N'humba there was no sign, much to their relief.

Eventually they arrived by the lake and discovered that the gazebo had a stall beside it serving ice cream, cool drinks, teas and cakes. A most convenient stopping place. Soon they were seated on the grass all sucking ice creams and gazing out over the lake at the little island.

'I wonder what's on it, besides plants?' said Stephen.

'Maybe there's a small summer house for her ladyship, and her servants would row her over when she wished to commune with nature and the deeper secrets of existence,' mused Sarah.

'More likely her husband had her put on it and left her there for a while when she got on his nerves with her vapid chatter!' retorted Sam.

'Beast!' said Sarah and punched him, causing him to stick his nose in his ice cream. There was a friendly tussle for a few moments until Stephen called their attention to the lake. 'Look!' he whispered, so that the grown-ups did not hear.

From near where they sat a line of ripples began to move out from the bank as if some invisible object was being propelled across the water. As they looked, a misty form appeared that gradually took on shape and definition. There, in a small African-type canoe, was N'humba, paddling his way towards the island. He saw them and waved back, calling:

'I go to find to out for you!'

'He must have overheard what we said,' groaned Stephen. 'I just hope there's nothing there that will cause more trouble.'

He looked round anxiously, for by now there were many groups of people taking advantage of the sun and beauty of the spot to sit and enjoy it.

The canoe disappeared round the island and a few moments later, with much noisy squawking, a flock of birds rose up as if scared by something. The children held their breath and wondered what would happen next. They did not have long to wait! The bushes now began to wave to and fro in an agitated manner, as if some large creature was forcing its way through them. Then through the greenery they caught a flash of brilliant colour; N'humba's clothing. It vanished, but following it they also saw a flash of the tawny hide of some large creature.

'A lion!' exclaimed Sam loudly.

'A wha?' said Derek sitting up suddenly and following his gaze.

'Er, nothing, Dad. I was just saying what a good place

to keep a lion.'

'Rubbish, who in their right minds would keep a lion on such a small island? What a foolish idea!'

Just then there was a loud shout of 'Oh my goodness me!' from the island and N'humba—visible to all—could be seen climbing up a slender tree, which swayed most alarmingly as he scrambled higher. Beneath, also plainly visible to all, was a large lion leaping at the trunk in an attempt to reach him. People on the bank scrambled to their feet. Some shouted instructions, others screamed, or yelled, children howled, dogs barked and the whole peaceful scene was swiftly transformed into one of total chaos.

A land rover with 'Park Warden' on its side came screeching down the road and two hefty khaki-clad wardens jumped out. One held a megaphone and was shouting through it:

'Calm down everybody, there is no lion on the island, I tell you there is no lion on the island. There is no...'

Here he stopped because he had just seen what was on the island! The next moment he continued, 'All right folks, don't panic! There *is* a lion on the island, but everything is under control; preventive measures are being taken.'

By now a second vehicle had arrived and four even heftier wardens emerged carrying an inflatable dingy, which they proceeded to pump up, hurl into the water and leap into. One carried a stun gun. The two on the bank now began to move the people back and away from the spot.

'Right folks, we must ask you to leave this area for your own safety. Please do so in an orderly manner.'

Most people were only too glad to leave, orderly or otherwise. Derek looked at the children.

'Is it?' he asked.

They nodded.

The dingy was now halfway to the island, but N'humba had seemingly had enough. He leapt from the tree, arms and legs flailing and fell into the undergrowth with a crash.

The next moment his canoe came shooting round a small promontory. Head down, he paddled furiously while a frustrated roar of rage echoed across the waters. The lion showed itself briefly at the water's edge then vanished. N'humba also became invisible to all except the children's eyes. They watched fascinated as his canoe streaked across the lake straight towards the dingy, the crew of which, nonplussed by the disappearance of hunted and hunter, had stopped, uncertain of what to do next. They soon knew. The canoe hit them squarely amidships and having a sharp prow, punctured their boat, which made a sound like a bursting balloon and promptly sank.

'Please move away NOW!' ordered the wardens and they joined the others drifting back to the manor.

'I wonder if they'll offer these people a third off *their* entrance fee?' asked Derek.

Apparently not. Another megaphone was being used to ask people to leave, as, 'owing to unforeseen circumstances', the park was closing early.

It was half past three, so they decided it was worth going on to Ascon House to at least get some idea of what it was like.

'If we think it's worth a longer visit we can always go there another day,' said Doreen.

'Yes, without our uninvited and somewhat troublesome guest,' added Derek.

There was no sign of N'humba. Jane thought he might have given up and made his way back to Bidford Manor. The others hoped she was right. The drive to Ascon House was easy. They followed the road on from Pittington Manor, under the railway line, then towards Curry Hatch, turning east just before they reached it. The entrance to Ascon House was where the road came to a 'Y' junction. Another long straight drive led them to an even larger house than the previous ones. The building was 'Queen Anne' style and rather like a miniature edition of Blenheim Palace. By local standards it was huge. There were not many people around, and the couple on the ticket checking table told them that business had been slow.

'It seems people went to the other two first and then decided they'd had enough,' one of them remarked.

'The management is thinking of opening specially for the May Day holiday,' the other told them.

'Good idea, we'll definitely come then,' said Derek.

They gave Binky a run round, deciding that the sheer size and scope of the grounds and house would need more than the hour or so left before it closed.

'Let's go home,' said Doreen, 'my feet are beginning to ache walking up and down all these gravel paths.' They returned to the car, drove out and headed for home.

On arrival they discovered that Cleo had not been idle. In the back kitchen a very disgruntled young thrush was perched on top of the curtain rail and the floor was covered in bird droppings and feathers. Having lost the bird, that young madam had gone out and come back with a mouse, which had also escaped and hidden in the cupboard under the sink, which Cleo was now trying to get into. A butterfly net dealt with the thrush, releasing it to the outside world, and after a protesting cat had been removed from the room, the mouse was caught in a Wellington boot and also popped out. Cleo was highly indignant at this treatment of her prey and refused to have anything to do with any of them until she'd had her supper. They felt the same until they'd had theirs. Later, in the sitting room, they were still wondering what had happened to N'humba when he appeared in the company of Bill, looking somewhat chastened.

'He wishes to apologise for the trouble he caused today,' said Bill with a faint smile upon his face. He did not realise there were so many different rules and customs here!'

'It was rather embarrassing, at times,' understated Derek.

'He assures me if he travels with you again he will make sure to ask before doing anything. But he would like you to know that Sir Brian's potion was not as effective as he had been led to believe. Sir Brian thinks he might have made a minor error in the strength of the mix, thus causing the unexpected appearances to others. He is working on it,' added Bill with a grin.

Sir Brian was well known for 'working on' things that had not turned out quite as expected.

'But what happened with the lion?' asked Jane.

N'humba told them. 'When you expressed the wish to know what was on the island I thought to please you I would find out. I always have my canoe handy and so I soon arrived at the island. It is very overgrown and when I reached the centre I found the remains of a large iron cage. Then I found its last occupant. It seems long ago the master of that house had brought back a captive lion from Southern Africa and kept it on the island because all his servants were afraid of the creature. The poor lion was *very* bored and sadly he died of loneliness and was buried there. But his soul was still chained to the island as he was far from his lion-soul pride. He suggested we played a game of catch, so I agreed, to cheer him up. And I promised to get in touch with his group when I return to Africa so that they can release him.'

'You mean,' said Derek slowly, 'that all that drama we saw was just a *game?*'

'Yes.'

Derek subsided into his favourite chair gasping, 'I need a drink.'

'So all is well?' N'humba queried.

'Oh yes, of course,' replied Doreen. 'Thank you for coming to explain things to us. Now I think it's bedtime, for everybody.' Surprisingly, nobody disagreed.

CHAPTER TEN

The next day it rained, heavily and solidly the whole time.

'Well at least it didn't do it yesterday,' said Sarah as she gazed through the window, which had a miniature waterfall running down it.

'What shall we do today?'

Derek came into the sitting room. He didn't look too cheerful either.

'You can help me clean out the car,' he said. 'There's an accumulation of rubbish and junk in it dating back to Noah's Ark and I shall need all the space I can get, as I'm helping Michelle's grandmother return to Tankerville Road this morning.'

This was received with mixed feelings, as it meant Michelle would be leaving the day after tomorrow.

'We ought to do something *really* special tomorrow,' said Jane, adding, 'I know, you all come over to Southleigh and we'll, we'll, *well*, we'll think of something.'

'No need to do that,' said Sam. 'It's a special day anyway,' and he pointed to the calendar.'

They looked and said 'Ah!'

'When do you go home?' asked Michelle.

'Somewhen, and somehow today,' replied Stephen.

'I shall probably be taking you later,' said Derek. 'Now I'm taking Melissa over with some of her stuff; then this afternoon I shall take the remainder and you two as well.

If there's room the rest of you can come along. Melissa wants to see all of you today, so that might be a good time; I'll ask her. Now I must be off. Try not to cause your mother unnecessary grief or wreck the place.'

Before they could answer, or throw something at him, he was gone.

'What on earth does your grandmother want to see us for?' queried Sam. 'I'd have thought she wouldn't want anything to do with us; after all, we upset all her plans.'

'Yes,' said Michelle, 'but that's how she *was,* not how she *is now.* She's really changed and Erin's been helping her. She's quite different in the way she treats me, and for the first time in my life I feel comfortable with her. I don't think we've anything to worry about.'

When Derek arrived at the flat, Melissa was ready, and as they loaded some of her cases and boxes into the car, she apologised for the weather.

'That's not your fault,' replied Derek.

'It could have been,' she said with a twinkle in her eye.

When loaded up there were still a few bits and pieces remaining.

'Shall I bring them and the children over after lunch?'

'Yes, of course; I feel guilty that I haven't spoken with them earlier, but Erin thought it best to wait a while. I was too confused, but things are clearer now.' And they set off.

This time the curtains did not twitch on her arrival. Through some work Erin had done, the strange behaviour of Mrs Mouldyberry—er, Merryberry—was forgotten.

If you had asked any ladies of the Residents Association they would have told you that the lady in The Laurels was slightly eccentric, but had been away for 'treatment' and was now 'quite her old self again'. However they hadn't pressed the poor dear to join any of their activities, yet. Better let her settle in properly.

They unloaded her stuff, getting rather wet in the process, but a hot cuppa soon restored their spirits, and Derek left her to unpack, promising to be back with the remainder and the children around three.

In the meantime, up in the secret room, five heads had been close together, plotting!

Tomorrow was April the first, and plans had to be made to exploit every possibility until midday. This did not preclude playing tricks on each other, but the main thrust was that their parents should really benefit from April Fool's Day! Two programs were drawn up. One for Bidford Manor and one for Southleigh; there were minor differences, but the aim was *fun* for and with parents. What they did not realise was invisible ears were listening and noting. Why should the children have all the fun? Sir Brian and N'humba became most enthusiastic about the whole idea and soon won Bill and JJ over. As Stephen and Jane would be back in their own home, JJ was dispatched to tell Bob Binnacle of their plans and to suggest he do the same. Bob wholeheartedly agreed, as life had been rather dull of late. When called for lunch there was much giggling and whispering going on over the table and several outbursts of laughter. Doreen promptly became suspicious and asked what were they up to? This only provoked more laughter, so she gave up.

Derek arrived halfway through the meal, wet, but cheerful.

'It's bucketing down. We'll have to get up into the gardens after lunch to make sure your plots and the sown wheat patch aren't waterlogged or being washed away.'

They enjoyed sloshing about in boots, digging channels for the excess water to drain off, and building dams in other places to divert the flow. Then it was back to prepare for their visit to Melissa. While they argued over clothing standards with their mother, Derek went round to the flat and picked up the remaining items. When he returned they were waiting for him. The rain had eased a little and as they turned into Tankerville Road it stopped altogether.

Melissa met the children on the doorstep and told them to make themselves comfortable in the front room while she helped Derek unload. When finished they joined the children. There was an awkward silence for a minute or two, then Melissa spoke:

'Thank you for coming, I can understand why you may have been reluctant to do so; but now here you are! And I want to apologise to you all—also Michelle—for my behaviour and the way I treated you before Easter. When I think about it I feel very ashamed and I want you to know that it will never happen again. It may be hard for you to accept that I *have* changed; but changed I have with the help of Erin, Karen, Michelle, and you children, as well. I hope you will feel you can trust me and treat me as your friend.'

She paused, and they could see her eyes were moist. Stephen stood up and spoke for all.

'We *know* you are changed!' he said, 'And as for what happened, that's in the past now. We'd like to have you for a friend, not only because you are Michelle's grandmother, but because you are a friend of Erin's. We like collecting friends, don't we?' he added, turning to the others.

'Of course we do!' they chorused.

Melissa looked greatly relieved and murmured 'Bless you!' With that they all rushed forwards and hugged her.

'It's worse than being hugged by a grizzly bear, isn't it?' remarked Derek, when at last she emerged from the mass of youngsters.

'Now, sit down and we shall celebrate!' she said. 'Perhaps, Michelle, you would like to help me bring in the goodies for the guests!' and they left the room. Michelle returned in a moment pushing a heavily laden trolley, her grandmother following with an equally laden tray. It was an afternoon tea to be remembered for many a long year, festive and joyful. To crown it all, the sun broke through and shone brightly, as if adding its approval to the proceedings. At around five, when all the dishes, bowls, jugs and their plates and glasses were empty, Derek said — reluctantly — that they must be going, for the Southleighans had to be delivered home.

'You two are welcome to call in any time you want, and so are Sam and Sarah when in Tadbridge, or any other of your friends, like Chris and Fenella,' she said as they left.

There was more giggling in the car:

'Phone us tomorrow and tell us.'

'Yes, you too.'

This made the driver uneasy; what were the little dears plotting now? He glanced at the dashboard clock. The date showing was the thirty-first of March. Oh, so that was it, was it? Well, two could play at that game!

The next morning the children were up by six and set about their preparations for the 'fun'. They flitted round like ghosts, in front of their parents' bedroom, on the stairs, into the kitchen, the sitting room, even out into the yard and garage. Well pleased with their activities, they returned to dress and await results. However, when the girls entered their room, their clothes had mysteriously disappeared and the next minute Sam appeared demanding to know where his were. They searched, but with no result until Michelle suggested the secret room. Sure enough, there, neatly laid out on the table, were all the missing clothes. They looked at each other mystified, who could have done it? Hastily they dressed and gathered in Sam's room to await the events that should shortly follow. They heard their parents' door open and a muffled 'ouf!' Someone had been caught in their blanket booby trap. They made to rush out and shout 'April Fool!' but Sam's door would not open. Suddenly the handle gave and they pitched out on to the landing, falling over a series of threads that had been tied across the passage to trip them. This was all wrong, but … …?

The sound of tins and the like clattering down in the

kitchen hopefully meant Doreen was experiencing the preparations made in there. They crept down the stairs and peeped round the kitchen door. No sign of anyone, most odd. Then from behind them a hollow voice said 'beware!' They turned round quickly — no one in sight. At that moment what appeared to be an egg came hurtling towards them, followed by another and another. They ducked and the missiles went through into the kitchen. There were the inevitable squelchy sounds as they landed. They ran in to see the damage. Not a sign of an egg, whole or broken! Then it began to rain cornflakes from the ceiling; soon the floor was thick with them, and any movement they made was accompanied by crunchy sounds. By now they were *very* bewildered and beat a hasty retreat to the sitting room, getting caught in the drop-curtain device rigged up over the door — by them. When they'd struggled free, standing and grinning at them with great glee were Derek, Doreen, Sir Brian, Bill, JJ, and N'humba, who chanted, 'April Fool!'

Sam guessed at once. 'You, you!' he shouted pointing at Sir Brian and company. 'You overheard us planning yesterday!'

'True, true,' said Derek, 'and they let us in on their little plan. Mind you, I'd already realised what today was. All your giggling and whispering gave the game away.'

For a second everybody stared at each other and then began to laugh. They'd been well and truly caught out.

'That egg trick was great!' said Sarah.

'And the cornflakes,' added Michelle.

'Talking of food, I think we should go and have breakfast,' said Doreen.

Sir Brian, being the senior member, led the way, which was just as well, for as he entered the kitchen, a large jug of treacle suddenly materialised above him and poured its contents on to his head.

'Not on me! on *them*,' he yelled; but the jug had its own

idea and in spite of his efforts to dodge, followed him round, dousing him with its contents until empty. Then, saying, 'April Fool!' it vanished. By now everybody was helpless with laughter. Sir Brian fled, returning some minutes later cleaned up.

'At least *that* spell worked properly,' he grumbled.

Bill asked, 'Are there any more possible hazards around?'

'Don't think so.'

'Well we can always send you in first if we're not sure.'

With this the four of them disappeared, leaving the mortals to have their breakfast.

During the meal they played harmless tricks on each other, like pinching the toast off Derek's plate when he wasn't looking, or passing an empty jug when someone asked for milk. Doreen continually passed the wrong items with a fixed smile on her face. It was great fun. However, there was some concern as to what else Sir Brian might have prepared and forgotten about.

They soon found out. After breakfast and the usual tidy up, they decided to do some cycling round the grounds and show Michelle the best way to cycle there from her new home. The bikes were stored in the garage, as Derek reckoned it was the safest place, and was wired with a warning device should anyone try to break in. It was a pleasant morning after all the rain, just right for biking. They rushed out and opened the garage and stared in amazement. Instead of the car, a dilapidated old-fashioned carriage stood there—minus horses—and in place of their bikes were three penny-farthings.

Their yells brought Derek running. He stared in disbelief and promptly roared, 'Sir Brian, come here NOW!' at the top of his voice. This was carrying April foolery too far!

Sir Brian appeared very promptly, as he must have caught the sense of urgency in Derek's voice. He too stared, then said, 'Oh.'

'Don't just stand there saying "Oh". Do something!' demanded Derek.

'I, er, forgot about this,' said the prankster. He stood in thought for a moment and then said: 'Nruter ot ruoy reporp mrof!' (try it backwards!) A mist filled the garage and a moment later they found themselves looking at a very battered old tractor and three hoops. 'Wrong?' he said.

'Of course it's wrong!' howled Derek.

'Hm, don't get so excited, it doesn't help; I'll try again.' More deep thought and then: 'ekam eseht smeti sa yeht erew!'

The same mist and now the previous objects reappeared. Derek was speechless and the children were beginning to become concerned; what about their bikes? Sir Brian concentrated furiously and tried again: 'erotser esaelp ot rieht lanigiro epahs!' he chanted, and to everyone's relief, three brand new bikes and a car stood there. The prankster discreetly vanished as soon as they reappeared.

They had a good time racing round and up and down the drive. Then after snack they took the bridlepath across the fields to Bidcote and the flat. Naturally they stayed and chatted with Ingrid, inspecting the room that would be Michelle's—a nice light and airy one, which her mother was repainting for her. Then, as it was now past twelve, they made their way homewards. When they walked in, Doreen said, 'Jane phoned for you and asks that you phone her *straight away*.'

There was a rush to the phone, and after a minor scuffle, Michelle gained it and was soon talking to Jane. It appeared that Stephen and her had had similar experiences to theirs. Things they had prepared for their parents had not worked, but unexpected things had happened to them! They had also found out that Bob Binnacle was at the bottom of it. Luckily his tricks were more reliable than Sir Brian's. Both Jane and Stephen now wished Michelle all the best for her move and were pleased to hear she would have a nice newly painted room.

The remainder of the day was spent sorting out Michelle's clothes and oddments that seemed to have become hopelessly muddled up with Sarah's.

'Well, her things are so like mine and mine like hers that they sort of got put in the wrong drawers,' explained Sarah.

'And your shoes and your toys and your books, as well?' asked an exasperated Doreen. 'Lucky for you she's not moving miles away; at least we can return anything of hers left behind, and she can return anything taken by mistake.'

'Naturally,' thought Sarah, 'so what's all the fuss about?' Parents are so unreasonable at times.

Sam offered to help, but he would pick something up and say, 'Who owns this?' and when told, like as not would put it down on the wrong pile, causing more confusion. Eventually they suggested he just talk to them. This didn't work either, as his talk usually required answering, which distracted them even more. In the end they gave him the book of Norse Myths and he read a couple of the stories: 'Thor loses his Hammer' and 'Loki's Children'. However, these were so exciting they would often stop what they were doing to listen. Eventually, by supper time, Michelle and her belongings were — well, sort of ready.

The next morning was a sad one for them, though at least she would still be very much part of their lives. Doreen was also 'sad/glad'; when she compared the shy withdrawn little girl that had come into their home a few months back, she could hardly believe that this cheerful, friendly, outgoing child was the actually one and the same. Though in spite of all her good food she was still as skinny as a rake. She would be missed, for she acted as a balance between the twins and their parents. She also had a knack of tempering their wild ideas. Derek admitted he would miss her too. He loved his two dearly, but this child had shown a love for him that sometimes he felt was sadly lacking in his! So that morning everybody went round saying, 'After all, it's not as if I/you will be gone forever' or 'It's not as if I/you won't be able to visit each other whenever we want to.'

Just before lunch Sir Brian and company appeared to wish her well and assure her of a welcome *anytime* she returned. Bill offered to look into the question of a house guardian for the flat, which she gratefully accepted. After lunch Derek said he would take her stuff across in the car, while they cycled over. First they had to help load the car.

'How on earth did you collect so much stuff?' wondered Derek as the interior of car and boot filled up.

'I don't know,' said their owner, 'except that kind people gave me things!' and she looked hard at Derek, who promptly busied himself with fitting it all in. A short while later the car drove off and the children mounted their bikes and rode along the bridle path to the village. On the way they met Geoff, who offered to call for Michelle each morning when they came over to catch the school bus.

'A good idea,' remarked Sarah, 'then neither of you will be late.'

When they reached the flat Derek and Karen were already unloading stuff, and the children helped carry it up to her room. They offered to help her unpack, but remembering the hassles of packing, Michelle said she would rather do it herself. Instead they went down to the kitchen and had tea with a specially baked 'welcome home' cake.

'You must come with us when we go to meet Aunt Daisy,' said Sarah. 'We'll phone you when we know the train time.' The twins cycled back to a house that seemed to be missing someone!

CHAPTER ELEVEN

When they arrived back their mother greeted them with:

'Aunt Daisy has just rung; she's coming back earlier than intended, in fact tomorrow, as the conference has completed its business ahead of schedule. She's arriving on the twelve forty-eight West Coast Express.'

Loud cheers and leaping round, which Binky enthusiastically joined in.

'All right, all right! Don't go mad. Ring Stephen and Jane and see if they want to come to the station, also Michelle.'

This was done and after supper they spent a pleasant time discussing what they could and would do with Aunt Daisy during the remainder of her stay. Just as they were going up to bed the phone rang again.

This time it was Uncle Fred. 'Just phoning to check when the aunt returns,' he said to Sam, who'd reached the phone first. 'Tomorrow? Good, tell her I've tentatively arranged an outing for Saturday. As there will be five of you, besides your aunt and myself, I'm hiring a medium-sized Land Rover for the day. No point in having us all squeezed up in my old car. I'll phone again tomorrow evening to confirm arrangements... ... Where are we going? Ah, that would be telling, and I'm not. You'll just have to wait and see,' and he rang off.

Once ready for bed the twins sat on Sarah's and tried to

guess where this 'Magical Mystery Tour' would take them. They listed all the possible places but none of them seemed to sound right.

'Unless it's a sewage farm—though I should hardly think so,' said Sam.

'Well, we *shall* just have to wait and see,' said Sarah.

There was a gentle knock on the door and N'humba came through it. He looked somewhat apprehensive. 'My madam returns tomorrow?'

'Yes, she'll be here in time for a late lunch.' He looked uncomfortable. 'What is it N'humba?' asked Sam, 'You look really worried.'

'You won't tell the madam about the holiday? Please! She would be very cross if she knew I had behaved wrongly as a visitor.'

'Of course we won't tell!' said Sarah. 'Nor will Dad; he's probably forgotten all about it by now. We'll leave it to you to say what you think is best.'

'Wait until she's in a good mood,' added Sam.

N'humba looked relieved, adding he *would* tell the madam, but perhaps not straight away.

Next morning was all hustle and bustle as Doreen checked that the guest room was in order and the bed freshly made. The children made a large paper banner to hang over the door, saying, 'Welcome Back Aunt Daisy!' and managed to find enough early spring flowers in the garden to fill the vase on her bedside table.

Michelle turned up at eleven, having found her way with no problems. An early call from Jane, saying Reg would be bringing them to the station, as afterwards they would be going back to his place for a 'Mrs Blankenzee' lunch, solved the transport situation.

While they were having snack, N'humba appeared. 'Are you coming too?' asked Doreen.

'No,' he replied, 'I wait here for my madam to make sure

all is well for her.'

When he'd gone, Sam added, 'He's scared stiff she's going to find out about his fun and games on Monday. I reckon she can lay it on like the "awful aunt" if needs be.'

'Yes, she's a very determined lady; otherwise she wouldn't hold the position she does. I, for one, would not like to argue with her,' agreed Doreen, adding, 'Come on, hurry up with your snack. We must get going. The train may be on time, for a change.'

A little while later, with three exuberant children chattering nineteen to the dozen in the back, Doreen drove into Tadbridge and parked in the station yard. As they were disembarking Reg drew up beside them and the twins tumbled out. 'See you, Gramps!' they shouted as he drove off.

'He's in a hurry,' they explained. 'Some client or other he has to interview. We just go round to his flat after we've seen Aunt Daisy.'

'Well, let's get onto the platform,' said Doreen. 'It's nearly twelve thirty; we'd better see if the train's on time.'

According to the arrivals board the twelve forty-eight was running to time: 'But may be subject to possible delays caused by points work just before Tadbridge.'

'Just our luck!' said Sam.

'Well at least the snack bar is open. When I was here to pick her up everything was closed,' retorted their mother.

They sat and waited; after five minutes the indicator flashed up that 'the twelve forty-eight will be five minutes late.'

'*Almost* on time!' remarked Michelle.

Sure enough, at twelve fifty-three the 'West Coast Express' drew into the station. A few people got out and a few got on. They spotted Aunt Daisy, a tiny speck, down the far end of the platform; it appeared she had been in the last coach. The quintet let out a whoop of delight and set off at top speed towards her. Doreen followed at a more leisurely pace. Soon *the* aunt was enveloped in children, laughing and joking with them.

'I thought our trains were bad enough,' she said, 'but this one was bulging at the seams. I did have a reserved seat but had no chance of finding it. I was stuck in the corridor down the far end. It seems that *two* other expresses were cancelled, one because the engine broke down, the other because there was no driver or guard available. So they crammed all those passengers in as well. Some changed at Bristol, but most of them, poor souls, will have to change at Plymouth. I'm glad I was getting out here.'

'Well, let's get you home for a good lunch and a rest,' suggested her sister-in-law.

'Hands off the lady you lot. Make yourselves useful and carry her bags. No squabbling now; if you're that keen you can take turns.'

Outside the station, Stephen and Jane reluctantly said goodbye, but cheered up when Sarah reminded them of the Saturday excursion.

'Is it arranged?' asked their aunt.

'Oh yes, Uncle Fred has it all planned, but he won't tell us where we are going and what we'll see,' replied Sam.

'He'll ring up this evening to confirm it,' said their mum.

Michelle was dropped off on the way back to the manor. Then, seated as usual in the kitchen having lunch, they chatted, while Binky curled up against Aunt Daisy's legs and Cleo settled on her lap.

'The conference went well,' she told them. 'I won't bore you with the details; much of it was administrative stuff and changes of policy. I think some good decisions were taken and some others which I'm not so sure about; I shall just have to wait and see. I shall know more when I arrive back at the mission next Wednesday.'

Next Wednesday! The children were horrified, why that was almost tomorrow. Well, not quite, but as she would leave on the Tuesday they would only have *three whole days* with her. It wasn't fair!

As if anticipating their feelings she smiled, saying, 'Wherever you are and whatever is happening to you, make the best of the situation and gain as much from it as you can. That's what I intend to do for the next few days and that's what you're going to do too.'

They knew she was right and cheered up at once. 'Now Daisy, off you go for a rest,' said Doreen, 'while we tidy up.' Seeing the woeful looks on their faces, Aunt Daisy added, 'I'll meet you in the sitting room in an hour's time!' That cheered them up; after all, an hour is not *that* long.

True to her word, exactly an hour later Aunt Daisy came into the sitting room, where the three of them sat waiting—Michelle had cycled over after lunch. They were supposed to be playing UNO, but concentration kept wandering and in the end the game petered out. Still it helped to pass some of the time. Aunt Daisy sat down with them and said, 'When I entered my room for a rest N'humba was waiting for me. He welcomed me most effusively, but I could tell he was very uneasy about something, as afterwards he lapsed into an awkward silence and stood there shifting from one foot to the other, nervously clearing his throat. "All right," I said, "Tell me all about it. What have you done now?" It came out in a rush and I gather his behaviour on Bank Holiday Monday caused a trail of chaos through three of England's stately homes! I'd like to hear your version as well.'

They told her that N'humba's account was more or less correct, barring a few details.

'Did you punish him?' asked Michelle anxiously. 'I'm sure he didn't do it deliberately. It's just that being in a foreign land he doesn't know the customs.'

'True,' said Aunt Daisy, 'but he is impulsive and over eager at times, often getting himself into scrapes at home.

I've warned him that one more misdemeanour during this visit and that will be the last time I allow him to come away with me. He knows I mean it, too. I hope for the last few days he will behave.'

'In some ways it wasn't *all* his fault,' said Sam. 'You see, he was given a potion by Sir Brian, you remember Sir Brian?'

She grinned, 'Oh yes, very well. I presume it did not quite work as expected?'

'Yes, instead of keeping him invisible to everyone except us, he kept on visibilising unexpectedly. That's what caused the most trouble!'

'Hm, all the same, he should know better at his age! Why he's well over a hundred and fifty years old. Sometimes I despair of him *ever* learning to act in an adult manner.'

The children pleaded his case so earnestly that eventually she agreed to give him another chance.

Then it was a good old settle down to listen to more of her stories about life in Africa and the work she did. After hearing about the children in the school where she taught and the difficulties in providing adequate materials and books, Sam said,

'They speak and read English don't they?'

'Oh yes, it's now their main language apart from their tribal one.'

'Then we could write to them and maybe send them some of our old school books?'

'That would be wonderful, Sam. Perhaps your class would like to take that on as a project.'

'Sure, we can ask Mr Atkinson tomorrow.' Pen friends in Southern Africa sounded exciting! At that moment the gong went for supper.

Later that evening the phone went and Uncle Fred was on the line. Sarah had answered.

'Hi horror!' he joked, 'How's the h'awful h'aunt?'

'Supermendous!' she replied.

'Right, now listen carefully. The Land Rover is hired. I've arranged to pick up Stephen and Jane around nine. So we should be with you by nine thirty. Let Michelle know so she's there when we arrive. Tough outdoor clothes and sturdy boots or shoes. No need to worry about food and drink, that's all arranged. We should be back around six… No, Sarah! I am not answering *any* questions, you'll just have to wait and see. Must go, lesson preparation. See you all tomorrow.'

With that they had to be content, though afterwards they played a guessing game as to where the Magical Mystery Tour would take them. Aunt Daisy had some original suggestions, but they went to bed still mystified.

Everyone was up extra early next morning, Sam and Sarah because they just could not stay in bed a moment longer once awake. Their mother was also up early to make sure they were ready when Fred arrived. The twins had a habit of being ready when in fact they were not. On one memorable occasion when an early start was being made they both appeared still in their pyjamas. 'But we are ready, we've only got to put our clothes on!' they had protested.

Since then Doreen made a point of being around to see they were properly ready. This morning though, with Aunt Daisy up and helping to prepare breakfast, they soon put in an appearance fully clad, in their outdoor clothes, except for their boots. 'You see, Mum, were *are* ready for Uncle Fred.' It was with some difficulty they were persuaded to remove coats and hats before sitting down to eat. What contradictory beings adults are. They tell you to 'be ready' and when you are, they tell you not *that* ready. Why can't they make up their minds what they want?

As soon as breakfast was over the ringing of a bicycle bell announced Michelle's arrival. They rushed out to meet her and soon were chattering like parrots round Aunt Daisy until Doreen shooed them off to allow her to finish her own preparations. It was now nine o'clock so they went out on to the porch to wait for the Land Rover.

'It's coming, it's coming,' yelled Sam, who had caught a glimpse of a dark green vehicle gliding down the lane. A few minutes later it arrived, disgorging the twins and Fred, who greeted Aunt Daisy with:

'I hope you are ready to be "magicked and mystified" today.'

'Oh yes,' she replied, 'You have already mystified these children and I'm quite happy to be mystified and even magicked as well!'

'Right, everybody pile in. Got your stout boots, hats, coats? Excellent. *No!* Sarah, I'm *still* not answering any questions, you'll know soon enough.'

They bundled into the roomy vehicle, waved goodbye to Derek and Doreen and were off.

'We start by going due north,' their tour operator informed them. Which they did, up the Tadbridge Road, taking the bypass round past the school, under the railway and on the road to Curry Hatch. The ridge of hills that had blocked the building of the canal lay in front of them.

'By the way, we are calling in on Will Bennett and family on our return journey,' said Fred to Aunt Daisy. 'I thought it would interest you, and Will has a great fund of local knowledge.' She nodded in approval.

They followed the road, which wound through the hills. However, Fred stopped in a lay-by and they got out.

'We are going to climb up to that knoll on top of this ridge,' he explained, 'Now you know why I suggested stout boots.'

They gazed up to their objective. The way was pretty steep and would require some scrambling. Jane opened her mouth, but Fred cut her short with, 'No, Jane, this is not our goal, but from up there I can point it out and tell you something about it. Now what are you all standing about gawking at, have you never seen a hill before?'

He pointed to a narrow path snaking up from the road. 'Come on, Daisy, we'll show these youngsters what hiking really is,' and the two of them set off at a spanking pace.

'Hey that's not fair, wait for us,' the children shouted and set off in pursuit. They caught up in a few moments, but as the path became steeper the pace slowed, for their breath was needed for climbing, not talking!

At last they reached a more level area, though still continuing the upward climb. Ahead of them rose the knoll, still some distance off. They paused for a moment to regain their breath and to look back towards Tadbridge. The countryside was spread out below them. To their right the remains of the canal could be seen and beyond it the town and railway line; the distant countryside was lost in a haze, though Heane Hill with the Iron Age Fort lifted its head above it.

'On a clear day you can locate Bidford Manor,' remarked Fred. 'You can't see the house, but the Obelisk is visible.'

'You mean if I climbed to its top I could see these hills?' asked Sam.

'Yes, but I don't think you'd better try. Your father might object,' grinned Fred.

They stayed for a few more minutes, then he led them on to their objective. The last part of the climb was steep, but eventually they stood on top of the knoll and gasped at the view spread out around them.

Now they could see the countryside on both sides of the ridge.

'By the way, this place is called Crimson Hill, no doubt named after the facial colour of those who climb it, and looking at you lot, not ill-named,' remarked their guide.

'And you,' they replied.

They looked northwards. The country was much flatter as it stretched away in the direction of Taunton and Bridgewater. Down to the right the New Abbey's white buildings stood out clearly. Away to the far left the River

Tad wound its way north-west, passing through another gap in the hills, where, Fred reminded them, was the water mill they had visited. But not a word did he say about today's objective.

'You look around and tell *me!*' he instructed.

They looked, but what were they looking for? Then Michelle, who had been systematically scanning the north slopes of the left-hand side of the ridge said,

'What's that place down there?' pointing to a flat area with strange lines running across it and what appeared to be the remains of several buildings.

'Ah, good for you,' answered their guide; 'but what do *you* think it is?'

The children stared. Obviously it was disused, whatever it had been.

Stephen gazed and mused. 'A large open space. Buildings round the edge, lines, roads? running across it. Running, that's it, runways, it's a disused airfield!'

'Quite right, Stephen, it is. One used during World War II. It has an interesting history and British Heritage has recently acquired the site. I know one of the local officials and persuaded him to lend me the key so that we can go and have a look round. What do you say to that?'

There was a unanimous 'Yes!' and they started back for the Land Rover, the descent taking far less time than the ascent.

CHAPTER TWELVE

They piled in when they reached their vehicle and Fred drove through the pass, swinging sharp left along the road running parallel to the hills. Soon they reached a T-junction, where he turned right, and there, on their left was the wide expanse of the old airfield. After a short distance a tall wire fence began to enclose the buildings from the road, which now forked. Fred took the left one, coming to a stop in front of a large pair of gates, fastened with a heavy chain and a formidable looking padlock. There was also a large notice. 'MOD Property. No Admittance. Keep Out!' Underneath was a newer one reading, 'British Heritage. For information regarding access please contact our nearest regional office.'

Fred hopped out and, producing a large key, undid the padlock, removed the chain and pushed the gates open. After he'd driven through he relocked them and drove over to the group of old buildings. There were still traces of a road, or part of the runway, but much overgrown and in many places the surface was cracked and missing. They parked by the remains of the control tower and got out.

It was strange standing there in that empty space where the only sound was the wind rustling the grass.

Sarah expressed the general feeling, 'What was it like during the war?'

'Let's find a place where we can sit and have lunch,'

suggested Fred. 'Then I'll tell you what I know about it.'

They collected two very interesting hampers from the boot and wandered past the building complex and along another overgrown roadway until they reached a spot where a few trees and bushes grew next to some ruins. Here, to their surprise, they found two concrete benches looking out across the field. Behind were the remains of a wall that gave them some protection from the wind. The hampers were deposited and Fred began:

'This airfield was a temporary one built early in 1939. It was a base for the fighter aircraft used to protect Bristol and Avonmouth. There were two squadrons, each of ten aircraft — one of Hurricanes, the other Spitfires — kept in those hangers over there. Also there were the control tower and administrative offices. That building you can see at the southern end was the fire truck and ambulance station. Where we are sitting, or rather just behind us, were the airmen's living quarters and also quarters for the few non-combatants who worked in the offices. There was also accommodation for some officers' families as well. Away over to the north there was a small anti-aircraft unit, which was run by the army and totally separate.'

'By June 1940 it was completed and fully functioning. Just in time too, for in July the Luftwaffe began to launch its attacks over south-west England. The fighters here played their part in defending Bristol, but the airfield did not go unscathed. Twice it was attacked by bombers and on the first occasion nearly destroyed; and there was a heavy loss of life and equipment. But it was soon back in action. After the Battle of Britain it was gradually reduced in aircraft strength and finally closed down in 1944 after the successful invasion of Europe. Though the buildings have suffered neglect and some vandalism, the place is pretty well as it was in those days.'

'The plan is to restore it to its former condition and

possibly have a couple of the original fighters on display. For some reason the MOD held on to this land, so the airfield is complete. British Heritage has been able to purchase it for a very reasonable price. Also there is the remains of an ancient Celtic village in the middle of the field, which has never been properly excavated. This would be a fascinating combination of ancient and modern. But I've talked far too long.'

Protests of 'No, no, go on, go on!' 'No, I reckon it's lunchtime now. My stomach tells me so. After lunch you children can have a good explore while your aunt and I put the educational world to rights. Then if you have any more questions I'll do my best to answer them. We shall leave here around three thirty as Will is expecting us at four.'

Luckily the day was dry and mild with not a cloud in the sky — for the moment. They had lunch, a very good one that Fred had made himself. 'It's your mother's training,' he told Sam and Sarah, 'I've become a compulsive cooker and caterer.'

'Now remember to be back by the Land Rover at three fifteen,' he added, 'or you will have to walk to Will's place. Not that it's far, if you just went straight up this side of the ridge and down the other you'd come to the old canal.' 'We'll be there,' the children assured him. Such a walk did not appeal to them after the scramble up to the ridge.

Leaving Aunt Daisy and Fred deep in educational conversation, they set off to explore the remains of the aircrews' quarters. Some were Nissen Hut type buildings, others more substantial, brick and timber built. They were all empty, but had an air of waiting for something about to happen to them. They almost expected to see and hear people.

Having explored the huts, they noticed some distance away the remains of more buildings and went to investigate. These were much more solidly built, but lay in ruins. Some of the half-standing walls were smoke blackened. At first they were puzzled; then Stephen said, 'Remember the air raids? I reckon these places were bombed.'

They picked their way cautiously through the weed and brambled rubble, realizing there had been two or three houses standing here, looking across towards the control tower and hangers. The last house was less damaged than the others and most of its walls were standing up to first floor level, though it had no roof. There were even floorboards in one room, under all the weeds and rubbish.

'Be careful,' warned Sam, 'they could be pretty rotten!' As he spoke there was a cracking sound and his left foot disappeared. He soon hauled it out. The stout boot had protected his foot from any injury. But in so doing he dislodged a pile of rubble, which tumbled across the space he'd just made.

'Hey!' he called, 'Look!' Carefully the others joined him. From amongst the bricks and shattered tiles he was digging out a toy car, a very battered die-cast Dinky Toy. Its paint had mostly gone, but once it had been a bright red 1938 model MG.

Jane, peering into the spot he had pulled out the car said, 'There's something else, under those bricks. See, there's a doll's hand sticking out!'

The boys carefully removed the debris to reveal the remains of a doll made out of some early form of plastic. The cords holding the limbs and head on the body had rotted away, as had the clothes. However, apart from being filthy and dented in parts, it could probably be restored.

'There were families living here,' said Sarah. 'I wonder what happened to them?'

They left their finds on a flat stone to collect on their way back from some further exploring.

They wandered out of the ruins and made their way across the grass, meaning to go and look at the fire truck and ambulance shed. Suddenly it felt very warm and a strange mist drifted across the airfield, blotting out the buildings and surroundings.

They stopped. After a moment it thinned, but everything in the distance looked hazy and indistinct, shimmering in the heat. The sky above was an intense blue. Stephen looked up; high above them silver specks denoted planes — small planes — flying swiftly eastwards.

'What are they?' said Sam, 'I don't recognise them.'

'Nor do I,' replied Stephen, 'and yet they are sort of familiar.'

Noises began to penetrate the misty silence. An engine being warmed up. But it did not sound like a car, it was deeper, more powerful. Voices, faint and far away calling to each other. Though they could not hear the words there was no mistaking the laughter and jocular remarks being made. The whole place seemed to become shadowly alive.

Sarah pointed in the direction of the place they had been aiming for. Coming through the mist were two children, a boy of about nine, holding the hand of a girl of about six.

They walked up to them. 'Hello,' said the boy, 'You're new here, aren't you? Have your fathers just been posted? They are awfully short of pilots you know. Oh,' he added, 'I'm Peter and this is my sister, Patricia. We are on our way home for tea.'

He waved his hand in the direction of the *no longer* ruined houses. 'Nice to have met you, I expect we'll see you again,' and with a friendly smile he walked off, his sister trotting along beside him.

There was a silence, then Michelle spoke. 'Did you notice their clothes? They were *exactly* like those you see in pictures of children during the war!'

'Must be some kind of re-enactment,' suggested Sam.

'Yes, but if so, why didn't Uncle Fred tell us?' asked Sarah.

Stephen spoke, abruptly. 'Did you notice what those two were carrying?'

'What?'

'The boy had a Red MG Dinky Toy and the girl a doll

made out of some kind of plastic!'

There was silence, but not for long. Suddenly the air became full of a shrill whining sound and from out of that glorious blue sky came a flock of what they took to be great black evil-looking birds plummeting down.

Sam stared, then yelled 'Stukas! Throw yourselves flat.'

The whining rose to a shrill scream, coupled with the sound of the planes yanking out of their dive and climbing. Almost at the same time came a series of deafening explosions, and when they dared to look through the mist, flames and clouds of black smoke were rising. Voices, still faint and distant, but tinged with fear and alarm could be heard, then the roar of aircraft, taking off. One of them threw its shadow over the children as it zoomed over their heads. The air was full of confused engine noises and the taka-tak of machine guns, punctuated by explosions and the thump of the anti-aircraft guns away to the north. The shrill whining scream returned and again the explosions shook the ground under them—some much nearer than others.

They raised their heads; the mist cleared for a moment and they saw the three houses had received direct hits and were blazing furiously. The noise of the planes grew fainter as the dogfight moved away. There was the clanging of the fire truck's bell and the ambulance as they raced down the field towards the stricken buildings. Then, in a flash the mist and sounds were gone.

They stood up, feeling rather stupid. Everything looked so normal; the deserted airfield slept in the sun. Without a word they made their way back to the spot where the doll and car had been left. Gently, very gently, Sarah picked up the doll while Stephen carefully wrapped the car in his handkerchief. Both looked very pale and Sarah's eyes were full of tears. They all took hands; somehow it comforted them, and they made their way back towards the control tower and the Land Rover.

Aunt Daisy and Fred were seated on the running board still chatting. They looked up at their approach, rising to their feet, somewhat perplexed when they saw their solemn expressions.

'Whatever's the matter, you look as if you've seen a ghost,' said Aunt Daisy.

'We sort of have,' said Stephen and he carefully unwrapped the hanky and showed them the battered car. Sarah showed them the doll, and they recounted the experience that had just occurred.

Fred nodded, 'I've heard of such things repeating themselves in places where very dramatic events have occurred.'

'Collective experiences of this kind are common amongst the Africans as well,' added Aunt Daisy. 'In fact, so common it's often very hard to know whether folk are speaking about something that happened today or during the time of their grandparents.'

Fred was thinking. 'That Luftwaffe attack occurred on Sunday, August the fourth, 1940 at around four o'clock Double British Summer Time which for us today would be three o'clock, just about now, though it occurred four months ahead. But the conditions must have been 'right' for it to happen today.'

'But those children, and their house, it was *horrible*,' whispered Sarah. 'Were they killed?'

'I don't know,' Fred replied, 'but no doubt there are records; I could try to find out.'

'Please, please do,' they begged, 'we want to know what happened.'

'I will,' he replied, 'but it may take some time. And talking of time we must be on our way, as Will and tea are awaiting us.'

They clambered into the Land Rover, taking the road back the way they had come. The sun was already moving towards the west and it was no longer as warm as it had been. They drove through the gap in the ridge, over the River Ide, then turned off down towards Canal Lock House, crossing the river again and arriving in front of this unusual building. Aunt Daisy was enchanted by it.

Will was waiting on the steps for them, Judy and Nicky beside him. They greeted the children eagerly, and soon Judy was chatting away to Stephen, and Nicky talking with Michelle, their special friends. Before they went inside, Will suggested it might be best to do the canal walk, as evening was drawing in and the shadow thrown by Crimson Hill cooled things down pretty smartly. They strolled along the south stretch while he sketched the history of the canal project to Aunt Daisy.

For the children it was renewing acquaintance with a piece of countryside that they found fascinating. Soon the long shadow of the hill fell across them and he called, 'About turn.' They made their way back to the house, where Will guided the downstairs tour, and Judy, with Nicky as assistant, showed off the upstairs. Then it was all hands to the kitchen for tea.

As usual Joyce provided a tempting spread! 'How did your trip go?' she asked Fred.

'Oh fine, I kept them guessing until we were on Crimson Hill and it was practically under their noses!'

'How did you enjoy it?' Will said, turning to the others.

'Great!' they replied, not sure if they should tell him about their strange experience.

'We have a family connection with that airfield!' he continued. 'During the war a great-uncle of mine served in the rescue service unit stationed there. You know, fire prevention and an ambulance. He was the officer in charge.' He paused. 'It's rather a sad story. Do you want to hear it?' There was no hesitation; they knew it *had* to be heard.

He began. 'He was seconded to the base soon after it became operational, that was in spring 1940. Being an officer with a family he was given one of the houses on the airfield. He had two children, a boy and girl. Of course there were other children on the base too. When France fell, the Luftwaffe began their attacks on the West Country and one of their objectives was to try and knock out the fighter bases to give their bombers clear skies. At the beginning of August they made a lightning raid on the airfield. Why they weren't detected coming in is a mystery. The surprise was complete, and although some of the fighters managed to take off, the damage to buildings and planes was devastating. The causalities were also high. When the second wave of bombers came in they met with more resistance and instead of aiming for the hangers and control tower, loosed their load on the other buildings scattered round the perimeter. The three houses received direct hits and most of those in them were killed. Great-uncle had the harrowing task—as emergency officer—in searching through the wreckage of his own house. His wife and little girl were killed. The little boy was seriously injured; at one stage the doctors thought he would never recover, but he did.'

He paused and Jane asked the question they all had in mind. 'Mr Bennett, what were the names of those children?'

'Peter and Patricia, Peter was just nine and Patricia was six, but why do you ask?'

They told him of what had occurred to them that afternoon. Also of their finds in the ruins. Sarah and Stephen went to the Land Rover and brought in the doll and car for him to see. Will examined them for some time, then said:

'Peter ought to see these.'

'Peter?' they exclaimed.

'Yes, I told you he recovered and is still alive. He's my uncle and a very indulgent great-uncle to Judy and Nicky. He often says that Judy reminds him of his little sister. Though, looking at Patricia's photograph, they don't look alike.'

'Could we meet him?' they wanted to know.

'I can ask him, but he may not wish to be reminded of that terrible afternoon. It's something he very rarely speaks about, if at all.'

Fred spoke up. 'Is he the "Peter" who has become involved in the project to restore the airfield to its 1940s state?'

'Yes, he is, and in that case he might be willing to meet you. I'll give him a ring this evening and let you know.'

'Best you ring Derek,' suggested Fred, 'We'll organise it from there.'

Judy spoke up, 'Uncle Peter is *very* nice to us, but he doesn't laugh very much and sometimes doesn't speak for ages and just *ages*!'

'I think if your two were at this meeting as well it might help him,' remarked Daisy.

Fred looked at his watch. 'Help, we must leave, I promised to return this lot by sixish and the "ish" is coming up fast!'

'Nicky and Judy are coming to stay next weekend, aren't they?' said Sarah.

'Yes,' replied Will. 'Maybe I can arrange for a meeting with Peter then. He lives in Tadbridge.'

They left, arriving home just in time for the evening meal.

'And if you think you are going to sneak off, Fred, you are mistaken,' Doreen informed him. 'And as for you two,' addressing Stephen and Jane, 'you are not leaving either. In fact *all* of you are staying overnight, Michelle included. There's room for all of you. Binky has offered to share his basket with you, Fred. Be warned, he bites in his sleep.'

As usual there was uproar and confusion for a few moments. Then they settled down to the serious business of supper and telling Derek and Doreen about their day.

'If Will can persuade his uncle to meet with you he could come here next weekend,' suggested Derek. 'I'll find out if that's possible when he rings.'

After supper Fred went out to the Land Rover and returned

with sleeping gear for the Randell twins and himself.

'You knew *all* the time!' they accused him. The answer was a grin.

He didn't have to sleep with Binky. There was a foldaway bed in the study!

CHAPTER THIRTEEN

Breakfast was one of those very relaxed Sunday meals where there's no hurry to finish because nobody has to rush off anywhere. Fred and Aunt Daisy were already well into the continuation of their educational discussion, with Derek and Doreen joining in here and there. The meal was trying very hard to draw to a close when the phone rang; it was Will Bennett, wanting a word with Fred. He returned smiling:

'It's all fixed. Peter is willing to meet you and quite happy to come here, especially as Nicky and Judy will be staying over. I've arranged to pick him up on Saturday morning, around nine. He lives in the same suburb as I do, so that won't be a problem. As Will and Joyce are coming over later, they've offered to take him home if necessary.'

The children were pleased; they would clean up the toys and restring the doll, but otherwise they would be as they were found. Breakfast finished; Fred and Aunt Daisy helped clear away, then retired to the sitting room to continue their discussion while the children went to tidy up their rooms.

Having done this, they gathered in the secret room to discuss plans for the day. It looked like being a typical orthodox April one: mild, sunny and showery. Some exploration seemed indicated. The question was, where?

'Next weekend we should try to get your bikes here,' Sam

suggested to Stephen and Jane, 'and yours, Michelle, then we could go off for a real explore.'

'If Dad has any surveys to do over this way any time he could drop our bikes off,' replied Jane, 'We don't often use them much during the week.'

'Fine, but what shall we do this morning?' asked Sarah.

At that moment their mother called them. There was the usual stampede down to the kitchen to find out what she wanted.

'Roger Fisher has just phoned. Cherry is taking Wendy and Ann to a party they've been invited to, leaving Shirley on her own. She's asked him if you could go over for lunch. Roger has to take a trip out to inspect some places west of Bidcote, and he wondered if you'd like to go along?'

This sounded great and there was unanimous agreement. It would give them a chance to spy out the cycling possibilities in that direction.

'Michelle, would you like to phone Shirley and say you're coming?' asked Doreen. 'She seems to have taken a liking to you.'

A few moments later it was all arranged. They would walk over to arrive in time for mid-morning snack. Only one person was not pleased with this arrangement. Binky—he had been looking forward to a walk, and in spite of promises that he would have one when they returned, he was dubious. These humans had no sense of time and often came back too late for what he considered to be a good walk. He chased Cleo out into the yard to show them how much energy he had. All he received for his pains was a ticking off from Sarah.

They started across the fields at about ten fifteen. So far the sun had the upper hand and the clouds were few and scattered. There was a real feel of spring in the air, and everywhere in the hedgerows shoots of fresh green were showing and the birds were busy nest-building. It made them feel light and free. They chased each other along the bridle path playing an impromptu game of tag. In no time at all they reached Bidcote and were knocking on the post office door. Actually they hardly had to knock, as Shirley had been looking out for them and opened it at the first tap. She took them into the kitchen, where Roger was busy preparing a snack.

'I thought we could do a bit of an explore,' he told them. 'I have to check some of the postboxes in the area to the west of Bidcote to see if they need repainting or any repairing. There's an orchard out that way, and I thought we'd call in, as the chap sells stamps and also has a small PO collection box. Maybe we can eat our lunch there.' This met with everyone's approval and Sam explained how they were thinking of cycling round that part of the country, so this trip would be useful, as the 'ups and downs' could be studied.

Half an hour later they set off, driving due north past the village hall and football field. About a mile further on, the road forked left and right. Roger took the left one. A high brick wall ran alongside them on the right, rather dilapidated in parts. Glimpses of the grounds showed the trees and undergrowth were thick and unkempt. There were also tantalising views of a large red brick Gothic-style building.

'Whatever is that place?' asked Sarah, 'It looks very spooky.'

Roger grinned. 'That, Sarah, is the old Tadbridge Lunatic Asylum. Built in the 1820's and closed some ten years ago, though at that time it was a rehabilitation centre. Since then it's been empty. The Local Health Trust have been trying to let it as they don't want to part with the land. It could be the possible site for a new hospital. But nobody seems to want it. I don't blame them; places like that have seen too much sorrow and suffering.'

By now the road had swung under the railway line and they headed off towards the hills. For the next two hours Roger drove round narrow country lanes, stopping every so often to inspect postal collection boxes set in hedges, in old walls and once or twice free standing in tiny village streets. One had 'V.R.' emblazoned upon it.

Then he drove back towards Orchard Farm. Here the collection box was fixed to the gatepost. The trees were just about to come into blossom and they found the owner busy inspecting them. He greeted his unexpected visitors cheerfully and had no objection to them using one of the table-benches set out in the orchard.

'Only put them out yesterday,' he remarked. 'Thought I might get some customers, and you are the first.'

He insisted on giving them two large bottles of clear apple juice made from last year's harvest. 'On the orchard,' as he put it, then left them to eat in peace while he continued his inspection. It was an enjoyable meal, though as they finished, April lived up to its reputation. A large cloud suddenly appeared out of nowhere and heavy drops of rain began to fall. Hurriedly things were packed away and they ran for the shelter of the Land Rover.

'Time to return anyway,' said Roger. 'I've done all the necessary checking and I expect you would like to spend some time with Shirley before you set off for home. Cherry and the youngsters should be back shortly.'

When they returned to the post office Roger set about entering the information he had gathered onto a very official looking form. Meanwhile, Shirley took them outside to show what she had been doing in the garden. Everywhere green shoots were appearing and in a few weeks it would be a mass of colour. 'How's the corn doing that we planted?' she asked.

The twins looked embarrassed; they hadn't been up to see since the flood relief operation.

Sarah had an idea. 'Why don't you come over and look?' she said, adding, 'We could do with some advice about planting for our plots, couldn't we Sam?' she nudged him.

'What? Oh yes, indeed we could.'

Michelle turned to Shirley, 'Have you got a bike?'

'Yes,' was the reply, 'but I'm not allowed to ride it on the road, Daddy says it's too dangerous.'

'I was thinking that you could cycle over with me when I visit them; let's ask your dad.'

They trooped inside to find Roger just sealing up an envelope with a 'Thank goodness that job is done!' look on his face. He listened to their request and suggestion quietly, then said, 'I'd be very happy for Shirley to help you. She's a far better gardener than either Cherry or myself. It would be good for her to be with friends of her own age, as the two younger ones are so exuberant and demanding, she does tend to be pushed into the background. Your offer to cycle with her is a good idea, Michelle, and I'm sure Cherry will be delighted.'

On cue came the sound of the front door opening, and with much chatter and clatter Cherry and the children literally bounced in, all talking at once. From the hubbub it was gathered that the party was a huge success and Ann produced a much crumpled and sticky paper bag for her elder sister saying:

'I bought you a doggy-bag, Shirley!'

She solemnly thanked her sister and put it on the dresser.

'Aren't you going to eat some now?' bubbled Ann.

'Later, we had a late lunch.'

'Oh, well then can I have some of the fruit gums before they go too sticky?'

Shirley handed the bag over with a faint grin. 'You take what you want and I'll have the rest.'

Ann grabbed it and scooted off upstairs, Wendy in hot pursuit!

Cherry was delighted with the proposed gardener-tutor arrangement, and as there was nothing special happening tomorrow, Michelle would collect Shirley around ten o'clock and they would cycle over.

It was now late afternoon so they said goodbye and made their way home. Also, Michelle had to pick up her bike and cycle home before it became dark, while Stephen and Jane were returning with Uncle Fred, who would be leaving after supper. Binky was right; he didn't get his walk!

It turned out to be a hilarious meal. Aunt Daisy was at her best and entertained them with stories of her humorous experiences, and Fred related some of his, such as his first teaching post. At the end, a more serious note was struck when their aunt explained how they had worked out a plan to provide training and material support for the mission school. Their school would become totally involved — the Principal had been very enthusiastic when Fred put the idea to him — and they hoped other local schools might also take up the scheme.

'So when we start on Wednesday we'll have a class discussion as to the best way to go about it,' Fred told them.

School? In three days! Where had the holiday gone? There were no groans, just a feeling of anticipation as to what this last term in class four would bring, as it included the class camp.

As usual it was a rowdy send off with 'See you Wednesday!' dominating, and Fred making comments like, 'Really? I thought of taking a trip to the moon on the eighth!' As he drove off he called out:

'By the way there's another new pupil for us.' But before they could ask 'who' he was gone.

'Typical,' remarked Sarah, 'he's a real tease.'

They went to prepare for bed.

'The forecast for tomorrow is fine,' Derek told them, 'If you are thinking of working in the garden I think I'll join you. No, I won't get in your way,' he added, seeing the looks on their faces. 'There's plenty of just straightforward clearing to be done. I'll leave the planting to the experts.'

It was great to have Dad around, but he did tend to interfere: 'Why don't you plant this there, and that here?' Well meaning, but you know how misguided parents can be.

Monday dawned bright and clear, ideal for gardening. Doreen and Aunt Daisy decided to go into Tadbridge during the morning to do some shopping for items that were hard to obtain in Africa. They would have lunch out and maybe spend some time in the park, chatting. Oh yes, they would be back to prepare the evening meal. There were sandwiches and fruit for lunch, so those staying behind wouldn't starve.

As they waited for Michelle and Shirley, Sam remarked, 'We haven't seen Bill, Sir Brian or N'humba recently. I wonder what they've been up to?'

'Probably showing N'humba round and visiting other house guardians,' suggested Sarah. 'I wonder if Bill was able to find one for Ingrid's flat?'

'They may be in short supply at this time of the year,' said Sam.

His sister was just going to ask 'why so' at this particular season; but the cheerful ringing of bicycle bells and the sight of Michelle and Shirley pedalling up the drive left the question unsaid.

Shirley was glowing with excitement; they had never seen her so happy. Sam guessed there was more to it than just this particular day.

'What's making you so happy today?' he asked.

Shirley grinned mischievously at them. 'I know a secret,' she chanted, 'and I'm not allowed to tell anyone.'

Questioning produced nothing except more grins and giggles, so they gave up. Anyway, the gardens were waiting, and they wished to get started before Derek came out, just in case he did 'offer' to help. Tools were collected and Shirley produced some envelopes full of seeds.

'I thought you might like some of these,' she said, 'they come from our last garden. I saved them as I knew they would come in useful sometime.'

When they reached their plots a surprise awaited them. Another one had been cleared and a notice staked into the ground read 'Michelle's Plot'. Derek had been at work early. He now appeared from below carrying a strimmer and hedge trimmer. 'I'll be working up the top,' he told them, 'if you need any help just yell.'

In response to Michelle's thanks for her plot, he said, 'Well, I thought if I gave it to you there's one less patch I have to worry about.' He fled before they could take revenge.

Under Shirley's guidance they set to work with a will, fine-raking the soil and preparing trenches for the seeds. They cleared the weeds from the corn bed, for any day now the first green shoots would appear. Shirley worked as hard as any of them once she had instructed them. It was a very satisfying first part of the morning. At eleven they broke off, yelled for Derek, and made their way down to the kitchen, where the snack Doreen had made awaited them.

When finished they went outside and sat on the stone seat by the entrance of the old ornamental gardens, and were deep in discussion as to what would be best to plant for the summer when shadowy shadows fell across them. Looking up, there stood Bill, Sir Brian, JJ and N'humba; with them was another figure, one they had not seen before. Bill spoke to Michelle:

'I said I would see what could be done about a guardian for your flat. Well, this is Trevor, the house he used to work at has just been converted into flats and although he has no objection to them — as such — he is more in favour of a single dwelling. His references are impeccable. Years ago he guarded the stables complex at Ascon House. I took the liberty of showing him the exterior of the dwelling that contains your flat, and we met its guardian. He was also concerned about caring for two properties, so it has all worked out in a most satisfactory manner.'

Michelle was delighted and thanked Bill profusely. Introductions were made and though Trevor reminded the twins of someone like Jeeves in his manner; they noticed he had a merry twinkle in his eyes and so probably wasn't so stiff and starchy as he appeared. Bill and his companions now departed to help Trevor settle in his new abode, and the children went back to their gardening.

By lunchtime the seeds were planted and the plots had been tidied up. They also weeded the path and trimmed back overhanging bushes. Derek joined them and helped to fix up the hose so that the watering could be done without having to resort to plodding up and down the steps with watering cans.

They returned to the house for lunch feeling very satisfied with their progress and full of praise for Shirley's advice and help. Afterwards they returned to the stone bench to decide whether to go on gardening or do something else before Michelle and Shirley left after tea.

They had hardly settled down when Sir Brian and N'humba appeared.

'Been admiring your work,' said Sir Brian, 'Nice to see the gardens taken care of again. In my day there were ten gardeners. Needed them, didn't have all these devices your father has to do the work.'

N'humba nodded, 'In my country most of these tasks are still done by many people. We do not have all the machines, for they are expensive. We are lucky if we have enough ordinary tools.' He sighed, 'I have enjoyed my stay here and learnt much. I think I understand my madam better, now I have seen how she lived before coming to us. She is very brave, you know.'

The twins had already realised from what she had related that this was true.

'But I shall be glad to return to my homeland tomorrow,' he continued, 'Your weather is so difficult, it is never the same from one hour to the next!' They all laughed.

'Come on,' said Sir Brian, 'it's not as bad as all that. Anyhow I promised to show you some more of the surroundings—Did I tell you about the boundary stone?' and with a nod to the children they walked off. They returned to the gardens and pottered around for an hour or so until the sound of the car announced the return of Doreen and Aunt Daisy.

Very soon they were having tea in the ornamental garden, the first time that year. The shopping expedition had gone well and the two ladies had had a good old chat over lunch and afterwards in the park. However, as Aunt Daisy had to complete her packing they had not stayed away any longer. Michelle and Shirley left shortly afterwards, Shirley still giggling over her secret. All that she would say was, 'Wait and see!' Michelle would be back tomorrow, for she was coming with them to see Aunt Daisy off. Derek had volunteered to remain at home so there would be room for her. Stephen and Jane would meet them at the station.

When they went indoors the twins asked if they could be of any help with packing, but were politely refused, which for their aunt's sake was probably just as well.

Seeing their forlorn looks, Doreen said, 'Come on, you two and help me prepare the meal. For her last evening I think it should be rather special, don't you?' They brightened up at once and were soon bombarding her with ideas for doing so as they made to the kitchen.

Derek grinned at his sister. 'Well, you've made a big impression here, Daisy, and your arrival was superb. I won't forget it in a hurry; nor will the children! I wonder if Michelle's remark about you coming back sooner than you think will happen?'

'I don't know, children often have remarkable insights into people's lives. We shall just have to wait and see. Anyhow, I've really enjoyed my visit, what more can I say? Now I must really go and finish packing.'

The meal was a great success and the joy of that evening remained long in their memories.

CHAPTER FOURTEEN

Breakfast next morning was a rather silent affair; everyone was occupied with their own thoughts, mainly dealing with Aunt Daisy's departure. She would be catching the same afternoon train as before, but would have to change at Bristol. At least this meant they would still have the morning with her. However, their mother had other ideas! She instructed them to prepare their school things *now*. Naturally they protested, but she pointed out, with the logic that grown-ups are *so* good at, that should there be anything missing or needing replacement it could be purchased when they went to Tadbridge. 'Otherwise I'll have to take you in this morning.'

They promptly capitulated and by ten o'clock were well school prepared, discovering that—for once—they seemed to have everything. The rest of the morning was spent with their beloved aunt. At her suggestion they took Binky for a walk down to Church Wood and then back via the farm to say goodbye to the Game family.

As usual there was a great welcome from Jill and Brian, though he was disappointed 'his' Jane wasn't with them.

Jill was busy chatting to Sam when suddenly she said, with a twinkle in her eye, 'I know a secret,' adding quickly, 'but I'm not allowed to tell you!'

Another person with a secret? 'I'll tickle you all over if

you don't tell me,' he growled fiercely. But she laughed and skipped away from him. Sam pretended to look very sad and hid his face. In a moment he felt a hand slip into his, and looking up earnestly into his face, said, 'Sam, I would tell you, honest. But I *promised* not to, it's a surprise, you see.'

'Ah,' he replied, 'Why didn't you tell me that at first? Anyway, if I catch you I shall still tickle you!'

Bess and Aunt Daisy had a few words together and parted with an affectionate embrace; the two little ones hugged her as well. They walked back to the manor in time for lunch. Then Aunt Daisy and Doreen went off into the sitting room for a final chat, leaving the twins to deal with the lunch things. However, Michelle arrived just as they were starting the washing up, so she was pressed into service as chief drier while Sarah washed and Sam was the honourary putter away boy. They had only just finished when they had to get ready. The dreaded departure time had arrived, well, almost. As they got into the car they saw N'humba vanishing into the boot with the luggage, while Bill, JJ and Sir Brian stood nearby wishing him well. Then it was off to the station.

The train was scheduled 'on time'. Stephen and Jane were already on the platform with Reg, who'd come along too. To their amusement, seated on top of her luggage, N'humba looked like a four-legged spider, with a big grin on its face. He was pleased to be going home. The train arrived, and after the usual farewells, Aunt Daisy found her seat and waved to them from the window.

Although they were sad at her departure they did not feel miserable. For Michelle's words 'you will be back next year' echoed in their hearts, and though it seemed impossible—impossible things often happen! Reg was taking his twins home, as they were still preparing for school, and Doreen shooed her three into the car, as Michelle needed to be back in good time; no doubt she had some preparing to do. 'See you tomorrow morning,' she called as she cycled off.

When they went in, Derek reported Geoff had just rung to confirm if was it all right for him to leave his bike there.

'Naturally, I said, "yes, of course". Oh, Bess rang too. Jill won't be going in by bus tomorrow.' Was that part of Jill's secret, they wondered?

'Go and double check everything is in order while I prepare supper,' ordered Doreen.

'But it is, we've gone over our stuff *thousands* of times,' they protested, reluctantly going to their rooms. Which turned out just as well.

During their absence Binky and Cleo had slipped out of the kitchen, Derek having forgotten to shut the door properly, and made their way upstairs. They discovered two other doors also had been left open, so went in to investigate. Binky chose Sarah's room and Cleo, Sam's. Sarah's school bag was lying on her bed with a strap hanging down. A few sharp tugs at it and the bag tumbled to the floor. The catch was unfastened and her gym shoes, which she'd stuffed in on top, fell out. They had a nice 'footy' smell about them and very chewable laces. He had a satisfying hour of pretending the shoes were rats and the laces their tails. Luckily, he could not do much harm to the shoes, but the laces…!

Sam's bag was also on his bed, perched precariously on the edge. Cleo had soon toppled it over and a cascade of items fell out. Pencils, erasers, notebooks and best of all, a bag of marbles he was taking to do some swapping with Chris. Naturally they rolled everywhere and Cleo helped them roll even further. She chewed the pencils, nibbled the erasers and ripped the cover of the notebook with her claws. She had a glorious time. Hearing their little humans come in, they both scooted downstairs looking suitably innocent.

Their yells of horror, when they entered and saw the chaos, can well be imagined. It took them until suppertime to clear up and repack everything. Luckily, Doreen found a spare pair of gym shoelaces and Derek was able to replace some of the too-chewed pencils. The culprits received a good telling off. But the grown-ups were very short on sympathy.

'You should have done the bags up properly and not left them just flung on your beds, *and how many times have you been told to shut your bedroom doors!*'

Really it wasn't their fault. After all, who had left the kitchen door open? *He* didn't get told off!

Supper restored their humour and the animals back into favour. They discussed plans for the coming weekend, including the visit of Nicky and Judy, and also Peter, who would be coming with Fred on Saturday. However, Doreen had her eye on the clock, and at eight they were sent off to bed.

The details of the early part of Wednesday morning can be omitted! Everyone knows what it's like on the first day of a new term. They greeted their old friend the bus driver and on arrival at school found Stephen, Jane, Christopher and Fenella waiting for them. Geoff took Nola off to kindergarten and they started to walk towards their classroom.

Suddenly, Stephen stopped dead in his tracks and Sam bumped into him. He pointed at a gaggle of class one children grouped round their classroom entrance. Amongst them was a little girl with fair hair and pigtails, Judy! As soon as she saw them she ran over and gave Stephen a big hug.

'Daddy said I was coming to your school and here I am!' she beamed, 'It's ever so nice here, and I've already got lots and lots of friends. Bye!' and she ran back to the others.

'Well,' said Jane 'I suppose Nicky must be in kindergarten; we'll ask Jill this afternoon.' They went on to their classroom. As usual it was full of noisy chattering children all exchanging holiday news. The warning bell rang, and they went to their desks. Once everybody was in place it could be seen there was an empty desk in the room. Was someone away, or had someone left? A quick count showed that all who had been there at the end of last term were still present. Then Mr Atkinson walked in. They stood up to greet him. But all eyes were on the empty desk.

'Ah, you've noticed. Yes, we have a new pupil, recently moved to the district. Now I must tell you something about this child. As you know, every class has its eldest and youngest member. Christopher is our oldest and Stephanie, the youngest. Well — she *was* the youngest. Our newcomer is right on the lower age limit. But after some consultation with the parents, myself and the Principal, we decided this was the right class for her.' He moved over to the door and opened it. 'You may come in now.' And in walked Shirley, beaming from ear to ear.

'So that's the surprise,' said Sam to himself, 'I should have guessed.'

'As Shirley already knows some of the most notorious members of our gang, er class, it was almost a foregone conclusion she'd join us,' added their teacher. 'Now, perhaps we can begin. Good morning, class four.'

'Good morning, Mr Atkinson.' And the lesson was soon under way. At break time they carried Shirley off to a corner of the playground and plied her with questions. Yes, that had been the secret. Wendy was also here, in class one and Ann in kindergarten.

'Lucky we didn't see them on our way over,' remarked Sam, 'it would have given the game away.'

'We'll be travelling on the bus with you too. Dad will bring us to the bus stop each morning and either him or Mum will pick us up from your place in the afternoon.'

'We'll soon need a bus of our own,' laughed Sam. 'Michelle, Geoff, Jill, Shirley, Wendy, Ann, Sarah, myself, and I suppose we should include Nola. That's nine of us, nearly half the bus load.'

They returned to class still chattering nineteen to the

dozen.

The rest of the day flew by and in no time at all it seemed they were on the school bus heading home. The driver also agreed with Sam's idea.

'Any more of you and we'll need a double-decker or another bloomin' bus,' he said.

On this occasion Doreen, Bess and Cherry were waiting for them. Poor Cherry was swamped by her three, all trying to tell her what a wonderful time they'd had. For once she could hardly put in a word edgeways. On arriving home Doreen insisted they all stay for tea, Geoff and Michelle as well.

After the guests had gone the reality of being back at school hit them: homework to be done. Mr Atkinson did not believe in wasting any time in getting down to the new term's work, especially as this was the last term of class four. They were starting with a maths period, which would complete the requirements for that year. In their last school, the twins had tolerated maths as something that couldn't be avoided, like rain. It was no good complaining about it; it happened anyway. But with this teacher it had suddenly taken on a whole new meaning. It was *useful* and he showed them *how* to use it. It could be fun, too. Maths funny? Never!

Now they were discovering much more about it by themselves, not just being told what to do. They even enjoyed the homework he had set, for it dealt with fractions in the form of practical problems. One being to count up the number of rooms in the house and then find out the fraction that were: bedrooms, living rooms, utility rooms and the like. Puzzle, what did the room where Binky and Cleo slept count as? It had several names, scullery, back kitchen, or 'the animals' room'. How did it alter the fractions if taken as a bedroom, or a utility room? How about Derek's study? Did he live in it? Or as they often suspected—when he went in and closed the door — did he sleep in there? Anyhow, working all this out kept them occupied until supper, much to Doreen's relief and Derek's delight. He remembered the times when maths homework had meant hours of trying to explain the obscure mathematical conundrums their previous teacher dreamed up!

After supper they gave Binky a quick run round the grounds and then settled down to reading their current school reader: a book called *Landscapes*, which contained descriptions of contrasting landscapes and how, over the years, they changed. Sarah put down her copy after half an hour and said, 'Talking of landscapes — the cellar?'

Her brother was used to her 'jumping' approach to a subject, so said nothing but waited for the next leap.

'You know — the secret passage that's supposed to link into the cellars. We've not looked for it since the time Jane found the plan of the passages in the wall.' (see volume one)

'True,' said Sam, 'and now they are properly lit it will be much easier to search. So why don't we have a go this weekend. It would be a big thrill for Nicky and Judy!'

'But Nicky's only five and might be rather scared,' said Sarah, adding, 'Maybe if Jill and Brian came over he'd be happier playing with them.'

They decided to suggest this to their mother, which they did when she came in to remind them it was time for bed.

'We shall be rather crowded this weekend,' she reminded them, 'but if you arrange to do your explorations on Sunday morning, and if Nicky is unhappy, I'm sure I can occupy him for a while. I know it's a pity Stephen and Jane won't be here, but that can't be helped.' That was a pity, unless......? As they went up to bed the twins put their heads together to 'work something out'!

CHAPTER FIFTEEN

Saturday came far quicker than they expected, though Nicky and Judy did not come home with them on the bus as originally planned. Instead Will drove to school with their stuff and then brought them over. This was in case Nicky might suddenly feel homesick and not want to stay. He was a little uncertain when his dad came to leave, but Binky proved a useful distraction, and he was so busy playing with him that when Will actually said, 'Well, I'm off now,' he merely raised his head and, 'Bye, Dad, see you tomorrow.' So that was all right.

Originally Fred was bringing the twins over, but because he would now pick Peter up, John had stepped into the breach and would drop them off about ten. Fred would take them home. However, the plan Sam and Sarah had concocted also involved their teacher, but more of that later.

Supper went well and the guests pronounced that it had everything they liked and Doreen was a super cook. Sam and Sarah now decided to introduce them to the secret room and hopefully Bill, so Judy could meet another guardian and tell him about Jim Barrow. Both of them were delighted with the room, and Judy told them about a cupboard in their house which, when you entered it, had an opening at the back leading through to a tiny under the eaves space with a window.

Once settled down, Sam told them about exploring the passages on Sunday. Nicky was as eager as Judy, so there was no need to worry about him. Just as they finished talking, Bill appeared and introductions were made. He listened politely to Judy's description of Jim and told her something of his tasks at the manor. Then he made a suggestion:

'Perhaps tomorrow morning they would like to meet Sir Brian and JJ. I think it best that I tell him first. You know what he's like. At the moment he's busy with a special potion, and from what JJ tells me things are not going quite as he expected — as usual.'

Sarah explained about Sir Brian and how he could be rather intimidating, but was really very nice. 'He won't hurt you,' she added. Nicky was the one who showed the most eagerness. He'd always wanted to see a 'real' knight.

'I'll come here after breakfast,' said Bill, 'to let you know when we may visit. I don't think it will be difficult. He likes to meet new people.' With that he vanished.

'Jim does that too,' remarked Nicky.

'Yes, when he's talking to us and somebody comes in, whiz, and he's gone! What if I could do that too?' said Judy.

'Well it's lucky you can't, because we'd always be losing you,' laughed Sarah.

The two children were to sleep on foldaway beds in Sarah's room. The twins helped them get ready for bed, and Sam read a fairy tale. Then they settled down quite happily.

'It's nice here,' said Judy.

'Almost as nice as home,' added Nicky.

High praise indeed, the twins felt quite flattered, and promising to be up 'soon', went down to tell their parents of the morning's arrangements.

The next morning after breakfast they made their way to the secret room, and sure enough, Bill was waiting for them.

'It's fine,' he said, 'Sir Brian is getting fed up with his potion business. JJ believes a distraction would do him good, so let's go.'

They went up to the main attics and along the passage to where the brass-handled door should be. Of course it wasn't, and Bill had to go through the wall to activate it. Nicky and Judy were most impressed when this appeared and Bill ushered them in.

The usual chaos greeted them. A thick haze hung in the air, and on the table a remarkable selection of bottles, flasks and bowls full of different coloured liquids were linked together by glass tubes, some bubbling furiously over small braziers of glowing coals. Eventually a muddy coloured viscous fluid dripped from a tube into a small bowl. Sir Brian was busily adding a drop of something here and a dash of powder there, muttering away furiously to himself. JJ was standing beside him to hand over the items he requested

Now he discreetly cleared his throat and announced:

'The visitors have arrived, my Lord.'

'Eh, what? Oh, ah, yes,' and Sir Brian turned round to greet them. Nicky and Judy were staring open-mouthed at him, understandably too! His beard, face and hands were multi-coloured from the various liquids he had been splashing about. It looked as if most of them had gone over him rather than into the flasks. Upon seeing the children his ferocious look softened and he greeted them mildly.

'And what are your names, my dears?' adding, 'any friends of Sam and Sarah I count as my friends too.'

Shyly they told him 'I'm Nicky.' 'I'm Judy.'

'Nice sensible names,' he observed. 'How long are you staying?'

The answer was never given, for at that moment one of the stoppered flasks, which was bubbling away furiously, blew its cork and boiled over. Sir Brian let out a yell and swung round to save it. In doing so his elbow caught the next container in line, a tall tube. It swayed gently for a few seconds and then fell gracefully onto the liquid collecting bowl, emptying its contents into it. There was a loud hiss and a great cloud of steam shot ceilingwards. The contents of the bowl bubbled violently for a moment, then stopped, and the sweet scent of roses filled the air. The liquid turned golden and light glowed round the edge of it. All the mist and not-so-pleasant smells dissolved away and the room grew lighter.

Cautiously the experimenter picked up the bowl, examining the contents carefully. Then he picked up a spoon and extracted a spoonful, sniffed it, and tipped the contents down his throat. They watched with bated breath. JJ was heard to murmur, 'Oh no, not again!' A beauteous smile spread across Sir Brian's face, a look of sheer bliss.

'It's it!' he whispered, 'at last, at long last, it's it! The freeing potion I have struggled to make for the past three hundred years or more.'

He turned to the children, 'It's all thanks to you! If you had not visited and I had not turned to greet you, careless of the fact that the liquid was coming to the boil, the accident would not have happened and the potion would have failed yet again. I don't know how to thank you. Especially Nicky and Judy, you brought me good luck,' and carefully putting down the bowl, he shook both of them solemnly by the hand.

Sam and Sarah suddenly felt a pang of sorrow. If he could now free himself from the power that held him here, when would he leave? So if he left, what then? Bidford Manor without Sir Brian, his experiments and harebrained ideas and enthusiasms was unthinkable. And yet, he had laboured long and hard to free himself, so surely would want to take full advantage of it. Sam spoke for them both; and for the others.

'We are *so* glad you are now freed; when will you leave?'

Sir Brian stared at him and then at their solemn faces.

'Leave, leave? Who said anything about leaving? Surely

you don't think after all the kindnesses you've shown me and all the fun we've had I'm going to up and depart just like that? I have no intention of leaving. The fact that I now have the liquid so that I *can* leave if I wish to is quite enough for the moment. Now, JJ, help me untangle all this stuff and clear it away. Find a decent bottle with a cork and decant the potion into it, label it and put it somewhere safe, very safe.'

It was the old Sir Brian again. He'd forgotten they were there!

'The visitors are leaving now,' Bill informed him.

'Oh, oh yes, nice to have seen you, call again, goodbye!' he waved vaguely over his shoulder and that was that. Bill opened the door, winked at them, and closed it quietly once they had left.

They arrived downstairs just in time to greet Stephen and Jane, who'd been dropped off by their dad. Michelle turned up on her bike about the same time.

Naturally they told them the news. 'I'm glad he found his potion at last,' said Stephen, 'but I'm also very glad that he isn't going to leave you straight away. This place wouldn't be the same without him.'

Jane and Michelle nodded firmly in agreement.

At that moment Derek came out of his study saying, 'Fred has just phoned, he's been slightly delayed, but should be here with Peter around ten thirty.' They told him the news, too. 'I must confess,' he replied, 'that in spite of his unscientific approach to chemistry and his apparent flouting of the basic laws of physics, were he to leave, a certain element of the unexpected would be taken from our lives.' All agreed with his summing up.

In preparation for Uncle Peter, as Nicky and Judy called him, the car and the doll were put in special boxes that they had prepared. Now all they could do was wait.

'Uncle Peter is really very nice,' Judy informed them, 'it's just that he doesn't talk very much and often seems sad.'

After a while they heard the sound of Fred's 'old battleship', as he called it—amongst other things—approaching up the drive, and went out to meet him and their guest.

When the car stopped the Bennett children waved excitedly to the person sitting in the front passenger seat, who waved back. Then he opened the door and climbed out. They ran forward to hug him; this gave the others a chance to look at their guest.

They saw an elderly man of stocky build with grey curly hair and rather heavy features. His eyes were deep brown and had a far away look in them. He seemed to be gazing into the distance, searching for something, even when talking to them. His smile was pleasant, but restrained. Now he turned, and looking slightly nervous, gave each of them a rather flabby—as Stephen remarked later—handshake.

By now Derek and Doreen had joined the group to welcome him. While this was taking place the children hauled Uncle Fred to one side and told him about Sir Brian.

'What a surprise!' he remarked, 'But like you, I'm glad he's not going to leave for the moment. Life wouldn't be the same without him.'

'That's what Dad said,' grinned Sam.

'Let's go into the sitting room where we can talk in comfort,' said Doreen, and they followed her inside, Nicky and Judy each holding onto Peter's hands.

They noticed that he held Judy's very gently, as if he was afraid of hurting her. Once settled, Fred opened the proceedings.

'I believe Will has told you why we hoped this meeting could be arranged. But I'd like to tell you a little bit of what happened to bring it about.' He recounted their expedition to the disused airfield, adding, 'These children,' indicating the quintet, found two items in the ruins of one of the old houses. Then, crossing the field, they had an unusual experience, which I think you should hear. It may be painful, and if you wish them to stop, please do not hesitate to say so.'

Peter nodded and spoke, really for the first time since he'd arrived. His voice was slow and rather featureless.

'Will has told me a little about this, so I am prepared. You see it is something which I've known I would have to face one day, and looking round at all of you I realise I could not ask for a more sympathetic audience. Now perhaps one of you would like to tell me what happened?'

They nodded at Stephen, who began to recount the experience they had had that afternoon a week ago, the others, as usual, adding detail here and there. When he'd finished, Sam and Sarah gave him the boxes, saying, 'We thought you ought to have what we found.'

Peter took the boxes from them and gently smiled his thanks. He turned to Nicky and Judy.

'Here, my dears, will you open these and show me what they contain, please?'

They did so, placing them on his knee; for several moments he gazed into each, then gave a long sigh, almost of relief. He replaced the lids and spoke to his waiting listeners.

'What I am going to tell you now, I have never told to anyone else. Not even my father. Somehow these toys have unlocked a closed door in my soul and now I shall share with you what lies behind it.'

'That summer afternoon, the fourth of August 1940, was indeed a glorious one: the sky clear as crystal and the sun beating down. We had just moved into our new house and Patricia and I had been exploring. At that stage we were allowed a free run of the place. Everyone was very relaxed, and the men were friendly and kind to all the children on the base. It was like having a super collection of extra uncles! We were returning to our house on the edge of the field when we met five children I didn't remember seeing before, but then we were new and possibly hadn't met everybody yet. Funny, I don't remember much about them, though everything else that afternoon is still very clear in my memory. They were sort of vague, that's the only word to describe them, though we talked. I remember that. Then my sister and I went home. We'd just got in when the raid started. Dad was over at the rescue service place. Mum decided we should shelter under the stairs. So we did, then there was a lull and we thought it was all over, so we came out. Patricia started to go upstairs; she wanted to put her doll to bed. I'd been playing with the car and it had rolled under the stairs. Mum was at the foot calling to Patricia to hurry up and come down. Then there was a terrible whining sound directly above us… …' He shuddered and paused, then continued.

'The next thing I knew there was a most awful bang and everything around seemed to jump about. Something hit me on the head and I didn't remember anything else until somebody picked me up and carried me out of the wreckage. It was Dad, he'd come as soon as he could to find us. I opened my eyes and I'll never forget the look of pain, sorrow on his face. I couldn't speak and he said, "There, there, Peter, you'll be all right now." I lost consciousness again. After that it was weeks of semiconsciousness and pain. At last, when I began to recover, Dad came one day and sat by my bed, holding my hand. I wanted to ask him how Mum and Patricia were. He must have guessed, because he said, very quietly, "Peter, Patricia and your mother were killed when that bomb scored a direct hit on our house. You were very badly hurt, but because you were under the stairs, survived." He didn't say more, but gave me a big hug and left. I was terribly upset and it took months before I was really recovered. Dad had a new posting and we moved to Cirencester. The worst of the bombing was now over, so life gradually returned to normal. About a year later he remarried. My stepmother was a gentle understanding lady and devotedly cared for both of us. However, when I was old enough I left home and trained as a surveyor, working for the Inland Revenue Valuation Department until I retired some years ago. I married, but it didn't work out. It was an amicable parting; my wife married again and now lives in Canada.' He spread his hands. 'Well, that's it.'

There was silence until Fred said softly, 'Thanks, Peter, thank you for sharing this with us.'

'Yes,' added Doreen, 'and please feel welcome to visit us any time you have a need for company, or want to talk. Now, I'm going to prepare lunch and shall take this scullion with me.'

She grabbed Fred by the arm and marched him off, while he protested his ignorance of any culinary knowledge. Derek quietly vanished, to his study, no doubt, leaving the children to entertain Peter.

'Would you like to see round the house?' asked Sam, 'or would you prefer a walk in the grounds?'

'How about here, for a start?' said Peter. So they took him on a conducted tour, avoiding the kitchen for the moment. When they reached the attics they found the brass-handled door was plainly visible.'

'Hm, what an interesting door,' he said, 'what's in there?' and before they could answer, he opened it.

They held their breaths. 'Oh excuse me!' they heard him say, 'I did not realise there was anyone up here; I did not mean to disturb you,' and he stepped back into the passage, quietly closing the door behind him. 'I'm sorry, I should have asked you before just barging in. I must apologise to your grandfather when he comes down for lunch.'

The children were in a quandary, should they just keep quiet or should they tell him about Sir Brian? Judy solved the problem. 'Uncle Peter, he's lived here for a long, long time,' she said, 'he's like Jim who lives in our house.'

Peter smiled. 'Oh, is he?' he said and turned to look at

the door. It had vanished! 'I think you'd better tell me something of what is going on here, please!' he said to the children. They took him down to the sitting room and told him about Bill and Sir Brian.

'I'm a bit like your father,' he said to Sam and Sarah. 'I don't believe or disbelieve, and for years I've held that strange image of the five children on the airfield in my heart. Now I know that they were *you;* we met through a crack in time. So I can accept your other house occupants. Perhaps when I come again you will tell me more.'

At that moment the gong went for lunch and they made their way to the dining room. The spread awaiting them showed that Doreen and scullion Fred had not been idle in providing a feast for both eyes and stomachs.

Afterwards, as big folk and little folk made their way back to the sitting room, Sam and Sarah trapped Uncle Fred as he pushed the trolley back to the kitchen.

'Do you remember the secret passages?' Sarah began.

'Yes, why?'

Well, tomorrow we are going to look for the entrance to the cellars with Nicky and Judy.' Pause.

'And you want Stephen and Jane to be here as well, don't you?'

Sarah blushed; she never thought he would cotton on so quickly.

'Quite right and proper too, considering how much they've been in on all your adventures. What time would you like me to bring them over?'

'Uncle Fred, you are the most amazingly, wonderful, helpful person in the whole world; and a jolly good teacher, too!' and she gave him a big hug.

'Here, be careful! I'm full of your mother's cooking and don't want to lose it just yet. And you, young lady, as I've said before, must be the world's champion arm twister. Do you think you could put up with an interfering grown-up as well on this exploration?'

'Of course,' said Sam. 'It would be good if you came along too, because the little ones might get scared.'

'As I'm taking the Randells home, I'll speak with their mother about tomorrow,' he added. So it was settled, and they were able to go and tell Stephen and Jane the good news.

They went for a walk to help digest their meal—to make room for tea—and to show Peter the grounds. Binky much appreciated this, as he'd been feeling somewhat left out of things during the morning. As they returned to the house the Bennett's car came purring up the drive. Will's face showed relief when he saw how Peter was completely relaxed with everybody.

His offspring greeted him with, 'You haven't come to take us home, have you, because we're not coming back until tomorrow.'

'Yes, we're going egg-pouring in the under-paths in the morning,' announced Nicky.

Tea went, where tea usually goes, together with the scones, jam, cream and iced cupcakes! Then Will nodded at Peter, who nodded back, and said, 'I'm not so young as I was folks, and this has been quite a day! So I hope you will excuse me if I leave now with Will and Joyce.'

'Of course,' said Doreen, 'and remember any time you wish to visit just give us a call and we'll come and pick you up.'

'Give me a ring, too,' said Fred, 'and if I'm coming over I can give you a lift.'

Peter thanked them all, picked up the two precious boxes, hugged the Bennett children and shook hands with the others. They gathered on the steps to see him off.

Then Fred added, 'And we must go, too.' He winked at the twins, 'We'll be back, though. For I am permitted to return tomorrow, provided I deliver these two as well!' and off he went taking Stephen and Jane with him. It had been a pretty exciting day, and the two little ones began to yawn and yawn during supper. Soon they were tucked away in their beds. The twins, having discussed the plans for the morning went and plagued their father about ropes, and torches — for a start — before going to bed. All in all it had been a highly satisfactory day.

CHAPTER SIXTEEN

Nicky and Judy woke Sarah early on Sunday morning. They were both very excited and eager to start exploring the passages *now*. She managed to convince them it would be best to have breakfast first and also to wait for the others to join them, Uncle Fred, Stephen, Jane and Michelle. To say nothing of Binky and Cleo, who, she explained, were well acquainted with the passages. Sam, awakened by their chatter came through bringing a somewhat battered copy of the passage tracing they had made back in November. It did not mean much to the younger children but looking at it gave the twins an idea of the ground they hoped to cover.

'We'd better have a chat with the others when they come, and see what's the best approach,' suggested Sam.

'Maybe we should check with Dad, as well,' added Sarah.

Hearing noises below they dressed quickly—also helping the little ones—and then went down for breakfast.

When Derek arrived they asked him the state of things, since the builders had finished for the moment.

'Well,' he replied, 'the Obelisk entrance still has to be repaired and reconstructed, and proper entrances to the old boiler house and the ruined hunting lodge made. Though the latter we may leave until it's been thoroughly examined. But some sort of safety cover will have to be fixed inside the summer house until the Obelisk passage and the other ones are restored and lighted. As you know, the one to the Dell is bricked off and a temporary gate placed across the passage that's supposed to lead to the cellars.'

'Oh,' said Sam, 'I thought the whole lot had been wired for lighting!'

'No, that was just too much work and expense for the moment. However, the builders did check the safety of that passage and reported it is structurally sound, so there's no problem about you exploring it, and I can fix up a couple of lamps on cables so you won't have to rely on torches.' That was a relief!

Just as they finished Michelle arrived, and at nine thirty, Fred with the twins. A conference was held in the kitchen to decide the best way to tackle things. Fred took the chair.

'There are two things to consider,' he said. 'First: your young guests, they are eager to explore, so we should give them a proper tour. Second: you want to try to find the way leading into the cellars. It's possible we have a similar situation here to the business of the summer house, where it was the *old passage* and not the *later* one that concealed the entrance. Who knows how many alterations have been carried out in that part of the cellars? I think I should take Nicky and Judy on the tour while you work as follows: two in the cellars with Cleo and three in the passage with Binky. If the animals sense each other through the intervening stonework, I think we may find what we are looking for.'

'Let's stick to our old set up,' suggested Stephen, 'I'll go with Sarah in the cellars and you three in the passage.'

'What about Uncle Fred and the littlies when their tour is over?'

'Well, he could stay down there and perhaps Michelle could bring them back to the cellars. They haven't been in them, have they?'

Derek produced the necessary cables and lamps and they set off to their respective locations. Nicky and Judy were hanging on to Fred's hands, skipping and singing, 'We are going underground, we are going underground!'

Picking up Cleo, Sarah and Stephen made for the cellars. It seemed ages and ages since Sarah had last been down there. In fact, apart from odd visits to bring up apples and vegetables or other items stored there in the cool, no further explorations had been carried out. From the stair lobby they made their way through the storage rooms until they reached the farthest section on the left, where the partition had a door in it.

They had previously searched it and this was where Jane had discovered the passage plan. Shutting the door so that Cleo could not sneak off, they put her down and turned their attention to the old section of walling. Cleo poked around for a few moments, showing no interest in anything near the wall, then went to the door and demanded to be let out.

'A lot of help she is,' muttered Stephen. Then, turning to Sarah said, 'Look at this piece of walling; it goes beyond the partition. See, it's also in the space next door. We didn't look there last time. You never know, come on, let's see.'

They opened the door and Cleo shot out. For the moment they ignored her and went to look at the wall. Yes, it did continue along to the brick supporting one that met it at right angles. It was built of the same mixture of dressed stone and rubble and was obviously very old. Carefully they began to examine the surface. There was no sign of a filled in doorway or shifting stone; it all sounded very solid when tapped. Quite baffling. Stephen went over the whole surface once more.

'It's a strange thing,' he remarked, 'but this wall is weathered; that means once it was exposed to sun, wind and rain.'

'But how can that be?' asked Sarah, 'It's underground!'

'Yes, underground *now* but when it was built it was *above ground*!' he replied. 'Don't you see? If that is so, the entrance would be *lower, under* the wall level. This floor is *higher,* quite a bit higher than the floors of the passages!'

'Right. But how do they link up then?'

'I'm not... ....' he began, but was interrupted by Cleo. She was standing about a meter or so back from the wall near where the modern one joined it. Her back was arched and she seemed to be listening, for her head was on one side. Then she began to scratch at the floor. Stephen went to the spot and began tapping it with his foot. 'Listen!' Thud, thud, thud, solid deep thumps. Then *thud, thud,* a much lighter sound over an area about a meter square. He grinned at Sarah. 'I think we've found it!'

☙

Meanwhile, the others had made their way to the summer house entrance, which Derek had already unlocked. He was waiting for them and handed one light and cable to Fred and one to Sam.

'There are power points at intervals along the passages, all you have to do is plug in. I've switched on the toplights.'

They descended the steps and made their way along to the passage junction. Nicky and Judy had been reduced to open mouthed silence and were holding *very tightly* to Fred's hands!

'I'll just take them down towards the Obelisk entrance,' he said, 'then come back and join you.' He took the little ones onwards, while they turned right until they reached the gate. Sam had the key to open it while Jane plugged in and switched on the light. Michelle held Binky firmly on his lead. They didn't want him running off!

The passage was lined with a mixture of brick and stone with a good solid floor. It was not very long and ran in a slight curve to the right. As they progressed up it, searching for signs of a doorway, or the like, they saw it was now completely lined with stone. Then it came to a dead end. A solid stone wall built right across it and mortised into the sides. Binky sat down, panted, wagged his tail and looked hopefully at them.

Sam examined it closely. 'This was all built at the same time, there's nothing beyond it, I am sure.'

'But the description Uncle Fred found distinctly said there was a link from the cellars to the passages,' complained Jane, sounding somewhat frustrated.

'Well perhaps, like Uncle Fred has said, other work was done later and destroyed it,' Sam suggested.

They searched around just in case there was something they had missed. While doing this Fred and the littlies joined them. He too examined the walls closely and shook his head — most perplexing!

'Odd, why should someone take the trouble to build a dead end passage and finish it off with fine dressed stone? It doesn't make sense. Any old pieces of rubble would have done, after all, who is going to come up here?'

He held his light up and flashed it on the curved roof. 'Look, even a perfectly fitted roof, crazy! Hey, wait a minute, what are those?' He pointed his light up to where the solid wall and roof met. About six inches below the junction, two strong iron hoops projected. 'Did one hook something into them,' he murmured, 'but why?' Another puzzle.

Sam said slowly, 'The manor is built on a slope, isn't it?' Fred considered this for a moment. 'Yes, it appears that to give it a proper setting, an artificial mound was constructed and the house built on it.'

'But the passages were connected to the *old manor,* which was built at the old ground level.'

'Yes, that's true. What are you getting at?'

Just as he was about to reply, Binky sprang to life. He ran forward and began excitedly jumping up at the wall, barking loudly.

They stared upwards. 'Quiet Binky!' said Michelle sternly. Wonder of wonders, he stopped at once. 'Listen,' she said. At first they could hear nothing, but then Judy said, 'There's a noise up there,' and Nicky added, 'Pussycat!'

Now, very faintly, they could hear, thud, thud, thud—pause, repeated, followed by a scraping noise and a faint, but unmistakable 'miaow.'

Sam grinned, 'I was right! We are *under* the cellars. I bet that old wall where you found the plan, Jane, was once at ground level.'

'And those rings are to slip a ladder on!' added Fred. He took the stick he'd been carrying and tapped the roof three times, paused, and repeated it. There was silence for a moment, then came, thump, thump, thump—pause—thump, thump, thump. Contact had been made!

'Michelle,' said Fred, 'would you take Nicky and Judy up to the cellars, as we arranged? Tell Stephen and Sarah what we've found. I think they'd better not try any digging or moving of stones. We don't know how this entrance works and the last thing we want is a large stone crashing down onto us. I rather think flat headed teachers and pupils suffer certain disadvantages, and please ask Derek to come down here.'

Michelle set off with Binky and the youngsters. To be on the safe side the others returned to the main passage.

Stephen and Sarah managed to scrape away most of the loose dirt on the cellar floor over the entrance, with Cleo's assistance. After a few inches or so they reached smooth and solid stone. Stephen thumped it and they listened. Was there a faint distant sound of yapping? Cleo heard something, for she miaowed loudly. Then there came three taps, a pause, and three more, apparently on the underside of the stone they stood on. Stephen thumped back the same rhythm.

'They are in the passage and we are directly above them,' he said triumphantly. 'There must be an opening here.'

'Wait!' cautioned Sarah, 'We don't want to send a heavy stone crashing down on them! Let's stay here for the moment.

Remember, Michelle will be bringing Nicky and Judy up and she'll tell us what they have discovered and what we should do.'

Though Stephen would have liked to find the secret entrance unaided he realised that they would have to be careful. 'Let's stand by the wall, rather than standing on the stone,' he suggested and they moved away. Soon they heard the chatter of voices, and Michelle with the Bennett children and Binky came down the stairs to where they were.

The discoveries of both groups were soon told, and as there was nothing more to be done at the moment they showed Nicky and Judy round the cellars. Then went up to the kitchen to await the return of the others. After all, this kind of activity made one rather hungry and thirsty. The 'undergrounders' came trooping into the kitchen shortly afterwards, and Derek arrived a few minutes later. Everyone was very pleased and the talk flowed fast and furious until, during a pause, Michelle said, 'We know there is an entrance to the passages under the cellar floor, but *how* do we open it?'

There was a silence. Yes, how indeed? That was the thousand dollar question.

'I would imagine,' mused Derek, 'that the builders of the Obelisk entrance were also the builders of this one. So we should look for some lever, handle or protrusion that would activate the mechanism that moves the stone. I suggest we uncover what looks like the trap door in the cellar so we know how large it is and then, if there's no obvious mechanism, look in the passage.'

'But one must have been able to open it from above and below!' objected Fred, otherwise it wouldn't have been much use if you were on the wrong side of it; you'd be trapped.'

'True,' acknowledged Derek. 'Anyhow, let's start. We don't need too many folk in the cellars. I suggest, Fred, you take the others down again and fix up both lamps so the place is brightly illuminated, then watch and see if you notice any suspicious cracks or lines in the stone work.'

Derek, Stephen and Sarah went into the cellars and the rest returned to the passages, much to Nicky and Judy's delight. Binky and Cleo decided they had done their bit and preferred the kitchen with the smells of Sunday dinner preparation.

With the aid of a shovel, a bucket to put the dirt in, and a couple of brooms, they soon cleared the surface of the stone. It was a large slab, about a meter square, edged with a wide trim of beautifully close-fitting oblong stones; and though they could see a hair-line gap running all the way round, there was no handle or depression to indicate how it was raised. Maybe the trim? Each stone was pushed, pressed, and pulled, but with no result. Perplexed, they rested to consider what next.

In the depths, the others had heard the noise of clearing above them and had identified the area in the curved roof where the trapdoor should be. But there was no sign of the flat slab or how to get at it. Even when those above tapped and pried not a speck of dust came down. Very frustrating indeed.

Then Judy suddenly pointed at the metal hoops saying, 'Why is one of them crooked?'

They looked; the hoop on the left was at a sixty degree angle. 'I'm sure it wasn't like that before,' said Fred. 'But what has caused it to move, and why?' He shone the light nearer.

'It's not just fixed in the wall, it's in a metal socket,' he announced excitedly. 'If I can slip something through I should be able to turn it. Sam, run up to the house and warn the others what I'm going to do, and tell Derek to tap twice on the slab when everyone is well clear of it.'

Sam shot off at full speed, and after a few minutes they heard two sharp taps from above their heads. Fred inserted his stick into the hoop and turned it clockwise. Nothing happened, it wouldn't move. He tried anticlockwise and slowly the hoop rotated until it was at ninety degrees. There was a distinct 'click,' as if some mechanism had engaged, and a grating noise above their heads. Looking up, they saw that a portion of the curved roof had split in half and slid back into the sides, revealing a flat slab above, but still no clue as how to open it. Sam had rejoined them, reporting that as far as Derek knew they had not touched anything that could have caused the hoop to shift. Fred began an inch by inch examination of the surface where the stones had slid back.

In the cellars, Derek, Stephen and Sarah were just as perplexed. Derek had rigged up a strong portable light to see if it would help, but so far, no luck. Binky and Cleo had come down too, but found it all rather boring, so they began one of their usual chases round the cellar. Cleo naturally cheated, for whenever Binky cornered her, she would claw her way up the rough wall and jump over him. In vain would he leap up, trying to catch her tail. Then he craftily hid behind the bucket, and when she came by, charged out. Caught off guard, the little cat leapt up at the rough stone wall and scrabbled frantically to gain a foothold, her forepaws hanging on to a slightly projecting piece of stone. Suddenly it shifted, pitching her down on top of Binky, much to his surprise, and to everyone else's, for there was a rumbling noise and the stone slab slid out of sight!

A beam of light shone up through the opening and they gazed down on their companions looking up. There was a loud cheer and shouts of 'Good old Binks and Cleo, they've done it again!'

Derek kept a couple of short ladders in the cellars for getting at fuse boxes and the like. He hauled one over and lowered it down to Fred, who set it firmly against the side of the wall, and one by one they climbed up. Then everyone climbed down, and up again, just for the fun of it.

'Whoever invented this was a superb craftsman,' remarked Fred. 'Heaven knows when it was last opened, but it works as smoothly as the day it was put in. Now how does it close?'

'I think if you reach your stick down and give that hoop a twist, the ceiling will close,' said Derek. Fred tried, and it did. Then Derek moved over to the projecting stone and gently pulled it up, pushing it in at the same time, and the slab grated back into place.

'I'll go and turn the lights off and close up,' he said. 'You folks better go and clean up! By the delicious odours wafting down here, lunch must be nearly ready. We can talk about this while we eat.'

Luckily, as they surfaced in the back kitchen, hot water, soap and towels were readily available, and they entered the main kitchen in a reasonably tidy state, where lunch was already set out on the table. They were neat enough for the mistress of the house to approve!

It was a noisy meal, but after all the excitement of the morning, how could it have been otherwise?

Fred and Derek were now hot on the trail of the mysterious mason who had constructed the entrance, and in all probability the Obelisk as well.

'Bill may know something, or at least have a clue,' Fred suggested. 'Then there's Hugh Dawes. His folk and those of several of his workmen have been building in this area for generations. They may know something.'

'I'll give him a ring tomorrow,' announced Derek.

Nicky and Judy were now secret passage mad, asking question after question. Were there more tunnels? Where? Could they see them? Could they go down them? Could they? Could they, please!

'I think you'd better go on a trip round the grounds and show them the Dell and the ruins of the hunting lodge. Take Binky as well; he still needs to work off some of his energy,' said Doreen.

So that's how the afternoon was spent, tramping round the grounds introducing all the various spots connected with the passages. Unfortunately, Stephen, who had Judy hanging on his arm, happened to say, 'I wonder where the southern passage from the hunting lodge goes, down to the gates or…?' At once their guests wanted to go exploring and it took a great deal of their combined powers of persuasion to convince them that was not possible 'just now', but one day soon, when they came to stay again, another exploration would take place.

As they were returning a car came up the drive—Will and Joyce. With whoops of delight their two rushed to greet them and were soon excitedly telling them of their adventures. 'It seems they have had a glorious time,' said Will to the quintet. 'I thank you all for being so kind and patient with them.'

Now it was afternoon tea time. Then the Bennetts had to leave, followed very shortly by Fred with Stephen and Jane. Soon afterwards Michelle left on her bike. The twins suddenly felt very tired, and there were no protests when they were sent to bed earlier than usual—well, hardly any.

CHAPTER SEVENTEEN

School very quickly settled into its usual routine during the next three weeks, keeping them well occupied and as enthusiastic as ever. As April drew to a close they realised a long weekend was coming up because of the May Day holiday. The Monday was already booked, as that was the day of the Open Day and Fete at Ascon House. The parents had this well in hand. This left the Saturday and Sunday to fill. 'Mum suggests why don't you three come and stay with us?' said Jane to the twins and Michelle. 'She says she'd love to have you—she really means it!'

Phone calls were made midweek and it was settled that Doreen would take Sam and Sarah's and Michelle's stuff over to Southleigh when she went in to town to do the Friday shop; and the Randells would bring them and their goods to Ascon House on the Monday.

Only Jane was a little concerned. On Wednesday evening she said to her brother,

'But what shall we *do* with them? We haven't any ponds or secret passages; it must seem awfully dull for them here.'

'Let's get Chris and Fenella involved,' suggested Stephen, 'They might have some ideas.'

'We could also ask Bob Binnacle for ideas,' added Jane.

However, Michelle informed them the next morning that her grandmother had invited them for tea on Saturday, so one afternoon would be taken care of.

Chris and Fenella were consulted, and Chris came up with a plan that sounded promising. 'On Sunday, why not take a picnic lunch with us and follow Bardon Lane towards the Pickham Hills and the Tadbrook? I've always wanted to do that. Dad says it's about a two and a half mile walk. I'm sure we could manage that easily.'

'What about coming back?' inquired Jane.

'Perhaps Dad would drive out and pick us up,' said Stephen. On consulting John they found he was willing. (It had also turned out that both Reg and John knew Peter professionally, as they had had dealings with him in his capacity as an Inland Revenue Valuation Officer. 'A small world indeed,' Reg told them.)

Friday found them full of excitement at the prospect of the weekend. The whole class was so excited that Mr Atkinson wisely decided it was not the sort of day for concentrated work; so instead, having rounded off the maths period, he read to them from Gerald Durrell's *My Family and other Animals*, which was much appreciated by the class!

When school ended, Sam collected Jill, taking her to the bus; Geoff would keep an eye on her, but she insisted that Sam put her on it! As they walked up from the kindergarten she said, 'Nicky has been telling me all about the passages. He says there's one you are going to explore one day 'cos you don't know where it goes. Can I come too, please?' 'Of course you can,' he replied, and with that she seemed content.

What with piling into the Randell's car and the chatter, he forgot to mention Jill's request. They were soon established in their old rooms at Southleigh and having a snack in the kitchen and admiring the latest addition to the menagerie. Two kittens, one black and white and one white and tortoiseshell, called Perry and Polly. Their antics kept them amused for some time until the two little creatures suddenly flopped down on the mat and went to sleep, tired out from their play. Having finished eating it was up to the play room to discuss what they would do tomorrow morning before going to Melissa's for tea.

'Chris and Fenella will be coming round at nine,' said Stephen, 'so we ought to have something planned; we don't want to spend the whole morning trying to decide what to do.'

They got the ordnance map out; maybe that would give them some ideas. They looked at it for some while, then Jane said, 'From Fenella's house to the river isn't very far and there's a footpath that runs past the side of her place straight down to it. What about that?'

'An excellent idea, even though it's only fresh water, my hearties,' and there was a smiling Bob Binnacle. 'I'll join you and give some nautical tips on inland water sailing.'

'But we don't have a boat,' protested Michelle. 'Never mind, who knows what you may find when there,' he replied, adding, 'I'll meet you by the river between nine thirty and ten,' then vanished into the famous Golden Hind Beam.

'That sounds promising,' said Sam as they went down for supper. The others agreed; having Bob with them would definitely make a difference.

Afterwards the kittens staged an entertainment, as Perry had discovered he could climb up the green baize-covered door between the kitchen and the hall. He would climb to the top and hang there miaowing to be hauled down. Polly would sit underneath looking up at him with sisterly admiration.

They arranged with Phyllis to make sandwiches for their morning trek.

'As long as you're back by one, at the latest,' she told them. 'Remember you are expected at Melissa's around two thirty and no doubt, when you return, you'll need a good clean-up before I can let you loose for polite afternoon teas.'

They promised to be back in good time; Stephen and Michelle both had watches — the others had as well — but too much winding and removing the backs to examine the works had impaired their accuracy. For now it was — off to bed.

༄

That evening as Jill and her brother played in the bath she began to think seriously about the secret passages. Surely if she could find the one Nicky had talked about the other children would be pleased, especially Sam. And if there was one thing Jill definitely wanted it was to please him and win his approval.

'Are you going to sit in there daydreaming all night?' inquired Bess, who had already removed and dried Brian. Oh, yes, the water was becoming cooler. She scrambled out and continued her thoughts while her mother dried her. Bess knew that when Jill went into one of these moods, or states, she was busy thinking about something. Her parents had found it was best to let her work things out for herself. If she needed help she would ask. So she said nothing, except to point out she was now dry and could put her nightie on! Once the curtains were drawn and after a story and prayer, Brian soon fell asleep. So she concentrated her mind on their house guardian, the Civil War soldier. Often at night he would come and talk to her. He seemed to sense when she had a problem.

Now he appeared, smiled and sat down on the bed. 'Well, my little maid, what troubles you?'

'It's not exactly trouble,' she replied and went on to explain about the secret passages, especially the one her friends wished to explore, and how she wanted to help. He listened attentively and then said:

'Little maid, during that terrible war I was involved in, the passage you speak of originally went to the old hunting lodge. Then the Lord of the Manor decided it should be extended as an escape route, and with great secrecy this was accomplished.'

'Where to?' asked Jill.

He smiled, 'To this very farm. It was well used, I can tell you! After the war it was forgotten and even I am unsure whether it came into the house or one of the outbuildings. I rather think the latter. The house would have been too obvious.'

'Would you help me find it, please?' she begged.

He smiled, 'If it will make you happy, yes.'

'I am happy,' she replied, 'But I want to make Sam happy too.'

'You are a very thoughtful and caring child,' he said, bending forward and stroking her forehead. 'Now you must sleep. I shall meet you tomorrow morning inside the entrance to the great barn, for it is the oldest building on the farm and would be a good place to start.' He vanished. Contentedly she fell asleep.

※

All was hustle and bustle at Southleigh next morning as they prepared for the tramp to the river. It was sunny, but the wind was cool. Fine for walking, but not for sitting about. Not that any of them ever did much of that! Breakfast was soon over and the sandwich packs prepared. They took one backpack, which each would take their share in carrying. Fenella and Chris would bring their own food. As they would be following the footpath by Fenella's house, Chris came up from his place, and the six of them set off just before nine for Fenella's. She was waiting for them at the gate, muttering about brother Andrew as — usual. He had refused to lend her his knapsack.

'And I asked him nicely,' she said bitterly. 'I should have taken it without telling him, he'd never have known; his room's always in such a mess. I've had to make do with this stupid shoulder bag.'

Chris promptly took the contents out and added them to his. 'Plenty of room,' he exclaimed, 'the two of us can take turns in carrying it.'

Before they set off, Stephen explained that Bob would be joining them by the river to instruct them in the art of inland water sailing. Though how he was going to do it without a boat, they couldn't imagine. In single file the explorers started off down the path. Soon it ran through open fields, and in the distance they could see the river. On their right the railway embankment curved away to the town. After quarter of an hour's steady plodding they reached the river bank. The path followed it to the left. On the right a fence and the notice 'Private Property, Keep Out!' made its meaning very clear.

From the ordnance map that Stephen had borrowed from his father, they saw that the path followed the river until it reached a plantation and then rejoined Bardon Lane.

'Let's walk along a little way and then stop for refreshments,' suggested Sarah. 'There's a clump of trees about half a mile along. That should give us some shelter from this wretched wind.'

This had become rather more annoying since their start. Upon reaching the trees, they settled down overlooking the River Tad. Apart from the wind it was very pleasant.

'I wonder when Bob will arrive?' remarked Stephen, 'It's already quarter to ten; maybe we should wait a bit before snacking.'

'Ahoy!' said a cheery voice and there was Bob, seated amongst them. 'Just right for sailing, me hearties, a good wind.'

'But how?' said Sam, 'We haven't a boat.'

'Ah, I thought it would be good to give you an idea by a practical demonstration using images, thus.'

He made some swift hand movements and before their startled eyes an apparently full sized sailing dinghy was floating in midstream. Bob now began to explain the names and functions of the different parts, as he did so these lit up so they could follow his explanations.

'Rather like a computer program,' remarked Stephen.

They watched the boat sail into the wind, against the wind, and with the wind; it tacked and reefed sail. It was so real each wanted to run down, jump in and have a go.

'I think if you show a reasonable understanding of how to handle a boat your parents might allow you a try out,' he explained. 'Now it's time to visit the mess deck, all hands to the food.'

Realizing how hungry they felt by now, the sandwiches were soon being enjoyed, while Bob answered further questions on nautical matters.

༄

After breakfast Jill said, 'Mum, may I go and play in the yard?'

Bess paused and said, 'Are you sure you want to? I'm taking Brian for his dental checkup in Bidcote this morning. Do you mind staying here?'

'No, not at all, I have something to do, for Sam.'

Bess smiled, 'If that's the case I know you'll be all right. Dad will be in Church Wood Meadow if you want him. I shall do some local shopping afterwards, so we should be back by eleven.'

'All right, thanks, Mum,' and she ran off to put her shoes on.

Having waved goodbye to Bess and Brian, she made her way across the farmyard to the great barn. This massive stone building dwarfed all the surrounding sheds, pens and byres. Its wide entrance had two enormous buttresses on either side. The floor was of great stone slabs and the windows were tiny slits in the thick walls. The roof, covering the massive beams, was of Welsh slate. Jill had always been in awe of it and had never been inside on her own.

She hesitated in the shadow of the great open doors, then tiptoed over the threshold. To her immense relief the soldier stood there.

He held out his hand and she took it—that was much better. 'Now we must search round to see if we can find any trace of an entrance,' he said. 'It may be a trapdoor in the floor or a false section of wall. Use your keen young eyes and anything you see that looks unusual, tell me and we'll investigate.'

'Please, before we begin, what am I to call you?' she asked. 'I can't just call you "man" or "soldier", that's not polite.'

'If you wish you can call me Edwin; will that do?'

'Oh yes, thank you—Edwin!' she replied.

'What we'll do first is work our way round the walls, then the floor,' he explained.

As it was still early spring the place was comparatively empty, so it was easy to examine the walls and floor. Starting from the doorway they began working their way in a clockwise direction.

༄

When the sandwiches had vanished and the drink bottles were empty, Bob started to explain how a larger sailing vessel worked. He illustrated this with a two masted schooner—a truly magnificent sight on the river, though it was rather doubtful if any ship of that size had ever sailed *that* stretch of water. It looked so real the children wondered if anyone else, happening along by chance, would also be able to see it. This question was answered sooner than they expected. Round a slight bend downstream a small motorboat came chugging along towards Tadbridge; in it was seated an elderly man, towing a fishing line over the side. He had his back to the direction he was going, obviously not expecting to find any obstructions in those tranquil waters. Bob, flustered by his sudden appearance, muttered something, but instead of the schooner vanishing, its sails suddenly filled out and it began to move majestically downstream towards the unsuspecting fisherman. For a moment the children were paralysed. Then Fenella jumped to her feet and yelled, 'Ahoy! Look out, boat ahead!' The startled fisherman turned his head and his mouth dropped open in amazement, as anybody's would at the sight of a schooner in full sail bearing down upon them on a tranquil minor waterway. Once the initial shock was over he reacted swiftly, leaping for the controls of his outboard motor and the rudder. Unfortunately he accelerated too sharply and jerked the rudder at the same time. The boat yawed violently, cut across the bows of the schooner and rammed the bank and with the engine still running tried to climb up it. The occupant was flung over the bows by the force of the impact, luckily landing in a thick clump of grass. At the moment he crossed the schooner's bows it disappeared! The children ran down to help him, but he was already scrambling out of the grass and had jumped into the boat to switch the engine off.

'Are you all right?' they asked anxiously.

He scratched his head and looked at them, then up and down the river. Not a thing in sight, except for a couple of ducks and a moorhen.

'Did *you* see it?' he asked hesitantly.

'Er, yes!' they replied equally hesitantly.

He gave a sigh of relief. 'Thank goodness, I thought I must be hallucinating.' To their surprise he asked no further questions, but busied himself tidying up the boat. Then with their help he pushed it back into the water.

'Thanks,' he said, adding, 'There are more things to be seen on this stretch of water than you'd credit. Though I must admit *that* was a real surprise!' The engine chugged into life and he moved slowly away upstream.

Bob must have decided that discretion was the better part of valour, for he had vanished. Stephen looked at his watch. 'Oh, goodness, it's already twelve thirty, we'll have to step it out smartly if we're to be back in time for lunch.' They set off at a good pace, parting company with Fenella at her house and Chris outside Southleigh. 'See you tomorrow,' he yelled, 'I'll be up around nine.'

☙

Edwin and Jill worked their way slowly round the interior of the great barn, examining the wall surface and the flagstones that rested against it: clockwise from the entrance, down the shorter wall and then along the back. When the corner was reached they paused.

'Can't you remember where the entrance is?' asked Jill.

Edwin shook his head. 'Alas no, little maid. True I have been in the passage; but I had been badly wounded in a skirmish round the manor and was carried through it to the farm so that my wounds could be dressed. I fear I was only semi-conscious and so have no recollection at all of the exit.'

'Are you all right now?' she asked anxiously.

'Oh yes, I recovered very quickly. Come, we should continue our search.'

They worked along the right wall then back towards the doorway. Just as they approached it a kitten ran in and across the floor.

'Naughty thing!' scolded Jill, 'He's always sneaking out and getting into mischief.'

She ran over to pick it up. Holding the squeaking little fellow in her arms she started to walk back towards Edwin, who was waiting by the door. Light streamed through it, making the surrounding walls seem very dark, or were they? On the left an area of lighter stone almost seemed to glow. The outline of an arched doorway! To the right, on the massive doorpost beam, the light shone on one of the great bolts fixing it to the wall. She gasped and pointed. Edwin reacted at once. He turned and studied the wall surface, nodding excitedly, for the strange light still played round the stones.

Jill ran over to the doorway and, putting the kitten down,

found she could just reach the knob of the bolt. But what now? A voice spoke softly in her ear, 'In the King's name, push, push, my girl!' She pushed and the bolt head slid back into the post. There was a loud 'click,' followed by a rumbling sound, and when she ran back to Edwin's side he was gazing into the revealed opening with a flight of steps going down. He turned to her. 'My little maid, we've found it!' he said.

༄

They just made it, lunch was already on the table, but Phyllis offered no comments; she was thankful they had arrived *almost* on time. Afterwards came the preparation for Melissa's. It turned out to be a very pleasant afternoon and they returned home about six, feeling very satisfied, especially in the food intake regions. A light supper, then they prepared for their excursion — and now? Oh! Was it really bedtime? 'Yes! Off you go!'

༄

Jill was happy, the exit to the passage from the manor had been found. Sam would be pleased. She had no wish to venture down there just now and was glad when Edwin suggested it be closed, which he did by pulling the head of the bolt so that it projected like its fellows. As she went out into the yard Bess and Brian returned. She remarked that the look on her daughter's face was like that of a cat well contented with a saucer of cream, but knew better than to ask why!

CHAPTER EIGHTEEN

Next morning they were up early again, checking their gear and wheedling binoculars from John, plus the map. Phyllis was organising the provisions with Michelle's help. Sam and Sarah loaded and checked the backpacks. They were taking two this time.

'Lets hope Fenella manages to borrow her brother's,' said Jane, 'I doubt whether Chris would be able to fit her stuff in his as well.'

Having made sure all was ready they settled down to breakfast with an easy conscience, and, bearing in mind the trek being undertaken, ate heartily. Chris arrived just before nine and they set off for Fenella's place.

As they left John said, 'I'll meet you at the bridge around four thirty; and I'll wait until five. If you're not down by then you'll have to walk back.' They assured him they would be there.

Fenella met them at the gate with her brother's backpack on her back and a big grin on her face. 'I told Dad I *had* to have a proper bag,' she told them. 'He said I should borrow Andrew's, I said he wouldn't lend it. "We'll see about that!" said Dad, and he did.'

The weather was similar to yesterday's, but without the cool wind, instead a gentle breeze swayed the grass along the lane side. They set off at a brisk walk until Stephen pointed out they had quite a distance to go and it would be better not to rush, but to set a steady pace, which would be far less tiring. As Bardon Lane ended at the foot of the Pickham Hills, only local traffic used it, which meant it was ideal for walking. They took their time, enjoying the surrounding countryside, being young and full of life and above all, *friends!*

By ten thirty they had reached the bridge spanning the Tadbrook, a minor tributary of the River Tad. They settled down on the grassy bank beside it and ate their snack, then they took off shoes and socks to paddle and refresh their feet before facing the climb before them. They crossed the bridge; here the road petered out and became an unmade track going to the left and right at the foot of the Pickham Hills, which now loomed directly ahead and looked as steep, if not steeper, than Crimson Hill! The lower slopes were covered with pine forest, which made the initial going straightforward, as there was little or no undergrowth and the paths were easy to follow. After plodding steadily upwards for half an hour the trees began to thin out, and they emerged onto the uplands, an area covered with gorse, dead ferns and scrawny grass. The sun had warmed up by now and they stopped for a moment to remove pullovers, put them in the packs and carry on in shirtsleeves. Ah, that was much better! As they climbed higher the gorse and fern became sparser and the rocky bones of the hills showed through the thinning soil; the grass was now reduced to odd clumps where it could maintain a foothold. The breeze was stronger, but very welcome.

They paused at the foot of the final steep slope to the summit. The view, looking back the way they had come was spectacular. Using the binoculars Stephen could pick out their house, and much to Sam and Sarah's delight, the back roof of Bidford Manor was also visible. It was just before twelve, so they decided to make their assault on the main peak and have lunch up there. It was a strange exhilarating feeling being so high, and their energy seemed boundless, though when the summit was gained everyone flung themselves down and just laid there—panting—for five minutes. Upon recovering they stood up and let the breeze cool them down before starting on the serious business of eating. It was pleasant sitting up there looking northwards with Hidding-cum-Stanton nestling against the northern slopes, which, they noticed, were not so steep as the southern side. Still it didn't really matter, as they had no plans for going down there at the moment. They felt rather drowsy, and the sun had turned hazy; the landscape became indistinct, and one by one they dozed off... ...

For how long they were never sure, but all awoke with a start. Something had disturbed them, but what? Then the sound came again, a rattle and crash of? Guns, rifles?

'It sounds like muskets,' remarked Stephen, who remembered when John had taken them to a Sealed Knot display last year. The sounds came from the lower slopes of the hills away to their right. There was another volley and faint shouting drifted up to them. The haze had become thicker and it was difficult to make out any detail of the land below. More sounds and shouts, this time nearer, as if those involved were drawing closer.

They hesitated, wondering what to do. Then out of the haze a figure came quickly towards them along the crest.

'Gather your things up, children, and follow me,' he commanded. 'You are in grave danger if you remain here!'

There was something in his voice and manner, which, without a word, they obeyed. He led them back the way he had come until they reached a gap between the peak they had climbed and the next. Soon they were in the cover of the trees again. Here he paused, saying, 'Rest a moment.' They were glad for a chance to regain their breath. Now they had time to look at their rescuer. He was dressed in old-fashioned clothes, a heavy leather jacket, baggy breeches and sturdy calf-length boots. A scabbard with a sword clanked at his side and in his wide belt there was a flintlock pistol. A broad brimmed hat completed his outfit. Seeing the bewildered expressions on their faces, he smiled, saying:

'The little maid of the farm begged me to come. She sensed you were in danger. I could not refuse her...'

He stopped and listened; faint noises could still be heard away to the right and slightly above them.

'We must continue down to the stream and the bridge,' he said. 'Once you are on the other side of it you are safe; come.'

They weaved their way down through the trees and soon could make out the sparkling Tadbrook far beneath them. The slope was not so steep here, and the trees started to thin out. They were crossing a fairly bare patch when there were shouts from above and behind. Voices crying:

'There they go, stop them!' and someone shouting, 'In the name of the Lord Protector I command you to surrender yourselves!'

'Dodge and run,' ordered their companion. 'When you reach the track run for the bridge and do not stop or look back until you have crossed it. I shall do my best to slow them down!' They hesitated. 'Go!' he commanded so fiercely that they ran.

Behind there came a rattle of shots and something zipped through the trees above their heads.

'There's one of them,' the voices shouted. 'After him!'

There was a loud 'crack' and cries of alarm. Their rescuer had fired his pistol. Now the sounds were moving away to the right. He was drawing them off. They came to the track and pounded along it. The bridge was in sight. More shouts from the hillside above them, but they had reached it and were swiftly across to the other side, sliding down the bank under the cover of its stonework, where they huddled under the arch wondering what would happen next.

There was a sudden 'snap', that's the only word they could

find to describe it. Before, everything had been hazy and vague; now it was all sharp and clear. They were fully in the present. The fear lifted and life returned to normal. Crawling out from under the arch they took off the packs and sat on the bank as they had done earlier. All of them were somewhat grubby; the scramble/slide down the hillside through the dusty forest floor had left them dirty and dishevelled. Removing shoes and socks they paddled in the stream and attempted to wash the dirt and dust off, using hankies to dry themselves — not very successfully, but it made them feel better. Then they sat on the bank again and talked about what had just happened.

'It was a time-warp thing,' said Sam, 'like we had at the airfield.'

'Yes, right back to the Civil War!' Chris remarked. 'But why and what, and who was chasing whom?'

'It was all so confusing!' added Fenella.

'What did he mean by the "little farm maid"?' queried Michelle.

'I expect Dad may know something about it,' said Jane. 'He's into all that Civil War stuff. He would have joined the Sealed Knot lot, but Mum wouldn't have it. Running round all dressed up and playing at soldiers isn't her idea of spending the weekend!'

At that moment they heard a car approaching. Goodness gracious, it had already gone half past four! They scrambled up the bank as John drew the car up by the bridge.

'My, you *do* look a scruffy lot!' he exclaimed, 'but I suppose that means you've had a good time! Pile in and we'll soon be home. Oh, by the way, Chris and Fenella are staying for supper. Your mother thought you'd approve.' Loud were the cheers for Phyllis!

Supper was held in the kitchen, and after further attempts at tidying themselves up they gathered round the table, doing full justice to its contents. Then, once past the pudding winning post, Stephen tackled his dad with their Civil War question. Phyllis rolled her eyes and groaned. 'It's all right, Mum, we just need some information,' her son explained.

'Strange you should ask that today of all days,' John began. 'It happens to be the anniversary of a minor action fought in this area in 1643 on May 3rd.'

'From February to June of that year there was quite a lot of activity in this area and the south-west. It appears that a group of Royalists fleeing from Taunton were making their way towards Lyme Regis but were surprised by a large troop of Cromwell's Horse as they left Hidding-cum-Stanton. They tried to escape over the Pickham Hills, but their pursuers split up and while one group chased after them, the remainder rode round towards the Tadbrook bridge in an attempt to cut them off. It seems the fighting took place on the eastern slopes of the first peak and then between it and the one to the west. It appears there were some civilians with the Royalists, even children, and one party only just managed to escape capture because the soldier who was escorting them put up such a determined rearguard action the pursuers had to send for reinforcements, which meant diverting the second patrol, so the bridge was left clear and most of the Royalists escaped.'

'What happened to that soldier?' asked Jane.

'He was wounded, but managed to evade capture, and with the help of local folk made his way to Bidford Manor. Unfortunately, it was attacked a few days later, but he escaped again. After the war he lived in the district. Some say he worked on the Manor Farm.'

They looked at each other; now who the 'little maid of the farm' was became clear.

'We can find out more tomorrow,' said Michelle, 'when we all meet up at Ascon House.'

☙

In the early hours of that morning Jill had stirred restlessly in her sleep. She was dreaming a very strange, and for her, vivid dream. In it she saw a steep hillside bare at the top and tree-covered on its lower slopes. She felt she was above it and yet at the same time on it. On the summit there was a group of people. They were resting, yet alert. Their clothes were very dusty and some were torn. There were children amongst the adults. Some of the clothing reminded her of Edwin's. One, who was acting as lookout shouted something, and the whole party staggered up and began to descend the slope towards the trees. Then she saw coming round the right side of the hill another band of men, definitely soldiers, all dressed in similar uniforms and holding long 'funny looking' guns (muskets). As soon as they saw the other group, commands were shouted and the people began to run for cover. Some of the soldiers unslung their muskets and began firing. She saw a man drop and lie still. She saw the children, running for their lives. One boy looked familiar, very familiar. It was Sam! running as fast as he could. One of the musketeers took aim and fired in his direction; she heard the explosion of the weapon. She screamed, 'Sam, look out!' All went dark and she woke up, trembling and crying. Brian, startled out of his sleep by her scream, seeing his sister sobbing, joined in. In a flash Bess was in the room comforting and soothing them both. But Jill was so upset it took a long time before she quietened down enough to tell her mother coherently about the dream. 'It's Sam, Sam!' she kept saying. 'He's in danger, terrible danger! He must be warned!' In vain did Bess explain that Sam, Sarah and Michelle were staying with Stephen and Jane and she would see them tomorrow at the Fete. 'He must be told!' she kept on saying. At last her mother promised to ring up the Randell's after breakfast so she could speak to him. With this the child calmed down. However, breakfast was late and by the time Bess remembered and rang Phyllis the children had already left on their trek. Jill almost became hysterical, and her mother was at her wits end what to do with her. Was she sickening for something?

Then, as if by magic, she stopped crying and a determined look appeared on her face. 'Edwin,' she said, 'He'll know what to do.' Before her mother could stop her, she dashed out of the kitchen and across to the barn, calling loudly as she went, 'Edwin, Edwin, I need you, quick, quick!' There he was, standing just inside the doorway. Almost sobbing with relief she flung herself at him, and, hanging on tightly, poured out the story of her dream. When she had finished, he said, 'Do not worry, little maid. I will go there myself, for alas, I know it all too well. I was one of those fugitives you saw.

There is danger, but your good friend shall not be harmed, nor his companions! Now go in to your mother and tell her all is well. When I return I shall come and let you know what took place.' 'I *knew* you would help,' she replied, and giving him a quick hug, ran back to her mother. Bess saw her coming and noted the change of expression. She gave a sigh of relief; whoever he was, 'Edwin' had obviously allayed her fears.

'It's all right, Mum!' she said as she entered the kitchen. 'Edwin will go and protect Sam and the others. He'll come back and tell me what happened, too.'

'That's kind of him,' said Bess. She wanted to ask who 'Edwin' was, but was not quite sure how to frame the question.

'Edwin's our soldier-guardian, you know,' Jill added conversationally, 'Oh, where's Brian? I want to play with him for a bit 'cos I didn't mean to wake him up all of a sudden this morning.'

'He's in the lounge,' Bess replied, and her little daughter skipped off as if she hadn't a care in the world.

That afternoon around four o'clock Jill was seated at the

kitchen table making a big drawing for Sam; she was trying to draw her dream. Suddenly she stopped and listened. Somebody was calling her; it must be Edwin. 'I won't be a moment,' she told her mother and ran out to the barn. There was Edwin, just as he'd promised. He looked pleased and relieved.

'All is well!' he told her. 'I arrived in time to guide them to safety. Nobody was hurt and now they are on their way back to the Randell's house. You will see them tomorrow for sure!'

She thanked him gravely and returned to her drawing, remarking to Bess as she did so, 'Mum, we are lucky to have a house guardian, aren't we!'

CHAPTER NINETEEN

The May Day holiday dawned bright and clear and the forecast was favourable, a most unusual event! The Grounds of Ascon House would be opened at ten thirty and the Fete was due to begin at eleven. As the grounds were extensive they could have a good wander round before meeting up with those coming from the Bidcote area. Fenella had persuaded her mother to take her — and Chris.

What the Southleighans did not know was that Fred was coming and bringing Peter with him. In fact it was going to be quite a gathering, and Derek had already booked a large table on the terrace for a special Grand May Day Lunch, which was being served by the Ascon House Catering Department. As it was likely to be very popular, John decided to leave early so they could find a decent parking spot. By nine fifteen everyone was ready to depart. As they drove out of the gates, Dorothy Steuart's old Morris Oxford squealed to a halt to let them out and then trailed along behind occasionally letting off loud bangs and weird choking noises, but still kept going!

Quite a few people had had the same idea, and when they reached the entrance gates there was a slowly moving queue of vehicles waiting to buy their admission tickets. However, they were not kept waiting too long and soon found a nice shady parking spot. Dorothy's car chugged in beside them.

'If you lot want to have a look round the grounds be off now and meet us back in front of the main house at eleven thirty,' said John, 'I believe the gardens are well worth looking round; afterwards we can wander round the fete and have lunch, which, Derek tells me, will be at one fifteen.' As the park now spread out before them looked very interesting, the children were off like a shot.

The estate was long and narrow, stretching for some five miles or more. It had been planted and landscaped in such a way that one was not aware of its narrowness, and there were small rockeries, water gardens, little glades and spinnies with paths that wound hither and thither — an altogether fascinating place. As they came round a bend by a large lily pond with a waterfall at one end, they encountered five familiar faces: Roger, Cherry, Shirley, Wendy and Ann. From the way she was talking and gesticulating, Shirley was explaining something to do with the water plants. They ran over to join them.

'Just the person we need!' remarked Stephen, 'to explain all these different plants and things. We know they are all beautiful and unique, but we don't really know much about them.'

'Now you've done it!' said Roger in mock despair, 'Once Shirley gets going there's no stopping her, she'll have your heads spinning in no time at all.'

Cherry looked at her watch. 'No time now,' she said briskly, 'we have to get back to meet the others.'

'Never mind,' said Stephen. 'Maybe we can come back after lunch for a while.' Shirley nodded and they all started back to the main house. The place was now milling with visitors and it took them several minutes to spot John and Phyllis and with them, Reg, Fred, Peter, Will, Joyce, Erin, Harry, Bess, Derek, Doreen, Ingrid, Melissa, Dorothy and of course *all* the younger children — what a gathering! According to Fenella's calculations there were thirty of them all told!

The fete was held in the grounds behind the house and had just been opened by the owner of Ascon House, who was also the local MP. The younger children were eager to go to the stalls and a roundabout rather than trailing round the interior of the house. It wasn't only the younger children who were keen either. For the older ones reasoned that the house would still be there after the fete was over so — they won! To their amazement — and joy — their teacher announced: 'OK, I'll go with them, after all I'm used to school excursions, and keeping an eye on an unruly bunch of young hooligans.'

'You're certainly not going to be left with that mob on your own,' said Reg, 'I'll come with you.'

Peter also nodded his head and joined the group.

'So will I,' added Melissa, and Dorothy decided to come along too, for being a journalist, she could probably write something about it for the 'Tadbridge Times'. A head count revealed fourteen children from three to nine.

'Stick together, and you older ones keep an eye on the younger ones,' said Fred, and they set off towards the stalls, booths and swings. Meanwhile, the remaining grown-ups joined the line of people waiting for conducted tours round the house.

The fete was a high quality one, and many of the stalls catered more for grown-ups than children. Knitted tea cosies, raffia napkin rings and odd shaped embroidered tablecloths abounded. There was a second-hand book and record stall. An 'antique' stall was selling at exorbitant prices things 'that were two a penny in my young days!' as Reg remarked. There were jam and cake stalls a plenty, a couple of garden and plant stalls and a childrens' stall with odd bits and pieces, 'nothing over 5p' a sign announced.

However, the fair section was better, with a coconut shy, hoopla, Aunt Sally and various other games of skill. There were swings, slides, two merry-go-rounds and a dodgems car set up. This was much more in their line. The older children went for the games of skill and did very well. In fact Sarah, Jane and Michelle were so good at tossing tennis balls in buckets that the stall keeper began to get quite agitated, as her supply of prizes was dwindling rapidly.

'Why don't you little girls go and try your luck somewhere else?' she remarked rather pointedly after their fourth round of 'good luck'.

The winnings, mainly woolly animals of doubtful species, were distributed amongst the younger ones. The others had also done well. Sam, Stephen and Christopher had been working one of the grab cranes where things have to be caught in its claws and dropped down a chute. They were also doing fine! Fred watched with a big grin on his face. The owner of the device began to look very sour-faced.

'Them your lot, Mister?' he said to him. 'Too clever by half, the little so-and-sos.'

'Co-ordination. They learn it at school — head, heart and hand,' replied their teacher.

'Cor, well get them away from here, they'll ruin me!' was the response. These winnings were also distributed to the younger ones.

Then it was hurrah for the swings, slides and roundabouts, which the grown-ups enjoyed as well. Melissa felt that Ann and Brian would be scared if they went by themselves, so insisted on going with them and paying for every ride, swing or slide they wanted. Reg, out of a sense of duty beyond the call of reason, went with Nicky and Wendy, though after one or two rides he looked slightly green in the face. Jill and Judy went with Sam and Stephen. But when the older ones tried the dodgem cars, they politely declined a ride and preferred to watch. By now, having exhausted all the various possibilities, Reg informed them it was time to make their way back to the terrace, where lunch would shortly be served.

The terrace faced south and was now bathed in sunlight and comfortably warm. Their party had been given a long table down one end, conveniently near the serving area. The seating of everybody took some time as the children kept on swapping round because they wanted to be near someone who was seated at the far end or on the other side. But eventually places were sorted out to the satisfaction of all. The service and the meal were excellent, and an hour or so later there was a pushing back of chairs and general sighs of contentment.

The adults had enjoyed their tour of the house and compared notes as to which of the items they had seen were most appealing, while the children compared fairground experiences and the smaller ones played with the toys they'd been given.

Sam had a chat with Jill about their experience on the Pickham Hills, and she told him of her dream and Edwin's assistance. 'So it was through you we were helped,' he said and took her to tell the others. They praised the little girl for her quick thinking, then she scampered back to play with the younger ones. After a short while the older children grew restless, and remembering their promise to Shirley, asked if they could go off to the water gardens for a while. Their parents agreed, provided they kept together and Fred agreed to come and fetch them when it was time to leave. This would not be too late in the afternoon, as it was 'you know what' tomorrow.

With Shirley in the lead, they made their way to the lily pond and waterfall.

'Could we make something like that out of our pond?' asked Sarah. 'It would be great to have lilies growing on it and those lovely feathery reeds round the edge.'

Shirley considered for a moment. 'Yes, I suppose it could be made like this, but there would be a lot of cleaning up work to be done first and landscaping of the sides. I don't think we could do it on our own. But we could put in various water plants to help clean the water and that would improve the general plant growth. But it would be better to wait until the autumn before making any changes.'

They stood at the side of the pond and realised they were the only people there. The sun shone on the water, making it sparkle, and reflections danced on the leaves of the trees above. Suddenly a haze descended, enclosing them for a moment in its cool embrace, then lifted. Everything looked the same, but was it?

The pond shimmered through a delicate veil of mist. A voice whispered in their ears,

'Dip your hands in the water, then close your eyes and place your wet fingers over them. Do the the same for your ears, then you will be able to see and hear!'

The children obeyed and when they opened their eyes the plant world stood out sharp and clear around them. When they gazed into the pond it was full of mobile weaving shapes. About the plants were similar forms, like a fine mist, slipping in and out and passing through the foliage.

The voice spoke again. 'What you see are the Elementals of natural liquids and moisture. They are known as Undines. Kneel down by the water's edge and one of them will speak to you.' Eagerly they did so. In the clear water a spot, rather like a patch of oil, moved lazily around. First a blob, then elongated, until it seemed thin enough to break. But instead it flowed together like some fantastic fish. Swimming over and lifting itself slightly from the water, it spoke to them in a soft liquid-like voice. It did not appear to have any features, as everything about it was continually flowing and merging into itself.

'Welcome, earth-walking beings to my realm, the Kingdom of Life.'

'I've never seen a picture of you in any books,' remarked Jane.

'I never knew you existed, I thought you were just made up in stories,' said Chris.

The Undine laughed, a sound like clear running bubbling water.

'Those you call artists try to depict us, but in truth they know nothing of our true nature. If they cannot draw a gnome properly, how can they draw us? Also their eyes are closed; they only see what they believe to be real. Once, during the Earth's childhood, we were known and treated with respect and veneration. Even today, in some remote places, there are still folk who possess this ancient heritage, such as those known as the Rain-Makers. We obey their call. Sometimes there are faint memories of us in old half-forgotten stories and legends set around old streams, ponds or wells. We have been called Nixies, beings with evil associations, caused by our true nature not being understood and being wrongly used. Today we are being driven out of our realm by the evil substances poured into it by humans. When the water becomes too tainted we look for cleaner places. But if we leave or diminish in numbers, the water also becomes lifeless.'

'What *is* your task?' they asked.

'Liquid is an important part of life, water in particular; we channel it, mainly to the plant world, though unbeknown to humans and animals we also work within you! Look around and you will see what I mean.'

They did so, and saw Undine beings moving into and flowing round the roots of plants beside the pool, carrying the life-giving water, silently, smoothly. They watched, entranced; it gave them a feeling of intense wonder. In the surrounding undergrowth they noticed how the Undines worked in harmony with the Gnomes, who made tunnels so they could reach the roots. Swirling round the trees were others collecting moisture given off by the leaves. After a while the vision began to dissolve.

The Undine spoke: 'What you have seen you may not have fully understood, but now you have an awareness that few humans are blessed with. As you tread your life-paths you will be able to relate this to others in a way that they can clearly understand. Now I shall leave you, farewell!'

'Farewell, and thanks!' they replied.

The haziness closed round them again for a few moments and then everything was normal. Two or three people walked past them. 'Lovely place, isn't it?' said one couple as they passed. 'Yes,' they replied, '*very* lovely and wonderful!' The couple looked quite surprised at their earnestness and quickly moved on.

They slowly walked back to where the children and adults were now gathered on the lawns in front of the terrace.

'That was something,' mused Shirley, 'I feel I understand much more about plants than I did before.'

'I think all of us will see them in a different light in future,' added Stephen, and the others nodded in agreement.

Their subdued approach was noticed by Fred and Peter, who came to meet them.

'Was it an "experience"?' asked their teacher.

'Yes!' they replied and told him briefly what had happened.

'Do you think between the seven of you, you could write a description of it and perhaps make a drawing or two?' he asked.

'I think we could,' said Fenella.

'Right, I'll tell you why. As you know, we return to school tomorrow, May the fifth, and break up for half-term on Ascension Day, May the fourteenth. Seven days of school. I thought of allowing the class to divide into three or four groups and each of them takes something connected with the work we have done so far this year and prepares a report and a short talk on it. What do you think? Yours could be connected with the environment.'

'What a super idea!' said Chris, and the others agreed.

They rejoined their group and spent another half hour or so playing with the younger children. Then a bell summoned them back to the terrace for afternoon tea. All discovered they had just the right amount of space for a Devonshire Cream Tea supplemented by ice cream produced from the Jersey herd on the estate. Then it was a series of hugs, kisses and handshakes as everybody said 'goodbye'. The general opinion was that they should do this again in the not too distant future. Now each and all went their own way. Peter with Fred, Ingrid and Michelle with Roger's family and so on, the children saying to each other, 'See you tomorrow at school!' It had been a highly successful day all round.

༺༻

Note: At school the following day Mr Atkinson introduced the project scheme that was to occupy them for the remainder of that week and the days of the following one before half-term. The class divided up into three groups, each undertaking some aspect of the work they had done in the course of the year. As suggested, the octet — they could hardly leave Shirley out, could they! — undertook 'Water in our Environment'. The other groups did their projects on 'Historic Tadbridge' and 'Local Wildlife.' The results were a highly successful day of presentations which, as the Principal, who attended, remarked, was 'A credit to all concerned.'

༺༻

For the original quintet, the last days before half-term were hectic, as preparations were under way for their coastal holiday with Reg. This included one *very* important change. They would be a sextet, for Shirley was joining them. Somehow they felt they could not leave her out, as her sisters were going to stay with an aunt for that week. So Jane had — somewhat forcefully — put the situation to her grandfather.

'We just can't leave her on her own!' she explained.

Luckily, Reg had been impressed by the child's knowledge of plants, and, provided her parents agreed, was very willing to include her.

'It's a good thing the cottage has an expanding bed system,' he told Jane, 'so we can easily accommodate her.'

Roger and Cherry raised no objections, so much to their delight, and Shirley's, it was arranged for her to come. Packing and preparation started over the weekend and by Wednesday evening all was ready. Reg would pick them up from school at midday Thursday, drive them out to Bidford Manor to load up and they would leave after lunch.

CHAPTER TWENTY

School on Thursday morning ended with a brief assembly in the hall on the theme of Ascension in the widest possible sense. Then they were dismissed. Reg met them at the pickup spot driving a very smart royal blue four-wheel drive.

'My car is getting on,' he told them, 'OK for puttering round the district but not so good on longer trips and it would be rather cramped for six of you, plus myself and all our gear. So I've borrowed this from a business acquaintance of mine. He's away for the coming week and delighted that it will really be put to the test. He reckons any vehicle that can survive *six* nine-year-olds for a week, can stand up to any amount of punishment.'

Other arrangements had also been made. As Charmouth, where they were going, was only some twenty-five miles from Tadbridge, they would be having day visits from: the Game family, and the Bennett family with Peter and Fred, who would bring Chris and Fenella with him. There was one other event of great importance. The day of their return, Saturday, May the twenty-third, happened to be Stephen and Jane's tenth birthday. They knew from the gatherings and whispering the grown-ups had *something* under preparation, but what? Well, they would have to wait and see!

Reg drove rapidly to Bidford Manor, and Doreen had lunch ready for the hungry six. Binky and Cleo both sensed something was in the air and insisted on being 'in' on and into everything. 'When we come down to see you, we'll bring Binky,' said Derek. Doreen glared at him.

'You never said you were coming down, when?' asked Sarah. Derek went rather red and muttered, 'Oh, ah, er, um, one day, you know,' and with that they had to be content.

'Imagine if Binky found a dinosaur bone,' said Michelle, and they all laughed at the though of the little fellow trying to chew such a thing.

As soon as lunch was over the task of stowing all their gear began. Though it was all ready, it still took some time to fit everything in and yet leave space for the usual extra items, to say nothing of the passengers. By just after two they were ready. The seating plan was sorted out and there were frantic waving and shouts of 'goodbye!' And they were off!

The good weather that blessed the fete had continued through the following weeks, and the forecast for the coming week was more of the same. It wasn't hot; temperatures were normal or slightly below normal for the time of year, but a slow-moving ridge of high pressure meant there would be no dramatic change.

'Couldn't be better,' Reg told them as they drove along the southbound road. The first stop — after all there was no tearing hurry — was in Chard, where they partook of *early* afternoon tea, or rather ice cream. Then on to Axminster where, much to their delight, there was the Thursday livestock market being held by St Mary's Church. They wandered amongst the pens and stalls looking at sheep, lambs, cows and calves.

The lambs were particularly attractive, and if certain young ladies had had their way, a lamb or two would have joined them on holiday. However, as Reg pointed out, looking after them, bottle feeding them regularly and clearing up their mess and such, would severely curtail their movements during the week. So reluctantly they said goodbye to them.

There was a quick peek in the museum, which showed the history of the carpet making industry in the town and then came *late* afternoon tea: scones, jam, cream and tea. When they were on the way again Jane suddenly said:

'Gramps, *who* is doing the cooking?'

He looked at her, very straight faced, saying, 'Who do you think?'

'Er, you don't mean *us* do you?'

'Well, I was considering that... ...(a long pause) but then I decided... ...(yet another pause) to have someone local come in to cook our evening meal (sighs of relief). We shall get our own breakfast; the good lady I've employed will arrive at nine, generally clean up and make a packed lunch for us; or if we are going to be back at lunchtime, leave it all ready. She'll return in the afternoon to prepare the main meal and all we shall have to do is warm it and wash up. Agreed?' This sounded reasonable enough, so they agreed.

The route was now through increasingly hilly country and eventually they reached the coast, going through Charmouth and up the steep road that led to the cliff tops, which then became a narrow lane ending in an unmade track.

Here, nestling amongst the woods, stood the cottage. Behind it lay a National Trust reserve.

As they drew up, the door opened and a cheery young woman came down the steps to greet them. She spoke with a broad Dorsetshire accent, which was markedly different from the Somersetshire one. The next half-hour was occupied with unpacking the vehicle and being shown their rooms. There were four bedrooms, three with bunk beds and one obviously for grown-ups.

'I furnished it that way,' Reg told them. There was a modern bathroom and kitchen built on the back, with a medium sized dining area off and the large sitting room entered directly by the front door. All very simple and basic, but what more did one need? The children thought it perfect.

Mrs Milne, or Brenda, as she preferred to be called, had made a most excellent shepherd's pie for supper, followed by apple pie and cream. When finished, as it was their first evening, she insisted on washing up for — as she said, 'You must be tired after your long journey.'

They assured her they weren't, and fully intended to do their share, but she shooed them out.

'Let's go for an evening stroll,' suggested Reg, 'and we can talk over what we intend to do tomorrow.'

They walked back along the track and then followed a footpath that led them on to the Southwest Coast Path just above a spot called Cain's Folly. From here they had a good view of the coastline. To the west they could see Lyme Regis, and to the east the Golden Cap, some six hundred and twenty feet high, the highest cliffs on the Channel Coast.

The sun was already setting to the west, casting its reddish tinge over the cliffs and sea. Sea gulls circled, calling and crying overhead. A sense of timelessness settled on them. From time immemorial the sun had set over this scene. For a while they stood silent watching the lengthening shadows and absorbing the peaceful atmosphere.

There was a bench a little further along, upon which they sat.

After a few moments Reg said, 'I think for starters we should visit Lyme Regis tomorrow to have a good look round to find out what's worth seeing. As you know, there are famous fossil bearing cliffs here and in certain places one is allowed to go fossil hunting. I thought that might be a good activity for early Saturday morning. Then after lunch we could visit one of the old churches or historical sites along this part of the coast. On Sunday, when the Game family arrives, we could have lunch on the beach at Charmouth, and work our way along towards the Golden Cap, where it will be less crowded. If it's warm enough we could swim, or at least paddle!'

These ideas were enthusiastically received, and having sat there until the first stars and the moon appeared, they made their way back to the cottage. Brenda had left, leaving a note saying she would be in at nine and if there was anything special they wanted, please to let her know. The air was much cooler now and they gathered in the kitchen, which, with its Aga stove, was pleasantly warm. Cocoa was made and drunk, then it was off to bed: Shirley and Michelle in one room, Jane and Sarah in another and the boys in the third. 'I shan't be long after you,' said Reg, 'It's been a busy day for all of us.' He was right, and although sleeping in a new place in strange beds, it wasn't long before all that could be heard were gentle snores.

They were up early, including Reg, next morning. It was a brilliantly sunny start and staying in bed or indoors was out of the question. Originally Reg had thought of driving into Lyme Regis, but at breakfast they decided to walk, taking the footpath down to Charmouth, crossing the River Char by the footbridge and then following the path along the cliffs into town, a walk of about two miles. They ate a good breakfast, and as lunch would be had in town, there was no need to take more than an empty backpack for any purchases. Just before eight they left the cottage and ambled down the track. Why hurry? They had *all* day and the surroundings were too full of interest to be rushed by.

Reg had a fund of information about the area and could answer most of their questions. 'I think he must have swallowed a guidebook!' Jane confided to Shirley.

There was a steep descent to the river crossing and an equally steep ascent on the other side. But they made it without any difficulty, Reg too, which showed, as Stephen explained to Michelle, 'How we keep him in good health.'

They reached town centre by nine o'clock and they made their way down to the harbour and walked out along the Cobb, a thirteenth century breakwater, from which there was a wonderful view of the Golden Cap and its surroundings. Then went to the museum, which told something of the history of the place and also housed a fine local fossil collection. They discovered that in the Middle Ages Lyme had been a salt producing town; but later, when East Anglia began to take over the trade, it became a fishing port. The Duke of Monmouth had landed there in 1685 in his abortive attempt to wrest the throne from James II. The town's fortunes declined as fish stocks dwindled, but in 1760 it became a popular place for sea bathing, which was supposed to cure many ailments. This attracted royalty, thus Regis was added to its name and famous people began to 'take the cure', Henry Fielding and Jane Austin, for example.

Afterwards they went to look at the house where she was believed to have stayed in 1818 while writing *Persuasion*.

By now the town was filling up with tourists and they decided to have lunch before the restaurants became too crowded. Afterwards they spent half an hour on the seafront watching some of the hilariously dressed holidaymakers parade up and down. Then at two o'clock they made their way to 'Dinosaurland', which was housed in an old eighteenth century chapel. Here were more fossil finds, reconstructions and dioramas. Also it included a fine Plesiosaur skeleton and biographical information about Mary Anning, who found the first complete skeleton in 1811, and spent eight years excavating it.

'What patience,' exclaimed Sarah. 'I bet lots of people told her she was wasting her time and why didn't she do something useful!'

'People used to think that fossils were either stones fallen from the sky or the remains of creatures who drowned in the Flood.' Reg told them. 'It was pioneers like her who began to make scientists take them more seriously and try to find out *how* they came to be buried.'

'It would have been interesting to talk with her,' said

Stephen,' I bet she could tell lots of exciting stories about her finds.'

'She had the reputation in later life of being a rather difficult and cantankerous person,' said Reg. 'Though now they think it was because she was unwell, and often in pain, but refused to let it stop her hunting for more fossils.'

The display was so fascinating that they wandered round it for at least another hour. Reg had a chat with the lady at the information desk and was given a leaflet on 'Local fossil hunting, where and what to look for'.

'This will be useful,' he told them, 'There's been considerable erosion on the cliffs here and the last thing needed is hoards of fossil hunters hacking and digging away at their fragile foundations. Not only for their own safety, but further cliff falls could destroy valuable fossils and properties on the cliffs.'

Upon leaving the place they went back into the town centre and bought postcards to send to Aunt Daisy and some for their friends. Next they found a tea shop, for the usual reasons. Then it was back to the cottage. Naturally the return journey took some time, as they were somewhat weary after tramping round streets most of the day. By six thirty they were indoors and waiting for the meal that Brenda had prepared to warm up. Afterwards they wrote cards and chatted about the plans for tomorrow. Reg decreed an early night if they wanted to go on a dawn fossil hunt the next morning. So two backpacks were prepared: one for sandwiches, fruit and drink, and one with geological hammers (which Reg thoughtfully supplied) brushes and plenty of paper towels to wrap their finds in. By nine the cottage was in darkness.

They had aimed to wake as soon after sunrise as possible, which was around five o'clock *and* they managed it! By six they were on their way down the track to Charmouth, but instead of going up the cliff path, having crossed the river, they made their way along the beach towards Black Ven and the Spittles. The sun had not yet dispersed the sea mist and they were glad of pullovers and jeans. When they reached the area where fossil hunting was permitted, Reg found a sheltered spot and made himself comfortable.

'I'll stay here while you go fossil fossicking,' he said. 'Remember, before you start hammering or removing material, make sure there's nothing loose or overhanging above you. I forgot to bring my bulldozer with me today!'

They left him and made their way further along the beach then moved up to the cliff face. The rock was loose and crumbly and among the fragments on the beach, fossil pieces could be found, but most were badly damaged or eroded by the action of the sea. Their hope was to find some good specimens in situ which they could prise loose and take home to clean.

Shirley spotted the first hopeful find, an ammonite shell partially exposed about three feet up from beach level. This was soon wrapped and placed in the pack. Now their eyes grew accustomed to what to look for and it was not long before they had quite a collection. Where they had been working a small gully ran back into the cliff face and looked hopeful, as the sides were steep and well exposed. They started cautiously up it.

Then, as so often happens, a sea mist rolled in and they found themselves unable to see more than a few feet on front of them.

'We'd better stay here until this lifts,' said Stephen, 'It shouldn't take long.'

They found a comfortable spot between two rocks, and to pass the time, examined some of their finds. Suddenly Sam paused and said, 'Hush a moment, what's that?' They listened; faintly, from further up the gully came a distinct 'tap, tap'.

'It must be a fossil hunter up there,' said Jane.

'But when we looked up the gully before starting to explore it there was nobody to be seen,' said Michelle.

'Surely they didn't climb down from the top,' exclaimed Sarah, 'that would be far too dangerous.'

The noise of tapping continued. 'Well, let's go and see,' suggested Stephen. 'If it's a regular hunter he or she may be able to give us some tips.'

They put their finds back in the bag and made their way cautiously forwards. The mist was still thick but every now and again it would thin, then close up again. As it cleared for a moment, some twenty feet ahead they could make out a figure crouched over a large flat rock. Sam cleared his throat loudly, in what he hoped was a polite manner.

The tapping ceased abruptly. 'Who's there?' a woman's voice called out sharply.

'We're looking for fossils,' called Sam. 'May we come and talk to you?'

'I suppose so,' was the grudging reply.

They made their way through the mist and were soon standing beside the rock. To their amazement, on its surface the top of a Plesiosaur skull and backbone were visible, obviously still being carefully chiselled out. She stood up, hammer and chisel in hand. Seeing their spellbound faces she smiled wryly.

'I don't suppose you've seen anything like that afore!' she said in a strong Dorsetshire accent.

'Only in the museum,' said Jane, 'and that was only a replica.'

'Museum, replica? What are you talking about, child? This is unique, the only one; six years I've worked to remove it from its prison of stone. "You're wasting your time" they say, "Who wants a lot of old bones? Throw them into the sea." I have to cover this up every time I leave for fear some ignoramus will come and smash it. It was bad enough getting help to shift this rock from the beach to a spot where the winter storms wouldn't destroy it! So you keep your mouths shut. Not a word to anyone!' She said this in a half threatening, half wheedling tone.

'We won't tell anybody if you don't want us to,' Michelle reassured her.

'You are doing scientific work of great importance,' added Sarah.

The woman looked hard at them. 'You be a strange lot, surely not local?' she remarked.

'No, we come from Tadbridge,' explained Stephen.

'Tadbridge, where's that?'

'About twenty five miles north from here.'

'Never heard of it. Never been further than Bridport,' she said.

Suddenly her face crumpled in pain, she gasped and doubled up as if struck in the stomach. After a moment she took a deep breath and relaxed.

'Are you all right?' asked Michelle anxiously.

'It's nothing child, nothing that any barber-surgeon can do anything for. But I have this.' She took a small dark blue bottle from her pocket and swallowed a small quantity of the contents. 'Laudanum, it kills the pain.'

The mist was clearing and they could see her better. Her dress was long, reaching to below her ankles. She had an old-fashioned straw bonnet on her head. These contrasted strongly with a pair of wooden clogs on her feet. By the rock was a heavy canvas bag into which she would put her finds. Curled up beside it was a small black and white dog. It looked at them briefly, wagged its feathery tail and went back to sleep.

Seeing their bag she asked, 'What have you found?' They showed her, 'Not bad, not bad, where did you find them?' They explained. 'If you want some really fine specimens go back to that spot but then go some ten yards towards Lyme. About four feet up there's a fine band of fossils. Good luck!'

The mist swirled down again and they heard the tap of

the hammer recommence.

'What's your name, please?' Jane called out.

A strangely bodiless voice answered from the mist. 'My name, child? Mary Anning of course, who else?'

For a moment the children stood silent, then called back 'Thank you!' There was no reply and the mist rolled away. Where they had seen her there was no large flat rock, but a mass of smaller pieces, which may have been the remains of it.

'Let's go and look where she suggested before we return to Gramps,' said Jane.

Sure enough the spot proved to be a treasure trove of fossils, easy to remove and in tip-top condition. The backpack was soon not only full, but almost too heavy to lift.

Reg was busy reading a book when they returned. He put it down and opened the pack with the food. 'Fossil hunting is a hungry job, I believe?' he said. They agreed it was. Once the food had been eaten that bag could be used to take some of the fossils. After a brief rest they started back, arriving at the cottage in time for lunch. 'This afternoon we'll take the car,' said Reg. There were no objections.

After lunch they piled into the sturdy vehicle and drove along the unmade track until it conveniently became a proper country lane that led to the main road. They swung off through the nearby village then followed another lane that climbed steeply to another, smaller one. Its church lay just off the high street and overlooked the river Char in the valley below. It was a small, very old Norman style building and is unique for it has one of the only shrines left in England that still holds the relics of a saint. The sides round the top were pierced with holes big enough to put one's arm in and round the base were another series which could take a foot and even the lower part of a leg.

'Whatever for?' asked Shirley. 'Many believed that the relics of a saint possessed miraculous healing powers,' said

Reg. 'If you could touch them or even place the afflicted part of your body near them you could be cured, provided your belief in miracles and faith in God was firm. That's what those holes are for, to thrust arms and legs in. People with damaged bones or sores that did not heal would light a candle to the saint, pray at the shrine, then place the damaged or diseased limb into one of those holes. The priest would tell them when to remove it.'

'But that would *never* cure anything!' protested Sam.

'If it didn't, then it was because your faith was not strong enough,' said Reg.

'That's a good let out for the priest,' observed Stephen.

'True, but in spite of that, there are persistent stories of cures. Also, this shrine was famous for over four hundred years. If it had produced no cures, or was shown to be a fake, people would not have come here. Our ancestors may appear simple-minded to us, but they were shrewd and not likely to be taken in that easily!'

The atmosphere was restful and they explored the building thoroughly before going for a stroll round the village, and by chance found the inevitable tea room. On the way back they stopped off in the first village, which has a famous biscuit bakery and bought tins for their parents and two special ones for Reg and Uncle Fred.

Then back to the cottage. Once again the Good Fairy Brenda had performed her task well. The evening was clear, so once more they watched the sun set before going to bed.

'We won't have to hurry up tomorrow,' said Reg, 'I don't think the Games will be here before ten at the earliest.'

'You never know,' replied Sarah. 'Harry's a farmer and used to getting up early, as is Bess, and I bet Jill and Brian will be so excited they'll be up early!'

'Right,' said Reg, 'breakfast at eight thirty, latest. But now, bed.'

CHAPTER TWENTY-ONE

Though they did not actually oversleep next morning, everyone was up later and a degree of sleepiness seemed to prevail. For example, at breakfast:

'Sam, pass the milk, please,' pause.

'Sam, pass the milk, please,' said louder and more urgently.

Longer pause, 'SAM, WAKE UP AND PASS THE MILK, PLEASE!'

'Sorry, Sarah, did you ask for something?'

Luckily, by the end of the meal normal day consciousness was attained by everyone. As it was Whit Sunday, after breakfast they gathered in the front room and Reg read chapter two, verses one to twelve, from the Acts of the Apostles and all sang a Whitsuntide Carol, 'Song of the Spirit', which they had practised secretly as a surprise and Whitsun gift for Reg. He was duly impressed, and touched when they also presented him with the tin of biscuits.

Now all hands were assembled in the kitchen to prepare a picnic lunch to take to the beach. They had just packed it into the backpacks when there was the sound of a van coming up the track. Nine thirty and here they were! There was a mad scramble to be outside to greet them. Reg was already directing Harry into the parking space beside his vehicle. As soon as it came to a stop a door opened and out shot Brian and Jill, charging at full speed for Jane and Sam.

'We've arrived!' they shouted, gleefully sending both of them staggering back when contact was made. Bess got out bearing a large basket.

'They're so excited,' she said, 'I thought they would explode before we arrived.'

Harry's comment, on looking round was: 'What a glorious place.'

Naturally the little ones had to be shown round the cottage first. This gave the adults a chance to relax and have the inevitable cup of tea before being called upon to prepare for the walk to the beach. The children had some of Bess's homemade lemonade and then, having collected towels, a rug and their backpacks, were off down the path to Charmouth.

Instead of crossing the bridge they took the path leading to the beach, starting to walk towards the Golden Cap. The weather was performing as forecast and although there was a fresh breeze blowing off the sea the sun was warming things up nicely. They went a short distance back to where Cain's Folly began and found a suitable spot to picnic and ideal sand for sand castles. Jill and Brian had brought buckets and spades and the others had discovered Reg had a collection in the cottage. Soon construction was in full swing and a mighty fortress began to arise, complete with an impressive moat and drawbridge. The engineering detachment, Stephen, Sam, Jill, Michelle, Jane and Sarah dug canals from the water's edge to fill the moat. Brian had taken occupation of the castle even before it was finished; squatting in the middle he directed the building team.

'Big, big tower here! Everso big wall this side! Want a door there!' and so on.

By lunchtime it was complete, decorated with pebbles and shells from the beach and Harry took a photo of them kneeling round it with 'Lord Brian' proudly seated in the middle with a bucket on his head and a spade, held like a sword, in his hand. Now it was time for lunch, and the builders were sure ready for it! Afterwards the adults settled down for a rest, as did Brian, who suddenly became very sleepy.

The older children were far from sleepy and decided to walk further along the beach to examine Cain's Folly. There was a purpose in this. In the booklet Reg had picked up from Dinosaurland it mentioned that:

'Fossils may sometimes be found along the cliff base from Cain's Folly to the Golden Cap.'

So they decided it would be good to explore there — taking Jill — so she could find some fossils of her own — with their help. They had brought along her bucket and spade, just in case. There were very few people about, in spite of the good weather. Most folk preferred to stay on the beach nearer Charmouth, not venturing to such remote spots. Having gone some two hundred yards or so they moved up from the water's edge to the cliff base and began to search along it. 'Look for pretty stones,' they told Jill. They walked slowly, eyes searching amongst the cliff debris.

Something made Sam look up. He wasn't quite sure of what he saw, but it appeared to him that a few yards ahead a vaguely familiar figure with a little dog at its heels, stood pointing to a particular place at the cliff base.

Jill's exclamation of, 'Sam, is this anything?' made him turn his head for the moment and when he looked back, the figure had gone. Had Mary Anning been helping them?

'Let's try there,' he said, and taking Jill by the hand went to the spot. The others followed. They had hardly been searching for a few minutes when Jill let out a gasp of delight, and picked up a small ammonite that had obviously just fallen out of the cliff. Then Jane found one, for Brian, and Shirley managed to dislodge two that were projecting from the cliff. A moment later Jill picked up a bivalve shell and another good ammonite.

They were just about to return when Stephen said, 'Look at that!' There, still partially covered by soil and loose rock fragments was a large ammonite about eighteen inches across. Keeping an eye on the cliff above, they carefully dug it out with their hands, moving it down the beach to examine it. 'Wow. What a beauty!' said Michelle, as they admired their find. Now came the problem of carrying it back to the grown-ups. For it was no lightweight and not big enough for two to carry easily without getting their feet tangled up.

Luckily, Harry had decided to stroll along to see how they were getting on, and with his help it was soon being admired by Bess, Brian and Reg. 'I'm sure Mary Anning pointed out a good place for us,' Sam told the others later, and they agreed.

The original intention had been to go into Charmouth on the way back to have a quick look round and possibly to track down that item known as ice cream.

The fossil presented a problem until Reg suggested they hid it in the bushes at the foot of the cliff path by the bridge. This done, they went into the town, which had some pleasant Georgian Houses and provided the other item as well! Then it was back to the cottage: Harry and Reg taking turns with the fossil, Jill on Sam's back, Brian on Jane's, Bess with the lunch basket, and the other children taking turns with the backpacks. They were glad when they reached 'home' and could sit in the front room drinking tea and eating biscuits from Reg's tin.

Shortly after five as the Games prepared to leave, Jill pulled Sam aside and whispered, 'Edwin and I are going to explore the passage. So when you come home I'll be able to tell you all about it.'

This rather alarmed him. After all it was fine when the four of them had done it, but a five-year-old and a house guardian didn't seem quite the best of combinations.

'You should tell your mummy and daddy what you are going to do,' he told her.

'But I want it to be a surprise!' she said and her bottom lip began to quiver. Then Sam had an idea. 'Wait a minute,' he said and ran inside, returning with an envelope.

'There, Jill, I've written something for your mummy and daddy. When you go exploring with Edwin leave this on your bed, then if you are not back when you should be, they will find it and know where you are. Promise me you will do that?'

Jill looked offended. 'Of course I will, if you ask me to!' she replied. Taking the envelope she put it in her pocket and giving him a hug, clambered into the van.

'That was a very pleasant and successful day,' remarked Reg over supper. 'Our next guests are due on Tuesday, the Bennetts and Peter. Then Fred with Chris and Fenella on Thursday.'

'What about Mum, Dad and Binky?' asked Sarah.

'I'm not sure; Derek rather gave the game away. You see he's got some publisher's meeting later on somewhen this week and may have to go to London at short notice. Let's hope that turns out to be early in the week. Anyway, your mum will phone either tonight or tomorrow, as soon as she has definite news.'

'What shall we do tomorrow?' asked Stephen.

'Well, as the weather seems to be holding I thought we could walk along the cliffs to the Golden Cap, and then visit a couple of places nearby; from one we can catch a bus back to 'our' village, then walk home down the track. How does that sound?' It sounded fine. They had another evening walk along the cliff and then retired for the night.

Somewhat to their surprise the morning dawned cool and cloudy. The forecasters had either forecast the wrong day, month or year for the eighteenth. However, it did not look like rain so the expedition was still on. The cliff top walk along the Southwest Coast Path proved eventful even if view was hazy. From the top of the Golden Cap they could see as far as Start Point in Devon to the west, Portland Bill to the east and inland to the rugged hills of Dartmoor. It was spectacular and Reg was trying to take a panoramic photo of it with his camera.

'I'm always hopeful I'll get a good result, but am usually disappointed when it's printed,' he remarked. 'But I keep on trying. Once when I was about seventeen I was up in the Lake District at Ambleside and took a picture of an old stone bridge with my mother's Brownie box camera. According to the experts it should not have come out, but it did. What's more, I entered it in a local photo competition and it received a commendation! I've taken thousands of photos since with all kinds of expensive cameras and none of them have turned out half so good.'

After resting for a while and snacking they went on, and down from the six hundred and twenty six feet to the 'town' at sea level, which boasted a public house, telephone and convenience, plus a camping site and caravan park. Though called a town, it hardly qualified for one.

They did not stay long, but made their way up the road to their next objective, a walk of just under a mile. Though more of a village and possessing a post office and church—as well as a public house, there was not much else. To find a spot for lunch they followed the road going north to its local manor house and sat in a field. A hazy sun had broken through the clouds and warmed things up. They returned to the village to catch the bus back and had a gentle walk down the track to the cottage.

It had not been an exciting day, but a very enjoyable one and they felt ready for the arrival of the Bennetts tomorrow. Reg suggested it might be a good idea, if the weather was uncertain, to go into Lyme Regis, as there was a good pool on the western side of the harbour and the aquarium that could be visited if the weather was very uncooperative. They could also walk a section of the Coastal Path if they wished.

'Final decision tomorrow when we see how the weather turns out and have consulted our guests,' he said.

'Maybe we should have a more local plan in case it turns out really nice?' suggested Shirley.

'Yes, I suppose we could go to the beach again like we did on Sunday,' he replied.

The remainder of the evening was spent with their fossils spread out on the kitchen table for closer examination and cleaning, though they soon realised they needed more advice and better instruments to do the job properly without damaging the specimens. Still, it was exciting to be handling items one had found oneself that were probably millions of years old.

'I wonder what it looked like round here all those years ago?' said Jane.

'The geologists and paleontologists think they have a pretty good idea,' replied Reg.

'The land was much lower, flatter and covered with a shallow sea, swarming with marine life. It was much warmer, probably semitropical.'

'I wish it was semitropical now, then we could swim!' sighed Michelle.

'I don't think you would have enjoyed swimming in those waters. There were large poisonous jellyfishes, the ancestors of sharks and many other rather unpleasant creatures, plus a few harmless ones. Whilst overhead the giant pterosaurs swooped down to seize fish from the sea. Considering some had a twenty foot wingspan they would have probably snatched you up, too, as you floated there. Luckily all this took place in the Cretaceous Period about seventy-nine million years ago. Humans weren't around then, at least not in their present form.'

'Still, it would have been fascinating to see it,' Michelle persisted.

'Only in dreams, or on TV, I fear,' said Reg, adding, 'You'd better pack up now. Let's have one last turn on the cliff before closing down.'

Next morning the weather was not sure what it was going to do. The sun would appear, then disappear behind ominous clouds and it looked certain to rain; suddenly the clouds would vanish and the sun would pop out again. They regarded this with exasperation.

'We'll just have to wait until the Bennetts arrive and see what they think,' sighed Reg.

'Do we prepare sandwiches?' queried Sarah, who was in charge of lunch preparations that day. This was an arrangement they had come to on Friday, as it meant less reliance on Brenda.

'Might as well,' said Stephen, 'we've got to eat anyway.'

'Fine, come on then, I appoint you my assistant,' she replied. He pulled a face but followed her meekly into the kitchen. The Bennetts arrived around ten. The weather still showed no sign of settling down to sun or showers.

'What do you think, Will?' asked Reg. 'Town or beach?'

'I reckon the beach,' he replied. 'Our two don't go to town often. They tend to get over-excited and end up fractious or being sick in the car! I'm sure when they are a little older things will be different. But all the way down they've been talking of nothing but beach, beach, and more beach! They would be very disappointed if they can't go. We came well prepared for any weather, so they can be warmly dressed and at least may paddle and use their buckets and spades.'

He turned to the older children. 'Do you mind?' he asked.

'Of course not!' they replied. 'We enjoy being down there anyway.' That settled it; and after making sure they were warmly dressed, the whole party set off down the path to the beach: Judy hanging onto Stephen talking nineteen to the dozen and Nicky trotting along beside Shirley, to whom he seemed to have taken a fancy. The sun had decided to generally be present, but every now and then would hide behind a large cloud. The wind blew off the sea and was — like the other day — rather chilly. But as soon as the little ones saw the water they let out a whoop of joy, and if Joyce hadn't caught them, would have charged straight in it without removing shoes and socks!

On Reg's advice they settled in the same spot as Sunday, which was semi-protected from the wind and nicely in the sun — when it shone. Uncle Peter was very quiet but seemed to enjoy being with them and watching the children. After getting ready for paddling and sand castle building they went to work with zest. Will helped them, for with his knowledge of canals, he showed how to channel the water into the moat. Peter joined in too, giving some practical advice. Young Nicky took a more active role than Brian had done. As the structure neared completion, Judy announced that she was going to be its queen and positioned herself regally in it. Nicky was inclined to object but was content when she announced he was her 'chiefest knight'. She kept them all very busy, as this queen had very definite ideas about decoration, rejecting pebbles which she considered were the wrong colour or shape to enhance the royal structure! They were surprised to find out how quickly time had gone when called to lunch.

Afterwards, as the breeze had dropped a little, they paddled and poked about in some of the rock pools. Then Sam suggested they try to find some fossils in the same spot where they'd had such luck before. Judy and Nicky soon understood what they were looking for, although Judy kept up a barrage of questions:

'If it's a seashell, how can it be stone? Who made it stone, had it been naughty? If it's lived in the sea, why is it in the cliff, how did it get there? Seashells can't walk. How could the sea gulls eat it if it's stone?' and suchlike!

However, when — by luck — she was the first to find a

fossil bivalve, she was so entranced she eagerly looked for more. They did not find anything as spectacular as the large ammonite, but after a couple of hours had a reasonable number of specimens for the youngsters to take home. Then they ran back along the beach to show the grown-ups their spoils. Just as they arrived a cloud covered the sun and a few spots of rain began to fall. There was hurried packing up and a brisk trot up the path back to the cottage. The rain spat at them all the way and hardly had they got inside when the heavens opened and it poured down!

It was now fourish, so it's easy to guess what happened next. Afterwards the Bennetts left with many 'thank yous' and 'goodbyes'. They found Brenda had made a nice and welcoming supper; her sense of variety was very satisfying!

'Tomorrow I think we should aim for Bridport and Symonsbury,' said Reg.

As he spoke, the phone rang. 'Ah, your mother, I hope!' he said to Sam and Sarah.

He was back in a few minutes. 'Yes, it's worked out as expected. They'll be down on Friday and will bring your mum too, Michelle.' She was delighted at this news.

However, Sam and Sarah had mixed feelings; it depended very much on what kind of a mood Derek was in.

So Bridport would be the objective for tomorrow as Uncle Fred, Fenella and Chris would be with them on Thursday.

'I hope we have some really good warm weather soon!' said Jane. The others agreed with her.

CHAPTER TWENTY-TWO

On Wednesday the weather was still unsettled, with more than a hint of rain in the air, so it was probably just as well they had chosen to go to Bridport, some five miles along the road to Dorchester. Though it had 'port' in its name, the town was situated a good mile back from the coast, West Bay being the actual harbour. However, the river Brit, which flows through the town, could be navigated from the sea by fairly large vessels, though it was no longer used for commercial purposes. Yachts and motor cruisers were moored along the quayside instead. The old town was quite interesting and had an excellent museum. Here they discovered that in past times, Bridport had, for many years, been the centre of the hemp making trade. Here, most of the rope that kept the British men-o'-war on the high seas had been produced until hemp began to be grown and processed elsewhere; then the town had suffered an inevitable decline.

One rather ghoulish sideline for hemp was the so-called 'Bridport dagger,' or hangman's rope, which was almost exclusively produced there right into the nineteenth century.

A further wander round after lunch drew their attention to an outlying area on the Mangerton, a tributary of the Brit, which joined it just below the town. This was called 'St Andrew's Well' and they wondered whether it had any connection with the St Andrew of the Tadbridge Well. But as they also wanted to visit Symondsbury, had to leave this mystery unsolved for the moment.

That village lay just half a mile off the main road on their return journey. Its fame rested on its thatchers and the thatching industry. Between the wars and until fairly recently, the art of thatching had almost died out, but a band of devoted thatchers had kept the craft alive and now it was a thriving business once more. They were shown examples of different kinds and methods of thatching and watched some demonstrations of these skills.

'We could try that at home,' suggested Sam, 'I'm sure Harry could supply us with straw. We could make a thatched shelter by the pond.'

Sarah was not quite so sure. It looked easy when you saw an expert doing it. Still, it was a challenge and the twins enjoyed challenges. One could always discard them if they proved too awkward and try something else. Their last garden had been full of such enterprises, from flying foxes to suspension bridges that didn't; also various excavations for underground ice storage houses and other such oddities as Derek used to find out to his cost. On one occasion when mowing the lawn, the machine had literally disappeared at his feet when it plunged through into a masterfully constructed tiger trap complete with sharpened stakes, which played havoc with its blades and machinery. Anyhow, Sam spent the sum of £4.99 on a handbook entitled *Simple Thatching*, which, when Derek saw it, would certainly set his alarm bells ringing.

There was a tea room in the tiny village where they had a very satisfactory tea and then motored back to the cottage. The forecast for Thursday promised a change for the better and they spent the evening planning and replanning what they would do with Fred and their friends the next day. They were supposed to arrive *early*, which meant between eight and nine o'clock.

Sarah and Jane had a plan. Setting their alarm for five thirty they dressed quietly, and letting themselves out of the cottage, made their way to the cliff top viewpoint, as they had named their favourite spot. The sun had just risen and was throwing long shadows westwards. The birds were beginning their dawn chorus here and there; otherwise all was very still and calm. They sat silently on the bench and watched as the light slowly lost the dawn tinge and grew stronger. It was very peaceful, as no hum of traffic or other human sounds could be heard. They gazed out over the mirror-like sea surface, which was a glorious pale blue, as if it wished to be at one with the heavens. For a moment both closed their eyes; it was almost too much, such beauty, such peace.

A warm gust of air swept along the cliff top, causing them to open their eyes in surprise. The sea still stretched before them but looked different. The sun seemed much higher and the water now had a burnished bronze look about it. They looked towards Lyme Regis. It wasn't there! The land appeared flatter and incredibly green and there was the same view when they looked towards the Golden Cap. Suddenly, a great shadow passed above them. Looking up they saw an enormous bat-like shape glide silently over and out to sea. The whole scene shimmered and was gone. Once more they looked onto the usual landscape.

'Do you think we... ...?' said Jane.

'Yes, that's what it must have been like in those far off times,' replied Sarah.

'I wonder if we could show it to the others and Uncle Fred?'

'I don't know, but I've the feeling we've been given a preview. Maybe if we all thought about how it was, it would happen again. Lets ask them to try.'

They left the bench and returned to the cottage, meeting Reg, who was just coming out.

'You two are up early!' he remarked, 'Been enjoying the view in the peace of the morning?'

'Something like that,' replied Jane.

'Well it looks like being one of the best days we've had so far for sun and warmth. Let's hope it doesn't vanish before our guests arrive.'

Vague noises from inside told them the others were astir. They found Shirley and Stephen busy setting the breakfast table while Sam watched the toaster, which had a sneaky habit of jamming and sending forth clouds of black smoke and then adding insult to injury by ejecting two pieces of charred and blackened bread. Michelle was boiling eggs and hoping she'd set the timer correctly for well boiled. Reg returned and they sat down to eat and review plans.

'They should be here in half an hour or so,' he said. 'I think fossil hunting is our first priority. Then we can spend the rest of the day in a more relaxed manner, or walk to the Golden Cap—or whatsoever takes our fancy. Fred sees no reason to leave before seven, eight at the latest. So I've asked Brenda to prepare a meal for ten ravenous mouths tonight. She was delighted. It appears she enjoys cooking in quantity; it improves the quality. We nearly meet her standards, but not quite. Ten of us after a day on the beach should be a challenge to anybody's cooking!'

Having done the usual after breakfast chores, they gathered their equipment and backpacks for the fossil hunt. By just before eight all was ready and they were waiting outside for Fred and company to arrive, passing the time by playing catch.

The sound of an approaching car brought the game to a rapid conclusion, and as it pulled up alongside Reg's, the guests were here! Fenella and Chris tumbled out to meet the barrage of chatter, while Fred made a more dignified appearance, shaking hands with Reg, inquiring how he was surviving under the strain.

Jane caught these words and promptly interrupted. 'What strain? What do you mean? We've been looking after Gramps very well and he hasn't been any bother at all.'

The others nodded in agreement. No, he'd been very good — on the whole.

'Well I think he deserves a break!' was Fred's comment. 'So I've given him the morning off and shall take responsibility for you lot until lunchtime. We'll come back for it so we can review options for the afternoon. As it looks like being a warm morning, I suggest you put your bathers on under your work clothes so we can have a swim after our hunt. I'm sure we'll be hot and dusty by then.'

There was a concerted rush to go and change. Fred was lucky, he got the bathroom all to himself. Reg announced he was going to spend a peaceful morning with the book he'd brought to read, but to date, owing to other occurrences, hadn't passed the opening page of the first chapter. Picking up their gear, the children wished him luck, and setting Uncle Fred in their midst, so he couldn't escape, set off down the path to the beach.

They went down and across the River Char's footbridge and onto the beach towards the Black Ven. They had chosen this area because the Canary Ledges were visible at low tide — flat rocks with pools and crannies that they could explore.

'Do you think we shall meet Mary Anning again?' Shirley asked Jane.

'I don't think so,' she replied. 'After all, she gave us some good indications and I'm sure we'll find plenty of specimens.'

When they gathered at the foot of the cliff, Stephen explained what they should look for and what precautions to take to avoid too much loosening of the cliff face. Sarah then told them about the glimpse Jane and she had experienced that morning, adding,

'If we all think hard about what it was like, it's just

possible we might experience that crack in time again, like the one we had on the Pickham Hills.'

'It's worth a try,' said Fred. 'But I suggest we fossil hunt first. Once you are actually holding a shell thought to be a few million years old there is something latent in it which could bring about the right conditions.'

Today, as the weather was already so fine, there were a few people exercising dogs or jogging along the beach, but it certainly wasn't crowded and there was nobody walking near the cliffs. As they moved along, Sam stopped and pointed: 'Look.'

Under the shadow of a large fallen piece of sandstone a figure stood, small and slight, with a little dog by its side; as they gazed it beckoned—and then? One minute it was there, for they all saw it, and the next it was gone.

'Mary Anning *did* come!' exclaimed Michelle, 'Let's go and see what she wants us to find.'

When they reached the fallen rock there was a narrow gap between it and the cliff face. The bands of strata showed very clearly. 'Like a jam sponge layer cake' as Chris put it. There were the usual heaps of loose rubble at the base and they picked these over first, as they would give a good indication if the rock face would yield anything. After a few minutes, Fenella, down on hands and knees, let out a loud whoop and jumped to her feet holding a reasonably undamaged bivalve shell. In a few minutes Chris and Shirley had found more. Then it was Fred's turn. Now they centred their attention on the actual rock face and discovered that the fossil bearing band was only about two feet above the ground. This meant working in crouching position, but the results were worth it, and after an hour and a half they had a reasonable collection which filled the backpacks and, as Fred put it, 'I'm glad you're carrying them and not me,' though he hastily offered to carry their towels and other items instead.

Even working in the shade had made them hot, and

dusty. So having consumed their snack and drink it was off with their clothes and into the cool waters. They were cool, too! For it was still early in the year, but after the initial shock they swam happily for some time and then scrambled over Canary Ledge, letting the sun dry them off while they examined the nooks, crannies and rock pools. Fred joined them, swimming and searching, but did not stay in the water as long as them. 'I might shrink,' he explained 'and you wouldn't want a midget for a teacher, would you?'

Gathering on the beach again they towelled themselves down and sat there enjoying the sun, gazing out towards the Golden Cap and beyond. A warm gust of air struck them, similar to the one Sarah and Jane had experienced earlier. Canary Ledge looked different, much flatter, while the sea stretched away under a sun that was far hotter than a few moments ago. There was no sign of the cliffs to their left, just a long, flat coastline covered with thick green vegetation. When they looked behind it was a similar picture.

Something broke the surface some way out to sea. They could not make out what it was, but obviously a very large creature. Then to the right, several long snake-like necks lifted above the surface for a few seconds, one carrying a wriggling fish in its jaws. Nearer inshore the waters parted again and a large fishlike creature, with enormous jaws like a crocodile's, and lined with exceedingly nasty looking teeth, leapt up, making a futile grab at a large flying reptile that was skimming the sea surface for fish. At the same time they became aware that several similar, and much larger, flying beasts were hovering overhead, possibly having spotted them as something for breakfast.

'Into the undergrowth,' snapped Fred. 'Now, run, never mind our stuff!' There was no hesitation and in a flash they were crouching under some strange bushy plants with great umbrella type leaves, which gave ample cover. The Pterosaurs, who were not blessed with overmuch brain, circled a few times over the spot where they had been, then flew off. It was cooler under the plants, so they settled down to watch the scene before them. A huge crab scuttled across the sand into the water. Another crustacean, looking like an oversized parody of a lobster, came out of it and was promptly seized by a flying reptile. A crocodile—hardly any different from a present-day one—except it was considerably larger, came ashore with an enormous octopus in its mouth and ate it in a leisurely way on the sand, then stretched out in the sun and sank into a digestive sleep.

They were greatly tempted to go out on to the beach to see what other wonders could be discovered, but Fred was definitely not in favour.

'We may be in a time warp, but the interest those Pterosaurs showed in us proves we are tangible to these creatures as a possible part of their diet. I would find it exceedingly hard to account for the lack of one or two of you upon our return, just as you would be if I were consumed. So we remain here!'

Hardly had he spoken when there came a loud snuffling noise from somewhere behind them, and the sound of something large and heavy moving through the undergrowth. Two small dinosaurs, running on long hind legs, scuttled under their bush, saw them and bolted—twittering.

'They're scared of something and I think it's coming this way,' whispered Fred.

Indeed, the ground was beginning to vibrate under the tread of the intruder. Fred lifted his head cautiously. 'There's an awful lot of bush waving to the right, and a large outcrop of rock to our left. Keep your heads down and follow me.'

He started off at a good pace towards the rocks. Behind them there was something that sounded like the cross between a sneeze and a roar and the thumping and crashing grew louder—and rapidly nearer! The rocks loomed up ahead—a craggy jumble with lots of cracks and crannies. Fred aimed for the largest one and herded the children inside.

'Get as far back as you can,' he ordered, then bent down and picked up a large nasty looking lump of rock. They didn't have long to wait. The thunder of the approaching beast was now directly in front of their hiding place. The entrance darkened as a huge head bent down to peer in and an enormous pair of twitching nostrils appeared. Fred hurled the rock with all his strength, striking squarely between them. There was a deafening howl of pain. Then the light streamed in as the creature blundered off, crashing through the undergrowth still complaining loudly about the treatment it had received.

'The point is, what do we do now?' Fred queried. 'Stay here, or venture out to be gobbled up by some other ghastly beast or —?'

At that moment the gust of warm air flowed through their hiding place and they found themselves back on the familiar beach. There was a universal sigh of relief all round. Gathering up their goods, they made their way back to the cottage to find Reg just putting the finishing touches to lunch.

'You look as if you've been chased by wild beasts,' he remarked. They told him briefly of their experiences.

'Now I know why it was better for me to stay here,' he remarked. 'Anyhow, come and have lunch, then we'll see what's next on the agenda.'

They were well and truly hungry, so having changed into clean clothes, rinsed and hung their costumes up to dry, everybody settled down to a hearty meal. Afterwards, seated outside enjoying the sun, they told Reg of their adventure in greater detail, Uncle Fred adding his usual wry remarks.

'Honestly, Reg, when I took on your grandchildren, then these two (indicating the Courts), to say nothing of already having two first class terrors in the shape of Chris and Fenella in the class, and then to allow myself to be inveigled into having a witch's granddaughter—to say nothing of the daughter of an engineering postmaster—I should have known that my life of peace and tranquillity was gone forever. Since last October I have been involved in more supernatural scrapes and murky mysteries than is good for schoolteachers. But,' he added, seeing the looks on the eight faces staring at him, 'I'm no doubt repaying for some terrible misdemeanour committed in my last life. So I'll just have to grin and bear you!'

He smiled at Sarah. 'It's all your fault, you little arm-twister,' and ruffled her hair. 'I feel better now I've got that off my chest.' Then he added, 'What shall we do for the remainder of the afternoon?' Reg suggested a stroll to the Golden Cap and a visit to an old church nearby. 'We can walk back over the hills and rejoin the track back to the cottage,' he explained.

And that's what they did, Fred warning them to look out for pterosaurs hovering over the Golden Cap. It was a pleasant walk, enlivened by both the grown-ups, who had a host of stories and useless information to impart to their young listeners. When the highest point was reached they admired the view, now sparklingly clear in the late afternoon sun, then made their way to the old church, had a look round and followed the path that led along hills, over the top and down to the track. They were greeted at the cottage by Brenda, whose eyes lit up with delight when she saw she had so many prospective mouths to feed.

'Supper will be ready in an hour,' she informed them. 'But in case you're a bit peckish after your walk, I've put out a wee snack on the picnic table and some drink.'

Her idea of a 'wee snack' can best be described as preliminary skirmish to put the digestive organs in shape for what would follow. It satisfied and built up anticipation for what was to come. The main meal was also eaten outside, and in spite of their offers to help Brenda would have none of it.

'You've had a busy, tiring day, and here am I as fresh as a daisy. Just you stay where you are!'

Who were they to argue with such a determined lady?

However, when Sam suggested they should buy her a present, the others agreed. Fred, Chris and Fenella insisted on making their contribution. 'You can tell us what you got her when we see you again,' they said. After the meal those who had to depart were reluctant to do so, or just too full to move.

'It's been a super day, thanks very much,' announced Chris.

'Yes, indeed,' added Fenella, 'in spite of the prehistoric you-know-what that nearly ate us!'

'I'm glad I don't know what it was,' said Fred as he climbed into the driver's seat. 'This has been a day I won't forget in a hurry.' The usual farewells were made, then the sextet made its way inside and bed suddenly became a very welcome thought.

Mary Anning

CHAPTER TWENTY-THREE

The following day was something of an anticlimax: Derek, Doreen and Binky, plus Michelle's mum. Not that Sam and Sarah didn't want theirs to come. It was just that—well, parents, you know. They do so often make a fuss! Their mothers would look them up and down and ask things like:

'Have you washed behind your ears?' and 'Did you clean your teeth properly this morning?'

Or worse still, 'Sarah, why aren't you wearing that nice pink top I packed? That white T shirt is grubby.'

'Sam, dear, I do wish you'd change your socks every day, otherwise they get so filthy.'

'Michelle, look at those nice new sandals. You've got tar *all* over them!'

All the sort of questions grown-ups like Reg never bothered with. Parents were all right—at home!

The day looked as if it might be fine, though not as warm as yesterday. The visitors were supposed to arrive around nine thirty and then plans for the day would be made. After breakfast they pottered round doing some initial packing of the stuff that could go back with the Courts, like the fossils and dirty clothes. Nine thirty came, and went. No sign of the car. Ten o'clock did the same and still no sign of them. This was annoying; a large chunk of their last full day had been taken up with doing nothing except hanging around.

At last, just after ten forty, they heard the car approaching and rushed to meet it. As soon as it stopped Binky shot out and raced to them, barking for joy and leaping all over the twins, licking them happily. Doreen got out looking rather irritated. The twins recognised the signs. A moment later Derek emerged, looking slightly bewildered.

'Sorry we are late, folks,' he began, but Doreen interrupted him. 'We—we? You! I, as your passenger, had no control over our time of arrival. But if you had listened to me and followed the directions I gave you from the map we would not have been so late!'

'Yes, dear, I know I took the wrong turning, but I thought…' While this was going on, Ingrid stood by with an embarrassed smile on her face.

Sarah decided enough was enough. 'Well, you are here, and that's what counts,' she said, giving them both a hug. 'Tea's ready,' sang out Reg, 'Come and get it.'

They went into the front room and after tea everybody was more relaxed and the day's course of action could be settled.

Reg came up with a surprise. 'How about a drive to Abbotsbury?' he suggested. 'There's St Peter's Abbey and the Abbey Barn, St Catherine's Chapel and the old Abbotsbury Swannery. Also, we shall be at the beginning of Chesil Beach, a place well worth seeing. It's only about thirteen miles and a fairly direct route, via Bridport. You'll be able to swim as well, so bathers on, you lot!'

The children disappeared and soon reappeared with ruffled hair, but ready. Binky thoroughly approved of all the hustle and bustle. Things had been far too quiet at home the last few days. Now he was in his element, rushing round after first one, then the other, barking cheerfully the whole time.

'There's an inn at Abbotsbury; I'll ring them up and see if they can do lunch for us,' said Reg, 'That will save time, as we shan't have to prepare sandwiches.'

The inn folk were most obliging and lunch for ten, plus dog, was arranged for one o'clock. Things were gathered up and cars started.

'Follow me,' Reg called to Derek.

'And a good job, too,' said Doreen, 'At least we shan't get lost!'

The road after Bridport ran along the top of the coastal ridge, which four miles along was just over over four hundred feet, rising to six hundred and ninety by the old hill fort known as Abbotsbury Castle. At this point there was a wonderful view looking down on Abbotsbury and the whole length of Chesil Beach to Portland Bill—a breathtaking sight on such a beautiful day. They then descended into the village and visited the ruins of the abbey. The only portion still intact was the huge tithe barn where the abbey used to store the produce that came to it as dues. The West and East Fleets, the lagoons separating the beach from the coast, were full of swans from the Abbey Swannery and they spent some time admiring these majestic birds. Then they climbed the hill upon which St Catherine's Chapel was built, giving a fine view of the Fleets and coast. The children were now eager for a swim, so they drove down to the beach a little way from the lagoons and had a dip before lunch. This time on the beach allowed Binky to work off some of his energy. He was highly suspicious of the sea and kept well away from it until his little master and mistress went in. Then he came to the water's edge barking furiously and running up and down. No amount of persuasion would entice him to enter and he was plainly relieved when they came out. The sun soon dried the swimmers and then it was off to the inn for lunch. It was an excellent, leisurely meal, taken outside in the pleasant courtyard.

Derek had noticed a sign as they drove in pointing to 'The Subtropical Gardens', which they visited afterwards. Shirley was in her element and her excitement and enthusiasm was so infectious they stayed much longer than intended. Their guide was very impressed with her knowledge and insisted on giving her two potted plants she could grow in a sunny spot in her own sheltered backyard.

They also discussed what plants could be grown round the pond at the manor.

Derek was also intrigued, as he had plans to get the old greenhouses going again.

By now it was late afternoon and they started back for the cottage. Derek, Doreen and Ingrid did not want to leave too late, and so decided not to stay for supper. Doreen was still suspicious of Derek's powers of navigation, especially at night! The surplus and unwanted goods were loaded into the car and just after six they left. As it disappeared down the track — with Binky peering out of the back window — Sam, Sarah and Michelle let out an audible sigh of relief, which made Reg chuckle. 'You all love your parents dearly — but!' he quietly remarked.

'Oh, yes,' they replied, 'but they are a sort of liability, for you never know what they'll be up to next.'

Stephen and Jane were the supper preparers that evening, and while they were busy, Reg beckoned to the others to come outside for a moment.

'As you know, it's 'the horrors' tenth birthday tomorrow. The party is on Sunday, at home, and you'll receive your invitations tomorrow. They know when the actual celebration will be, but I thought it would be nice to give them a surprise on the way home. So I've arranged a special birthday tea at a rather nice cafe in Chard. Now don't say anything about it, all right?'

'Of course not!' they promised. On the quiet, cards had already been made, though how they found the time and place to do them was a mystery.

Supper was a cheerful meal, though secretly they all

were wishing that the holiday could go on, and on, and on! It had been such fun and there was no doubt about it, Reg had been a most wonderful host, knowing exactly when to turn a blind eye to their antics and yet still keeping things within reason. They hoped he would invite them again.

At the end of the meal, Brenda appeared to clear up; she *insisted* on doing this on their last evening. The children begged her to sit down for a moment, and left the room to return, a few minutes later, carrying a brightly wrapped parcel for her and a selection of homemade 'thank you' cards. She was quite taken aback, especially when she opened it and found a beautiful linen apron and a selection of colourful ladies' hankies. They had noticed she liked these.

'Well,' she gasped, 'I don't know how to thank you all.'

'But it's us, we wanted to thank you!' they explained.

She insisted on giving everyone a hug, including Reg, and promised to come back in the morning to see them off and tidy up. 'Now I *must* get back to the kitchen,' she said, and was gone.

'What time do we leave, Gramps?' asked Jane.

'After lunch, there's no hurry to get back before supper. It means if the weather is good we can nip down to the beach and you can have a last dip. Approved?'

Approved, very definitely! Some more packing was done and then to bed, as they wanted to be up as early as possible to enjoy to the full the last morning.

As a result the children were up at six, but decided to be very quiet so that Reg could sleep on until seven. They managed to creep out of the cottage with the minimum amount of disturbance and went to the cliff 'view point' to enjoy their last look at the sea and cliffs, then back to make tea. However, Reg was already up and had made not only tea, but breakfast as well. Now Stephen and Jane received their 'semi-official' birthday greetings from their friends and congratulations from Reg.

'Of course the real celebrations will be tomorrow,' explained Stephen, while Jane handed out invitations to everyone. He continued, 'Mum thought that with being away and coming back today it was too much to have a party as well, so although we are ten today it's unofficial; tomorrow it will be official. Anyhow, let's finish breakfast and go for that last swim and morning on the beach.'

'Before we go down, and there's plenty of time,' said Reg, 'will you go and pack everything except what you need for this morning? Then check that nothing has been overlooked in the bedrooms and put all your stuff in the front room by the door. This will make loading up easier after lunch. To make sure nothing does get left behind, Sam and Stephen check Jane and Sarah's room. They check Michelle's and Shirley's and they check the boys' one. Right, off you go. Let's try to be ready in half an hour!'

It took slightly longer, as in each case, looking under the beds revealed odd items like socks, a pencil, a notebook and some peppermints. In each room something was found. They then descended upon Reg's room. But he was an old hand at packing, and not a whisker did they find! Brenda appeared just as they were going to the beach and promised to have a prepared lunch on the table ready for their return. She said goodbye, as she would have probably left by the time they got back.

It was breezier today but they swam and enjoyed the time poking about the rock pools again, though there was no specimen collecting today!

Jane and Stephen were paddling through a large shallow pool when Jane let out an 'ouch!'

'What is it? Has a crab nipped you?' grinned her brother.

'No, silly, I trod on something hard.' She bent down and began clearing the sand away. Stephen joined her.

'It's just a piece of old rock,' he said, as a roughly square slab was uncovered.

'No it, isn't,' retorted his sister, 'look.'

She had lifted up a flat heart-shaped object, about six inches long. 'It's metal, very rusty though.'

They examined it, but the surface was so pitted and covered with grime it was difficult to make out what it was. They took it over to show the others and then Reg.

'Hm, some token or maybe an old insurance sign,' he suggested. 'They used to fix them to houses that were insured. When you get it home, try to clean it up. But be careful not to use any strong cleaners on it.'

'We could take it to school,' said Stephen, 'Uncle Fred will know how best to do that, and some of his friends in the Historical Society may be able to tell us what it is.'

They wrapped their strange find up in a piece of paper and left it by him.

'Another half hour and we'll have to go,' he called out.

They made the most of it, you can be sure! Now came the long pull up the cliff path back to the cottage. Jane carried their find, but as they walked on she lagged further and further behind until Sarah went back to see why. She looked very pale and exhausted. Her steps were uncertain and she hardly seemed to know where she was going.

Sarah was alarmed. Was Jane ill? Had she been stung by something and was allergic to it? All manner of thoughts flashed through her mind.

'Jane! What's the matter, aren't you well? Here, let me help you!'

She took her friend by the arm and tried to assist her along. Jane shook her head.

'It's not me,' she whispered, 'it's this,' indicating the paper-wrapped object. 'I feel as if it's draining me of energy. It wants something, though I don't know what!'

'Here, give it to me, I'll carry it,' Sarah responded, and she took it from Jane's listless fingers. The moment she touched it, she felt a strange sensation pass through her body. There *was* something strange about it, as if it wanted, or needed energy from some source.

'You're *not* having it from me!' she said very firmly, and at once the sensation lessened.

'Come on, Jane, let's catch up with the others.' Jane already looked better and her normal energy seemed to have returned. They caught up just before the level piece that led to the cottage. As soon as they were back and while lunch was being set out, for Brenda had left, Sarah drew Reg aside and told him what had happened to Jane.

'Strange,' he remarked. 'When I had that thing beside me every now and then I felt 'odd' as if I was falling asleep against my will.'

'What shall we do with it, then?' she asked.

'It let itself be found by Jane, so there must be some purpose in this. However, it does seem to have an unfortunate effect upon people,' he replied. 'There's an old metal box in the boot. I think it would be best to put it in that, and when back home we can decide what to do with it. One thing's for certain, we don't want tomorrow to be spoilt in any way.'

He took the package and went out to the four-wheel drive. When he returned lunch was ready. Afterwards came the packing of their stuff and the final goodbye to the cottage.

'Now homewards,' announced Reg, 'But I've some business to do in Chard on the way, you don't mind, do you?'

'Oh, no!' said the children, those who knew what the business was and those who didn't!

'Afterwards we'll go back via Bidford Manor, Bidcote and eventually Bardon Lane,' he added.

It took about half an hour to reach Chard and they were there by three thirty, in the old part of the town. There was some difficulty in finding a parking spot, but eventually did so.

'Now this business may take some time,' Reg informed them, 'so I think you'd better come along too. I may need your advice on certain matters.'

Off they went through the winding streets that formed the original town on top of the hill.

It seemed that Reg was deliberately going the longest way round to reach his objective, but after ten minutes of brisk walking he dived down an alleyway, into a courtyard and through an old fashioned broad and low door. They followed him. They were in a tea room!

As soon as Stephen and Jane entered they gasped, for there before them was a long table festively set for seven. On it — in full view — was a large iced birthday cake with ten candles and 'Happy Birthday Stephen and Jane' in blue and pink icing. Behind it stood several waitresses and kitchen staff who promptly launched into 'Happy Birthday to both of You!'

'You see what I meant when I said I would need your help,' grinned Reg.

It was one of those rare occasions when both Randell twins were lost for words; all they could say was 'Oh, Gramps!' and hug him.

Soon they were all seated, the candles were lit and the party was in full swing. Several other guests came over and congratulated them, and besides all the usual things to eat there were birthday crackers as well. It was a glorious end to a wonderful week and six very contented children climbed back into the four-wheel drive some two hours later. Then it was back to Bidford Manor.

'See you tomorrow, though,' they called to each other. Shirley and Michelle were dropped off in Bidcote and Reg drove his remaining passengers to Southleigh.

As they unpacked the remaining bags and bits from the boot, Reg remembered the strange plaque, or badge. He scooped it into an old canvas bag so he avoided touching it and took it, with some remaining items, up to their play room.

'Listen you two, after the experience Jane had this morning when carrying this, I think it best you leave well alone until we can find out more about it.'

Stephen looked rather surprised, as he knew nothing of what had happened, but when told, agreed with Reg. There was an old iron hook in one of the beams (not the 'Golden Hind' one) and Reg hung the bag on this.

'Iron, that should hold it! Now don't forget what I said!' They nodded and the three of them went back downstairs.

A few minutes later Bob Binnacle appeared in the room and stood staring at the bag.

'Now why on earth did they have to get muddled up with something like this?' he said to himself. 'I shall have my work cut out dealing with it! Still, I didn't take this job on for a rest cure. But it's going to be all hands on deck, or to the pumps, Bob, my boy!'

CHAPTER TWENTY-FOUR

Stephen and Jane woke early the next morning and were soon up and dressed, eager to find out what was going to happen today. However, their mother and father were up before them, and when they arrived downstairs for breakfast they were hustled into the kitchen and firmly told there was to be no poking or prying around.

'But we want to help get things ready!' they protested.

'The best way you can help is to keep out of the way!' Phyllis told them.

'But... ...!' began Stephen.

'No buts, I want you two to go up to the playroom and sort out the things you'll need for school. This is an ideal time to do it. You certainly won't be in the mood or even capable of that this evening. So now's just right; and it will keep you from getting under our feet. Now off you go and don't come down until I call you for snack. Afterwards you can go back there until lunch and *then* we shall have to get you ready.'

They groaned; 'getting ready' was one of the 'most subtle' forms of torture ever invented by grown-ups. However, there was no escaping it! They made their way up to the playroom.

'It's being treated like when we were little,' said Stephen. 'We used to be sent up here when we were supposed to have been naughty, to think about it.'

'Yes,' said Jane 'Or if we'd been unkind to each other, like when you pulled my hair and made me cry.'

'Or you bit me,' added Stephen.

'I never bit you,' she replied indignantly.

'Yes, you did.'

'Well, you *did* pull my hair!'

Well, you deserved it, because you bit me!'

How long this argument would have gone on it's hard to tell, but at that moment another voice broke in, 'No doubt it was half a dozen of one and six of the other. But I'm glad to find you up here, for I urgently need a word with you about the contents of that bag,' and Bob indicated the canvas bag holding the object Jane had found in the rock pool swinging gently from the iron hook above their heads.

'Tell me, where and how did you find this object, and do you know what it is?'

They told him how they had come across the piece of metal and Jane added that it was so weathered and worn they had no idea what it was, but their grandfather thought it might be an old insurance plaque or tradesman's mark. She mentioned Sarah and her experience with it and Reg's remarks as well.

'That's why it's up here, out of the way, because we don't know whether it's safe or not,' Stephen explained.

Bob looked serious. 'After what you have just said about the effect on Jane, and what I myself felt when the bag was hung here, I believe we must treat this thing with great caution. It could be harmless, though I very much doubt it. I fear it is extremely dangerous!'

'But why, why should we have found it, why us?' queried Stephen.

'Why you? I can think of several reasons. With your friends, you drove away the Enchainers from Bidford Manor. You helped the Hill Folk retain their talisman. You stopped the destruction of the boundary stone and recently you helped to keep the Primal Power under control, *and* reformed a witch! In each case, evil, and its dark forces were thwarted. There are those who see you as a threat to their very existence and to their future plans. This object, whatever it may appear to be, saps your energy and weakens you. What better way to render you harmless? On the other hand, it may contain the residue of some ancient charm and all it is doing is trying to regain its strength. You chanced upon it and brought it home, so it's drawing energy from you. But until we know for sure it's best left well alone.'

'We thought of showing it to our teacher,' said Stephen, 'he knows about old things like this.'

'Better it remains here and is not touched more than necessary and moved as little as possible—at any rate for the moment—perhaps your father could make a picture of it with one of those 'picture making' machines to show your teacher.

'Picture making machine?' Oh, I know, you mean a camera?' said Stephen.

'Yes,' he replied, 'and this afternoon make sure none of your guests come up here alone. The last thing we need is someone interfering with it.'

He sounded so serious they must have looked very crestfallen; was their party going to be spoilt?

Suddenly Bob smiled, 'Don't worry! I'll make sure nothing unpleasant happens today. I shall remain here to keep an eye on things. I reckon I can handle it. Now you must forget all about this.' He moved his hands in front of their faces and at once their anxiety faded away. They did not forget about the object, but it no longer seemed so important. At that moment their mother called them for snack.

'Have you sorted your school things out?' she asked.

'Not yet, Mum, we were talking to Bob about the thing we found in a rock pool yesterday.'

'Gossiping, eh! Well as soon as snack is finished, back

you go and sort and pack your school stuff. It will be no good coming moaning to me tomorrow morning if you haven't got something.

'Yes, Mum, we won't!'

Knowing you two, you'll give it a jolly good try, now scoot!'

They scooted back to the play room—Bob had disappeared—so they set about looking for their school things and soon the room was in complete chaos, for they had to empty every shelf and cupboard to find them.

'Goodness knows how they managed to become so all over the place!' bewailed Jane.

Just before lunch they had their bags packed and ready and were waiting for their mother's call when Bob reappeared.

'I've been thinking about this business,' he said. 'And I'd like to get the opinion of someone like Bill Bluff or Sir Brian. They have more experience in such matters. Now if it had been a sea-going object I would have been more at home—or at sea with it.'

'We'll ask Sam or Sarah to tell Bill to contact you,' they said.

'Good, then we can arrange a meeting.'

The call for lunch interrupted any further conversation. Bob disappeared and they thundered downstairs. By now the excitement was really beginning to build up and they could hardly eat a thing—well not much—only half a dozen sandwiches each instead of the usual dozen. After lunch the refined torture began as Phyllis supervised their dressing.

'Jane, you can't wear that T shirt, it's got a dirty collar! Stephen, those jeans have a split at the back! No, I can't stop to mend them now. Well, if you knew they were split why didn't you show them to me last night? Jane, what *have* you done to your hair? It's full of straw! Your sandals were in the hayloft? What on earth were they doing up there? No,

Stephen, I don't have any spare white shoe laces! Where do you expect me to find some on Sunday afternoon? You'll just have to tie that one, as best you can!' And so on and so on.

At last they were ready and went down to the front porch to receive their guests and to relieve them of any packages they might be carrying. Again they were forestalled by their mother.

'All packages go by the lounge door,' she instructed, 'and keep your hands off them.'

It was now quarter to three. The guests would start arriving at three. As it was school the following day the party would finish at six thirty. Quite long enough John reckoned; he hoped he would still be comparatively sane at the end of it.

A look at the guest list may be a good idea before things become too hectic. Reg of course, Sam, Sarah and their parents. They were also bringing Erin, Michelle and Ingrid. Jill and Brian with their parents. They would be bringing Shirley and Geoffrey. Judy and Nicky, their parents and Uncle Peter, if he felt like coming. Chris and Fenella. *And,* naturally, Uncle Fred. Eleven children and eleven grown-ups. Quite a gathering!

At three the guests began to arrive and by ten past all were gathered. John stood in the porch and addressed them.

'Dear friends, we are gathered here today to celebrate the birthdays of our two... ...er two?' He paused.

'Children?' suggested Phyllis.

'Ah, yes, now I remember, children! First I want to thank you all for coming. Will the guests now please enter the lounge while I hold these two back until you are settled.'

He grabbed Jane and Stephen round the waist and hung on to his giggling, wriggling offspring until Phyllis called out, 'All set.' Taking them by the hand he escorted them in. Upon entering all they could do was gasp, 'Oh!'

In front of the fireplace a long occasional table had been

placed. On it was a white linen cloth and on that was a mound of brightly wrapped packages and envelopes. Overhead hung a paper banner reading, 'Happy Birthday Jane and Stephen, may you have a wonderful year!'

They noticed there were two chairs decorated to look like thrones a short way back from the table. Both had large labels. One read, 'Her Royal Highness Queen Jane'. The other, 'His Royal Highness King Stephen'.

'Will Your Majesties pray be seated!' said John and they did so.

Sam and Sarah now stepped forward and stood at either end of the table. Brian and Judy now came forward and stood before Their Majesties, bowing low, while Michelle and Geoff, each bearing a large wastepaper basket, came and stood one on each side of them.

'These are your royal loyal servants'—indicating Brian and Judy—'who will bring you your gifts, and we are the Royal Rubbish Collectors!' they chanted. Shirley came and bowed before them. 'Let the royal present presentation begin!' she announced in clear ringing tones, and it did.

There were many different gifts, too many to mention in detail. Suffice to say: from Reg each received a camera. From their parents, hiking outfits and boots. From Sam and Sarah, proper hiking rucksacks and from the Game, Evard and Fisher families, two lightweight sleeping bags. Fred gave them a set of local 'Explorer' Ordnance maps and there were various books and other items from relatives. From their Australian cousins came two Bush hats, very much appreciated! Erin's gift was a pair of binoculars. 'I'll tell you more about them later,' she said.

Finally the table was cleared and the Royal Rubbish Collectors had very full baskets. Derek now approached the thrones and bowed low before them.

'If your most Royal Highnesses would condescend to follow me into the garden, something further awaits your pleasure!' he announced.

They rose and there was a movement among the guests towards the door.

'Oy, you lot stay where you are until royalty has passed,' he ordered. '*Then* you may follow!'

He walked backwards, only colliding with the doorpost once. Judy and Brian held the Royal hands, while behind came Sam, Sarah, Michelle, Geoff and the other children, followed by a gaggle of grown-ups. Derek backed carefully down the steps and round the house and over to the gate into the orchard.

'Close your Royal eyes,' he requested, 'your servants will lead you.' Judy and Brian did so, taking them through the gate.

'Now open them!' Their Majesties were standing before two one-person brightly coloured lightweight tents. Each was complete with its own attached groundsheet.

'When packed they are so small and light you can easily pop them in your rucksack or tie them on,' John explained. Naturally everyone, grown-ups included, had to crawl in and out of them just for the fun of it. 'You two are well equipped for our class camp!' laughed Fred. 'I just hope the others are.' Seeing the worried look on Geoff's face he added, 'Though if anyone is short of camping gear I have a contact in a firm that hires out camping equipment, so can usually borrow anything we need.'

The new cameras were now used to take photos of the tents and children in, out and grouped around them. Reg also produced his and took a couple of birthday group pictures, which he was also in — by using the self-timer.

'Now, Your Majesties and other assorted royalty and non-royalty, I request you all follow me to the banqueting hall, or if you prefer it, the dining room!' announced Derek.

The procession moved speedily. It's amazing how hungry one can become just sitting or standing round watching people unwrap presents.

The dining room was very festive with balloons and streamers and another large banner over the table saying, 'Go on! Don't be shy!' Not that the guests needed any encouragement. There was a cake of massive proportions in the shape of a mountain with icing sugar snowy peaks and miniature candy mountaineers, goats and suchlike all over it. The ten candles formed a ring at the peak. Round the base was a ring of crackers.

At last, when most plates only had crumbs left on them and most of the glasses only had drops in them and the cake resembled a geological cataclysm, did they realise the feast was over.

John, who was feeling rather full, rose slowly to his feet. 'Now, for those who can still move, even a little, I have to announce a treasure hunt in the back garden. Hey! Wait a minute, you haven't been given your instructions yet! First, all those under seven join with an older child (no prizes for guessing who went with whom!). They will read the clues to you. Yes, there is a treasure for everyone. *But*! There is one extra treasure; each of you will have one clue to help you find it. Good luck and off you go!'

He quickly pressed himself back against the wall until the torrent of children had swept past.

'I'll go and keep an eye on things,' said Fred and followed them.

'Now for some peace,' said Phyllis. 'To the sitting room everybody, make yourselves comfortable, tea and coffee and stronger brews are coming!'

There was a dignified rush of the grown-up variety to secure comfortable seats. Actually they were all *very* comfortable. 'Do we barricade ourselves in?' asked Derek.

'No, but I think I can guarantee at least three quarters of an hour before they return!' grinned John. 'Ah, here are the drinks!'

In the back garden children were flitting in all directions like sanguine butterflies — peering and poking under shrubs and bushes, looking up trees, under flower pots and in the garden shed. Every so often there would be a shout of triumph as another clue was found. Occasionally Fred would sidle up to a worried looking participant and drop a hint. 'Oh, I never thought of looking there, thanks, Uncle Fred,' and they would scurry off.

The birthday children found their treasure first. 'Which is as it should be,' remarked Sarah. Their treasure was a small robust torch, ideal for camping.

Brian also found, with Jane's help, his 'twesser,' a soft toy 'Tigger' which delighted him.

Stephen and Jane now helped the others to interpret their clues while they kept an eye open to see if their remaining clue, the extra treasure clue, would lead to it. Gradually others found their own treasures. Soon all had completed their personal treasure hunt. Jill's was also a torch, just what she needed for her passage exploration. Only the special one now remained unsolved, as the clues they had found did not seem to give enough information on their own.

Fred gathered everyone round him. 'If we read the cards out, I think we shall find that each leads on to the next. Is there any other marking on them?' They looked carefully.

'Hey,' cried Geoff, 'look in the bottom left-hand corner. Mine has a tiny six there.'

The others looked, and sure enough, each card carried a number. When put in sequence the clues made sense.

'Whoa a minute,' cautioned Fred, 'Remember, this treasure is meant for all of you. Ready, come on, let's go!' The clues, eleven of them, led them a fine old dance round the garden, ending up in the hayloft. There, sticking out from under a pile of straw was the corner of a box. Eagerly it was hauled out and opened.

'A real treasure chest!' marvelled Jill. In it were eleven

little canvas bags containing chocolate money, fruit gums, a balloon and a small toy—little Chinese dolls for the girls, and little Chinese Mandarins for the boys. Cheerfully and cheering they made their way back to the house.

Their arrival had been prepared for, and when they entered the sitting room, cool drinks and biscuits awaited them. Now, all too soon, it was time for the party to finish. The twins thanked their guests for a wonderful time and the guests thanked them for such a super party. Then everyone began to say goodbye to everyone else. While this was going on, Stephen and Jane drew Sam and Sarah aside and gave them Bob's message for Bill and Sir Brian.

'Right, we'll tell them as soon as we get back,' Sam promised.

The Royal Host and Hostess stood on the front steps and graciously waved regal goodbyes as the cars drove off. Peter had come quietly up to them as he prepared to leave. He shook each warmly by the hand and said:

'Thanks for inviting me, I really enjoyed it.' They knew by his voice that it had meant a great deal to him.

'Please, may we call you Uncle Peter?' asked Jane. He looked surprised, but replied,

'Why, of course, if you so wish.'

'Well, please come again, Uncle Peter!' they said eagerly.

'Indeed, I will,' he replied and they knew he meant it.

When the last car had driven away and they had helped with the clearing up, the twins rushed up to the play room to tell Bob how things had gone.

They found him seated at the table looking very pale and tired.

'Are you all right?' they asked anxiously.

'Yes, my dears, but it's been quite a struggle. The entity, or whatever it is, wants to get out. Naturally it couldn't draw energy from me, as we are of a similar incorporeality, but it nagged and nagged the whole time.'

'In words?' asked Jane.

'No, that's just it. You feel it's trying to speak, but it can't form words, so it's like having a noise going round and round inside your head the whole time and it's impossible to shut it out.'

They reported they had delivered his message via Sam and Sarah and hoped that Bill would soon contact him.

'Good,' he said. 'Now remember, leave well alone and once I've consulted with Bill and Sir Brian we may be in a better position to know how to deal with it. Now, my dears, I'm going to get some rest,' and he disappeared into the Golden Hind beam.

The children went down to prepare for bed. While they were doing so Stephen said, 'Jane, tomorrow we'll get up early to take our school things from the play room. *But,* we'll take our cameras up with us. My film is nearly finished so I'll use the last few shots on the object.'

'Good idea,' she replied, 'I'll set my alarm so we don't oversleep.'

CHAPTER TWENTY-FIVE

When Sam and Sarah arrived home they went straight up to the attics and called for Bill. He appeared in the passage by his room and they gave him Bob's message. He listened with interest and promised to have a word with Sir Brian.

'For he is the one who can travel between here and Southleigh easily and possesses enough knowledge to do something about finding out what this entity wants,' he told them. 'Now off you go to bed, you look worn out, otherwise you won't be ready for school in the morning.' For once they went almost gladly.

In the meantime, Bill invited himself into Sir Brian's study and relayed Bob's concerns to him.

'Wants me to have a look, eh? No harm in that. I've heard of these things. Used to be some kind of good luck and protection charm for one's house or trade. Sometimes the spell—though simple—can be tricky; you had to have everything absolutely correct or other unpleasant powers could slip in. Sounds as if that's the case here. I'll pop over tomorrow morning and take a look.'

'Fine,' said Bill, 'if your surmise is correct we shall have to find the source and try to deal with it, no doubt?'

'Yes, but who knows how long ago this object was empowered and who did it? That's not so easy to discover.'

Bill nodded, this looked like being one of those tasks that

was going to turn out far more complicated than it appeared.

'Let me know when you return, then we can discuss what is best for us and the children to do.'

Early Monday morning Stephen and Jane were up, and, armed with their cameras, made their way to the play room. Jane had borrowed a pair of thick oven gloves from the kitchen, as she thought it best neither of them touched the plaque with bare hands. She also collected a pair of coal tongs from the dining room for lifting down and replacing the bag.

'Lucky our cameras have a flash,' remarked her brother, 'it's still pretty dark up here.'

They laid a sheet of blank white paper on the table and got the bag down with the tongs, which proved quite a tricky task. Then Jane removed the object wearing the gloves. Even so, she felt a tingling in her fingers when she took it to place on the paper. Once this was done Stephen took several pictures from various angles, using up the remainder of his film.

'I hope at least one comes out!' he remarked.

'You took about eight, so you should have something!' replied his sister.

She also took a couple, just in case. They slid the plaque back into the bag and hung it up again.

They went down to dress. Stephen gave the exposed film to John, who promised to take it to one of those 'Swift Print' places so possibly he would be able to bring it home that evening.

The return to school was hectic; the pupils were sort of ready, but in a sense they weren't. This was complicated by the fact that Easter had been early, causing various public holidays *and* their half-term to come in a bunch. There had been the May Day Holiday at the beginning of the month and now, at the end of May, the Spring Holiday on Monday the first of June. So they would have a week at school and then a long weekend. Mr Atkinson had prepared a concentrated maths revision main lesson slanted towards practical work. Then on return after the break a two week English period before the class camping trip. Once the class had settled down, after the morning verse and usual exercises he gave a brief outline of the plans for the latter.

'Right, I hope you all washed your ears out well this morning because I want you to listen *very* carefully. In fact, have a piece of paper and a pencil handy to jot down the important points!'

'We leave by coach on Friday the nineteenth of June for a farm near Selworthy on the North Somerset Coast. It's a few miles beyond Minehead near to the Southwest Coastal Path, and to the south lies the Exmoor National Park. The main emphasis on this trip is self-sufficiency and orientation. We shall make several day hikes round the district and one overnight hike into the National Park, staying in a ranger's hut. However, if you think I'm trying to wear you out with walking, note that on the Wednesday we shall have a coach trip down the North Cornish Coast to Tintagel Head. I've prepared a full list of the equipment you need to bring with you and one of optional items. Take this home and get your parents to tick off the items you have, both required and optional. They should also indicate the ones they still intend to obtain. Once I have *all* the lists back I can contact the camping hire company to loan us any missing equipment. So, lists back by Friday without fail! Any questions or problems I'll deal with after main lesson each morning. Here, Chris, Michelle, hand out these lists, please. There's also a permission slip attached.'

After that it was down to work. The practical maths involved compass reading and plotting. This proved great fun as they tried to plot the position of their classroom on a plan of the school. It finished up in some rather odd places, such as on the roof of the school hall. However, by the end of the lesson they had a much better grasp of how to read co-ordinates.

In the meantime, Sir Brian made his trip to Southleigh. Apart from landing on top of a cherry tree in the orchard, rather than *in* the orchard, he managed quite well and made his invisible way up to the play room, where Bob was waiting. He was shown the bag hanging on the beam that contained the object. Gingerly, Sir Brian took it down and shook the contents onto the table. Producing a short wand from the folds of his robe, he cautiously prodded the heart-shaped piece of rusted metal. Nothing happened. Using the wand he carefully flipped it over, though it was difficult to tell the back from the front. Now he produced a large magnifying glass and examined the surface closely, also sniffing it. Turned it over again, repeating the process. Then he looked at Bob.

'Any clues, Sir Brian?' he asked.

'None,' was the reply. 'But I must say there's something about it I don't feel at all happy with. Can't put my finger on it, but I suspect it's connected with the *old* magic. For what purpose, I don't know. Let's consider; why did these youngsters pick it up? Or, for what reason did it choose them?'

Bob reiterated his thoughts about the work the children had performed against the Dark Forces and whether this was to try and curb their activities.

'Could be, could very well be,' agreed Sir Brian, 'but honestly, I don't know.'

He pushed the plaque back into the bag with his wand and hung it up again.

'Keep away from it as much as possible. I'll have a chat with Bill and we'll see if we can trace where it came from and how it got into that rock pool. I have a funny feeling it originated from round here; that's why it's returned. Well, best be off. Nice to have met you. Let us know if anything out of the ordinary happens, odd or suspicious.'

He twirled himself round rapidly, muttering furiously, and vanished, landing in the old boiler house owing to a slight miscalculation and went to find Bill.

When both lots of twins arrived home from school their house guardians reported on Sir Brian's excursion to Southleigh. For the moment 'leave well alone' was the message, which they were quite happy to do.

With the long weekend approaching the children wanted to make the most of it. Stephen and Jane could not come over for the whole time, as on Saturday various relatives who had been unable to come to their party were visiting, and naturally they would have to be present. However, they would be brought over on Sunday with their bikes. John had meant to bring these over before, but had either forgotten or just did not have time.

On Friday, when school finished, they decided for Monday they would go for a day's cycle ride and investigate the old asylum. On Sunday? Well, it depended on what time the twins arrived. Possibly passage exploration, the one leading to the farm that Jill and Edwin had discovered the entrance to?

The problem for Sam, Sarah and Michelle was what to do on Saturday, not really a big problem, but they wanted to do something useful and preferably exciting. Derek pointed out the gardens needed some attention and perhaps Shirley would like to come over with Michelle. A phone call ascertained she would — and could — as her sisters were off to a party. It was arranged for Michelle to call for her at nine thirty and they would stay until seven thirty.

As they prepared for bed that evening there was a knock on Sarah's door and Bill, with Sir Brian close on his heels, entered.

'Sir Brian has been doing some research,' Bill announced, 'and thinks you should know what he's found out.'

They sat on Sarah's bed while the noble lord took up a

position on the hearthrug, cleared his throat and began:

'I spent the remainder of today doing some visiting. There's an old fellow in Bidcote church, sort of verger-cum-ghost, or ghost-cum-verger. I asked him if he had any knowledge of one who used to make plaque charms. He was rather reticent about the whole business, but eventually told me that about a hundred and fifty years ago an old woman lived in the village who was—as he put it—"very powerful" and could "do a might of good, but maybe a might of bad as well!" It seems she fell foul of one of the local gentry named Absolom Brockfield. More than that he flatly refused to say—at first. However, I persisted and it appeared the cause was a plaque she made for him. He was a wealthy merchant with his own merchant ship berthed at Bristol Docks. He went to her for a charm to protect the vessel on its voyages and offered her a handsome sum of gold for it. She made a special one, though how, he had no idea. Anyway when this fellow collected it he refused to pay her the agreed price, saying it was a poor piece of workmanship and not worth any gold. She grew very angry and threatened to place a malefic influence on it. He snatched it from her—laughed—and threw down a couple of pieces of silver, then left.'

'The ship had a voyage the likes of which its owner had never had before. It returned loaded to the decks with precious merchandise. The captain intended to unload some of the cargo at West Bay and then sail for their homeport—Bristol. As he sailed up the Channel a freak storm swept down at night. The ship foundered off Lyme Regis, all hands were lost and not one scrap of the cargo was ever washed up. The sea took it all! Now Absolom's son, Isador—a proud young upstart—promptly accused the woman of causing his father's loss of wealth. One night she vanished from her cottage. The place was all overturned and upset, but the neighbours swore they heard nothing. The narrator reckoned their lips had been sealed — with gold.'

'That's his story and I believe it gives us a partial answer to the source of the plaque. Something *was* washed up from the wreck. And Jane found it. Now it's come back to the district where it was made, no doubt seeking its mistress. But where or what happened to her we don't know — for the moment. I shall continue to make enquiries and you might have a word with Erin; she may have some ideas.' He bowed and did a vertical take off through the ceiling.

Bill smiled, 'I think his research has been really helpful, let's hope it will be possible to find out more before this thing becomes really dangerous.'

'Do you think it will? asked Sarah.

'I'm afraid so, there's a force impelling it, and as you heard, not a very pleasant one. But it's in good hands. Bob Binnacle is a reliable fellow and will keep an eagle eye on it. So put it out of your minds for the moment, good night,' and he too disappeared — through the door. Sam and Sarah tried to put the matter out of their minds, but it was not easy. Uncertainty is far more difficult to deal with than certainty. However, eventually they fell asleep.

Next morning they were up early and spent some time before breakfast collecting the necessary tools for their garden work. Derek was also pottering around, though he intended to work in the ornamental garden. After breakfast they took Binky and Cleo out to play on the lawn while waiting for Michelle and Shirley to arrive. It was a good day for outside work, sunny, but not too hot.

The girls arrived on time and the four of them went up to the gardens. There was a fair amount of weeding and tidying up to be done. However, most of what they had previously planted was doing well. Shirley was concerned over the drainage of the terrace beds, for rubbish had blocked some of the outlets. So there was a grand clean out and realignment of the channels to cope with any flow resulting from a heavy downpour. This kept them happily occupied until lunch, after which they went up to the secret room for a chat. When Shirley heard they were going to investigate the passage leading to the farm tomorrow, she asked if she could accompany them.

'What about your sisters?' asked Sarah.

'Oh, they won't want to come,' she replied. 'They don't like dark or dirty places and Mum wants to take them to some "do" at the church for under eights mid-morning. So I'd be left on my own.'

It was arranged for Michelle to collect her.

They heard the phone ring and Doreen calling, 'One of you come down please, Jane's on the line!' Sam galloped off, returning a few minutes later with a wide grin on his face.

'Jane says they should be here by ten at the latest. Their dad has an appointment in Hidding-cum-Stanton at ten thirty. Someone is coming down from London to look at that house we went over. I hope Eli Wrink approves of them—or they *will* be in for a shock!'

'Try to be here by quarter to ten,' Sarah told the cyclists, 'Then we can collect what we need and be ready to start as soon as they arrive.'

'Let's go and check with Dad now about lights, cables and whatever else we may want,' suggested Sam.

Derek was still in the ornamental garden, struggling to clear the weeds and brambles off the paths, which were badly overgrown and damaged by their intrusion, so he was glad for an excuse to stop. They sat on the old stone seat and asked him for what they thought would be required.

'I don't think there should be any problems,' he replied. 'But be sure to take your torches, for if that passage *does* go to the farm, the cables will not be long enough. If you come across any fallen bricks or masonry, don't try to go any further. One of you report back to me and I'll come and take a look. It might be an idea to ring Harry before you start so that he can be around if you reach the way out Jill found.'

They couldn't think of anything else for the moment, so helped with the path clearing until tea time. Then they went and started a game of Scrabble, which did not reach a conclusion, as Binky chased Cleo into the sitting room, and in her attempt to escape she took a flying leap onto the table, scattering the board and letters. There was only one thing to do, chase Binky and Cleo, which kept them going until supper. After Michelle and Shirley had left, the twins collected the items they needed for the morning.

The passage would be entered from the old boiler house. Derek had already connected up the cables and lights. One very important question was, did they take provisions with them? It was decided, 'yes', because as Sarah remarked:

'You never know, it might not lead directly to the farm and there could be just *miles* of passages, so we would need something to sustain our energy.'

'Then you can make a pile of sandwiches in the morning,' Doreen told them. 'Now off to bed with you and make sure you wear your oldest clothes tomorrow, *not* your Sunday best!'

'You mean our Sunday *worst*?' said Sarah.

'Yes, for once I do!'

CHAPTER TWENTY-SIX

Several things happened on Sunday morning that had a bearing on subsequent events. The first occurred as the Randell twins left Southleigh, their bikes safely strapped onto the cycle rack.

Up in the playroom the canvas bag began to swing to and fro under its own momentum. Bob was not there. He had remained on hand for most of the week and nothing had happened. So he felt justified in taking a bit of time off, nipping over to have a quick chat with Joshua Reynolds at Fenella's place.

The bag swung faster and faster until with a tearing noise the cloth handles gave way and it fell to the floor. The plaque slithered out and started to cross it, looking like a weird scuttling crab. There was a fairly wide crack between the floor and the skirting board, which it slipped into. A soft malicious chuckle sounded, then all was quiet.

☙

At the farm Jill was up early; she'd made up her mind. She was going to investigate the passage herself! She knew Sam and the others intended to explore it today, but was not sure when.

'It would be nice if we met,' she thought to herself.

Her torch was ready and Harry had given her two spare batteries that she would take along. She'd practised taking them out and putting them in under the bedclothes so she could do it in the dark. The only thing now was to be able to slip into the barn without being noticed or missed. Sunday morning was a good time, perhaps? Harry always checked his herd of cows down near Church Wood on Sunday morning. And this Sunday morning Bess was taking Brian to play with a little friend of his and to have coffee and a chat with his mum.

'You'll be all right, won't you, poppet?' she said to her daughter. 'You know where Dad will be and Bindle will stay with you!'

'I'll be fine!' replied the little girl.

Bess thought, 'A few months ago she'd have been in floods of tears if I left her alone in a room for a couple of minutes. Sam and that school have done wonders for her self-confidence!'

Bindle? Well Bindle is an elderly sheep dog with many years of faithful service behind him. Now he was too old and stiff in the joints to round up sheep. So he was the 'guard dog' round the farm. He was a quiet and gentle old fellow who had soon decided that the children were his sheep and followed them everywhere.

Bess left with Brian around ten, and Harry was already in the fields. She played in the yard for a while then went to collect her torch, the batteries and a few biscuits from the kitchen. She left the note that Sam had written for her on her bed, as he had told her to do. As she crossed to the barn Bindle joined her. She had an inspiration; she would take him along.

The phone rang in the house but there was nobody to answer it. The answering machine clicked on, so Sam left a brief message: 'We are going to explore the passage to the farm. Hope to see you shortly!'

Michelle and Shirley turned up on time and John's car rolled up just before ten.

'See you lot tomorrow,' he said, 'I'll be over about seven, so *be* ready.'

'Of course we will, Dad,' said in slightly injured tones; they were *always* ready. Well nearly always!

'We've brought our cameras and the binoculars Erin gave us,' said Jane. 'We haven't had a chance to use them yet, and as she said there was something special about them we thought this might be a good opportunity to find out what.'

'We've also got the pictures we took of the plaque,' added Stephen, 'though it's so battered it's difficult to see what it is. Maybe Uncle Fred's historical friends may know something about it.'

'It was odd about them,' continued Jane. 'Dad took the film to one of those 'Swift Print' places and went to pick them up after work — that was Monday — they couldn't find the prints even though the technician had the batch number and everything. They were awfully embarrassed and offered Dad a replacement film, which he accepted. Then on Friday morning they rang to say the print folder had turned up. So he went and got it. They said he could keep the film and didn't even charge him for the developing and printing. No one in the shop could explain what had happened, either!'

'Anyway, the place can't have the film back,' grinned Stephen. 'It's already in my camera.'

Dumping their stuff in the hall, they picked up the items they were taking on their passage exploration and made for the old boiler house. Derek was waiting for them also; with tail going full speed a wag in anticipation, was Binky.

They paused. 'Do we take him?' queried Stephen.

Jane sprung to the little dog's defence. 'Binky has been with us before. Remember how he and Cleo frightened off those Enchainers? Who found the summer house entrance? Who... ...?

'All right Jane, I was only asking,' he said hastily.

'I think it's a good idea if he goes with you, in any case,' said Derek, so that settled it!

The cables were all ready and they switched on the lights. Derek handed them two spare bulbs. 'You never know, you may need them, you may not,' he remarked.

Torches were checked and they prepared to descend the steps. 'If you're not back or haven't reached the farm by lunchtime I shall come searching for you,' he told them.

'Thanks, Dad, see you!' and they started off.

☙

Jill and Bindle entered the semi-light of the barn. She found the bolt and pulled it. The arched entrance appeared; she shone her torch down the steps. At the bottom, projecting from the wall was another bolt head.

'Come on, Bindle,' she said, 'we're going on an adventure.'

The old dog looked suspiciously at the steps, but obediently followed her. She pushed the lower bolt in and the entrance above swung shut. For a moment she felt afraid, but Bindle pushed his wet nose into her hand as if to say:

'Don't be frightened, little mistress, I'll protect you!' She took hold of his collar and they started off down the passage.

☙

At the foot of the steps the children transferred the cables into the passage power point. Derek had told them there was another down by the old hunting lodge ruin, and if they used the adaptor he had given them they could plug one cable into the other, giving them double the length, though they would only have one light. Full of confidence they set off.

☙

At Southleigh the play room door, which had been left ajar, was pushed open; a little black and white face peered round it, while behind, a white and tortoiseshell one peeped over its shoulder. Then the kittens Perry and Polly crept in and began a thorough examination of the room and its contents.

The canvas bag, lying on the floor, soon attracted their attention and a wonderful game of hiding and scuffling with — and in it — began.

Then Polly caught a glimpse of a flicker of light from under the nearby skirting board. In a flash she was there, poking her paw into the crack to find out what it was. It was something hard and rough, so she gave it a hefty bat with her paw, causing it to skid out across the floor, where Perry promptly leapt on it. In a moment they were both having a great game!

Bob appeared, having returned from his visit. He gasped when he saw what was going on, and quickly grabbed the object from them and dropped it onto the table. He picked up the bag and looked at the remains of the handles still on the hook.

'Hm, those rascals certainly didn't knock it down, far too high for them to reach. So it must have done it itself!'

He bent down and examined the floor. From approximately where the bag would have fallen he could make out faint scratches running across the floorboards to the crack in the skirting.

'So, it tried to hide, possibly escape? Luckily for us those kittens sneaked up here. There would have been a right old do if I'd returned and found it gone!'

He looked at the plaque lying on the table, dark, dirty, battered and rusty. Even as he did so he distinctly saw it rotate slightly, as if somebody had pushed it with their finger. He looked round the room. An old-fashioned cake tin caught his eye. Not one of those flimsy modern ones, but a good solid metal box. It was full of the children's odd bits and pieces. He carefully emptied them into a handy bowl and picking up the canvas bag, used it to push the plaque into the tin. He dropped the bag on top of it and tightly closed the lid. Then he placed it on top of a high bookcase, well out of reach of the children — and cats. The kittens watched all this with great interest. He spoke-thought with them (the usual way entities like house guardians communicate with animals).

'Your naughtiness has brought about good; I thank you. I want you to keep an eye on this room and should you hear, see or sense anything strange, call me at once; and I'll tell your little mistress and master to give you a saucer of cream every evening.'

'Miaow!' — There was instant agreement!

ಌ

The passage was narrow, but stonelined, about eight feet high with a paved floor. It ran straight ahead for as far as Jill's torch could show. The air was fresh and cool, a slight draft meant it must be entering from somewhere. She plodded on for what seemed to her to be a long time when it began to curve to the left, and she was confronted by a double archway, *two* passages! Which one should she take? She switched off her torch and sat down to consider. Bindle settled down beside her; she hugged him.

'Which way, Bindle, which is the way to Sam?'

Bindle wagged his tail. He liked Sam, although he'd only met him a few times. He was a nice boy and cared a lot for his little mistress as well. Jill suddenly felt very tired. Bindle lay beside her; she rested her head on his silky back and in a few moments was fast asleep.

ಌ

The sextet soon reached the old hunting lodge entrance. 'Do you remember when we fell through it?' Jane reminded Sam.

'Yes, and how lucky we were to escape from those Enchainers,' he replied.

'Well, at least there won't be any down here now,' said Sarah.

Binky had been put on his lead. They did not want him

running off chasing whatever scent he'd picked up. It was Stephen who now realised that Derek had overlooked one important point regarding the cables. It was all very well to say they could put the two cables together with the adaptor at this power point, but *how* could they if one cable was plugged in at the boiler house entrance without going back to fetch it?

Derek's scientific thinking had gone somewhat astray, he told the others.

'Well we shall just have to take this one as far as it will go and then use our torches,' said Michelle. 'At least with six of them we should be all right.'

They plugged the cable in and set off. The passage now narrowed and the roof was lower. It was still stonelined with a paved floor, all beautifully finished, and the air was fresh.

'I bet the same masons built this as the ones who made the cellar entrance passage,' remarked Sarah.

Now the cable reached its limit. Stephen put it on the floor. The wire frame round the bulb enabled him to point it the way they were going so the torches would not be necessary just yet, as the passage was absolutely straight. Later they would have to walk in single file following the leader's torch. Binky was also at the head of the line, straining on his lead and snuffling furiously.

They went on for some twenty minutes in this fashion and had fallen into a steady rhythm when Binky suddenly pulled up short, nose twitching, tail erect.

'What is it, Binks?' asked Sarah. They bunched up behind him just in case.

'He usually behaves like that when he scents a strange dog,' remarked Sam.

'He must be nuts,' Stephen replied, 'A dog down here? Impossible, unless it's a ghostly one.'

That thought brought them up sharply. After all they did not know what might lurk in these passages. Like the

Primal Force it could be something that had been hiding down here for hundreds of years and perhaps they had disturbed it. They listened and then began to move cautiously forwards. However, this was not easy, as Binky refused to budge. Then they noticed that the passage ahead of them curved slightly away to the right. However, there appeared to be a junction because the right-hand wall had a gap in it. A low soft growl reached their ears. It came from the part they could not see. Binky also growled. Now — as they all knew — he would tackle *any* dog, no matter how large or how ghostly.

'Should we let him off?' Sarah whispered to her brother.

'Not yet,' he replied. 'We must try to get nearer first.' Slowly, carefully, they edged their way along. As a precaution Sarah picked up Binky. His little body was taut with excitement.

Jill stirred and woke. Goodness, she'd been asleep! Bindle was still at her side, but she could feel his body was tense and no longer relaxed. He lifted his head, sniffed and let out a low growl from the back of his throat. She noticed it was no longer pitch dark. A very faint light glimmered to her left; there was something or someone in that passage. The light wavered up and down. The old dog growled louder and she thought she heard an answering one. Then whispering sounds. Should she switch her torch on? She became aware of a thumping noise beside her, it was Bindle's tail going up and down. He was wagging it! At once she realised everything was all right and scrambled to her feet, switching on her torch and, more for comfort than to restrain him, took hold of Bindle's collar.

☙

The children crept nearer and nearer to the opening. Sarah became aware that Binky had suddenly relaxed and his tail was wagging. At the same moment a light appeared in front of them, illuminating the passage wall, obviously from a torch! As they watched, two shapes came into view: one a small figure, the other a medium-sized dog. A childish voice echoed towards them.

'Hello, is that you, Sam, with the others?'

'Good heavens!' he exclaimed, 'It's Jill!' and ran forwards. In a trice he was being hugged and a rather muffled voice—because it was buried in his midriff—was saying,

'I knew it must be you, I came to find you and I did as you said, I left the note on my bed!'

☙

Harry returned from the lower fields and walked into the kitchen. 'Jill, Jill,' he called. No reply. He went to the yard door and called again. Strange, where was she? He returned to the house. Was she playing hide-and-go-seek? She did that sometimes.

'Wherever you are, I'm coming to find you,' he called, then listened. Often she would giggle because she wanted to be found. Not this time, silence. He began to feel uneasy. This was unlike her. He made his way upstairs to the children's bedroom. No, not in here. Wait a moment, there was an envelope on her pillow. He picked it up, and taking out a piece of paper, read the contents.

'I have gone into the secret passage to see where it goes.'

He recognised the writing as Sam's. What secret passage? But where, and how? He had no idea where it started. But wait a minute, she'd been in the barn recently and talked about 'a passage'. He ran downstairs, and as he went into the kitchen, noticed the answering machine was blinking. He set it going and heard Sam's message. Then he dialled the manor. Derek answered; he told Harry what had happened.

'There's a chance they will meet up, if there are no side branches for her to wander into,' he replied. 'I'll go down and try to find them. Can you find the way in from the barn? The entrance is there, I remember Sam saying so.'

Harry ran to the barn, as he did so he became aware that

Bindle was not in the yard. She must have taken him with her. At least she was not alone; that made him feel a little easier. Oh, he'd need a torch! Luckily, he kept a large one in the kitchen for emergencies — he was soon back. But *where* in the barn *was* the entrance? Just inside the doorway on the right he saw something white on the ground. It was a child's hanky. Shining the torch on the wall above he could just make out the outline of an arched opening. But how on earth did one open it? Something fluttering on the doorpost caught his eye. He went to look. On a bolt hung a piece of green thread, and Jill had been wearing a green jersey that morning! Looking closer he saw the bolt was not driven straight into the woodwork but rested in a metal socket. Taking hold of the projecting head, he pulled. There was a slight rumbling, grating noise, and there was the opening and steps going down. Switching on his torch he was soon striding along the passage calling, 'Jill, Bindle! Where are you? Can you hear me?'

༄

In the space between the two entrances the children gathered round Jill and Bindle. Binky pranced round them all, wagging his tail with glee, telling Bindle how glad he was to see him. The question was, what now? They could go on, as originally planned, to the farm. They knew that's what *should* be done... ... But facing them was another passage, unexpected and unexplored! Surely it would do no harm to at least investigate it — maybe just a little way? There were the remains of a rotting wooden frame, which indicated it once had a door. They shone a torch through, noticing it curved away to the left, and entered in single file. It was not so well constructed as the other. The floor was uneven and the stonework much rougher, looking as if it had been built in a hurry.

'Probably it's an escape way made during the Civil War,' suggested Shirley.

'Could be, but why the door?' asked Sam.

'Prisoners could have been kept in it?' she hazarded.

'That's not much good, if you could sneak out the other end!' said Stephen.

'How much further are we going?' asked Michelle.

'Why?'

'Look at the dogs.'

When they had entered, Binky and Bindle had been eagerly running on in front. Now they were behind the children, slinking along very reluctantly and constantly having to be encouraged to keep up.

'Something's worrying them,' said Jane. 'Best stop for a moment.'

They did so. The passage had turned into a tunnel; it was very narrow and the roof was so low they often had to duck. Also the air was no longer fresh, but smelt stale and dank. Stephen shone his torch on the floor. Ahead of them it was damp and muddy. Water dripped from the roof. Even as he did this, a slight tremor shook the tunnel. Binky and Bindle let out frightened yelps, turned tail and fled.

'It's not safe, back!' cried Stephen.

They turned and began to stumble back. Another tremor, small stones fell from the roof. The evil smelling air washed over them like a great wave as if something was pushing it from behind. It made them gag and choke. They staggered on, feeling that a malignant entity was trying to catch up with them.

☙

Derek made good progress down the passage and congratulated himself that he had snatched up a torch before he left.

'How stupid of me,' he muttered when he saw the cables. Soon he was heading down towards the passage's junction and as he neared it saw a light coming towards him. He met Harry there.

'Any sign of Jill?' he asked. 'Nothing, nor Bindle.'
'What about the others?'
'Not a sign of them!'
They looked at the other passage. 'Do you think?'
'Yes, I do! It's highly probably they met up here and decided to do some further exploring. Come on, we'd better take a look.'

They had not progressed very far when a tremor shook the tunnel and there were sounds of a rapid approach. Binky and Bindle literally ran into them and were overjoyed to find their adult humans; they were also pleased, for it meant the children could not be too far ahead. The wave of fetid air swept over them, urging them forward. A wavering torch beam appeared and in a few minutes they were all reunited.

But this was no place to stop and chat, so they stumbled back to the safety of the main passage. As they neared it, the smell and the sounds grew fainter. However, they did not pause, but carried on to the barn exit and then to the farmhouse kitchen. Harry made tea while they raided the cake tin and the children recounted their experiences.

'I'll board up that tunnel entrance for the moment,' said Harry.

'I think it should be investigated,' suggested Derek. 'But *not* by you children!' he quickly added.

'The way from the manor to the farm seems safe enough,' remarked Harry, 'But until the lighting system is extended, I think it's best you children keep out of it. Especially you, young lady!' He grinned at his daughter. The children, having recovered from their fright, now decided it was time to consume the snack they had brought with them for emergencies.

In the midst of all this Bess and Brian returned. Brian was delighted to find Jane there and very impressed to learn she had come all the way underground. Bess insisted they stay for lunch and sent Derek off to collect Doreen, who had just been wondering what to do about lunch, as she had no idea where her brood was.

Afterwards they retired to the lounge and spent a very lazy afternoon, returning to the manor after tea. Michelle and Shirley cycled home a little after six. Shirley would have loved to have been with them on the following day but her parents had already arranged a family outing.

That evening they prepared for their cycle trip. Bikes were thoroughly checked over, tires pumped up and oil liberally squirted over all moving parts, and a few others as well. Then they retired for the night.

CHAPTER TWENTY-SEVEN

Early next morning Sam phoned Michelle, suggesting they should meet up in the village rather than her cycling over, as in any case they would have to come her way.

'Meet you about nine thirty,' he told her. In the meantime Stephen was pouring over the local explorer map of the district. Their route was obvious, but he was also looking for the possible direction of the strange tunnel.

'There are no streams running across it as far as I can make out,' he mused. 'That dampness could be from an underground spring. What I can't understand is what the tunnel leads to. There's nothing I can see on the map that would make sense.'

The girls had joined him by now, and looking over his shoulder Sarah suggested,

'Maybe it went to some place that no longer exists, so it won't be shown.'

'That's true,' admitted Stephen, 'I think we'll have to see what Uncle Fred turns up via his Historical Society friends.'

The call to breakfast interrupted this conversation and they hurried down, as there were still some necessary items to be collected.

'We must take our binoculars,' reminded Jane. 'I want to find out what Erin meant by saying they are special.'

'We could call in and see her,' said Sarah.

'Let's do that *after* we've been to our objective and used them,' suggested Stephen.

Backpacks were gathered, plus sandwiches and drink bottles, as they raced through the kitchen, shouting, 'Goodbye, see you later!'

'Supper's at six thirty; anyone not here by then won't get it!' warned Doreen, though she knew it would fall on deaf ears.

They decided it would be best to use the road into Bidcote. The bridle path was quicker, but the chances of a puncture were greater and that was the last thing they needed right now. Traffic was light on the short stretch of main road they used and the Bidcote road was deserted. At nine twenty-five they drew up outside the entrance to the apartment. Michelle waved from an upstairs window and in a moment she was with them.

'Which way shall we go?' asked Stephen.

Once more they consulted the map. There were two possibilities; the road leading north out of the village would take them directly to the asylum in about twenty minutes. Or they could do a sort of tour by taking the westwards road, going under the railway and cycling back along the road to Tadbridge that passed the front entrance of the place.

They chose the longer route, as this would give them more exercise and a chance to explore the countryside as well.

'If we reach it around twelve we can have lunch and then explore,' said Sam.

Sarah looked at the map again. 'When we cross the Tadbridge Road we could drop in on Orchard Farm and say "Hello". If we are there around eleven it would be a good chance for a break.'

This idea was accepted and they set off, though before they left Stephen insisted on taking a photo of them 'ready to depart'. Jane took one as well so that he could be in the picture.

It was a good day for cycling, sunny, but not too hot, and they made good progress to the railway bridge. On their left was a wood that had an inviting and sign-posted 'bicycles and horses' track leading through it. As they had time to spare, they pushed their bikes in that direction. For a while it followed the railway embankment then swung southwards. This was more interesting. The trees were sporting fresh green leaves and squirrels ran up the trunks chattering angrily at them for disturbing their nut hunts ('I know I buried them somewhere round here, my dear!'). Then the track petered out in a small clearing. They sniffed; there was a strange smell in the air, a musty dampness. On closer examination it was obvious the ground was very waterlogged. They worked their way around the edge to see if the path continued, but there was no further sign of it.

'Why should anybody make a path that leads into a smelly old bog?' grumbled Michelle.

'It does seem odd,' mused Sarah. 'Ouch!' at that moment her shin encountered something hard. She had bumped into the overgrown remains of a brick wall, banging her shin against a projecting brick. The others gathered round, and searching about found a few more scattered remains. It appeared the structure had jutted out into the boggy area, for they could see its remnants out there as well.

'Who on earth would want to build a building *here* and what for?' exclaimed Sam.

'Wait a minute, wait a minute!' Stephen was struggling to get the map out of his backpack.

'Look!' He stabbed his finger on the wood and then on Bidford Farm. 'See what I mean?'

It was obvious; the tunnel could have possibly come in this direction. Indeed the smell was very similar to the one they had encountered while in it. Sarah hauled out her sketchbook and made a rough drawing of the place. Then they worked their way back to the road. This was something that would need adult assistance they decided.

The quintet cycled up to Orchard Farm. The stall was open and the owner, recognising Sam and Sarah, greeted them and their friends heartily, especially as he could sell them some of his excellent local ice cream. They sat at one of the picnic tables to enjoy it. More photos were taken. The owner strolled over for a chat, for it was early in the season and business was not very brisk. They told him where they had just come from.

'It's called Morton's Wood on the map,' remarked Stephen.

'Ha,' he replied, 'Morton was the fellow who owned it about the middle of the nineteenth century. Named every piece of property he owned after himself, he did! My father told me that in *his* father's time it had another name. Of course it was bigger then; the coming of the railway destroyed a great deal of it. It used to be known as 'Cavaliers Covert', as the owner prior to Morton kept game there. Before that it was known as 'Cavaliers Wood'.

The children looked at each other. If that was so, then the tunnel could have indeed run to it! They would tell Uncle Fred tomorrow and see what he could find out. They chatted for a little while longer, and after promising to return later in the summer, cycled back to the Tadbridge Road, heading in the direction of the asylum.

They passed the second railway bridge, and there it was. Or rather, there were the grounds, thick and tangled behind the high spike-lined brick walls. Soon the main entrance was reached, which they had not passed previously. The great wrought iron gates were closed and padlocked; but there was a small side gate by the old lodge that looked as if it would open. They tried it — yes — it yielded protestingly to pressure.

Then Michelle pointed out, on one of the pillars of the main gate, a Countryway arrow denoting a footpath through the property.

'That's why there are no 'Keep Out' signs, I suppose,' she said.

This put them at ease. At least they wouldn't be trespassing as long as they kept to the path. Unfortunately, although it went some way down the drive it veered off to the left to link up with the road to Bidcote. They paused at this point and gazed at the massive frontage of the asylum — Red Victorian Gothic at its most extravagant. Stephen fumbled in his backpack and brought out the binoculars to examine it more closely.

'Jolly good glasses!' he remarked, 'they make everything really clear. Hey, there's somebody in there. I saw a movement by a window. Up there on the third floor, towards the far right, under that pinnacle.'

'Let me see,' said Jane. She focussed the glasses on the window he indicated. 'Yes, there is somebody there! I can see them moving about. Funny, there are curtains at the window, and at some of the others.' She lowered the glasses. 'But now I can't see them.'

'Perhaps we are too far away?' suggested Sarah. At the same moment they simultaneously shouted, 'Look!' For all of them saw the window in question open, and somebody leaned out, waving their arms wildly.

'They must be in trouble,' exclaimed Michelle. 'Perhaps they wandered inside and hurt themselves or lost their way.'

'It's no good just standing here,' said Sam, 'Let's go and see.'

They started down the drive to the massive entrance.

'It looks much more dilapidated than it did through the glasses,' said Jane.

Dilapidated or not, the front doors were firmly closed, barred and bolted.

'We shall have to go round the place and see if there's another way in,' said Stephen.

They set off round the outside working anticlockwise.

There was no other entrance along the front or down the side, but as they reached the rear an unlatched ground floor window swung idly in the breeze.

'That must be how the person got in,' said Sarah. Stephen was boosted up first and with his help they were soon inside.

The room they found themselves in had been a storage room for cleaning equipment. There was a large old-fashioned deep sink in one corner, a broom cupboard and another one, which had probably held cleaning items like polish, dusters and such. The place was very dusty and originally had been painted a tasteful shade of battleship grey. They cautiously opened the door and peered out. It led to a long passage extending in both directions with numerous doors off on either side.

'What now?' asked Jane.

'We must search for the stairs,' replied Stephen.

'This passage must run across the building,' said Sam, who had been trying to work out the geography of the place. 'So we must find one at right angles to it. On the right if we go left.'

'Or on the left if we go right?' added his sister.

'Stop being so confusing,' begged Michelle, 'or I think I'll have to walk on the ceiling!'

However, they turned left and after a few minutes reached another passage on the same side that led to some imposing double doors.

'I bet that goes through to the entrance hall,' said Sam, 'come on.' They hurried on and sure enough it did. This looked even more desolate in its state of unkemptness. Dust and grime were everywhere. Some of the banisters were missing; plaster from the ornate ceiling had fallen here and there. But the wide stairway, a magnificent marvel of elaborately carved oak, still managed to preserve an air of faded grandeur about itself. The stairs were firm and did not creak as they climbed up to the first floor. From the landing another flight, not quite so fine, led to the second floor. Before going up them they went a short distance down a passage. Off this on either side were small rooms with barred windows.

'It's like a prison,' remarked Jane.

'That's how most of the so-called insane were kept,' informed Sam, 'locked up, or in padded cells and straightjackets.'

They shuddered, for the place still retained an atmosphere of gloom and hopelessness.

'Let's get on and find that person, then get out of here, it's giving me the creeps!' muttered Michelle.

'You're not the only one,' retorted Sam.

So it was up the next flight of stairs. A window looking out over the drive helped them to orientate themselves and they set off to the left. As they passed another window, the sun, which had been behind a cloud, broke forth and shone brilliantly; blinding them for a second. When they could see again, all was different. The passage had highly polished linoleum on it. The grey walls gleamed dully, as if they were freshly painted. There were noises, too. People talking, strange sounds — sobbing, laughing, jabbering, howling — coming from the rooms they passed. Then the passage reached a 'T' junction, and as they were debating which way to go, they heard footsteps approaching. A door stood ajar at the corner.

'Quick, in there!' mouthed Jane. It was a large broom cupboard. They pulled the door until it was almost shut. The footsteps stopped at the passage junction. There were two people.

'I thank you, indeed, Doctor for being so accommodating. I'm much obliged to you. I hope the 'fee' is adequate? Of course monthly payments will be made for her upkeep, but she's an old woman and not in the best of health, eh!' There was an evil chuckle.

'If she should die within a year or so, she will have been

forgotten by those who knew her in the village. You have a graveyard for paupers and I believe many of the occupants are nameless. Of course, as the only mourner, I shall see to it that you and the institution receive suitable recompense for your assistance in dealing discreetly with such a sensitive matter.'

'You are indeed generous, Mr Isador Brockfield; I shall do all I can to carry out your wishes within a reasonable time. Meanwhile, she will make an interesting case study. Suffering from hallucinations and delusions. No more charms and plaques for superstitious villagers!'

The voices and footsteps died away. After waiting for a few moments the children emerged from their hiding place.

'So *that's* what happened to her!' exclaimed Sam.

'Of all the mean, evil and cruel things to do!' cried Sarah.

'No wonder she wants revenge,' said Michelle grimly.

'So you could be locked away as "insane" if somebody wanted to get rid of you?' asked Jane.

'Yes, especially if your persecutor had money and influence. Doctors working in places like this probably weren't well paid; so if an opportunity came along to earn a little extra money, you didn't ask too many questions,' explained Stephen.

'What shall we do now?' asked Sam.

'Find her and try to talk with her, of course,' retorted Sarah.

'But she's locked away!'

Michelle dived back into the store cupboard and came out holding a large bunch of keys. 'I noticed these when we hid,' she said, 'I think they fit the cell doors so the staff can clean them when the inmates are taken out for treatment — ugh! — or exercise.'

'Good, let's start searching,' and Sam strode off along the passage, which they hoped would lead to the cell in question. It came to an abrupt end with a barred door facing them. By standing on tiptoe, Michelle could just peep through the grille.

'This is it!' she called excitedly. 'There's an old woman sitting all huddled up in a corner.'

'Call to her,' suggested Sarah.

'Er, madam, lady, good dame?' How to address her was a problem, for the old woman took no notice.

'Let me try,' said Stephen. He peered in, then said very softly and clearly, 'Plaques.'

The result was startling. She looked up, leapt to her feet and rushed over, pressing her face against the grille.

'What do you mean, boy, has it been found, has it? Tell me!'

'Yes, in a rock pool near Lyme.'

'Where is it, where is it?'

'We've got it at our home, our house guardian Bob Binnacle is keeping an eye on it.'

'Bring it here, you *must* bring it here!'

'But we can't, you see we are from over a hundred years hence.'

'It's as I feared! It has become too powerful; it wants its own way. Boy, you must… '

But at that moment they heard footsteps coming down the passage and a rough voice broke in. 'Ho there, what are you doing, you young varmints? This section is forbidden to visitors. Wait until I lay my hands on you, you'll be sorry for this.' They were trapped — it was a dead end, there was no escape!

But from the other side of the door the old woman's voice rose shrill and vengeful.

'Leave them alone, you evil wretch. May the plaque-curse that destroyed Captain Absolom Brockfield destroy you too, Doctor Ignatus Proctor! May you die disgraced and in poverty! May its power annihilate all who would do away with poor old Grace Goodridge. May it…!'

The doctor let out a roar of rage, which diverted him from the children for a moment; pushing Stephen aside he thrust his purpling face to the grille. 'Be silent, you old hag. You can do nothing, nothing, I tell you. You are in my power!'

This was greeted by a shrill laugh and she spat in his face. The doctor reeled back, wiping the spittle from it.

'Power, power, you don't know what power is! I have more power in one hair of my head than you have in your gross body. I have links to the Ancient Ones! Those who cross them and their servants meet a terrible end and suffer even more after death. Beware, you are warned!'

Suddenly she spoke in a perfectly normal voice. 'Why are you children still standing there? Run, run to the sunlight.'

This jerked them out of the paralysis that had seized them. For when the doctor had forced his way to the grille it meant they were now *behind* him. Sam gave the doctor a hefty push, which sent him cannoning into the door, and they fled back down the passage.

'To the front, where the windows are,' shouted Jane.

They ran into the wide corridor leading to the stairs. Coming up these were a motley crew of so-called attendants; the children had never seen such a villainous looking bunch. But the sunlight was streaming through the windows; in a flash they were bathed in it and temporarily blinded.

When they could see again the corridor was empty, deserted, dusty and forlorn. The echo of a wild shriek died away in their ears. They stood for a moment, hearts beating wildly. Then they made their way to the ground floor and to the window by which they had entered. In a few minutes they were on the grass and running down the drive to where they had left their bikes.

'What do we do now?' asked Sarah.

'Have lunch,' retorted her brother.

'Let's follow this path and find a spot where we don't have to look at *that* place,' said Jane.

Luckily the track led through the trees and then ran alongside the road for quite a way before reaching a gate that gave access to the road. They found a pleasant spot amidst the undergrowth where they could sit in reasonable comfort. The bikes were propped against a nearby tree, and they settled down to eat and talk about what they had just witnessed.

'We can tell Bill what happened to Grace Goodridge, anyway,' said Sam.

'True, but it doesn't help us to know what to do with the plaque, or how to handle it,' said Stephen. 'From what Grace was yelling and screaming about, it's got some pretty nasty powers. Especially that part about it no longer being under her control.' He looked at his sister. 'Do you still feel happy with such a thing in our house?'

'No,' she replied. 'I'm afraid it will harm Bob, or anyone else who touches it by accident.'

'But where *will* it be safe?' asked Michelle. That was indeed a problem.

'It's like the brooch; it attached itself to us and we had to get it back to the Hill Folk. This thing wants us to help it, but somehow I don't think it wants to be reunited with its creator. There's something else tied up in all this, but for the moment we don't know what,' added Sarah.

They sat silently for a while, absent-mindedly consuming sandwiches and trying to work out what would be best to do.

Sam looked at his watch, 'It's half past two, so what…?'

Jane interrupted him. 'I know! Let's go and do what we said we might do when we set off—visit Erin. We've lots more to tell her now, and I'm sure she'll be able to help us. If it hadn't been for those binoculars, we would never have found out about Grace.'

The idea of talking with their old friend cheered them up and a short while later they left the asylum grounds and set off down the road for Bidcote, through the village and on to Croft Corner Cottage. As they propped their bikes up inside the gate, Sarah said, 'Do you think she'll mind us calling in like this, all unexpected?'

'Let's find out,' said Sam and he knocked on the front door, not too loudly. In a trice it opened and Erin stood there smiling a welcome at them. 'Come in, come in,' she said, 'I was expecting you any time now.'

By the hearth a tray with tea and cakes stood ready; Rosie was curled up on the rug. The chairs were arranged in a semi-circle. Erin motioned to them to sit down and took her place by the teapot.

'Not a word until you've had a bite to eat and a mite to drink,' she told them.

Being obedient children (some of the time) they did as they were told.

After a while Sam asked, 'How did you know we were coming?' She pointed a foot at the rabbit curled up on the rug.

'Oh, of course,' said Sam, 'Rosie told you!'

'Rosie informed me you were coming because you have a problem and some questions to ask. So tell me all about it.'

They did, tracing the story from the finding of the plaque to today's events. Erin listened intently and when they related Sir Brian's story, placed Rosie on her lap, so she could listen as well. When they were finished there was a long pause. Then she spoke.

'I must say you children seem to land in the most unlikely situations. This one is particularly complex. We have a frustrated Grey-One, her spirit form chained to an unmarked grave in the asylum grounds, and we have a plaque-charm that was made in good faith and then distorted to take revenge on the perfidy of the greedy ship-owning merchant. This seems to have given it a far greater power for harm than was intended. Evil begets evil, just as good begets good. The problem is we don't know what it intends to do and why you are involved. I agree that your home, Stephen and Jane, is not an ideal place for such an object. It could cause trouble, not only for Bob, but for all of you.'

She continued, 'The question is, where would be a safe place for it? I suggest you consult with Sir Brian; I shall see if I can find out anything as well. But we must act quickly to counter any possible harm. Finding out, "why you?" may take somewhat longer.'

She spoke so calmly, and her common sense manner made them feel more at ease.

'Now to more serious matters,' she said with a twinkle in her eye, 'More tea and cake?'

The conversation became lighter as they told her about the coming big event, the class camp. Jane asked if she could take a picture of Rosie and her mistress. It ended up being a real photo session. Rosie solo, Rosie and Erin, Rosie, Erin and the children individually and in a group.

Around five o'clock they said goodbye and parted company by the boundary stone. Michelle cycled back to Bidcote, while the others returned to the manor along the bridle path. By the time they were cleaned up, ('Clean up? But why, we're not really dirty.' 'Go and look in the mirror.' 'Oh!') had eaten, and gathered Stephen and Jane's stuff together, John had arrived. So there was no time to consult with Sir Brian. The Randell's bikes would remain at the manor for now 'for future use'. They decided tomorrow they would ask Uncle Fred for his help and advice. It was a pity they did not talk to Sir Brian that evening, for this omission had far-reaching consequences later.

CHAPTER TWENTY-EIGHT

How they managed to catch the school bus was a wonder, for everything seemed to go in slow motion next morning, except the clock, which went at twice its usual speed. Stephen and Jane reported the same phenomena. They reached the classroom just as the first bell went, and Mr Atkinson wasn't there as the Principal had waylaid him over an administrative matter and *he* only just made it a few seconds before the second bell. Several people were late. Not late, late, but late enough to disturb the morning verse and exercises. So it was a scrappy beginning. There was now the business of checking the final arrangements for the camp. There were still a few 'wants' lists missing and their teacher grew very emphatic about this.

'If one or two people cannot, or will not make the effort to prepare a list, or nag their parents into returning permission forms and the deposit on time, not only do they put their chances of going in jeopardy, but that of the whole camp. They also make it less likely that the organisers will have the enthusiasm to undertake such a project next year.' Pretty strong stuff!

Then in a softer tone: 'I've told you *all* that if there are any problems you should tell me so that if necessary I can contact your parents to discuss them. Now, notebooks out; we've a challenge, three week's work crammed into two. Or you'll be packing your school books as well!'

At break time they blocked his 'coffee run'.

'Please, can we talk with you, it's ever so urgent.'

'Let me get my coffee, you tyrants, and I'll join you on the playing field.'

Which he did, in two minutes flat. Stephen handed him a photo of the plaque and explained what they wished to know. Then the further history of its creator and her fate *plus* the possible consequences were outlined.

'I'll see what I can find out,' he promised, 'but the most important thing is for you to get hold of Sir Brian *as soon as possible;* it's imperative this device is put out of harm's way.'

'We'll talk with him as soon as we get home,' promised Sam and Sarah.

The remainder of the day passed uneventfully, though at the end of the final lesson he reminded everybody again to check and double check their camping gear.

'It's no good remembering your camera and forgetting your swimming towel, you can't dry yourself on a camera!' he told them.

As soon as the twins were indoors — well, after snack — they went up to the attics and hopefully rapped on the wall in the vicinity of the brass-handled door, which promptly appeared and was opened by JJ.

'Pray enter,' he intoned, 'Sir Brian is at home.'

From the puffing and grunting going on at the desk it was apparent that he was struggling with some profound problem. They approached with due caution and respect so as not to disturb him. The desk's top was littered with scraps of paper covered with abstruse calculations mixed up, or in, with several pieces of bread and a jar of jam, which added to the clutter. However, the latter had tipped over and the lid had come off. A small lava flow of blackcurrant jam was meandering slowly across the desk and papers to gradually drip into the wide sleeve of Sir Brian's robe.

'Got it!' he suddenly shouted. 'JJ, in future cut the bread to a quarter inch or six millimeters thickness; spread a sixteenth of an inch or one millimeter of butter and two eighths or three millimeters of jam on it. The perfect sandwich!'

He thumped the desk, which was unfortunate, as the jam jar rolled down its surface and into his sleeve where it emptied the remainder of its contents. It took a good five minutes to sort things out; but once he was re-robed and seated again he turned his attention to the children. Quickly they explained the reason for their visit and the point that both Erin and Fred had stressed, the need to do something quickly to restrain the plaque's negative influence.

'Hum, yes, awkward what? Thought when I saw it on my visit to Bob there was more in it than met the eye. Nasty business when a benevolent charm is transformed into a malevolent one. Risky, one should first cancel the former. Mixing the two often causes unexpected results. From what you've just told me, it looks as if the curse fed off the charm and absorbed its energies. It's like a witch hiding herself in the guise of a beautiful woman. The plaque looks harmless enough… …but!'

'Have you any suggestions?' asked Sam.

'Been thinking, found in water wasn't it?'

'Yes, in a rock pool covered with sand.'

'So if we can find similar conditions it should restrain its energies — at least for a while. It's worth a try.' The old fellow was on the ball! His eyes sparkled and his voice grew firm and decisive.

'Yes, but *where* and *how*?' inquired Sarah.

'Tell me more about your tunnel experiences and the possible exit you found in the woods,' he requested.

They gave him as much detail as they could remember. He considered this. 'You say the object is in a tin box now under Bob's care. Sensible fellow, Bob; knows that the "tin" of an old box is usually made of tin-plated iron! As you know, iron is something most of these beings can't stand. I suggest it remains shut in the box and is placed in that tunnel. There it will be safe, giving us time to find out how to deal with this problem, and the restless spirit of its creator.'

'So you believe it should be brought over *this* weekend and hidden in the tunnel?' said Sam who liked to have things nice and clear.

'Yes, I know it should be done quickly, but as it's confined in the tin, I don't think a few days will make much difference. Tell Stephen and Jane and arrange for them to bring it here on Saturday. It will be necessary to have at least one grown-up to help, as I believe Harry has boarded up the tunnel's entrance. I shall be there and so will Bill. Gather the others who have also been involved. Michelle, Shirley and little Jill. It would be good to ask Erin if she can be there. The more positive power we can muster, the better.'

Then, as usual, he turned back to his desk and started muttering about sandwich thicknesses again.

'Thank you, Sir Brian,' they chorused and left.

'That seems pretty straightforward,' remarked Sam. 'You ring Jane and then I'll ring Harry. We'll check with Mum about them staying overnight. We can tell Michelle and Shirley tomorrow. Maybe we should invite Uncle Fred as well.'

It may have *appeared* straightforward, but it was far from so! At every turn they met problems. Jane and Stephen were unable to come *at all* that weekend as it was their Great Aunt Agatha's ninetieth birthday and there was to be a great family gathering at her home in Blandford Forum. They would be staying overnight, places having been booked for long-distance guests in a local hotel. Derek had an appointment in Taunton that day. Harry was attending an all day farmers' conference in Chard and Fred had a teachers' workshop kindly booked for him (without his prior knowledge) by the Principal. Michelle was spending the weekend with her grandmother and the Fisher family was also visiting relatives!

Sam and Sarah were appalled; what could they do? The grown-ups were deaf to their pleas and the business of moving the plaque was dismissed as being relatively unimportant.

However, there was one exception: Erin. 'But I am not in a position to influence your, or anyone else's parents!' she told the twins firmly. 'All we can do is take the opportunity if it occurs.' Both sets of twins had the feeling that some force was actively trying to block and thwart their plans.

It was intangible, but nevertheless there and malevolent. It penetrated their dreams with a sensation of vague fear. They had similar dreams, where they stood before a partially open door leading into a well-lit room, but they *knew* something lurked behind the door, waiting for them and they dared not enter in spite of a gentle voice calling, 'Do come in, my dear child!'

At big break on Thursday the sextet gathered in the shade of the trees bordering the playing field to discuss the situation.

'What *are* we going to do?' asked Stephen. 'If we don't do something to curb the plaque's influence, anything could happen!'

'I think it's already been left far too long,' added Sam.

'Yes, I'm sure it's gaining strength, just as it tried to gain energy from us, and I feel it's found another way to do it,' said Jane.

Michelle looked at Sam and Sarah. 'If you two are the only ones here this Saturday then *you* will have to do it!'

'But how can they if the tin containing the plaque is still at Southleigh?' asked Shirley.

It was indeed a problem—how to get it to Bidford Manor? Not only that, how to move it safely and who could help them?

At last Sam spoke up, 'There's only one person I can think

of who may be able to do it—Erin.'

'Why Erin?' asked Sarah.

'Because she has a broomstick.'

'You mean...?'

'Yes, if she could fly over tomorrow night and either you or Bob give her the box. She could bring it to us, or Sir Brian. It could always be put in the old boiler house. We don't actually have to have it inside.'

'But what about Saturday, how do we do it? Especially as Harry has boarded up the tunnel.'

'We'll just have to take a crowbar, a hammer and some nails, undo it and board it up again as best we can.' He brightened up, 'I know you lot can't be there, but at least Jill can.'

'Jill? But...'

'Remember Erin said she should be; I'll take responsibility for her. In fact if we could enter from the barn it would be better, there's not so much passage. I reckon the quicker it's done, the better, before the thing realises what we are up to.'

As there seemed to be no other way, this scheme was adopted.

'Just keep us in your thoughts,' begged Sarah. Their companions solemnly promised to do so.

When the twins arrived home they found Bess waiting for Jill. 'Can we come down to the farm on Saturday?' they asked. 'Of course, any time you want,' she told them. 'You don't even have to ask, just come. Jill will be delighted.' She already was!

'I have to take Brian for another dental visit in the morning. She'll be far happier with you.'

After she'd left they asked if they could cycle down to Erin's. 'Fine, as long as you have no homework and are back in time for supper.'

Off they went. 'I feel a bit rotten taking advantage of Bess like that,' said Sam.

'I know, but what else could we do?' replied Sarah.

Erin was waiting for them; Rosie had forewarned her. Quickly, Sam explained the plan.

'It's bold and drastic,' she said. 'Full of hazards, but I too see no other way. I am willing to get the box and bring it over. But I have a better idea as to where to leave it. I shall take it directly to the barn. Tell Jill to warn Edwin. I think he can help us in this matter more than Sir Brian, as he has first-hand knowledge of the tunnels. As you say, it means a shorter distance to carry it. The less we handle it, even in the box, the better!'

They returned home feeling that things were improving—for a change. In a way, Doreen confirmed this.

'If you are going to be at the farm on Saturday I shall go with your father to Taunton,' she said, 'We shall be back late afternoon.'

That evening they called Bill and explained the revised plan. He was dubious, but as there were no other possibilities, he agreed.

'Sir Brian and I will be there on Saturday morning,' he said. 'We'll come down the passage from the old hunting lodge, just as a precaution. I wish there was an adult with you, but your determination to carry out this task convinces me that it will work.'

The next morning Sam spoke to Jill when she was dropped off. He told her what was planned. Her eyes sparkled with excitement. 'Bindle can come too,' she exclaimed.

'She's right,' thought Sam, 'and Binky!' He asked her to tell Edwin that they would also need his help and she promised to do so.

The others were relieved when they heard Erin would help and Jane undertook to tell Bob to be ready with the box for her to collect. All that could be done now was to hope everything would go according to plan.

Before they went to bed that night the twins prepared

a backpack with torches, a rope, crowbar, hammer and a small bag of nails.

As soon as darkness fell, Erin wrapped herself up warmly and took her trusty broom outside. It was a cool, clear night with a sickle moon. 'I'm getting too old for this kind of night-flying stuff,' she muttered as she took off and headed for Southleigh. She was concerned about her ability to carry out her task and anxious for the children. There were so many risks and uncertainties involved. In fact she was so busy thinking about all this she nearly overshot her destination. Carefully she circled the house, noticing that the right-hand attic room in the front had a lighted candle in its window. She edged as near as she could, hovered and peered in. Ah, there was Bob. He came over to the window and opened it. In his hands he held a square, old-fashioned cake tin.

'Here,' he said. 'Be careful, good luck!'

She grasped it and tucked it under her arm and swung her broomstick towards the farm. So far, so good!

However, after a few minutes there was a violent jerk from the box that nearly unseated her. The plaque was throwing itself against the sides, bottom and lid of the tin. Clank, clank. It was trying to escape! Each time it struck the tin she had the greatest difficulty in controlling her flight. At the same time, a strange lassitude began to steal over her. Her eyes grew heavy and her head kept on nodding forward. But her mind remained alert, telling her that this thing was trying to work its power on her.

'Faster,' she whispered to the broom. It quickly responded and the ground flew under her feet. At last Bidford Manor came into view; she flashed over it and began to descend towards the barn. The thing struggled even harder. Clank, clank, clunk; her side and arm felt quite bruised and sore from the constant battering. Swooping over the roof of the barn, she spotted Edwin standing in the great doorway. She motioned to him to stand in the yard. He guessed her intention and did so, holding out his arms. She hovered briefly over him and allowed the tin to drop from under her arm. To her delight he deftly caught it, quickly wrapping something round the box. She waved and set course for home. On arrival she made herself some remedial tea, then went and soaked her bruised side and arm in a good steaming hot bath containing soothing, healing herbs.

Edwin had wrapped a strip of stout linen round the tin, then hurried into the barn. By the secret passage entrance he had discovered a hiding place in the wall. An odd shape block of stone merely fitted, it was not cemented in. Behind lay a small recess. No doubt it had been used for secret messages and the like. Carefully pulling out the stone, he thrust the box inside. Before replacing the stone, he placed a short bar of iron on the tin's lid. A shuddering sigh echoed through the barn. 'That should keep you quiet,' he muttered as he pushed the stone back, then returned to the house.

He went to the children's bedroom. Jill was still awake, her big eyes peeping out from under the bedclothes. As soon as he entered she sat up tousle-haired. Sam had told her what was going to happen.

'Did Erin bring it?' she whispered.

'Yes, it's safe in the secret hiding place I told you about. Tomorrow, when the twins come, we shall take it out and do what has to be done.'

'Good,' she said and settled down under the sheets. 'Good night, Edwin.'

He ruffled her hair, 'Good night, little maid,' and vanished. But he did not go to his usual niche. Instead, he returned to the yard and took up a position on the barn roof. From here he could look across and beyond Bidcote to the grounds of the asylum.

He sensed something was stirring there, rising, wavering, seeking. Faintly on the night air a sound reached him.

A cry of anguish, of unfulfilled ambitions, of desolation and despair. The call of a lost soul, which knew no peace. Edwin tensed; it was coming nearer. It had felt the power of the plaque. Tomorrow they would have to deal with not one malignant energy, but two.

In Bidford Manor the twins slept uneasily. Though their dreams were vague, they were still full of uncertainty. At Southleigh it was the same for Stephen and Jane. Strange cloud forms floated in the skies above both houses, taking on shifting and fantastic shapes. Bob noticed them, as did Edwin from his place on the barn roof.

In the manor itself Bill was talking with Sir Brian as they tried to work out the best procedure for the morning. Sir Brian was all for taking one of his 'infallible' devices, including a catapult machine that would fire the tin into the tunnel.

'Fine,' remarked Bill, 'but as the machine requires three men to work it and is wider and higher than the passage to the tunnel, I don't think it can be of much help. Now what would be useful, in fact *very* useful, would be something that could remove all the nails and bolts that Harry has used to secure boards over the entrance. It would be even more useful if it could put them back when we have finished. But it would have to be small, light and portable.'

'Ho, you don't think I can do it, do you?' snorted the inventor, 'I'll show you. Simple, all we need is an attractor and a detractor. No, I mean repellent! Um—oh you know what I mean, something that does the opposite. I'll go and see what I can do right now,' and he disappeared into his study, from which strange clattering and banging noises were soon heard. Down below, Derek half woke up. 'I must fix those loose windows in the attics,' he murmured and went back to sleep.

Later, Bill, patrolling round, also heard the distant cries and guessed their import. 'I'm not looking forward to tomorrow,' he confessed to himself. 'I just hope the children's courage and determination are more than a match for what they have to face!'

After her bath, Erin sat up in bed with Rosie curled up beside her. 'I think, Rosie, Sir Brian is right; we shall definitely attend tomorrow. We'll be up early and do some investigating in the fields first, just to keep an eye on things above ground as well. Yes, I'm sure we'll be needed.'

CHAPTER TWENTY-NINE

The following morning most of those who would be involved in today's drama woke early. Erin and Rosie were up at dawn, for her main concern was Grace Goodridge, or rather the spirit of Grace Goodridge. What was she after and — most importantly — what state or mood was she in? Could she manage to speak with her? It would be a risk, but one well worth taking.

Bill was also up at dawn. JJ let him into the master's study. Loud snores came from the desk where the great inventor was sprawled, his head resting on a heap of bits of metal, screws, nails, bent pins, glue and various other pieces of inventing stuff. However, by his out flung arm stood a brass cylinder, about a foot long, with a nozzle at one end. From its side projected a lever that ran in a groove. Below this was a switch.

'Is that *it*?' Bill quietly asked JJ.

'Yes!' he replied, adding awesomely, 'It works, it actually works! He took all the screws out of that cupboard early this morning so it fell apart, then reversed it.' Bill stared at the cupboard; it looked fine.

At that moment Sir Brian awoke, yawned and sat up. 'Breakfast?' he said hopefully and JJ set about preparing it for him.

Seeing Bill he indicated the machine, saying: 'Told you

I could do it!'

'Yes,' Bill agreed, 'great!'

'When do we start?'

'As soon as the children walk down to the farm. I'll go and warn them now.'

The twins were just getting up when Bill popped in. 'Sir Brian and I will meet you at the passage junction. He has invented a device that will enable us to remove and replace the boarding without damage to it.' Seeing the incredulous looks on their faces he hastened to add, 'It *really* works.'

'I still think we'd still better take the tools I packed,' said Sam.

'I agree,' replied Bill, 'after all, you never know, they may come in handy. Also bring an empty bag; it may be needed for the tin. See you later.'

They went down to breakfast and told Binky he was coming with them to the farm. After the usual tidying up was done they gathered the backpack, a spare bag and Binky's lead. Derek and Doreen were just about to leave.

Derek gave them a spare key 'Just in case you come back before us,' adding laughingly, 'Whatever have you got in your backpack? It sounds as if it's full of old iron!' The children giggled nervously, 'Er, well, sort of,' replied Sarah. But their parents wanted to be off, so no further questions were asked — much to their relief. They waved goodbye and then set off along the lane towards the farm.

Jill had also wakened early; for a while she lay there thinking. Today her Sam would be coming and they were going to do a terribly important thing. Like the time before when in subduing the Primal Power she had special movements to make. She wondered what she would have to do this time? She was sure there would be something.

Then Edwin was sitting on her bed. 'Little maid, I must tell you there is one who badly wants what we are going to store for safety in the tunnel. She may try to stop us.

Should she appear—and I believe she will—speak to her. Say whatever comes into your mind. She will listen to you. Do you understand?'

'Is that the special sort of thing I have to do?' she asked.

'Yes, I suppose it is,' he replied. 'Make sure Bindle goes with you; the others will be bringing their little white dog too.'

He left saying, 'I shall join you when they arrive and we are ready to perform our task.'

When he had gone Jill woke Brian up and dressed him, then herself. They went down to the kitchen for breakfast. Her father was just leaving. 'Have fun with your friends, Mousie!' he called as he went out the door.

'Brian and I will leave as soon as the twins arrive,' Bess told her. 'Be sure to be a good girl and do as Sam tells you. I know you will,' she added hastily, seeing the look of outrage on her daughter's face. As if she would not do what Sam told her!

'There's some cake and cookies in those tins on the table, and of course they must stay for lunch.' With that she went to get Brian and herself ready, as they would be walking to the village. Jill put on her outdoor shoes and went to the yard gate to await Sam and Sarah's arrival.

As they walked to the farm, Sam remarked, 'Sir Brian's invention sounds great; I only hope it *does* work in the way Bill says. You never know how his devices are going to turn out.'

'Even if it only works once it will help,' said Sarah, 'and if it's a real success he could patent it and make lots of money.'

'But what could he do with it? In his state he doesn't need or use the stuff. Oh, there's Jill by the gate. We'd better hurry, I expect Bess wants to leave.'

They hastened on; Jill had already run into the kitchen to tell her mother they were here. After a quick exchange of greetings Bess and Brian left.

'Edwin says we are to meet him in the barn when you are ready,' Jill told them.

'Just better check we have everything we need,' and Sam rummaged around in his backpack. 'Jill, have you got your torch?'

She nodded and from her little shoulder bag she produced it and two spare batteries. Sam rechecked theirs and they set out across the yard for the looming bulk of the barn.

Bindle joined them as they did so and gave Binky a warm welcome, which was enthusiastically reciprocated.

As soon as he saw the twins leave Bill went and called Sir Brian, who thanks to JJ's administrations was up and ready, clutching his new invention in one hand and a string bag in the other, from which various objects protruded.

'Just in case, you know,' he remarked, airily. He did not say in case of what. 'Then let's be off,' said Bill and they hurried down the drive to the old hunting lodge ruin.

JJ, tidying up after his master had left, was startled to hear a crash and clatter of wood. Upon investigating he found the cupboard, on which his master had experimented, had fallen apart; all the screws and nails had come out of their own accord.

～

Edwin was waiting for them in the doorway. 'I wish that our first meeting could have been under different circumstances,' he told the twins. 'But I am *very* glad to meet you and shall do all I can to assist in this task. The tin lies behind that stone in the wall by the entrance. Let us not waste time. You have a bag? Good. I shall drop it in and I suggest you carry it on the end of a stick, so we touch it as little as possible.'

'I'll get one of Daddy's walking sticks, you can hook the bag handles round it,' said Jill and raced off; she was soon back.

Binky and Bindle had been getting more and more excited

as they prepared, though the old dog stayed close to Jill. Edwin now removed the stone and eased the tin out, dropping it into the bag, which Sam held open. Sarah thrust the curved end of the stick through the loops so she could now carry it over her shoulder, well away from her body. Jill pulled the bolt and the passage entrance appeared. Sam switched on his torch, took a firm grip of Binky's lead and started down the steps. Sarah followed him, then Jill with her hand on Bindle's collar, and Edwin brought up the rear. As they entered the passage he pulled the door to, but did not close it. The barn was now empty apart from the rustling of a mouse in the hayloft.

☙

Erin also set off early with Rosie in her basket. However, she did not take her broomstick. Her objective was the boundary stone and to remain there for a while to see if Grace came that way, though she had no idea how she was going to handle matters if she did.

Bill and Sir Brian entered the passage by the hunting lodge ruins and started towards the junction. Sir Brain was very uneasy and confessed to his companion he didn't mind the dark 'outside' but in a passage he found it very claustrophobic.

'But you don't need a light to see your way,' argued Bill.

'I know, but once, owing to a slight disagreement with one of Good Queen Bess's advisors I spent a few very uncomfortable days in one of the Tower's dungeons. It affected my psyche.'

'Your *what?*'

'Soul, or something like that. I heard a chap use the word once and rather liked the sound of it.'

'Well, if your psyche doesn't get going at a good pace down this passage now, lots of other psyches are going to be upset!' retorted Bill and he set off at a good speed with Sir Brian stumbling along behind him, muttering away as usual.

※

The children made slow but steady progress towards the junction. The two dogs trotted happily along and the atmosphere was calm. Suddenly Sarah nearly fell over. The bag on the end of the stick had swung savagely, causing her to almost lose her balance. It continued to do so as she tried to walk on.

'It has sensed what we intend to do with it,' said Edwin. 'Give me the stick for a moment.' He took from his pocket the small iron bar he had placed upon the tin and dropped it into the bag. There was a 'clang' as it struck it. The movement ceased. 'It will still swing, but you should be able to handle it,' he said.

They plodded on. But whether the iron had slipped down to the bottom of the bag or whether the plaque's malignant power was increasing as they neared the junction, they did not know. Again and again it threatened to throw Sarah down. They halted, uncertain what to do.

Then Jill spoke up. 'I know, give it to Bindle. He'll carry it, won't you boy?'

Sarah lowered the stick and as the bag slid off Bindle seized it between his jaws. He let out a menacing low growl and the bag hung inert as he trotted along beside his little mistress once more. The junction came into view and as they reached it two figures approached from the other passage, Bill and Sir Brian.

The look of relief on the latter's face was comic. 'Light! light!' he exclaimed, 'Now my psyche will be happy.'

Bill was more businesslike. 'Now we are together and Sir Brian has his invention here, let's get going. I don't like the atmosphere of this place.'

Indeed they were all beginning to notice that a less than subtle change was occurring. The place began to grow hot and oppressive. A dank odour began to issue from behind the boarded up tunnel and strange vibrations of air swirled round them. Bindle dropped the bag and sat by it, growling softly. Binky strained at his lead to sit by him and was making his own little rumbling noises in his throat.

'Move back, please!' announced the inventor and he stepped forward, pointing the nozzle of the cylinder towards the boarded up tunnel. Being Sir Brian he could not, even under these circumstances, resist giving a lecture.

'This device of which I am the sole inventor, uses the magnetic properties of metal. Like a magnifying glass it focusses these magnetic properties and thus draws iron and the like to it. By reversing this process they are driven back into the wood they were drawn out of. Now, I set the power I require, 'full' in this case, then move the lever to 'on,' and he prepared to do so.

☙

Erin noticed a sudden chill in the air as she waited by the stone. Rosie popped her head out of the basket, sniffed a couple of times then snuggled down under her cover.

Her mistress looked to the north. From some point beyond the village a black cloud was boiling up, rising ever higher in the sky. It resembled a small whirlwind. Already strong gusts of wind were sweeping leaves and debris through the air. The cloud spread rapidly southwards and at the same time the sun vanished behind a great bank of threatening storm clouds. The whole sky grew dark. The wind was now whistling and howling through the tress. She realised she was in an exposed position. A large dead tree branch came hurtling past her, tossed through the air like a piece of matchwood.

'The ditch,' she said to herself and climbing over the stile, dropped into it. Luckily it was dry and gave good cover. The sky continued to darken as the whirling cloud swept overhead. The noise of the wind rose to new heights and mingled with it she could hear other sounds. Voices crying, wailing, sobbing—or was it only the wind? Then in the semi-light something darkened the place where she lay. She sensed a presence looming over her and looked up. Against the shifting, purpling cloud wrack hovered an unearthly figure. Tall and attenuated it swayed to and fro emitting a strange greenish glow. She saw it was that of an old woman, wild-eyed, with long unkempt hair, arms raised as if in triumph over her. A voice, whether real—or within her head—sounded.

'You thought you could stop me. No one or thing can stop me. You with your puny magic! I *shall* regain what is mine and take the revenge that is my due before I rest. All who stand in my way shall be swept aside. Oppose me at your peril!'

Then the spectre was gone, carried away by the wind. The sky cleared and the sun came out. Erin scrambled out of the ditch and was just in time to see the strange cloud funnel itself and disappear into the ground somewhere between the manor and the farm. 'Come on, Rosie, we have work to do,' she said and set off across the fields towards the farm.

☙

'Before you let that thing off we must be ready to put the tin within the tunnel,' warned Edwin. 'Place the bag with its opening facing the tunnel entrance, and Sam, take the stick. As soon as the boards are down, hook the tin out. Did you say you had some heavy gloves with you?'

'Yes, in our backpack.' He opened it and took out a heavy pair of padded workman's gloves, which he'd picked up at the last moment, thinking they might be useful.

'Excellent. Put them on, and be ready to hurl the tin into the passage. Then Sir Brian, put your machine into reverse as quickly as possible.'

'I know what to do,' said the old warrior testily, 'you don't have to tell me. Stand well back, all of you,' he added.

The children and dogs drew back. Bill and Edwin stood behind Sir Brian. The cylinder was pointed and its inventor set the lever and pulled the switch. A loud hum filled the air briefly, followed by a series of pinging noises as the nails left their holes and the boards fell in a heap at the foot of the tunnel.

Sam was just about to step forwards when a strange rushing sound was heard coming down the passage from the manor. An icy blast of air struck them as it streamed forth making a mournful wailing sound that froze the soul. They stood transfixed. In the passage mouth appeared the apparition Erin had seen. Sam and Sarah recognised her at once — it was Grace, or rather, her restless spirit.

'So you *do* have it,' she crowed. 'It's mine. I made it, I blessed it, I cursed it, and now through that power all those and their descendants who have wronged me shall suffer!'

Long skinny hands reached out. 'You, boy, *give it to me!*' These words were spoken slowly with great emphasis to Sam, who slowly began to bend down towards the open mouth of the bag. The others remained seemingly paralysed, except Jill. Remembering what Edwin had told her, she stepped forward. How dare this strange and not very nice old lady speak to her Sam like that; never a 'please' or 'by your leave' either.

She did not understand the words she uttered, they just came: 'Go away you old witch, you have no business to do that!'

Grace gaped and staggered back as if struck by an invisible force. She stared at Jill, wild-eyed. 'A child, *the* girl child!' she muttered in an anguished whisper.

Jill's action broke the spell that held the others. Someone else did not approve of Grace's tone. It reminded him too much of the Enchainers. Binky, whose lead Sam had put down when he put the gloves on, shot forwards barking furiously. Bindle did not move from Jill's side but added his rich bass voice to Binky's treble.

Pandemonium ensued; Grace could be heard screaming,

'The dog, *the* white dog!' Jill was still saying 'Go away!' in a loud voice and Sir Brian was bellowing, 'When do I reverse the lever?'

Sam came to life. He grabbed the tin from the bag and flung it with all his might into the tunnel, at the same time shouting, 'Now, Sir Brian, now!' There was a loud 'ker-click' followed by what sounded like a speeded up hammering noise. Planks and boards sprang back into position and nails pinged into their holes.

Another sound was heard, someone approaching rapidly along the passage from the barn and Erin popped out of it! She glanced round and a smile of satisfaction spread over her face.

'Congratulations, Sir Brian,' she said. That gentleman turned a rosy pink and stuttered, 'Think nothing of it, dear lady, just a little thing I happened to think up, you know.'

'When *are* you going?' Jill was still confronting Grace. 'I've told you to, ever so many times!'

Binky was still standing in front of the old lady, barring her way, while Bill and Edwin stood protectively in front of the other children.

Erin stepped in front of Jill and spoke to Grace. 'I think you had better take this child's advice, and leave,' she said very quietly.

The figure snarled at her. 'Think you're clever, don't you? Let me tell you I *shall* have what is mine by rights and neither you nor any child or dog shall stop me! You may have it shut away safely for the moment, but *it* won't lay quiet. Little do you know what you have become involved in. Yes, I *shall* go, but don't think you have seen the last of me.' She paused and said in a placating tone, 'Unless, of course you hand it over now, like any sensible person would.'

She was met by silence. 'Very well; may the consequences rest fully upon you all.' With a harsh laugh she vanished up the passage, the howling wind accompanying her. There was a last echo of '...on you all!' Then silence.

'I always said witches were an uncouth lot,' remarked Sir Brian. 'No manners, no sense of how to address their superiors and betters. I'm glad she's gone.'

'Well done, you three,' exclaimed Bill. 'Yes, indeed,' chimed in Erin.

Edwin smiled at Jill. 'You see, little maid, you did as I said you would and the right words came. If *you* had not spoken out, her words would have bound us all and she would have been able to snatch away the plaque.' He now turned to the dogs. 'Without you, faithful hounds, things would not have gone so well. Little white dog with the heart of a lion and Bindle, a noble old warrior. Loyal animals like you can also check the power she tries to wield. But why do we stand talking in this dismal place? Let us return to the daylight.'

He led them back down the passage and into the yard. The sun shone brightly, the air was sweet and fresh. All that had just happened was like a bad dream. Indeed it seemed no more than that now.

'Rosie and I must be getting along,' said Erin. 'We are very lucky things worked out so well. It was also essential that I was able to speak directly to Grace. Now I am confident I can match her power. As for her threats, I'm not sure how much weight they carry. However, we must still be careful, this business is far from finished!' With that she left.

'Suppose we better be going too,' added Sir Brian. 'Want to make a few adjustments to this!' he said, proudly waving his invention around.

'Hey, be careful with that thing,' warned Bill, 'If you press the switch accidentally heaven knows what may happen.'

'Of course I won't!' he retorted and did. Luckily he was pointing it at the gate to the yard. All the screws from the hinges came out and the gate fell with a spectacular crash to the ground. After some fumbling the inventor managed to pull the lever back, and the gate, plus screws, sprang back into place.

'Do you think it needs a safety catch?' he asked. They agreed it did.

The three children and two dogs stood in the yard. 'I shall leave you now,' said Edwin. 'There are one or two things I want to look into as well.' He smiled at them and was gone. Binky and Bindle wagged their tails in appreciation.

'I'm hungry and thirsty, how about you two?' said Sam.

'Let's go into the kitchen, Mummy left some cake and cookies for us,' announced Jill.

'And I could do with something nice and warm and soothing to drink,' said Sarah.

They made their way inside and were soon seated round the table — relaxing.

'I wonder what Grace meant by her "little do we know what we've become involved in" business?' remarked Sam.

'I expect we'll soon find out!' said Sarah, 'Anyway, let's forget all about it for the moment. I feel like a nice walk in the sun, how about you two? — and Binky, and Bindle!'

'Yes, down to the ruined church,' said Jill firmly. So that is where they went.

As usual they sang the 'Alleluia for all Things' standing before the altar. Brother Andrew did not appear, but they felt much easier in their minds, and stayed for a while just enjoying the peace and beauty of the place.

When they returned Bess and Brian were back and Brian insisted on showing them his new filling. Lunch preparation was already well under way and Bess asked, 'Did you have a nice time, dears?'

'Oh yes, well sort of,' they replied; luckily there were no more questions.

The remainder of the day passed quietly. Sam was concerned for Jill, as she suddenly looked very pale and tired. Her confrontation with Grace had proved very draining.

They settled in the lounge, Jill on his lap while he read her fairy tales. After a while she fell asleep, waking quite refreshed an hour or so later. Around five Harry returned. They did not tell him anything about the morning for the moment, deciding to wait until a more suitable occasion. Just before six Doreen phoned to say they were back, so Sam, Sarah and Binky — the boisterous — made their way home.

CHAPTER THIRTY

As soon as supper was over Sarah phoned Melissa's and asked to speak to Michelle; when she came on she told her of the morning's happenings. Michelle was greatly relieved at the good news, but when she heard of Grace's threats her delight was sobered.

'We shall have to be very careful, Sarah! I'm going straight to school from Gran's on Monday. See you there and then you can tell me more.'

Sarah had hardly put the phone down when it rang. She picked it up; it was Jane.

'Thank goodness I've got you, Sarah! Dad said I could phone, but must keep it brief; what happened?' Quickly Sarah told her. 'Phew, you'll have to tell us the full story on Monday. What's it like here? Boring, boring, nothing but old, old and older relatives all talking about ancient times and saying, "Do you remember this time last year Aunt Cynthia and Uncle Hubert were still with us?" Then they all look miserable and call for another round of drinks. None of them can remember our names for more than a few seconds and will call us *little girl* and *little boy* when they can't think of them. Oops! Dad's coming, I'd better go!'

Shirley would not be back until Sunday evening so they'd have to wait until then to let her know what happened — which they did.

On Monday the usual update was held at school so all were aware of the present situation. However, the remainder of that week and much of the following one were taken up with completing the main lesson work before the camp—and the final preparations for this. One of the tasks arising from their expedition would be the writing of a report on the week. So! As a first-hand description from somebody on the spot is better than my second-hand one, below is one of the children's reports—Fenella Steuart's. It was quite difficult to know which one to choose, but as that young lady has a journalist for a mother, there is good reason to believe she was born with a pen in her mouth and and ink and paper in her hands—so to speak. This gives her account a certain extra zest!

CLASS FOUR'S **CAMPING** TRIP TO SELWORTHY.

June 19th to June 27th.

BY

FENELLA STEUART.

INTRODUCTION.

The pupils who went on this trip — just so you know — were:

Christopher, 'Chris' Shelley — He's the oldest in the class and a chatterbox.

Margaret Himmelhoch — She's awfully nice, but has two left hands, like my mother says when I drop anything.

Fenella Steuart — That's me, I didn't put myself first because that's not polite, though I think I should, as I'm writing this.

Barbara Hoaks — She's ever so quiet, but pleasant.

Bernard Schultz — His dad and mum are

German. He has diabetes.

Adrian Hart — The biggest and toughest boy in the class (he thinks). But he's quite a softie really!

Leland Green — He's the sleepiest boy in the class and only wakes up at snack time.

Vanessa Turner — She's like Barbara, only she has darker hair.

Rebecca Stehli — Her hair is ever so long and always in a tangle!

Julian Naughton — He makes smashing paper darts!

Marion Foster — She's rather posh, but you should hear the words she uses when she gets really angry!

Gillian Thomas — She gets asthma, but is a real brain box.

Stephen and Jane Randell — Twins, two of my best friends.

Sam and Sarah Court — Also twins and also my best friends. They joined the class last year after Hallowe'en.

Michelle Evard — She's ever so skinny, but really super, I like her. Her grandmother used to be a witch. She, Michelle — not her grandmother — joined the class in January.

Stephanie Struckett — She used to be the baby of the class, the youngest, and still is, the baby I mean. Gosh, you've only got to stick your tongue out at her from two hundred yards away and she bursts into tears!

Tanya Taousis — Her dad's Greek and her mum Dutch. But Tanya speaks English.

Jonathan Wilson — He's another real brain box and a worrier. If he hasn't got something to worry about he's unhappy!

Geoffrey Neeley — The last school he went to was

awful, he joined in January and is Jonathan's buddy, so they both worry along together.

Billy Jones — He's the smallest boy in the class, but makes up for it in noise. His voice is well over safety decibel level.

Shirley Fisher — She only joined us this term and is also my friend. She knows masses and masses about gardening. She's now the youngest in the class, but she's no crybaby.

That's us, class four, ten boys and thirteen girls (hurrah!).

I must also mention our teacher Mr Frederick Atkinson, or 'Atty' — when he's not listening. He's been our teacher since class one and knows us really well. Of course we know him better, but don't let on. He's the most super teacher one could ever wish for. He expects us to work hard but makes lessons such fun and so interesting you can't help learning. He tells stories like no one else and can be ever so funny. Anyway, you'll read lots more about him in this report.

We also had a student teacher along to help. She was Dutch, spending a month at our school to improve her English and see how to teach a mob like us. Her name, well, it was very hard to pronounce, it sounded like 'Vinegar Treaclebug' but she didn't seem to mind if we called her 'Miss Treaclebug,' so we did.

She was supposed to be looking after us girls on camp. But on the first day she caught a dreadful cold and we spent more time looking after her than she did looking after us! Still it all worked out well in the end and she was fine for the last three days.

We were camping on a farm. There was a field we were allowed to pitch our tents in and there was a toilet block at one end so we didn't have to dig latrines like Mr Atkinson said we would, or wash in a horse trough. I told you he likes making jokes. There were also safe places for us to cook our food. But there were porta-gas burners too, so if it rained or our fires wouldn't go properly, we could still cook. There was also a barn that had been made into a sort of recreation room so we had somewhere to go if it was rainy. It was a super place, right up on a hill overlooking the sea with a path down to the beach, leading to a little cove where we could swim, providing we had an adult with us.

Now I'll give you a day by day account of what happened starting with:

Friday, June the 19th.

We met at school around ten o'clock. Everybody was loaded with gear and parents telling them to do this and not to do that. Poor Miss Treaclebug was getting an earful from Stephanie's mum. I bet she couldn't understand half of it! 'Atty' was buzzing round, quite unflappable, getting stuff stowed in the coach luggage bays and checking pupils' bags off on his list. As soon as our gear was loaded we had to get on the coach and *stay* on so he knew where we were. Steph's mum got on too, still issuing last minute instructions, but had to get off because she was blocking the gangway. So she hopped up and down outside.

A headcount revealed we were one short. Guess who—Leland. He'd overslept and his mum let him sleep in because she didn't want him to be exhausted for the trip! Anyway he turned up about ten seconds before we were due to leave. I bet he's never moved so fast before in his whole life.

At ten thirty-one and eleven seconds we were off.

Nobody was to leave their seat — on pain of death or no lunch, the choice was theirs — except to go to the loo. Our journey was about forty miles. The coach went via Taunton, then took the Minehead Road. We stopped at a village for our snack and then went on to another one, where we had to stop because Billy was sick — yuk! There we joined the coastal road to Minehead and so on to our destination Selworthy, arriving at the camping site about twelve thirty.

We ate our packed lunches at the picnic tables then started to set up camp. It was chaotic for there was this enormous pile of gear dumped by the gate of the field and we had to sort it out, find our tents and pitch them. Atty had made a plan, but at first people were setting up tents here, there and everywhere! Treaclebug got awfully upset; apparently where she comes from they 'do it otherwise'. But good old Atty didn't turn a hair. He called us together and explained how you pitched your tent so that you didn't have the wind blowing in the front, and how to use the lie of the land on the site. He tore up his plan and suggested we camp in a big circle with the cooking area as its centre point. That made sense and by mid-afternoon we were all camp-shape and ready. The farmer came to inspect it and said he hoped we'd keep it that tidy *all* the time! He also told us the rules and the do's and don'ts round the farm.

Afterwards we strolled into Selworthy to get to know the place, as it was the source of our food supplies. It's one of those quaint thatched villages. We visited the general store and post office. Some people bought cards and sent them off to their parents. I'm not going to do that until Monday, then I can tell them how things are going. We didn't have to cook that night as Atty had arranged for a takeaway meal to be delivered from Minehead. It was a 'dip and mix' affair and jolly good. Then we lit a campfire, though it wasn't really cold. But we sat round it while Atty told us a smashing tale about the olden days in Minehead. Then he suggested that each evening one of us told a story. 'It only needs seven volunteers,' he said, and he got them. Now it was off to the loo block to wash and clean our teeth. Then we gathered round the dying fire again and he said an evening verse. Then it was: 'Into your sleeping bags, you lot!' I didn't feel one teeny bit tired but once I'd snuggled down in mine I felt really weary and was soon asleep. So was everyone else.

Saturday, June the 20th.

There were lots of people who claimed they didn't sleep a wink all night. But I don't believe them! After breakfast we held a camp meeting to share out tasks and arrange a cooking and cleaning roster. Then the rest of the morning was our own. We could go down to the beach with Miss Treaclebug, stay in camp or go to the village with Atty. A group of us decided to stay in camp because we had something very important to discuss. Tomorrow is Atty's birthday and we wanted to organise a celebration for it. Lots of the children have brought gifts for him and the parent-birds are sending a thumping big cake by special delivery to the farm. Stephen and Jane thought something like the way their party was organised might be a good plan. 'Emperor Atkinson' sounded fine, so each of us would tell those not at the meeting what the idea was. We knew that a walk along the Coastal Path was scheduled for Sunday, but as we'd have to be back in time for the cooking squad to prepare the evening meal, it would give us time to set up for the celebration. Michelle and I went to ask the farmer if we could use the barn for it. He was most amused at the thought of children actually doing this for — of all people — their teacher, and willingly gave his consent. He also supplied us with some big sheets of paper and felt pens to make banners. The morning went by awfully quickly. After lunch we walked to Selworthy Beacon, one thousand and fourteen feet above sea level and North Hill, eight hundred and forty-three feet up. From here there was a spectacular view of the coast. Sarah tried to sketch it but she wouldn't show anyone the results. Billy was sick behind some bushes; he ate too many sausage rolls too fast at lunchtime. When we got back everybody went for a swim. Then supper was prepared. In spite of the fact certain people were rostered to do it, everybody helped. I think some of us were afraid we wouldn't get a decent meal if we left it to just a few. Although there were really 'too many cooks' it turned out quite well. Stephanie nearly got stung by a wasp — it passed within six feet of her. She howled for the rest of the meal until she realised it was ice cream for dessert. We lit the fire again and Chris told a story. He's very good at it, that boy sure has a vivid imagination! Then it was heigh-ho for bed. During the evening we managed to have a word with everybody, so the plans were all set for tomorrow.

Sunday, June the 21st.

We had breakfast at seven thirty and it was what Atty called 'fresh' or jolly cold. His plan was for us to walk the path to West Porlock to have lunch and a swim before returning. When the sun got higher it began to warm up and some children stopped complaining about being too cold and complained they were too hot. Stephen and Jane took their cameras and a pair of binoculars, which they said were 'special'. They looked quite ordinary to me. However, before we started we stood round our teacher in a big circle and sang 'Happy Birthday' to him. He tried not to look too pleased, but we could tell he enjoyed it.

The walk was lovely. The sea was a deep blue and we saw masses of sea gulls and other birds. One big black-headed gull zoomed over us and did a dropping on... Yes, Stephanie's hat! She howled until someone stuck a peppermint in her mouth. When we reached West Porlock we had lunch on the beach and then a swim. Afterwards came the return march. The whole walk was, including ups and downs, about ten miles. By the time we got back it felt like ten hundred.

Now we had to make our preparations without Atty knowing. Luckily he was called to the farmhouse. His sister was phoning to wish him 'all the best'. So we could get everything ready. By arrangement the farmer kept him chatting as well. We sneaked the cake in and soon had everything set up. Supper was eaten at the picnic tables as usual. After we'd cleared away, Chris and Michelle detained him while the rest of us went into the barn. He was now blindfolded and led in. Seating him on his 'throne' — a deckchair with arms — Stephen placed a paper crown on his head, Jane pulled the blindfold off and we all cheered and whooped like mad. In front of him was a trestle table with his presents on it and the enormous cake in the middle. It didn't have any candles because we couldn't find out how old he was. I suppose grown-ups like to keep _some_ secrets. Sam and Sarah did the honour of bringing his gifts to him so he could open them on his throne and when that was finished he cut the cake and we all had a piece, it was terrific, with masses of cream and icing. Billy was... ...as usual. Afterwards we sat round, sang songs and told jokes, some of which were pretty awful. Gosh, it was already bedtime! By now we were used to sleeping in our tents and some people had to be woken up in the morning. Atty had brought along an old bugle and he started to blow this at seven every morning; after _that_ it was impossible to go on sleeping.

Monday, June the 22nd.

Yesterday was the summer solstice, so today we are going on a hike to Dunkery Beacon, one thousand seven hundred and seven feet high, on the fringe of Exmoor. We went via Luccombe. This was a _real_ trek, though the actual distance was only four and a half miles. But there were masses of downs and ups. I think everyone enjoyed it, even Billy, in spite of being you-know-what. Atty made us fill up our backpacks so we'll be used to carrying quite a load when we go on our trek into the Exmoor National Park and stay overnight from Thursday to Friday. We were really bushed when we returned, but good old teacher had arranged for the farm to provide us with an evening meal, which we ate in the barn. Afterwards we played guessing games and charades. Then had a story told by Michelle, _not_ about witches.

Tuesday, June the 23rd.

The weather pooped on us today! It was rainy with squally showers, but it gave everyone a chance to try out their rain gear and find out how waterproof our waterproofs and boots really were! We walked into Minehead and took a ride on the West Somerset Railway to Wachet and did some rock scrambling on the beach. Things brightened up in the afternoon so we took the train back to Dunster station and went into the town, but didn't go to the castle. Instead we had ice creams and caught the train back to Minehead. The weather promises to be better tomorrow.

Wednesday, June the 24th.

I was on cookhouse duty this morning, the very morning we had to make piles and piles of sandwiches because we are going by coach to Tintagel. I would land a rotten job like that! Luckily Michelle and Shirley were on too, so we had a good fun time together. I hope the sandwiches were all right ('They were!' — Chris). ~~Teh~~ The coach arrived at eight thirty, as it's quite a long journey down the North Devon and Cornish Coast. About ninety miles. But the scenery was terrific. Wild and rocky, just the place for smugglers and pirates. Atty used the coach PA system to tell us a real blood and thunder story and before we knew it we were in Tintagel. Lunch was eaten overlooking the castle ruins and we had another story about King Arthur and Merlin. This was followed by a guided tour of the ruins. That was a bit boring, as we weren't allowed to explore where we wanted, but had to keep together. Though in one place if you strayed off the path and slipped there was a three hundred foot drop onto the jagged rocks below. One look at that and Billy was sick again and Stephanie started to cry.

We had a look round the village and bought cards

at the 'Old Post Office' and local souvenirs. Then it was back to the coach and 'home'. You know camp really does feel like home now. That evening we had to pack to have everything ready for an early start in the morning. Our sleeping bags would be the last items to pack. Tomorrow we'd be using our compasses to navigate our way across Exmoor. I hope we don't get lost!

Thursday, June the 25th to Friday, June the 26th.

I'm back in camp, and so is everyone else (Friday evening). It was quite a trip! Nothing terrible happened. There was an awful lot of just slogging along, putting one foot in front of the other. Then stopping to look round and wonder at the wildness of the place. We saw lots of wild deer and ponies; it was something I don't think I'll ever forget, even if I live to a hundred. (My brother reckons I'll be bumped off long before then). On Thursday our objective — by evening — was Windsford Hill, one thousand four hundred and five feet high. The plan was to reach Dunkery Beacon and strike due south across country using our compasses and map to keep on course. This proved to be quite exciting and Atty made us use co-ordinates every so often to check our progress. We ate our packed lunches at a place called Gutthorne, about halfway. Had an hour's rest and then tramped on.

'We are supposed to reach the Ranger's Hut on the south slope of Windsford Hill between four and five,' he told us. The last few miles were hard going, but we made it by quarter to five and the ranger was there waiting. The hut ~~wsa~~ was quite big, with a large room that had an enormous fireplace in it and off there was a kitchen and a bathroom. But the loo was <u>outside</u>—round the back. That was fine in daylight, but at night when you're sleepy and have only a little torch, not so good. As soon as we arrived the cooking team—yes that was us again—started to prepare the evening meal. We'd brought dried veg' and stuff to make a big stew and soon the kitchen was full of good smells. People kept popping in and saying, 'Isn't it ready yet?' Michelle soon got fed up with this and said, 'No, it isn't and the more you keep on interrupting us the longer it will take. So shut up and go away!' That did the trick.

The ranger had supper with us and then explained about his work on the moors, especially the part about dealing with scrub fires. That was exciting! Then he left, bumping off in his four-wheel drive. We had to sleep on the floor that night. At first it seemed awfully hard, but we were so tired that, hard floor or not, we were soon fast asleep! To be wakened from our slumbers by a familiar howl, Steph' again! She'd gone to the loo and dropped her torch on the way back. Luckily Atty was sleeping by the door so he shot out to rescue her and the torch. She sniffled for a while then fell asleep.

Next morning we were up early and after breakfast spent the morning map reading round Windsford Hill and plotting the position of the hut from different points. Jonathan took so many bearings his plan looked like a crazy spider's web. We had an early lunch and then prepared to leave. The ranger arrived and checked out the hut, locked it up. Wished us a 'good trek back' and drove off. Some of us wished we could have had a lift. But once we got going it wasn't nearly so bad. The weather was fine and it was interesting to see things from the other side. I mean when you walk south, like we did, you have one view and when you walk north, as we did going back, you see it differently.

Camp was reached just after nine and the farmer had a meal ready for us in the barn, and there was a birthday table and cake. Modesty prevented me from mentioning this earlier, but now I'll have to. You see it was my birthday today! They did sing 'Happy Birthday' and gave me handmade cards this morning, but our minds — mine too — were taken up with preparing for our return march. Though Chris kept on saying, 'I wonder what you'll find when we get back?' After the twelfth time I told him to save his breath for scrambling, otherwise he would never know because he wouldn't get back if I had anything to do with it. Like a good boy he shut up.

Anyhow, in spite of us all being weary, the sight of the meal *and* the cake, not to mention the birthday table, drove away our weariness. The meal was excellent, so was the cake and the lashings of ice cream that went with it. Then I was let loose on the presents. There were some pretty good things, like a really super compass and a neat pair of folding binoculars, which would slip easily into a shirt or shorts pocket. Dad had sent a box of top quality coloured pencils and Mum a folder-cum-bag to carry all my art stuff in. There was also a note promising 'more' when I got home. My ratbag of a brother had added a line saying 'if I did.' Cheek! There were also gifts from both pairs of twins, Michelle and Chris. His card was a masterpiece of chaos, just like him; but he means so well and is so good-hearted that I can never be angry with him for long. Atty gave me a book, *Mistress Masham's Repose*, by T.H. White, the chap who wrote *The Sword in Stone*. This is different but looks good. By now it was ten o'clock and we were shooed off to bed and shortly after it was, snore, snore, snore!

Saturday, June the 27th.

This was it, our last morning. The coach was coming at two to take us back to our parent-birds and civilisation. As the morning was warm and sunny we all went down to the beach for a swim and to lounge around. Miss Treaclebug was asking a lot of questions about us and of us. She seemed to think English people were a bit strange.

'In Holland we have what are called "free schools" which are run similar to this.' She spread out her hands, 'But it is you English who are so, how do you say? Odd!'

Atty wasn't at all perturbed. 'It's the way we do it and it's suited to our children,' he told her. She just sat there shaking her head. I wonder how I would find a 'free school' in Holland? I suppose I'd have to learn Dutch!

Over our sandwiches Atty told us that the first school like ours had been evacuated from London to Minehead during the Second World War. But the house where it was accommodated no longer existed. Now we had to do our final packing and move all the stuff down to the gates ready for the coach. We said goodbye to the farmer and he said we could come again any time, because we were some of the best campers he'd ever had, even better than some adults.

The coach arrived and we loaded it. Billy was... ...—excited I suppose—even before he got into it. During the journey back we sang songs and chatted. At four o'clock we drove into the school car park, which was swarming with parent-birds. Stephanie started howling because she couldn't see her mum, but she was there all right. We all said goodbye to Vinegar Treaclebug who was going back to Holland the next day and we thanked Atty for such a wonderful trip. He's funny; he _thanked us_ for being such a great bunch of kids. Still it is rather nice to be one of a 'great bunch'! I said goodbye to my friends and Mum drove Chris and me home. Andrew was greenly jealous when he heard what a super time I'd had. But his group is going to France next week anyway.

That's my report; I don't think the school journal will print it. But maybe future generations of pupils will read it and wonder. Wonder whether we were just plain crazy or always carried on like that!

Fenella Steuart.

CHAPTER THIRTY-ONE

For the campers Sunday was a day of recounting all that had happened during that eventful week to sympathetic parents and the adoration of younger brothers and sisters. Though as Fenella mentioned, *not* the older ones! They also luxuriated in the comforts of home and spent a lazy day — recovering!

Sam and Sarah dawdled like the rest, but had hardly finished breakfast when Sir Brian appeared, eager to demonstrate the new improved model of his machine. They were just in time to stop him from 'de-screwing' the kitchen dresser, which was loaded with china. Then he was all for using the breakfast laden kitchen table for his demonstration. At last they persuaded him to come to the secret room where the bedside cupboard they had borrowed proved to be an ideal object. It fell apart dramatically and came back together with a most satisfying 'kerklunk'. The children were very impressed and the inventor was overjoyed at his success.

Now Bill and JJ arrived, so they gave them a blow-by-blow account of the camp. The same thing was happening at Southleigh, where Bob listened approvingly to Stephen and Jane's account. He was especially delighted that they were learning to read the compass and was full of praise for their teacher.

Doreen called up the stairs, 'You have visitors.' They ran down to see who it was. Actually, it was quite a gathering: Bess with Jill and Brian, Will Bennett with Nicky and Judy, Erin with Rosie all eager to hear of their adventures. Jill naturally wanted to know how her Sam got on and sat on his lap listening open-mouthed as he described their trek across the moors.

'When I'm in class four shall I do that?' she asked.

'I expect so,' he replied.

'Will you please teach me how to use a compass, so I shan't get lost?' she begged.

'When you are older,' he replied.

Soon I shall be,' she announced triumphantly, 'I shall be *six* on Saturday!'

'Oh,' exclaimed Sarah, turning to her brother, 'and we shall be ten!'

Their parents grinned. 'That's one reason for this gathering,' said Doreen. 'Now, my dears, it's a perfectly good morning, no need for any of you children to hang around indoors. Binky has really missed you; so do him — and us — a favour by taking him for a walk while we discuss 'certain matters'. Eavesdropping is strictly forbidden, shoo!'

It was great to walk round the familiar grounds again with the four younger ones. Binky also thought it great; four extra stick throwers was his ideal of the sport and he had a wow of a time. They wandered through the ornamental gardens and round the coppice past the old hunting lodge ruins.

Suddenly Jill tugged at Sam's sleeve. 'What's that?' she asked.

'What?'

'Listen!'

They stopped and listened, even Binky.

'It's a funny noise,' remarked Judy. Indeed it was, a very

faint but distinct sound.

'Like somebody wearing metal flip-flops,' said Sarah. She looked at Sam. 'Do you think it may be… …?' Her voice trailed off.

'I don't know,' he replied. 'When we get back let's ask Erin.'

Once they were away from the spot they cheered up and circled the park, ending up by the pond. 'It would be great if we had a proper boat,' mused Sam, 'Not just an old pallet.' Sarah agreed with him. Neither of them noticed a little secret smile flit across Jill's face.

When they returned to the kitchen, having announced their return by singing 'Frere Jaques' loudly—and being told they could enter—Sam told Erin about the noise, asking if it might be to do with the plaque.

'It might be, but on the other hand it could be Grace. I don't know. But Rosie doesn't seem perturbed, which means things are well under control. But perhaps it would be as well to put the "rabbit watch" on the alert, so that anything unusual in this area is promptly reported.'

This made them feel easier. After some general talk the visitors left and the children suddenly felt very tired.

'Your week's catching up on you,' smiled Doreen. 'I suggest both of you take a nap after lunch. I'll wake you for tea.'

They protested they would be awake *long* before that. At four fifteen she wakened two soundly sleeping youngsters for tea. Afterwards they prepared their school bags and collected the notes and sketches they had made on the trip—exactly what all their classmates were doing that evening!

The return to school was quite a shock for the class, but under Atty's guidance they soon recovered! The remainder of the week was busy with working on the maps they were building up from their compass exercises and writing their own descriptions of the class treks, the visit to Tintagel and so forth. The week flew by. As they boarded the school bus for home on Friday Stephen called out, 'See you tomorrow.' They looked puzzled for a moment until Jill nudged Sam saying, 'Our birthdays!'

While North America — the United States part of it — was letting off fireworks and holding Fourth of July parades, Sam and Sarah were just getting up and wondering how different life would be having reached double figures.

'We'll have them for the rest of our lives unless we live to be an hundred,' remarked Sam at breakfast.

'Heaven forbid!' exclaimed Derek, 'There are enough disasters in the world already.'

'Oh Da-ad!' they chorused.

In front of their places had been a beeswax candle surrounded by a wreath of flowers and the birthday cards from many relatives and friends. The presents part would be in the afternoon. However, much to their amusement, Binky suddenly trotted in with a red ribbon round his neck carrying a small gaily wrapped package in his mouth, bearing a label saying: 'Happy Birthday, Sam and Sarah, from Binky and Cleo'. However, he was very reluctant to part with it and they had to chase him round the kitchen several times before he was cornered and relinquished his hold. Upon opening they found two small hardbound surveyor's notebooks. Ideal for the practical work they would still be doing during main lesson.

'We hoped to get Cleo to carry one,' said Derek, 'but all she would do is try to tear the wrapping off!'

The rest of the morning, which was bright and sunny, they spent up in the gardens, pottering round, doing some tidying up, weeding, watering and bush trimming. Bothering Derek — a favourite occupation — and examining the currant bushes to see if there was any ripe fruit yet — there wasn't.

Suddenly it was lunch and then time to get ready to

receive their guests. Jill's party was going to be combined with theirs and she would be having two of her little kindergarten friends along as well. 'But everybody knows us, why do we have to dress up?' they protested. They were reclothed, but luckily not too much. 'At least we can still move,' remarked Sarah.

The guest list read the same as for Stephen and Jane's party, which isn't surprising. Only Peter didn't come this time, as he'd had to go to Bristol on business. Jill's extra guests were Nola and a little boy called Tom, who was very quiet. 'He's shy, like I was,' she told Sam. The guests, having parked cars or bikes by the garage or in the courtyard were conducted round to the front where the birthday children greeted them. Jill stood happily beside Sam. She was dressed in a pale pink frock with a similar ribbon in her hair. He felt strangely proud of her.

When all were assembled in front of the porch the birthday children were instructed to stand on the top step. Stephen, Jane and Wendy came and placed paper crowns on their heads and they were each given a 'golden staff' to carry. The odd thing was that the two for the twins had hooks at the end. John stepped forward and requested that their 'Royal Highnesses' should follow him to the 'Royal Banqueting Hall' and he led them to the summer house, which had been specially decorated for the occasion. Inside was a long table down the middle for the guests, and at one end a smaller one laden with presents. After Their Majesties had taken their places at the head of the main table and the guests were seated, their presents were handed to them by Nola and Tom for Jill and Chris, Michelle, Fenella, plus Shirley for the twins.

Jill revelled in new paints, colour pencils and modelling wax, a beautiful handmade rag doll and some glorious picture books with moving pictures. She also received a waterproof walking jacket and a pair of sturdy boots. 'Now

I can come walking with you!' she exclaimed delightedly to Sam. He grinned while she scuffled about among the wrapping paper to find the label, and let out a shriek of joy when she saw it was 'S-A-M' who had given her the jacket.

Amongst the twins' parcels there were several with warning notices on them. 'Do not open until instructed to!' They were of the most interesting shapes. When the present table was emptied and the debris cleared away, Doreen announced:

'Before we cut the cake and have tea I must request that you follow me. Your Highnesses first and then the hoi polloi — you lot — at a respectful distance behind.'

Everybody got up and followed her. She led them out and along the side of the stream towards the pond, which looked very peaceful; its surface was like a mirror. Three paving stones had been placed at the edge and by them were three fishing nets, a small one for Jill and larger ones for the twins.

'Plunge your nets directly into the water in front of you,' Doreen instructed, 'until they reach the bottom, it's not very deep here. You will feel an object, which if you are careful, you can catch in your net. Once all three have been caught, tell me and I shall count one, two, three! On three, lift them out.'

The Royalty followed her instructions. Sure enough they felt something and Jill, with a little help from Sam, caught hers too. 'Ready!' they said. 'Right! One, two, three, lift!' They lifted and gasped with surprise. In each net was a beautifully sculptured stone fish, quite heavy for they caused the rods to bend and the children really had to strain to lift them out. But why fish, what for?

A shout from the onlookers made them turn their attention to the pond again. Something was stirring on the bottom, slowly moving upwards, something that wallowed like a great fish from the depths.

'Your Royal Rods, Your Majesties!' called Derek. Of course, they had large hooks! Quickly they plunged them into the water and found there were tabs they could push them into. 'Heave-ho,' shouted the guests. 'One, two, three, heave!' Slowly they dragged and hauled the object up onto the bank. It was a large bag made of plastic; along one side was a zip. Eagerly they unzipped it and pulled out — an inflatable dinghy! Like Stephen and Jane, all they could say was 'Wow!'

Derek stepped forward, bowed, and presented them with a medium-sized box wrapped in nautically styled paper.

'Here, Jill, you open it,' said Sam. When done, a foot pump for inflation was revealed.

'Now, now, do it now!' everybody yelled.

Within a few minutes the dinghy lay on the bank ready for the water. The other mystery parcels that had been brought along were now opened. A pair of collapsible oars, two life jackets, a waterproof box for storing food, etc., a first aid kit and a real lightweight nautical compass in gimbals. Stephen, Jane, Michelle, Shirley, Chris and Fenella ran forward to help slide the dinghy into the water, but left the bow still on shore. Derek handed Sarah a plastic bottle with some yellow liquid in it saying, 'You must christen her.'

'But what?' she asked, then after a pause, turned to Will.

'Mr Bennett, do you think Uncle Peter would mind if I christened her 'Patricia'? I feel that's the right kind of name to give her. He sent us such a nice birthday letter saying he didn't know what to give us. The name would be a lovely gift!'

'I'm sure he will be pleased and touched,' was the reply.

So Sarah tapped the bow with the bottle and said, 'I christen you 'Patricia', and the others carefully eased her into the water. Then Their Highnesses clambered in, and taking the oars, set out to navigate uncharted waters. It took them a little while to get the hang of using the oars.

At first they tended to go round in circles, not helped by everybody shouting contrary instructions from all sides of the shore! But after a while they got the hang of it and paddled round the pond in fine style. Then it was back to the summer house for the birthday tea, which was described as 'superb' by the participants. Afterwards there were games for the little ones—and bigger ones—ending with them trooping over the bridge and down to one of the large oaks. From its lower branches hung several large gaily-coloured balloon-like objects made from papier mache. Each child was provided with a stick and two lines were formed. One was for the younger children, whose 'balloons' hung lower. The other was for the older ones.

'These are a festive idea from Mexico,' Fred explained. 'I thought they would make a fitting end to the day. Each is filled with goodies and small gifts. As you walk by, give it a good bash with your stick. The person whose stick breaks one open distributes the contents to the others, retaining one item for themselves. Right, are you ready? Go!'

It was wonderful fun and a great way to end the party. 'What's it called?' asked Chris.

'The nearest I can get to the Mexican is 'Pen' or 'Pinata', said Fred. That was good enough for Chris, who liked collecting strange or unusual words, which he often used in stranger and even more unusual ways!

The party was over! The guests said their farewells and eventually only the Game family remained. One last surprise awaited the youngest birthday child. Sarah handed her a soft package. 'For tonight,' she explained. Puzzled, Jill opened it. There was a lovely fluffy dog pyjama case, and in it a pair of pale lilac pyjamas, her favourite colour. Jill still looked puzzled until Sarah said, 'You see, you didn't bring your night- clothes with you.' Then it dawned on her, she was staying the night! 'That's because you are now six!' said Sam. Brian would have no doubt protested, but he was already asleep on his father's shoulder. Her parents left and a very proud little six-year-old, under Sam and Sarah's supervision, cleaned her teeth and got ready for bed. She slept on a put-away bed in Sam's room.

Sunday was a peaceful day. They tried the dinghy out again and had a great time all morning learning how to handle it. Jill managed remarkably well at steering and even had a go at taking an oar. The only member of the family who did not approve of it was Binky. When they tried to put him in he jumped straight out and refused to go anywhere near it. As they paddled round he ran up and down the bank barking in an agitated manner. When it was pulled out and deflated he ran off to a safe distance and growled furiously at this monstrous creature. He never really approved of it, though an ordinary wooden boat presented no such problems.

'It may be the smell and the way the air-filled material yields to the touch,' suggested Derek.

They took Jill home in the late afternoon and, as she had been so good, promised she could come for another sleepover 'soon'.

There were eight more days of school before they broke up for the summer holidays. Eight days full of rounding off the year's work and sorting through the piles of material it had produced. Every afternoon during the last few days they went home laden with main lesson books and various work folders. 'We'll have to build a couple of extra rooms on to house all this,' joked Derek.

On Tuesday there was a dress rehearsal for the end of the year festival and a final 'clean up' of the classrooms. Then came the move to their new classroom for next year. The actual breaking up was on Wednesday with the festival. This was in two parts. In the latter part of the morning it was an internal affair for the classes when each teacher addressed them, briefly reviewing the year's achievements and looking forward to the coming one. After lunch came the open part, for parents to attend, where each class, and the school choir and orchestra would perform. This was quite a lengthy business with an interval after class eight's turn. Even so, it was past five o'clock before it was all over. Then it was goodbyes to classmates and various teachers until September.

'You won't shake me off that easily,' said Fred. 'I'll be over to keep an eye on you now and then.'

'Aren't you going away?' they asked.

'For a few days to visit my sister, but that's all. I've lots to do here and round the school—also preparation for next year. Got to keep you lot on your toes!'

When he'd gone to talk with another group of children and parents Jane said, 'It's a shame he can't go away for a proper holiday and have a real rest and change.'

'But why doesn't he?' asked Sarah.

'Because he can't afford it on his salary,' announced Stephen. 'Dad says the teachers get paid peanuts, just enough to live on.'

'There ought to be a fund or something so there *is* money for them to go away!' said Sam. 'Maybe we could do something to raise some?'

'We could think about it during the holidays,' said Jane. 'But,' she added, 'what about the holidays anyway? We'd better start making plans.'

'There you are,' said Doreen, 'I've been looking for you all over the place. We are going back to Southleigh for a meal. Phyllis has prepared an end of school year celebration. Come on, or we'll be late.'

It was a grand gathering with all the 'regulars' including Fenella's parents and Chris's, Ingrid, Karen and so on. The now *nearly* class five children gathered in a corner to talk over the "Holidays for Teachers" plan and how to pass the summer. After tossing a few ideas around Sam suddenly

exclaimed, 'I know! We've all got camping gear, haven't we?'
'Yes.'
'Well, why don't we camp at our place in the grounds?'
'Brilliant!' said Chris.
'We've all got bikes as well, haven't we?' asked Sarah. 'So we could go for day outings and then our parents won't say we're hanging around like a smell on the landing the whole time.'

The more they talked it over the more enthusiastic they became about the idea.

'When shall we ask?' queried Michelle.

Sam looked at the group of parents and other grown-ups.

'They're all here. So let's ask *now*, there's no time like the present!'

Before the others could stop him he walked forward, cleared his throat and said, 'We have a holiday proposition.' Then before they had time to recover he launched into their idea.

When he'd finished, Fred, who was standing at the back of the room, murmured, 'That boy should go into parliament.' The parents looked at Doreen, after all... ...!

'Well, I am perfectly willing to have them,' she began, only to be drowned out by a burst of cheering from the children. When silence was restored she continued, 'Providing I have some assistance from all of you. If the weather is fine I foresee no problems, but if it is wet we shall need a backup programme.'

She turned to the eager children. 'Idea accepted; leave the practical side to us. There'll be quite a bit of organising to be done. I think we could provisionally say from Saturday, July the twenty fifth to Saturday, August the eighth, agreed?'

Everyone agreed. Shortly afterwards the gathering broke up. The sextet pronounced themselves the childrens' committee and arranged to have a meeting this coming weekend.

'Stephen and Jane can come over, can't they, Mum?'

'Yes, of course.' So that was settled!

As they were preparing for bed Sarah said, 'You know the plaque and Grace's threats?'

'Yes.'

'I think your idea came up because something *is* going to happen and we shall need all the help we can get.'

Sam considered this for a moment. 'You know, Sis, I believe you are right. But what about the others, how will they take it?'

'Well, apart from Geoff, Chris and Fenella, they are all involved.'

'What about the suggestion Mum just made about having some of the younger ones over for a few days, like Shirley's sisters, Nicky and Judy, also Jill and Brian?'

'I don't see any problems if we keep an eagle eye on them and organise games and the like.'

'I suppose not.'

'Aren't you two in bed yet? Quit gossiping and get on with it.'

'Yes, Mum, G'night!'

୯ଓ

Some distance away in the bowels of the earth a rhythmic tapping continued as a shell-like object slithered its way slowly through the mud and slime of the tunnel towards the one who had called it into being and caused it to be 'ensouled' in a lifeless metal plaque. The call of its creator had been heard and it was seeking, seeking.

In the passage outside the boarded up tunnel, eddies of air swirled round brushing against the timbers. A voice-sound was carried by them.

'Soon I shall be stronger, soon I shall be stronger. Then I shall achieve my revenge on those who wronged me, and find peace at last!'